I0652285

"STEBBINS IS THE MASTER OF THE THINKING READER'S TECHNO-THRILLER."
—Internet Review of Books

Four Action Packed Political Thrillers. Three End of the World Scenarios. Two Unusual Love Stories. One Secretive Intelligence Branch.

The *Intel 1* Global Thrillers

"A MONSTER NEW TALENT IN THE THRILLER GENRE."
—Allan Leverone,
author of *Final Vector*

An

ARMAGEDDON
DUOLOGY

Books three and four of the *Intel 1* novels
The Anonymous Signal and *The Nash Criterion* combined

Erec Stebbins

TWICE PI PRESS
New York, NY, USA

Only one thing is impossible for God: to find any sense in any copyright law on the planet. —Mark Twain

This book is a work of fiction. Any references to historical events, real people, or real locales are used fictitiously. Other names, characters, places, and incidents are the product of the author's imagination, and any resemblance to actual events or locales or persons, living or dead, is entirely coincidental.

An Armageddon Duology. Copyright © 2016 Erec Stebbins
www.erecstebbinsbooks.com

Unless otherwise indicated, all materials on these pages are copyrighted by Erec Stebbins. All rights reserved. No part of these pages, either text or image, may be used for any purpose other than personal use. Therefore, reproduction, modification, storage in a retrieval system or retransmission, in any form or by any means, electronic, mechanical or otherwise, for reasons other than personal use, is strictly prohibited without prior written permission.

Paperback CS
ISBN-10: 1942360142
ISBN-13: 978-1-942360-14-8

Hardback
ISBN-10: 1942360169
ISBN-13: 978-1-942360-16-2

Paperback LS
ISBN-10: 1942360150
ISBN-13: 978-1-942360-15-5

E-book:
ISBN-10: 1942360177
ISBN-13: 978-1-942360-17-9

Published 2016 by Twice Pi Press
TwicePiPress@gmail.com

Cover designs by Erec Stebbins
Images licensed from Shutterstock.com, Pond5.com, Adobe Stock images, and individual artists. Copyrighted artists GlebStock, Milan Ristic, Nik Merkulov, Krasowit, Olga Nikonova, isak55, Zoom Team, and flywish.

Lyrics from "Supremacy" by Muse used with permission from Alfred Music Publishing.

Edited by Michael Matheson.

Wake to see
Your true emancipation is a fantasy

—Muse, *Supremacy*

THE ANONYMOUS SIGNAL

NO FORGIVENESS. NO FORGETTING.   EXPECT IT.

EREC STEBBINS

The

ANONYMOUS
SIGNAL

Book Three in the INTEL 1 Novels

Erec Stebbins

Twice Pi Press
New York, NY, USA

Only one thing is impossible for God: to find any sense in any copyright law on the planet. —Mark Twain

This book is a work of fiction. Any references to historical events, real people, or real locales are used fictitiously. Other names, characters, places, and incidents are the product of the author's imagination, and any resemblance to actual events or locales or persons, living or dead, is entirely coincidental.

The Anonymous Signal. Copyright © 2015 Erec Stebbins
www.erecstebbinsbooks.com

Unless otherwise indicated, all materials on these pages are copyrighted by Erec Stebbins. All rights reserved. No part of these pages, either text or image, may be used for any purpose other than personal use. Therefore, reproduction, modification, storage in a retrieval system or retransmission, in any form or by any means, electronic, mechanical or otherwise, for reasons other than personal use, is strictly prohibited without prior written permission.

Paperback CS
ISBN-10: 1942360096
ISBN-13: 978-1-942360-09-4

Hardback
ISBN-10: 194236010X
ISBN-13: 978-1-942360-10-0

E-book:
ISBN-10: 1942360088
ISBN-13: 978-1-942360-08-7

Published 2015 by Twice Pi Press
TwicePiPress@gmail.com

TWICE PI PRESS

Cover designs by Erec Stebbins

Images licensed from Shutterstock.com, Pond5.com, and individual artists. Copyrighted artists GlebStock, Milan Ristic.

Edited by Michael Matheson.

To Nina and Billy

A thousand years scarce serve to form a state;
An hour may lay it in the dust.

—Lord Byron
Childe Harold's Pilgrimage
Canto II (1812), Stanza 84.

PROLOGUE

THE BABY pulled on a string and the toy's small disk chimed. A lion roared and birds tweeted. A dog barked, and the disk stopped spinning. The baby giggled and pulled again.

The room was dark except for multicolored stars projected onto the ceiling. A window was cracked open, letting in crisp spring air. Across the room, a tired-looking woman rested, eyes half-closed, in a rocking chair, watching the child.

The baby grew bored with his toy and turned to a mobile above. A panda-headed cord dangled there, and he could just reach it. Lights blinked and a tune played. The baby smiled.

He pulled himself up awkwardly, legs wobbly. With one hand the baby grasped the panda, with the other the thick string hanging from the disk. With jerky movements, he pulled back and forth on each, nearly stumbling as each mechanism activated in succession. A light shone on the child's face, an obsessive gleam in his eyes as they darted between the two chiming toys.

Jenny smiled and suppressed a laugh. Even so late at night, when really all she wanted to do was crawl back into bed with her husband, watching her son play was magical. She'd suffer tomorrow for another interrupted night, but it was worth it. He was so happy!

She rubbed her eyes and sat up stiffly in the chair, getting a better view into the crib. Her expression clouded as the toys continued to chime, her son now sitting again on the mattress, bouncing lightly as the racket continued.

Shivering, Jenny draped a shawl around her shoulders and stood up, stumbled to the window and closed it. She turned to the crib and yawned. "How you reaching them down there, pooh-bear?"

She stopped and stared as the baby pulled on the string to the animal disk again. The mechanism clicked and the heads began to rotate. At the same time, the mobile above lit up and played its little tune. The baby smiled and giggled.

"How did you do that?"

The string with the panda was wrapped around one of the animal heads of the disk, so as the disk advanced slightly with each pull, the tug on the mobile activated the second toy, the mechanisms now linked. There wasn't any slack left in the mobile string, and she detached it from the lion head the string had looped behind.

"There," she said. "You'll break it, silly boy."

13

The baby pulled on the animal disk string and it moved. He stared at the mobile expectantly. Nothing happened. He pulled on the string again. His lip quivered, and he began to cry.

"Shh. Sorry, pooh-bear, but you got it all tangled." She smiled and cooed at him. He didn't seem to notice her and continued to tug on the string in frustration. The woman sighed. "We got to get some sleep, sweetie. Mommy's tired."

She walked back to the rocking chair. "Mommy's just going to close her eyes for a few minutes."

She slumped down and exhaled deeply, the chair swallowing her whole like an ocean pulling her down into slumber.

And then the sounds again. Animal noises followed by the little tune. Dancing, dancing together in her mind one after the other. The patter of them landing on her like rain. Where had she heard them before? Oh, yes. But the string would break...

Jenny snapped awake and knuckled at her eyes. Sure enough, the baby had done it again. The string from the mobile was fixed to the other toy disk mounted on the side of the crib.

She got up slowly and walked to the bed, reaching in to untangle the devices again. The baby began to cry.

"Sweetie," she began and then stopped, staring quizzically at the child. She reached up and slowly detached the string, letting the panda head drop downward back under the mobile. She watched her son closely. His complaining slowed and then he toddled up, reaching deliberately over to the panda head to pull it to the side, and yanked the string clumsily to the disk. After several failures, the string latched around one of the animal heads. The baby squealed and dropped back down. He pulled the string and the two toys danced in unison.

She repeated the process to the same effect.

Then she ran from the room.

"Look, Henry, just look!"

Jenny stood beside the crib, Henry, the boy's father, yawning. He watched his son.

"See? He's hooked them together. They both play when he pulls one string!"

"Okay, Jenny? So he tangled them up. We just undo it and it'll be

fine."

"No. Don't you get it? It's on purpose."

His forehead creased. "On purpose?"

"Yes! He likes it when they both play. He figured out a way to link them together."

"At nine months? Jenny, come on. You need sleep."

"No, listen! I undid it like three times. He keeps putting them back together."

"Honey, how about I take over tonight and you get some rest?"

She pushed forward, the wild look in her eyes causing him to backpedal unconsciously. "Henry, do you know what this means? Do you?"

The man shook his head.

"It means he's a genius, Henry."

The father had reached the doorway, yet she pursued him, grasping the folds of his robe and pulling him toward her.

"Our baby is a genius!"

PART 1

Remember remember
The fifth of November!
Gunpowder, Treason and Plot!
I see no reason
Why Gunpowder Treason,
Should ever be forgot!

—English Folk Verse (c.1870)

BEFORE:
THE ANONYMOUS EVENT COMMISSION

DEPOSITION IN THE MATTER OF:
UNITED STATES ARMED FORCES SPECIAL TRIBUNAL,
Plaintiff,
v.
JOHN SAVAS, Defendant
Case No. M120039E-007X

DEPOSITION OF:
FRANKLIN JOESEPH MILLER
called for examination by Counsel for the
Defendant, pursuant to Notice of Deposition, at
the Independent Council Offices, located at
[REDACTED] Washington, D.C.,
when were present on behalf of the
respective parties: [REDACTED]

Counsel on Behalf of Defendant (CBD): Will you
please identify yourself for the record?
MR. MILLER: Franklin J. Miller, Special Agent,
Counterterrorism. Intel 1 division.

CBD: You have a service record?
MR. MILLER: Yes. Three tours in Afghanistan.
Honorably discharged.

CBD: Honorably? I'd say that is an
understatement. Medal of Honor, if I'm not
mistaken? Second Battle of Fallujah, according
to your records here.
MR. MILLER: That's correct.
CBD: Would you care to elaborate for the panel?
MR. MILLER: I would prefer not to.

CBD: Thank you, Mr. Miller. You understand that
your testimony here is on the record, and your
words might later be used to charge and try you
as an enemy combatant of the United States?
MR. MILLER: No, I don't understand that.

[REDACTED]: Have you not been informed of your
rights and requirements under the new Tribunal
Act?
MR. MILLER: Yes, sir. But none of this makes
any sense to me.
[REDACTED]: You have been informed of the law?
MR. Miller: Yes. Jesus.

CBD: Mr. Miller, how long have you worked with the defendant?
MR. MILLER: Nearly a decade.

CBD: And in what capacity?
MR. MILLER: First I was a special agent in the Intel 1 division under the umbrella of Larry Kanter's counter-terrorism branch. After the attacks on our division, I served under him in the restructured Intel 1.

CBD: And it was serving in this role during which the events in question occurred?
MR. MILLER: Yes.

CBD: And how did you and the Intel 1 division become involved?
MR. MILLER: John likely knows the chronology better. But-

CBD: You mean the defendant, former agent Savas?
MR. MILLER: Former?
CBD: Agent Savas.
MR. MILLER: Yes. Special agent in Charge, *John* Savas.

CBD: Continue.
MR. MILLER: I mean for the rest of us it was a relatively normal day, if you can ever consider counterterrorism a normal job. We had our usual reports, chatter, kidnappings by more extremists, talks of retaliation for the French raid in Algeria. It was also the ceremony for John's medal, and that morning we were all in front of the Mayor and Attorney General.

[REDACTED]: And the Anonymous case? Please focus your responses to material relevant to this inquiry.
MR. MILLER: Right. It started with the bombing, obviously. As far as I know, NYPD was the first on the scene but they called us in fairly quickly.
[REDACTED]: You know this because?
MR. MILLER: John told us.

CBD: Can we just back up and get the events from you one step at a time. Tell us from what

you remember what happened.
MR. MILLER: I wasn't there for a lot of it, but
we were all briefed.
CBD: That's fine. Just your words, please.
MR. MILLER: All right. Like I said, it started
just like any other day.

OCTOBER 17

1

"MR. CRAIG, SIR."

A man in a chauffeur's uniform held a door open patiently. The CEO of Goldman Sachs stalked toward the car. Silver-haired, dressed in a tailored business suit with a golden watch that glinted in the sunlight, his thin-framed glasses gave his harsh features a predatory intelligence. The black leather handle of his briefcase contrasted sharply with his golden wedding ring. Two bodyguards left his side and walked to a second car parked immediately behind.

Jack Craig nodded to the chauffeur and stepped into the limo. He dropped his briefcase onto the leather seat, pulled out his cell phone, and dialed as his driver shut the door. The interior was spartan compared to the cars kept by many of his equals at the top echelons of corporate power. But Craig had never taken to the ostentatious bravado that infected so many of his peers. To his mind, there was no surer sign of dominance than the refusal to flaunt it.

The driver entered and started the engine. "World Financial Center, Miles." The driver nodded and pulled the car out into midday Manhattan traffic. Craig engaged the auditory dampening system, sealing him off from the driver. "*Yes*, Heidi. I understand that there are midterms coming, but this bill cannot come up for a vote. It's got Warren's dirty paw prints all over it and it's a step in the wrong direction." He paused, listening. "No, it doesn't matter. You won't lose your position on the committee. Hell, given how much you lot have gerrymandered things I doubt I'll be alive the next time you lose the House. We've got you more than covered with the advertising, believe me. Kill this vote. You've got nothing to fear." He pulled the phone away from his head to mitigate the shouting on the other end of the line. "For fuck's sake, Heidi! Least of all the press! Not even the *Times* has anyone off the payroll now."

Craig nodded several times, satisfied. He ended the call and sighed. *No one in Congress has any balls except that damn bitch Warren!* And they hadn't been able to find a price for her. He doubted there was one, but they still had many years to find out.

Especially if they could couple it with some dirty laundry and rattle her cage a little. He swiped across the phone and hit an entry, placing a call.

"Hi, sweetheart!" For the first time that day, Jack Craig smiled. "No, I can't make your show today, I'm sorry. Daddy's got a very important meeting with the *President*. Tell that to your friends!" He frowned as a whining pitch escaped from the speaker. "I know, I know, honey. I'll bring you something special tonight, from that new toy store they opened, what's it called? The one with the giant bear?" There was a sound on the other end. "Right. That one. A surprise, okay?"

The vehicle pulled out onto FDR Drive and sped south beneath the Hospital for Special Surgery, the sun glinting off the East River on his left. Craig cracked the window open a wedge, gazing toward the looming mass of the Queensboro Bridge and the white sailboats bobbing along the currents.

"Now, Daddy's got to go. You give him a kiss." A pop sounded on the speaker. "Thanks, honey. Talk to you later." He closed the connection.

Continuing to stare outside his window, Craig felt a weariness descend. Soon, he knew, they would reach their exit and the nasty courting ritual would begin at the hotel. A presidential speech on financial reform, dutiful agreements from the top managers, handshakes, TV moments, and reporters' questions. Too much money had changed hands for there to be any real concern. They owned the committees. The damn politicians had to trot them out every few years, give them a public tongue-lashing, and then it was back to business as usual.

A black spot in the sky in front of them caught his eye. *What the hell?* He disengaged the sound suppression.

"Miles, can you see that thing in front of us? I thought it was a plane, but it's something else."

While he was accustomed to the low-flying aircraft along this route—helicopters heading to the Hamptons and tourist planes lumbering overhead—something was wrong. The craft, whatever it was, seemed way too low. *Too small.*

"Look at it—it's off the river and over the damned FDR."

He could see his driver straining upward and nodding. "Some kid's remote control helicopter or something, Mr. Craig."

Craig shook his head. "Maybe. Damn if it's not going to hit us."

The object careened straight for them, slowing its approach until it paced the car. He could see it better now: four helicopter-like blades spun equidistant from each other separated like the points on a square. A mass of spidery arms underneath held what looked like a cylinder, the bottom shining like a large metallic disk. Craig felt a strange unease. *It's like some giant insect from Mars.*

"Miles, take the next exit. There. The sign that says 53rd. Take that exit."

"But sir, we'll get snarled in the local traffic."

"Just do it!"

Craig wasn't sure what was happening, but his instincts were never wrong. He had lived too long as a predator and master of the games of power. When soldiers around him died in Vietnam, he made it out alive. It was a sixth sense, background processing, *something* that always alerted him to danger and opportunity. Right now, his alarms were ringing frantically.

The limo darted across lanes toward the exit to a chorus of horns. The small flying thing matched their motion and continued to close the distance.

Miles grumbled as the wheels hit the exit ramp. "This some new paparazzi thing?"

Then, the impossible! The small craft accelerated and slammed directly onto the roof of the car.

Craig jumped. *Shit!* "Pull us over, Miles. Now!"

But there wasn't a place to stop the car. Still exiting the off-ramp, the driver accelerated and hurtled toward a curbside ahead.

"Goddamn thing is stuck to the rooftop," yelled Craig, grabbing the handle of his door. He prepared to leap out of the vehicle.

A large explosion rocked the corner of 53rd and Sutton Place. Windows of surrounding buildings shattered, facade stone fractured and fell, and debris from a black limo blasted outward with a fireball that set nearby trees and garbage on fire. Smoke surged upward from the demolished vehicle, only a chassis and partial skeleton remaining. Alarms sounded from cars parked near to the blast radius, and voices screamed over the din. Bodies were strewn motionless around the inferno. Wounded screamed for help.

Above the growing chaos, unseen by anyone below, a frenetic buzzing purred. An apple-sized object hovered hundreds of feet above the fire, a propeller whirling above an octagonal hardware collection ending with a downward-pointing lens. The mechanical insect observed the scene with a cold stillness. As the first sounds of sirens began to spill toward the carnage, it climbed above the buildings and disappeared into the sky.

2

"SO IT IS only fitting that today, five years after the events in New York and around the world that brought us to the brink of international conflict, we honor a man who was instrumental in bringing us back from that cliff."

Special agent John Savas squirmed in his metal fold-out chair and prayed that this horrific political pageantry would reach its inevitable and dreaded climax. His salt-and-pepper hair was trimmed similarly to that time five years back, a time when the home-grown terrorists of Mjolnir had aimed a nuclear warhead at the Muslim holy city of Mecca during the great Hajj pilgrimage. But no amount of self-delusion could hide the fact that it was considerably more *salty* now than it had been. While he still worked to keep himself in shape, at fifty-five, age was beginning to finally have the upper hand, and his increased desk time as the director of Intel 1 hadn't helped.

But it was more than simply age. As for the nightmares—Savas was too mired in a dying male culture to do much about them. PTSD was what psychologists talked about on cable news, not what men had or admitted to. Only his wife of three years, agent Rebecca Cohen, truly knew the extent of the damage. And that because she shared the trauma as well.

Savas watched the new Attorney General of the United States bring the speech to a point of tension and transition. The former prosecutor looked in his direction and nodded.

"And without further delay, here to receive the Award for Exceptional Heroism, please welcome a true American hero and pride of New York City, John Savas!"

Savas surged to his feet, flashbulbs exploding around him, applause drowning his thoughts like a churning waterfall. He moved as confidently as he could toward the stage, remembering to paste a reserved smile on his face for the evening news. A row of officers from the NYPD and local FBI branches greeted him with handshakes and pats on the back. Nearing the podium, reporters' cameras pummeling him like strobe lights, and he shook hands with the Attorney General with one hand while grasping the medallion case and plaque in the other.

As they paused for the photographers, Savas instinctively searched among the front row of FBI agents for a diminutive brunette. Her long hair would be secured formally behind her. For events like this she usually wore her blue pantsuit. He would see her radiant smile beaming toward him, his desire to impress her flooding him with energy.

But she wasn't there. He knew she wouldn't be there, but looked anyway. She was hundreds of miles away in a secret location only a handful of people knew, checking up on two charges that Savas had personally assumed responsibility for. Deep in a forest, high in the mountains, Rebecca Cohen was at this very moment in the company of the nation's most wanted fugitives.

Savas shifted his focus back to the Attorney General. He smiled for the cameras.

———

Exhausted, Savas dropped into his office chair and stared forward blankly. The medal and certificate stared back at him from his desk. He didn't want them. He didn't join the FBI after his son's death on 9/11 for honors, and he hadn't risked everything, even Rebecca, to stop Mjolnir to get a damned medal. He could think of thousands of victims of terrorism who deserved much more than he did. Who would repay them and their families? He could think of one man, Husaam Jordan, who had stopped a nuclear holocaust by sacrificing his own life. But what good were medals to the dead?

He grasped the award materials and unlocked a key-coded drawer in his desk. He yanked it open and pulled out a thick file folder, dropped the medal into it, and closed the drawer. It clicked loudly as it locked. The label on the file, bold black ink on white, left an afterimage in his mind: *The Ragnarök Conspiracy*.

Savas loosened his tie and sighed deeply. Now for just five minutes of peace.

"Captain Overlord, sir, transitional paperwork is now one hundred percent completed."

He startled at a bald woman framed by his office door, her arms grasping the metal frame above her head. Savas tried not to gawk at her toned body, hammered and stretched by several years of intense combat training. Gone were the waist-length orange hair and the Amish dresses. Piercings ran up her ears, in her lips and eyebrows. Today she wore fatigues and a green tank revealing rippling muscles on a thin frame—some punk version of Sigourney Weaver in *Alien 3*, but with orange eyebrows, green eyes, and a more spaced-out glare.

Another casualty. The meek girl he had known was gone, murdered just as surely as many in the ground. In her place stood something far more potent.

"Morning, Angel. Here to ruin my day?"

"It's part of my mission statement," she said.

"You know, agent Lightfoote, I've spent every favor I had left to let you parade around here like GI Jane. A little protocol every now and then would be nice."

"Stopping a madman and saving the world buys some unique capital, Fearless Leader." Her face darkened. "Steals other things though."

Savas absorbed her words silently. The losses could never be measured. Talented people, good people who could never be replaced.

"John, it's not your fault they died. Not your fault that you're the best to run Intel 1. Trial by fire," she said, nodding to herself. "They cut the fat. Axed all those 9/11 counter-terrorism toys or put them under you. Larry couldn't have done a better job."

Visions of a house bomb rushed through his mind.

"I don't know about that. He was a genius."

"And things are different now. Larry didn't know shit about cybercrimes. *You* set up the Operations Center under Manuel, not Larry. After what happened, you knew where crime and national security were headed: *digital.*"

Savas shook his head. "Big picture only, Angel. I still can't figure out my email sometimes."

"Boss Man is supposed to be big picture."

"At least making you head of cybercrimes means someone can call you Captain Overlord or whatever for a change. How is your command and control center coming along?"

Lightfoote pouted. "John, there's no budget! We cannibalized the Operations Center, but it's not nearly enough. It's outdated. We need server farms to handle the loads of searches and to fend off digital attacks. DNS floods are *daily*. Everyone wants to bring down FBI or get in our systems."

Savas nodded. "I know, Angel. But times are tight. Budgets are bleeding. You're going to have to be creative. If the criminals can do it, so can you." He smiled.

"So Mr. Big Picture is telling me to emulate cybercriminals? You know blowing things up is a lot easier than building them."

"Angel, don't twist—" An alert tone rang on his phone. He scanned the message. "It's Rebecca."

"Yeah? How's her *special assignment*?"

Savas frowned. "It's very *special*. Now I need to take this." Lightfoote beamed at him. "*In private.*" She grinned more broadly and left the room, closing the door behind her.

Savas sighed and opened the connection. A woman's face appeared on his smartphone, brown hair and eyes, a smile on her lips. *God, it's good to see her.*

"Agent Cohen, it's been too long."

"Yes, I've been stuck with babysitting duty. *In the mountains.* Now, who was it that stuck me here?"

"A heartless boss."

"No doubt. If he hadn't, Agent Savas, I could be there now. Next to you. Much *closer*." Her eyes smoldered.

"Yeah, definitely way too long. I hope this call means you'll be coming home tonight?"

Her smile was mischievous. "Booked my flight. In by ten."

"*Good.* There's *a lot* to catch up on." His face darkened. "And how is Gabriel?"

Cohen looked to her side. "Gone now. Back to the cabin. They're adapting, but getting restless. They've made it a home. But the world has made it a prison."

There was a long pause as he considered her words. "No one said this would be easy for either of them. It's wrong, but the setup was too good. A fight we couldn't win."

"I think they need to continue to fight, even a guerrilla war."

"It's on the agenda. We've finally put things back together over here and I'm coordinating with Fred Simon at CIA. We won't leave them hanging. There's a lot to be done."

The landline on his desk buzzed. *Now what?*

"Hang on, Rebecca. This is from NYPD, on my red line." He pressed the button to go to speaker. "Hi, Will. Don't hear from you often."

"John, we need you and a crime unit up to the East Side, Sutton Place. *ASAP.*"

"You sound rattled. Boys in blue don't want this?"

"It's a car bomb. A big one with some collateral damage."

Car bomb? "Anyone killed?"

"Several bystanders and those in the car."

Savas furrowed his brows. "Your crews are about as good as ours. Why me?"

"This one's different."

"Might be a challenge to ID those in the car if the fire was bad."

"That's just it, John. We know who was in that car. Phone GPS confirms it."

Savas glanced to his smartphone. Cohen's face looked tense. He turned back to the speaker on his landline. "Well, who was it?"

"Jack Craig, CEO of Goldman Sachs."

"Ah, hell. Are you sure?"

"Unless someone else had his phone, it was him and the driver."

"Dammit. A car bomb?"

"So it looks. That's why we're calling you in. It's getting out already and it will stir all the hornets' nests. And a car bomb, Goldman CEO? Whatever it is, it's big. Mafia, some Unabomber type, or maybe one of these new terrorist groups. Too radioactive for us."

"Understood. Moving on it now. Where are we headed?"

"Sutton Place south, fifty-three. Or just follow the GPS coordinates on all the photos flooding the internet. There's no hiding this."

DEPOSITION IN THE MATTER OF:
UNITED STATES ARMED FORCES SPECIAL TRIBUNAL,
Plaintiff,
v.
JOHN SAVAS, Defendant
Case No. M120039E-007X

CONTINUED DEPOSITION OF:
FRANKLIN JOESEPH MILLER

MR. MILLER: We sent a crime unit. I was there,
too. Jesus, what a mess. I hadn't seen anything
like that up-close since Afghanistan. I think
without the GPS data we'd have spent a while
trying to figure out just who the hell was hit.

CBD: And the target was confirmed by location
data and DNA analysis to be Jack Craig, CEO of
Goldman Sachs?
MR. MILLER: That's right. There was no
question.

CBD: And how did the defendant react to this
event and information?
MR. MILLER: Well, sir, John Savas is a good as
they come. Everyone was shocked. John, too, but
he was professional. Got the division primed
and assigned several agents to the case. They-

CBD: The agents assigned would be you and Agent
Cohen?
MR. MILLER: Yes, that's right.

[REDACTED]: What about the other members of
Intel 1?
MR. MILLER: They were on other duties.

[REDACTED]: Why didn't Savas treat the bombing
with the full attention of the division?
MR. MILLER: Well, we didn't know then what it
was all linked to. I mean, it was a car bombing
in Manhattan. That's pretty fucking serious but
still isolated. Still with more unknowns than
knowns. There were a lot of serious things with
unknowns going on in the world and we were
charged with keeping tabs on a lot of it. I

mean, it wasn't long before the whole finance thing started to go FUBAR and that ate our cybercrimes subdivision.

CBD: We'll get to that. Let's focus on how this began and what you remember. So, how did Intel 1 respond at this point?
MR. MILLER: Well, John—Agent Savas—personally got involved with the footwork.

[REDACTED]: Why?
MR. MILLER: He's like that. I mean he can't do it in every case, but he's very hands on. Goldman CEO? This had PR nightmare all over it. John went personally.

CBD: Went where?
MR. MILLER: To talk to the employees at Goldman about our investigation. To try and find out if they could shed any light on the situation.

CBD: He went alone?
MR. MILLER: No, he and Agent Cohen.

[REDACTED]: For the record, let it be noted that Agent Rebecca Cohen is the defendant's spouse. Mr. Miller, can you comment on FBI policy with respect to employees and nepotism laws? Romantic associations?
MR. MILLER: I don't much read the regs, sir.
[REDACTED]: Can you or can you not tell us if you know that it is against Bureau policy to have superiors and those under their authority in personal relationships?
MR. MILLER: No. That stuff never mattered to me. Besides, we always did everything a little different at Intel 1.
[REDACTED]: Yes, that is becoming more and more clear.

CBD: Let's return to the events immediately after the bombing. You say Savas and Cohen went to Goldman.
MR. MILLER: Yes. The morning after. We had already pulled a late night and put together some interesting information we had to run by them.

OCTOBER 18

3

SAVAS AND COHEN stepped out of the Crown Victoria in front of 200 West Street in Lower Manhattan. A towering glass skyscraper rose into the sky before them. Known as the Goldman Sachs Tower, the new forty-four story structure gleamed in the morning sun as it looked down from the northernmost end of Battery Park toward the World Financial Center. Savas could almost feel the power radiating from the monolith.

He closed the door and stared upward. "No logo. Not a letter or word on it. World's most influential financial institution, and it's basically anonymous."

Cohen stepped beside him. "It is kind of eerie, that's for sure. But I'll take it over yesterday's carnage, thank you. Forensics was picking things up with tweezers. I've had enough bombings for one lifetime."

"Hits too close to home." He turned to look behind them. "Look at those playing fields. Still brand new. This whole area was rubble and soot."

Cohen looped her hand under his arm. "It's hard to take, I know."

"Thanos died a few blocks from here. A lot of people did. Sometimes I think they should have left it like that. Broken. Raw." Kids squealed as they kicked a soccer ball across the field. "World moves on, and somehow we're all supposed to be okay with that."

"John, here they come."

Representatives from the bank rushed out to greet them. Two men and a woman, they wore appropriately moderate smiles for an occasion that consisted of their CEO having been blown up the day before, ushering them politely inside. Savas paused momentarily as they entered the lobby.

"That's impressive."

It was spectacularly cavernous, the ceiling higher than an opera house, works of modern art draped thirty feet in the air above them. It reminded him of standing in some of the newer airport terminals, only that everything was fashioned at several notches above the quality required for mass transportation hubs.

The woman nodded. "We're very proud of our new building and contributions to the revitalized financial center," she began, the delivery so perfect it seemed long rehearsed. "There are twenty-one million square feet and six trading floors, each larger than a football field. It's a very environmentally friendly building with floor ventilation, cooled by a hundred storage tanks containing nearly two million pounds of ice. Views of the Hudson River and New York Harbor are available for our most senior members."

"Like CEO Craig," said Savas.

The woman's faced paled. "Yes. Please, follow me."

The building spanned two city blocks, and to Savas it felt like the walk to the elevator took them across the length of it. No one followed them inside, and the three Goldman employees were silent as the elevator sped upwards and stopped on the eleventh floor. Stepping out, they found themselves in a second, less gargantuan lobby, which required yet another trek to a second bank of elevators. Windows covered the walls and portions of the ceiling, bathing their path in light.

They passed the second bank of elevators and stopped in front of a doorway. The woman swiped a card over a reader and then keyed in a passcode. The door opened, revealing a short corridor to a smaller, lone elevator door.

"For our top executives," she began as the elevator opened, "we have implemented enhanced privacy and security protocols. This elevator leads to the offices of the CEO and other top Goldman Sachs staff." Her eyes darted away. "Unfortunately, we do not control the security outside of Goldman."

Savas could see pain in the woman's face. "You seem to have known Jack Craig well, Ms.?"

"Greenwald. Susan Greenwald. Yes, I was his personal administrator. His right-hand woman, you might say. Geoffrey and Kendall here are my assistants." She nodded toward the two men. "As we discussed on the phone, you will be meeting with our interim CEO Donald Freiheit."

The elevator doors opened. Before them an expansive conference room ran across the floor, centered on an enormous table of cherry wood. A man at the end of a polished, wooden table rose and ambled over in their direction.

Susan Greenwald reached over and tugged on Savas' jacket, whispering to him. "I don't care what you hear about us in the press, but Jack was a good man. He's done more for this country, for this city than anyone I know. Find his killer." With that she turned on her sharp heels and entered the elevator, the doors closing quickly as she vanished from view.

"Agents Savas and Cohen," came the voice of Donald Freiheit. "Two names that need no introduction."

Freiheit shook their hands, an expression of genuine interest on his face. He was a short man, bordering on stout, with thick glasses and a mass of gray and black curls that gave him more the look of an elder artist at a poetry slam than a new CEO. He led them to the table and poured water for each, sitting next to them like a professor before two students at office hours.

"We've had several rounds with the NYPD and FBI since yesterday. All of Jack's scheduling data, emails, phone logs—they're now in your hands one way or the other, either from us or your national databases. I'm not sure what else I can tell you, but I'm honored by the visit."

Savas nodded to Cohen and she got immediately to the point, removing several photographs from her briefcase and placing them before Freiheit. "Surveillance footage from a handful of operating CCTV cameras identified some very unusual elements in the bombing."

Freiheit glanced at the images. They were grainy, the black limo blurred in the still shot, even the street signs hard to read at the resolution afforded. However, his eyes immediately gravitated to the anomalies she referred to.

"What is this black thing on the top of the car?"

"That's what we're trying to find out, Mr. Freiheit," she said. "Look at this image, taken from another camera closer to the exit ramp from FDR Drive."

"It looks like some giant bird or something. What's it doing?"

Cohen shook her head. "We don't know, and we were hoping that you might could shed some light on it."

The CEO adjusted his glasses. "Me? How?"

Savas bent forward motioning between the images. "Between the time when the vehicle containing Mr. Craig took the exit ramp and the time the bomb exploded, something descended onto the roof of the car. Our analysts are still conferring with the military, but our best hypothesis is that we're looking at some sort of remotely piloted aircraft, an unmanned aerial vehicle that was tracking the CEO's position and then moved to intercept the car immediately before the explosion."

"Unmanned aerial vehicle?" Freiheit seemed stunned. "You mean a drone?"

"Yes," said Cohen, "a drone."

"Doesn't look like a drone."

"Not like the military aircraft shown on TV," said Cohen, "but there are hundreds of other military and civilian models of more designs than you could imagine out there. We can't get enough information from these low-quality images to positively ID the model, or even establish that it is a drone, but it's our best working model right now."

Savas focused intently on the new CEO. "Is there any way this could have been Goldman surveillance? Your Ms. Greenwald was extremely protective of Mr. Craig. Does your company use drones to monitor or keep tabs on Goldman execs?"

Freiheit shook his head vigorously. "Absolutely not. I've never even heard it floated as an idea. I'm not sure it would even be legal."

"It wouldn't," said Savas. "Not yet anyway, but the laws on domestic drone use are in dramatic flux. Some honest mistakes could have been made."

"Not by us, I can assure you. We've never had such a security effort and currently have no plans for one. I find these images very disturbing."

"So do we, Mr. Freiheit. But before we went on any wild-drone chases, the obvious step would be to see if Goldman was in the business. The topic is sensitive, and, I hope I don't need to emphasize, confidential. So we did need your time today."

He nodded. "I understand."

Cohen placed the images back in a folder. "A final item. FBI analysis of phone logs indicates that Mr. Craig made a series of calls to

Washington the morning he died. The numbers were resolved to those used by Heidi Moss, the Utah Senator. Since these calls were only minutes before he died, they are of special interest to us. Do you know his relationship with the Senator?"

Freiheit licked his lips quickly and shook his head. "No. I mean, Goldman has many supporters, as well as enemies, on Capitol Hill. It's not unusual for some of our most important lobbying efforts to come straight from the top, as it were. Business, you understand?" He smiled wanly. "Beyond that, I really have no idea what those conversations might be about."

———————

The interim CEO walked the agents to the elevator. "Susan will meet you on the Sky Lobby, the eleventh-floor lobby. You should take some time there if you can. It's quite a view." Freiheit smiled as the doors closed.

Cohen smirked as the elevator descended. "Bad actor."

"Yeah, he's lying," said Savas. "Not about the drones—I think he was honest there. But there's something going on with the senator."

She began typing into her phone. "Next shuttle to DC?"

"Think so. Have the team give Moss the heads up that we'll need to speak with her today."

"You going to run it through the Washington branch?"

Savas grimaced. "I should. But that will delay everything. I'm so used to the autonomy at Intel 1. I can't stand the bureaucratic dances, anymore. It's likely a dead end, so no harm, no foul. Right?"

"Okay," said Cohen raising her eyebrows. "You know best."

Savas frowned at her.

BEFORE:
THE ANONYMOUS EVENT COMMISSION

DEPOSITION IN THE MATTER OF:
UNITED STATES ARMED FORCES SPECIAL TRIBUNAL,
Plaintiff,
v.
JOHN SAVAS, Defendant
Case No. M120039E-007X

CONTINUED DEPOSITION OF:
FRANKLIN JOESEPH MILLER

[REDACTED]: Why did Savas purposefully keep other FBI divisions in the dark?
MR. MILLER: I'm not sure. That was a judgment call, maybe the wrong one. But it would have cost time and John felt he was on the scent.

CBD: And that's why the two agents immediately flew to D.C.?
MR. MILLER: Yes. At that point we didn't know what was happening. Just got a text message that they were following up on a lead that led them there. Ring the senator's office and let them know.

CBD: That would be Senator Moss?
MR. MILLER: Yes.

CBD: What did the senator say?
MR. MILLER: I wasn't there, but we were briefed when they returned.

CBD: And what were you told in that briefing?

4

DUSK HAD ARRIVED in Washington. Street lamps engaged, drivers switched their headlights on, and the buildings took on a checkerboard pattern of light and dark. The large window before the FBI agents looked down to the busy streets, the view blocked by the form of an older woman before them.

"This is highly irregular and very short notice, but I understand the circumstances are unusual," said Senator Moss.

Savas and Cohen had rushed to meet with the congresswoman as fast as possible, but extracting themselves from New York and navigating the D.C. rush-hour traffic had put them in much later than they would have preferred. They were lucky to catch Moss before she left for the day. High-level phone calls had helped constrain the situation—when the CEO of Goldman Sachs is blown up in Manhattan, normal etiquette is suspended.

"Indeed they are, Senator," said Savas as they took seats around her desk. Moss was nearing sixty, yet still carried the grace and self-assured mannerisms of the opera singer she had been a lifetime ago. Cohen had quickly filled out her resume for them on the way over. A fourth-term Republican from Utah, she had been a vocal critic of internet freedoms because of cyber-threats to national security and had worked to enact laws to bring the wild online world under increasing surveillance and regulation. As chair of the Subcommittee on Science, Technology, and Innovation, she now exercised enormous influence on national telecommunications.

Cohen leaned forward toward the senator. "Only minutes before he was killed, Goldman Sachs CEO Jack Craig made several phone calls to your office number, Senator. Can you tell us what these calls were about?"

"Those are privileged communications. Unless we want to get very messy with the lawyers, I can't divulge what was discussed. However, it was nothing out of the ordinary. Issues of business and telecom, with Mr. Craig arguing for certain approaches that he felt would be beneficial to the country and his business."

She smiled. For far too long. Savas picked up the thread.

"Could it perhaps have something to do with the highly unusual series of votes that have come from you the last month, Senator?" Moss' smiled faltered. "My colleague here has tallied not only a surprising reversal of several positions on the congressional floor, but also an increasing number of articles in the press trying to figure out just what exactly is going on."

"I'm not sure what you are talking about. The press is always looking for a critical angle, you know that. My positions have always been clear. Certainly, different pieces of legislation can embody my positions to different degrees of satisfaction, and voting for or against a bill is often complicated by the sausage-like production methods of these laws, where the good and bad can be mixed together."

Cohen didn't mask her annoyance. "I'm sure that's true. But there are bills that hardly changed where your votes have flipped. For example, Murdock-Holsen. A bill that would have denied the NSA certain access to internet communications. You initially opposed that bill, gave speeches against it, opposing the very nature of limited access by our surveillance branches." Cohen read from her tablet. "To quote from your speech, you called it 'A dangerous bill that would tie the hands of our law enforcement agencies and aid the work of criminals and terrorists.' Yet three weeks ago you stopped speaking against it and have voted twice to move the bill through committee to a vote."

"I believe that the concerns I had were adequately addressed in the revised version."

Savas could see the woman's lip trembling, the tightness in her hand grasping the side of her desk. Cohen seemed to notice as well. This topic had put Senator Moss under tremendous stress, and his instincts told him she was lying to them. *What are you so afraid of, Senator Moss?*

"Has the topic of domestic drones ever been part of your conversations with Goldman Sachs?" asked Cohen.

The terrified look intensified, and the senator glanced quickly toward photo frames on her desk. She seemed to half-whisper the next words. "No. Never. Why do you ask?" The false smile almost seemed macabre, now.

Cohen ignored her question. "You are on the record as supporting their use."

"Yes," she said distractedly, seeming not to see the FBI agents anymore and gazing behind them. "They are needed for homeland security. To make us safe. That's what I thought."

Savas furrowed his brows. "What you *thought?*"

She blinked quickly and regained focus. "What I *think*, yes, agent Savas. Law enforcement can make great use of drones to pursue criminals when vehicle chases would be impossible or dangerous, take surveillance without endangering officers, many things."

"And what of arming them?"

She cocked her head to the side. "That has been discussed in closed-door sessions, but I don't see that as necessary or likely in the near future."

Savas sensed her resolve returning and saw that they were losing the advantage. He spoke on a hunch. "Are those your daughters?"

Instantly, an anxiety seemed to spread over her features. She smiled stiffly. "Why, yes, yes. Margaret and Sophia. Twins. They're in college now, opposite sides of the country." Her fingers curled inward toward her palm, the nails digging slightly into the wood. "Identical twins and so different. Isn't that strange?"

"How are they doing?" he continued.

"Well!" she nearly shouted. Cohen leaned backward, and the senator adjusted her tone instantly. "Sophia's pre-med, 4.0. Margaret's still finding her way, but she's doing great. Absolutely great." That smile again.

"Well, try to appreciate every minute, senator," said Savas earnestly. "I can tell you, you never know what you have until it's gone."

Her face blanched. "Yes. You know all too well, agent Savas. I will. I promise you."

They stepped out of the Russell Senate Office Building into the brisk October evening, a black town car before them, waiting by the curb. Savas pulled his collar up and turned to Cohen.

"Well, what do you make of *that*?"

She shook her head, a cool breeze tossing brown hair about her face. "She's been compromised, John. Did you see the terror in her eyes? You pushed a very bad button with her kids."

"But who? And what? And why with fear? Don't the players just buy their way to influence these days? Corporations are people, all that?"

She nodded. "This doesn't make sense, and it feels very dark. Moss is a believer, John. You can see it all over her record. I'm not saying she's above lobbying or influence, but nothing in her twenty years in the Senate compares with what's happened the last few weeks. She's either had a mental breakdown, a stroke or something, or what we saw means somebody has her in a very bad vice."

"Her kids?"

"We should look into them. Check on their whereabouts, status. Start tonight with social media, get some shoes on the ground at their schools."

"If they were snatched, we'd know."

"True. But maybe something will come out of it if there has been some kind of threat."

"Political? Dirty laundry?"

"Always in play with these folks."

They arrived at the vehicle, and Savas opened the back door for Cohen. They got in and he slammed it shut distractedly.

"Reagan National," he told the driver. He whispered to Cohen. "A CEO car bombed. A US senator looking blackmailed and changing her votes. What's going on?"

She stared out the window. "Nothing good, that's for sure."

5

HALFWAY AROUND THE world, off the tip of the Malay Peninsula, the city-state of Singapore was an engine churning into morning overdrive. Businesses hummed, planes were launched around the world, financial transactions from hundreds of nations sped through the computer systems of their exchanges.

In a gleaming new building of blue and gray, on a wide and open floor lit by a bank of windows facing toward the front of the structure, rows of digital detectives sat in front of their computers. Near the middle of the floor, a short, gray-haired man of European descent hunched arthritically beside the desk of a young Asian woman. He wore a stunned expression as he stared at her screen.

"Are you sure about this?"

Yi Ling nodded to her superior. The thin fingers of her right hand drummed nervously on her keyboard. She reflexively tugged at her chest-length hair with her left. She could not afford to be wrong about this.

It was only two months ago that she had landed this job at the newly opened INTERPOL Digital Crime Centre in Singapore. The DCC was a dream job, letting her use her computer skills in her home country under the auspices of one of the largest and most respected law enforcement agencies in the world. Her friends were all impressed. It paid very well. But now, everything was threatened by the discoveries she had made over the last two days. It had taken her all of yesterday to convince herself that should risk raising the issue with her superiors.

"Yes, Mr. Rosenfeld," her perfect English hardly accented by her native Mandarin. "It's always on the derivative bets. All off-market."

The older man coughed and adjusted his glasses. "Nothing from the exchanges?"

"No," she said, wetting her lips with her tongue. "See these modifications to the contracts? They occur after the parties have established the contract terms but before the instrument is finalized."

Rosenfeld nodded. "That's incredible. How are they not noticing the modifications?"

"I don't know, sir, except that few check the source code anymore. Everything is automated these days, everything comes out of code. Maybe that's why nothing was tried on the exchanges since there'd be too many eyes on the trades. There's a code injection into the contract scripts here." She indicated a row of text on one side of the display. "The siphoning is minimal and scaled to the return on the instrument. They'd have to dig through the layers of fees and clauses to root it out."

"God damned penny shaving. But these are pretty big pennies. How on earth are these modifications getting in there?"

"I'm not sure, but look at this. The losses don't show except for hundredths of a second because an equal amount of money comes into the account."

"From where?"

"It's random. Shell-accounts, investment banks, everywhere. And that's what happens in every instance. There is a loss and nearly immediate plug of the deficit." She didn't want to say more and hoped Rosenfeld would reach the conclusion she had.

"I'll be damned. It's some sort of light-speed Ponzi-scheme."

Yes. "I think so, sir. And I think it works because of the epic nature of the worm infection. There are so many compromised accounts, tens of thousands, that the code left on the systems can continuously shuffle money, even in these increased amounts, so that for no length of time does any one account report much of a loss. It's fantastically complicated, but there is so much unregulated and unmonitored in these dark markets. I think that explains how it's gotten away with this for so long and with so much money involved."

"Just how bad is the spread?"

"I don't know for sure, but unprecedented. I couldn't believe how systematic it is. I've been using the NSA share-data on the known financial OTC trading, and I haven't found any derivative contracts of significance in the last six months that haven't been modified. It's got to total in the trillions."

"Incredible."

"And as long as the contract is viable, it's funneling the money. Untraceable. The money trail disappears in one offshore account after another."

"Like some damn invisible parasite. Thank God we have access to the OTC bids. We'd never have known. Chalk up a success story to the NSA octopus."

The woman swallowed. "Well, that may be part of the problem, sir."

The old man looked at her face and pulled a chair over. He sighed, sitting down. "I'm not going to like this, am I? Go on."

"I'm not sure yet, but there seems to be an association with the NSA data hacks and the timing of the code penetration." God, she hoped she wasn't making a fool of herself. She was prodding a dragon. She knew that.

Rosenfeld removed his glasses. "Wait. You mean that whoever is behind this might be piggy-backing on the NSA worms and backdoors?"

"I think so, sir."

"*Oy vey.*" He put a hand to his head. "This is going to explode."

Yi Ling felt her stomach churn.

After a silent moment, the old man replaced his glasses and patted her on the back. "This is incredible work. I'm going straight to Richards with this, getting this off my plate as fast as possible. We'll see how the bigwigs are going to handle it. I need you to prepare a presentation. I'm going to put you as point. This is going to bring in all the agencies and spooks. Governments are going to freak out, especially the US. We're looking at a game-changer here."

The slight Asian woman trembled with excitement. "Yes, sir. Immediately."

The old man stared grimly forward. "You might just have uncovered the biggest financial cybercrime in history."

6

"JEN, WHAT THE hell is your son doing at my computer?"

The black hair of a young boy popped up from behind a monitor, his eyes wide behind oversized glasses. Several books were positioned around him on the desk, and his hand clutched a computer mouse in an iron grip.

A red-faced man stood in the doorway to the home office, his teeth bared, high-end casual clothing draping an athletic form. A woman rushed past him into the room, placing herself between the boy and the man, hands up as if to ward off a blow.

"Now, Richard, he just wanted to try some programming. It's for his class presentation." She smiled wildly. "His will be so much better than all the other children's! He's a genius, you know!"

"A genius. Am I hearing this right?" He stepped into the room deliberately. The woman's smile faded. "Your second-grade brat is fucking up my workstation for a goddamned school project? I have trades on that machine, client information, our taxes! Important documents! Where do you think all this comes from, lady?" He gestured dramatically around the room. "Your nice clothes? Your car? That bitch therapist? Or those ritzy lunches you have with your girlfriends?"

Her shoulders slumped and she backed away from him. 'Richard, it's only—"

"How many times have we talked about this? I don't know what his father let him get away with, but the little prince has got to learn the rules around here! My desk and my things are off limits! They're not toys! Do you understand that, kid?"

"He is doing serious work, Richard!" The wild smile returned. "See? He wants to be like you. He's got your books out and he's learning to write those programs like you do! I'm so proud of him!"

"So you're defending him in spite of what I just said?"

"Yes?" she said, her face falling.

Richard lurched forward, left arm whipping across his body to backhand Jenny across the face. Her head snapped back with a crunch, and she dropped to the ground, catching herself on her palms.

"Mom!" The boy leapt up from the chair, then froze. Without turning his face away from his mother, his wide eyes darted toward the broad shape in the middle of the room. He began to shake.

Richard stared down at the crumpled form of the woman, drops of blood falling to the floor from the back of her hand, the overturned palm already filled like a bowl with a thick, crimson fluid. The anger drained from his face.

"Fuck!" he said, turning to the boy. "This is your fault, you know, you little brat. I don't want to see you touching anything of mine again without my permission, or I'll beat the shit out of you, too." He spun and stormed out of the room. "I won't be back till late. Try to clean that mess up."

There was a jangle of keys and then a door slam. The house fell silent.

"Mom," said the boy again, moving away from the desk. His hands reached out hesitantly toward her.

"No, no!" she said loudly, keeping her face angled away from him, her voice distorted, mouth full. "It's okay, pooh-bear. Don't come closer. Mommy's okay."

"Mom, your nose—"

The woman tried to stand, swayed and steadied herself on a chair nearby. Her face and shirt were stained red, her nose bent gruesomely.

"Can't get blood on his chairs," she mumbled, stumbling sideways with her hands cupped under her face. She reached the bathroom just off the office and closed the door behind her. The boy heard her retching.

For several moments he didn't move. Just faced the door of the bathroom, breathing labored, body shaking. He closed his eyes. Water ran behind the door and the sounds of muffled sobs leaked into the office space. His breathing slowed.

Exhaling, he opened his eyes. His upper lip twitched. He turned to the computer and sat down in the chair, pushing his glasses up the bridge of his nose.

Richard was too big. He knew that. He couldn't punch him the way Richard had hit his mother, not unless he wanted a worse beating. He couldn't hurt him that way. But if he didn't do something, he would hate himself forever. He knew that. He couldn't just let him get away with it. His mind raced.

His stepfather didn't like anyone to use his things. His stepfather's computer was important. *The things on the computer were* serious work. *Maybe it was true, maybe he didn't know how to code like a grown up yet. He wasn't sure. No one would teach him at school and his programs didn't always work like he wanted. He knew he needed to learn more.*

But he could delete files. He knew how to do that.

He could delete ALL his stepfather's files.

He opened a terminal window and began typing.

BEFORE:
THE ANONYMOUS EVENT COMMISSION

DEPOSITION IN THE MATTER OF:
UNITED STATES ARMED FORCES SPECIAL TRIBUNAL,
Plaintiff,
v.
JOHN SAVAS, Defendant
Case No. M120039E-007X

DEPOSITION OF:
REBECCA RUTH COHEN
called for examination by Counsel for the
Defendant, pursuant to Notice of Deposition, at
the Independent Council Offices, located at
[REDACTED] Washington, D.C.,
when were present on behalf of the
respective parties: [REDACTED]

Counsel on Behalf of Defendant (CBD): Will you
please identify yourself for the record?
MS. COHEN: Rebecca Cohen, FBI special agent,
Intel 1.

CBD: You understand that your testimony here is
on the record, and your words might later be
used to charge and try you as an enemy
combatant of the United States?
MS. COHEN: I want to petition for a civilian
lawyer and habeas corpus.

[REDACTED]: Your requests have already been
noted and processed. Until such a time as they
are ruled upon, please focus on the inquiry at
hand. Do you understand the law as it applies
to you?
MS. COHEN: I was told that this is a
deposition. Isn't it a bit unusual to have
[REDACTED] with my counsel? Cross-examination?
[REDACTED]: Please answer the question. Do you
understand the law as it applies to you?
MS. COHEN: Oh, I understand, all right. This is
a damned inquisition.

CBD: To the matter at hand, Ms. Cohen.
MS. COHEN: Do I have a choice?

CBD: There is some discrepancy about when and
how the Washington FBI divisions were informed

59

of your suspicions concerning Senator Heidi
Moss.
MS. COHEN: Clarification. By "your" you mean
Agent Savas and myself?
CBD: That is correct. Can you shed light on
this?

[REDACTED]: Enough! Damn the protocol issues.
Agent Cohen, it seems pretty clear that Intel 1
kept this information to itself for some time.
Now, when you and Savas returned from D.C.,
what were his actions at Intel 1?
MS. COHEN: We didn't have any time to do much.
All hell was starting to break loose. The virus
was already eating through the world financial
system, and the first big break on that, hell,
the discovery of it, was made in Singapore.

CBD: You knew this then?
MS. COHEN: No. But that's the timeline.
CBD: Let's stick with what you knew at the time
and how the defendant behaved.
MS. COHEN: How did he behave? We were both
exhausted from racing around trying to piece
together what the hell was happening with the
car bombing, when bam! A VIP kidnapping spree
and a fucking boat-bomb!

CBD: Wait, one thing at a-
MS. COHEN: We were hardly given a moment's rest
and then I'm racing to midtown while John and
Frank are landing back in D.C. to interface
with the local FBI divisions on the snatches
there. My work cell is firing like a
receptionist's and our division is split across
the city and between cities. Then, the next
thing you know it's the NSA on the line and-

CBD: Ms. Cohen, please! One thing at a time. We
need things to be clear.
MS. COHEN: You want clarity? You have us
isolated and jailed under military law, asking
all sorts of questions about our protocol
during those days! Protocol! You want clarity?
Try following protocol when VIPs are
disappearing and blowing up in real time around
you, when you get informed that a cyberworm is
chewing through the modern monetary system!

CBD: We understand that this was a difficult

time, Ms. Cohen, but-
MS. COHEN: You don't understand anything!
CBD: Please. I'm his counsel, I'm on your side,
here.
MS. COHEN: Are you?

CBD: All right, let's calm this down and try
again. After your return from D.C., what
happened?
MS. COHEN: What happened? Everything happened.

OCTOBER 19

7

CITIGROUP CEO MITCHELL O'Kelly glared across his desk at his chief of security. He couldn't believe they were wasting his time on this, but the directors had insisted and there was one thing even the CEO couldn't ignore, and that was the Board.

He had known Jack Craig personally, of course. They'd been sparring frenemies for their entire careers across a slew of different corporate locations. O'Kelly had always found Craig an uptight puritan who couldn't help but judge everyone else around him. But he had respected Jack. The man was a fucking genius with the nose of a shark, and you were a fool to bet against him unless you were holding one hell of a hand.

What had happened last week was indeed disturbing. Certainly O'Kelly was worried for his own safety, but the odds that this was something corporate CEOs in general were going to have to be concerned about were very low. He still didn't have a working model for who could have committed such an act—nor had law enforcement as far as he could tell—but it was most likely related to specifics of Craig's business dealings, his personal life, or a random nut job like John Hinckley or Mark Chapman. Sure, beef up the security, scramble the schedules, and then get on with business.

If only.

"Mr. O'Kelly, we have contacted a private security firm that was active in Iraq for VIPs."

"Active in *Iraq*?" This was getting ridiculous!

"Yes, sir. They have a lot of experience dealing with threats of violence against vulnerable and important targets. They are mostly former military, highly trained, experienced with this sort of thing."

"This is *Manhattan*, gentlemen, not Kabul or Baghdad. We're not going to be driving around in bombproof Humvees. Let's get a grip."

"Sir, we've been personally contacted by the Chairman. He supports our recommendations. With threats of this nature—bombings, IEDs, whatever—we need people who have clocked hours with this sort of thing. The landscape changes."

Holy shit. "What does this mean? Armored vehicles? SWAT escorts? Can I go to my son's soccer games without a parent shakedown?"

The two security men glanced at each other anxiously. The older man spoke. "We don't know yet what they will recommend, but we have scheduled a meeting with them tomorrow, first thing in the morning. They're eager to find work in the States, sir."

"I'm sure they are."

"We'll get recommendations and then brief you and schedule a second meeting all together to iron out a course of action."

Ah, to hell with it. "Fine. Do what you need to do. Now, out. This nonsense has taken enough of my time today."

The two men excused themselves with apologies and quickly exited the CEO's office. O'Kelly swiveled his chair away from the closing door and glared up at the dim ceiling of the executive suite. The second floor design hadn't been renovated for years and still possessed the wood and metal, mirrors and leather sensibility of a previous era of financial power. He found the stately atmosphere helped clear his mind, focus his thoughts on the tasks at hand.

His cell phone rang. He scanned the caller ID.

Franklin?

His son had grown up with a special rule in the house: Dad isn't to be bothered during the work day unless it's an emergency. In sixteen years he had never called. Not once. Not during his parents divorce. Not even when he had smashed his first BMW on the Long Island Expressway. Why was he calling now?

"Franklin, what's going on?"

A harsh voice cut through the speaker. "We have your son, O'Kelly. Don't do anything rash, anything stupid, or we will not hesitate to kill him."

O'Kelly jerked upward and stood at attention, his gaze wild. "Who is this?"

"You know what we did to your partner in crime, Jack Craig. We blew him to bits. His bones litter the streets of this city, one of many he robbed for so many years. We will do much worse to your brat if you do not follow our instructions to the letter."

His pulse racing, sweat building on his brow, O'Kelly paced the plush floors of the executive suite in panic. "How do I know—"

"Dad?"

It was Franklin. O'Kelly closed his eyes.

"Dad, God, please. They're not kidding." He seemed to be choking up. "They *killed* Coach Larsen. Shot him. *Dead!* It's my fault, Dad! He was just trying to—"

Abruptly his son's voice was cut off.

"Convincing enough for you?"

"Yes," he whispered, his mind racing for solutions. He walked to his desk and the red panic button.

"You have two choices, O'Kelly. The first is that you kill you son by calling the cops, the Feds, your new military men," said the harsh voice.

"How do you know—"

"*Or*, you act normally, alert no one, and do exactly what we say. You have no guarantees from us except that we will kill him. I think you know we are willing. But we don't give a damn about your son. Only about *you*."

A voice cried from the background.

"Dad! No, don't—"

O'Kelly heard a slap, then silence.

"We are more than willing to let your spawn escape to gain increased cooperation from you. Because we have a special use for you. And you will be helpful to us because you know that your son will never be safe."

"What do you want?"

"There will be no ransom. There will be no stalling. There is a black SUV waiting below on Park Avenue. If you are not in that vehicle in five minutes, your son dies. You are to come down from your second-floor perch. Do not bring your armed muscle."

"They will follow me once they see I'm leaving."

"Make sure you get outside. Then whatever happens, do not pause, do not stop, do not seek to do anything except find your way to that vehicle. Do you understand?"

Thoughts and scenarios flew through his mind, options and risks and assessments that could not be made with any confidence without data, without time.

"This is not something the both of you are going to get out of, O'Kelly. Make your choice: your life or your son's. In four minutes, a decision will be made one way or the other."

The connection was broken.

Mitchell O'Kelly did not hesitate. He had been presented with an impossible choice, and he didn't need any more deliberation to make his decision.

Outwardly calm, he walked quickly out of his office and down the hall. Luckily the ground floor was only two flights down, otherwise there would be no chance to escape without being closely followed. Completely contrary to habit, he entered the stairway to the surprised expressions of the secretaries and leapt down the steps in painful bounds. His aging frame wasn't up to this sort of shock, but it seemed likely he would soon have more serious concerns.

The CEO of Citigroup burst out from the lobby stairwell and walked like a man possessed toward the main entrance. He was not spotted until he had crossed nearly two-thirds of the distance. Shouts came from the voices of his security team, and his peripheral vision sensed several shapes converging from behind. They would reach him in seconds.

He was through the doorway, the sunlight of the clear October day blinding him momentarily, his eyes squinting desperately to find the black SUV.

There. Blackened windows hid the occupants. O'Kelly surrendered all pretense of casualness and sprinted toward the truck.

"Mr. O'Kelly!"

His bodyguards cried behind him. The men were under the strictest orders. They would have him in their arms within seconds for this dangerous breach of protocol, especially after recent events. The black vehicle was still fifty yards away. He'd never make it.

Hornets buzzed past his head. There were screams. He heard bodies fall heavily to the ground. He didn't look back. He ran harder, the back door of the SUV opening, arms grabbing his, pulling him in violently. The vehicle lurched forward with screeching tires and he was thrown backward into a seat.

But he had seen. In a split second upon entering the truck and turning his head toward the plaza in front of the building, it was all too clear.

The fiends had shot and killed the men that had been charged to protect him. Their bodies were strewn across the cement and steps, people racing in panic away from the scene.

O'Kelly closed his eyes. God only knew what they were going to do to him.

8

REBECCA COHEN SAT in the back of the FBI vehicle, nearly sick from the lurching dash through traffic. Staring at the choppy video feed on her phone was surely not helping the situation. They should have just called. But they needed to see each other.

"On the tarmac, Rebecca," said a pixelated Savas, his phrases peppered with staccato pauses. "This is getting a bit insane."

They had not been back a day before the next crisis had pulled them apart again. This time it was sudden disappearances of important people both in New York and in Washington. Congressman, aides, more CEOs, workers at the Federal Reserve Board. Whatever theories they had before were jettisoned. Whatever was going on, it was highly coordinated and professionally implemented.

"Feels like we're back under siege from Mjolnir," she said to the frozen face of Savas. "John?"

There was a pause, and then the connection reestablished. "Lost most of that except for Thor's Hammer. But I think I know what you were saying."

They had split their team at Intel 1. Savas had taken ex-Marine Frank Miller with him to DC. They would soon be on their way to the Capitol. Cohen had called another agent on their team, JP Rideout, and they were going to meet at the headquarters of Citigroup. The other cases were reported disappearances, no shows and quiet vanishings. But not at Citi. There were witnesses. There were bodies. There had been a failed pursuit by NYPD.

The sedan jerked to a stop and Cohen dropped the phone, the connection with Savas lost. She quickly texted him that she had arrived and would talk to him later. He would soon be busy as well.

The driver opened the door for her and she stepped out quickly, heading for the crowd of police and decorations of yellow tape in front of the building. The glass and steel structure towered above her. Horns blared like a strong wind from the snarled traffic of rubberneckers. *Here to see the bloodbath.* She counted four bodies.

Two were near the exits, and two had moved toward Park Avenue before they were cut down. A black NYPD detective met her.

"Agent Cohen?" he asked. "I'm Tyrell Sacker. You're it for the Feds?"

"No, we have a crime group en route and another special agent from my division."

"Which is?"

"Intel 1."

The cops eyes opened wider. "Well, we need the best. Reports are coming in from all over the city. The radio's total chaos."

"I know. Look, we're going to go through this thoroughly, but can you tell me what you've put together? Is there enough for a summary?"

Sacker nodded. "A crowd of witnesses, and security cams to go back to and verify. But it still doesn't make sense, even if the testimony agrees so far. Their CEO literally comes sprinting out of the building, ignoring the calls of his security team, running straight for a van or SUV. He was scheduled for meetings all day and was already late for one in the building. It's like he went nuts. His team bolted after him, and, well, you can see what happened to them."

"Shots came from the vehicle?"

"Doesn't seem so. None of the witnesses reported seeing anything in the truck but some dark figures pulling O'Kelly inside. The shots were professional, agent Cohen," Sacker said, looking back toward the bodies. "No evidence of misses. I mean, how often does that happen? I'd bet there were gunman positioned and waiting."

"We'll have our ballistics teams here soon, and we'll need to get all the CCTV footage from all security cameras in the area."

"On that. I'm point for this scene, so you'll be talking to me."

Cohen smiled. She liked Sacker immediately. He was gritty yet polite, sharp with an underlying empathic feel. She hoped that she could trust him.

"All right, we'll work out the coordination of this investigation soon. For now, take me up to the crime scene. I want to get a look at the victims."

The Capitol Police officers glared at the hulking form of Frank Miller with suspicion. Savas stood with him before the grand entrance of the Russell Senate Office Building. The stately marble, lofted steps, and the presence of twenty to thirty uniformed officers in combat gear sporting military-grade automatic weapons made an undeniable impression. He was as polite as possible.

"Yes, special agents Savas and Miller. These are our IDs. We're en route from New York because of an apparent coordinated abduction connected to those here."

A nervous officer stood several steps above them. "We have explicit instructions not to allow anyone except approved law enforcement officers into the building."

"We *are* approved law enforcement officers!" growled Miller. "We're here *by request* of the agency acting on orders from the fucking president! The little headsets you're wearing with mics—try them out and contact your damn superiors."

Several weapons were pointed their way.

Miller was losing his temper, as he tended to do. A decorated former soldier, he had been shot twice saving Savas' life in the line of duty as an FBI agent. He didn't suffer fools well, and there wasn't much that scared the man. Which is what frightened Savas.

"Okay, Frank, let's just back off and wait for the red tape to unspool. There's a lot of tension right now. We're all on the same side."

They returned to their car and waited out the next half hour. Evening began to fall, and the streets were a ghost town. The Capitol had been completely locked down.

The wall of police opened and a figure in a suit shuffled down the steps. Savas immediately recognized him—Tim Cox, Assistant Director in Charge, a lanky, bespectacled man and former Secret Service agent. The local branch had brought in the big guns on this scene. People were shook up.

"Agent Savas," said Cox extending his hand with a surprisingly strong grip. "Your reputation precedes you of course, but you're a long way from home."

"Things are moving very fast, sir, and there hasn't been time to coordinate investigations. But the murder of Goldman CEO Jack Craig may be tied in some fashion to Senator Heidi Moss."

The Assistant Director squinted. "How so?"

"His last phone calls, minutes before his death, were to her. We paid her a visit and while nothing concrete came up, it was clear that she was under some sort of threat of some kind."

"And you did not bring this to the attention of my office, because?"

Great. Miller glanced at him and Savas tried hard to ignore it. "It was a hunch, sir. And if not for the kidnappings of other CEOs and members of Congress today, it would have remained a completely unsubstantiated hunch. We can't bother you with every possible idea."

"Still, Savas, this is our turf. Let us decide what is worthy of our attention."

"Point taken, Assistant Director." Savas hoped they would be cooperative. "As you know, we have multiple events in New York, some still coming in as people are reported missing. I'm back here to begin coordinating with you on this seemingly related set of disappearances."

Cox nodded. "It's unprecedented. We have three missing Congressman, a high-level official at the Securities and Exchange Commission, and just as of ten minutes ago, it seems that the head of the Federal Reserve did not get off her plane at Reagan National."

"Louise Lelann?"

Cox sighed. "So now you see the magnitude of this. Homeland Security is descending like a storm cloud, as if they didn't eat up enough of our departments already. We're on lockdown, the president's day has been scrambled. I'm not sure who knows where he is. It feels like a terrorist attack."

"I think it is," said Miller.

"Well, then you folks are the right ones for the job."

"There's no one claiming responsibility? No ransom demands? Anything?"

Cox shook his head. "Nothing. But the game is still early. It's certainly different than anything before. The murder of Craig—it could have been anything. But it was *murder*. A car bomb. A terrorist-y thing. Abductions of state officials? Corporate CEOs? What the hell is the play here?"

Savas looked at Miller and back to Cox, the cold night air bringing more of a chill than was warranted.

"I'm sorry to say, Assistant Director, I have no idea."

9

"SENATOR, MR. AVRAM'S yacht is probably the *safest* place you can be today," said a gorgeous blonde hanging on the old man's arm. She turned toward him conspiratorially, whispering in his ear. "They say it even has a radar system to detect missiles." The senator reddened as her ruby lips brushed his earlobe.

The boat carved its way through New York harbor like a titan. Nebula was the world's most expensive privately owned yacht, three years in the making and boasting a pool studded with Havana bars, a helipad, five water jets, a cinema, and a four thousand square foot master suite. Nine decks, each with entry and exit points, rose from the waterline and gave the vessel more the appearance of an aerodynamic condo than a private cruise boat.

"Truly," came the deep voice of Robert Avram, "she's the safest boat in the waters today."

They stood on the upper deck, lower Manhattan a frozen collection of ten thousand Will-o'-the-wisps of skyscrapers, apartments, and bridge lights. A full moon rose into the night sky and painted the gleaming surfaces on the yacht in luminescent hues. The blonde escort smiled broadly at the CEO, her sequined dress a light show reflecting the moonlight, the plunge of her neckline scandalous. Soft jazz floated on the crisp air from below.

"I hope so," said the senator, vacillating between the seduction hanging on his arm and a set of internal worries that he could not completely dismiss. "I'm actually scared to go home tonight. People have disappeared from their own houses!"

The woman purred. "Maybe you don't have to go home tonight."

Avram smirked and left the pair to their courting dance. He had no doubts the woman would be in the old fool's bed this evening. He had hired the cream of the crop. And he had made sure that useful photos would be taken discretely at opportune moments. Robert Avram ran his business like an old Mafia boss, and he was proud of that fact.

Stepping down the stairway toward the floor below, he felt a buzz in his shirt pocket. He removed his phone and answered. Almost immediately his face turned ashen.

"You can't be serious?" He closed his mouth quickly, glancing around the harbor in panic. "Yes, I'm listening." His eyes widened as a man's voice spoke on the other end. "You want me to what? This is crazy! Why should I—"

At that moment, a light flashed above him. A second later the event repeated. "Yes, I see it. No, you're right. Our radar can't detect objects that small. Yes. I see. Yes, of course you are." He looked down to the guests mingling below. "Can I at least warn the others?"

His face grimaced as he placed the phone in his shirt pocket again. His hands gripped the railing tightly, and he breathed in and out slowly several times. *This is not happening.*

But it was. And he had been told he had little time. He rushed down the stairway. Several people approached him, but he ignored them, darting into the heart of the vessel. Forgoing the crowded stairways, he would avoid being seen this way. No one would bother him, ask questions. He would not have to think about what was happening. He pressed his thumb to the scanner by the elevator.

The doors opened immediately. He entered and hit the button to the sea-level floor. The elevator descended, the doors opened, and he dashed toward the back of the vessel.

The area was empty, all the guests and staff concentrated on decks above with better views of the harbor. Avram removed his jacket and tie, kicking off his shoes and socks as well. He dropped his phone and Rolex on the deck beside a railing at the stern of the Nebula, the engines below softly churning the dark waters.

He gazed back at the boat. He had never been in love. He appreciated women, their beauty, enjoyed sex. But *love?* He hadn't been raised on love. But the Nebula—that was a beauty to be loved. His design, his testament to everything he had accomplished and would do. He stared at it as a man would a lover on her death bed.

Then he climbed the railing, standing unbalanced at the corner of the stern, as far from the engines as possible. The lights of New Jersey and Manhattan formed a dizzying panorama of radiance around him. Placing his hands out to the sides, he leapt forcefully into the darkness.

The harbor was frigid, and he gasped for air as he struggled to tread water. Fortunately he had been a talented swimmer at Harvard, and despite the numbness creeping over his limbs, he was able to orient himself onto his back, his feet pointed back toward the Nebula, its music and soft lights fading as it sped away from him. A minute passed. Then two, and he worked to keep his arms and legs moving, the circulation flowing, retarding the hypothermia that had begun to freeze his muscles.

What sounded like a series of humming hornets' nests streaked over his head and toward the boat. He spied small shadows cross over the lights of lower Manhattan, but he could not be sure it was anything more than his imagination.

But then the Nebula erupted in flame. A series of fireballs ignited around the boat, consuming his lady in a hideous light. The sound rushed over him, one-two-three punches of compressed air and ear-splitting detonations. Burning debris flew into the sky, then rained back down on the dimming skeleton of the boat.

Robert Avram wept. He knew in that explosion he had lost not only the symbol of his greatness, but everything. Confirmation arrived with little delay as he felt hands grasp his shoulders and lift him out of the water, dumping him harshly onto the deck of a small motorboat. Burly shadows manhandled him like livestock, binding his arms and legs, toting him to one end of the vessel, and casting him painfully into a corner. His captors revved the engine, and turned the boat southward toward Staten Island, racing into the darkness.

OCTOBER 20

10

SAVAS WATCHED THE faint light of the morning grow over the East River. He sped down the FDR en route from La Guardia airport in an FBI vehicle, retracing part of the path Goldman CEO Craig had taken right before he died. The lights of the Queensboro Bridge were still bright enough to be easily seen in the creeping dawn, the tram lifting sleepy commuters into Manhattan from Roosevelt Island like a floating cabin in the sky. To his right, the concrete redwoods of the city flew by him with trails of light.

He was hardly awake himself. Last night an explosion had occurred in New York Harbor, before the eyes of Lady Liberty herself. Another CEO of a powerful multinational financial company was dead, his luxury liner blown to pieces where the fresh water of the Hudson mixed with the sea. The agency branches in Washington could work on their disappearing governmental employee problem themselves. New York, *his* city, was under siege again.

He had spent the better part of a night arranging his travel and for Frank Miller to stay in DC to coordinate between the coupled investigations. An early plane landed him in New York with the first businessmen. His driver flew down the East Side highway, traffic still minimal at this hour, their destination lower Manhattan. Cohen was waiting for him there.

The thin tower of the UN building darted past on the right, the reddening sky casting an infernal hue across its glass facade. For Savas, it seemed prescient, foreboding. His instincts told him that something subterranean and evil was brewing. He only hoped that they could find a break in their endless game of catchup with these dark forces and find a way to prevent further attacks.

The car passed NYU Medical Center and soon entered lower Manhattan. Lost in his own ruminations, he failed to notice as they darted into the Battery Park Underpass and emerged on the western tip of the island. He was surprised to sense the car slowing as it pulled into North Cove Marina.

Cohen was immediately at his side as he stepped out of the

vehicle.

"God, John, you look like crap."

He laughed and fingered the lapel of her coat. "Always good to be home." They walked toward the dock and the Coast Guard boat waiting there. "We've lost three CEOs in a week."

"There's still no claim for the attacks or abductions. The JP Morgan CEO, Robert Avram, is presumed dead, although his body hasn't been found. Most of the bodies on the ship manifest haven't been found."

"But Senator McDougal?" He asked. "I heard that he was found."

"Confirmed an hour ago at the morgue."

"*Jesus*. I've heard talk of the National Guard, although I can't imagine what good it would do outside of giving the public and news shows some sense that we aren't sitting here helpless."

"But we are, John."

They neared the boat and several members of the Coast Guard approached them. He gritted his teeth. "Let's see if we can change that. Gentlemen!" They walked forward and shook hands. "Agents Savas and Cohen."

"You're the man who took down Gunn," said one of the sailors. "Honored to meet you, sir. I know about your son. I was here on 9/11, evacuating folks trapped on the south end after the towers fell."

Savas swallowed. "Then *I'm* honored. You guys moved more than half a million, if I remember right."

"Maybe more. Papers said it was bigger than Dunkirk in WWII. Somehow feels like we're always at war."

Savas understood completely. "Let's get out there and see what we can see."

They stepped onto the boat, the sailor gave instructions, and they pushed off from shore. "We towed it to Governors Island. Used to be a Coast Guard base. Boat was sinking, even with all the technology built into it to prevent that. I read up on it. The owner was a paranoid son-of-a-bitch."

Within minutes they had arrived on the small island. The wreckage of what had once been a luxury yacht was awkwardly tethered to the dock, wisps of smoke still trailing upwards from her, the smell of melted plastic overpowering. It was obvious why no one had survived.

Police and fire crews worked with investigators combing the remainder of the vessel. A sharply dressed man, attired in a suit, with black hair and a French nose walked up to the FBI agents.

"JP," said Savas. "What do we have?"

Rideout squinted in the light of the rising sun. "Well, this is big league forensics. Half the evidence is at the bottom of the harbor. But from what we've found and working with witnesses on shore and in other boats who saw the explosion, we're talking about multiple detonations spaced a few seconds apart. Odd for a bomb planted on the boat, but there you go. The fireball was hot enough that we can assume synthetics and a big payload. But it will take some time to analyze the residue and debris." He indicated a small boat pulling out nearby. "We're still relocating the bodies, the remains. It will take some time to identify them all. In some cases DNA matching might be the only way—there isn't much left to go on. NYPD and several university labs with the required equipment are pitching in. Avram threw a big party."

Savas shook his head. "Grim work."

Cohen shuddered and rubbed her hands together in the morning chill. "You said multiple blasts. Could it have been explosives delivered externally?"

Rideout nodded. "Drone idea again? I think it's likely. Missiles are out, as crazy as it is to even say something like that. Avram had a pretty sophisticated radar system that not only detected incoming birds but automatically would send the data out encrypted on military and police frequencies. I guess he had some issues, but the fact is that the boat didn't squeak last night. But I don't think it could pick up fliers as small as many drones. They'd be invisible to the radar."

"I guess he didn't modernize his paranoia," said Cohen. "Who would have thought to protect their assets from drone strikes?"

"Why aren't there more agents here?" asked Savas, glancing around the dock.

"It's a bit chaotic," said Rideout, "and you've been in transit for the last two days. Commands from on high have all agencies scrambling to put bodies on people and places. The Bureau is like a ghost ship, if you'll excuse the juxtaposition."

Cohen turned to Savas. "It's all been in the last twelve hours. The kidnappings and killings have a lot of powerful people very frightened. Pressure is being put on all governmental and state agencies to secure them. Favors are being called in. People are starting to panic."

Savas nodded. "Should have seen it coming. You'll have to excuse me—I'm running on about negative three hours of sleep. Hopefully I can get some shuteye soon, that is if nothing else goes FUBAR in the next few hours."

His cell rang.

Rideout and Cohen stared at him. He just sighed. "Here we go." He tapped the screen and placed the phone to his ear. "Hi, Angel. What blew up now?"

BEFORE:
THE ANONYMOUS EVENT COMMISSION

DEPOSITION IN THE MATTER OF:
UNITED STATES ARMED FORCES SPECIAL TRIBUNAL,
Plaintiff,
v.
JOHN SAVAS, Defendant
Case No. M120039E-007X

Continued DEPOSITION OF:
JEAN PAUL RIDEOUT

MR. RIDEOUT: John had just flown back. He and Rebecca met me at the dock and we got our first look at the boat. What remained of it.

[REDACTED]: Is this when Agent Lightfoote became involved in the investigation?
MR. RIDEOUT: Angel? No.
[REDACTED]: Statements from other members of your division state that she was.
MR. RIDEOUT: Why would she be involved in the bombing case? She was cybercrimes.

CBD: But she called at the dock? We have cell phone records and the testimony of Agent Cohen.
MR. RIDEOUT: Yeah, she called. So what? The virus was completely unknown to us at that point. Angel didn't know why they were calling. She took the call and passed the message on to John.

CBD: Is that normal?
MR. RIDEOUT: NSA called. She's cybercrimes. What's the mystery?

CBD: But Savas took her along with him to the meeting?
MR. RIDEOUT: Of course. Again, she's *cybercrimes*. Why wouldn't she go?

[REDACTED]: But you said you didn't know about the virus.
MR. RIDEOUT: That's what the NSA meeting was about! So, no!
[REDACTED]: So, why bring your cybercrimes leader?
MR. RIDEOUT: Because NSA, duh? Angel is our

87

digital guru. We're retreading this thing like you've never heard of a circle.

[REDACTED]: And now she's AWOL.
MR. RIDEOUT: AWOL? What the hell? She's not conscripted! She doesn't owe you guys anything. Just because your goons failed to grab her doesn't mean she's up to anything bad. If I hadn't been shot, I might be out there with her, deep in hiding from this mess.
[REDACTED]: She's breaking the law.
MR. RIDEOUT: Not any laws I know about. But you all have new laws now, don't you? Just making them up as you go. Christ, I had a bad feeling when martial law was declared. Little did I know!

[REDACTED]: There have been extraordinary events. Unprecedented threats to the nation. We are doing what we can to preserve order.
MR. RIDEOUT: Don't you think I know that? But you're shooting at friendlies, dammit!

CBD: Then you can understand our need to get to the bottom of things. Tell us about Lightfoote.
MR. RIDEOUT: Why are you so obsessed with her? Don't you have one hundred dossiers and film surveillance and case records? What the hell am I going to tell you that you don't know?

[REDACTED]: How about where she is?
MR. RIDEOUT: If I knew, that'd be the last thing I'd tell you.

11

"Joe, Jesus, it's the middle of the trading day. What the hell is this about?"

Two men huddled underneath a pedestrian walkway in a quiet London park. They had both approached the location independently, secretively, without informing anyone of their destination. Both had exercised extreme vigilance in their journey, checking for pursuit or other surveillance, doubling back and changing routes several times, increasing by three-fold the amount of time it would take to reach the rendezvous. One man was dressed in a suit and sported closely cropped gray hair. The other, a younger man by two decades, wore slacks and a button down shirt as well as sunglasses. Both appeared anxious, their British accents cutting like daggers through the conversation.

"I'm taking a huge risk even showing up here," said the young man.

"And I'm not? Spit it out. Is it this virus you've been talking about?"

"Worm," he corrected.

"Whatever."

"The difference is important."

"That's because you're a computer programmer."

He shook his head. "It *matters*. Look, a virus is a file, you have to execute it, infect your computer with it. A worm digs in by itself, and can lay a lot of viral eggs and do other things. But it spreads itself. This worm is spreading *everywhere*."

"What's everywhere?"

The programmer's arms danced through the air. "By now, half the machines on the London exchange are likely infected. By next week, nearly all of them will be."

The older man straightened slightly. "What will it do?"

"We don't know!" he shouted, quickly catching himself and lowering his voice. "Look, my division at Interpol got the first information from Singapore a few days ago. Since then, all hell's broken loose. We're finding it everywhere, chasing it everywhere. No one has a handle on it, not the Americans, the Chinese, or the Russians. Hell, if the Russians can't take it down, we're in a fucking boatload of trouble!"

"Brilliant. Let's calm down. What do you know?"

The Interpol programmer wiped his brow, sweat glistening and beginning to pool in his eyebrows despite the cool autumn day. "It's global. Initially we thought that it was only a finance worm, now we're finding it other places. It actually seems to have used NSA backdoors and code as gateways to infiltrate the machines the damn Americans were already spying on. It hides well. We mainly find what it leaves behind."

"Which is?"

"Lots of really nasty code. The thing is injecting subroutines and entire programs into existing software or between two pieces of software and handshaking them. Gave itself away when large sums of money started to funnel through the infected systems into offshore accounts."

"How much money?"

"I don't know. Billions. Maybe more. But that's one thing. Billions from the derivative market isn't going to be missed, really. But recent findings are looking a lot more scary. Your machines, your trading algorithms that run the damn exchanges, they are all compromised."

The older man narrowed his eyes harshly. "Compromised? How?"

"We're still trying to figure that out! We'd need full access to your machines, *today*, to get to the meat of it quickly. We can't lock this down with you running the programs. You're going to have to halt trading."

"Out of the question! We aren't going to shut down the London Exchange so Interpol can go rummaging through our systems."

"You don't get it! This is preliminary, but if it's verified, if what we're seeing is real or even looks like it might harm the exchanges, Downing will pull the plug on the exchanges anyway! A stop in trading on purpose is better than a system meltdown."

"There isn't going to be a system meltdown!"

"We don't know *what's* going to happen."

"Every few years you fools cry wolf over some Millennium bug, Heartbleed this, or Shellshock that, and all manner of bloody apocalypse is about to descend on us. Every time the markets kept going just fine and the only thing hurt has been your reputations."

"You know, most of the time the money you guys send my way is all I need for motivation to talk to you. And I've more than paid for myself in the information I've delivered. But this is *different!* I'm scared shitless right now by this thing, and so are half the people in my division. The Americans are scrambling and the Asian markets as well."

"And I don't see them shutting down in panic, do you?" The programmer said nothing, but stared toward the other end of the tunnel, exhaling a cloud of vapor. "Look, we'll do a complete IT sweep, antivirus everything. We've handled these types of things before."

"I'm telling you, this isn't like—"

"Bring me back something *concrete*, with concrete effects and predictions, and then I can make a financial assessment of how much is to be lost from the thing as compared to the absolutely huge losses that we'll be *sure* to take for shutting down the exchange. *Shut down* is the panic button. The fail-safe. Bring me real data, not doomsday maybes. Understand?" He fired a harsh gaze toward the programmer and stormed off into the park.

The man remaining in the tunnel shook his head and lit a cigarette. He smoked it under the walkway for several minutes before leaving, spacing his exit with that of his contact at the exchange. He also needed to clear his head and calm down. It was always like this, he told himself. Investors had profit on the brain and a foresight of a goldfish. All that mattered were next quarter's returns.

I could be wrong. The truth was that they really didn't know what this thing was yet or what it would do. He *hoped* they were all wrong about the dangers. He dropped the bud on the concrete and crushed it out with his shoe, turning up his lapels and entering the chaos of children's shouts.

———————

A boy stared toward the man as he exited, his gaze focused slightly above him and the bridge under which he had stood for the last half hour. He tugged on his mother's arm and pointed into the sky. A small, blurred ball danced in the air above the park.

"Look, mummy. It's a helicopter! It's remote control!"

His mother nodded her head and tapped onto her smartphone. "Yes, dear, that's nice."

The boy continued tracking the object as it moved away from the bridge. "Herman has one. It's wicked. It can do anything and...oh no!"

"What is it, dear?" his mother asked, her eyes never leaving the screen in her hand.

"It's just going up and up. It's too high!" He looked frantically around the park for the child who was trying to control it. His face dropped. "It's going to be lost."

And soon enough it was. The small object disappeared from view as it ascended into the sky. It did not return. The boy continued to look around the park, but there were no children in distress or racing after an out-of-control toy. His shoulders sank and he dug into the soil with his shoe.

The woman looked up from her phone. "What was that you said, dear?"

12

"SO IT SEEMS the internet is going to blow up."

Savas sat in front of a table in the computer science department at NYU. The academic setting was made all the more surreal by the presence of NSA staff, Interpol officers, and members of the Secret Service alongside several professors and students.

The NSA man tried again to assume command of the conversation. "That's a rather dramatic way to put it, Agent Savas." The representative of the agency was stiff in his gray suit, looking down his nose at the students and especially Lightfoote. However galling, Savas had to admit, she looked the part of a freedom fighter from some post-apocalyptic dystopian teen film. Eyes tended to wander toward her.

Savas was still trying to parse the odd collection of people around him. The NYU students had stumbled upon something. Fine. They had called, of all places, specific *NSA branches*. Why? Because along with Homeland Security, the NSA was funding their research. They were a "National Center of Academic Excellence in Information Assurance and Cyber Defense." *Information Assurance.* He liked that.

Then there was the presence of the Secret Service which had been explained by the financial end of this story. Yes, Agent Savas *was* aware that the Secret Service was responsible for investigations into financial fraud, in addition to its protective function for governmental VIPs. *But still.*

Finally, *Interpol!* But that is where things really got interesting and expanded from a local to a distinctly global problem. In fact, it was the Interpol officer who cut in on the NSA suit.

"Drama, Mr. Teller, may in fact be warranted here." His thick Scottish brogue worked as an aural spotlight. "Our offices in Singapore have this worm penetrating systems all over the world, including major financial institutions and governmental entities. We believe upwards of ninety percent of machines exposed to it are vulnerable."

The NSA man cut in quickly. "There hasn't been time to ascertain how widespread it is."

"With all due respect, I think the NSA has a lot of reasons to minimize the threat of this code." The Interpol and NSA representatives stared each other down.

Savas leaned forward toward the European. "Why is that?"

"Because the worm has gotten the most mileage out of piggy-backing on the NSA's own spyware—*their* worms—used for hacking and stealing the secrets of everyone from the UN to foreign leaders. And don't even try to deny your agency's actions," he said, cutting off an attempted protest by Teller. "Snowden let that cat out of the bag a while ago."

The Secret Service agent spoke. "It's a financial instrument," she said. "Once into the system, there are a set of specific programs it looks for. When it finds them, it adds modules of code that relate to options trading on the derivative market."

"What does this code do?" asked Savas.

The Interpol officer spoke. "From what we can tell, it's funneling enormous sums of money from the off-market derivatives trading."

"Off-market?"

"Yes," he continued. "Contracts, *bets* if you will, that do not show up on any exchanges and are poorly regulated. In fact, we don't even know how much money is tied up in those deals. But it dwarfs the imagination. Estimates are in the hundreds of trillions of dollars."

Savas tried not to let his jaw drop. "I didn't know that much money even existed in the world."

"It's all in bits and bytes, not in gold or cash," said Lightfoote.

"Virtual money that isn't so virtual." Savas leaned back in his chair. "And how much money is being stolen?"

A white-haired professor from the computer science group flipped pages on a notepad. "We've been following the thing for three days now. There's no way to know how much was siphoned before that, but our estimates are in the hundreds of millions of dollars."

"That's a hell of a lot."

"Per *day*."

A silence filled the room. Savas looked at Lightfoote, who just laughed.

"Does you intern think something is funny, agent Savas?" asked

Teller.

Lightfoote spoke for herself. "You *idiots*. Did you ever stop to think that if it was so easy for you to tear through the world's firewalls that others couldn't? Did you stop to think how fragile everything is now, everything online, everything in bytes—money, electricity, nuclear power systems? And now someone is using your own black hat code to leech from an underground financial market that should have been shut down after 2008? You're like a bunch of fucking twelve-year-olds wandering around an arms factory and pushing buttons."

"Your division has been included in this briefing because of your track record, Agent Savas," said the NSA official, "but the disrespect and frankly treasonous attitude of your staff cannot be tolerated."

"Are you insane?" asked the Interpol officer. "This is not a US governmental matter only. You aren't in authority here, whatever God-complex your organization has developed. The lady is right. This is *big*. This is a disaster!"

"Look, people," said Savas, standing up. "I'm inclined to agree with that assessment, and I thank you for including us in this briefing. Our team will get to it immediately. Anything we find with we'll pass your way. But, you may have noticed that we have our plate full right now. Matters of life and death, not just money and taxes. Our resources are stretched to the breaking point." He turned to the Scot. "This is a big threat. We'll help, but we're going put out the fire in our house, first." He turned to leave.

"We need countermeasures," said Lightfoote. Eyes turned toward her. "This is something new. Something truly dangerous. You can't just rely on the software companies to develop and issue patches. There isn't time."

"What do you mean there isn't time?" said Teller.

"I mean that whoever is behind this is not playing for a criminal unit or nation-state. Those groups have long-term ends in mind, stability of the system. You can't make a living off the system as a criminal if you bring it down."

"The *system*, whatever that might be, isn't going down!" Teller looked incredulous.

"That's where you're wrong." Her green eyes burned. "This is major artery damage. You can't wait to patch it. The patient will bleed to death. Organ systems will malfunction. You've got to go in aggressively and root the damn thing out. If you don't, at the rates the professor mentions, come November you're going to have an economic *catastrophe* on your hands."

13

A FOUR-BY-five panel of giant flat-screen monitors covered a wall in a dark room. News stations spanning the content of the major networks to cable providers flashed a diversity of images. One by one, sound was associated with a given monitor and channel, large speakers on the sides of the array of screens projecting audio, the brightness on the other nineteen monitors dropping dramatically to emphasize the featured screen. Centered before the dizzying display was a lone chair containing a shadowed figure.

"This is Monica Grayford from CNN," began the short-haired brunette standing before the Capitol building in Washington, DC. "Chaos has swept over the House of Representatives as a rebellion in the GOP threatens to bring the legislative branch to a standstill. Key members of House committees have suddenly switched their votes on multiple issues central to several pressing pieces of legislation. Among them are a host of financial reform bills including raising the marginal tax rate on the wealthiest Americans, legislation to remove corporate tax loopholes, and challenges to overturn the Supreme Court rulings on campaign finance reform and the personhood of corporations. In addition, numerous laws aiming to regulate the internet have found their support shifting dramatically, with numerous Democratic and Republican Congressman now supporting net neutrality and opposing governmental regulation and internet monitoring. For more on this developing story, we go to—"

The screen dimmed and the audio cutoff. A monitor on the upper right brightened, and a panel of men and women on Fox News were yelling at each other across a common table. A stout man in a suit centered in the middle screamed over the group.

"None of these theories makes sense! With elections nearly here, you aren't going to see members of both parties suddenly reversing their long-held positions on important issues! I think that we need to step back and ask what is really going on here. What backroom deals are being made and has the White House been involved to try and throw the results in November into chaos? We all know the polls show that the midterms are not going to go their way, so they have to be involved!"

A woman near the end of the table on the left cut in. "Based on what? Why do you always have to turn everything into a conspiracy of foul play by this administration?"

A black man near the center raised his hands in the air. "This is all speculation at this point. We don't know what is going on. Neither do the leaders of *either* party. Until we can get explanations from the members of Congress themselves, all this is just hot air."

The viewpoint shifted, jumping to a monitor on the lower level in the middle of the array. A heavyset man in a suit with gray hair paced about a television stage, waving his arms and gesticulating. Behind him was an enormous chalkboard, names of important political figures and organizations written and boxed in various locations, numerous arrows studded with short phrases and comments connecting the various names. The commentator was shouting.

"A Democratic Super PAC with ties to a billionaire is suddenly bankrupt? Why? Where did all that money go? A week later, we find one member of Congress after another switching their votes, always in the direction of the liberal agenda. Always decreasing our ability to monitor communications for terrorist activity and attacking the earnings of the job-creating class. Am I the only one seeing this? I mean, could it be more obvious? My fellow Americans, we are poised on the edge of a terrible cliff, where the terrorist sympathizing, Marxist left-wing agenda has put our very freedoms in the crosshairs." His voice caught, and he wiped his eyes. "There might not be much more time. I don't know how many times I'll be allowed to address you when the new world order is imposed. I've never said this before, but I'm scared. Scared for America. Scared for the world. Because, in the end, it is we Americans that stand between order and chaos on this planet."

The image and sound jumped to the upper left of the screens, a dour, bald man centered in the camera before a microphone. A woman's voice spoke over the images.

"The Russian president has just begun a press conference. This is Russia Today with an exclusive video feed of the event called in response to reported violations of international treaties this week by the US Congress."

The sound switched to the figure behind the podium. An angry voice speaking in Russian, muffled beneath the words of a man translating the speech into English.

"...are extremely destabilizing and foolish. We urge party leaders in US House of Representatives to stop extremist wings and put stop to many bills now on floor. We call to United States President to veto laws passing. Russia will not tolerate more US imperialism over regions and resources international law has divided."

The focus point shifted to a monitor in the middle of the array, a young woman of Middle Eastern appearance interviewing a cabbie on the streets of New York.

"Miss, what's to say? It's open season on the one percent. It's bombs and guns in New York. All the VIPs are disappearing or going nuts in Congress. You know what I think? I think it's the antichrist. I think it's the goddamned end of the fucking world. First we're gonna eat each other and everything's gonna fall apart. Then all those angels with fire and lightning are gonna come down and fry us. You know what I'm gonna do tonight? I'm gonna go to church. I'm gonna light some goddamned candles and pray my ass off that God's got a place for me in heaven."

The man rolled up his window and the cab sped off. The reporter turned to the camera, her face troubled, her words stuttered.

"This is Maryam Tavazoie, Al Jazeera America, in New York."

All the monitors went dark and the figure in the chair brooded in silence for several moments. From the faint afterglow of the screens, a weak line reflected off a hard surface.

A toothless smirk.

OCTOBER 21

14

ANGEL LIGHTFOOTE POKED her head around the doorframe. "John, the kids—they're not all right."

Savas sat behind his desk and held up his index finger with one hand and cradled the landline receiver in the other. The digits of his free hand also tapped onto a cell phone as he texted.

"Right. Ronald, look, I have to go. Thanks for the report and I'll share it with the group." He hung up the phone.

"Forensics?"

Savas nodded. "Yes. Residues found at the car and boat bombings match. Synthetics. Nothing special that we can trace."

She nodded, the fluorescent lighting reflecting brightly off her scalp. "Come with me. We need to talk."

—————

Five minutes later they were exiting an elevator and stepping onto the basement floor. Savas smiled as he looked around the maze of monitors and racks of computers.

"Love what you're doing with the place, Angel. Looks more and more like the Bat Cave."

Lightfoote gestured toward several rows of servers. "That's the Hernandez pile, all Manuel's machines that can still keep up. Most of the connections to law enforcement and other agencies—not to mention the satellite uplinks—are now ported to the Great Wall." Her hand swept toward a much large bank of computers racked in metallic girders, floor to ceiling.

"Glad to see the money's well spent."

Lightfoote shook her head. "Everything's been augmented, enhanced. More aggressive than the old crises center. *Militarized*. It's cyberwarfare out there now." Lightfoote sat at a long table with several monitors. "We've been stalking both of Senator Moss' girls. One is at UCSF, the other Georgetown."

He sat down next to her, watching windows displaying two young women's faces. Video footage streamed and maps and other surveillance software recorded locations and other information. "So there's a problem, or I wouldn't be down here. Disappearance?"

"No, it's a lot more subtle. The women are fine. So far. No sign of anything on their social media, personal emails, or phone conversations. We correlated their routines to video surveillance footage over the last few months. Nothing to indicate that they are functioning under duress." She turned toward Savas and winked, the piercings running across her face inches from him. "But we're playing with some inside information."

She cleared the active windows and opened several CCTV montages displaying footage from numerous cameras. There seemed little relationship between the locations, angles, or time the video was captured. Lightfoote stared at one intensely and then hit a key, freezing the playback.

"There. See, that's Anna Moss, right there, backpack, ponytail. She usually takes this route on Wednesdays. This is footage from two weeks ago. Look there," she indicated on the screen.

Savas squinted. A dark blur was above and behind the student, but he could not make out what it was. "What is it?"

She stared at him with her eyes angled upward, nearly rolling them. "Watch." Frame by frame, she advanced the footage. The Moss daughter moved jerkily as if caught by a strobe light, pedestrians and cars around her as well.

And so did the blur. Savas felt his pulse quicken. "It's tracking her," he whispered. "It's a drone."

Lightfoote smiled. "He can be taught! Watch closely. It shadows her up the street and then, *there*, lifts off into the air and is gone. We've got hundreds of hours of footage of the sisters. That let us catch the drones in ten or fifteen events. No doubts, John. We've tried to use image enhancement but didn't get much. We're also taking known drone models and creating cross-sections at different angles and using image recognition software to score similarity. But whatever the models, these women are being stalked. By drones."

"That's it, then," he said. "Imagine the kinds of photos you could get with these things. The kind of photos that when sent to a parent with the right note attached would petrify them."

Lightfoote nodded. "And you don't even have to put organic assets in play or touch the ground around the targets."

"Wouldn't someone notice these things?"

"Probably, but what would they think? There are kids' toys as big as some of these, and in several states law enforcement groups are beginning to use drones. And whoever is behind this isn't stupid. They don't hang around long. So, somebody sees one? Then what? Before they can do much it's gone. Not much to report without sounding like a UFO nut."

"No wonder she jumped when I asked about drones. She's a smart woman. She would have connected the bombing and these drones shadowing her daughters. And it's almost a certainty that Craig from Goldman was calling her about her vote flip-flops. If it hadn't been for the other CEO murders and kidnappings, I might have thought he was killed for that."

He stood up and placed his hands on his hips. "That's great work, Angel. You've linked the killing to the threats on Congress. With the meltdown there yesterday, it looks like she was the canary in the coal mine. We can use this to pressure the rest, make them open up about the blackmail."

"You'd think that the victims would have noticed their peers' behavior. Teamed up. Gotten some crowd bravery and brought the blackmail to the attention of someone by now."

Savas nodded. "Maybe. But it just happened. They probably thought they were the only ones, working in a panic, tunnel visioned and focused on whatever personal nightmare was threatening to consume their life."

Lightfoote stood up as well, continuing to stare at the blurry drone images on her monitors. "Drones of all sizes exist. Some able to handle large payloads. Some able to be mounted with weapons. And they're invisible to radar. They could fly right up to the president with a bar of Semtex strapped to them. Or pop over to the Indian Point nuclear plant. They can go anywhere, John. They can photograph people's bedroom windows, follow their kids, spy on the routes of world leaders. I'd be worried if I were you."

A chill ran through him. "I am, Angel. I think we need to find out who is making drones in this country, what they're making, and who the hell they are selling them to. Look for patterns in purchase and shipment. *Anything.*"

"Already beginning that search. What I'm worried about is that our drone-master is too smart for that. He wouldn't have left such an easy trail, but would likely buy them in small amounts and change shipping locations, payment methods. Or under the table purchases from dealers who aren't listed in the Better Business Bureau. That's what I would do."

"You know what Angel," said Savas, eyeing her suspiciously. "You are frighteningly good at thinking like a psychopath."

Her face darkened in a manner that unsettled Savas. She spoke hoarsely. "Thanks, John. It's good to be noticed."

"Well, I want you to keep doing that. In fact, you have my explicit permission to go full madwoman down here and follow any idea you think might be interesting. Don't tell me when you fail. Don't tell me missteps. Just do it. Find out what in the name of all that's holy is happening."

15

"No fucking *way*, man."

Two young men sat in the middle of a nearly empty warehouse, a dense clustering of high-tech equipment forming an isolated island in the middle of the space. Three to four rows of nested black towers formed a maze around them, the cabinets housing shelf upon shelf of computer banks. A thick series of cables and power cords snaked across the dusty cement floor like an obscene vasculature bringing nutrients to a gestating embryo. In the center of the maze was a set of tables holding five or six large flat screen monitors.

"No way, Chen."

The contrasting pair sat in front of the monitors, typing on keyboards, staring at a scrolling data stream. Chen was dressed in fatigues, close-cropped hair topping off a thin and angular frame, a tight tank-top revealing tattoos painted across his arms and back. He sat upright, tense, tapping the screen in front of him.

"I'm not shitting you, Dave, these are *his* accounts! Offshore, unregulated. It took me this whole week to get to them."

Dave swept his long, unruly hair out of his face, a tangled mass of brown and blond, greasy and unwashed. His general appearance was slovenly, and he slouched forward gazing at the screen. He shook his head in disbelief.

"Can't believe Fawkes left a security hole."

"Well, he's not running the bank servers, now is he?" said Chen, his voice defiant.

"Five hundred million? I mean, *what the fuck?*"

Chen shook his head. "I dunno, man. Something's up with this. Something really not cool."

"Yeah, how does Fawkes get half a billion dollars? You think it's related to all this shit going down?"

"Look at the withdrawals!" Chen scrolled through the banking records. "It's like five million here, ten million here. Restore Our Future. American Crossroads. Strong America Now."

"Sounds like student council assholes," Dave said, upturning a bag of chips into his mouth, his words garbled.

"They're conservative SuperPacs, you fuck."

"SuperPacs?"

Chen rolled his eyes. "You're such a fucking pothead, Dave."

"Amen and praise Jesus, you bet!" said Dave, smiling.

"Whatever. Look, there are transfers to Europe, China, India. It's like he's some multinational! These transfers are totally laundered. No transaction codes, no IDs, nothing!"

"Ain't no money for nothing, dude."

Chen nodded. "Something is *really* not cool here."

A loud scraping noise startled the pair. They spun in their chairs and looked behind them, through an opening in the maze of the server farm. The large door of the warehouse had been yanked open, and three men walked into the cavernous space. In the middle was a young man, thin, nearly gaunt, dressed casually in a black T-shirt and jeans. His short-cropped black hair and pencil-thin goatee were offset by a pair of shaded smart glasses. He constantly fiddled with a smartphone affixed to his belt. Flanking him on either side were two much larger, muscled men. They wore nondescript business attire, their eyes hidden behind black sunglasses. Their expressions were indecipherable.

"Shit," said Chen under his breath, spinning slightly to position his hand over the keyboard and enter several strokes. The windows on the screen disappeared. He turned back quickly to the approaching men as they neared. The three stopped a few feet in front of the hacker pair, silence lingering for several moments.

"Yo, Fawkes!" said Dave awkwardly. "What's this? Fucking Terminator Ten?" His smiled floundered against the stony gazes of the three men.

Hands continuously tapping the smartphone, Fawkes appeared to stare straight ahead at something outside the room. "You were always such a fucking waste, Dave. You could've been the best black hat to ever crawl out of 4chan. You know, when that shit-hole was actually worth something."

Dave flipped him the bird. "Up yours. I still am."

Fawkes ignored him. "Chen. It's too bad you had to be so curious.

Killed a lot of cats. I thought you'd be more grateful after I gifted you this little playground."

Chen licked his lips, glancing between Fawkes and the two men on his sides. "What's up, Fawkes? We're just hanging."

Fawkes finally took off his glasses, his gray eyes burning into Chen. "I've had a tick on you for weeks, Chen. I know you've been poking around the offshore accounts."

Chen sat utterly still. The large room was silent except for the constant hum of the server farm around them. Dave broke the eerie stillness.

"So the fuck what, man? It's not like you haven't hacked your way through a hundred accounts."

"But those are *my* accounts, Dave. Accounts that are too important to be messed with. Or for anyone to know about."

"Fawkes, what's going on?" asked Chen, his face grave. "Hundreds of millions? What are you up to? What's with the bodyguards?"

Fawkes laughed. "You stupid fucks still don't get it. You actually think a hundred million is a lot! Try seven-hundred *trillion*—that's the size of the derivative market. Did you know that? And it's *all* virtual money." He gestured vaguely to the walls of computers around them. "It doesn't exist except inside investment bank computers and people's very active imaginations. When things are bytes in compiled data structures, they are *meant* to be hacked. It's fucking righteous deeds." He laughed. "I've got *trillions* of dollars, you clueless ass. Those accounts you stumbled on were early, poorly secured penetration tests."

Chen blinked. "Trillions? That's not possible. What's the game, Fawkes? This doesn't make sense. We were against all this stuff!"

Fawkes fit his glasses back on, his voice growing slightly distanced. "I don't have the time to explain to you losers. You never had the balls, Chen. None of you did. We hacked our way to the truth, but it didn't set us free. We found out their dirty little secrets, and all of you panicked. *Pissed your fucking pants!* You wouldn't dare do what had to be done. You hit *MasterCard* or outed bad cops."

Dave and Chen looked at each other anxiously. Chen spoke again. "What has to be done?"

Fawkes began fiddling with his smartphone, staring off into space.

With his other hand, he lifted a black and white object, a tight string hanging off the back. Placing it on his head, he pulled downward, the elastic string tightening around the back of his head, the object fitting tightly over his face: a mask of a smirking man stared back at them.

"What the fuck?" whispered Dave.

Fawkes motioned toward the two men beside him, who nodded. His voice was muffled. "Core dump, bros. The system software is too corrupted. Time for a reboot." He turned his back on them and began to walk away.

Chen shifted nervously in his chair as the large forms of the bodyguards approached the two hackers. "My God, it *is* you! All of this!" His voice rose dramatically in pitch. "Are you insane? Do you understand what will happen?" Silence. "That's not what we were about! No one reboots the fucking world!"

Fawkes stopped and sighed, his fiddling paused. The mask turned back toward them. "I do. And nothing is going to get in the way of that, not even Anonymous. *I'm* Anonymous now—what you all should have been." He laughed. "You'd be amazed what you can do with a trillion dollars."

Fawkes resumed his distracted gait and headed for the exit. The bodyguards who had entered with him reached into their jackets and removed pistols. Bulging suppressors were attached to the ends.

"Ah, man, no way, no way, no way! This isn't happening!" cried Dave, his eyes large. He stood up trembling in his chair, looking around the wall of computer cabinets hemming them in. Chen didn't move, but simply closed his eyes.

A sudden scream ripped through the warehouse, punctuated by a series of sharp spits. The following silence was disrupted only by the echoing clap of shoes on hard concrete.

BEFORE:
THE ANONYMOUS EVENT COMMISSION

DEPOSITION IN THE MATTER OF:
UNITED STATES ARMED FORCES SPECIAL TRIBUNAL,
Plaintiff,
v.
JOHN SAVAS, Defendant
Case No. M120039E-007X

Continued DEPOSITION OF:
JEAN PAUL RIDEOUT

CBD: And so this was the first hard evidence that drones were being used?
MR. RIDEOUT: Right. But we all believed it was drones from the start. Nothing else fit.

[REDACTED]: And yet your division, led by Savas, still refused to share this information with other FBI divisions and national agencies.
MR. RIDEOUT: Refused? We didn't refuse anything. This was all unfolding in real time. Do you understand how that works? We'd barely get a chance to breathe before the next shock wave hit. We had barely just put this together. And the evidence wasn't going to win any court cases. I'm sure John would have been happy to share more. In fact that's what we did!
CBD: When he contacted NSA?
MR. RIDEOUT: Exactly. Angel made a breakthrough.

[REDACTED]: This is when Lightfoote broke numerous cybercrimes laws and released dangerous viral codes into the internet?
Mr. RIDEOUT: Worms. They were worms. Yeah, damn. She sure as hell did. And it worked! But the damned NSA just blew us off, right when the whole thing went to shit.

OCTOBER 22

16

IT WAS PAST midnight, and the basement at the FBI building was staffed only by three people. Two women and a man hunched over monitors as the steady buzz of computer servers churned around them. The bald woman stared across at the other two, her expression grave.

"Well, John, there was something about 'explicit permission to go full madwoman.'"

"I didn't know you were going to turn everything back on us!"

"It's a logical byproduct of the search algorithms."

Cohen placed her hand on Savas' shoulder and yawned. "Can we just have one night without another crisis?"

Lightfoote stood up, a short tank exposing her midriff and rows of chiseled abdominal muscles. She walked over to the banks of servers and ran her hands over them like a nurse would a sick child.

"That meeting at the NYU computer science department spooked me. They weren't coming clean with how bad things were, and what was said was bad enough. I knew then we couldn't trust any of the other agencies to handle this. Worst of all was the NSA. They know the most and share the least." She patted the metal shelving holding the individual units of the server farm. "So, assuming the worst, I let loose some worms of my own."

"What?" said Savas, his eyes wide.

She turned her green eyes toward them. "*Full* madwoman, remember?"

"Yeah, breaking Federal law?"

"Well, that's all not going to matter much longer anyway if we don't get this under control soon."

Savas swiveled in his chair to face Lightfoote. "Angel, what are you talking about?"

"My little wigglies reported back. It's *everywhere*, John. Gone fucking viral is the phrase. All my babies," she leaned her head against the machines, "they're all infected. We're infected—FBI is infected."

"Damn." Savas rubbed his temples. "Okay, so what—"

"The whole goddamned world is infected! This thing has simultaneously exploited every known security whole in the underlying operating systems. It's like a MIRV missile for the internet with multiple warheads. Each one hits something, somewhere, in every system. And that's all it needs. One weakness. Then the worm is in."

Cohen whispered softly. "What is it doing?"

"Nothing yet. Nothing active. Or, whatever it's done was done before we began monitoring it and it has covered its tracks. There's a bunch of encrypted code that comes along with the thing in every infestation. That's got to be the heart of it. Whatever it's up to, I'd bet it's contained there."

"Can you get into it?" asked Cohen.

"Not yet. But I'm worried that when I do, it won't be straightforward. Whoever did this has made an attack that is sophisticated beyond anything the internet has ever seen. The code isn't complete or standardized."

"I don't understand," said Savas.

"Those encrypted modules? They're really diverse. Not one the same size on each system. I think it's distributed. It's like a P2P system where pieces of the file to be shared are stored all over the internet in different places. When you download your pirated film, the software at the end assembles a composite file from hundreds, sometimes thousands of independent file elements. *That's* what's going on here. The worm has spread to tens of thousands, probably millions of computers. Each infection is one of a large set of different worms— let's call them strains like for viruses. Each strain carries a different piece of the code."

"Then if we can kill some of the strains, it can't put the full program back together and we stop it?" asked Savas.

Cohen shook her head. "If I understand this, then each strain will have thousands of copies of itself all around the world. We'd have to hunt every one of them down."

Lightfoote nodded. "Exactly. It's too distributed. It's like having a million backups on different servers where literally every computer is a potential backup system once infected. We'll never stop it that way."

"Then how?" asked Savas.

Lightfoote shook her head. "I don't know."

"Okay, then what does that code do when assembled?"

"I don't know that either. I haven't cracked any of the encryptions, and there are already hundreds of different packages I've found with the worms. We need the NSA computers to be working full time on this."

"You think they know?"

"Yes. Definitely. They're poking around infected systems, just like I did. So many computers are poorly secured, it's easy to get into them and find things out. They *have* to know by now, or they shouldn't have the keys to their computer arsenal."

Savas stood up. "Then it's about damn time they opened up and worked with us. Tomorrow morning we'll get this moving."

Cohen grabbed his arm. "Are you sure about that? I think you might be overestimating the influence the FBI has on the NSA. They're so frighteningly close to Big Brother, we're not going to have much pull."

Lightfoote nodded. "And they aren't going to look at my little enterprise as anything remotely useful compared to the fleet of processors they have. From a certain perspective, they're right."

"So, what then? We wait here helplessly for the NSA to formulate a cure and perhaps share it with us? If this thing shuts us down, we're crippled to investigate the killings and abductions, anything at all really. We can't remain that vulnerable!"

"Try the NSA, John," said Cohen, walking up to Lightfoote. "Meanwhile, I suggest that you leave the leash off Angel. Don't rescind your madwoman decree." Cohen took Lightfoote's shoulders in her hands, squaring up to face her. "Angel, why don't you see what you can do about this thing. Assume we're on our own. Assume it's a matter of life and death."

Savas nodded. Lightfoote stared between them and then back at her server.

"Okay. But be careful what you ask for."

17

CHAOS ROILS WALL STREET AS WORLD MARKETS SHUTTERED

By Christina Patrikia, *Washington Post*

In an unprecedented turn of events, the major world stock exchanges were forced to suspend trading as markets oscillated wildly and company fortunes were obliterated and made in instants.

Beginning almost immediately after the opening bell was rung at the New York Stock Exchange, and despite normal after-hours trading the night before, chaos hit the floor as share prices of everything from Fortune 500 companies to bundled options on the futures market dropped or increased thousands of percentage points in seconds. The changes swung back and forth, even on individual stocks, at the speed of the electronic trading computers.

"The system went haywire," said Brian Gunter, an analyst from Brookmans. "It was faster than the human mind could follow. All in electronic trading, across the board stock dumps and purchases, seemingly at random."

It appears that automated trade-halting safeguards designed to prevent massive stock fluctuations either did not function as expected or were unable to handle the volume and nature of the spurious trades.

"We are assuming a major malfunction," said Gordon Jones, a technical support specialist working for the NASDAQ exchange. "Either the safeguards to prevent market meltdowns failed or something more systematic occurred. With current software, trades are executed in less than a half a millionth of a second. Feedback loops at those speeds can lead to major problems on time scales human beings can't react to. It's a very nonlinear system."

While there had been previous scares such as the rogue program from Knight Capital that nearly halted trading in 2012, no glitch in the now-ubiquitous trading computers had caused anything approaching what took place today. Representatives from the world exchanges have been in conference calls since trading was halted in the early morning.

Washington Post financial correspondent Angela Kong explained: "World leaders are involved. It is an unusual crisis. You have a majority of the largest companies in the world now worth pennies on paper, or rather, worth nothing in the digital systems storing their valuations. We're talking IBM, Apple, Google, GE—you name it. They're wiped out. Meanwhile, there are a host of nothing companies, green energy, solar, drug companies in India that have instantly grown to the size of Google. It's economic chaos. There is talk of a market reset."

Kong quoted several sources within the administration stating that, once the market software had been fixed, there were plans to resume trading at the prices on shares at which the exchanges had opened this morning. The move would be unprecedented, and is not without vocal critics in the government and private sector. However, consensus seemed to be building that only through such action could an unparalleled market collapse be staved off.

In an ominous repeat, the malfunction of the trading software that led to the trading halt in the US markets spread to every exchange across the world. One by one, as each of the major exchanges opened, chaos ensued and trading was stopped. Markets in Asia have not yet opened, but already the Nikkei and Shanghai Stock Exchange are being prepared for an unscheduled shut down to prevent further chaos in the world financial system.

First term senator and political firebrand Nathan Schelot—who rose to power on an election in California rocked by accusations of fraud—was vocal on Capitol Hill following the Press Secretary's minimal statement on the crisis at noon.

"And is this the leadership we need in a time of turmoil? Now you see the product of a runaway, capitalistic system. When will we regulate the bidding bots, the electronic microsecond trading that has turned our once human economy into a cyborg market? Robots take our jobs and now they are taking over our corporate structures. We are not in control anymore, and if something isn't done soon, everything this nation has built will come crashing down."

BUGS IN AUTOMATED WRITING SYSTEMS FLOOD ONLINE NEWS
By Anna Zeabee, *Wired*

They have been heralded for years as the next wave in machine displacement of human workers. They are the programs that have been written to produce news articles, financial reports, sports summaries, even law briefs. Light years ahead of the clumsy text and speech generators of a generation ago, they are now increasingly used by all the major media outlets to fill the seemingly insatiable appetite for online content.

They are even the seeds of new businesses, as Image Council's Jeff Philips has deluged the publishing industry with manuals and fact guides created only by computer algorithms that write books based on the contents of databases and fact lists.

But today a major bug has turned these time-saving tools into seemingly independent intelligences as thousands of unapproved and propagandistic news stories swamped online publishing sites, hijacking a significant fraction of the news reported.

While the chaos on Wall Street was the story of the day, for several hours the *New York Times* sported a headline criticizing income inequality in a thousand-word manifesto.

"It's clear that we have some hackers playing with our system," said Executive editor Jerry Wilbur. "The writing seems to be similar to taking a fourth grader's dictionary and throwing it into a dishwasher. Nevertheless, it took some time to pull it."

Despite the high profile nature of the breach, the *Times* was hardly alone. Most of the major news feeds and even news flagship websites were drowned in a cascade of articles focused on financial statistics and world economic problems. The automated systems adopted a Marxist bent that seemed funny to many except for the problems caused.

"Income inequality? Corporate welfare? Lobbying and money? All very interesting to some left-wingers and it was cute to see the *Wall Street Journal's* editorial page moaning about the evils of capitalism," said a source at a competing publication. "But this shut down our news systems as well. This was a global problem that cost man-hours and will total in the millions to fix. We're still flushing these bot-articles out. They haven't stopped. Only when the companies running them shut things down will it end. Meanwhile, we're unplugging from their services. Right now, they're drowning us."

18

EVENING HAD FALLEN on the crowds in Times Square, but the streets were bathed in electric hues from multiple monitors displaying ads and streaming video from numerous locations. Horns blared as cars piled along curbs waiting for an opportunity to turn into adjacent streets through the flood of pedestrians. Some walked in groups. Many seemed tuned out and into their digital devices. All were dressed in jackets to ward off the late October chill.

One by one, those walking the streets began to slow down, staring at their phones or tablets. Others began to crane their necks upward, interrupting their conversations, staring puzzled at the glowing behemoths of dancing images around them. Within a minute, nearly all the motion in the square had come to a halt, and the blaring of horns increased ten-fold as roadways were completely blocked.

Like dominoes, all the monitors in the square flipped jerkily to the same static image: a circle with a globe depicted in grid lines, leaves of a plant along the sides, the figure of a headless man in a black and white suit with a question mark over him.

Out of a window, a taxi driver stuck his head and gazed up at the bizarre tiling of images across the buildings around him. He tugged on a baseball cap.

"What the hell?"

"John, you'd better come with me."

Cohen stood in his doorway, a sharp glint in her eyes. Savas prepared for the worst. "Another attack?"

She shook her head. "Something different. But I think related. Media across the country, maybe worldwide, is being hijacked. It's cable, network, online streaming sites like YouTube and Hulu. It's systematic."

"Systematic? The worm?"

"Don't know. But this sure sounds like something it could be up to."

Savas sprang from his chair and followed her into the floor's common room. Normally a place for coffee and a break from work, the small space was packed as agents and staff stared up at a flat-panel screen. A strange black-and-white image of a headless man in a suit took the place of all programming on nearly all stations. Savas and Cohen stood outside the door looking in.

A man's voice came up over the din of buzzing conversation. "That's Anonymous!"

Cohen turned to Savas. "He's right! I knew I had seen it before."

"Anonymous? Those kids who do social justice hacking?"

The voice of Lightfoote startled them from behind. "Kids, maybe. No one really knows who they are, how they organize, where they are. A few caught were high schoolers. Others older. Some established, even corporate. They're everyone and no one. The name really does mean something. Unknown, distributed anarchy. Probably why they never achieved anything really big."

"Until now, maybe," said Savas as he started at the disconcerting image.

"Uh oh, there it goes," said Lightfoote.

The screen pixelated horribly, and then locked onto another video feed. The crowds at FBI, in Times Square, and in millions of homes across the nation stared at two rows of chairs in a dark room. Harsh lighting fell directly on those seated in the chairs, the space behind them and to their sides too dark for any details to be made out. The men and women were tied to the seats, their arms and legs lashed with rope, gags in their mouths, and terrified expressions on their faces as their eyes darted.

"Oh, my God," whispered Cohen. "The abductions."

Savas felt his stomach drop as he began to recognize faces. The CEO of GE. Congressmen. The Chair of the Federal Reserve. Luminaries in business, finance, and politics. What the hell was happening?

Lightfoote spoke. "I'm going to the basement. They've compromised major digital distribution hubs. I bet it's the worm. We might be able to catch it in action and see what it looks like!" She darted from the crowd and headed toward the stairway.

A mask appeared in front of the screen. Black-and-white, smirking, a thin goatee etched across the upper lip and chin. Savas had seen it before. It was a symbol of underground resistance to established powers—the mask of Guy Fawkes.

"Greetings sheeple of America, Europe, and beyond," came a digitally distorted voice. "We are Anonymous and today is a day of judgment."

The masked speaker stepped back from the camera. The figure was of indeterminate frame and size, dressed in a black suit and tie. It walked confidently toward the double row of hostages. Their eyes looked hopeless and panicked.

"Already we have targeted some of the worst criminals in our malignant society. Robber barons, plutocrats who pull the strings of the drugged masses. The architects of a feudal world increasingly of a few elements of royalty standing on the backs of millions of slaves."

"Jesus," said Savas. He picked up his mobile phone and dialed. "Yeah, Angel. You got *anything* on this? Location?" He grimaced. "I *know* there hasn't been time! But what I'm seeing—it's *not* good. I think these people are in danger."

The masked man continued. "Today, as a taste of things to come, we again pass judgment on a group of criminals whose status in society is the only thing separating them from the mafia. Because in their greed they have killed like common thugs."

He slapped the face of a man next to him. Savas recognized the captive as CEO O'Kelly.

The masked man continued. "They have poisoned our world, our rivers, our air, our very bodies as they profit. They have drilled and dug and burned and buried. They have denied health and home and peace to billions so they could luxuriate in ten thousand times more than they could ever require."

Several shapes in dark clothing moved into the view frame of the camera. They wore Guy Fawkes masks. They carried automatic weapons.

"Oh, Christ," whispered Savas. Murmurs ran through the crowd at FBI.

Several of the hostages in the chairs let loose gagged screams, twisting and wrenching their arms and legs in attempts to free themselves. Other seemed resigned, staring forward blankly.

"Today, we reject the weakness of fools. Of the failed Occupy Movement. Of the false Anonymous. Of corrupt nation-states who claim to serve the people but serve only their masters. Today we reject the foul words of the pundits, the professors, the activists, and the politicians who spout lies about change as they bathe in the status quo. Today, a real change comes. Today, we begin to put down a sick and broken system."

There was a pause, and then he nodded toward the gunman. "Remember. Remember the fifth of November. This time there will be no providence of God."

The men raised their weapons. Shouts came from some of the FBI onlookers.

Cohen turned to Savas. "John, Tell me he isn't—"

Bursts of light erupted from the muzzles of the automatic weapons, blurs of static from the flatscreen. Puffs of fabric and blood exploded outward from the clothes of the hostages, their forms shaking from the projectile impacts and reflex action, muffled screams bursting from their gagged lips.

Then silence.

The murderers with guns were gone. Only the bodies of the dead stared back into the camera with vacant eyes or tortured final expressions. The grinning plastic of the man with the Guy Fawkes mask approached the camera, until the mocking face filled the entire screen.

"We are the *real* Anonymous. We are indeed Legion. We do not forgive. We do not forget. Expect us."

The video feed switched to a set of multiple views arranged in an array across the screen. In each case, the camera floated above the ground at what seemed to be disparate locations, darkness punctured by the lights of cars and buildings in the cities below.

The viewpoints descended. With increasing speed the ground dashed upward toward the viewer as the land sped by underneath, buildings whipping past. A disorienting collection of sub-screens careened wildly together.

But there was guided purpose to the movements. A zeroing in

towards defined goals. Familiar and famous objects swam into view. The Capitol. The New York Stock Exchange. The Citibank building.

Savas gasped. "Oh, my God, Rebecca. They're drones. They're drones flying in for the kill."

The screens went black. Outside the FBI windows, light pierced the darkness. The crowd turned toward the flash, an orange fireball climbing in the evening sky from Midtown. An explosion rattled the windows of their building.

OCTOBER 23

BEFORE:
THE ANONYMOUS EVENT COMMISSION

DEPOSITION IN THE MATTER OF:
UNITED STATES ARMED FORCES SPECIAL TRIBUNAL,
Plaintiff,
v.
JOHN SAVAS, Defendant
Case No. M120039E-007X

CONTINUED DEPOSITION OF:
JOHN SAVAS

[REDACTED]: Again we remind you that you are
under oath, Mr. Savas. You understand that this
is not a Federal or Civilian court, that the
jurisdiction of this case is considered outside
the Constitution and to be part of the armed
forces in a service in time of war and public
danger?
Mr. SAVAS: I have been made to understand that
all too clearly, [REDACTED].

[REDACTED]: Please answer the question posed.
Do you understand the law as it pertains to you
in this tribunal?
MR. SAVAS: I forfeit my rights to the 5th
Amendment and others. No grand jury or due
process. And I can be compelled to be a witness
against myself.
[REDACTED]: Counsel may continue the
questioning.

CBD: Mr. Savas, let's pick up where we left off
yesterday, shall we?
MR. SAVAS: Or why don't you go fuck yourself,
instead?

CBD: Cooperation will save you time and
mitigate further inquiry.
MR. SAVAS: Inquiry? Is that the latest term? I
thought it was enhanced interrogation.

CBD: [Inaudible] Would you please just continue
your account from yesterday?
MR. SAVAS: Remind me. My brain is a mush.
Isolation for a month, sleep dep. Just staring
at gray walls. Messes with your mind. So will

near drowning.

CBD: The executions.
MR. SAVAS: Right. Jesus, yes. The executions.
[Inaudible] Live and HDTV for all to see. Well,
as horrible as that all was, it was our first
real break.
CBD: How so?
MR. SAVAS: The worm. Angel's spyware reported
back. The television hijack was tied directly
to it. So, there it was. What we had been
pursuing as unrelated cases, the murders, the
kidnappings, and the financial meltdown. It was
all tied together by the worm. By Anonymous. It
was part of the same thing. And it all made
sense.

CBD: What made sense?
MR. SAVAS: I mean it all fit together.
Anonymous had set its eyes on bringing down the
world financial system. It was fighting on
several fronts from the virus wrecking the
markets to the drones killing financial
tycoons. The blackmail of congressmen changing
laws was another front. It was incredible,
really. Amazingly orchestrated. Diabolical
genius.

[REDACTED]: You sound inspired.
MR. SAVAS: You sound like a goddamned Nazi.
Inspired? Well, we all had to be. The world had
been caught with its pants down and effectively
castrated. Anonymous had played us like fools.

CBD: And you are so sure it was the hacker
group Anonymous? Who was their leader again?
MR. SAVAS: I've told you already, there isn't
one Anonymous. There are legions. It's more an
idea than an organization. And Fawkes, well, he
was the inevitable, the instability that takes
over any distributed authority.

[REDACTED]: Fawkes. This is the one found in
your office. That you claim you caught and who
single-handedly masterminded the Event?
MR. SAVAS: Yes. It was his worm. His plan. His
signal that was to bring it all down once and
for all. But I didn't know that then, when he
murdered them all.

[REDACTED]: And that is when you contacted Lopez?
MR. SAVAS: That is correct.
[REDACTED]: Can you tell us why you thought it prudent, let alone legal, to search for and enlist the aid of the nation's most notorious outlaws? Murderers of hundreds, including some of the most important persons in our nation?
MR. SAVAS: Because I knew they weren't murderers. I knew that they had been framed.
[REDACTED]: This is ridiculous. You only reveal your own involvement with these terrorists!
CBD: This is not a trial, [REDACTED]!
[REDACTED]: There isn't going to be a trial.
CBD: This is a deposition and we are instructed to take it. [Inaudible] May I continue? Thank you.

CBD: We will ascertain how you knew the pair later. For now, can you tell us please how they got involved?
MR. SAVAS: We had setup a safe house for them.
[REDACTED]: Who is we?
MR. SAVAS: You'll have to waterboard me some more to get near that. Let's just say there are many forces at work here that you don't know about. Forces that believe in this nation. What it used to be, anyway.

CBD: Mr. Savas, look. As your counsel I am trying to help you, but you are making that a challenging assignment. Can you help this panel understand why you would bring in two wanted terrorists and murderers?
MR. SAVAS: After we put together the bigger picture, when I saw where Anonymous was headed, I knew then what was at stake. So did my team.

CBD: And what was at stake, Mr. Savas?
MR. SAVAS: Civilization itself.

19

CHAOS STORMED THROUGH New York and the world.

After the feed from Anonymous, network programming returned to something quite different than normal. Broadcasters replayed the carnage over and over, whipping themselves and the public into a frenzy.

At FBI, Savas had steered his people back to work. They would be slogging through the night. Schedules, family, *health* would suffer, but until the crisis could be controlled, he didn't see any other choice. His phone rang constantly. From his superiors came a barrage of commands. Most of these came from above as the governmental apparatus went into war mode. Contacts and numerous agencies checked in with him, provided small pieces of useless information, and asked for favors of investigation and protection in return. He had nothing to give. His staff was already depleted even before the televised mass assassination.

In the middle of the chaos, he received a message on his private cell. He stared at the number. It made sense. In all that was happening, now was one of the greater periods of danger from a government eating itself, going too far, forgetting its principles. Now would be a time for the Watchmen to call.

The group had formed during the Bush years when some in the FBI and CIA had grown concerned about the powers the executive branch and other governmental agencies had begun to assume under antiterrorism laws. Under the increasingly paranoid Obama administration, they had only redoubled their efforts to exert a more sane response to threats. Indefinite detention and torture were one thing, but secretive decisions for assassination of Americans without trial, endless spying on citizens by governmental organizations—for some of them, it had gone too far. With the national scandal of the Priest and Whore last year, they had finally pooled their meager resources and acted. And thus had Gabriel been created.

"Alice. To what do I owe the pleasure?" His smile faded. "What? Are you sure? *When?*" Savas looked around the floor. "Jesus. What will that mean? How far is the decree?" He nodded scribbling on a notepad. "Understood. Right. Thank you."

He put the phone away and stared forward, seeing nothing except images of the city in his mind. A New York surrounded by military vehicles.

Savas jumped from his chair and exited his office, finding Cohen on the floor. She was coordinating with several agents on the requests —or rather *demands*—for even more of his staff to be reassigned to protective functions for VIPs. Very soon, they would be running Intel 1 on pure air.

"Everybody listen up," he said, cutting into the middle of their conversation. "Very serious newsflash. I just got a call in from some sources, reliable ones. The president is going to declare martial law."

Cohen blinked. "*Martial law?*"

Savas nodded. "Within the hour. In the city for sure, maybe the whole tri-state area. They're panicking. I guess I understand that, although I don't know how locking down the city is going to help much. They must know about the worm, and now with additional threats of terrorist bombings and killings, they needed to act. They decided to lock everything down."

"Anonymous isn't stuck walking the streets of New York, John!" shouted Cohen. "This won't achieve anything except to cause a real panic. People are going to start bolting from the city."

"They won't be able to."

"And you know how that's going to turn out, right?"

"God, I hope not. We can't let this panic us, too, okay? At the root of this is a core organization, people orchestrating everything. If we can find that core, flush out or corner those people, we can put a stop to this. And for that we need—"

"Here, Commander," said Lightfoote, panting from a run.

"We need Angel."

"It's probably going to be both New York and DC," said Lightfoote, catching her breath. "I'm intercepting a lot of chatter. People aren't using secure lines. They're freaking. They've also got a lot of the Cabinet and Congress going underground, presuming continual threats."

"Word on the Capitol?"

Lightfoote nodded. "You've seen the footage on the news. Main entrance and steps are blown to hell and back. Few were hurt at this time of night, but the point sure was made. The building is structurally sound, however. It would take a lot more firepower than these little drones can carry to seriously damage it."

"And what if they have bigger drones?" asked Cohen.

Angel bit her lip. "Then it could be a lot worse. But the scurrying of governmental staff is creating power vacuums. Basically, we're moving to a crisis mode unlike anything except during the Cold War. Not even 9/11 approached this. The apparatus is gearing up for siege."

"This is not going to end well," muttered Savas. "Update me on the worm."

"It had to get visible, and wow, what a beauty." Cohen arched her eyebrow. "Seriously, Rebecca, this is the Michelangelo of hackers. The damn thing *self-assembled* from thousands of computers around the world on some mysterious signal."

"Self-assembled?" asked Savas.

"Yes! We thought that it was hiding on various computers. Only *parts* of it were. Like the distributed code I mentioned? I didn't realize that the *entire worm* was networked. In other words, it doesn't exist as a single piece of code on *any* computer, but like a neural network that's the sum of a bunch of minor worms on millions of computers. It's incredible. Powerful. Unstoppable."

"Unstoppable?" said Cohen.

"Well, *I* don't know how to stop it. I don't think anybody would. It's unprecedented. It's a distributed AI that's taking over the distributed brain we call the internet."

"But it was activated with the Anonymous broadcast?" asked Savas.

"It *ran* the damn broadcast, John! I tried to get inside the code that activated, but it quickly detected my efforts and erased itself from my computer and shut down the computer's internet access. Wiped the hard drive. I'm reinstalling from backups."

"Wouldn't that cutoff part of itself, if it's some distributed thing over computers?" asked Cohen.

"Yes, but it's like killing some of your brain cells by a night of heavy drinking. The brain overall isn't hurt much by that afterward. And the thing is everywhere from finance to military computers. We can thank God that the nuclear arsenal is still mainly run off five-and-a-quarter inch floppies and machines from the 1970's. But every other damn thing is infested. We don't control the digital world, anymore. The worm does."

Savas felt his head pounding. He needed something concrete, something practical. "Tell me what the threat is."

Lightfoote looked at him in shock. "John, it can do anything. Write any code, erase data, create data, shut systems down, modulate system function. Turn off the water and lights. Open the Hoover Dam. Drop half the airplanes from the sky. Delete the world's money supply. *Anything*. What's the threat? It's fucking digital Armageddon."

Cohen turned to Savas. "John, this is too big for us."

He nodded. "I'll call in every contact I have at the CIA and NSA with what we have. We'll run a shadow agency. Meanwhile, let's see what's left here."

"We're down to the core group and a few extra hands," said Cohen. "They've pulled all the assistant agents and trainees. It's mostly us. We're the boutique group. Expendable in this crisis."

His mind raced. "Let's break this down into tasks. Overall, we need to provide some kind of quick break into the worm and who is behind it. We're a small team, a talented team. We can move quickly whereas other agencies will just be reactive. We need to go after the worm first." He nodded to Lightfoote. "We'll get JP down with Angel in the basement, and they'll try to trace the origins of this thing, find out its weaknesses. Rebecca, you, me, and Frank will find everything we can on this Anonymous group. But Intel 1 doesn't have much firepower right now."

"We do have an ace-in-the-hole," said Cohen.

"Yes," said Savas wearily. He rubbed his hand across his brow. "I'm not sure they're ready to wade back into things—they're still radioactive. But we don't have a choice. Once they defied an entire nation. Maybe now they can help us save it."

20

SARA HOUSTON, WRAPPED in a dark coat, trudged across a white field carrying a pile of firewood. The pines behind her circled a small cabin, smoke rising from its chimney, a warm yellow glow spilling through the windows, reflected on the snow crunching under her boots. Clouds of vapor escaped her lips as she marched forward, a serene expression on her face, crisp blue eyes peering outward from a face framed in brown hair.

She climbed onto the porch and dropped the wood into a bin. She ran a gloved finger across the door, tracing the vines that trailed up the wood. The leaves had fallen, and only cordons and trunk remained, hardly more than thin stems. But Houston had planted them only a year ago and was satisfied with the progress.

Dusting off her boots and coat, she opened the door and stepped into the warmth of the small cabin—a single room with bed, table, and miniature kitchen. A sofa beside the window overlooked the porch, and the fireplace crackled loudly on her right, casting red and orange light across her chiseled features. She lowered her hood, chin-length brown hair dancing in a disheveled mess about her face. She smiled at Francisco Lopez walking toward her with a pair of tumblers holding caramel liquid.

The light showed the breadth of him, muscles filling out a black sweater, short and curled black hair and a dark beard masking much of his face. His features were a sharp contrast to hers, his skin a rich copper, features Aztec. He held a glass toward Houston and smiled back at her. She brought the drink to her lips.

"Mmmmm, Francisco," she said, downing a quarter of the two inches in the tumbler. "Cask strength?" He nodded. "Nice and warm. That shed is going to get further and further away as the winter comes."

Lopez grunted. "I think we'll spend a lot of time just clearing a path to it. I didn't realize the snows came so early here. The mountains in Alabama weren't all that high or cold."

"How's the buck?" she said, walking into the small kitchen.

"Biggest one we've bagged. You've got your work cut out for you to top that one."

"You're one competitive girl, Sara," he said, laughing and shaking his head. "But he's coming along well. Should be dinner for two weeks with the last veggie run."

She nodded. "Runs are going to get harder with the weather. We need a strategy for supplies. I don't think the Outback can handle what might be coming on these lousy roads. Next trip into town we need to make sure we have enough fuel for the generator."

"By then we'll have natural refrigeration and drain less power. We can fill the shelter with things. We're remote, Sara, but not that remote."

Houston placed her tumbler on the table and walked up to Lopez, draping her arms around his neck. "I'm getting used to a certain rustic luxury up here, Francisco. Nothing ruins rustic luxury like a few weeks of rationing."

They kissed. Houston wasn't sure what felt warmer, his lips or the whiskey. As his hands moved over her waist, she realized that both could spin her head around in the most delicious ways.

A device buzzed from a table beside the sofa.

Both Lopez and Houston turned quickly to the sound, the warmth draining from their faces, softer expressions replaced with intense eyes and set jaws.

Lopez rumbled deeply. "My guess is that it's for you."

Houston smirked and walked toward the landline. It looked like a receptionist's business phone, rows of buttons and an LCD display glowing back at her. The phone cable ran through a black box with a pair of lights. The red light glowed. "They sure know how to ruin a girl's evening."

Lopez downed the rest of this whiskey and followed her to the phone, ignoring the device and staring out the window. He seemed to focus on objects thousands of miles away.

"Mary here," said Houston, using the false identities they had been given. "Gabriel's fine." She pushed a button and the device went to speaker. A woman's voice spoke from the other end.

"It is said: 'Do not meddle in the affairs of Wizards, for they are subtle and quick to anger.'"

Houston replied. "And it is also said, 'Go not to the elves for counsel, for they will say both no and yes.'" She watched a series of numbers changing across the LCD. They locked in a particular sequence, and she continued. "Handshake completed. Hi, Rebecca."

"Hello, Sara," said Cohen, her voice strained.

"This isn't going to be a good call, is it? Are we blown?"

"No. Nothing like that. Something much worse."

Lopez turned his head and met Houston's eyes. His voice was curt. "What's going on?"

There was a sigh and long pause on the line. "Be glad you're in the mountains. Down here, it's chaos. Short story is that there seems to be a hacker group called Anonymous that has suddenly mutated into a full-bore terrorist group. Attacks have ripped through the virtual world and bombings and assassinations in the real world."

Houston crossed her arms over her chest. "What's that got to do with us?"

"Sara, this is a national security threat. We've had major figures in business and finance and in the US Congress blown up or gunned down in the last week. At the same time, some kind of Armageddon worm has been secretly eating its way through world networks, siphoning off huge sums of money, controlling international media, and insinuating itself on every computer from academia to the Pentagon. It's already caused havoc and we're pretty sure it's just getting warmed up."

Lopez leaned over toward the phone. "That doesn't answer the question. Why on earth are you calling us? What could we do? If we show our faces down there, we'll just end up in a cell. More likely just dead."

"The President has declared a state of martial law in New York and Washington."

"What the fuck?" said Houston. "Are you kidding me? It's that bad?"

Cohen sounded tense. "They've used drones to bomb the Pentagon, Wall Street. They took over the networks to televise the execution of business and political leaders. Military units are already moving into the city. Curfew is in place. So yeah, it's pretty damn bad."

Houston shook her head. "How does the world go to hell in a week's time? You were just here!"

Lopez pressed her. "Look, if what you say is true, then what could we possibly do? Seems better that two hunted fugitives wait it out in hiding. Law enforcement will be looking suspiciously at everyone. That's some attention we don't need."

"Most of our staff has been annexed by Homeland Security and put into bodyguard roles for the powerful. It's the same all over NYPD and other FBI divisions. All kinds of 9/11 laws are getting dusted off and put into use. HS is calling all the shots. It's ludicrous!" Cohen barked a laugh. "Right now, all we've got is the core of Intel 1: me, John, Angel, JP, and Frank. The other agencies seem paralyzed. We need you. The *country* needs you."

"The country needs us," said Lopez. "Would that be the same country that wants us dead? The same government that slandered our names and has us on *your* most wanted list?"

"Francisco, today's not the day to seek justice for what happened to you. You know there are plenty of good people who deserve our best. Some of those risked their lives so that you and Sara could find a new life up there."

"And now you want to take that away from us."

Cohen sighed. "If we don't stop Anonymous—I don't know how far they'll go. I'm *afraid*, Francisco. Soon, there might not even be a country to establish your innocence in!"

"This is crazy," said Houston.

"I know it is, but aren't most disasters as they unfold? 9/11? The attack on Mecca with one of our own nukes? Please. You two have unique skills. Highly valuable skills. And you're ghosts. You have no obligation to the US government or anyone else. You can do what we can't. Even Anonymous can't find out who you are. Tools we can use to turn this around."

"Tools," said Lopez.

"Dammit, Francisco, you know what I'm saying! You've been screwed, yes. But don't you feel the least bit of obligation to the people of this nation?"

Houston looked painfully toward Lopez, who turned his head away as he spoke. "You know I do. I was a priest once."

"Then help us! We need everything we can get right now!"

Lopez looked at Houston. He nodded and closed his eyes.

"The activation protocol?" Houston asked.

They could almost hear the relief in Cohen's voice. "Yes. I'll rendezvous with you at the specified location. Thank you. Both of you."

"You're welcome," said Houston.

"And Sara, make sure you come prepared."

The light on the phone switched to green and the LCD went blank.

———————

Lopez silently grabbed his coat and walked to the door. Houston followed suit and took an LED lantern from the mantle. Together they walked outside and around to the back of the cabin. Lopez approached the cabin wall and knelt down. He brushed away several inches of snow, revealing a set of padlocked doors embedded in the ground. Houston removed the key from a chain around her neck and inserted it into the lock. They pulled together on the doors, the sound of them swinging on their hinges muffled by the deep snow around them.

A short flight of steps ended at the bottom of what appeared to be a surprisingly large wine cellar for a mountain getaway. Houston stepped from behind him and held up the lantern, pressing a button to intensify the light. Sharp shadows were cast across the room. The light spilled over crates and suitcases, canisters and body armor.

Lopez flipped open one case. Dark vestments, black gloves, and masks were folded neatly into sections. Houston ran her fingers over one of the masks and sighed.

"Never thought I'd be wearing these in the States. Never dreamed we'd be activated here."

"Well, it'll shoot facial recognition to all hell and back. We have to assume the targets will all be wired with a hundred cameras, and half of them might be governmental for all we know."

"Blended in better in Islamic countries. That's where all the action is these days. Or used to be."

"From Rebecca's tone, disguise will be the least of our issues. We'll need something more serious than clothes."

They both turned to an open wooden box, the top of the crate slightly off position. Houston tossed the lid to the ground and they stared inside. The light of the lantern glinted off black metal.

The interior was filled with guns.

PART 2

Guy Fawkes, Guy Fawkes, 'twas his intent
To blow up the King and the Parliament
Three score barrels of powder below
Poor old England to overthrow

—English Folk Verse (c.1870)

21

"WHY DO WE have to call you Fawkes, anyway?"

Three teenagers crouched in a dark hallway, whispering sharply to each other. Mark and Violetta slunk behind the third, a lanky boy with unkempt hair. He turned back to them with his finger on his lips.

"Because I said so," he whispered. "Now, be quiet. Boot camp library is around the corner."

"But it's locked," said Violetta. Fawkes reached into the back pocket of his jeans and removed several small, metal rods. "You're gonna pick it?" Her eyes widened.

"Come on."

The three moved quickly down the hallway. The building was still and silent, only the emergency exit signs providing light in the corridor. At the end of the hallway a set of double doors framed by windows on each side awaited, a soft glow from computer monitors in screen-saver mode spilling through.

Fawkes knelt down beside the lock and quickly worked the tools as the other two watched in awe. Less than a minute and the mechanism clicked. He reached up and pulled the handle down and the door opened.

"Inside."

The three rushed in, Fawkes closing the door quietly behind them. He motioned with his hand for them to follow, and he led them away from the windows toward the recessed counter where the librarian worked. He went behind a computer monitor at the book checkout and wiggled the mouse. A login screen appeared.

"What are you going to do?" asked Violetta.

"I told you. Get us all out of here," he said with a smirk.

"With the computer? Come on."

He used one of his tools to open the chassis of the machine as he spoke. "These old junkyard machines have BIOS holes you can drive a truck through." He toggled from working on the circuit board to typing at the login prompt and back again.

"I hate this place," said Mark, looking around the dark room. "All I *did was one joint. I didn't even want it. Then it's undercover cops and detention and mom sending me to this stupid place to save me, or whatever. It's all my brother's fault."*

"It seriously sucks," Violetta agreed. "Caught me with a boy in the attic. Shamed the family, you know. I'm fifteen! They think I'm a baby."

Mark swept his eyes over her body. "You're not a baby."

She ignored him. "So, Fawkes, why are you here? You never said."

The computer beeped and he typed furiously at a prompt on a black background. "Stepdad. Got tired of beating on me. Decided the ex-marine who runs this place would get my ass straightened out." He clacked the enter key and the screen went dark. A second later it lit up with a bright image of a field of green grass. "We're in."

His companions crowded around the screen. Fawkes worked quickly, searching through file systems and applications.

Violetta continued questioning. "How can you do anything from the library computer?"

"It connects to the others. See, look. I'm using this terminal window to remote login on the other system. They're so stupid. All the passwords are related. So I'm in there, too. Admin office computer. And these," he said smiling as text scrolled through the window, "are files on all of us. What's your last name, Violetta?"

"Rayon," she said.

"There you are. Born in Mexico City? What, you illegal?"

"Shut up."

"Maybe you were born in LA."

The girl gasped as the text changed at his keystrokes.

"You can do that?"

"And, looks like you're here for the month program. That's a long time."

"Yeah." Her face fell.

"But since the last day is tomorrow, you'll be going home."

She squinted at the screen. "You changed the dates!"

Fawkes opened another window and keyed in lines of code.

"Take too long to do this by hand," he said. "This little script—wait, gotta save it—it will do them all." He typed the name of the new file into the other command window.

"What's it doing?" asked the boy.

"Reading all the files in this directory, looking for the dates, and changing them. There, all done. Everyone goes home tomorrow."

"Fucking awesome!" The boy shouted.

"They'll figure it out, dumbshit," said Fawkes. "Don't get too excited. But we'll have a few days of chaos. I wonder how many parents will get calls and show up?" They laughed.

"What else can you do? Can you like put naked pictures on the screens or something?"

"Yeah, sure. We'll need to download some. And—wait, what's this?" Fawkes stared at the screen and the file he just opened. "Oh, this is good. See the dollar signs? This is budget stuff! Financials! Same format my stepdad uses for his accounts. Okay. We can do some serious damage here."

The girl's eyes darted. "Fawkes, maybe we should leave. We could really get in big trouble for this."

"Hold on, hold on." He tuned her out, opening other files, scanning the numbers and accounts at light speed. "What the hell? Ah, no, no, no, no, no. Ah, man. Tonight's fucking lotto. Oh, Mr. Harrison, you've been a very bad man!"

Mark backed away slightly. "Mr. Harrison? Don't mess with him, Fawkes. Scares the shit out of me."

Fawkes laughed. "Boot camp marine man? Yeah, but right now, I got his balls in a vice. Oh, man. My stepdad's gonna love seeing where his money went! The tuition? All the fees? It's all transferred. It goes from the school account to this one. And look whose it is!"

"Wait," said Violetta. "Mr. Harrison is stealing?"

"What's stealing? Dumbass parents send them the money. Fix us and all that. He already stole it. But that's not how the world works. I've seen my stepdad with his money. Taxes and shit. You have to do it right or the FEDs come down on you. You can go to jail, even. Mr. Harrison's gonna be in a world of hurt if this gets out—which it's going to!"

"Don't!" said Violetta. "Fawkes, don't. He'll do something. The man is messed up or something."

"Yeah," said Mark. "Look man, this was fun, but I don't want to end up somewhere worse than this. You get him in trouble, then what's he gonna to do?"

Fawkes froze a moment in thought, a half-smirk on his face.

"Excellent points, friends. But it's a crime to let this go. So, there's only one option left. And I think it's a much, much better option."

"Get the hell out of here?" said Mark.

"No. Blackmail."

BEFORE:
THE ANONYMOUS EVENT COMMISSION

DEPOSITION IN THE MATTER OF:
UNITED STATES ARMED FORCES SPECIAL TRIBUNAL,
Plaintiff,
v.
JOHN SAVAS, Defendant
Case No. M120039E-007X

DEPOSITION OF:
TYRELL SACKER
called for examination by Counsel for the
Defendant, pursuant to Notice of Deposition, at
the Independent Council Offices, located at
[REDACTED] Washington, D.C.,
when were present on behalf of the
respective parties: [REDACTED]

CBD: Will you please identify yourself for the
record?
MR. SACKER: Tyrell Sacker, Detective, NYPD.

CBD: And your background? How long have you
been with the NYPD?
MR. SACKER: Four years. I signed up after my
Iraq tour. Promoted to detective two years ago,
detective second-grade this year. Military
service and cracking cases clear a lot of
paperwork.

CBD: Congratulations to you, Mr. Sacker. Can
you tell us how you came to know the defendant,
Mr. Savas?
MR. SACKER: Professional interactions. I served
as the point of contact between FBI and the
NYPD on the kidnappings and murders by
Anonymous.

CBD: How did that come to be?
MR. SACKER: I was on site at the bank
kidnapping of Mitchell O'Kelly. Agent Cohen
from Intel 1 led the FBI team. I worked with
her and her division from that point on.

CBD: You worked exclusively with Intel 1? No
other agencies at FBI?
MR. SACKER: That's right.

CBD: Why is this? Why only Intel 1?
MR. SACKER: I'm not sure. With all the chaos,
it was just easier to set up a clear protocol
to pipe information back and forth between the
agencies. Things seemed to fall into place. You
know, it was all getting crazy and manpower was
being sucked up for a hundred security cases
and events. Ladner, my captain, barely had time
to go for a piss. The setup was working, so why
fix it?

CBD: So you were exclusively shuttling
information from NYPD on the events to Intel 1?
MR. SACKER: That's right.

CBD: Do you know whether they shared this
information with other divisions?
MR. SACKER: I assume so.

CBD: But you have no evidence for that?
MR. SACKER: No. But why wouldn't they?

CBD: Please take a look at these photographs.
In your interactions with the FBI, did you ever
come across either this man or this woman?
MR. SACKER: No. I don't think so. Who are they?

CBD: Known terrorists. Francisco Lopez and Sara
Houston. You might know them better as the
Priest and the Whore.
MR. SACKER: [INAUDIBLE] Why would they be with
the FBI?

[REDACTED]: I'll be frank with you, Detective.
You have been summoned to this tribunal to help
us figure out some highly irregular actions on
the part of the Intel 1 division led by Mr.
Savas. It is for some of these actions that he
is the subject of this inquiry.
MR. SACKER: Irregular?

[REDACTED]: Illegal. Treasonous.
MR. SACKER: No. I don't believe that. These
were good people. I didn't work day-to-day with
them, but I interacted with them enough to see
their dedication. Look, I don't know what was
going on, but they aren't traitors.

[REDACTED]: But as you noted, you were not
closely involved with them. You need to

understand the seriousness of this inquiry, and the consequences for not being completely forthcoming.
MR. SACKER: What does that mean?

CBD: The site in Connecticut—how was NYPD involved?
MR. SACKER: That was a coordination between New York and local police, as well as FBI. Most of the victims were from the city financial district. We had been filling our offices with new case files on their disappearances. We had a pretty big stake in it. FBI helped bring some of us on board in Bridgeport.

[REDACTED]: But neither you nor the local police handled any evidence?
MR. SACKER: No, it was local and NYC FBI forensics teams. Mostly the New York guys, I think. They were much better equipped to do the work.

[REDACTED]: So NYPD never saw any of the alleged evidence?
MR. SACKER: Alleged?

[REDACTED]: Can you answer the question, please.
MR. SACKER: No. Like I said, the evidence was all handled by FBI. They kept us updated on the results.

CBD: You mean the Intel 1 division?
MR. SACKER: I don't know whose forensics team was involved. I think the results were handled by that division, yes.

CBD: But Cohen kept you informed?
MR. SACKER: She did. I mean, with everything going down, it wasn't like I had her piping information to me on an hourly basis! But all things considered, they were pretty good about keeping us in the loop.

[REDACTED]: But you knew nothing about the fugitives Lopez and Houston?
MR. SACKER: No, I didn't.
[REDACTED]: Or about the Intel 1 division hacking into governmental agencies?
MR. SACKER: Sorry, what?

[REDACTED]: Or about the disappearances of the fugitives and the head of their cybercrimes division after these hacking events?
MR. SACKER: No! What are you talking about?

[REDACTED]: Would you characterize all the NYPD interactions with FBI in this case in a similar fashion?
MR. SACKER: I'm not following you.

[REDACTED]: The raid on the Anonymous group. The capture of the hackers. The hit on the warehouses and ship. NYPD had involvement, but is it not true that all evidence, all prisoners, all aspects of the case were tightly control by Intel 1?
MR. SACKER: Yes, but—

[REDACTED]: And in all of this, you would describe John Savas as masterminding all the activities at FBI during this crisis?
MR. SACKER: He was head of the division. I don't think masterminding is a good word, but he—

[REDACTED]: Thank you, Mr. Sacker. We appreciate your time in this inquiry.

CBD: [REDACTED], there are still several questions—
[REDACTED]: That will be all, Mr. Sacker.

MR. SACKER: But wait a minute! What's this all about? What hacking? What treason? You can't just drag me in here and ask me questions without telling me anything!

[REDACTED]: The tribunal reminds you that the entire proceeding is classified under past and more recent national security laws: The Patriot Acts, the Terrorist Surveillance Order, the Obama Doctrines. You are to be reminded that we are at war and under martial law. You may not speak to anyone about any of this or even acknowledge that you have been here or that this tribunal exists. The recent NSA authorizations for tracking and recording citizens means that you will be monitored via your new nation identity card through all electronic devices, both public and private.

Failure to abide by these instructions will be
discovered and may be construed as action
hostile to the United States of America. Do you
understand?

MR. SACKER: Jesus.
[REDACTED]: Do you understand?
MR. SACKER: Yes.

CBD: You are free to go.

OCTOBER 24

22

MILLER BLASTED THROUGH the left-most toll lane with lights flashing as he and Savas raced down Interstate 95 on their way to Bridgeport, Connecticut. The NSA finally seemed to be playing nice with the other agencies and had come through in a big way. With their eyes nearly everywhere in the digital world, they had been able to trace the feed for the streaming video of the assassinations to a boardwalk section of the port town.

"Near Captain's Cove," said Savas, mapping the location on his phone. "Seems to be some minor touristy location by a marina. Move a bit out from it and things deteriorate quickly. A lot of abandoned buildings."

"Buildings with serious bandwidth, it seems," said Miller. He cast a sharp look toward Savas. "Rebecca's where again? We could use her today."

Savas sighed. "Tell me about it. Look, I know I've been keeping this in a black box, Frank, but there are some very good reasons. Things will be clearer soon. Current events have complicated things, but she's tending to something important."

"Your call, John. But I can't say there hasn't been a lot of interest and speculation."

"Answers are coming. Meanwhile, we focus on today."

Miller stared a moment more at Savas, then turned his eyes back to the road. "Sure."

Savas continued. "We're going to have local and state police at the scene, and some agents from the New Haven Division. But they've saved the crime scene for us, and I've got a forensics unit en route. This is our first real physical connection to Anonymous."

"Well, let's hope these digital ghosts leave real-world footprints."

They stepped out of the car in front of a faded orange building.

159

Sandwiched between several dilapidated and shuttered structures, it hardly seemed the location for the broadcast of the most devastating video in the history of the internet. They were met by representatives of the local FBI division and surrounded by police. Bystanders stood behind police tape, gawking at the uniformed presence, cell phones raised like torches, beaming images around the world.

"Assistant Special Agents in Charge Jimmy Onda and Maggie Linven," said a tall woman wrapped in a coat and indicating a wiry man with thinning hair. Both of the New Haven agents appeared anxious and fearful.

Savas shook their hands. "John Savas and Frank Miller, Intel 1. I take it you've been inside?"

Their wide-eyed expressions gave Savas his answer.

"Yes, agent Savas. The bodies are still there. They haven't been disturbed. I was told your New York crime units are coming."

He nodded. "Yes. They should be here any minute. Mind if we have a look ourselves?"

"No. But it's pretty grim."

The four of them entered the building, a narrow hallway leading back to what might have been a storage room for a small business decades ago. Photographers continued to take pictures, and the strobing of the flashes in the dark space created a strange, discontinuous visual effect as he and Miller snapped on nitrile gloves.

Even walking in the space was hazardous. Clotted pools of blood had seeped from the center of the room outward, coating the floor in an expanse of red goo. The staging was as it had been in the video: two rows of ten chairs, corpses tied to them, stage lights affixed to stands around the massacred, and a dark cloth framing the nightmare in a semicircle of black.

"There seems to be some rigor mortis remaining in the bodies," said agent Liven. "That's consistent with the timing of the broadcast last night."

"So it was live," mumbled Miller, a scowl on his face. "Like to tie down the bastard that did this and see how he likes the treatment."

The accompanying agents eyed Miller cautiously. Savas turned the conversation back to Anonymous.

"That speech on TV sounded like talking points from a

manifesto. They truly hated the people here, saw them as criminals and murderers that deserved their punishment."

"Sounds like you're empathizing with them," growled agent Onda.

"Not at all," said Savas. "But we can't sit here getting off on righteous indignation. We need to understand them, get in their heads. We need to anticipate them. And we can't do that if we can't think like they do. Basic criminal psychology 101."

A glint of light caught his attention. Moving in a wide arc around the crime scene to avoid the blood, he approached the left side of the chairs and crouched beside a white object on the ground. One side of it was dyed red from blood that had run alongside the plastic.

"The Guy Fawkes mask," said Savas.

The head of the New Haven division stared between Savas and the mask. "I wondered what that was all about in the video. Who's Guy Fawkes?"

Savas shook his head. "Too much FBI training is still in the analog years." He stood up and continued to move parallel to the chair rows, examining the layout. "Historically, he's a figure from British religious wars in the sixteenth century. Led a failed Catholic rebellion against the English. Fast forward. Now, amazingly, he's become a general symbol of resistance to oppressive systems. Started with a graphic novel. The hacker community in particular has adopted him as a symbol. Anonymous often uses iconography of him —the mask in particular—when putting a public face on their activities. It literally keeps them anonymous and gives them some kind of mythic power."

The New Haven agent shook her head. "That doesn't make any sense."

"Yeah, well, since when do sociopathic revolutionaries have to make sense?" asked Miller. "But the idiot left the mask here."

"Exactly," said Savas, a glint in his eye. "And look, behind the chairs," he pointed with a blue finger. "Some masks from the shooters. They wore them for the entire video." He smiled. "Maybe Anonymous is made up of geniuses, but their intelligence is limited to the digital realm. They're rookies here."

At that moment, several additional agents entered the room

carrying equipment and evidence bags. One waved to Savas as he approached.

"Just in time," said Savas. "Our NYC crime unit. And it looks like Anonymous has left some interesting Easter eggs for us to open."

OCTOBER 25

23

AN UNREMARKABLE BLUE sedan pulled up to a tollbooth on the George Washington Bridge on the Jersey side. The booth officer watched as a man with blond hair and a youngish face shoved a fist out the window, offering a ten and a five from inside. The officer could see her face reflected in his mirrored glasses. She glanced inside at his companion as she took the bills, glimpsing a woman with short black hair and dark sunglasses. The man looked away as the gate swung upward, and the car dashed off, lost in the traffic swarming onto the bridge.

Lopez rubbed his hand across his face as he steered the vehicle toward the right lanes, glancing upward to a sign for the Harlem River Drive.

Houston smiled. "Miss the beard?"

"Not sure. Just getting used to it. Nervous habits and all." He took the offramp from the bridge and forced his way into the gaggle of vehicles queuing up for the East Side Highway. "I'm sure we got our photos taken back there."

Houston stared outside the window at the merging traffic. "The image-recognition solutions still struggle with facial hair, so I'm the bigger danger. We *are* number one on the most-wanted list. Anyone would want to make their career bringing us in." She looked behind them and studied the vehicles. "These giant sunglasses should mask my forehead and cheekbones some. I kept the visor down as well as we approached the toll booth. Which reminds me: fifteen bucks for a car?"

"Getting a bit ridiculous. Cheaper with EZ-Pass, but we have to stay off the grid." Lopez grunted. "So how do we fight a digital terrorist group when we stay off the grid?"

"First, they stopped being digital. Rebecca's encrypted data was informative: Bombings, shootings—nothing virtual there. Second, there are ways to get online without alerting the world to your presence. We've done it."

"*You've* done it. But these guys put the Feds to shame. It's different."

"They aren't omniscient. They don't know what to look for. We don't exist for them. Not yet, anyway. We'll be targeted later."

"They seem pretty good at that."

Houston turned her body toward Lopez, swinging a leg onto the seat to stabilize herself. "I've been thinking about that, Francisco. How the hell did these guys remotely pilot these things so skillfully? They aren't drone operators."

"Maybe they recruited some. Besides, it's not like people don't know where the Capitol is. Just punch in the GPS coordinates and off you go."

"And how do you explain hitting a moving vehicle like the CEO's car?"

Lopez nodded. "Got me there. They'd have to steer it. In real time."

"Pretty tough with an evasive target. I doubt the best drone pilots in the CIA could do that."

"Then how?"

"Same thing you said. GPS coordinates."

Lopez furrowed his brows. "I see. Mobile devices."

"Right. Even CEOs have their damn smartphones these days. If they could hack into one or more of the Big Brother databases out there, they might be able to get the target's phone GPS feed. It's like shining a laser beam for a missile. Even a *moving* target. Individualized. It's perfect. They were using this in Pakistan and other locations for al-Qaeda honchos. But it should work even better in Western nations."

"You're right. It's perfect for assassinations: auto-piloted drones coupled to the real-time coordinates of the target."

Houston spun back around as Lopez exited the Harlem River Drive and entered the streets of Harlem itself. "For now. If this is what is happening, you can bet every figure of importance will ditch their GPS-enabled tech."

"By then, it might be too late."

Rebecca Cohen was standing outside the rundown brownstone as they pulled up. Lopez and Houston exited the car quickly and scaled the steps to meet her at the doorway.

Houston glanced around them. "You're on a burner cell? No GPS?"

Cohen nodded. "As you asked. It's a cheap model, but it makes calls. You might be right about how the hits were made. It's so simple it's frightening." She motioned them to the entrance. "Let's get in and I'll let John know you're here." Cohen unlocked the door and the three entered rapidly.

"What a dump," said Houston. Cohen shut the door behind them.

The wreckage of the former living room was strewn with broken furniture, blankets, and litter. Grime coated the walls and floor. It stank.

"Former crack house that was shut down and left to die," said Cohen as she handed Lopez the keys. "Gentrification hasn't made it this far north yet."

He nodded. "It's perfect. I'll be right back."

The ex-priest returned quickly with a heavy suitcase in each hand and a backpack strapped over his shoulders. Cohen glanced briefly at the bags as she dialed. She didn't need any guesses as to what they held within. She punched a key on her phone.

"John? It's Rebecca. They're here. Yes, okay. Go ahead."

She was silent for a few moments as muffled sounds came from the speaker. Meanwhile, Lopez and Houston opened one of the suitcases, removing body armor and firearms. They stripped to their underwear, Houston with a tight sports bra, Lopez's rippling musculature distracting the FBI woman. They donned tight black tanks and black pants, strapping on shoulder harnesses with holsters for handguns and knives. Cohen thought she saw stun grenades as well in the suitcase, but it was closed before she could be sure.

She hung up the phone and approached the pair. "Some interesting news."

Houston slipped a loose black shirt on, the rough fabric concealing all evidence of the weaponry within. "The crime scene?" Lopez seemed to be tying together a long robe or coat of some kind.

"Yes," said Cohen. "The executions. Looks like our hackers left considerable physical evidence behind in their getaway. The crime unit just went through things and it's preliminary, but there are prints and hair."

Houston's face was set. "Well, it's a start. How soon until we have something?"

"This is priority one. John and Frank are on their way back with them. They'll do this right. Best people, best labs. Everything is nearby. Bottlenecks should be travel time to the labs and lab work. We'll get the fingerprints first. DNA tests in some hours plus time to search databases."

"If things go well," said Lopez. He stepped beside her.

His demeanor had changed completely. Outwardly, he was covered in black vestments, modified and tightened so as not to restrict his movements. Along with the monastic garb came a stern expression on his face, one Cohen had never seen before. For the first time, she noticed clearly the scar on his forehead, branded there by the hot barrel of a weapon held by a vengeful madman, a circle of white tissue with a cross from the site at the top. It almost seemed to glow.

Cohen cleared her throat "Yes, if things go well. Listen, I want to thank you both for coming. I know you didn't have to."

Lopez slammed a magazine into the butt of a gun and holstered the weapon within the folds of the vestments. Even his gloves and boots were black. As Houston unconsciously moved to his side, Cohen noted how similar they seemed, how coordinated their motions, like two black cats stalking prey.

"Let's get to work," Houston said. "When do we get to meet the gang?"

24

THE LOCATION WAS ideal. The overpass was large, the tunnel and space underneath deep and shadowed. They were concealed from nearby residential windows by the thundering highway above and from other eyes by the East River at their backs. The dark evening created numerous pockets of gloom away from any direct lighting. There had been a contingent of homeless, but at the sight of the figures entering the dark underpass, they seemed to sense danger, and one by one they filed out and seemed to dissolve into the flow of the city.

Savas had used Intel 1's access to city camera systems and determined that the area was poorly covered, a patchwork of lenses crossing nearby but leaving considerable holes, including the space underneath. It was not difficult to arrange for separate approaches that would avoid nearly all surveillance.

Miller, Lightfoote, and Rideout stood like statues in the cool air and watched three shadows approach from the opposite side of the tunnel. The distance was only fifty yards, and it was easy to identify one of the shapes. Cohen walked at a brisk pace several paces in front of the two other figures, her eyes locked on Savas. Behind her glided a lithe woman with a confident, feline gait, her body remaining shrouded in black even as she approached close enough for light to spill over her form. Her face was covered completely by a veil or mask. A slit in the dark fabric revealed a pair of intense, blue eyes. Beside her strode a powerfully built man, also black-clad but with his face uncovered, dark eyes and raven hair blending into the night. He seemed to possess an underlying tension that caught on the air like static.

Miller spoke quietly to Savas as the three neared. "Is that a cassock?"

"Maybe," Savas growled.

Rideout cut in. "If you mean the one next to the hot burqa-ninja, I would say yes. Definitely a cassock."

Miller shook his head. "John's mystery project. Who are these

169

ghosts?"

Lightfoote laughed, tipping her head to Miller's. "Avenging spirits, Frank."

The pair behind her stopped several feet in front of the others. Cohen stepped up to Savas and placed her hand gently on his shoulder. She glanced backward.

"They weren't happy to come, John. But they're here. They're ready." She slipped alongside him and turned to face the ciphers.

Savas spoke to his team. "I'm sorry for this secrecy, but it was necessary for reasons I can't go into. But they're here to help." He gestured toward the pair. "Gabriel and Mary. You're to know them by these names. They're professionals. They are off the radar. They have no ties or allegiances to anyone. But they're allies."

Savas saw Miller and Rideout appraising the pair. Lightfoote only smiled.

Cohen continued the introductions. "Mary is an experienced field operative. She's smart and can handle herself in just about any situation. Gabriel has a unique history, but he is unparalleled in combat and crisis."

Rideout cut in. "Gabriel and Mary? What's next, the Holy Spirit? Christ child?"

Lopez walked up to Rideout, who could not suppress an instinct to step backward. As Gabriel, he offered his hand. "We'll need all the help from God we can get, if what Rebecca has told us is true. You can trust us."

Rideout extended his hand cautiously. The two men shook. There followed a repeat of the ritual with the other members of the team. Houston paused a moment looking Lightfoote up and down.

"This the one? Your white hat hacker?"

Savas nodded. "I don't know what color she is. Red, by the color of her butchered hair." He gestured toward Houston. "Angel, meet Mary. You and JP will be paired with her and Gabriel to form a team to look into the drones and computer end of this case. The rest of us will pursue the human angle and try to dig out the members of Anonymous."

The two women shook hands.

Houston stared quietly a moment longer. The fabric around her mouth pulled tightly from a smirk. "I like this one. She's hardcore."

Lightfoote looked deeply into Houston's eyes. "We all have to be. Now the nightmare really begins."

Lopez moved between Savas and Lightfoote. "You said she was special."

Savas shook his head. "You have no idea."

"Now that we're one big, happy family," said Lightfoote, "Let's get the hell out of here. Meeting together is a bad idea. For all of us, because of Anonymous. For you," she said, indicating Lopez and Houston, "because of, well, everyone else. Right, Fearless Leader?"

Miller and Rideout looked over sharply, but Savas ignored them. "As usual, Angel is correct. But I felt to get us through this email wouldn't cut it. Sometimes face-to-face is required. So, the drone data?"

Lightfoote pulled out a black binder filled with paper and handed it to Houston. "Mary, your homework for tonight."

"What is it?" Houston asked.

Savas answered. "Angel's been digging into the drones. Records of the sales and trades of the major manufactures in the country. Hardcopy in case we'd transfer the worm to your computers. You said yours are scrubbed?"

Houston nodded. "Re-virginized."

"I think you'll find this interesting," said Angel, a sly look on her face, indicating the binder.

"Once you've had a chance to digest it, we can plan the next steps," said Savas. "Meanwhile, we split up again, contact only through burner cells without GPS. Anonymous may have compromised telecommunications, and we can't afford to tip our hands."

Miller grunted. "Or you may find a drone up your ass with an unfriendly payload."

"Who's our contact point?" Lopez asked.

"You'll have all our numbers, and should we need to dump a phone we'll update as we go. But you'll funnel all communications through Angel. The rest of you, outside of an emergency, straight to me. We believe Anonymous is using the NSA-developed snooping tools, piggy-backing on US surveillance. That means anything and everything is possibly an eye or ear for them. Angel is monitoring those tools for any hint that we've been compromised. Unlikely given our precautions, but we need to be careful, so let's keep communication minimal."

"See, you aren't the only ones hiding from Big Brother," said Lightfoote, smiling toward Lopez and Houston.

Lopez arched an eyebrow and Savas cut in. "Frighteningly intuitive, as I mentioned. I'm still calling it a feature, not a bug."

Houston half turned to leave. "Okay then. Let's break and communicate when we're ready to move."

Savas nodded, and with a last look across the members of Intel 1, Lopez and Houston walked back through the tunnel and disappeared into the darkness.

Rideout let out a long breath that condensed in the air. "Well, that was intense!"

"Trusting your judgment on this, John," Miller said. "But I know death when I see it. And it was just standing in front of me."

"They've been through hell and back," said Savas. "Believe me, you wouldn't want to walk in their shoes."

They turned to exit the tunnel in different directions, each to take a different path and avoid detection. Before leaving, Lightfoote dropped alongside Savas and pecked his cheek with a kiss.

"Explanation?" Savas had known her for too long to hope to guess.

"The Priest and the Whore." She nodded approvingly. "Good catch, Aging Overlord."

Savas sighed. "Damn, Angel, sometimes I don't know whether you're our only hope or our doom. How the hell did—"

"And it's really something that you did for them." Her expression turned serious. "But don't forget—I'm the only Angel."

25

IT WAS THREE in the morning, and a bleary-eyed Sara Houston lay back against the filthy wall of the abandoned brownstone. Small lamps were placed on the floor around a crouched figure in front of her. Cords ran to outlets in the wall at her left. Lopez sat cross-legged in the middle of the circle of light, his dark features giving him the appearance of some ancient priest petitioning the gods. Instead he bowed over reams of paper and rubbed his eyes.

"It's so obvious if anyone had been looking." His voice was deeper than usual, rough from lack of sleep.

Houston spoke over the wailing of an ambulance siren as the flashing lights played across the windows. "So, we've got records for six major drone manufacturers in the US. Every single one of them has seen a marked increase in sales over the last six months. No wonder Angel thought we'd find it 'interesting.'"

Lopez nodded, stood up, and stretched. "But we could be jumping to conclusions. Maybe the market has picked up for drones? More and more police and news stations want to get their hands on these things. Doesn't mean it's Anonymous-related. Would they even shop local? Leave that kind of trail?"

"I don't know, but they haven't shown the same talents in real world crime as they have online. Anyway, we can't visit all these places across the country. Not in time to hope to contribute meaningfully to this case. But from what I can see, four of the six plants only ship smaller scale drones. I think we can forget those. The drones carrying explosives—they'd have to be much larger."

"Agreed."

"There are only two providing models of that size in any number in the US. And guess what? One of them happens to be across the Hudson in New Jersey."

Lopez stared down at her. "I suppose you're interested in paying that place a visit?"

Houston smiled. "And there's no time like the present. What do you say we make a little excursion to Jersey?"

173

Lopez began to pace. "We're not ready. We need to do recon. Find out what this place is, try to determine the security, what we'll be up against. And what's our target? We won't have access to the guided tour."

"We'll need to be in and out in under half an hour to be sure the police don't arrive. We need their records. What they've been selling and to whom. Hopefully, we can use that to trace the drones to Anonymous. In the real world, you always leave footprints."

"So we need to identify their offices, determine how to penetrate their perimeter and security, how to get into the records, all from outside with no computer access."

"We can't do it without online access."

Lopez raised his hands. "But that opens our computers to the worm. Right now they're wiped. Pristine. Who knows how long before we're infected online."

"From what Angel said, not long."

"Then we might as well be televising what we're doing. At some point we risk opening ourselves to discovery by that thing. Best case they blow our data. Worst case they send assassins."

"So we don't use our computers."

"Then what?"

Houston stood up, stretching slowly in different yoga positions as she spoke. "Public library. We'll disable some of their safe-browsing settings, install TOR for anonymity, and get what we need and hope for the best."

"All those computers are infected."

"Yes, but the worm isn't omniscient. It's also latent until activated. Is there a trigger keyword in every strain on every computer about everything that might be a threat to them? Anonymous can't anticipate all the threats."

"And if they have anticipated that one?"

"We'll lose the computer and connection as the worm is activated. Then we go back to the drawing board, or head into the plant blind."

"With somebody alerted to our interest."

She sighed. "A risk we have to take."

Lopez nodded. "We need building specs. Satellite info. How do we get that from the library computer connections?"

Houston laughed. "More than you think is publicly available. But for the details, we need governmental access." She picked up her phone. "Angel must not be getting much sleep these days." She dialed.

Lopez walked to the window and stared out into the night. The streetlights took on a hazy blur from the soiled glass. The occasional passing car was enveloped in a glowing fog that seemed to give it a phantasmal quality. Sleep deprived and anxious, the images stirred his primitive emotions. To add to the suspense, a whistle rose and fell from a wind picking up and blowing through the alleyways.

"Hi Angel. Mary here." Houston made her way to their weapons cache. "We have a lead on a manufacturing plant in Jersey. No, not far. South of Newark. Yes. Look, we need to do some serious recon before we hit that place. We need access to FBI databases, satellite scans, building schematics. Anything on the site." She paused, listening. "We don't have time to wait until John's back. Yeah, I know you'd like his approval, but he's not my daddy. You're point for us, remember? And don't tell me permission from the boss ever got in your way!" Houston picked up a large handgun, a Browning 1911, and sighed. "Look, can you do this, give us access or not? Okay, then just do it." She nodded and checked the magazine on the weapon. "Thanks. And tell John we'll be careful."

She closed and pocketed the phone as Lopez approached. He glanced down at the weapon in her hand.

"Tell your dad to watch over us."

She smiled at the .45 caliber, semiautomatic. "He always does. Believe that."

Lopez checked his watch. "So, what time does the library open?"

BEFORE:
THE ANONYMOUS EVENT COMMISSION

DEPOSITION IN THE MATTER OF:
UNITED STATES ARMED FORCES SPECIAL TRIBUNAL,
Plaintiff,
v.
JOHN SAVAS, Defendant
Case No. M120039E-007X

CONTINUED DEPOSITION OF:
REBECCA RUTH COHEN

CBD: And it was at this point that you began to question the individual members of Anonymous.
MS. COHEN: Yes. We had compiled a list of known and suspected members that were in custody, serving time for hacking-related crimes. Other offenses. We could get immediate access to those.

CBD: How many were in custody?
MS. COHEN: In the tristate area? At that time, four. Three were minor hackers. One was a central figure in the underground community, Laurens Hanert, who had just been transferred from FCI Manchester in Kentucky. We focused on him.

CBD: Who is Hanert?
MS COHEN: An online activist, mainly. Started a hacker site open to the public. Criminal record consisted of a few Mary Jane possessions and participation in protests. Riled up a bunch of people by working with Wikileaks. Then in 2012 he was busted by the FBI in a sting operation using an informant who was a former member of Anonymous. Basically, he was set up for a hack of an intelligence company. Borderline entrapment but it worked. Pleaded guilty and got fifteen years. Longer than most murder sentences.

CBD: Did you speak to the other hackers in custody?
MS. COHEN: No. We were low on personnel. We didn't have the manpower to question them all. We thought that Hanert was our best bet.

[REDACTED]: And so the other members of Anonymous remained free.
MS. COHEN: Free? Those we knew anything about were in lockup! Free from our rushed and crazy inquiry as the world fell apart, sure. But Hanert was important. We were right to zero in on him.

CBD: How so?
MS. COHEN: He led us to some of the local hacker cells, cells that were unknown, underground. And he was the first to clue us in to Fawkes.

[REDACTED]: The mythical Fawkes, again.
MS. COHEN: I don't know what this witch hunt is about, but you're missing the elephant in the room. It's not John! Fawkes was real and nearly got us all killed as we hunted him down. If you want to understand this thing, you'd better start taking that seriously.

CBD: And where did you meet this Hanert?
MS. COHEN: FCI Ray Brook, up in the Adirondacks. Long five-hour drive from the city.

CBD: Why drive? Why not fly?
MS. COHEN: We considered it, but with the risks of the worm to air traffic and guidance systems, if we were blown it seemed an easy way to get us out of the picture to bring an aircraft down. Paranoid, sure, but staying off the grid as much as possible, that was our plan. We tried hard to stick to it. Which makes the end result so ironic. But Hanert was worth it, even if it almost cost us our lives.

OCTOBER 26

26

THE GUARD SAT the prisoner down across from them on the other side of the plexiglass. There was a voice activated speaker that did away with the antiquated two-phone system of the past. Cameras were perched on the ceiling in multiple locations. The armed guards did not leave.

Savas and Cohen had driven north from the city into the heart of Upstate New York, the scenic Adirondack mountains. Miller remained at Intel 1, serving to coordinate the division's activities in their absence as they waited for the results of the forensics. On the way up, Lightfoote had informed them of the progress on the drones and Lopez and Houston's plans to infiltrate the New Jersey plant. It was reckless, but Savas had to concede that it was necessary. The finer points of legality and admissibility seemed to matter little when the city was locked down by the National Guard. It had taken them an hour simply to get permission to leave Manhattan.

The prisoner stared across the composite glass with apparent bemusement. He was lanky and his posture slovenly, body nearly vanishing in the folds of his overlarge gray and tan uniform. A baby face aged by a short growth of beard grinned at them as his fingers drummed incessantly.

"Laurens Hanert?" began Savas as the pair of FBI agents settled into chairs. Cohen swiped across her tablet and opened several files.

Hanert smiled. "Who wants to know?"

"FBI Special agents Savas and Cohen. New York."

Hanert leaned forward with a smile. "Federal special agents. Well, well, well. What brings you two all the way up here? Don't you have a national crisis to solve?"

Cohen scowled. "I'm sure you can imagine why."

"An-on-y-mous." He broke out each syllable in slow motion, seeming to relish every moment. "Remind me why I'm locked up in here?"

Cohen set her lips in a line. "Hanert, the judge slammed you, no doubt. But you weren't a nihilist. You were an activist. You can't tell

181

me you approve of what has happened."

"FBI girl with a heart. I like that. You must be good cop. In fact, you remind me of the lady that cuffed me when they flash-bombed my bong-session at home. America is lucky to have you folks on the job."

Savas cut in. "Why do you have any loyalty to Anonymous? They ratted you out."

"Please, at least pretend you're not as stupid as you sound. It's a distributed group, Einstein. Anarchist. There isn't *an Anonymous*. There are as many as there are people and groups within it. I was sold out by one motherfucker who decided to protect his own ass when he fucked up. He set me up to cut time served. *You folks* gave him that deal. I don't blame Anonymous for this," he said, rapping on the glass and gesturing around him. "And you shouldn't blame them for what's happening now."

Cohen tilted her head to one side. "What do you mean?"

"I mean, pretty agent girl, that you need to take that bloodbath broadcast seriously. One very disturbed dude with an *I'm-the-real-Anonymous* delusion of grandeur. The rest of us are as *Oh Shit!* as you FEDs are."

"Do you know who he is?" asked Savas.

"We all know who he is. Those of us who were in deep. There is only one nut job with the chops to pull this off."

Savas leaned forward. "And who is that?"

Hanert smiled. "What's Batman say? 'If you make yourself more than just a man'?"

"That was Ducard," said Cohen. "And it's *a legend*."

"No fake geek girl here!" Hanert paused and looked between them. "Interesting. There's some chemistry between you two! Tell me, gramps, you banging this one? You getting some? 'Cause she's hot."

"What legend?" asked Savas, his voice strained.

The prisoner's smile fell. "Right now I should be asking for early parole or something. But honestly, I think this damn place might be safer than being on the outside from here on out." He leaned forward, his expression serious for the first time. "You know why communism never worked?"

Savas blinked. "I don't see what—"

"Because it's based on perching society at the top of an unstable equilibrium. I mean, forget all that 'give to those in need from what you have' Marxist ivory tower bullshit. Sounds nice. Would be a good Sunday school lesson if people understood a fucking thing in the Bible. But it's a god-damned local maxima!"

"I'm not following," said Savas, who looked to Cohen. She was staring intently at Hanert.

"Jesus, don't they teach even basic math to you *special agents*? How are you going to understand the economy or cybercrime? Look, for an economic system you want stability. Communism ain't it, because all it takes is one person—a single fucking non-saint—to start being a selfish asshole and the whole thing collapses. Of course, usually you get groups of selfish assholes that form parties and blocks and structures to protect their power. But I digress. It's inherently unstable! Like a car perched at the top of a hill. Release the brakes and zoom! That's Anonymous."

"How's that?" asked Cohen.

"It's a leaderless, structureless anarchy. That's nice for flexibility and isolating different cells when you Feds come knocking. But its weakness is in the Selfish Asshole. One person can assume control of it before it can be stopped. This new *real Anonymous* of live televised massacre notoriety. And that person is Fawkes."

"Fawkes?" asked Savas. "As in Guy Fawkes?"

Hanert slumped back in his chair. "Yeah. I mean who takes that handle? Mt. Everest ego. But this wacko was like Mozart. He could play the hell out of the code."

Savas shook his head. "You're telling me that there is a single individual—this Fawkes—who is responsible for what is happening? I don't believe you."

"Look man, I don't care what you believe."

Savas continued. "Who is he, then?"

"Hell if I know. It's not like we all got around and passed the hash pipe. It's called *Anonymous* for a reason, you know."

Cohen pressed. "Doesn't this Fawkes need other members of Anonymous to help? An infrastructure? You can't orchestrate multiple bombings, kidnappings, and hackings without money and people. A small army."

"No doubt."

"And so?"

"So, it isn't Anonymous. None of the main players anyway."

"And how would you know that?" asked Savas.

Hanert smirked. "I have my ways of knowing. Even in here. Believe me when I tell you that the main hacker groups aren't involved. It's a ridiculous idea, anyway. They aren't terrorists. Most wouldn't know which way to point a fucking gun."

"I want contact information on all of these groups. How can we find them?"

"Fuck you, man."

Cohen spoke. "Hanert, one of them might know something that can lead us to this Fawkes. We're not interested in them right now. They may have broken one hundred federal statutes, but in the larger context that's background noise. You can see how serious this is. You know about the worm, I assume?"

He nodded. "Yeah. We all do now."

"Then you know what's at stake. *Please*. You have to trust us. And we need to trust you to tell us what we need to know. Anonymous was about changing a corrupt system. But right now the entire system is about to be blown up."

"That's Fawkes. His conclusion. Some agreed with him."

"Do you?" Cohen locked eyes with him.

"No. Far more damage than gain. We could go back to the Stone Age."

"Then you'll give us names?" asked Savas.

Hanert looked at him and back to Cohen. "Yeah, but only because she's so damn pretty. I wouldn't give grandfather here jack."

"Go to hell, Hanert," said Savas.

The hacker smiled and tapped his index finger repeatedly, nail to vinyl on the short shelf between him and the glass. "I said we didn't know each other. That was mostly true. But there's online and there's the real world. Some of us did pass the hash pipe. Maybe more."

Cohen tapped on her tablet and looked up. "Well, I'm ready when you are."

27

COHEN SPED DOWN I-87 toward New York City, the black Dodge Charger clearing one hundred without seeming to break a sweat. She glanced from the speedometer over to the impressive LCD screen flashing information on the cellular signal as Savas continued to speak through the hands-free system. The hidden flashing lights had been activated, but she had left the siren off—she'd have a migraine by the time they entered the City otherwise.

"Several of the prints returned with hits." It was Miller's voice. "They're all over the place—security firms, prison guards. One was ex-military, then worked for a contractor that provided muscle in Iraq and Syria for VIPs."

"I'm smelling mercenary," said Savas, his expression grim.

"Possible. But it's not very helpful. No recent addresses. We'll fish with relatives and last known residences, but—"

"But we don't have the time for that. What else?"

"The mask was better."

"How so?"

"Hair. They got DNA sequence—likely the mask ripped out some strands with roots."

"A match?"

"No, and that's the interesting part. Doesn't match the prints. The DNA sequence is an unknown. But some genotyping gives us a first sketch of the leader: Caucasian male, brown eyes, black hair that matched the hair color found, so a good control."

"Fawkes," whispered Cohen, staring ahead at the blurred road. The dash display flickered oddly. She hoped that she wasn't pushing the car too hard.

"Sorry?" asked Miller.

Savas answered. "We'll fill you in soon, Frank. Thanks. I'm getting an alert of an incoming call from Angel. We'll get more details in an hour when we arrive."

"Right. Out for now."

185

The connection was severed and Savas punched the touch screen on the dash to take the call from Lightfoote.

"Shoot, Angel."

"John, pull the damn car over!"

"Sorry—repeat that, Angel?"

The dash screen pixelated and froze. Cohen spoke coldly.

"John, the steering wheel is locked."

Lightfoote's voice still came in over the speakers. "The worm! You're on a system with an online connection. Your car cell is tracked. Worm activity lit up on my monitors and it's you two!"

Savas felt his stomach clench. "The car?"

Cohen gasped. "Oh God."

Savas didn't have to see the needle on the speedometer begin to spin clockwise, he could feel the acceleration in his gut. Cohen frantically stomped on the brake.

"Nothing's responding!"

The speed climbed toward one-hundred and twenty. Cohen flipped the switch to engage the sirens. They were not part of the car's system, installed independently, and they blared out. Cars in front began to swerve to the side as the blue and red lights bore down on them.

"Disconnect the motherboard!" came Lightfoote's voice. "Under the steering wheel, wires lead to the circuitry. Yank them! You'll get manual, maybe. Or the car will shut down. I don't know! But disconnect, now!"

There was a loud pop from the speakers. The control panel went dark.

"Angel?" called Savas. There was no response.

"No time, John. Connection's severed. Do what she said. Get over here."

The car shuddered and Cohen gasped. Her hands were white with pressure and her shoulders hunched as she struggled with the wheel.

"John, hurry! It's trying to turn!"

Turn? At that speed, they'd flip over and roll to their deaths.

There was no time for finesse. He removed his sidearm and fired several shots into the casing of the dash near Cohen's legs. He saw her flinch as the plastic exploded only inches from her knees. His ears rang. He released his seatbelt and fell onto his back toward the driver's seat. His feet worked their way up the window and he pushed himself between the steering wheel and the floor board, body crushed into the tight space.

"One forty! It keeps trying to turn! John, hurry!"

Jesus. Grasping the smoking and shattered plastic, he ripped with all his strength. Toxic fumes from melted insulation choked him, but he reached in and grasped elements of the circuitry and wires, praying that he wouldn't electrocute himself.

Cohen screamed and he felt the car lurch back and forth and barely remain under her control. He felt sick from the motion and stench, but forced himself to focus. He ripped backward from the electronics, snapping wires and yanking pieces of the computer boards out with them, static pops exploding beside his face.

The car stalled.

"John, no control. No brakes, no wheel. Key is locked! I can't start it!"

"Is the computer control dead?"

"I don't know!"

Ahead of them construction arrows indicated a merge of traffic. Cohen could see a small bottleneck approaching and a single-file line of cars. The car continued to slow down, but it wouldn't be enough.

"John, hotwire it. Now. Construction!"

"Shit! Can you hotwire these cars?"

"Try!"

In his wild efforts to disconnect the computers of the dash, he had smashed part of the paneling around the steering column. He reached up and beat on the loosed parts, crushing several elements and the ignition cover. By now his hands were bloody, but he hardly noticed, running on pure adrenaline.

Three wire pairs. "Battery, lights, ignition," he spoke numbly as his slick fingers worked to strip the wiring, bring the leads to this mouth where his teeth ripped at the insulation.

"John, now!"

He didn't have time to figure it. He'd have to guess. He grasped two wires which he prayed were the power to the car. He disconnected them from the cylinder, twisting them together.

Cohen cried out. "We've got the dash and lights. Start it, John!"

He took the two remaining wires and touched them together. There was a spark and the engine roared. Cohen slammed on the brakes and steered the Charger. The car shuddered and leapt into the air. From his vantage point he could see nothing, only imagining her veering away from the obstacles ahead and likely off road. If the shoulder was not forgiving, they were likely dead.

A machine gun sound beside his ear announced the engagement of the antilock brakes, and the car began to spin. Cohen screamed. They wrenched sideways, glass shattered, and everything went dark.

28

"JOHN, CAN YOU hear me?"

A woman's voice. Probably his mother's.

He was at the seaside. A strong wind was blowing, waves crashing, muffling sound. No, he was in the water, floating on his back, incoming waves smashing against him, up and down, right and left. Dizzy.

His whole body hurt.

"John?"

"Please, ma'am." A male. "You shouldn't even be here." That would be dad.

Sirens. Why were there sirens at the sea?

Another jolt and his eyes opened. He was staring up at a ceiling, a blurry sphere above him condensing slowly into a fluid-filled bag. A tube ran from it to his right arm. Across from him was a shape on a gurney. A woman with brown hair. Her leg was immobilized with a metal shell of some kind. Blood soaked bandages on her head and shoulder.

"Rebecca."

He tried to sit up but found himself unable to move.

"Hold still, Captain Overlord," came the woman's voice again. "You're strapped down or you would have bounced all over the place. Highway infrastructure deterioration and all that."

"Angel?" he turned his head painfully to the side. The motion was restricted and stiff. There was something fitted around his neck.

"Rebecca's banged up, but she's okay. Well, broken leg, I think. Maybe a concussion. We're inbound to the hospital and will be there in twenty if the traffic opens some. Frank will meet us there. I was lucky to catch a ride. Not policy you know, but with the world going to shit the plumbers get some perks."

Savas looked down at his body on the gurney. A few bandages. Ripped clothing. Otherwise, he seemed to have escaped any serious injury. He let himself settle back into the padding of the gurney. He closed his eyes. "What the hell happened?"

"You don't remember?"

"They hacked the damn car. Nearly killed us. We spun out and crashed."

"That's about it," she said. "You were lucky she steered into a row of construction barriers and attenuators. Course you were going nearly seventy at that point, so it was still a mess."

"Yeah, that part I don't remember."

"Frank and I followed the last known GPS pinging from your car and alerted local emergency responders. We got up here as they were extracting you from the car. A really twisted cage you two were stuck in."

"Jesus." He looked toward Lightfoote, her bald and pierced image surreal in the sounds of the siren. "And the worm?"

She smiled. "Well, it was likely not your plan, but that act of crazy on the highway may be a breakthrough."

"How?"

"The worm in the car's system—it never got a chance to go into hiding again, to erase itself from memory and go latent. Bang, you cut the power and froze everything in place. We've got a crew extracting the computer elements from the Charger. We might get lucky."

"What does latent mean?" He just wanted to sleep.

"It's like Herpes."

"Herpes."

"Yes. Cold sores come out every now and then. Not from new virus you get exposed to, but from virus hiding out in your cells. The genetic material is dormant, *latent*. Waiting to be activated. Usually for herpes it's stress of some kind. For the worm—well, we don't know all the things that might wake it. But the programmers have established some flags. Apparently investigating Anonymous members like Hanert was one of them."

"Wake it up?"

"Well, not really wake. It's not sleeping. That's just scientific vernacular. For viruses, there are proteins that react to signals or stresses and then go and start making the virus again from the genetic code hiding out in the cells. That's waking up."

"Uh-huh."

"For the worm, the signals are detected by smaller pieces of code floating about, placed there by the initial infection, and they wake up the worm, which then assembles, like the parts of a mature virus particle, from various pieces of code across the net."

This would have given him a headache on a good day. Now it was torture.

She continued. "Usually, after that, the worm disintegrates, so the active, fully functional copy is lost, and the encrypted genome hides out latent. That's the problem getting at it. I couldn't get my hands on anything functional. Until now. Just maybe your automotive catastrophe trapped our little monster in a cage."

"So you can study it." His voice was hoarse.

"It's going to be tricky. As soon as I try to connect a live computer with functioning operating system to the thing, the worm is going to try and go active. Like melting the ice off *The Thing*. Look out. I've got to prevent that, prevent it from taking over whatever system I'm using to study it. And prevent it from erasing itself before I can look inside."

"Can you?"

Lightfoote stared into space. "I don't know." She turned her intense eyes on Savas. "But I'm going to try."

He was beginning to drift off. He fought the currents dragging him under.

"Lopez, I mean Gabriel and Mary. Have you heard anything?"

Lightfoote shook her head. "They've gone dark since we gave them the keys to the databases. My guess is they're prepping."

He nodded. "How's the world doing?"

"A few days of martial law sure has an effect on a town. It's like some apocalyptic thriller. But no zombies, sadly. The worm's been quiet since the massacre. Well, quiet is a relative word. It's still spreading, penetrating more and more systems. No one has a solution to that yet. But so far no direct attacks. No other mischief."

Her voice seemed to fade. He was staring up a deep well, trying to communicate. "That's good. That's good."

"But I think everyone knows it's a calm before the next storm. Someone has a grand scheme. Phase one is done. Phase two will be worse, I bet."

She looked down at Savas, but he was already back under. Her hand found his. "Goodnight, John. Rest up. We're going to need it."

29

A LANKY ADOLESCENT male slouched in a baroque chair, the office around him out of a seventeenth-century painting. He sported shoulder length black hair and rumpled denim attire, square prescription sunglasses masking his eyes. Across from him, a young woman with a shawl over her bare shoulders scribbled notes and nodded her head. The boy hardly looked at her.

"I will have to submit my evaluation next week, Tony," she said.

"That's not my name."

The woman nodded. "And I will continue to use it as per the juvenile privacy laws. Tony. I will not know your real identity. We protect those under custody."

"Jesus Christ. How long do we play this game?"

The therapist sighed. "You do want me to write you a good report, I assume? You want to go home?"

"Home? You've got to be kidding. Don't you read the files they send you?"

"Foster home. You ran away from home and your mother is a recovering alcoholic. Yes, I know. I meant, don't you want out of here?"

The boy completely repositioned his frame in the chair, whipping a leg across the other and folding his arms across his chest.

"It doesn't matter. I'll be out very soon no matter what you write. I've made sure of it."

"Hacking the city council's computers is a serious offense. Hasn't this experience humbled you at all?"

The boy laughed. "It was an experiment. Not for the hack. That was all too easy. For the effects. Learned a lot about cybercrime investigations and protocol. I'll follow up on the outside. But I've gotten all the data I can from this, so there isn't much of point in continuing here. And, you know, what I found on their servers was a thousand times worse than anything I've done. And they know it. I squirreled it all away where they can't touch it. They're not going to fuck with me."

The woman stopped writing. "I'm worried about you, Tony. You manifest a collection of antisocial behaviors and extreme, nearly delusional idealizations."

"Don't forget boundary issues. I think you still show too much cleavage for a doc. Go with the more discrete pushups from Victoria's. I like small and well-made. You don't have to look like you have implants, you know."

The woman buttoned the top of her blouse and angled her body to the boy. "Yes, that is what I mean. You are alienating. Hostile. Even to those you know mean you well. Psych profiles place you in the top percentiles for intelligence. If you would have cooperated on the examinations we could have placed you more accurately. But you don't use that intelligence wisely. You purposefully lash out and degrade those around you."

"Or, you could just be more honest and say that people want to maintain the facade of comfortable lies and masks they use. Jesus, don't you all get tired of it? Or is it that you're all just so fucking scared all the time? Fuck all your boxes. Fuck all your strata and rules and cages. Look at you! Borderline anorexic, overly made-up, over-slutted, and probably thinking to get a boob job. Honestly, did you sign up for this shit when God handed out the double X's?"

The woman looked away from him. "Is that why the girl left you? Did you treat her like this?"

The boy turned to face her for the first time. "Seriously? You know my fuck-buddies? Is that why they picked you?"

"We receive detailed dossiers on our patients. Personal relationships are often part of that. All anonymous. We try to understand and we need backgrounds to see the big picture."

He laughed, throwing his head back. "You lying motherfuckers. You're a goddamned Fed! I should have known it. All this therapy for juvenile offenders! You're profiling me!"

The woman froze slack-jawed but said nothing.

"I can't believe I didn't see through it sooner. I guess they picked you for that. I kinda trusted you. It was like instinct. All those pheromones and those boobs and the neural pathways—zap! They fuck you up. You really want to know? Zap! That's what the girl was. Lots of research you can read online. It's like heroin, you know? Same brain pathways. Same high. Same addiction and withdrawal. Except it also plugs into all these *emotional pathways. So it's a hundred times worse than heroin. Hormones and receptors and neural pathways designed over ten million years to get chunks of meat to fuck and make more chunks of meat."*

The woman paled and pulled back slightly in her chair.

"These thoughts, Tony, I am concerned—"

"You are concerned," *he barked, chuckling. "You don't give a fuck except for what kind of checklist of personality traits you can enter into a database for your puppet masters. Fingerprints, blood type, you likely got my DNA. Now it's gonna be some kind of brain-print. You need a pattern, profiles, data for the algorithms to train on. Not really there yet, are you, though? But let me help. I can tell you all about our relationship." He leaned forward toward the woman. "I think you like talking about sex. I think it arouses you." He held his face steady in front of hers. "Maybe that's why you do this."*

The woman licked her lips.

The teen pivoted his body again and looked away from her. "Anyway, that fucking girl. I can tell you, heaven and hell, love and loss. All that. Damn, that panic. Lost, lost, lost." He replaced his glasses. "But that's the withdrawal. You're sick, all the hormones fucked to hell. Then, you finally come out of it. Then you see. You finally know the truth."

"Which is?" Her voice was hoarse and dry

"That there is no love. No destiny. No meaning to these stupid feelings. That's the delusional thinking, doc. Then you understand that emotion is the problem."

She shook her head vigorously. "Don't you see, Tony? This is just another form of extreme idealization. You went from an extreme belief in transcendent love to an extreme disbelief in all love, a rejection of all meaning in human emotion."

His voice turned cold. "Look, dogs love us. Cats nurture their young. Birds have emotions. The only thing that distinguishes us from the rest of the animals is a small first step in abstract thought. That's it. With emotion, we're puppets to our dicks, our ovaries, some asshole with a shiny car or a promise that you'll live forever. Cut the emotion! Engage the fucking homunculus."

He stood up and pressed his jacket flat, buttoning it closed.

"We're done here," he said. "You go write your report. Like I said, they're not going to do anything with me. They wouldn't dare. File it. It

won't matter. In ten years, it won't even exist."

The woman's eyebrows arched upward, but he didn't pause to consider her confusion. With confident steps, he walked to the door of the office and left.

OCTOBER 27

30

IT WAS ONE of the largest water filtration plants in the United States. Twelve acres, drilled through bedrock to a depth of over four stories in the Bronx's Van Cortlandt Park, it sat over one of the main supply lines feeding water from the Croton Reservoir into New York City. Water flowed from the force of gravity upstate through two eight-thousand-foot-long tunnels into the plant, where particulates were removed, solids dewatered by centrifuges, and the filtered water disinfected with ultraviolet light and chlorine. Chemical alterations were then made to control corrosion and add fluoride.

The entire process utilized several networked controllers, twelve workstations, five separate operator interfaces and numerous 'intelligent' devices, including flow meters, pressure and temperature sensors, transmitters, and automated chlorination analyzers. Everything was networked, highly modernized, automatic, and requiring far less human oversight than anything else like it ever produced.

On the evening of October 27th, the first sign of problems was detected by a skeleton crew manning the equipment to analyze the quality of the final water to leave the facility. A young woman with Indian features and lush black hair gazed at the readings from a dilapidated sensor, a relic from the early testing of the computer systems. Her body was tense, the white of her lab coat contrasting with the deep caramel of her skin. The readings from the other sensors were normal. She felt that she shouldn't care about this artifact of older tech, one that management had never given the order to remove. While it had never acted up before, common sense told you that someday it would fail. It shouldn't bother her when all else appeared normal.

But it did. She spoke into a mobile phone.

"No, Larry. Everything reports nominal. It's only the older ovation monitor. It's screaming on the chlorine and fluorine levels. Look, I didn't want to get you out of bed for this. Probably just the old unit has finally gone senile on us."

There was a pause in her speech as she listened intently. "No, really, no need to come in. Look, I know your close, it's just I...Okay. All right. Fine. I'm happy just to log it, but if you want...Okay. Yeah, I'll call the chemists on three."

She walked up to the bank of computer monitors to check once more the readings from the chemical sensors. Satisfied that all was within normal parameters, she sat down to open a video call with the staff upstairs.

"What the hell?"

The computer was unresponsive. She moved to a nearby terminal, but it too had completely locked up. The unease that had buzzed in the background of her mind at the anomalous readings came much more strongly to the fore. *Is there a computer problem?* In all the years she had worked here, there had never been a glitch affecting more than one unit. Multiple computers down alongside the dangerous readings coming from the other unit—she whipped out her cell phone and called the upstairs number directly.

"This is Deepta from Analysis. Look, are you guys having any computer problems?" Her brow furrowed and she listened. "Yeah, me too. Look, I need to ask you a favor. I'm getting some ridiculous readings on an older sensor. It's not networked with the others; it's probably just failing. But all this has me nervous. Is there a way you can monitor your additive levels? Yeah? Sure, I'll wait. I'll put you on speaker while I recheck that damn unit."

She pressed a button on the mobile phone as she walked to the far wall and crouched in front of the older equipment again.

A voice erupted with distortion from the small speaker of the phone. "Okay, Deepta. Give us a few minutes here. There is a panel of sensors directly on the additive pipes. They *should* be read by the main software—and all that looks good—but they also display the values on the sensor units themselves. We can read them off directly. Hang on."

"I'll be right here."

She shook her head. The anomalous readings had not normalized. In fact, they were shooting up. It was like they were unloading their entire store of toxic chemicals into the New York City drinking water!

The door to the operations center burst open. A middle-aged man with a crop of silver hair dashed into the room. He was roughly dressed, clothes obviously thrown on in a hurry, hair uncombed. He rushed straight to the computer monitors as he put on his glasses.

"Mike, wait that's no good. There—"

"Deepta! What the hell's wrong with the interface?"

"It's down! I'm trying to tell you. All the machines! And not only here, but on other floors."

"But the software's still running. I just can't access anything. God, we'll have to reboot everything!"

"Mike, come look at these readings." Her superior shuffled over and bent down to examine the older unit. "Please tell me this is malfunctioning."

His face paled. "I grew up on these things, Deepta. When they fail, they don't give readings like this. The checks are too thorough in the logic. This is not failure behavior. We need to find out what's going on with the treatment chemicals."

"Right. I'm on the line with—"

The phone popped. "Deepta? Mike? This is Herman Richards upstairs. We have several people double-checking, but your aberrant sensor is *not*, I repeat *not* malfunctioning. Our pipe sensors are screaming. The valves are completely open. We're dumping everything into the supply!"

"Can you shut things down from there?"

"So far no! All computer control is locked. We can't get into the system. We're force rebooting a few to see if that clears the problem. Meanwhile we're poisoning the water supply for millions in the city! We've got to get a public health message out. Get this on the news. Something!"

"Calm down! We follow protocol. Deepta, get the manual open and let's go by the book on this."

"We went paperless three months ago, Mike. The hard copies were recycled."

"Jesus!" He shook his head. "Then go from memory! Meanwhile, we've got to shut it down before too much gets out there."

The voice on the phone sounded panicked. "I know! What if we can't?"

"Then we're going to have a hell of a lot of sick people come tomorrow."

BEFORE:
THE ANONYMOUS EVENT COMMISSION

DEPOSITION IN THE MATTER OF:
UNITED STATES ARMED FORCES SPECIAL TRIBUNAL,
Plaintiff,
v.
JOHN SAVAS, Defendant
Case No. M120039E-007X

CONTINUED DEPOSITION OF:
JOHN SAVAS

CBD: And what was the result of the filtration plant failure?
MR. SAVAS: Minor. New York only got about 10% of its water from the Croton pipeline. They manually shut off the flow before much of the tainted water got into the main supply into the City. What did was diluted out. We got lucky.

CBD: And this was the worm?
MR. SAVAS: Yes. The computers running the plant were all infected, of course. They lost control of them. Like with our car. Everything is plugged in now, even things that are life and death. Something as basic and driving, as basic as water.

CBD: So, it's your belief that Anonymous tried to murder you by hacking your car?
MR. SAVAS: Not Anonymous. We were learning better than that. Fawkes.

CBD: But you have said that he called himself Anonymous.
MR. SAVAS: I could call myself the Pope, but it wouldn't mean I could lead services at the Vatican.

CBD: You claim you were nearly killed by this Fawkes. How could he hack your car?
MR. SAVAS: Turns out it's not that hard. We were in a brand-spanking new Dodge Charger model outfitted for police work. One of the most powerful engines in a production model— seemed some great wheels to make time upstate. What a bunch of idiots we were. Like the civilian models, it came standard with a new

high-tech digital interface. Everything from
GPS navigation and mobile apps to handsfree
phone calls. Probably would do your dishes if
you asked nicely. Used the latest mobile phone
tech to connect to the internet. Ran one of
several operating systems vulnerable to the
worm. QED. Infected.

[REDACTED]: And how would you know all this?
MR. SAVAS: You do remember I have a cybercrimes
group? Angel filled us in once we got back, as
luck would have it in one piece. We went back
to older Crown Vics from the garage after that.
They weren't networked and so were isolated
from infection.

CBD: How would Anonymous know to target you?
MR. SAVAS: *Fawkes*, not Anonymous. And that one
is a bit of a mystery. Maybe by pairing our FBI
origin coordinates with the prison destination.
Hanert could have been a trigger, a flag, and
once raised, they could monitor our phone calls
made from the car system. We were really
stupid. So much for off-grid. We ignored the OS
backdoor in the car we were sitting in. And we
knew that wasn't going to be the end. The clock
was ticking. Fawkes knew we were poking around.
It was just a matter of time before they tried
something else to slow us down.

CBD: Wouldn't the break-in at the drone factory
have had the same result?
MR. SAVAS: No. Lopez and Houston, they were
ciphers. No ties to anything. Sure, it would
have given Fawkes a jolt, but nothing to bring
FBI, and our division in particular, into the
cross-hairs. They were in and out like ghosts.
And thank God Houston took the paper copies.

CBD: Please elaborate.
MR. SAVAS: On what? The break-in?
CBD: Yes.

MR. SAVAS: This is second-hand, but they had
the same problem we were facing, this
dependence on digital technology for nearly
everything, and now behind it all, the worm, of
course. So, they worked off public computers, I
think the library. Angel gave them temporary
codes to the federal databases, access to

names, locations, sat imagery, and more. Down
to the positions of the guards on an hourly
basis as I understand it. They even had the
specs on the security system. Not sure what
happened, if anything, to the computer systems
they used to do all this research on.

CBD: And they used this information to break
into the factory?
MR. SAVAS: Yes. They had schematics for the
buildings, and Angel had put a trace on orders
coming in and out to verify the likely center
of operations and data storage at the facility.

CBD: Which was your target?
MR. SAVAS: If we could get the buyer info, we
might find leads. Those drones had to go
somewhere. Someone had to get them at a
specific address. All this would leave a trail.
It was worth a shot.

[REDACTED]: So you ordered a commando-style hit
on a civilian manufacturer without
authorization of any kind?
MR. SAVAS: I did. But since the fugitives
didn't work under me or anyone else, you might
say that they acted on their own recognizance.

[REDACTED]: Are you saying you had no authority
in this? Didn't you lead the investigation and
bring these criminals into this?
MR. SAVAS: Lopez and Houston helped bust this
case open. They were instrumental then and
later in bringing Fawkes to justice. Just who
do you think the criminals were in all this?

[REDACTED]: Well, that indeed, Mr. Savas, is
why you are here. And until you give us what we
want, we have no option but to assume that you
are implicated in a bigger conspiracy.
MR. SAVAS: What is this nonsense? I've told you
—you've made me tell you over and over—I don't
know where Angel is. I don't know where Houston
and Lopez are. When you sent the cavalry to pry
us out of our own offices, by the time the
smoke cleared they were gone.

[REDACTED]: We want the file.
MR. SAVAS: You have it! It was on her damn
computer! I don't understand any of this!

[REDACTED]: A copy was made. A thumb drive was connected to that computer and the file was copied.

MR. SAVAS: I can't help you with that. You have your copy, you can try to decrypt it as well as they could. Unless. Wait a minute. [INAUDIBLE] This isn't about trying to figure out what Fawkes was trying to tell her, is it?

CBD: Let's proceed to the next set of questions, Mr. Savas.

MR. SAVAS: I'll be damned. It's about the file! You don't want that file in her hands. In anyone's hands! You're trying to bury the information!

CBD: Let's take up what you have said Houston found in the factory records. First—

MR. SAVAS: That's it, isn't it? What the hell is going on here? What are you trying to cover up?

OCTOBER 28

31

A HEAVY COLD front had rolled in a thick layer of clouds, and the evening was without moon or starlight. Lopez and Houston lay prone at the top of a small hill overlooking a factory. Inside, thousands of drone unmanned aerial vehicles were assembled for governmental and civilian buyers, loaded at a wide dock, to be shipped across the country. The factory was isolated in a relatively undeveloped region in New Jersey east of Newark, nestled in a minor valley. The small facility was surrounded by tall fences and wire, imaged by numerous cameras, and protected by a small crew of five security guards at several stations scattered around the compound.

The two fugitives wore dark clothing and gazed down through night vision scopes mounted on rifles. Houston pulled her head back from the lens and whispered.

"I think we've got shots at three guards from here."

"Should be four," grumbled Lopez. "The info is outdated, so our guard count is wrong. Other things could be off."

"You didn't expect a briefing from them, did you?" she smirked. "Three down is a big win. I doubt they'll have added many more guards. Maybe one is out to piss."

"Things could get messy. These guys are naive hires. They don't deserve a grave for this gig."

Houston sighed. "So we'll do our best, Francisco. Right now the big game is threatening many more lives. Even theirs."

"I know. So, let's bring them down. One should do it. Two for sure with plenty of margin for safety on the overdose."

They bent to the rifles, aiming down the hillside. The sounds were soft, muffled expulsions of pressured gas. Each of the guards jerked when hit, twitching again from a second impact. Within seconds, each fell to the ground, unmoving.

Houston pressed a button on her wristwatch. "Clocks running."

Lopez donned a ski mask and they sprinted down the hill, arriving at a central transformer near the fence line. Houston removed a small pack, placed it on the metal casing with a clang as the magnet took. They dashed away from the location as a red light blinked on and off behind them, putting several hundred feet between themselves and the pack when it blew. A small explosion lit the dark night orange with a shower of sparks. The facility lost power, and they quickly cut through the fence and raced toward the central office building.

The structure was the size of a residential home, lined with corporate dark glass, dwarfed by the manufacturing buildings and warehouses around it. They passed two guards on their way in. Large darts in their thighs left them unconscious, drugged. As they neared the entrance, the door opened and two figures stepped out.

The two guards were disoriented, the blast and light drawing their attention. The blurred motion of their assailants was glimpsed too late, part of a distraction of violence and prone figures, two shadows blending into the night.

The intruders engaged without weapons. In a flurry of hands and feet, the guards were disarmed, their weapons sent flying, sudden blows to the abdomen and head stunning them. Before they could even cry out, both were down, unconscious in front of the doors of the office. Lopez emptied the guards' weapons, slinging the ammunition into the night. Removing wires from their belts, the two shadows secured the guards, tying their arms and roping their ankles together. Duct tape sealed their mouths. Houston grabbed a keycard from one of the men and tried it on the front door. It opened.

"Emergency power's up," Lopez noted.

They headed inside. Weak illumination spilled from corners in the room and green lights from some of the older cameras.

"Smile pretty. Just keep your mask on," said Houston.

Passing the reception desk and moving down a hallway, they stopped in front of a door labeled 'Records.' An alphanumeric keypad was embedded in the door beside the handle.

"I don't recall any of the files mentioning a code for this, do you?" she asked. Lopez shook his head. "Didn't think so. Hinges?"

Lopez reached behind his back and unslung a short-barreled pump-action shotgun. Houston stepped backward as he aimed. He fired blasts near the top, middle, and bottom of the door across from the handle. Wood splintered and metallic fragments rained around them. He spun and kicked the door inward, the wood hanging to the frame weakly from the keypad and lock mechanism, then ripping free and thudding to the floor.

Inside were a set of computers and floor to ceiling filing cabinets. They moved quickly.

"Grab all the hard drives," said Houston, pulling out what looked like a large pocketbook. She unzipped the leather and removed several tools. "We'll deal with them later. I'm going to go for paper."

Lopez knelt down and pulled the chassis off one of the computers. "That wasn't part of the plan."

Houston went to work with several microtools on the locks of the cabinets. "Neither was the fact that they still had paper records."

"The disks will be fast! It will take you forever to get the records."

"We've got twenty minutes. A little more if they're out for donuts."

The shell popped off one of the units as Lopez reached inside to disconnect the wires to the hard drive. "Cutting it close, Sara!"

There was a click, and the large cabinet door was slung open. Houston shone a small flashlight on the folders and began scanning their content. "Paper, Francisco. No bytes. No worms. No worries. I'll be done before you."

Grunting, he dropped one drive into a bag and moved to the next computer. Within ten minutes, Lopez had removed all the drives and placed them in the bag. Houston called him over, showing him regions in three cabinets where purchase orders over the last six months were filed.

"That's three full boxes!"

"So, a transport!" she said, pointing to the far end of the narrow room.

Lopez rushed over and wheeled a wobbly cart to her side. Together they hefted three large boxes full of files onto the slight metal surface.

"This is definitely not my idea of stealth. I hope this doesn't collapse."

They sped out of the building as fast as possible, Houston with one hand stabilizing the boxes, Lopez pushing the cart from behind as they navigated prone bodies, ramps, and the sharp rise of the hill.

They were forced to remove the boxes and fit them through the hole in the fence one by one, bringing the cart awkwardly through at the end.

"It's no good. We can't get that thing up the hill," said Lopez.

"Okay, bring the car around. Tape the plate, but we'll have to lose it tonight."

He nodded and sprinted up the hill. Houston waited in the cold night air, her fogged breaths coming quickly. She heard the engine cough.

Lopez rounded the corner of the hill and braked hard beside her, popping the trunk. They worked quickly, flinging the boxes in, the car bouncing with each impact. Houston slammed the trunk and ran to the passenger side, Lopez already seated. He gunned the engine.

Red and blue lights flickered in the distance, reflecting off the low lying clouds.

"Wait, Francisco! We'll need a back road. Listen!"

Sirens. The police were converging on their position from the main route. Lopez spun the car in a one-eighty and tore down the road in the opposite direction.

He laughed ruefully. "Well, this sure feels familiar."

BEFORE:
THE ANONYMOUS EVENT COMMISSION

DEPOSITION IN THE MATTER OF:
UNITED STATES ARMED FORCES SPECIAL TRIBUNAL,
Plaintiff,
v.
JOHN SAVAS, Defendant
Case No. M120039E-007X

CONTINUED DEPOSITION OF:
JOHN SAVAS

CBD: And so the computer records led you to the warehouse on Long Island?
MR. SAVAS: No. The hard drives melted down.

CBD: I'm sorry?
MR. SAVAS: Well, not literally. But all the facility's computers were infected. Turns out, the worm was indeed monitoring the records of the drone sales, so Fawkes at least saw that as a potential vulnerability.

CBD: The worm erased the files?
MR. SAVAS: Nuked all the drives. One after the other as they tried to access them. Maybe Angel could have prevented it, although I doubt it. But Lopez and Houston didn't have the digital chops to even try.

CBD: Then it was the paper records you mentioned.
MR. SAVAS: Yes. Can you imagine? Two burglars with the police bearing down on them toting six months of paperwork out of a secured facility? I don't know if Sara guessed there might be a problem or it was just instinct to get everything they could get, but it saved our investigation. They must have spent hours going through that crap. But they knew what they were looking for: shipments of large drone models, likely in quantity. And they found them.

CBD: So, all of them went to the Long Island facility.
MR. SAVAS: No, they weren't that reckless. In the end we'd find that they ordered multiple drones from several facilities, using a series of aliases for each order, often multiple

orders under different names from the same
facility. Then they'd ship them to one of five
or ten storage locations, then re-mail them.

CBD: How did you discover this?
MR. SAVAS: You'll have to ask Lopez and
Houston. Too bad they aren't here.

OCTOBER 29

32

A MISTING RAIN partially solubilized the grime on the gray Ford Taurus that pulled alongside a nondescript brick warehouse in Long Island City. Lopez and Houston exited, both dressed in dark trench coats and shades. Passing underneath the "Your Storage!" sign and the security cameras, they entered the small business.

The office was more a glorified hallway outfitted with a narrow countertop and secretarial equipment on the right side. Behind the counter was a receptionist, a slight African American woman, with thick glasses and makeup obscuring much of her face. She spoke into a microphone on a headpiece as she motioned for them to sit. Houston turned to look behind her at a small and uncomfortable looking bench. She shook her head at Lopez.

Reaching over the counter, Lopez removed the headset in one quick motion, tossing it to the side. The receptionist looked stunned.

"Hey! Just what do you think you're doing?"

Houston placed a hundred dollar bill on the counter. "We'd like to purchase the expedited service."

"The expedited...?"

"Just get your manager out here now and you'll get another one."

Grabbing the bill in her hand, she stood up slowly, her eyes ludicrously exaggerated in the strong lenses, her bright purple eyeshadow giving her features a slightly alien quality. "Just a second." She stepped out from behind the counter and clicked to the end of the room in impossible heels. She opened a flimsy door. "Hey, Ryan. A man and a woman need to speak with you."

"What do I pay you for, bitch? You deal with it!"

The receptionist startled as Houston handed her another hundred. "Go on back to the call. We've got it from here." The woman took the bill and scampered away.

Lopez opened the door and stepped into a crowded room. Likely an addition to the hallway, the walls were a temporary attachment, the flooring added over part of the cement below it. He canvassed the ceiling and corners, the desk surface and walls. There were no cameras.

A bald man sat over a terminal and flashed them a puzzled expression.

"Who the hell are you?"

He gasped as Houston pointed her Browning at him. Lopez closed the door.

"We're the ones with the guns. Don't scream. Keep your hands over the desk."

"Oh God, oh God, oh God. Please. Take what you want. I have a safe, there!"

"Shut up," said Houston, ignoring his gesture. "I'm going to ask you a few questions. You are going to answer them truthfully and quickly. Or I'll let my partner deal with you." Lopez held a hunting knife in his hand.

The man swallowed, struggling to speak. "Yes."

"So, Ryan," she began. "What do you do here?"

"We, ah, store things."

"What things?"

"We don't ask. It's like a remailing service. People ship here, we get another address for the item and ship it there. Keeps buyers and sellers separate. Anonymous."

"Anonymous?" said Lopez.

The man stared at the knife, terrified. "Yeah. Private. That's why we don't ask what's in the boxes. It's all perfectly legal."

"So you don't know where the boxes come from. How do you know where to send them?"

"Paired codes. The sender has a code that has to match the buyer's code before we ship to the buyer's address. They get those from whatever exchanges they make their deals on. That way nothing can be traced."

"But you put the items in the mail. In their original boxes?"

"Oh, yes. We never open a box."

"Then you must know the weight of the items. For postage."

He nodded. "Yes."

"And you have records of that?" Houston asked.

"Of course. That's our main expense. Why are you asking this?"

"The people with guns ask the questions, Ryan."

The man shrank into his chair. Houston removed a set of folded papers from inside her coat and looked them over. As the seconds ticked by the manager began to sweat. Beads of perspiration dripped down his forehead, and his underarms stained.

Houston grabbed a pen and circled several regions on the paper. "Ryan, I need you to find shipments that match these weight specifications."

"Now?"

"Yes, now."

The manager typed furiously on his computer keyboard. Within seconds, his face relaxed. "Yes, I have a bunch of them. Lots of orders match those specs exactly."

"Where are they shipped to?"

"Um. That's interesting. All shipped to the same place. Some address in Jersey."

"We would like you to print out one of those records, Ryan, with the address."

"Yeah, okay." He clicked several times with his mouse. A small printer behind Houston whirred to life.

She grabbed the printout and stared at it. Nodding to Lopez, she grabbed the papers she had given the manager and then pocketed all of them. A wad of cash thudded on his desktop.

"You wouldn't lie to us, would you, Ryan?"

He looked at the knife again. "No way." He licked his lips.

"We were never here, and you can enjoy the fee for this priority service." The man nodded dumbly, taking the money. "But this is a discrete service, right?" She glanced at Lopez, who twirled the knife slowly, staring at the serrated edges. "There isn't going to be any need for us to come back and register a complaint that our privacy has been violated, is there? Nobody would like that."

Again the man swallowed. "No. I never saw you. I never want to see you again."

"That's good," she said smiling, opening the door.

Lopez sheathed the knife, staring fixedly at the bewildered man. "It was a pleasure doing business with you."

33

"YOU SURE YOU'RE up to this, John?"

Savas shifted his position in the car once again. It didn't help. He was bruised all over his body, several lacerations still quite painful to the touch. He stared at Miller and ground his teeth. Of course he was *up to it*.

"Frank, I'd have to lose a leg or worse to have an excuse not to be on the ground in this crisis. Are you going to tell me otherwise?"

"You are literally the boss, so okay." The ex-Marine continued to focus ahead as he drove. "And Rebecca?"

"Tibia was snapped. Soft tissue damage from the bone as well. It's set, she's stitched up. But it's going to be a serious cast and crutches for a couple months. She'll heal. She's tough."

Miller nodded. "It always seems to get personal with us, doesn't it?"

Images of a gray-haired man swept through Savas' mind. They came with explosions and collapsing buildings, a sniper round buried in the shoulder of the man driving next to him. A massacre of an FBI division. A threat to Rebecca's life.

"Yeah, and I'm getting kinda tired of it."

"We sure know how to make friends." Miller's smiled faded as they pulled alongside a black van in an abandoned parking lot. "Don't think this club is going to be very taken with us today. I hope this intel is worth it."

"Highest level contact in Anonymous we have. Rebecca seems to trust him. Let's see if she's right."

A commuter train rumbled overhead along the Queens subway line. Nestled underneath, a rusted warehouse waited before them. Heavily armed FBI agents in body armor stepped out of the dark van and grouped around them.

Savas limped toward the group. "I'm sorry to pull you from every which division, but you know what we're up against. FBI—now the damn Federal Bodyguard Institute." The men laughed. "Thank you for coming on such short notice. We might already be too late, but we

221

have to try. Police are inbound, but we'll be without their backup for the dangerous parts. I'll let our vet from Kabul fill you in."

Miller stepped forward. "There was no time and no data to recon this right. I don't know what we'll find in there. Might well be empty. Might be an armed engagement with as many as ten hostiles. But if our intelligence is right, it's going to be a bunch of hackers scared shitless about what's going down. We don't need them dead— understood? We need information. They need to be able to talk, and dead men don't. Defend yourselves but keep a level head. We'll go in through the main door with a volley of flash bangs and tear gas. Unless they're trained militia, that ought to have most of them rolling on the ground crying for mommy. Bag them and into the van. Make sure you canvas the interior and clear it. We don't want any surprises. Questions?"

"Yes, sir," came a voice of a young blond to the right. "Is this Anonymous? Are these the guys?"

"We don't know, but not likely. But we think they can get us to the real criminals. So remember—*alive*. Understood?"

The men nodded. Along with Savas and Miller, they donned gas masks. Savas drew his weapon. "Okay, boys, your show."

The SWAT team filed off in a quick jog, splitting into two groups on either side of the door, weapons at the ready, quickly reaching the wall of the warehouse and using it as cover from the building windows. They slid along the sides, Miller and Savas at the far end of the lines. An officer nearest the door pulled slightly on the handle near the ground. The roll-up door moved slightly, and he gave the thumbs up. Miller nodded, the other officers set, and the door was raised.

The men dashed inside and out of sight. Savas ran forward and could just discern the arc of canisters being lobbed into the air and over a set of dark obstacles inside the building. The flash bangs flashed and banged. It was nearly stunning even from their position. Several canisters of tear gas filled the space inside with a cloud of burning vapor.

For a moment, there was no other sound. Then the screams began.

The SWAT team pulled out the last member of Anonymous just as their police backup finally arrived. They had never been in any danger. The disoriented and snot dripping youth that were dragged out of the warehouse were never going to put up any kind of a fight. Some of the SWAT team administered first aid to those who had suffered most from the chemicals and shock. It looked to Savas that the agents felt sorry for them.

The blond leader of the SWAT team came out of the warehouse, mask in hand.

"Secured?" asked Miller.

"Yeah," he said, coughing. "Most of the gas is gone. And you need to come and see this."

Savas arched an eyebrow. "Right behind you."

He led the special agents into the warehouse. The dark obstacles Savas had seen were revealed to be rows of computer hardware stacked six feet high in places. The SWAT officer zig-zagged through it like a maze and brought them to the center, a space occupied with several large monitors. And two decomposing bodies.

"Jesus, that ruins your lunch," said Miller, scowling.

Savas stepped forward and stared at the bodies. Flies danced around the forms and maggots were slithering over the decayed faces. "They've been here a while. Likely rules out a killing by our friends."

"Today, anyway," said the SWAT officer.

"I doubt they'd have come back here," said Miller. "Division in the ranks?"

Savas nodded. "Looks like a hacking bunker. I'd say these poor jerks pissed somebody off."

"Fawkes," said Miller. "He's turning out to be one ruthless bastard."

"Okay, let's get a forensics team in here and see what we can find. My guess is the computers are all wiped. But we need to check them all. Meanwhile," he said, turning toward the door, "I've got a few questions for our hogtied friends outside."

He strode back out the door, Miller close behind. The members of Anonymous were placed in a circle in front of the FBI van facing outwards. Their eyes were red, faces flushed, one with bandages over his head. Groups of NYPD and SWAT officers mingled in haphazard groups around them. He stopped in front of the circle.

"I think you know that all of you are fucking screwed," he began. "Basically anyone connected to Anonymous right now likely goes straight to jail without their $200. Not to mention, as you surely saw inside, the real problem is still out there on the loose turning you folks into corpses."

He could tell the last remark struck a raw nerve as several bodies jerked and heads turned toward him. He hoped to God he could reach the sane part of someone in the group.

"Now, we have a global catastrophe looming. We know about the worm." More heads turned. "We know about Fawkes. But we don't know where he is or what the endgame is. But I think it's clear it's going to be ugly. As in civilization-ending ugly. We're going to get you all back to lockup to question you there, but time is not our friend. So I'm going to give you the opportunity to talk right here, right now. Right now there's no Miranda. There's just me and you and getting us all out of this mess."

"Fuck you, pigs!" yelled one of the group, a long-haired man across the circle. He spat at Savas.

"Anyone else? Anyone else with parents? Friends? Kids? Anyone who wants to help us stop this before it's too late? Right now I couldn't give a rat's ass about you, your amateur cybercrimes, or the Anonymous Manifesto, or whatever you have. I need answers now! I need to stop this. Help me."

There was only silence. Police red and blue flickered over them like washed out club lights, the setting sun beginning to dip below the taller buildings in midtown across the river. Officers in heavy gear shifted weight, the friction of thick Kevlar on rubber popping around them. Savas looked up into the sky with his hands on his hips. A crimson scab ran down the left side of his face.

"No one?" He shook his head and turned to the SWAT team. "Okay. Load them up. We'll try again back home."

"Wait!" A female voice. Savas turned to his right. A black-haired woman with deep black eyeliner stared back at him, the goth makeup running down her face as her eyes watered.

"Yes?"

"Shut up, Poison! Don't make this personal!" said the long-haired man.

"Up yours, Protos. Fawkes is into some fucked up shit. Pig's right. Somebody has to end this."

Savas crouched down beside her, several agents stepping forward with weapons at the ready.

"You know Fawkes?"

She laughed. "Yeah, you might say. Better than all these losers here, anyway. Better than you Protos and your group of ass-wipes."

"Fuck you, Poison. We'll remember this."

She laughed. "Remember this? You gonna remember Dave and Chen? Yeah? You don't get it. He's burning everything to the ground. Us, too! There ain't gonna be nothing to remember, you dumb fuck!"

Savas tried to control his voice. "How do you know Fawkes? What can you tell me about him?"

She looked Savas in the eye and smiled. "What do you need to know? His favorite food? Fetishes? Size of his dick?"

Several members of Anonymous laughed. Some of the police officers smirked as well.

"Look, if you want to help, I need you to be serious. What can you tell me about his whereabouts? How do you know him?"

"Whereabouts? I don't know jack. He's too careful. But how do I know him? That I can tell you. I was his lover."

"His lover?"

"Yeah, you know, Anonymous cock. Hackers do it through the back door. Fawkes' fuck buddy. On top, underneath, sideways." She angled her head to the side and ran her tongue over her teeth, leering at him. "Fucking yoga position. I was his right-hand girl, you know what I mean? That answer your question?"

Savas stood up. "Yeah."

"Then let them go, and I'll tell you more than you want to know."

34

LIGHTFOOTE AND POISON were hitting it off charmingly.

Savas had agreed to release the other prisoners if and when she responded to their questions back in Manhattan. They had carted the entire crew back into the city, once again subjected to the delays and authority conflicts from the declaration of martial law. However, having claimed to have bagged key members of Anonymous opened the gates more quickly, and they soon had Poison isolated in an interrogation room. The rest were being held in lockup.

Poison was actually Tabitha Ivy, 'Poison' her own hacker handle used from the time she was fourteen. A quick database search revealed that she was now nineteen, a repeat offender having been busted for several hacks of corporate websites, having served nine months behind bars for one job on Pepsi. There was an additional list of minor infractions from possession to vandalizing a parking meter.

It was no wonder she hit it off so well with Angel.

"From what I can tell," said Lightfoote, "about half the code is just to execute this biological like replication and camouflage system." She sat next to Poison at the table, Savas and Miller across in a more standard adversarial position. "Another quarter is still just a black box. Finally about another quarter for ending the world as we know it."

Poison sounded impressed. "How the hell did you get all that? We couldn't even get near the thing."

Lightfoote looked at the battered visage of Savas and smiled. "Mr. I-tried-to- shave-during-an-earthquake over there trapped a live worm for me."

Poison's eyes grew wide. "How the fuck did he do that? I'm surprised he can log into his own computer."

"An unusual technique, but it worked. I have an activated worm trapped on a hard drive. The hardest part was dissecting it without it sending everything to hell and back. That's when I thought, oh, *VMS*."

"VMS? Like your great-grandfather's OS?" The hacker looked

confused.

"It's 1970s stuff, for sure, but it kicks serious ass. It's a hacker's worst nightmare. Amazon uses it for shipping. Some stock exchanges. Pretty rare and pretty secure."

"And the worm wasn't designed to hack those machines?"

"Bingo!" Lightfoote beamed.

The two men stared at each other in confusion.

"I don't get it," said Miller.

Poison scowled at him as Lightfoote elaborated. "Fawkes found hacks into a bunch of the world's computer operating systems: Microsoft, all the flavors of UNIX including Apple. The worm bundles all the tools to hit each of them. But he didn't waste his time finding security holes in something so rare and hard to hack as VMS."

Miller shrugged his shoulders. "And?"

"So it's fucking *immune*, you thug," spat Poison.

"Wait," said Savas. "So you could use it to look at the worm? The worm can't operate in this VMS machine?"

Lightfoote clapped her hands together. "Correct! But interfacing with the hard drive was a nightmare. We only had a few 1990s era VMS machines left around here. They weren't designed to handle modern hard drives. I practically had to solder half the spare parts we owned, and cannibalize several perfectly functional computers, to rig something to read the data. Piece by piece. The older machine doesn't have a lot of memory. But we're doing it. JP is down there now with some of the rest of the unit. Active worm, but frozen on my lab table!"

"What else have you learned from it?"

Lightfoote's face fell. "Nothing good. Names. Important names. Politicians. More CEOs. I think they're targets."

"Jesus, here we go," said Miller.

"We need those names now, Angel," said Savas.

"JP's getting the list. But just wait. This is only one active worm, and every worm is different, remember? These were the names we were lucky to get. And we don't have dates or other information. Just names."

"There could be other targets?" asked Miller.

"Almost certainly. But there's more. I don't think the main course has even been served."

"And that means?" asked Savas.

"That last 25%. The really bad part? It does a lot of things. It infiltrates, copies, and reports out to address that are relays to relays: I can't track them, but it's pooling information somewhere, likely ending at his terminal. But the weird part is that this region *always* has empty space. In the code, nonsense. It's filler. But no way this guy would write junk code. That code is something else. I think it's a marker for new code. The virus is waiting for new command modules, something that is going to come down the road."

"Why?" asked Savas. "Why not just hide it all around like the rest of the code?"

Lightfoote shook her head. "I don't know."

Poison rested her head on the table and spoke through a mumble. "Fawkes. It's Fawkes. He's paranoid. A total douche about it, too. Never get involved with a paranoid. Fucking misery."

"What do you mean?" Savas asked her.

"It must be the kill shot," she said, her eyes closed. "He's too paranoid to ever trust his code. He thinks he can hack anything—that anything can be hacked. So he's worried he'll get hacked."

Miller looked at Lightfoote and chuckled. "He was right."

Poison's eyes flashed open. "So, he's saving the best for last, just in case."

Lightfoote nodded. "Now I see. The relay system to the worm. He's going to use it to upload a final code sequence."

Poison slammed her hand on the table, causing the others to jump. "And then we're fucked. Once he sends that signal, it's over. You can't let him send that signal. You've got to stop him or the worm will carry out his final instructions."

"And what might those be?" asked Savas.

"Who the hell knows?" said Poison, her arms out to her sides. "But seriously, Einstein, after all this shit, how do you think his kill shot is going to go down?"

Savas looked toward Lightfoote. "I hope you have some good news about stopping it."

"Sorry, John—no. That's a whole other story. But, I've sent out my little spies to find out as much as they can."

"Little spies?" asked Miller.

Lightfoote beamed at Savas. "The virus I used to discover we'd been hacked? Well, I'm a few generations down the road with it and it's spreading across the net. The worm gave me a few ideas of using NSA backdoors and we're using them. They're looking for worm activations and taking what snapshots they can, sending them back to me. Real time. You should come down and see the data. Like some war going on out there."

Poison stared at her. "Beautiful."

Miller held his hands up. "You're infecting computers now? That makes us hackers, too?"

"You're amateurs compared to the NSA," said Poison. "As American as apple pie."

"Too true," said Lightfoote. "But we're not looking for stealth or long term stability. We're going in full bore. But don't worry, Frank. It's a good virus. A pet virus. It's on God's side." She smiled.

Miller stared incredulously at her. "Jesus. John? What do you say to this?"

Savas appeared not to have heard him. He stared intently at Poison, his eyes focused, seemingly both near and far away.

"John?"

He glanced toward Miller. "Yeah. I've green-lighted Angel's shenanigans. Paying off, I'd say." Then he turned back to the hacker. "You stopped seeing him?"

Poison frowned. "Fawkes? Yeah. Look, I told you, I don't know his real identity. He only trusted me with his dick."

"But you said he pursued you."

"Jeez, yeah. And you know, when you have the world's best hacker stalking you online, it's a fucking nightmare. I spent months shaking him off. I mean, he said it was over, so get the fuck out of my life, right? I think he finally gave up."

Savas held up a small cylinder. "Are you sure?"

She reached over and grabbed it from his hand. "What's that?"

"GPS tracking device. An agent pulled it off your car at the warehouse. It's not in our records. Not a model we use." Savas stared intently at her. "Anyone else you think might be interested in following your every move?"

"Oh, Christ, that fuck!" She stared furiously at it.

"He likely knows you're here by now."

"Yeah, well, so what? He won't be tracking me anymore."

"He might try to get you out."

Poison laughed. "You're kidding right? Why would he do that?"

Miller leaned forward. "Because he's obsessed with you. Maybe he thinks it's love. But it's obsession for sure."

Savas nodded. "And that makes me wonder just what we're going to do with you."

Poison shook her head. "You really think he'll come after me?"

Savas smiled for the first time. "I'm counting on it."

OCTOBER 30

35

A DEEP VOICE chanted in the darkness beside the candle flames.

"God of power and mercy, maker and lover of peace, to know you is to live, and to serve you is to reign."

Houston observed the flickering light from a distance, giving Lopez space as he dressed. Body armor under vestments, belts and holsters for guns, magazines, knives, and grenades. All the while he chanted. She would never understand. He reached out to a God who had rejected him. He sang the song of a priest when the Church had cast him out. It was his way.

"Through the intercession of St. Michael, the archangel, be our protection in battle against all evil."

Michael. The older Lopez brother. The man whose death had brought her together with Francisco. The man whose life had upturned theirs and so many others. The man whose actions had created a monster of terrible vengeance that had burned like acid through the Central Intelligence Agency. *The wraith.* A killer whose life ended before the barrel of the man before her.

Michael. An archangel. Like his brother, *Gabriel.*

"May our cause be just. May we have clear vision. May our courage not falter. May our efforts bring lasting peace. Should we perish in the struggle, may God embrace us and find for us a place in His Kingdom. Amen."

Crossing himself in front of an icon of St. George slaying the dragon, he blew out the votives and turned toward her, his black cassock a flowing shroud over layers of death. She waited as he approached, a shadow herself in dark camouflage, an energy anticipating the coming violence burning within her.

Lopez spoke softly, staring into her eyes, black to blue. "Everything will depend on removing the sentries on the roof. Those snipers will pick us off if we try to enter. We'll have to be fast and accurate. The diversion will buy us only moments."

She smiled beneath the covering of the mask. "Amen."

Lopez frowned. "Let's hope our recon remains accurate, that they don't change anything."

"Lord hear our prayer."

He watched her silently for a moment and then pulled down the fabric of the mask covering her mouth. He kissed her, lingering until they pulled away for breath.

"In case it's the last kiss," he said. "I want to make it count."

She reached her hand up to his face and cupped his cheek. "Every mission you do that. And every time I want you to. Because one day, we won't come back, Francisco."

He nodded, turning with her toward the door. "But let it not be this night, O Lord."

36

THEY CALLED HIM simply Alpha. He was the point man, the de facto leader of this group of men wrapped around and above, guarding the warehouse. The building was a squat little thing, about half a city block. Isolated in the northern New Jersey countryside, it attracted little attention, was not easily accessed, and unregistered in any business directories. It was a ghost.

Like they were. All their real names were scrubbed. They adopted spy thriller handles. Former soldiers and contractors, all of them, hired secretively by a company many in his team began to suspect was involved in some of the attacks occurring around the country. That suspicion led some to leave. But most stayed. The company had done its homework. Like Alpha, most of them would point the gun for whoever paid them the most.

But tensions had escalated dramatically. Five additional guards had been added bringing the total to fifteen. Powers that be were getting rattled about what was inside the metallic walls of the structure. Alpha didn't know what was in there, and he didn't want to know. A few times each month, a small convoy of trucks would show up and pull into what he presumed was an enclosed loading dock, the doors closing and sealing off everything from view. Shortly afterward, the trucks would drive off, whether having unloaded or loaded a mystery that was not part of his job description. A job that paid ridiculous money for guard duty in the states. Iraq had been one thing, but Jersey? Retirement gig.

Until things started blowing up. Until more and more trucks had come. Until more former soldiers had been brought on to fortify a rural building like something in the green zone. Just the presence of that many guns raised the temperature.

"Main gate, clear," came a voice through static on his headset.

"Roger that."

It was Delta. There was only one way by vehicle into the building, through a gate lodged in the electrified fence, then down a broad, truck-friendly road to the loading dock. Three guards patrolled the gate, two at the dock entrance, four moving about the perimeter fence. Six took to the roof, four at the corners and two on the longer sides of the building. Those on the roof were trained snipers. Alpha was one of them, positioned at the front on the right-hand side facing the gate.

"Perimeter report."

Several voices spoke in order of established protocol. The roof snipers followed suit. The space was clear. As it was half an hour ago. As it was at dusk. As it was every night for the last six months that he had worked this job.

That's why when he spotted the headlights at the top of the hill in front of the gate, he didn't quite believe his eyes.

"Delta, check scheduled arrivals."

It looked like a smaller delivery truck, not the massive eighteen wheelers that they tended to get. He zoomed his night-vision goggles. The truck was nondescript, no insignia, the plate damaged and unreadable. The windows seemed opaque or blacked out. Something was wrong.

The vehicle began to accelerate down the hill. Alpha didn't hear the telltale sounds of torque in the engine, the changing pitch as the rpms increased. The steering was odd. His alarm bells were ringing

"Log's empty, Alpha. Nothing due until tomorrow afternoon."

He powered up his scope and set his transmission signal to maximum. "Unidentified vehicle approaching from the road. Treat as hostile. Repeat, treat as hostile!"

Automatic gunfire erupted from the gate. The flashes lit the dark night, strobing the gatehouse, glinting off the chain-links in the fence, reflecting back from the glass in the truck that was now barrelling down the hill. The windshield of the truck exploded, glass spraying inwards, the metal of the hood pocketed with bullet holes. It only accelerated.

"Perimeter guards move forward to engage. Anyone up top with a view, take a shot if you have one. Gamma and Omega, hold the dock!"

The maniacs! Whatever crazed assault this was, it was only going to end one way, and that was with the occupants filled with holes. A foregone conclusion that didn't give him any comfort—madmen always maimed and killed. How many men would he lose tonight?

He settled into a crouch on the roof's ledge, stabilizing his rifle, knowing that the snipers around him were doing the same. The night-vision scope zoomed in on the rushing vehicle. Alpha focused on the cabin, determined to take out the driver himself.

The cabin was empty.

Shit! "Delta, all crews, break off! Repeat, break off!"

But it was too late. His eyes were seared by a bright light and a blast of air that nearly knocked him backward. Stunned, he shielded his eyes as an orange fireball climbed into the sky, quickly darkening in a blanket of smoke and falling embers. The screams hit him now. Just like he remembered. Just like in Mosul when the trucks came and the bombs blew and men and pieces of men lay strewn in the street.

The afterimage of the blast partially blinded him, but he strained to see the gate below. It was gone. The metal ripped and melted like cotton candy, flaming chunks of truck and gatehouse scattered radially around the scene of destruction. Only those bodies that were not close to the explosion were visible, but all of the men he had sent to converge on the intruders were now corpses, or as good as. Three at the gate, four wrecked forms from the perimeter guards. It was a slaughter.

"Roof report." His voice was strained and husked.

Silence.

He spun around the rooftop, dropping the goggles over his eyes again. Motionless forms were draped in various positions across the asphalt. They were all dead. Sniped themselves while distracted by the commotion and chaos at the gate.

Alpha stood up fully now, heedless of the danger, removing his goggles. It was just a matter of time now. Light flickered from the burning debris behind him. He stared up into the sky, looking for some heavenly object, the moon, even a single star to glimpse before the final darkness came.

But it came without mercy. His head snapped backward, a bullet tearing through the soft flesh of his face, a clean hit to the brain stem that unplugged his basic physiological functions in an instant. For a second, his eyes empty, he stood staring stupidly forward. Then the electrochemical signals ceased completely, and he dropped straight to

the rooftop with a thud.
Then, only silence.

37

LOPEZ AND HOUSTON entered the burning compound. Their forms wrapped in black, packs strapped to their backs, and pistols in their hands as they jogged cautiously among the scrap and human remains scattered before them. They paused over several bodies, checked them, and moved on toward the compound's entrance.

With weapons raised they approached, stairs on either side leading to a loading platform in front of the enormous roll-up shutter door. Two bodies lay on either side of the stairway, blood pooling underneath them. Houston sprinted up the right-hand steps and examined the large locks barring entrance. Lopez continuously scanned around them with his weapon raised.

"Francisco, it's no good!" she cried. "We're going to have to blow it."

"I counted fifteen. They can't have had more, could they?"

Houston sprinted down the steps, unstrapping her pack. "I don't know. Paranoid as all fuck, so I won't put anything past them. We need the charges from your pack."

Lopez slung his bag to the ground and removed several gray blocks with detonators. He handed them to Houston who returned to the door as he resumed his scanning. Placing the explosive on the locks, she set the charge and sprinted down the steps. They grabbed their bags and rounded the corner of the building, constantly alert for hostile movements or sounds. Houston raised a controller.

"Three, two, one..."

She pressed the bottom and a blast shook the building. After several seconds, they came back around the wall and ran to the loading platform. Twisted steel and smoke greeted them, as did an enormous hole in the shutter door the width of a small car.

Houston laughed. "Just meant to break the locks. I need a course on explosive yields."

She removed a flashlight and they stepped into the building through the hole, careful to avoid the sharp and smoking edges. The air inside the place was stale, almost metallic tasting, the acrid smoke from the blast mingling with the stored smells of machines and dust. The echoing of their footsteps made it clear that the space was vast and open, but it was too dark to see much beyond the direct beam of the light, which only revealed the reflective hulls of large shapes.

Lopez led her arm. "Try the wall. Lights."

Houston scanned the beam across the nearby wall and located a set of switches. Lopez faced away from her with his gun raised in anticipation. She flipped the switches together in one motion.

Ceiling-high bulbs winked to life with a buzz. Dim at first, the bulbs slowly waxed to full brightness, their combined numbers across the length of the warehouse causing the pair to squint as their eyes adjusted.

"Holy shit, Francisco."

They stared down rows and rows of enormous bladed aircraft. The machines were variable, all devoid of a cockpit or other indication of a pilot's chair. Some of the smaller units sported large cameras. The larger drones were outfitted with an array of cargo, all of it dangerous.

Lopez walked up to one of the larger ones, bulbous, metallic shapes strapped to its underside. "Bombs."

"Looks like," said Houston. "And those are aircraft sized machine guns on that one. Can you imagine the bullets?" She swung her gaze across the interior. "There's got to be forty or fifty in here. It's the drone motherlode."

Lopez got to one knee and crossed himself. "At least it wasn't for nothing." Houston placed her hand on his shoulder.

"It had to be done," she said, staring across the warehouse, seeming to see beyond it.

"It makes us as much murderers as them."

"And the alternative?" She knelt down beside him. "We knew the moment we canvased this place that the drones were here. Stupid to put the place surrounded by hills, but it was muscled up. We weren't going to be able to convert them to our cause. It was either more drone attacks or we fight this war."

"Killing in war only makes it necessary, not moral." He stood up, his composure returning. "It's still killing, and we just left the biggest body count we ever have."

She placed her hand on his face and looked into his eyes. "I know. I know it hurts you. And I know you do this only because you see that we had to. You'll ask your God for forgiveness. And I know you'll mean it. But, meanwhile, we need to bring in the cavalry."

"FBI?"

"Yes. This changes everything." She held up a plastic bag with several phones. "And we got these."

"You don't think they'd be stupid enough to leave a trail?"

Houston shook her head. "Not Fawkes, but he's got an army now. You're only as secure as your weakest link." She looked back outside toward the carnage. "Lots of bodies. Lots of hires. Lots of potential weak links." She pulled out her phone.

"How much time do we have?"

"I don't think the local police or fire will be out here quickly. It's the middle of nowhere, and these guys weren't plugged into their systems with a burglar alarm. No, just the opposite. I bet this place is off the grid completely." She punched a number. "I think our Intel 1 pals will be the first on the scene."

A voice crackled on the other end.

"Angel? This is Mary. We hit the jackpot. Tell John and the others to get to the address we sent you. And bring fire and a cleanup crew. And body bags. Lots of body bags."

———————

Hours later an army of police cars, FBI vehicles, SWAT vans, and emergency response crews were stationed around the smoldering scene. Spotlights were trained around the compound, and forensics teams darted around the bodies like fireflies with their flashlights and cameras.

Cohen slowly exited one of the black Crown Victorias. She hopped beside the door, removing a pair of crutches, and then proceeded to swing herself toward the stairways. Refusing the aid of several agents and police, she forced her way clumsily up the steps and into the warehouse.

Inside, a group of men stood marveling at the building's inventory. Flashbulbs exploded around them, documenting the scene.

"John. Frank. Sorry I'm late."

Savas turned around and the lines of his mouth tightened. It was hard to see her like this. The bruises had only begun to leave her face, the hideous black and green fading to a sickening yellow, scabs slowly being absorbed, hair lost from her left side where stitches ran over her scalp like laces on a game ball. Cohen limped toward them, her breath ragged, her eyes fatigued, yet a light burning within them.

"You didn't miss anything," said Savas, taking her arm. She relented and let him help her. "Or rather, we all missed the same thing. Hell of a fireworks display. And just look what Pandora's box has inside it."

Cohen whistled. "And no one noticed that someone was piling up large drone orders like this?"

Miller shook his head. "It didn't look that way on paper. Our two shadows tracked it all down, like tributaries piling into a big river. Then they came here and did this," he said, gesturing outside. "Who did you say those folks were?"

"I didn't," said Savas.

"Mmmm."

"We've counted twenty-five of the largest models," said Savas, "most equipped to bomb or shoot anything to smithereens. The rest are reconnaissance setups, smaller models with different imaging equipment ranging from cameras to infrared, audio—you name it."

"The bodies outside?"

Savas nodded. "Need to confirm, but facial recognition from snapshots IDed two of them. Former contractors that worked in the Middle East, one ex-army."

"More mercenaries," growled Miller. "Fifteen of them, it seems. Your ghosts are better than Jason Bourne."

"Moving on," said Savas. "We'll ID all we can and see what we can find from it."

"Meanwhile, we've put a dent in their attack plans," said Cohen.

"I hope so."

"What do you mean?"

Savas sighed. "Fawkes used a bunch of shell companies, crisscrossing aliased orders to stock this place. It was to hide his tracks, hide this place from prying eyes. But I'm starting to think that he's not the kind of guy to put all his eggs in one basket."

Miller looked gravely at him. "You think he has more drones."

"I know he does."

Savas didn't want to believe his own words. He needed a win, the kind of win that would let him believe he had declawed this nebulous monster. But the truth was too obvious.

Cohen changed tact. "You said there was a call from Gabriel?"

"Yes. They have a bag of phones. You can guess from where. Angel's on it now, but it's beyond her resources. I'm going to go long on this and bring in Simon."

"Fred Simon of CIA?" she asked. "We haven't contacted him since—" She caught herself. "Not for a while."

Miller smiled. "Who's he?"

"Someone who might can help," said Savas. "We might also need the NSA to work those phones."

"More Watchmen?" asked Cohen.

He nodded to her and stared at Miller a moment. "Why don't you fill in Frank a bit on the group while I get this show wrapped up here. I think the usefulness of certain secrets has diminished greatly given the current circumstances."

"About damn time," whispered Miller under his breath.

Savas smiled wanly. "Be careful what you ask for, Frank. Ignorance can be bliss."

OCTOBER 31

38

SAVAS AND COHEN sat in the back of one of the old Crown Vics as it sped toward Manhattan on I-80. The sun arced over the factories and former swamplands, pouring a bronze coating over the buildings and waterways. Savas found it increasingly difficult to keep track of the days, one rolling into another on minimal sleep and maximal stress. But now, finally, there were some real breaks in the case.

They had insisted that the car be swept for digital technology, and screened their drivers, allowing only those who agreed to leave their smartphones and similar equipment behind. There was no point in spending the time to explain why. The turn to Luddites had hampered them severely, however, as the attempt to establish a conference call with Fred Simon had demonstrated. They had tried to have two phones on speaker, Lightfoote on Cohen's phone, Simon on Savas' cheap model. But it had proved unworkable, the sound quality rendering much of the dialogue incomprehensible. They had settled on speaking to Simon alone.

The CIA agent's voice was energized. "Our mutual contact at the NSA has managed to make rapid progress. All the calls and texts from the numbers you gave were grabbed over the last week. There wasn't much to go on. They were careful, but not careful enough. Two of the phones had sent text messages to the same number. I don't think it was because they were brothers and contacting mom."

"What was that number?" asked Savas.

"An unregistered phone. Likely a burner. But we don't need a name to track it."

"GPS?"

"No. They weren't that careless. But with enough activity, we can triangulate from the cell towers. They didn't check the fine print on this model. It checks with the home company a lot for service performance. Pinging back on an hourly basis. They might as well be flashing a light."

Savas sat up in the seat. He turned to Cohen. "Do you think it could be Fawkes?"

"I doubt it, John." She swept the crutches from between them and leaned them against the window. "You never know, but my guess is a mid-level operator. But he could lead us to the boss."

The speaker crackled. "My thoughts exactly."

Savas nodded. "So where is this phone?"

"Long Island Sound near Glen Cove."

"In the water? They ditched it?"

"Unlikely," said Simon. "It's moving. Speed and direction consistent with a maritime vessel following the coastline."

Savas and Cohen exchanged glances as she spoke. "Well, that isn't likely for some low-level grunt. Maybe we have something interesting."

"Want real-time footage?"

"Are you serious?"

"Soon as we had the coordinates, we dispatched a chopper."

"An agency chopper in the US? Where from?"

"Need-to-know basis, John."

"I thought the CIA didn't operate within US borders."

"Clinton said it best: it all depends on the definitions of words like 'is' or 'operate.'"

"Mmm-hmmm. You bet your ass I want footage, but we're pre-smartphone era here, Fred. When the AI in our car tried to kill us, we decided to go Amish."

Simon barked a laugh. "I understand. NSA has found a way to firewall the damn worm. Slowing them the hell down to fence everything off, but they've got server farms now with serious prophylactics. I'm watching real time. It's a nice boat."

"I bet it is."

"With a bunch of folks on it. Hard to make out high-res detail—the bird is at a distance and altitude that won't give it away. But I can tell you they aren't milling about socially. Positioned strategically."

"Bodyguards," said Cohen.

"Who needs a ship full of muscle?" chipped Simon.

Savas felt the adrenaline kick in. "Fawkes." He turned to Cohen. "We need a rapid response team. They'll lose that phone or the owner soon."

She nodded. "That means air. We're out of choppers. Too busy flying the VIPs out of the city still."

"Dammit!"

Simon cut in. "Well, remember those contractors that the CIA doesn't hire under aliases for work inside the country? Well, why have one chopper when you can have three for ten times the price? The fact that they don't exist creates some budget magic."

"You've got a spare bird?"

"Already routed toward you."

Savas punched the seat in front of him, startling the driver. "I owe you big, Fred."

"Don't think so, John. I've got a ways to go on that other debt I owe you. Speaking of which, how are my kids?"

"They're good. Spooking my team with their ninja-assassin program. Even Frank was impressed. But they're delivering big time." He glanced at Cohen. "We're a bit busted up and we've got a full plate of hackers in the City. I think I know who I'd send for a rendezvous with the boat."

"I agree," said Simon, "but we're pushing them. They're human, whatever they seem to accomplish."

Savas sat back in the chair and closed his eyes. "I know, Fred. But right now we all need to be a little superhuman. There's a monster to fight. I don't have the manpower to do this. Maybe Frank, but he's one. And there are some important people we need to question as of several hours ago."

"I'm with you. Tell them the chopper's been loaded with some useful gear. But getting on that boat and surviving isn't going to be as easy as the warehouse."

"Easy. Right. I'll tell them. I'm glad you're with us, Fred."

"I'm not the only one, John. The Watchmen still have some kick left. Until soon."

The connection was closed. Savas dialed and held the phone to his ear.

"Yeah, Mary? This is John. That bag of phones? Well, they might have bagged some big game. The guards called a number. Fred Simon traced it. It's zipping along the Long Island Sound as we talk. We need you two to intercept a boat."

A muffled voice sounded through the other end. Savas nodded.

"Not to worry. Give me your current position. We've got that covered."

DEPOSITION IN THE MATTER OF:
UNITED STATES ARMED FORCES SPECIAL TRIBUNAL,
Plaintiff,
v.
JOHN SAVAS, Defendant
Case No. M120039E-007X

Continued DEPOSITION OF:
JEAN PAUL RIDEOUT

CBD: I want to read for you some documentation from the archives of the NSA. Prepared specifically for this inquiry.
MR. RIDEOUT: This should be fun.

CBD: As of 30 October, more than a third of the agency's computers were wiped and placed behind a newly designed firewall, code-named ROUNDUP. This firewall successfully prevented further infections and those machines took on the bulk of NSA computing tasks, both internally and externally. This was not a "cure" of any kind. It served as a preventive measure for infection and allowed the agency to resume increasingly normal levels of operations. However, due to national security concerns, it was decided not to share this information with outside agencies, private or public institutions, or the personal computing world for fear that release of the code would allow Anonymous to develop countermeasures.

MR. RIDEOUT: Hang on! So they had a block—they could fence it out—but kept it to themselves? Genius! How did the asses there feel when the Boeing plants blew themselves to bits? Robots slinging parts every which way, killing hundreds of workers, crippling aircraft construction for years? Jesus! Or the General Dynamics tanks and trucks? So sophisticated with their fully wired innards! The worm had them turning on their operators and blowing holes in the army bases! Bet those guys would have liked a peek at that firewall!

CBD: There was debate. For example, it says

here—

MR. RIDEOUT: Debate! I love it. How about the
farm belt catastrophes? Irrigation and
treatment systems poisoning tens of millions of
acres? Chinese air traffic control going to
shit and nearly leading to a launch of
missiles? Taiwan is lucky to still be here,
honestly. And of course, who can forget the
digital money supply of the world banks
literally disappearing before our eyes?

CBD: The NSA isn't the focus of this inquiry!
MR. RIDEOUT: Then why bring them up at all?

CBD: I was getting to this point. The document
continues.

CBD: Debate on this topic intensified during
the next few days as the worm caused
accelerating damage to civilian and
governmental infrastructure. However,
increasing concern developed over a second, and
unrelated series of malicious code attacks that
were eventually determined to have originated
from offices of the FBI in New York City.

MR. RIDEOUT: Oh, here it is! Angel. Now I see
what this is about. So the NSA began to spy on
the FBI as well.

[REDACTED]: Because your division had gone
rogue and was releasing viral code into the
internet!
MR. RIDEOUT: Because it was the only way to
fight the damn thing! Fight, well, that came
later. At this point, we'd only begun to see
the worm's activity through Angel's code. We
didn't have time to get permissions or test the
friendliness of this stuff! As you read so
eloquently, the damn world was falling apart
around us!

[REDACTED]: Many find it intriguing that at the
same time as Anonymous was bringing down the
world's digital economy, military, even food
and water production, your group at FBI was
engaging in a simultaneous release of hostile
code.

MR. RIDEOUT: It wasn't hostile to—

[REDACTED]: And that it was your small division in an obscure branch of the FBI that managed to bring in the leader of Anonymous. A hacker who personally communicated with your chief programmer before and after the arrest—
MR. RIDEOUT: Communicated? He fucking wiped our server farm!
[REDACTED]: leaving her, and her only, encrypted messages and files.

MR. RIDEOUT: You're serious? You think we're in league with that fuck? He tried to kill us multiple times! We were trying to save the nation!

[REDACTED]: Did saving the nation require you to provide aid and comfort to enemies of the state?
MR. RIDEOUT: Aid and comfort? That's treason. What the hell are you talking about?

[REDACTED]: Francisco Lopez. Sara Houston. The Priest and the Whore. Surely you have heard of them?
MR. RIDEOUT: The Priest and Whore? [Inaudible] Oh, my God. Gabriel and Mary! Are you telling me those ciphers were Lopez and Houston?

[REDACTED]: It's charming that you are so ignorant of this.
MR. RIDEOUT: I didn't know who they were and I don't believe anything coming out of your mouth! All I know is that those two risked their lives over and over to bring Fawkes in. And they did! You should pin a fucking medal to their chests.

[REDACTED]: Perhaps they'll receive what's coming to them if you would tell us where they and Angel Lightfoote are hiding.
MR. RIDEOUT: I have no idea! Neither does anyone else in Intel 1. For all I know they're dead in the chaos. The city was on fire when you took us underground, when your thugs knocked our doors down and grabbed us. They were already gone into that mayhem. From what I'm seeing here, I'm thinking that was maybe the best outcome.

CBD: You say this Mary and Gabriel risked their lives several times. Can you elaborate?

MR. RIDEOUT: I've told you about the warehouse raid. Jesus, that was straight out of Call of Duty. That's where we found the drone stash. They took down a bunch of armed guards to get into that place. Of course, that fuck had more than one location. But I can at least say that there is no way their raid didn't save lives and infrastructure. Some bridges are still standing and some people still walking around because of that raid.

CBD: Who else was in on it?

MR. RIDEOUT: No one. Two on like fifty, I don't know. Bodies were everywhere. I saw the photos. Of course, the craziest was the boat.

CBD: Boat?

MR. RIDEOUT: Yeah, the very next day. Airlifted them like battle bots and dropped them in. And we almost had him, dammit. We could have prevented so much if they had caught him. So many deaths. But it wasn't to be.

CBD: Fawkes? How did you know he was there?

MR. RIDEOUT: We tracked some phones. Dead guards had contacted people. Led to the boat.

[REDACTED]: How was the FBI able to track this boat without computers, without the technology? Where did you get the vehicles to airlift the fugitives?

MR. RIDEOUT: John had connections. In fact, I think some were in your vaunted NSA. Some good guys. I don't know. But they made it happen, tracked the calls, got Mary and Gabriel in there. Would have been something to see in the flesh, I have no doubt.

39

A DARK-HAIRED man handed Lopez a tablet and swiped through several photos. Although dimmed, the glow of the screen was nearly blinding in the dark interior of the aircraft, the thundering sound of the blades and engine suffocating auditory senses as well. They were flying just over the low cloud cover on a moonless night, shadowing the boat by matching speed and direction, remaining well out of earshot.

The two men were young, barely out of their twenties, and Lopez wondered where Fred Simon had found them. Breaking agency protocol, even in this crisis environment, likely meant they were not mere tools, but a part of the loose network united by Savas and Simon. *The Watchmen.* Lopez didn't know whether to respect their efforts or consider them hopeless idealists.

He turned his attention to the tablet. The images showed increasing zooms toward an unusual-looking boat. Lopez strained to hear the CIA man over the sounds of the helicopter and the strong headwind that rocked the craft mercilessly. Even with the headphones, he found himself using hand signals to get Houston's attention as he handed her the device.

The CIA man repeated what he had said. "It looks like one of the newer anti-pirating vessels. Aluminum hulls and cabins designed to withstand small-arms fire. Dual-engines to bring top speeds of around sixty miles per hour. They can turn on a dime and chase down anything that isn't a speed boat. Or outrun it."

"Good thing we're in a helicopter," said Houston, smiling.

The CIA man wasn't amused. "Look, I don't know who you are and what strings you pulled, but his isn't a day trip. Look at these."

He scrolled past several photos that centered on the boat and its hull, pausing over a pair that focused on the deck.

Houston interrupted. "We see them. Guards fore and aft, automatic weapons, even a fairly large machine gun mounted there," she pointed. "If I were you, I wouldn't bring this bird in too close. The gun might almost qualify as anti-aircraft depending on the rounds."

"But if we are going to have you near enough that thing, the approach is going to have to be close," he scowled. "They'll make us for sure by sight as well as sound. There's nothing identifying on the outside, especially at night, but that in itself will likely send up flags."

Lopez nodded to the side door. "What is this thing? I assume it's for us?"

"The best we could manage on extremely short notice. We aren't the Navy Seals, and to be quite honest, this is our first and I hope only sky-to-sea assault mission. Usually we do things with a bit more stealth."

The man edged over and unzipped one of the bags. Black fiberglass gleamed back at them, reflecting the light of the tablet and cockpit instrument panel.

"But this will get some points for that."

"It's a jet ski?" asked Houston.

"Yes," said the CIA agent. "Electric. Good for the environment."

Houston nodded. "*Silent*, in other words."

"Next to the motors on the boat, most definitely. It's pitch out there on the open sea and they're not running all that dark, so you should almost be invisible. We disabled the safety lights. It's a two-seater, so you'll both fit with some minimal gear. You stay in their wake and you should be able to grapple on before they know you're there."

"Except for the thundering helicopter drop-off, of course," said Lopez.

"We'll try to keep as far out as possible, so there will be some distance. You can hit 50 on this thing. Boat tops off at 60 and they aren't pushing it that hard right now. Nowhere close. You can close the gap." He looked Houston up-and-down. "It's not us I'm worried about. Getting on the boat is one thing. Then what? I hope Simon hasn't lost his mind."

Houston used the silence to loudly slap a fresh clip into her browning. "Just get us on the water and watch your own ass. We aren't outfitted for a sea mission. Put us low to avoid a bath and we'll preserve more function in the gear."

The CIA man motioned to a rope and pulley. "Thirty feet already laid out. In this blackness, well, that's pushing it, and the downwash is going to be a problem."

"We'll make do," she answered, wrapping a tactical vest around her.

The pilot spoke through the noise. "Target has decelerated. Down to 30 miles per hour."

"We do it now," said Lopez.

The CIA man nodded. "Drop us down, Charlie."

They felt a tug inside and the helicopter buried itself in the cloud layer, additional turbulence rocking the small craft back and forth violently. The pilot was flying dark except for instrumentation. They plunged below the clouds and the sea swelled into view. Light from the boat ahead bobbed like a beacon.

Houston and Lopez removed the remainder of the tarp on the jet ski. Without a combustion engine, it was surprisingly light, and they positioned it in front of the door. They were dressed in black with protective vests, ski masks and dark gloves, packs on their backs and weapons strapped to utility belts. Night vision goggles dangled from their necks.

The helicopter plunged toward the sea, the pilot speaking in their headsets. "Wind's a bitch! Be quick."

They lurched to a hover. The pair removed the headphones and fastened the rope to the jet ski. The CIA man opened the side door and they lowered the watercraft quickly. The gears on the pulley hummed as the rope flew through the mechanism, the smell of burnt leaves filling the small space. Far below, they watched the water splash outward from the impact on the surface.

"Go, go, go!" cried the pilot.

Houston leapt onto the rope and wrapped her feet around it. She descended swiftly down its length and vanished below. Lopez paused a split second to give her space to clear, then dropped straight into the wind and night.

It was all completed in less than a minute. The pilot was skilled and held the helicopter in position. Feet firmly planted on the jet ski, they detached the rope as Houston slipped into the driver's seat and fired it up, the engine purring softly.

The craft leapt forward toward the dancing lights of the yacht. Lopez removed a high-powered assault weapon and focused ahead as the helicopter darted upward, heading back toward the cloud bank and safety.

Only it would not make it. Operators on the boat had seen the craft. Through the washed-out green of the night-vision, Lopez saw a volley of infrared tracers converge on the aircraft. He remembered the large weapon in the recon photos. He removed his goggles and stared helplessly.

A bright light erupted above them, painting the ceiling of cloud-cover in orange and white, the water reflecting the growing fireball. The sound shook them as they sped forward, the rending of metal and air pressure from the ignited fuel. In the dimming fireball the wreckage could be seen to careen toward the open sea and slam into the water like the surface was made of concrete, the helicopter crushed and sinking. It vanished below the waves.

Lopez felt all ambivalence evaporate.

"Let's get these bastards."

40

THEIR TARGET ACCELERATED. Houston gunned the jet ski and pushed it to the breaking point. The boat took no evasive action and even angled toward them to narrow the distance somewhat of their approach.

"They haven't spotted us," screamed Lopez behind her. "Running from the crash site!"

Houston nodded vigorously and continued to push the ski full out. The high waves gut-punched them as they sliced through the water, but they gained on the yacht. Lopez began to see just how fortified it was. *Anti-pirate, indeed.* While it possessed a superficial resemblance to the luxury powerboats decorating many docks, the fiberglass was replaced with thick aluminum, the windows black and refracting light unnaturally, the bullet-resistant composition altering the optical properties. And of course the guards and their weapons, in addition to the churning motors kicking a spray like a comet's tail behind the craft.

They were within ten yards and still gaining on the starboard side. Now came the true insanity: The boat had accelerated beyond fifty miles per hour and the jet ski was barely holding together. The angle had decreased, reducing their relative velocity, but also affording the only way to try to board. Lopez shouldered the automatic rifle and removed two stun grenades.

"Flash bangs ready!" he called to Houston. They were nearly alongside the yacht.

She nodded and he flung the bombs one at a time toward the bow of the ship. Both landed and rattled across the surface, ricocheting off the gunwale, then exploding. Even from the side of the ship, the sound and light were startling.

Lopez heaved a grappling ladder against the side and it caught, the roped steps unfurling against the hull. Just then the boat lurched starboard slamming into the jet ski. Instinctively, both of them leapt off the doomed craft and grabbed the sides of the ladder, one on each side, their legs half-submerged in the sea. The friction of the water threatened to pull the grapple from the boat and deposit them into the propeller blades.

Lopez placed a foot on the roped ladder and violently swung himself toward the gunwale, grasping the side of the boat with his hands. He tucked his legs underneath his torso like a gymnast and planted his boots on the uppermost portion of the hull, a powerful thrust of his legs propelling him over the side to land in the stern on top of the engine box.

Two men were positioned near the cabin looking ahead at the commotion caused by the still smoking flash grenades. At the sound of his awkward landing, they turned too slowly, the shock of the unexpected attack leaving them off guard.

The distance was only a few feet, and Lopez placed his hands on the engine box and swept his leg through the air like a switchblade. His boot connected with the head of the leftmost guard, the neck snapping to the side, teeth raining sideways against the metal. The man fell with a crash and didn't move.

But it left Lopez open for a strike from the second guard. He prepared for the worst, hoping Houston would be there in time to engage.

And she was. As he spun away from the guard and onto his feet, he crouched and pulled a handgun from his belt. In front of him there was a blur of hands and feet as Houston's lithe form pummeled the thick hulk of the other guard. The results were devastating. Blows to the neck and groin incapacitated him while she drew a knife. Using the momentum of his failing retreat, she toppled him onto the prone form of the other guard and plunged the blade into his neck, wrenching it several inches, sidestepping a jet of blood that bathed the floor of the boat.

It was over in seconds. In the cacophony surrounding the boat, the melee had barely risen above the chaos.

"I'll take the cabin," she said, twitching her head toward the interior. "There are two guards at the bow. I doubt the flash bangs did much more than knock them sideways."

"Be careful, Sara," said Lopez. "I don't want to lose you now."

"Move, priest," she said and darted toward the door.

Their actions played in counterpoint. Lopez sprang forward, his weapon raised, back sliding along the wall of the cabin. The acrid smell of smoke from the lingering grenades burned in his nose as he approached the front of the ship. He turned the corner of the cabin and crouched to one knee, steadying the pistol with his left hand as he scanned the deck.

One of the guards remained positioned on the gun turret, checking the skies as if awaiting another attack. The other had tossed one of the smoking remains of the grenades over the side of the boat, aiming his weapon downward, anticipating an assault from the water.

The assault came from behind. Lopez fired two shots before the man could turn. Both connected. The guard slipped over the railing and disappeared into darkness.

The other guard heard the shots. Lopez walked casually toward the turret, his weapon aimed at the man, the guard releasing the controls of the large machine gun, realizing it couldn't be used at close range. He desperately tried to draw a pistol.

Lopez blasted his right shoulder, the man's obvious gun arm. The guard screamed and clutched the wound, terror in his eyes as the masked assailant approached.

Lopez grabbed the wrist of his uninjured arm and twisted. Again the man screamed, his body paralyzed in pain, eyes shut harshly.

"How many guards?" yelled Lopez. "Don't think! Tell me! How many guards?"

Like a programmed machine, the man stuttered his answers: "Two here. Two in the back. Two in the cabin with Fawkes." Tears streamed down his face.

Fawkes? It wasn't to be believed. The architect of Anonymous was *on the boat*. "Sara's in the cabin with him," he whispered, the frightened man looking on in distress.

Lopez brought the handle of the pistol down on the man's temple, the body collapsing into the turret. He sprinted back to the stern of the boat.

———

At the same time, Houston stood over the bodies of two men.

She had entered the cabin forcefully, kicking in the flimsy door to find three men looking through the front window at the aftermath of the flash bangs. Two were obviously hired protection—broad in the back, towering over the middle figure who could otherwise have been mistaken for a scrawny teen. They turned at the sound of her entrance.

Fawkes. It was the glasses that sealed the identification. The female hacker's words—her *lover*—the lanky body, the darting motions, the smart glasses: it was Fawkes. But she had no time to consider the implications.

The men held guns in their hands. They turned to engage, but she held the advantage. She fired twice, each shot aimed quickly at the moving targets across from her. The first shot hit true to rip through the forehead of the bodyguard on her left, his blood splattering the window and ceiling. The second shot drifted right from her momentum. The bullet hit the man in the chest, too high for the heart, but he cried out, dropped his weapon, and careened toward the window.

But he wasn't down. As Fawkes screamed and darted left, the guard faced her and rushed, the crazed look of a wounded animal on his face.

She pivoted, side-stepping, and grasped his outstretched arm, using his momentum against him. He missed, and she thrust him toward the window in the back of the cabin. His face smashed the glass, a spiderweb of fractures erupting from the bullet-resistant material. Leaving nothing to chance, Houston fired once into the back of his head. She turned quickly to subdue Fawkes.

But he was gone. Wind and a salty mist poured in from an opening in the roof. A short ladder led from the cabin upward. Fawkes had gone up.

She ejected the magazine and pulled another from her belt. Slamming it in place, she darted to the stairway, weapon raised to the ceiling. She could see no one. At the same time, the whirring of an engine could be heard, changing in pitch from low to high.

"No!" she whispered under her breath and sprinted up the ladder.

A loud voice exploded throughout the cabin as Lopez charged inside.

"Sara!"

She was climbing a ladder across the room and didn't hear him. Her feet lifted from the steps and out of sight. Ignoring the bodies around him, he dashed to the ladder and ascended. Houston was there, firing her gun madly as she aimed out over the open water.

He followed the barrel of her gun. In the distance, a form was suspended over the ocean, legs dangling and kicking, arms grasping desperately above him. Overhead, a shadow hummed, a black object the size of a bed, the pitch dropping as the man accelerated away and faded into the blackness.

"*Fuck!*" cried Houston as the object disappeared, her mag emptied.

They both stood there in silence, spindrift coating the dead bodies scattered below them, the boat hurled back and forth in the wind.

All for nothing!

Fawkes had escaped by drone into the night.

DEPOSITION IN THE MATTER OF:
UNITED STATES ARMED FORCES SPECIAL TRIBUNAL,
Plaintiff,
v.
JOHN SAVAS, Defendant
Case No. M120039E-007X

CONTINUED DEPOSITION OF:
REBECCA RUTH COHEN

MS. COHEN: We almost had him. It could all have
ended right there. But we had the boat. And a
lot of bodies to examine. Also one survivor to
question.

CBD: They killed the others?
MS. COHEN: Yes.

CBD: You don't look okay with that.
MS. COHEN: [INAUDIBLE] Not really. Violence
isn't really my thing, you know? But sometimes
there isn't another choice. Those were hired
guns that would have killed them—tried to kill
them—without a second thought. God! Why am I
explaining this?

CBD: I'm interested in understanding the
motivations behind each member of your team.
MS. COHEN: The motivation was the same: to stop
what Fawkes was doing!

CBD: Did the survivor provide any useful intel?
MS. COHEN: Not much, but some. Once isolated,
it was clear to him that the money he had
received wasn't worth what he was going to get.
We didn't even have to lean on him.

CBD: And?
MS. COHEN: Unfortunately, most of it was what
we had guessed, but confirmation was nice.
Hired mercenaries. Paid ridiculously well.
Never privy to anything important—Fawkes kept
them completely in the dark. They were there to
follow his direct orders and serve as
protection. He was one paranoid monster.
Anyway, we learned that Fawkes was spending

more and more time at sea.

CBD: Why was that?
MS. COHEN: The bodyguard thought it was to avoid law enforcement. I think it was more than that. I think Fawkes was planning to ride out offshore the societal chaos he was inducing. With everything Angel began to put together, it was clear that he was planning some big event, and it would go down soon.

CBD: What else?
MS. COHEN: Print and DNA samples linked two of the men onboard to the public assassinations. And we matched Fawkes' DNA as well—same as in the mask in the Bridgeport scene.

CBD: Where the shootings occurred?
MS. COHEN: Right.

CBD: But you still hadn't found him in any database?
MS. COHEN: No. Might be he was off the radar. He was young, maybe never caught in criminal activity. Another possibility we considered is that he scrubbed his files.

CBD: Scrubbed them?
MS. COHEN: Fawkes was a master hacker. Databases are often too easily accessible online. Really—do you know of a single major private or governmental organization that *hasn't* been hacked in the last ten years? If he knew he was in certain systems, he might have found his way into them and deleted all information about himself. He could do it, I don't doubt that. Either way, we had nothing. And now we had stirred the hornet's nest.

CBD: Meaning?
MS. COHEN: Until that point, we had been only a blip on his radar. Someone probing too much in the wrong places. Even that was enough to try and kill us. But now—we'd entered his space, killed his bodyguards, nearly grabbed him off that damn boat. If he didn't have that escape drone on the roof, we would have. Now he was pissed, and he came after us.

CBD: First with Angel?

MS. COHEN: Well, she was the thorn in his side that kept getting worse. But everything just began to escalate at that point. Within the next few days we'd be hit, and absolutely devastating attacks happened across the world. And if it hadn't been for the information Angel obtained from the worm dissection, we would have lost even more.

CBD: So she was key.
MS. COHEN: [INAUDIBLE] Here we go again. Yes, she was key. So were John, and Frank, and JP. And certainly Gabriel and Mary.

CBD: The aliases—
MS. COHEN: Just stop. I'm not going there. Look, we worked as a team. A damn good team. What happened next just motivated us more. That's when John's idea took root, when we agreed to try it. Fawkes was hitting the world where it hurt. This time, we were going to hit *him* where it hurt.

NOVEMBER 1

41

HE SPOKE TO them on five different encrypted video conferencing calls. They were hired guns and bombers, assassins trained under diverse conditions spanning the military to organized crime. He'd baited them through the underground online marketplaces with money few could refuse. He'd filtered through information searches, background checks, and video chat interviews. He'd tested each of them with small-scale operations, sifting the wheat from the chaff, identifying the unreliable, the unstable, the less competent, and those who reported back to others and revealed themselves as informants. Sometimes he was forced to erase those who could pose a threat.

The few who survived the process were moved like chess pieces, directed remotely so that groups were formed, hierarchies established, rules set and punished harshly when broken. And always there was money. Hard to comprehend amounts of money, accounts protected from the worm scattered across the world. Houses and lands were purchased. Protected lives and identities created and promised. All for the taking should a final set of missions be accomplished. And all to be snatched away once the missions completed. He was fighting against the plutocracy and he was sure as hell not going to create another one.

Fawkes adjusted the mask over his face. A mask of a smiling, goateed madman from another age, always in place, his identity revealed only to those bodyguards who worked directly with him. He prepared a final address. Now he would move the strikes forward quickly in time. Now he would give a last set of instructions for the beginning stages of the end. Dangerous people at the FBI and other agencies had forced his hand sooner than he would have liked. He preferred careful probing of systems and weakness, test shots and stress tests that allowed him to screen his people as much as the target systems. He liked to thoroughly debug the code.

But the time for precise experimentation was gone. The time for drastic action had revealed itself. He could not afford another near disaster like that on the boat. How had they found him so quickly? Attacked him so easily? He had taken every precaution! Every trace erased from the digital world. But he was clearly not careful enough. Which meant he had to hurry. There was no telling from what direction they were coming, what flaws in the program were still lurking, waiting to collapse like poorly designed walls under siege.

Chaos was his ally. The more dysfunctional the world became around them, the less the governmental apparatus could use its considerable firepower to find and kill him. The attacks would begin there with the heads of the hydra in Washington. They thought they *had* been attacked! But they had seen only the weak pieces, a feint to test the strength of their defenses. And those defenses had been found lacking.

But the hydra's handlers were not in Washington, but Europe and Asia. And so he would begin the dismantling of the European society and destabilization of China and the lesser economies. There could be war. These disturbances might be enough.

Otherwise, he would bring the final direct attack. He would darken America and plunge the nation into complete anarchy. Moments before the lights went off in the centers of power in the United States, the signal would be given for the worm to complete its final function. The digital mind of the planet, on which all the modern societies rested, that calculated trade and commerce, that built buildings and cars, that became nearly a higher order organism of parsing ideas and thoughts in a fiber-optic neural network, a brain beyond anything the solar system had likely ever seen—it would die. Erased. Unmade in a cascade of deletion that would render them beyond salvage. Once the signal was given, the mad mind of Earth would die.

Only then might there be a chance for something more worthy, more pure to rise from the ashes. Fawkes didn't care if it was Humans 2.0 or the dolphin beta release. It had to be something new. Utterly new. The corrupt, cancerous, and insane thing called modern culture, what the deluded called modern civilization, had to be sterilized. Every cell wiped to prevent reinfection.

The worm would do that. The final cargo to be uploaded was designed and long perfected. It would exploit the enormous security and logical holes in the neuronal system of the world mind and scramble it, then like an acid eat away at the fibers and proteins until even the very DNA was digested.

Fawkes smiled behind the mask as he spoke to his blind tools. The FBI group had nearly ended it, but had only accelerated the date of doom.

He would start with them. He would pay that bitch in the bowels of Manhattan a short visit. Then he would show her who really ran things in cyberspace.

"Knock, knock, Angel."

42

THE NAMES UNFURLED across the screen like entries in some doomsday book.

It was the new month, November first at three in the morning, and Angel had spent it deep in the basement of the FBI building. She rubbed her eyes. The holes across her left ear were swollen and red from the piercings that had been squashed as she slept during the last worm decryption job. Running one hand over the orange stubble of hair on her scalp, she clicked with the other to silence the alert tone from the computer that had called her out of some murky dream—only to stare at another nightmare.

She read through it again. The list was a who's who of the power brokers in Congress and business.

"Oh, look—there's the president herself!"

Of course. If you're going to bring down the US in one blitzkrieg, you ought to have her on the list. That made sense.

But did any of it really make sense? Angel knew her brain was close to oatmeal at this point, but were these really hit lists? What madman would try to off that many high-profile people? What lunatic could ever think something like that was even possible? And to what end?

Chaos. She shook her head. It all seemed to point in that direction. The banking meltdown. The attacks. This list of powerful names. Fawkes had made no demands. He hadn't tried to leverage the threats into anything. He seemed to be running by a playbook no one had ever seen before. No one could anticipate his moves.

Until now. Her virus was functioning, reporting on the worm's activities. And her little digital operating room had revealed more and more of the inner workings of the worm. Like any code, it was a series of instructions, fragile logic and loops calling out to be hacked. All she needed was time. But there was precious little of that left.

Angel sat upright and gulped down a wash of cold coffee. She'd bring this directly to Savas in the morning. Those names had serious protection, especially after events of the last two weeks. But was it enough? Could the secret service, the military, private contractors, could any of them anticipate what attacks might come from a man that was as diabolical as he was creative? Could anyone?

Her screen went dark.

"What the hell?"

She clicked on keys and the mouse, but there was no response. *Wonderful.* It was a very bad time for a device failure. She began to reach around for the power switch to forcibly reboot the machine when a line of green text ran across her screen.

"HELLO, ANGEL."

It was like some old mainframe terminal, letters appearing left to right revealing words, then phrases. Carriage returns advancing text. A knot formed in the pit of her stomach. Someone else had hijacked her computer, and she had no doubts about who that was.

The GUI was gone, but she found that she could type.

"HI, FAWKES."

She jumped up and disconnected the VMS machine from the internal network. She hoped to God he didn't have any inkling of what she was doing with it.

More text appeared.

"LIKE THE MATRIX, RIGHT? IT'S BEEN INTERESTING WATCHING YOU WORK. BUT I'VE GOT THINGS TO DO AND YOU'RE CRAMPING MY STYLE."

A green light appeared on the upper lip of the screen indicating that the camera was on. She ignored it and the video image that appeared on the screen. She raced toward the bank of computers along the wall.

A mocking voice came over the speakers.

"No use, Angel, baby. I've turned all the drives to goo already. You don't think I'd give you the chance to shut them down first, do you?"

She reached the first machines and scanned for the main power connector.

"Thorough, aren't you? Look at your pretty little ass wiggle! Here, I'll just put a stop to all this unnecessary work so we can chat a little bit."

The cluster of computers switched off. Machine-gun like clicks of the system shutting down, the lowering pitch of hundreds of disk drives spinning to a stop—it was like some sonic rush of wind through the room.

"There. That's better."

She turned to face the only active monitor left. A masked figure stared back at her, smile frozen in place. She walked up to the terminal and sat down.

"Practical. I like that," came the distorted voice. "Butch, too. You swing both ways?"

"I'll be swinging at you."

He laughed, the sound crackling as the distorted audio maxed out the dynamic range of the electronics.

"Feisty! I should'a known that, though. I knew right off that those bugs crawling up my ass weren't NSA. Not close to their style. Crude, self-taught. More clever. You weren't raised in some dot gov hacking camp."

Angel resisted the urge to look at the VMS machine. Everything might depend on whether he had discovered it. It loomed like a presence behind her, some spirit that waited for her attention that she had to ignore. Until this asshole had his gloat and finished the wipe.

"It's not over, Fawkes."

"That's where you're wrong, Angel Lightfoote, special agent Intel 1. Angel Lightfoote of the scrubbed records."

She bit her lip and tried to keep her composure.

"What? You thought I wouldn't do my homework? You got *history*, girl! Most of it wiped. Somebody wanted you cleaned up and made presentable. Would that be this Savas guy? No? Probably the other one, Kanter, the one blown up a while back?"

"Fuck you," she hissed.

"Oh, emotions, Angel. Not a girl's best friend in this game. Don't get attached. Don't feel bad for Blown-Up Man. Slows you down. Blinds you."

"Makes you human. He was a hundred times the man you are."

"A man who was into other men, huh? Hundreds of times, I bet."

She flipped him off.

"Well, good old *Larry* must have gone the extra mile. I was scraping the digital basements. *Nothing*. But then I found all that stuff on dear old *dad*."

Tears welled in her eyes as she ground her teeth.

"That all had to suck, yeah? Tell me, were you really there, in that cage when he bit it? Yeah? I thought so. Fucked you up good, didn't it? Did dear old dad have to watch what they did to you? Every little thing? I can imagine the next few years. No wonder they had to bleach your record! Is that what they did upstairs in that shiny little head of yours, too?"

The sly face on the mask, the smirk of Guy Fawkes, the tormenting knowledge this sociopath had about her life, it was too much. Angel reached down and picked up a metallic wastebasket from the ground.

"Angel, darling, let's not fight."

"It's not over, you bastard. I promise you. *Never* make it personal? Well, you just sure as hell did! And I'm coming for you!"

She swung the basket at the monitor. Again and again she pummeled the screen, plastic cracking, pixels shattering. The monitor fell to the ground, a black circle from the impact in the middle of the masked face, blocking it out. Still she smashed it. Over and over on the ground, a fissure opening in the screen, the dark circle expanding like some black hole to swallow the entire image.

All the while, laughter.

Fawkes' wild laughter spilled like acid from the speakers into her ears. Finally, she turned to the power cord and grabbed it with both hands, yanking it from the socket, releasing a tormented scream.

The sound ceased. What little was still glowing on the screen went black. The room was plunged into near darkness, the glow of the EXIT sign over the side door painting the room dimly in an infernal red.

She wiped sweat and tears from her face and stumbled over to the VMS machine. Her right hand was bloodied. She crouched and touched the surface of the old computer with her left, resting her head against the cold metal.

Her head nodded rhythmically as she began to rock back and forth on the ground. She repeated words over and over, her voice much higher, nearly that of a child's.

"I'm sorry, Dad. I'm so sorry. I'm so sorry."

She wept.

43

THE MARINE CONTINGENCY posted around 1600 Pennsylvania Avenue had swelled beyond anything Elaine York had ever experienced. A former army field officer, one of the few women to be deployed into live hostilities in the first Iraq War, she didn't shrink from conflict, armed or not. But to see the White House nearly obscured by flak jackets and fatigues was to enter into the kind of nightmare reserved for over-the-top Hollywood blockbusters. That it could become real had never truly entered into her imagination.

President York stepped away from the window and turned back to her desk. Her last images of a figure sprinting down the circular roadway in front of the main doors—George Tooze, her Secretary of Homeland Security. She sat down and tried to compose herself. Her head throbbed from two straight days without sleep. Her mind still reeled from continuous updates, each more alarming than the last, from every corner of the globe. And now Tooze racing over like a high school sprinter, his sixty-five-year old body likely straining under the duress. This was not going to be good.

And yet, what had been? The latest report from the NSA couldn't have been worse. The damned worm had begun to disrupt vital elements of the world's infrastructure. Haphazardly, to be sure, but her advisors, and her own gut, spoke to the possibility that what they had seen so far had only been feints. *Tests* to optimize the monster running through the cortex of the modern world and yet which had, even on their own, produced planetary chaos.

Food and oil supply chains were disrupted from agribusiness farms to the international shipping systems on which a hungry world depended. Sea and air systems were scrambled, systems that transported the world's goods, including the ever-critical supply of oil. Hospitals were running out of supplies. Telecoms were unreliable. The world was losing its collective mind.

She half-expected red lights to be flashing around her and sirens wailing. The National Terrorism Advisory System threat assessment was at "IMMINENT." All branches of the military were at

DEFCON 2 or higher, the birds in international airspace with different flags buzzing around each other nearly an invitation to a catastrophic mistake. The Force Protection Condition was DELTA nearly everywhere. INFOCON was at 1 and might as well have just put up a white flag and shut down.

And here was Tooze.

The flushed face of her trusted adviser burst into the Oval Office. He held an envelope in one hand that he brandished before him like a radioactive substance.

"A number," he gasped, resting a hand on the other side of her desk. He held up the letter again. "Limited lifespan. It's from Bilderberg."

Time seemed to stop and she felt her mind disengage. She remembered the first time that she had experienced death. Her mother had been braiding her hair one morning, and by afternoon she had been a seven-year-old raised by a single-parent father. The moment had been just as immediate as the rush of Tooze into the room. One minute, she could hear the sounds of her mother talking on the phone in the kitchen while she played in the living room. The next, a crash and house-jolting thud. She had run in to find her mother unconscious on the floor. She would never wake. A brain aneurysm, or a big balloon that popped in her head as one of the doctors had tried to explain it to her. She had feared balloons ever since. It could happen so fast. Pressure. Weakness. Then—pop.

She rose, turned away from Tooze, and walked back to the window to stare at the troops outside. So much firepower. Such an apparatus in the nation's military. And, in the face of the forces that truly controlled the world, so powerless.

Had it come to this? This new land and new dream of not even three centuries, of miracle cures, trips to the moon, supercomputers in your pocket—had its time come so soon? All because of this terrorist and his devil worm?

Pop.

"Ms. President? Elaine?"

She turned back to Tooze and felt the room sway, barely keeping her balance. "Thank you, George," she said, pulling the paper from his hand and trying to remove a tear discreetly. "I will need to be alone for this call."

He nodded, his face telling her all she needed to know, that he too understood the significance of what she was about to do.

"I'll be outside," he said. "Don't lose hope."

He turned and walked out of the room, closing the door softly behind him.

Sighing, she approached the grand desk and pressed her thumb against a fingerprint-reader on a drawer, then entered a code into a keypad next to it. There was a clear click, and she pulled the drawer open. Inside was what looked to be a bulked up cellular phone from decades past. She knew it to be a special device, engineered to work through a covert collection of satellites, encrypting transmissions through means not even the worm could break. At least some things were beyond its reach. In the realm of monsters, the worm was just another fiend.

Bilderberg. So it had finally come to this. Like ghosts, powers that many felt but never saw, sometimes they became incarnate. Like the beginning of her presidency, they had come and impressed upon her their reality. Sometimes the phantoms moved objects around a haunted home. Or a nation. Sometimes they killed.

She read the number off the paper in the envelope and keyed it in. A series of strange sounds of static and digital processing harshly burbled from the speaker. Then a loud click.

She exhaled slowly.

"This is Elaine York calling from the White House."

BEFORE:
THE ANONYMOUS EVENT COMMISSION

DEPOSITION IN THE MATTER OF:
UNITED STATES ARMED FORCES SPECIAL TRIBUNAL,
Plaintiff,
v.
JOHN SAVAS, Defendant
Case No. M120039E-007X

CONTINUED DEPOSITION OF:
JOHN SAVAS

CBD: And it was at this point that you put your trap in motion?
MR. SAVAS: Yes.

[REDACTED]: Why did you trust this criminal?
MR. SAVAS: To be quite honest, I didn't. Maybe the trap was going to be reversed and sprung on us. I was flying on instinct, and something resonated as truthful about her dislike of Fawkes and what he was doing. Anyway, I didn't feel I had much of a choice. We had to act fast or things might get beyond the point of fixing. The disaster with Angel just confirmed how vulnerable we and the entire world were to this maniac.

[REDACTED]: The purported accident with your computers.
MR. SAVAS: Not accident, sabotage. It was a cyberattack.

[REDACTED]: Conveniently timed to cripple you at a moment, to use your words, where things were so serious that they might not be fixed.
MR. SAVAS: Which is exactly what Fawkes would have wanted. We'd shaken him. He responded to protect his plans.

[REDACTED]: But no one else was with agent Lightfoote when the alleged hacking attack occurred?
MR. SAVAS: Alleged?

CBD: Why don't you tell us about Angel Lightfoote, Mr. Savas.
MR. SAVAS: Can you be a little more vague, please.

CBD: Why did you put her in charge of your cybercrimes unit? Her records do not indicate any experience in digital technology or training of any kind.

MR. SAVAS: She showed an aptitude. After we lost Manuel—agent Manuel Hernandez—we needed someone in the chaos of the time to handle the system he had set up, our operations room at Intel 1. Angel was one of those to step up. After a short time she was running things by herself.

CBD: Is it common practice at FBI to promote people into positions for which they clearly have no training, no experience?

MR. SAVAS: Of course not. But it wasn't common occurrence to lose half your people to a vengeful tycoon plotting a global genocide. John Gunn and Mjolnir massacred half our division. The regs didn't mean a hell of a lot in those moments. We were battered. We survived as a team. More than a team. As a family. Screw the fucking protocol.

[REDACTED]: Again, we are to understand that you were able to *ignore* policies and procedures because of your division's vaunted status at FBI and elsewhere?

MR. SAVAS: We were cut a lot of slack.

[REDACTED]: Which you used to promote an unstable personality into the prime position overseeing your cybercrime investigations just as the world was to suffer an unprecedented digital terrorist attack.

MR. SAVAS: Unstable? Look, Angel was weird, but she was a damn fine agent. Became a better one after Mjolnir. The trial by fire chars some, brings out the gold in others. She was gold.

[REDACTED]: These photos, Mr. Savas. This is Lightfoote?

MR. SAVAS: Yes.

[REDACTED]: How can you possibly justify this?

MR. SAVAS: So she's got short hair and some piercings. She saved the damned world, you idiots! You want to turn that back so you can dress her like a Stepford girl?

[REDACTED]: Saved the world. Only she could do
it. Only she had the power to stop the virus, a
virus she was instrumental in discovering, that
she claims wiped her computers and all previous
records of cyber-activity in your division. A
woman contacted by the very man you assert was
the prime terrorist in the events last fall. A
woman with a diagnosed mental illness, hired
and promoted without following basic FBI
protocols.
MR. SAVAS: What do you mean a diagnosed mental
illness?

[REDACTED]: Don't play ignorant with us now.
MR. SAVAS: What diagnosed mental illness?
There's nothing like that in her file.

[REDACTED]: Of course not, because as our
research has uncovered, FBI computers were used
to wipe national databases, medical records
destroyed. Or so it was thought. But you were
not thorough enough.
MR. SAVAS: Deleted records? [INAUDIBLE] Larry.
Dammit, Larry, you should have told me.

[REDACTED]: Now you wish to pass the buck to a
dead boss, is that it?
MR. SAVAS: Never mind. You're going to twist
and fit everything into your preconceived
notions in this witch hunt. I can tell you I
didn't know, but I don't much care even knowing
now. Larry made some unorthodox hires,
including yours truly. Those choices wouldn't
look good on paper in front of a committee like
yours. And those choices put together a group
of damaged yet exceptional people that have
saved all your asses on more occasions than we
have time for!

[REDACTED]: So you would justify this?
MR. SAVAS: I'll justify it with our record.

[REDACTED]: That is exactly what we are here to
examine. Not the fantasy you put forth as you
actions, but what really happened.
MR. SAVAS: What really happened.

[REDACTED]: Yes. And we know that Angel
Lightfoote is at the center of this. Placed at

the center of digital operations immediately
before the chaos by you, escaping from custody
with two known terrorists and enemies of the
state that you sheltered and aided.
MR. SAVAS: Oh, good God.

[REDACTED]: You might ought to pray to your
God, Mr. Savas, because as things are shaping
up, that is the only place you can expect to
find any mercy.

CBD: Can we turn this back to the so-called
trap?
MR. SAVAS: [INAUDIBLE]

CBD: So, this "Poison", real name Tabitha Ivy,
she agreed to serve as bait for Fawkes?
MR. SAVAS: Yes. She was bait. We'd make it
clear we were holding her, that we would
extract information by any means necessary,
threatening to expose Fawkes, to harm someone
he possessed an emotional attachment to.

CBD: And by any means you mean torture?
MR. SAVAS: We faked interrogation scenes,
placed them on poorly secured servers. Sent
unencrypted emails revealing that we held her,
provided information that we could possess only
if we did. We believed this would get back to
him and he would respond.

CBD: Which you claim he did?
MR. SAVAS: With a vengeance. We weren't
actually prepared for how swift and devastating
the response would be. We were naive about just
how much manpower he had amassed and how
obsessed he was with Poison. But afterward, we
knew the plan would work. He gave us the
confidence to set it up by those actions.

CBD: And so that was the next event in the
chronology, the warehouse in Brooklyn?
MR. SAVAS: The plans for that were set in
motion, but everything was exploding at that
point. Lopez and Houston were sent to D.C. You
know, your two terrorist enemies of the state?
They *volunteered* to try and stop the
assassinations we deduced were coming. They
saved the president.

[CBD]: Let the record show that Mr. Savas
refers to former president Elaine York.
MR. SAVAS: Former?

[CBD]: She has been charged with treason and is
a most wanted fugitive under the current
authorities.
MR. SAVAS: Current authorities? What does that
mean? Who is running the damn country?

[CBD]: We are not at liberty to convey such
information to you.
MR. SAVAS: Jesus Christ! What the hell is
happening topside? What have you people done?

PART 3

By God's providence he was catched
With a dark lantern and burning match
Holloa boys, holloa boys
God save the King!
Holloa boys, holloa boys
make the bells ring!

—English Folk Verse (c.1870)

44

"LOOK, YOU NEED to understand. This comes from way up—from Sergei. We need those users in China. If we don't expand into those markets, we're going to end up on the wrong side of history in tech."

The bald suit behind the desk looked down at his desk as he spoke. Across from him, a dark-haired man with smart glasses stared forward with intense eyes. His fingers drummed on the armrests of the chair.

"Wrong side of history? What the fuck is 'Don't be evil' then? We censor and keep information from people? Information should be free for everyone! You know, even the Chinese! I thought that's what this company was about!"

"We have to make compromises. Find the right balance."

The young man stood up, his voice seemingly focused on the conversation, but his fingers on a smartphone and tapping furiously. He began to pace the small office space.

"And what about the backdoors to NSA and others?"

The superior finally did look at the younger man. "What are you talking about?"

"Don't play dumb with me. I've got enough access to source that I can recognize a backdoor when I meet it. Fucking sloppy code too, if you asked me. Some Russian mobster is going to rape you up the ass for it someday if you don't clean it up."

"I think you're definitely poking around in places you don't need to be," he said, swiveling around in his chair to fully face the young man.

The pacing continued. "Oh, look at that. Suddenly we're all serious like. Well, I'm into free information. Nothing is off limits."

"Then you're going to have to find yourself another job. I don't know why we tolerated you as long as we did."

"Because I can code circles around anyone here."

"No one is irreplaceable."

His step uninterrupted, the youth laughed. "Oh, a threat. From the internet's biggest, baddest company."

"You should take that seriously. We can make you. Or break you.

Don't fuck with us or you'll never work in the valley again."

Finally the pacing stopped and the man stood over the desk, facing his superior. "Make me? What, move up the ladder? To what? Chief of sucking China's dick? You dumb ass, I can make more money hacking clueless banks than you pay me here. I thought maybe there was something good in the corporate cesspool. Man, you guys have let me down."

The man behind the desk looked stunned. "There will be no more talk of illegal activity in my office."

"'Cause the NSA is on the line, you mean. How much of your soul did you sell for this shit?" He laughed and shook his head. "Let's get this straight. You're actually upset about me tapping the evaporation *off these big companies while you prostitute yourselves to a dictatorship? Keeping information from its own people? Allowing our government to spy on its own citizens? Okay, this place is actually* seriously evil. *God, I didn't see it. I didn't want to see it. I mean, what's left? I can be a legal criminal here or a black hat out there? This whole tech industry is in deep with the devil." He threw a chair across the room. "Fuck you! And fuck the slave masters. The entire system's corrupt."*

The bald man stood up behind his desk and pointed to the door of his office. "Get out of here. You're fired! No, as of today, I can promise you, you're finished in this industry."

The youth laughed again. "You fucking moron. I'm just getting started."

NOVEMBER 2

45

Sara Houston stared through the window of the helicopter at Washington, D.C. The familiar landmarks were gone. The bejeweled arteries of transportation dark, the lights extinguished by a city-wide blackout. Along with the loss of the grid, the monuments vanished as the spotlights winked out—the Capitol, the Lincoln Memorial, the pillar of the Washington Monument. Gone.

But there was light—orange, glowing in a primitive anger rising from the ground. *Fires.*

The pilot's voice rang in her headphones.

"I'm going to put you down as close to 1600 as I can. I'm broadcasting on all frequencies—if anyone is listening we've got the codes to prove we're friendlies."

"Maybe they're shooting first and asking for ID later," mumbled Lopez beside her, his words barely discernible in the thunder of the blades above them.

"Might be," said the former Blackhawk pilot. "But the rest of the city is chaos. The food riots from the lockdown last week exploded earlier tonight when the power cut. It's like something out of a zombie flick. You'll never make it through the streets."

Houston shouted over the noise, "The President is still there? Are we sure?"

"As of twenty ago, yes. They've had a marine contingent keeping the mobs at bay."

"Why hasn't she been evac'ed?" asked Lopez.

"Got me. Word was filtering through that they were going to. They were flying missions in. Marine One should have choppered her out, but something happened."

Lopez looked at Houston and mouthed, "The Worm." She nodded staring back down to the patches of red and orange flickering below.

The pilot continued. "But I don't know why they haven't been able to get a military mission in there. Someone must be running interference."

Houston gasped, pointing vigorously below. "Maybe those?"

Lopez and the pilot glanced downward. Over the dark city, underneath and in front of them, structured like a migrating flock, small objects reflecting the moonlight sped along their vector. The outlines of the White House could be made out, approaching quickly, the building still illuminated by emergency power. The objects raced straight for it.

"Look!" cried Lopez. "The ones in the back—they're carrying people."

"Drones," said Houston. "They're dropping in a hit squad. Can you outrun them?"

The pilot shook his head. "We're too close. This old shit heap you forced me to fly can't compete with the new birds. It's too slow."

"Gun it!" she yelled, releasing her safety harness and grabbing a machine gun from the back. "Just gun it. Bring us into firing range."

The pilot accelerated sickeningly. Houston was nearly thrown against the back of the cabin. Lopez leapt up and steadied her, pulling her forward beside him near the side door. They mounted one of the weapons on a makeshift turret, Lopez slinging the other weapon against him.

The helicopter darted forward, closing the gap between it and the flock of drones. They approached the back rows, human forms dangling from the larger machines, a strike team of nearly ten black shapes descending with the flock toward the growing form of the President's house.

Houston slung the door open. "Keep it steady!"

They fired. At their distance accuracy was poor, but they compensated with a full spray of bullets. Houston worked the larger, mounted gun, the ordnance dramatically blowing apart machines and men. Between them, they managed to take down more than half the team before the killers realized their peril. The rest dove straight to the ground and out of range.

The remaining drones ignored the helicopter and accelerated downward. Houston and Lopez fired maniacally at them, but only managed to down a handful more. The remaining plunged like kamikazes toward the White House.

"Aerial strike!" said the pilot.

Around the property, explosions erupted. The fireballs lit the drone's targets—military trucks, fortified gunners, the power generators. The building was plunged into total darkness.

"Setting you two down!" came the pilot's frantic words.

The chopper dropped like a brick, the lurch in their stomachs only matched by the strength of the crush to the ceiling. They held on for dear life. The aircraft came to a bone-shaking stop as the landing skid struck the grass on the front lawn, hopped, and slammed down again.

"Go!"

They leapt out of the helicopter and crouched, automatic weapons at the ready. The chopper climbed quickly to an altitude the pilot hoped would be safe from the madness below, prepared to return and retrieve them once Houston and Lopez had located the President.

They'd taken no friendly fire on landing, and it was quickly obvious why. Flames raged around them and smoke filled the air. The initial wave of explosive drones had more than neutralized the military defenses, leaving no one to guard of the nation's First House.

Lopez pointed to the blasted remains of the fence in front of the building. Bodies of rioters were strewn everywhere. It was unclear whether they had been killed by the deceased marines or by the blast that had torn the barrier down. He screamed over the cacophony around them: "The assassins landed back there! They'll be coming through the front gate."

Houston nodded, motioning for him to follow. They sprinted forward, and she made a beeline for the blasted remains of a military barricade. Soldiers and their remains littered the makeshift rampart. Houston heaved one off a mounted machine gun, pointing the weapon toward the street.

"They wanted shock and awe," she said, looking around. "They got it, but we punched a hole in their plan. We can stop them."

Lopez crouched beside her and removed pieces of a weapon from a backpack. He quickly assembled a rifle and attached a night-vision scope. Placing it on the cement barricade in front of him, he aimed through it.

"They're here!" he said. "Four. No, five! I can get several before they react."

"Wait!" said Houston scanning around them. "Let them get through the fence."

"That's too close, Sara!" he said. "Less than a hundred feet. Anything could happen!"

"But if some rabbit and come at us from other directions, we might be sitting ducks hunting for York. Draw them in," she said, pulling out two grenades. "Pick off as many as you can. The others will hunker down for a few seconds before making a run for shelter."

He nodded. "Throw deep, girl."

They didn't have to wait long. In the dancing light of the flames, Houston was soon able to spot the shadows approaching. They were moving swiftly, in a tight formation, cautious yet still seemingly confident of the outcome. *Overconfident.*

Lopez squeezed the trigger. One of the five arched backward, paused a second frozen, then tipped like a bowling pin to the ground. Before he'd hit the asphalt the man beside him took a shot to the head as well.

The others dropped quickly to the ground. Houston hurled one grenade after another at their location. Her motion drew the attention of the attackers, but she continued to throw, even as shots whizzed by. She'd launched four grenades in quick succession when Lopez tackled her before she could remove more. As they fell, the explosions began.

"Dammit, Francisco!" she screamed over the series of detonations.

He ignored her and aimed the rifle again, staring through the scope. "All five down, you crazy fool!" he said, removing the weapon from the barricade and planting the butt on the ground beside him. He sighed. "What a mess."

She smiled and grabbed him roughly by the cassock. "No more foreplay. Need to find POTUS."

They turned to the entrance, preparing to run into the damaged building. A rapid fluttering sound whipped over their heads and two shadows dropped to the ground in front of them, catching them unprepared. They stared into gun barrels.

"Sara, down!"

Automatic fire erupted as they dove for cover. Houston felt two rounds slam into her stomach, the flak jacket absorbing the most dangerous energies. She rolled desperately away and then sprang to her feet, leveling her weapon. She expected to die.

A pair of women stood in front of them, the bodies of the assassins at their feet, smoke trailing upward from their weapons. One was a female Marine, bloodied, and with a fire burning in her eyes. Houston moved her finger off the trigger and raised her gun skyward. She stared at the other figure, an older woman in a dark suit, short gray hair in disarray, a gun in her hands.

"Well, I'll be goddamned."

It was the president.

46

"MADAM PRESIDENT," SAID Houston as she stood up, grass stains and soot plastering her face. "You look like you know your way around a war zone."

Elaine York scowled and handed the weapon to the marine. "*Ms.*, please. I don't run a brothel. Your friend's hurt."

Houston's eyes darted across to Lopez. He sat on the ground holding his left arm. "Shit!" She dashed over to him.

"It's okay, Sara," he said, seeing her wild eyes. "Just a graze. Not even my gun arm." Blood soaked his shoulder and dripped through the cuff of his sleeve.

"Dammit, Francisco, you're too much a linebacker to dodge!" Houston ripped open the fabric of the cassock and revealed an ugly laceration across his upper arm. "Graze or not, you're going to bleed out if we don't close this up."

"Get York out," said Lopez, glancing up as the president stood over him. "Call the pilot. We'll deal with it after."

A pained look in her eye, Houston pulled out a handheld radio. It cracked with static. "Extraction 1. Target is acquired. Retrieve immediately. There are wounded."

There was a short silence, then: "Roger that. On your position. On the ground in half a minute."

Houston thrust the handheld to the president who took it with stern eyes. Pulling the dark mask off her head, she ripped it lengthwise and wrapped it into a tight mass, pressing it to Lopez's shoulder wound.

The marine beside the President looked grimly over the field of battle. "Let's hope to God that's the last of those fucking deathbots."

The deep throb of the helicopter blades grew quickly. Lopez stood up as the craft hovered above the building, kicking up debris and nearly blinding them. It set down on the lawn fifty feet from their position. The pilot waved them over frantically.

They ran. There were no more surprise landings. No shots fired or bombs detonated. As Houston slammed the door, the four of them still moving to take seats, the bird rocketed up, the sound of the rushing air muted as the latches sealed. She reached over and pulled a first aid kit from underneath the seat. Within seconds it was open and she was dressing Lopez's wound.

"I was going to offer some help," said the marine, eyeing her carefully. "I'm certified as a medic. But it looks like you know what you're doing."

Houston didn't take her attention from Lopez, who grimaced unmoving as she worked the torn flesh. "We've had some experience."

The President spoke. "Okay, so who the hell are you people? I don't usually jump into moving aircraft with just any pair of armed personnel, but today has been a bit unusual."

Houston continued working on Lopez's shoulder. "The pilot will drop you off at Mount Weather. Plans were likely for NAOC or something, but given the buzzing drone armies, I think feet on the ground is the place to be."

The President furrowed her brow. "You aren't coming? What's going on here? Who are you?"

Houston paused a moment and turned her head toward York, expression strained. "We don't exist, Madam—Ms.—President."

"Let's not get cheeky, darling. Out with it. There are no government ciphers to me."

"We aren't government. We don't exist. Friends called us in. But we're out before the light of day." Houston returned to treating the bullet wound, hands covered in Lopez's blood.

York eyed her silently for several seconds. "Friends called you in, huh?" She shook her head. "Damn prescient friends you have and I'm not going to second guess them. Not after what just happened. I assume you're legit or I'd be dead by now."

Houston chuckled. "I wouldn't go so far as to say we're legit."

Lopez opened his eyes and fought to smile. "I'm Gabriel," he hissed between clenched teeth. He twitched his head at Houston. "This is Mary."

York nodded. "Praise the Lord. Whoever you really are, I'm pleased to meet you." She shuddered. "I thought we were goners down there. I hope to be able to thank you properly someday. Consider me very intrigued."

Houston spoke flatly. "Who else is left?"

York closed her eyes and sighed, the fatigue apparent on her face. "A few staff. I hope to God they retreat to the bunker. We were cut off from escape by the explosions. Caved in a good part of the White House. Killed most of the soldiers. Nearly killed us." She looked to the bruised and bloodied face of the marine. "We're barely standing up again and it's gunfire, more explosions, your helicopter in the mix. I thought you were the bad guys until the drones dropped off the last two." She looked at Lopez. "Saved your life right before we mowed them down. Anyway, I judged you were friendlies. The Vatican look might have helped."

"I meant, who's left in the government?"

York's face hardened. "It's not good. Confirmed killed are the VP and the most of the leaders of Congress. The cabinet is MIA." She opened her eyes and stared out at the receding flames below. "Damn. Look at her burn. Should take a photo for my presidential library." The others stared at her in silence. "Meanwhile, Mount Weather makes a lot of sense. It's close enough, secured like all hell, puts me in contact with all the governmental emergency systems. Better than airborne right now. Speaking of which, how safe are we?"

The helicopter began to descend. Houston finished taping off Lopez's shoulder and slumped next to him on the chair, drenched in sweat.

"We're not Air Force One, Ms. President," said Houston. "Just another helicopter flying around on doomsday. Who's to care?"

Lopez steeled himself and sat up as the craft neared the ground. "This is our drop off, Ms. York," he said with difficulty. "The pilot is in our circle of *friends*. He'll get you to the emergency operations center, assuming the little flying demons don't pick you off."

"Reassuring," muttered York.

Lopez smiled. "Oh ye of little faith."

The helicopter touched down and the pilot called out to them. Houston opened the door and prepared to jump. York grabbed her arm.

"Good luck," said the president, holding Houston's eyes in an intense stare.

She returned the gaze. "We're all going to need a lot of that."

47

THEY WATCHED THE helicopter disappear into the evening sky. Tall grasses spread over the remains of an abandoned farm and a dilapidated barn rose behind them, the property encircled with trees.

"Let's get moving, Francisco."

He nodded and they turned toward the barn, moving as quickly as the former priest's fatiguing body would allow. There wasn't a door to secure the building, the remains having fallen off and laying rotted to the side. Much of the ceiling had collapsed as well. The rank smell of rotting wood was overpowering.

In the center of the barn was a jeep, a canvas thrown over the vehicle hastily, barely covering the sides. Houston walked up to the driver's side and yanked it off, tossing the fabric behind the truck. She helped Lopez remove his backpack and stripped his body armor.

"Don't worry about it," she said as he began to protest. "We should be done with commando activity for the night. You need to conserve energy."

He acquiesced and entered the jeep, stowing the gear in the back. Keys were sitting in the ignition. "Savas has some connections," said Lopez, staring ahead of them as Houston started the vehicle.

"I don't think anyone is keeping score on favors right now," said Houston, gunning the engine and racing out of the structure.

She felt conspicuous with the lights on, the clandestine and dangerous mission still locking her mind into a paranoid state. But it was too dark to drive without them, too dangerous on this poorly kept country road to risk ending their efforts for something so irrational. The jeep leapt and shuddered over holes and mounds in the dirt road. With each impact, Lopez gasped, his face a mask of pain.

Near the rusted gate to the field, Houston pulled the jeep to a stop. She removed a mobile phone from her shirt pocket and switched it on.

"No signal," she said.

"Location bad?"

"No, this area was supposed to be blanketed, remember?"

"So the towers are dark. What's even functioning, do you think?"

She shook her head. "Not much. Washington's completely dark." She released the belt and turned to the back, digging through one of the packs. She spun back in her seat holding a large handheld device. "At least we have this. Unless the damn worm fried the satellites, it should work."

She switched on the device and let it power up. Within a minute she had punched in a call and was waiting for a response. A low click sounded as she put it on external speaker.

Savas' voice burst into the crisp, Virginia air. "Gabriel? Where the hell are you two? What happened? It looks like an invasion in DC!"

"Mary here, John. Gabriel's close, nursing a blasted shoulder."

"Jesus! The president?"

"POTUS is secured. En route to the agreed upon location. She's shook up, but okay. The lady can take care of herself."

"You should see the footage on the city."

"We were *there*, John. It's worse. Look, I'm heading to the landing strip. We need immediate evac for Gabriel. I'm not going to wander into a local hospital, I hope you'll understand. He needs stitches. Maybe some blood."

"Roger that. We'll get you two back here, however we can. It'll be a bitch, though. You think the lockdown was serious before? Right now it's not clear to anyone who's running the damn country. The Guard is not ready for this. Folks are going to get killed."

Lopez motioned to Houston for the phone and grabbed it with his good hand.

"John, Gabriel here. Look, we need to regroup. This is moving too fast. You need to circle the wagons and get that crazy idea of yours in motion. Something. *Anything*. I don't think there's much time left."

"Agreed. Damn! We need to get her out of here to a different location, one where they'll feel confident to make a move. FBI headquarters is likely not going to encourage them. We're scouting some places, but it's hard to imagine how to get around the way things are."

Houston took the phone back.

"Look, John. We'll figure that out soon enough. I'm closing this call and beelining to the strip. Please tell me something is waiting for us there and it has airfoils."

"Fueled and ready. Go. There's no way to say it right, but thanks to both of you. And I'm sorry. The worst is still coming."

The line went silent. Houston flung the device into the bag behind her, released the brake, and hammered the accelerator. The jeep jumped forward onto the main road, tires screaming as Houston veered sharply right. Within a minute the vehicle was lost from view, red tail lights winking like mad eyes in the dark, leaving the pastoral hills of Virginia to cricket song and the glow of distant fires.

48

A MORNING GLOW *seeped through the filthy window and spilled onto two naked forms entwined on a bed. The woman lay with her head on the chest of the man, short-cropped hair like a sea-urchin next to his long, black strands. Both rested unmoving, eyes half-lidded. The man spoke.*

"You know, Poison, it's finally hit me."

The woman frowned, her brow creasing, and sat upright in the bed, small breasts decorating the sculpted ribs of a thin body. She moved her hand down the man's torso.

"What's hitting you?"

The man grabbed her hand and sat up as well.

"I'm serious."

"Yeah, that's obvious." She turned away, to stare out the window.

"I finally realized something about us." Poison didn't say anything, just watched the growing light. "You want to know what that is?"

"Fuck you, Fawkes," she said rising from the bed and wrapping a tattered robe around her. "No games."

"Not a game." His eyes were intense. Almost wild. "I finally realized that something incredible has happened. Something I never, ever expected. Something that should be impossible for me. Really, man, if you knew. Should just be impossible now."

"What, dammit?"

"I realize that sometime over the last month I've fucking fallen in love with you."

Her face froze and then a smile crept outward, shyly.

"Yeah?"

"Yeah. I mean, it's happened once before. But I thought that was it, never again. I'm pretty much all fucked to hell and back, you know. Emotionally retarded and all that. Psych-ward material. But whatever. I'm fucking nuts about you. Suddenly, I don't care anymore about all that shit, all these damn plans our stupid groups have been putting together. I don't care. Right now, I realized all I want to do is just take

311

off with you. Disappear. Live in some trailer somewhere and forget the goddamned world."

She moved toward him with her hand extended, but he stood and turned away from her, slipping tight underpants on, grabbing a t-shirt from the floor.

"It came into focus and explained so much. Why I couldn't concentrate. Why I was losing motivation."

Her hand dropped to the side, her smile fading.

"And then I realized what I had to do."

He turned toward her, the shirt pulled down over his thin frame, yanking on a pair of jeans.

"So what do you have to do?"

He sighed, snapping his fly closed. "It's over, Poison. I'm leaving and not coming back. It's been fun." He held her eyes.

"I don't understand. Her tone rose, the pitch quavering, her eyes large. "Why?"

"Don't make it any harder. For either of us. Just let it hurt and die." He threw things into a duffle bag. "This is the hardest thing I've ever done."

"Then why are you doing it?" she shouted, tears in her eyes.

"Because it is so hard! Because I know! I know that all our feelings, this love and joy and soaring hope and wonder is all a lie!" He looked at her as some despised thing. "Bubbling broth of chemicals in our minds that will lead us astray. That will end in hurt." He zipped the bag and walked to the door as she stood rooted, turning her head stiffly to follow his motions. "Worse. It'll wreck my plans, erase my desire to achieve my goals, to impact a lasting change. And why? For love. For limbic lies. I will destroy everything I've worked so hard on, only to lie dazed and happy with you under some tree somewhere. Justice demands so much more."

"Justice?" her face was a mask of confusion.

"It will not be stopped. Not even by you, Poison. I will go, our love will die, and I can finish what I started. I'm sorry for the pain. But it's just withdrawal. Just your brain missing its biochemical fix. It'll be over soon."

With that he stormed out of the room, leaving Poison to sit on the bedside, her eyes red and wet, a snarl on her lips.

```
            BEFORE:
    THE ANONYMOUS EVENT COMMISSION

      DEPOSITION IN THE MATTER OF:
UNITED STATES ARMED FORCES SPECIAL TRIBUNAL,
              Plaintiff,
                  v.
        JOHN SAVAS, Defendant
        Case No. M120039E-007X

       CONTINUED DEPOSITION OF:
     FRANKLIN JOESEPH MILLER
```

CBD: So then, these fugitives were sent to rescue the nation's president?
MR. MILLER: Which they did. Poke any holes in your dumbfuck theory?

CBD: And what were you doing during these hours of chaos in Washington?
MR. MILLER: If only it was just Washington! You seem to be forgetting the hand basket Europe went to hell in.

CBD: Yes, the nuclear plants.
MR. MILLER: You want chaos? There you go! Chinese party leaders blasted, too. When the TV news wasn't streaming video of DC on fire, it was showing ten different reactors smoldering in France. All from aerial reconnaissance photographs, of course, because it was a radioactive clusterfuck on the ground. Did you know that the Germans were nearly nuclear free?

CBD: I'm sorry, I don't see the relevance of—
MR. MILLER: They had made it a fucking law that they'd end nuclear power in Germany by 2020 or something. You know those Krauts, damned if they didn't figure out how to do it! Nuclear free. Fossil fuel free. Sustainable energy. In five years they'd be there. No worries for meltdowns. Unless, of course, some psychopath flies a bunch of drones into your neighboring country's reactors, blowing that shit into the atmosphere. Ain't nuclear free no more.

CBD: Mr. Miller, let's get back to—

MR. MILLER: So, when you say 'what were you doing?', try to remember that, first of all we were all trying to stay sane. Stay focused. On task. Every single one of us was struggling not to lose his shit as the world literally burned right in front of our eyes.

CBD: Yes, as I said, it was chaotic.
MR. MILLER: And in our own backyard. The food riots were spreading. No deliveries into or out of the city for days. Even if the worm hadn't FUBARed the distribution economy, the lockdown of the city made things ten thousand times slower. People were hungry. What's that saying, even a good man is nine meals away from murder? It was getting scary just to go outside. Everyone was panicking about a blackout like in DC. But we didn't have time for that shit. John's plan. That's what was on our minds. We spent sleepless nights setting it up. Filming interrogation scenes worthy of a goddamned Oscar. Feeding it out through Angel's digital feints.

CBD: I thought her system had been sabotaged by Anonymous.
MR. MILLER: Yeah, that set us back. She quarantined the computers from the internet and wiped them to make sure all traces of the worm were gone.

CBD: How?
MR. MILLER: I don't know. She's the code-head. I just shoot stuff.

CBD: Her system was brought back online?
MR. MILLER: A part of it. Enough to hook back up to the net. By then John had gotten some of the code for the firewall from NSA, and Angel fortified our position, whatever that means. She had more space now to breathe, but we didn't seem to have much time.

CBD: These feints?
MR. MILLER: Right. So, she put the interrogation videos on some unsecured boxes, other shit. To piss Fawkes off. The idea was to find a location offsite that looked vulnerable, move the girl there, leak that we moved the girl there, then wait with the bait for that

fuck to show up.

CBD: Sounds like a good plan.
MR. MILLER: Yeah, you try to find a way to net
that ghost in a few days while everything went
to shit. But it *was* a good plan. The only
problem was that Fawkes had his own plans. And
we hadn't anticipated them.

NOVEMBER 3

49

THE ELEVATOR OPENED and Savas saw the broad form of Frank Miller filling the space between the doors. The ex-marine's suit bulged on each side and his shirt strained from the pressure of body armor underneath.

"Suiting up for a rough game, Frank?"

"Time to move," Miller said.

Savas stood beside Cohen and the woman who called herself Poison. No one moved for a moment, the air charged with the potential of what was to come. They were crossing a threshold, setting events into motion that could not be recalled.

"FEDs first," said Poison, grasping a USB disk hanging around her neck like a talisman.

Savas followed as Cohen limped into the car and turned around, watching the hacker intently. Poison continued to face them as Miller pressed a button to hold the doors open.

"It has to be done," said Cohen. "You know that."

Poison nodded, looking sideways around the room as if for an escape. "Yeah, but when it comes to it, leading the prick to the net seems low even for slamming your ex." She looked at them harshly. "Try not to hurt him."

With that she walked into the elevator and turned her back on them as the door closed. Savas felt it better to leave her last request unanswered.

"Gabriel and Mary?" he whispered to Cohen.

"On their way. He's okay, patched up."

"Once we're outbound, I'd like to talk to them."

Cohen nodded. Miller was silent, and the remaining ride to the basement garage was eerily quiet.

The doors separated to reveal an underground parking lot—gray walls, flickering fluorescents, and row upon row of vehicles blurring into monotony. Standing out dramatically from that background was a black FBI van. It was built for undercover work, devoid of any insignia or lettering, the communications equipment inside visible through the open side door. Only the telltale bulge of the black antenna by the back doors would announce an investigative presence to the trained eye.

Alongside the van was a row of four uniformed SWAT officers. They were fitted in black uniforms and external body armor with weapons at their sides. Poison looked them up and down with a scowl.

"I'm part of the matrix now," she said bitterly. "Is this all you could get?"

"You think Fawkes will throw worse at us?" asked Miller.

"I don't know what he might do anymore," she said. "I hope these Storm Troopers know what the fuck they're doing. He won't mind wasting any of them."

Cohen handed Savas her crutches and faced Poison, her brown hair like a shawl offsetting the angry fire in her eyes. Cohen startled the hacker by reaching up to her shirt collar and straightening it.

"Look, Ms. Ivy—*Poison*—whatever you want to imagine yourself to be *in the matrix*. A little appreciation for putting ourselves in harm's way would do you well. Appreciation for dedication, duty, public good and all that. Inside the suits are human beings, just like you. Try to remember that."

Poison stepped back from the intensity in Cohen's glare, but the agent had turned away. Savas tried to rescue the moment.

"We were lucky to find anyone. Fawkes has pressed all the panic buttons. Washington's on fire and New York might be next. We have what we have. Most importantly, we have you. I just hope Fawkes wants you badly enough to do something stupid."

Miller motioned to the SWAT personnel. "Poison will go in the van with the team. There shouldn't be any issues along the way, but if there are, they'll need a small army to get to her out."

"Assuming they want me alive," she said.

"That's the basis of the entire plan," said Cohen. "Otherwise, he'll just drop a drone on you when he gets your position."

Poison looked terrified.

Miller continued. "The rest of us will follow in the car. I've put through all the channels we can for clearance, without revealing exactly what we're doing of course. Hopefully we'll make it through the checkpoints without issues. There are a lot of ways to get to Brooklyn. If we're held up at one bridge or tunnel, we'll try another. Hopefully we won't waste too much time."

Savas nodded. "What this means, of course, is that we're on our own. No backup. This entire operation would never fly with the brass if they knew what we were trying. It's too unorthodox, too poorly planned, too risky."

Poison laughed. "You're giving me a whole lot of confidence."

Miller scowled. "You should worry about the warehouse. You'll be dug in with no place to go there. Like I said, I don't anticipate any issues in transit today. Fawkes doesn't know what we're up to, he won't know where you are without his GPS device. Angel will leak the location once we're ready."

"Unless he knows a lot more than you think he does," said Poison.

Tires screeched. The group turned toward the sound. From the exit ramp two white vans rushed recklessly into their level and came screaming to a halt. Savas cried out as the doors of the vans swung open and dark shadows leapt out, weapons drawn. Cohen grabbed onto Poison and fell with her to the ground behind a car as the FBI SWAT team faced the oncoming figures.

Miller drew his gun and concealed himself behind the back of the van. Savas rushed forward beside him, pulling out his Glock and crouching. The SWAT team remained exposed, flanking their right.

In the sudden chaos, the sounds of automatic gunfire echoed madly through the underground chamber.

50

THE HAPHAZARD POSITIONING of the participants ensured that the firefight would be quick. The SWAT team was exposed and took the brunt of the initial offensive, unable to find cover. They responded by advancing into the fray and opening fire. Despite their protective gear and powerful weapons, they were outnumbered, and the attackers cut them down mercilessly.

But not without cost. Savas had kept the van between him and the assailants. He swung his gun arm into the line of fire just as the last SWAT man fell in front of them. Multiple bodies of their attackers lay on the asphalt as well, shell casings littering the ground beside him and in front of the vans. Gunshots exploded above his head as Miller fired, and Savas saw a shape fall as it ran, a body striking the concrete only feet from the shelter of parked cars.

His peripheral vision caught other forms dashing for cover on his left and right. A magazine dropped to the ground beside him as Miller reloaded, sliding down the side of the van.

"How many?" Savas asked.

"Four or five more," Miller panted. "They're spread across."

Savas spotted movement behind a blue pickup. He blasted its windshield for effect more than any hope to strike a target.

"Right idea," Miller said. "But it won't stop them for long. They've got the firepower on us. And still the numbers. How the hell did they know?"

Savas shook his head. "No time for that. Take point."

Miller swung into position and fired several shots. He ducked back and a barrage of gunfire chased him, blowing out the tires on the far side of the van, the windows exploding. Glass rained down on them.

"So much for an escape," Savas muttered.

He had turned back toward Cohen. She was propped on one knee and the car, poised with a pistol, head barely over the hood. Poison crawled behind the Crown Vic, terrified. Savas wondered if she could be the target. Was Fawkes there to terminate her?

Harsh words disabused him of the notion.

"Send the girl!" a man's voice cried. "All we want is the girl!"

Savas saw Cohen shake her head vigorously in the negative. Miller sighed.

"We *might* bring them down, John," he said, "but not before we're bloodied up good."

"Any ideas?"

"If I had a few minutes, maybe."

Their assailants wouldn't give them thirty seconds.

"We've got one of your men!" came the voice. "He's wounded but not dead. Send the girl or we waste him!"

There was a scream and Savas thought he heard the word "name". A rattled voice could barely be heard.

"Agent Longwell. Special Weapons and Tactics."

The voice was gasped, in pain, heavy breaths between the words.

Savas dropped to the ground and slightly forward. For a moment he was able to see ahead, the presence of an armed intruder pointing a gun at the slumping body of a SWAT officer, a trail of blood across the floor from where he'd been dragged. He rolled back behind the van just as shots ripped open the asphalt where he'd been. "Hurt bad but still alive," he said to Miller. "*Damn!*"

"You got ten seconds!"

"John, whatever you do, don't negotiate with these killers!" Miller looked furious.

Savas looked back. Cohen had dropped her head, defeated. He had a second to make a decision weighing a man's life and a possible stop to a world terrorist event. He closed his eyes.

"Frank, take my gun and—"

"I'm coming!"

He opened his eyes and saw Poison standing up behind Cohen. The hacker moved her hands upward and danced around Cohen's clumsy attempt to grab her, trotting forward awkwardly with arms raised.

"Anyone else move and this pig is dead!" cried the voice.

Savas cursed. The girl had taken things into her own hands. They hadn't killed her, which ruled her out as a target. It looked like Fawkes had sent a retrieval team to get her out of FBI custody, that he wanted her alive and was willing to invest significant resources into saving her. *Dammit!* The plan would have worked!

Poison was now just in front of the van, walking slowly, eyes wide and face frozen. She was beyond the team's reach now, any actions they might take could be countered devastatingly.

"They've got her," Savas said to Miller, hand clenched into a fist.

Miller nodded. "She made the call. Damage control, John. We need to create a distraction."

"A distraction?" he asked, the truth dawning on him.

"To get Rebecca out," said Miller grimly. "No way we all walk. Not after those videos. Not after this bloodbath. We need to draw fire and get her the hell out of here. Somebody has to walk away and try to get assets on that van."

Savas nodded, the implications hitting him like a sledgehammer. "Maybe we can take enough of them down, damage the van. Trap them, slow them down."

"Good a plan as any," shrugged Miller.

"But she can barely walk."

Savas looked back toward Cohen. Her attention was focused on him. He motioned with his eyes to the stairwell, a bright EXIT sign over the door. She followed his gaze and nodded, grabbing the crutches beside her.

They heard a scream and thump. Savas assumed it was Poison being thrown into the van. They had only seconds now.

"Go!" he hissed to Miller, and the two spun toward the attackers, weapons drawn.

They opened fire.

51

WEAPONS DISCHARGE FILLED the reverberant chamber. It was several seconds before Savas could fully process what was happening. He'd locked on the shapes in front of the white van, the form of Poison glimpsed momentarily within as he took aim. From both sides figures were rushing toward the van in a blur of motion.

But something was wrong. The mass of figures was too large, and the flow of bodies counter to what would be expected of their attackers. Shapes were moving down from the access ramp, black fabric fluttering as they dashed.

They were firing on Fawkes' team.

"Friendlies!" screamed Miller beside him, his combat vision parsing the chaos more quickly than anyone.

Lopez and Houston. Savas didn't have time to consider how they had arrived and found their way to the conflict. That would come later.

"Sideways, John," Miller yelled. "Watch the cross-fire!"

They darted away from the center. The team sent to snatch Poison was caught between hailstorms of bullets. Lopez and Houston had drawn their attention, wounding several, just as Savas and Miller opened fire. In less than a minute, the firearms were silent. Shell casings tinkled to a stop on the hard surface below. The charred reek of gunpowder burned in their nostrils.

A mass of bodies was scattered around the white vans. Two of the forms jerked helplessly, one screaming in agony. The rest were silent and still. It was over.

"Poison!" cried Cohen. She hobbled on her crutches straight to the van.

Miller and Savas moved cautiously, training their weapons on the bodies below them while Cohen disappeared inside the transport. Lopez and Houston rounded the right side of the vehicle, the former priest's left arm in a sling, his right clutching a submachine gun. Houston holstered a large Browning.

"Fuck, Savas!" she said, out of breath. "This was supposed to be where we recuperated!"

He frowned at them. "Thanks for saving our asses. Now get topside and check that we aren't going to get another surprise. Call Angel when you get back and let's try to figure this out."

"Francisco can wait it out here," she said. "Doc isn't going to be happy with his recent exertions." She sprinted away and up the ramp, weapon drawn again.

Lopez looked toward the fallen men around them. "I'll see what's left here. Go check on our bait."

Savas nodded and ducked into the vehicle. Inside, Poison cowered at the far end, shaking, wedged into a corner by the back doors with her legs pulled up and her arms around them. Cohen crouched next to her, one hand resting on the hacker's arm.

"Poison," Cohen said. There was no response, just a wide-eyed and distant look on her face. "Tabitha." She turned to Cohen, still not speaking, and Cohen continued gently. "It's over. We need to get you out of here, now, in case more are on the way."

"He knew," Poison whispered, clutching her necklace. She grabbed Cohen's vest. "How did he know?"

Cohen shook her head. "I don't know, but we need to move."

"We aren't safe anywhere! He'll know. He'll follow." Her eyes were wild. "How could he know?"

Savas' baritone rumbled from the front of the van. "Maybe I can shed some light on it." He spun from the front seat to the pair in the back, holding up a smartphone. "Look. GPS app."

He held the device toward them. On the screen a bright sphere blinked on their position.

"You're bugged, Poison," Savas said grimly.

"Bugged?" Poison looked perplexed. Then a light flared in her eyes. She jerked her necklace hard enough to break the clasp, leaving two ribbons dangling from her hand. Inside her palm was the USB stick.

"The drive?" asked Savas.

She laughed bitterly. "My first hack. Backed up. Like a trophy for luck. He knew. The prick! He knew. He must have switched it with a tracking device. *Jesus!*"

With a wild motion, she flung herself through the van, forcing her way past Savas and outside. The two agents followed her out and watched her fling the device to the ground. She picked up one of the assault rifles beside a dead man and aimed the butt of the gun toward the USB stick.

Cohen extended one of her crutches and stopped her. "We want him to know where we are, remember?"

"You want another bloodbath?" Poison said, indicating the bodies at their feet. "He'll come again. Can't you see that?"

"No," Cohen said. "We'll shield it, jam it until we arrive at the warehouse."

Poison nodded. "Yeah. All right." Her breathing slowed. Her eyes flashed downward. "I still want to smash the damn thing."

The edges of Cohen's mouth twitched upward. "I'm sure you do."

Cohen reached down awkwardly and scooped the stick from the ground, her face momentarily lost in a cascade of brown hair. Houston came jogging around the two vans.

"All clear," she panted. "The guards at the front are dead and the gate mechanism's smashed to hell and back. I used the phone there to call for some backup. This building must be ghosted. There hasn't been any response!"

Savas nodded. "We're spread so thin across the city that we're losing function."

"I also got Angel on the phone. She says she's got some interesting news."

Savas turned his head. "What news?"

Houston shrugged. "Something about immune code or something for the virus? I have no idea. I turned the conversation to our little problem down here. She'll get some reinforcements to us soon."

"No need for a medkit, though," said Lopez, stepping back into their circle. There was blood on his hands. "Too much iron, too many holes. They're all dead. Your men and those from Fawkes. The last just bled out."

They all turned to look out over the bodies scattered around them. Savas grimaced at the sight of the downed FBI agents, and the pools of blood clotting underneath them.

"This bastard is building one hell of a body count."

Cohen held up the USB stick. "Yeah, and he still thinks he holds all the cards. But not this one. Not anymore. We make it go dark, move to the location, and set up. Then we switch it back on. After all this, is there any doubt?"

Houston smiled. "Moth to the flame."

DEPOSITION IN THE MATTER OF:
UNITED STATES ARMED FORCES SPECIAL TRIBUNAL,
Plaintiff,
v.
JOHN SAVAS, Defendant
Case No. M120039E-007X

CONTINUED DEPOSITION OF:
JOHN SAVAS

MR. SAVAS: Everything was happening at once. We worked to clear the parking level. There wasn't much point in turning it into a crime scene. The whole planet already was one. The bodies were moved, some of the mess fire-hosed away. Found another van, but that was it for a SWAT presence. We were on our own.

CBD: Who then headed to the warehouse?
MR. SAVAS: Me, agents Cohen and Miller. Lopez and Houston. Finally, the woman. Poison.

CBD: The convicted hacker?
MR. SAVAS: That's the one. Agents Rideout and Lightfoote stayed behind to handle the digital angle of this.

CBD: How did you prevent Fawkes from tracking you?
MR. SAVAS: Simple. We bagged the stick in a shielding case—no signal in or out. For good measure we brought onboard a jammer. We checked it carefully. It was gagged. We sent out three vans in different directions in case any of his drones were watching. Janitors drove them around the city for a while. Not sure what was the key element, but it worked. We weren't followed.

CBD: And you know that because?
MR. SAVAS: We're still alive.

CBD: So it was during this time that agent Lightfoote designed the prototype code that infected the entire internet?
MR. SAVAS: Her immune cells. Yes.

CBD: What does that mean?
MR. SAVAS: Go ask a biologist. I don't know. [INAUDIBLE] All right, look, the idea is simple, at least. Our bodies have immune cells that recognize different bugs and kill them, right? These cells float around inside us waiting for an infection then do their business. The way Angel explained it, she couldn't attack the worm directly. It was too distributed or something. All over the place. A hundred million computers. If you don't get all of them, all the parts, it reinfects and spreads like wildfire again. So, her idea was to mimic the immune system. Design programs that would spread themselves like the worm, copying themselves, hacking into computers. But their purpose wasn't going to be to fuck things up like Fawkes. Her worms were single-minded in going after his worm. She called them immune cells.

[REDACTED]: Then let me get this straight. Your agent created viral, self-replicating code that would break into computers all around the world, including classified networks, including governmental systems?
MR. SAVAS: It was the only way. Like an infection where you only kill 99% of the bugs with an antibiotic, it can come roaring back. We had to get close to sterilization.

[REDACTED]: And you gave her permission to release this code?
MR. SAVAS: You bet your ass, I did. I had no idea if it would work. I'm not sure she was confident it could work. But it was sure worth a shot. What was the downside? It fails? Back where we were. We accidentally blow up the internet with her code? Well, that's *where* we were *already*!

CBD: Why did she think it could work?
MR. SAVAS: You know, I'm not a programmer or a biologist. She used the worm she had trapped in-house and some other bits of it she had captured across the net, used that code as some sort of matching-recognition system. All of her immune cells, her worms, were randomized with different bits of the code. They would search for matching elements, worm signatures, on any

computer her code infected. Match meant two
things. Her code would copy itself like crazy
and spread the recognition element, amplifying
it. It would also erase the worm on that
computer, but not before copying the code of
that worm for identification elements to
spread. The idea was to find new bits of all
the different, variable worms around. Over time
it should recognize them all and erase them
all. Fawkes' worms had to sit around and wait
for his signal. It wasn't designed to fight off
something like Angel was making. If she did it
right, and if we had enough time—if it spread
fast enough—we might sterilize enough computers
so that whatever final action he was planning
would fail.

CBD: Sterilize. How can the computers be
sterilized if they are infected with her code?
MR. SAVAS: Okay, sterile as far as the
Anonymous signal was concerned.

CBD: The Anonymous signal?
MR. SAVAS: Yeah, what we were calling it, the
activation Fawkes was going to send to take
down civilization.

[REDACTED]: Sounds very far-fetched.
MR. SAVAS: Does it? You saw what was happening.
All the attacks on online systems from finance
to manufacturing—did all that not happen? And
those were test runs! Used to assess and refine
the hammer stroke. It was just a matter of
time.

[REDACTED]: Yet now all that remains is a
wrecked computer infrastructure the world is
trying to patch together again. And your
agent's code is the only thing on every
computer! No other malware. Nothing from some
imaginary mask-wearing global vigilante named
Fawkes. No Anonymous Signal.
MR. SAVAS: So now you're going to condemn her
because she made the damned thing work?

[REDACTED]: She isn't here, Mr. Savas. Which is
damning enough. Last seen in the company of the
two most wanted fugitives in this nation,
murderous terrorists the likes of which we have
never seen before. You are the one who has

orchestrated every element of this. It is not
Angel Lightfoote who is on trial now. But you.

MR. SAVAS: Unless I tell you where she is,
right? If I hand her and her damn file from
Fawkes over to you, then you'll cut me some
deal and I walk.

[REDACTED]: You won't be walking, Mr. Savas.
Not from this. But there are sentences and
there are sentences.
MR. SAVAS: You idiots. If she took the file, it
could be copied a million times by now and in a
million hands. The horse is out of the barn.
Closing the door won't matter now.

[REDACTED]: One fire at a time, Mr. Savas. One
fire at a time.

52

"WELL, HI THERE, Fawkes!"

Angel stared at the computer screen and smiled. Once again buried in the basement of the Javits Federal Building late in the night. Again the mask of Guy Fawkes stared back at her, floating on the screen in front of her.

But this time, the gloating was gone.

"You fucking cunt!"

She laughed. "Don't you swing that way, Fawkes? Or can I call you Guy? I thought you liked cunts. I *know* you liked Poison's cunt. She says you visited all the time."

"Fuck you!"

"And your pathetic attempt to grab her was as clumsy as your code, which, by the way, my programs are eating through right now. You notice?"

"You think you're safe behind the firewalls of your NSA overlords, but you aren't. I can't reach you right now, but it's just a matter of time before I'm back in and burn your fucking house down."

Angel nodded as she typed. "Not before I hunt down every last one of your worms, you mean. Dissect the motherfuckers. I know you've been keeping score out there. See that tide rising?"

"You're interfering in things you don't understand!"

"Really?" She shook her head. "You going to mansplain the situation to this poor, clueless little cunt?"

"Damn you! You don't know what I know. The power isn't where you think it is. It hasn't been for hundreds of years! I've hacked my way to it."

She put her chin on her hand. "Fawkes, seriously. Is this where you try to tell me how we can rule the galaxy together if I'll just embrace the dark side?"

The masked face in the video stream turned to the side. A scream sounded over the monitors.

Angel clicked her tongue. "You have major anger management issues."

The face was back.

"Every nation, every corporation, every standing army is marching to hidden orders. Events—they're all part of a big game board! Pieces—disposable pieces—moved by the few that really hold the power. We can't change it from within. We can't defeat them on their terms!" The face panted. "But they've made themselves dependent on the modern information system—and they can't control it. For the first time in hundreds of years, they've made a fatal mistake!"

Angel stared silently for a moment. "You're really a mental case, aren't you?"

The scream again. "No! I can show you. Prove it! Your fucking code—it's threatening everything! You have to listen to me!"

"Listen to you go full tin-foil-hat on me as you try to destroy the world? This crap's not even up to the bottom suckers of the worst chat room. If you wanted to make a good first impression, you lost the chance big time when you screwed over my servers, when you brought my dad into this!"

"I will bring your shitty code down!"

She was standing now, palms down on the table. The light of the monitor reflected off her scalp and the metal in her face. "And we still got your girl! She's singing, singing, singing like a fucking bird. Well, really, it's a bit more like screaming. Honestly, so far—it's just screaming. But we know we'll get enough out of her to come after you in the real world."

The mask hovered in the center of the monitor without speaking. Angel could hear his labored breathing. She twisted the knife.

"I can send you a live feed the next time we go at her. But do you really want to be there when we break her? Might fuck you up good, yeah? Watching what we do to her? Every little thing? Believe me, I can imagine how that'd make you feel."

His next words were slurred—hissing. "You're not the only one who can reach out in the real world."

She laughed again. "You hit us with everything you had and I'm back. It's worse for you than before. Really, Fawkes, you were an inspiration to write this code! Thank you for that."

"I will make you hurt for this."

"Oh, Guy," she said dismissively, "I'm not scared of you. And neither is my code. Expect it, fucker."

Lightfoote hit ENTER and sent a video feed through the connection. She watched a mirrored window on her monitor display the content—a young woman strapped to a table, men beating her, blood on her face and pouring from her nose. *Poison.*

She closed the connection and walled Fawkes out with the NSA module. The monitor went dark. She sat down and leaned back in the chair, disgusted with the lies they were sending him.

"But you made me get dirty, you fuck," she whispered. "Now, come get her."

NOVEMBER 4

53

FOR ELAINE YORK, the "SF" was as comforting as it was alarming.

The acronym-smiths of the bureaucracy had called the Mount Weather retreat the High Point Special Facility, HPSF, but the human beings it was designed for had digested that down to something more manageable. *High* in the Virginia mountains to be sure, it was *special* in ways only a self-contained, doomsday hideout could be. Replete with self-sustaining environmental processes for waste and water, military grade rations lining underground storage silos to feed hundreds for weeks to months of isolation—its soldiers, weaponry, and communications systems were rivaled only by NORAD. Prime vacation estate for the nation's leaders when the world went to shit.

And the world was definitely going to shit.

The Colonel—*which one was he?* She'd lost track in the chaos—droned importantly about the precariousness of their plight.

"Without the logistics software, Madam President, we risk an entire breakdown of the supply chain. Our recommendations are to secure all of the major air, land, and sea routes immediately for governmental use only."

President York stared outside the reinforced glass window at the color explosion of the surrounding forest. The morning sunrise crested over the mountains and flooded the compound with light. Waves of flaming red and orange, bright yellow and dim browns blurred in her mind with impressionistic artists' canvases. Patches within the tapestry, like flaking paint in a poorly maintained van Gogh, revealed the skeletal tree branches buttressing the display and hinted at the coming hardness of winter. York knew that this winter would be one of the hardest in memory.

The bald man behind her continued, his ghostly reflection in the glass distracting her. "It's not just food and fuel anymore. We're looking at a prolonged deficit in nearly every category needed to maintain defense functionality."

She now presided over a nation teetering toward dissolution. The major neural networks controlling the modern world were misfiring, clogged with corrupt code like amyloid plaques, rendering the body of the nation as disoriented and confused as an Alzheimer's patient. Beyond the psychological damage of losing most of the modern computer infrastructure—a loss utterly traumatizing to generations now raised on its presence and dependent on the very idea of a world entirely connected, ubiquitously digitized—the very tangible losses of computer regulated transport, manufacturing, scheduling, communications, and medical care had left increasingly large swaths of the country reeling.

"As per NSA analysis, the projections from the last few days, the attacks are intensifying, likely to reach a climax very soon."

Remember, remember the fifth of November.

It was November fourth, and York dreaded the passage of time like the helpless descent of a sleeper into a nightmare. "What about this anti-worm virus they were talking about?" she asked, turning around momentarily to face the officer.

"There's too much contradictory data, Ma'am. No one knows where it's coming from, who's behind it, if it even *is* working against the worm. Some are convinced of it, but others aren't. It might even be a feint by Anonymous to distract us. It is spreading, though. Pretty rapidly."

"And the drone attacks?"

"Those have tapered off. The worm is a replicating resource, but the drones are finite. Anonymous is running out of them."

"They seem to have done enough damage. And what of the reports of a lone mastermind—this *Fawkes* from the FBI data?"

The man shook his head. "Unconfirmed and isolated reports to a single division of FBI. Analysis casts a lot of doubt on the hypothesis."

"Intel 1, if I'm not mistaken."

The soldier nodded. "That is correct. But the consensus—"

"They trumped the consensus five years ago. You might remember." She rubbed her temples. "I wish we had more time to consult with them."

The lights flickered momentarily, then steadied. York glanced around the ceiling and then back at the Colonel.

"They're still working out some kinks in the new electrical regulators," he said.

York shook her head and turned back to the window. "Decades of prep time and what do we do? Repeat the same mistake the world over! The pretty digital magic, all wired up here, the Pentagon, White House! Look at the damn walls! Everything gutted now! 1970s wiring is our salvation! Sophisticated environmental, solar-powered-what-have-you duct-taped to rusted generators. I'm starting to think that when it's all said and done we're going to blow it all up and the damned forests out there are going to swallow what's left of us."

She tried to focus, but the crushing weight of the crisis and the lack of sleep was breaking down her will.

"It's not just us," the Colonel answered. "Every country is struggling with this. Some have it easier: North Korea was so damn paranoid that even the worm is slowed there. And the third world doesn't have enough of a modern architecture that they're relatively intact from the direct effects. But the indirect effects are equally crippling, Madam President."

"Yes, yes," she said, waving him off. "The world is *flat* as the pundits like to say. A sneeze in Beijing or Washington gives a cold to the world. You know what it feels like now? Not like a cold, but like that plague Ebola is eating its way through the arteries of civilization! It's like the world were a giant hive, and now it's degenerating into thousands of isolated and panicked islands." She tried again to focus. "Market report?"

"Securities trading restrictions have effectively brought them to a standstill. The viral bidding is completely out of control. Destabilizing. The evaporating monetary base, huge capital movements into and out of banks by the worm—they've frozen lending and shut down more and more banks. Liquidity is gone. Commerce has come to a standstill. The food riots are growing and taking root in some of the most populous regions of the globe. Hell, right here in America."

"More reports?"

"New York. Chicago. Atlanta." The Colonel paused. "We're losing control."

Remember, remember the fifth of November.

When York didn't answer, the Colonel coughed. "It is the consensus of the Joint Chiefs and what remains of the military advisement panel that we should implement Directive 51."

York glanced sharply over her shoulder to glare at the Colonel. The rest of her body followed and she walked deliberately to her desk. The temperature in the room seemed to drop several degrees, the scarred walls of hanging circuits and controllers feeling like violated strips of her own body.

"So it's come to that."

The Colonel spoke quickly. "The situation is critical. Standard Constitutional protocols are hampering our ability to respond to this crisis. It's urgent that we temporarily suspend the government and act under the emergency directive."

York nodded. "It's frightening how well prepared the United States government is to abolish the United States government."

"You would be overseeing all the branches, Madam President. Nothing is abolished. Power is only concentrated."

"Yes, with the executive. With *me*, as you note. That is exactly what frightens me." She sat down behind the desk and sighed. "I know about REX84, Colonel. You remember the Readiness Exercise of 1984? My father served on the Senate panel that authorized and buried it."

The military man stiffened. "That was an important first step, Ma'am, the first real plan to cover something outside of nuclear war. It was needed! We weren't ready for every contingency."

She nodded, her fingertips pressed against each other. "I know. We'd seen it happen to other nations. Well, after REX84, all a president had to do was declare a *State of National Emergency* and bang! The machine would kick into full gear. Martial law. Military control of state and local governments. Detention of citizens who were scored as national security threats."

"Simulations were run. It's the best way to contain such crises. Maybe the *only* way."

"But Directive 51 goes one step further, doesn't it? Bush and Cheney made sure of that. At least with 84 we had a Constitutional structure, a president answerable, in theory anyway, to Congress and the Judiciary. But here comes 51, *paying respects* to the three branches of government, to separation of powers. But bottom line? The president has unlimited power." She coughed. "At least I won't be called *chancellor*. But we don't kid ourselves, do we, Colonel? Not when survival is on the line."

Concentration camps. Military rule. Dictatorship.

"Everything's temporary. Reversible once the crisis is resolved. Meanwhile, we can have some breathing room. We can act without the delays of Congress and the fiscal limitations! The only other option is to invite collapse of this government!"

The man was red-faced. York arched an eyebrow.

"So the analysts predict," he said, passing his hand over his scalp.

"Here's a mouthful for you, Colonel: *Ermächtigungsgesetz*. German for Enabling Act. You heard of it?"

"No." His face appeared strained.

"Passed by the Nazi-controlled parliament in 1933. They called it the 'Law to Remedy the Distress of the People and the State.' My father also taught about it in law school. It suspended constitutional authority and placed absolute power in the hands of the Chancellor, whom you may have heard of."

"Ma'am, we aren't Nazi Germany."

"Neither was Rome, but it was easier for them, too. In hard times just turn over power to a strong leader. Doesn't usually end well." She laughed, closing her eyes. "Here we were the last twenty years, repeating the mistakes of the Weimar and serving as a script for George Lucas and Alan Moore. Do I make a better Susan or Palpatine, do you think?"

"This isn't fantasy. This is serious. Look what's happening! There's a lot of concern about how to maintain order and preserve the nation through this catastrophe, Madam President. There are growing and serious divisions in the military."

Her head cocked to one side. "Is that a threat, Colonel?"

He paled. "No, Madam President, what I mean is—"

She stood up from her desk, gripping its edge. "What you mean is that order—more to the point, *loyalty* to this office—is being lost. Whether you want to admit it to yourself or not, Colonel, what you're telling me is that the military no longer has confidence in civilian rule. I see the beginnings of a coup."

"You misunderstand—"

"Out!" she shouted, walking around the desk. "Go back to your handlers and tell them that they had better not underestimate my support. We're at a precipice, Colonel, both externally and internally. And I'll be damned if I'm going to bow to any pressure to burn our Constitution. Go back and tell them that I will ignore Directive 51. Tell them that they need to make their choices, and that those choices will define them for the rest of their lives!"

After a final, panicked stare, the man dashed out of the room. York stood in front of the door, trembling, pressing her fingertips to her temples again.

NORAD. The command structure there was solid, loyal. At least she *hoped* it still was. The location was even more secure. She would make arrangements to relocate the principle elements of government. But she had to move quickly. They were at a tipping point. *The irony.* She was as vulnerable here in this doomsday locker as anywhere.

Remember, remember the fifth of November.

The second line of the old song danced rebelliously in her mind.

Gunpowder, treason, and plot!

54

THE BRIGHT LIGHT of the sunrise was smothered by thick shutters that plunged the room into complete darkness. In the center of the space was a lone figure in dark robes, a shining Guy Fawkes mask reflecting the artificial light in front of him. The wall-panel of flat-screen monitors displayed multiple locations, scenes dim and sequestered. Figures stared back through the screens, their eyes wary and unsure, weapons and military-issue equipment surrounding them.

"What good is all your money if there ain't nowhere left to spend it?" came one voice.

The mask spoke. "Have you forgotten the plan? When power is taken from the forces controlling our world, my software will orchestrate a new order. An order where each of you will preside like kings over lands and treasure and people. Kingdoms for kings, if you want. Or whatever you want. There will be no interference. I hold the keys to this new order. Have you become such terrified children at the destruction we have spread that you long for the safe chains of your former lives?"

The groups could be heard talking in a cacophony amongst themselves. The mask waited patiently. Several screens clicked off, the images gone, the fearful opting out of this terrible and all too real multiplayer game. The mask keyed in codes. A few remaining solo drones switched on in their hidden hangars. They were preserved for just this contingency, this betrayal and danger to his efforts. Along with a sortie to finish the game, they were all that was left of a once impressive fleet. Images flashed on the darkened screens, a God's eye view of a takeoff and flight. The man behind the mask smiled. *Once in, never out.* They would be dead within minutes.

One by one, the remaining groups committed to the final missions or were similarly dispatched. The final plans were rehashed. Ports and landing strips. More nuclear power plants. Dams and oil rigs. And finally, a team recommissioned to the US electric grid. The mask closed all the connections save this last one.

"You have your new target?" it said.

A bearded man with a green army cap nodded. "I thought your damn worm was going to shut the grid down."

"It was, but the anti-worm code has substantially weakened our capabilities. I can't risk failure. The grid must fall and never rise again. America must be plunged into a final night."

"Some speech you gave," said the man, an automatic weapon in his hands.

"You are my most trusted allies. We have shared goals from the beginning. We do not hope to live as kings or queens. We know how vile and rotten the system is, how deeply the roots of the octopus dig. There is only one way to burn it out—wither the thing to the core."

"You like to talk," laughed the man. "We don't give a fuck about your politics. For us, it's just the high! Mutilation. Dissection. Destruction!" There was a loud cry in unison from the group. "You are the Dark Angel, masked man. You're the power to bring Hell to earth! See you in the flames!"

The figure pressed a button and a screeching recording of death metal thundered in the room. The masked man switched it off and sat silently in the darkness.

The gore-grinders weren't wrong. If all went according to plan, the nations would eat themselves. The violence would consume all power structures. Modern civilization would be laid waste by the very wires it used to hoist itself.

But it was of course not enough. True anarchy could not be achieved until they had erased the heart of corruption. And only his worm could achieve that. Only by completely liquidating all the modern elements of control could there be true freedom.

It was this very goal that was now in doubt. The FBI woman was tweaked, that was for sure. Only a deeply twisted mind could conceive of such a violent cure for the dying human enterprise. It broke all their laws. It was off leash and could possible turn on healthy systems. It was reckless and wild.

And it was winning. He had not counted on anyone with the talent or audacity to unleash the monsters that she had. She had his respect. He would not turn from the truth of it. Truth was the only thing left. *The truth of human corruption.* The truth of what needed to be done.

A screen opened revealing a set of black-clad men.

"Are you prepared?"

A man with intense eyes nodded onscreen. "It's a small unit. There isn't much left now. But it should be enough. We've been watching the building for days via the surveillance drone you spared us. Some boots on the ground, too. We could walk into the place without a problem. They're decimated."

"It must be done right. They have proven far more resilient than we imagined."

"We aren't taking this lightly after what happened to Bravo team."

"You're sure that several members of Intel 1 left the building?"

"Yes. Immediately after our extraction team failed. They sent decoys and used multiple evasive strategies. We didn't have the manpower to follow everything. We lost them."

"And Poison?"

"Signal was lost. They could have discovered the device. Or maybe they're underground too deep. There are mazes of old tunnels on this island. Rumor has it there's some kind of Fed bunker, too."

The mask nodded. "One they will need soon. I have other plans for dealing with Poison. Stay on mission. You have the blueprints."

The man laid out a building plan on a table, pointing to the lower portion of the paper. "Lower basement. These three rooms."

"Your priorities?" asked the mask.

"Seize the mainframes," he said, holding up a UBS stick, "and inject this code."

"And the personnel?"

"We're to kill them all, especially the bald woman."

"Then go. There isn't much time."

The screen went dark. Fawkes removed the mask and exhaled, his features hidden in the darkness. Everything was coming to its final iteration. His ammunition was nearly spent. Ten years of preparation, weeks of assault on the world, and now the final activation. A signal to be sent to every active computer on the planet, one that would induce a final and unstoppable chaos.

He smiled. He *did* respect the girl. That's why when he silenced her, insured her talented hands would not continue to wreak havoc on his plans, he would broadcast the signal from her very machines, thwarting her counter-code and symbolically triumphing over her impressive resistance.

He twirled the mask in his hands.

He was, after all, quite taken with the dramatic.

55

"ATTACKS ON THE power grid?" Cohen shouted into the phone as the car sped along the Shore Parkway, the waters of the Lower Bay tinted orange by the rising sun. Savas had engaged the switch boxes, running quietly unless hitting traffic, the red and blue flashing lights beginning to give Cohen a headache. Poison sat in the back of the vehicle with Miller, in silence. Behind them a second Crown Vic with Lopez and Houston followed closely.

"What's happening?" asked Savas.

"Okay, Angel, hold on. Let me tell John." She turned toward him and sighed. "Looks like the November fifth theory is right. Angel says all hell is breaking loose and major manufacturing and resource systems are under attack by the worm. The scariest is the power grid. You remember the briefings after 9/11?"

He nodded. "Yeah, craziest situation. What, ten critical power stations stand between us and the Stone Age? Six month black out?"

"Pretty much," said Cohen. "It was nine of them. Out of fifty thousand. Which ones were classified of course, so no terrorists could get them. Unless—"

"Unless you've hacked into every computer on the planet and gotten your paws on the files."

"Right. It would likely be down by now just from software attacks, but her crazy code seems to be slowing it. Maybe even turning the tide, she says."

"That's good, right?" He wove in and out of traffic, switching on the sirens to prompt cars out of their path.

Muffled sounds from the phone mixed with the wailing pitches. "Hold on, Angel. Yes, John, that's good. And a lot of good news on that front. Angel says she's working on a new iteration of her immune code, one she thinks will erase the worm once and for all. It can spread anywhere the worm has gone, using the worm to do so, and sterilize any machine that's infected."

"In time?"

Cohen shrugged. "She not done with it and Fawkes is putting

351

things in overdrive." There was more screaming from the phone as Cohen held it away from her ear. "Right! So, the *bad* news is that she's convinced there'll be a physical attack on the power grid, at what she's calling a weak node."

"And she knows this how?"

"She's intercepting more and more information from Fawkes' data stream, hacking more worm strains. She found blueprints, schematics for an assault strike on the power plant. It's in Jersey, routes huge amounts of power from the US and Canada." Angel called out loudly over the phone again. "And like Angel says, it was one of the weak links in the 2003 Northeast blackout. Caused by a software bug at a power plant, she reminds my battered ears."

"Great," said Savas, accelerating unconsciously. "They could already be there."

"And at who knows what other *weak nodes* across the country," said Miller from the back.

Savas shook his head. "No. I don't understand how he built up the resources to do as much as he did, but they're finite. It's clear his supply chain is gone. I don't think he planned to strike every weak grid point with a commando team. He couldn't. Angel's code might have just saved the lights."

The ex-marine shook his head. "Nothing is certain, John."

"We'll see. But I do think this is because of Angel. I think he meant for the worm to throw wrenches into all the electrical machinery like the industrial plants. Machinery tearing itself apart, transformers exploding. But now he's not *sure* anymore. His code might not be there or at enough locations. So he has to make sure, and the East Coast is the seat of government, finance. He's sending all his assets to make sure."

Holding the phone away from her ear again, Cohen nodded. "Angel agrees. She says you need to get Bonnie and Clyde on it."

"Bonnie and—right. Okay, tell Angel we'll call her back after we've explained things."

Cohen smiled, closing the phone. "No need. She called them first. They've agreed and were waiting for your instructions." The headlights of the car behind them blinked repeatedly. "I think she just informed them of your consent."

Savas shook his head. "She'll be running the damn place soon."

The car behind pulled right and exited at an approaching turn-off, the black vehicle disappearing behind an overpass. Lopez and Houston were gone.

Poison spoke from the back of the car. "So, wait. Now it's just us? I'm the bait for your trap and you three are going to face down all his killers?"

Cohen looked back in the review mirror at the frightened woman. "That's right."

"Well, fuck! Can't you call in some cops or army or something?"

Cohen turned around and placed her arm on the chair. "In case you haven't been paying attention, we're in a war zone. There *isn't* anyone who's going to hand over troops or police to some obscure FBI division because they have some unsubstantiated theory about a crazed madman and are unilaterally going to test it by playing a dangerous trap-the-terrorist game with his ex-girlfriend."

Poison simply gawked at her.

Cohen sighed. "We're betting that he's about out of muscle, and that most of it is headed to a power plant in Jersey."

"Betting with our *lives*," stressed Poison.

"Well, probably not yours, dear. He's trying to rescue you from the monsters at the FBI, remember? You'll be fine as long as some stray bullets don't find you." Her tone was impatient. "We'll be the ones filled with steel."

"Not if I can help it," said Savas. "We're going to set up carefully before we let that beacon out of the box. We'll make them come to us and take heavy damage. If he's as weak as we're hoping, that might be enough."

"Fawkes might not even come," said Poison. "Could all be for nothing."

"He'll come," said Savas.

"Why? He didn't last time. He sent people, but he didn't come. Why now?"

"Because you're off site. Because of the last failure he won't want to repeat. Because it's almost over: The fifth of November is tomorrow. I don't think he had much of a plan after that. Besides watching the world burn."

Savas hammered the accelerator, Coney Island and the New York Aquarium flying past them. The engine howled.

"He'll come."

56

THE ELECTRICAL SUBSTATION was located on the outskirts of Elizabeth, New Jersey. Houston had raced across Staten Island through a surreal apocalyptic landscape. Fires were raging around the ports, and Lopez thought he had seen Blackhawk helicopters launching missiles at boats and opening fire at the docks. Military vehicles from the National Guard were positioned at gateways—toll booths, tunnel and bridge entrances, certain exit ramps—but eerily, all were abandoned. News on their radio confirmed that rioting had spread through the tri-state area as essential functions continued to break down in the public and private sector. Law enforcement was completely overwhelmed.

They had crossed two bridges without incident and were now speeding past Elizabeth and into a decayed urban wasteland of rusted warehouses and closed factories. The power lines around them were beginning to converge. The substation was near.

Lightfoote's voice came over the speaker. Houston had wedged her phone inside a cup holder, the conical shape funneling the sound upwards and acting as a small megaphone.

"Power's still up, so they haven't hit it yet. Latest military data indicates a contingent of Guardsman are assigned there, maybe ten. The site was on a list to lock down in a national emergency. I don't know if they made it or are still there, but if so, you have to warn them, prepare them."

"And how do we do that without getting arrested?" asked Lopez. "They won't let us get near, and if anyone tries to get our story verified, too many questions will be raised. We'll be in a cell before nightfall."

"I don't know how!" cried Angel, "But we need all the help we can get. We don't know how large Fawkes' strike team is."

"Mother of God," whispered Lopez. "How many enemies do we have to fight?"

"Look, we'll improvise," Houston said. "Meanwhile, you were saying they would hit the transformers?"

"I've given myself a crash course in this the last few hours," said Lightfoote. "Power from several coal and gas plants, and the nuke plant south of you, are funneled through the substation. To handle it, they have these enormous transformers that link up the lines coming into the lines going out. Match up the power on them. For the size of the loads they're dealing with here, these are giant things. We're talking hundreds of tons, tens of thousands of gallons of fuel. This is one of the biggest in the country."

"Fuel?" asked Lopez. "Why does it need fuel?"

"To run all the coolant systems," said Lightfoote. "Ever had your outlet or computer heat up?"

"I think this phone is about to explode," said Houston.

"Well, just imagine this transformer that's bigger than a house and all the current running through it. Fawkes could take it out just by blowing the cooling units and waiting for the thing to burst into flames."

"Jesus," said Houston. "So, big as a house. Lots of big wires going in. We can't miss it."

"No, it will be obvious. And, from what I could find out, relatively unsecured. A chain link fence and some concrete barriers to stop suicide trucks."

"Wait," said Lopez, shaking his head. "Our electrical grid is dependent on a few of these behemoths and all we've done to keep modern civilization running is slap some cheap wire around it?"

"Pretty much, Holy Man," said Lightfoote. "Lots of congressional hearings after 9/11. Not much done. It's a sitting duck. If we lose it, it could be the entire Northeast and parts of Canada."

"That's unbelievable," Lopez said.

"They *did* fortify the transformer in 2015. Says here it's bullet resistant."

"Bullet *resistant*? What, to protect from transformer snipers?"

"In part," Angel continued. "There have been several incidents of lone wackos shooting at them. One guy caused an explosion that blacked out part of Texas for hours. Anyway, this one has reinforced concrete around it."

Lopez pointed ahead of the car. "That's it, Sara. Take that road."

The substation opened up in front of them. Several football fields in surface area, it looked like something from a dystopian film. Wires sprouted from it like tentacles, only to be contrasted by the harsh steel and Frankenstein-esque electrical devices that neither of them had names for.

The transformer was obvious. Enormous. It dominated the other structures within the compound. Thick, metallic arms erupted above a sloppy concrete girdle around the thing, giving the object the appearance of a colossal robot design project gone terribly wrong. Thick wires connected to the transformer through the ends of the arms to the chaos of wiring overhead that linked the substation to the rest of the grid.

"You found it?" called out Lightfoote.

"Yes," said Houston flatly.

"And the transformer? You see it?"

"Oh yes," she said.

"Great!" Lightfoote's relief was palpable.

"Not so great," said Lopez as Houston slowed the car in front of the twisted and mangled remains of a chain length fence.

"Why? What's wrong?"

Two National Guardsman lay by the wrecked gate, their bodies riddle with bullets. The gatehouse windows were shattered and the wood pocked with holes.

Lopez spoke in a rough baritone. "It's on fire."

Black smoke poured into the air in front them.

"THE TRANSFORMER'S BURNING?"

Lightfoote's voice rang out desperately over the phone. Lopez exited the car and stared forward, shielding his eyes from low-lying morning sun. Houston shut off the engine, grabbed the phone, and followed.

"I'm not sure," said Houston. "Lots of fires and smoke. Some around the transformer. But, no, it doesn't seem hit."

"Then there's still time!" cried Lightfoote. "We still have power. You still have a transformer. I need power to get the last code out! Hang up, get in there, and stop them!"

"Yes, ma'am." Houston closed the phone. "She's right. There's still a chance. They haven't managed to bring it down yet."

"Could happen any moment," said Lopez. "We don't know their numbers or how they're armed."

Houston removed her Browning and pulled the mask over her smile. "I'm a lady who loves surprises." She jogged down the small road from the gate, toward the flames.

Lopez reached inside his vestments and grabbed the submachine gun. His left shoulder was screaming, useless to help him aim his pistol. The submachine gun would blanket his targets and help compensate. He ran forward, chasing Houston.

They passed grassy lawns on both sides of the road. Ahead, rows of wired equipment intersected above them. In the middle of it all lay the concrete slab with the transformer inside. Keeping alongside a row of utility sheds, they remained concealed from anyone around the object. Apparently, the idea had occurred to others. The bodies of three men—not Guardsman—were strewn along the path of the sheds, gunned down while moving toward the transformer. The bodies of several soldiers were across from them, near the far corner of the sheds.

"They must have used the shelter of the sheds for a last stand."

Houston pressed her back against the cold metal, stepping over the body of one, and peered cautiously around the corner.

Her head snapped back and her eyes locked with Lopez. "More dead guards. Looks like grenades."

"The strike team?"

"They're there. Alive. Right next to the concrete around the transformer. One had his hands on the wall, fiddling with something. The other seemed to be yelling at him. That's all I got."

"Bomb," Lopez said.

"Likely they're wiring it up now. From the argument, we can only hope some of the dead bodies were their demolitions experts."

"Assuming those two are the last."

She nodded and spun around again, keeping her sights forward for several seconds before whipping back around.

"You think you can get me on top of that shed?"

Lopez frowned. "It's over fifty yards, Sara. That's a good shot, even for you."

"You have better ideas? It's all open field from here to the transformer. No way to sneak up on them. We could go in blazing and hope for the best, but odds are not good for a clean win. I'll stabilize on the roof edge. Three shots or less and you owe me a drink."

Lopez frowned and got on one knee. "Just don't step on the left shoulder, or you forfeit any winnings. I'll be ready for a sprint."

She holstered the weapon and he hoisted her toward the roof. She grabbed the edge, swinging herself over. Lopez couldn't follow with his bad arm, so he returned to the corner and crouched, weapon readied.

Houston kept low and crawled to the end of the shed overlooking the transformer. She could see the two men facing the concrete wall, oblivious to her actions as they worked on the explosives. She removed her Browning. The edge of the roof rose several inches from the base and she used it to steady her weapon. She sighted the two dark shapes, focusing on the one who seemed to be taking the lead. She calmed, steadied her breathing. His torso fused into an extension of the barrel. She felt the metal tube reach outward towards him, connecting, closing the space between them. She stopped breathing and pulled the trigger.

There was an explosion. The figure before them shuddered, hands jerking outward and away from the bomb. He fell to his knees, then onto his side. She repositioned the gun.

The man next to him froze for an instant and then wheeled in their direction, weapon raised. He scanned a small arc across the sheds, then centered on the roof, and Houston. He dropped to one knee and aimed his gun in her direction.

Two more shots burst in the compound, the sounds reverberating off the concrete and metal, echoing and blending in a dispersing chaos of noise. The man in front of them buckled but did not fall. He began to turn toward the wall slowly, gait lumbering, face toward the device fixed to the transformer.

A fourth shot rang, a third bullet embedding itself in his torso. This time he fell, his weapon dropped. His legs jerked as he tried vainly to rise. Houston saw the broad form of Lopez race toward the shape.

"Four," she said, sitting up and scanning around them for hostiles. The place was empty but for the dead and Lopez, who now stood beside the explosive device, waving her over. "Perfectly good glass of whiskey shot to hell."

58

HOUSTON SPRINTED ACROSS the lot toward the concrete security barrier. Two bodies lay beside the house-sized transformer, unmoving. Lopez had laid out several of their items: firearms, cell phones, and, most crucially, detonators and radio-controllers. He was studying an array of what looked like beige clay blocks taped across the concrete. Detonators and wires ran down from the blocks to a metal box.

"C-4?" Houston said, catching her breath.

"That, or something similar. Twelve blocks."

She examined them closely. "I'm guessing M112—military issue. Uncle Sam needs to keep his shit off the arms markets."

She crouched and examined the wiring. Above her, the huge expanse of two transformer arms cast a long shadow in the early light. The hum of the electricity flowing through the area was almost nauseating. Thick wires like oak limbs sprouted from the arms many tens of feet away.

"Look at this shape," she said, turning back to the molded plastique. "It's going to funnel the blast inward and up. Twelve blocks? Shit, this concrete wall will be turned into a weapon. Those humming arms are coming down, probably the whole thing will take major damage. No way this thing survives. Game over. Power gone."

"No timer, so we don't have to deal with that," said Lopez, eyeing the metallic box.

"Is it trapped?"

He shook his head. "Doesn't seem so. They didn't have time and weren't planning to leave it here long. Set it up, reach safe distance, maybe behind those sheds, radio the signal into this control box. Boom."

"Should be easy to disarm then." Houston frowned. "Why does that make me nervous?"

"Because nothing is ever for free."

Houston centered on the far-left block and placed her hand around the blasting cap wires. "Let's make sure and remove the detonators from each."

Lopez mirrored her actions. "Here goes."

They pulled on the wires. Thin metal tubes resembling smoothed hinge bolts came out of the soft material. As the end of the tube was cleared from the explosive, they paused and locked eyes.

"No boom," she said.

They repeated the process until all the detonators were removed, and tossed the blasting caps onto the ground beside the dead men. Lopez removed a large knife and cut through the thick tape sticking the blocks to the barrier. Soon there was a stack of clay blocks on the ground as well.

"All right," he said, wiping sweat from his face. "Always exciting. Let's call this in to Angel. We did our bit to preserve the lights."

Houston punched her contact number for Lightfoote's burner cell. She frowned and looked at the phone.

"Zero bars. No signal."

Lopez looked around. "This place should be blanketed. We had signal when we arrived."

"Check yours. Maybe this cheap thing's failing."

He removed his phone. "Nothing. No signal."

"Shit." Houston folded her arms over her chest. "No coincidences. The towers are down. Probably the worm."

"Or more of these guys," he said, nodding toward the bodies.

"I doubt it. No way he has an army. This was a strategic target. Too many towers for physical strikes on the cellular system. That's got to be the worm."

Lopez nodded. "Maybe it's just some of the carriers." He reached down beside the corpses and grabbed two phones.

"Everything's down. AT&T. Verizon. This guy had T-Mobile."

Houston scanned the horizon back toward New York City. "Everyone's cut off now. No voice, no data. I think this will trigger a real panic. After a few hours, it's going to be mayhem."

"There's more here," said Lopez working on one of the phones. "Messages. All about this raid. Has to be from Fawkes."

Houston stepped beside him and looked at the screen. "With those kind of details? Fawkes for sure. They were getting sloppy." She took the other man's phone and examined it as well.

"Well, tomorrow's the fifth, right?" said Lopez. "The end of the world as we know it. Security is so pre-apocalypse."

Houston continued scrolling intensely through the phone's messages. "Or maybe not. *Fuck*. Francisco, tell me you don't recognize this address."

The former priest stared at the small screen, brow furrowing. "That's the warehouse in Brooklyn. Where they're taking Poison. How—"

His eyes widened.

"They know, dammit!" said Houston. "Look at this message. 'Heading to the site. When finished double back there for backup.' They've known for a while!"

Lopez glanced up toward the car. A line of dark clouds was moving in from the south, promising to bring showers and possibly thunderstorms.

"Savas isn't setting the trap. Fawkes is."

"Jesus! No cell phones. We can't reach them. We have to get over to that warehouse!"

"We took out their strike team. That helps."

"Judging from the message, he wasn't counting on them. They're backup. He's got others."

"But what do we do with this mess? Dead men? Bombs?"

Houston stared down at the bodies with disgust. "Leave these assholes to rot." She began stuffing the plastique inside a bag lying on the ground beside them. "But we take the bomb. Could prove useful."

59

LIGHTFOOTE STARED AT hundreds of lines of code on her screen. She spoke in a distracted monotone. "All the carriers are down?"

Rideout nodded, tossing his phone on the table next to five others. "I checked them all. He's nuked the cellular system."

"Damn," she said. "Cut off from everyone. Power's still up so our Dynamic Duo hasn't let us down. But we need the coast power up or we'll never get this new worm out there with enough time to spread."

He grabbed two of the phones and held them up. "You guys want your phones back?"

Across the room three men were arguing animatedly over the scrolling text of a computer screen. They waved him away to continue their heated debate.

Rideout leaned over the computer desk and whispered into Lightfoote's ear. "I don't trust those yahoos."

She smiled, never removing her gaze from the screen. "John does. The older one, anyway. *Simon*. They have some kind of history. And to be honest, the coders from the NSA are really good. I'd never have gotten this finished in time without them."

"Thanks for the vote of confidence," said Rideout. "And *are* you finished, anyway?"

Her face clouded. "Getting there." She returned her gaze to the screen and typed furiously.

A stout man, near sixty, ambled over toward them and dropped heavily into a wheeled chair. He looked at Rideout.

"Look, Dietrich at NSA lent us these two programmers. Technically, they're not under our authority. I'm CIA. You're FBI. But with our connections, and dangling your project in front of them, they ate it up. But they're stuck on something now."

"Can't keep up?" asked Rideout.

"It's not a pissing contest, son. It's the new bit, the code randomizing thing."

"The mutagenesis," cut in Angel absentmindedly.

"Whatever you call it."

She turned to him. "It's important! It's key. I call it mutagenesis because the whole thing is based on mimicking biology."

"Is this going to be a graduate school lecture?" asked Simon, his face weary.

Lightfoote continued. "Look, we have code that hunts and recognizes Fawkes' worm like a white blood cell. In the body, one thing those cells do is *mutate* the parts of them that recognize the foreign invader. For some mutants it screws them up. They don't work anymore. But for a few, the mutations make them better or create variant cells that recognize mutant pathogens. And when you combine that with recognition-based replication, you quickly select for optimized cells and make lots of them. It's evolution!"

"I think I'm gonna fail this test, professor," said Simon.

The two NSA men stood behind him. One interjected. "Yeah, but you know what happens when you get a lot of mutants in a population? You get cancer. Or autoimmunity. *Bad* changes with the good. Things go south, you know?"

"Sometimes," admitted Lightfoote.

"And so what are we doing?" continued the man. "Unleashing rogue code, independent of any controls, that's designed to replicate and mutate? We could lose control over it."

The other coder chimed in. "We probably *will* lose control over it."

Rideout waved his arms animatedly. "Does what is happening now look like an abundance of *control*? Sounds like you're scared this thing might actually work, take down the worm. How about we put that fire out first, before it burns everything to the ground? We can worry about Angel's mutants afterward."

Simon nodded. "That's about how I see it. We either fire the new weapon and hope the collateral damage is low, or we watch as that thing out there tears our world apart." He stared at the two men. "But we need you two on this. Angel's nearly done, but she needs those modules from you. You in?"

They looked at each other. One sighed. "Yeah, I guess so. We have to do something."

The other nodded. "Okay. But we are literally letting a genie out of the bottle here. Remember that a year from now."

Lightfoote nodded. "If there still is a digital world left over for this code to haunt, we'll work on it."

"How close are you two?" asked Simon.

The men were back at their terminals. One called over. "We're done. That's the fight. We built a bomb, we're just pissing our pants about arming it."

Simon turned to Lightfoote. "Angel?"

"I'm debugging the mutation code. I don't have the time to fine-tune it, and that worries me. Too much and it will fuck itself to oblivion. Too little and it won't adapt fast enough to identify all Fawkes' worms. But I'm almost there! Then I just need to assemble the modules and fire it out."

An explosion rocked the building and the lights flickered.

"What the hell?" cried Rideout.

Dust filtered down from the ceiling and the lights completely cut out. Emergency lighting clicked on while the computers continued to hum. Shouts from floors above erupted, followed by gunfire.

"Fawkes," said Lightfoote, her face grim. "He's going to shut us down the old fashioned way."

"Jesus," mumbled Simon, rising stiffly to his feet.

Rideout unholstered his pistol and checked the magazine. "Thank God you put the servers on generator power. That explosion blew the main lines."

"But not the hard lines. They're buried too deep. We still have time!"

More gunfire. More screams above.

"Not much!" cried Rideout. "You two, you're done, right? So get your asses over here! Move those cabinets to the door—quickly!"

The NSA programmers shoved the two waist-high cabinets, computer paraphernalia spilling out of the poorly closed doors, to block the entry. Rideout overturned a long table, spilling workstations and monitors to the floor.

Lightfoote tossed him a holstered firearm. "Mine. Give it to them." She returned to the code.

"Spread this out!" said Rideout, waving his arms across the room. He frowned. "Either of you ever fired a weapon?"

Both shook their heads.

"Either of you ever *want* to fire a weapon?"

One put out his hand. Rideout gave him the black pistol.

"Safety's in the trigger, so don't point unless you mean to kill. Got it? Pull the trigger with follow-through, you'll feel the safety release and then the shot. Slow, steady, pull. No panic. Aim and pull slowly, even if Godzilla comes through." The NSA coder nodded frantically. "You," he yelled at the unarmed coder, "grab that large wrench over there. Hide behind the server wall. If the guns fail, beat the shit out of the first person who comes in range."

Simon braced himself on the wall beside the door, gun pointed at the entrance. "I'll have the first. They won't know what hit them."

Rideout crouched behind the overturned table and motioned the NSA man with the gun over. "They'll have to get past us to get to Angel, then get around the server farm between the door and her desk. We need to buy her all the time we can. Even if that means our lives, you understand? Her code has to get out!"

The programmer simply stared at him.

"What about the servers?" asked Simon.

Lightfoote called back. "I just need this computer, this one connection to send it out through the NSA backdoors. It's the end game now."

The door shuddered from a heavy blow. Rideout and the NSA man concealed themselves behind the table, positioning their weapons forward. Heavy objects slammed repeatedly into the door, rattling the metal cabinets. The drumming was offset by the maniacal clacking of Lightfoote's keys, the two percussions accompanied by the ever present hum of the server farm between them.

The thudding stopped. Dust continued to drift down from the ceiling. The sounds of muted shouts outside could be heard, along with muffled shuffling and scrapes. Several seconds of silence followed. Rideout and Simon aimed their weapons.

Then the door exploded.

60

THE POURING RAIN clattered angrily on the metal roof, the storm winds shaking the thin walls of the warehouse. Daylight faded, dimmed further by the clouds, still just managing to illuminate the interior through the high windows. The air tasted of mildew and rot, chased by a metallic tang. A low rumble shook the long structure, momentarily interrupting conversation within. Two figures stood perched atop a large, moveable platform.

"I can't reach anyone," Cohen said, flipping her phone closed with a snap. "Looks like we've lost all cellular. We're blind here."

Savas nodded, examining the readout on a small control unit. "Not completely blind," he muttered. "As long as the power holds."

Cohen limped over to Savas and wrapped an arm over his shoulders. "Frank got the motion sensors up?"

"Yeah," Savas said, turning toward her. There was another roll of thunder. "We'll at least get some advance notice."

"Crunch time, Johnny-boy." She ran her fingers through his hair. "I'm starting to get a little tired of the world ending around us."

He kissed her, cupping his hand behind her head. Her breath was warm in the frigid air of the unheated warehouse. A cloud escaped his mouth as he pulled away. "Don't ever say I didn't show you an exciting time, girl."

"Just don't make me climb any more ladders until this damned leg is healed."

A shout from across the expanse of the building brought them back to their surroundings. Their eyes caught sight of a figure slamming shut the main door, water dripping from his muscular form. Miller jogged back toward their position, an automatic rifle in one arm.

"Motion detectors mounted and signaling," he called.

The space within was long abandoned. Decaying, discarded crates the size of trucks littered the floor. The ex-marine dodged back and forth, zig-zagging as he approached. The detritus provided the perfect cover for their needs. Fawkes and his mercenaries would need

371

to expose themselves several times in order to get near.

Savas and Cohen looked down from a raised, metallic platform. Once used by a supervisor directing the traffic in the warehouse during better years, it now served an unintended strategic purpose. They had positioned several crates facing the entrance. Together with the advantage of height, the cover would ensure that only an elite commando force of some number would make it through. Whatever they would face, they were sure to do it much hurt.

Miller finished scaling the ladder and dropped heavily onto the platform, water scattering and dripping through the metallic mesh of the platform floor. He scanned the interior of the building and grunted.

"Of course, they could try blasting or cutting their way through any number of weak points in this flimsy structure. But I think that's giving them too much credit and time to plan. And only if they had the numbers." He pointed to the main entrance. "My money is on the front door. John and I can take positions on opposite sides of this platform—there and there. Rebecca, we could use your gun, but we can't trust that hacker. Keep it trained on her the entire time. We're vulnerable from behind."

Cohen smiled. "Good plan. I refuse to move this leg again." She turned behind them, looking down on the bound form of Poison. The hacker glared back. "Sorry about the cuffs."

"Fuck you Feds. Maybe I should help him kill you."

Savas crouched down beside her. "We don't know that you won't, Poison. Try to see it from our angle. There isn't much trust going around when it comes to Fawkes and Anonymous."

"He's not Anonymous. Not anymore."

"Who's to say? He claims he is. He's sprung several traps on us, tried to kill us. We can't assume you're on our side."

"Why would I be here?"

"Maybe the bait is to hook *us*."

She scowled at him but remained silent. At that moment, the monitor on the floor of the platform began to beep. Miller scooped it into his hands, glaring downward.

"They're here. Barely time to prepare. Ten yards in front of the door. We've got seconds."

Cohen leaned into one of the crutches, holding her firearm pointed at the platform near Poison's feet. She stared intensely at the other woman. Miller and Savas shook the platform as they rushed to the opposite corners, crouching behind wooden crates and aiming their weapons toward the door.

Miller called to Savas. "If they throw frags, look away until the blast. Then back and focus."

His anticipation proved correct. The door to the warehouse was slung open, the rusted metal screaming like something dying. Several black shapes outside hurled objects into the warehouse. Savas and Miller turned their heads as the grenades exploded, the sound rivaling the thunder outside. They recovered quickly and reoriented, training their guns on the men rushing inside. And opened fire.

61

THE INCOMING SOLDIERS were dropped quickly, their position impossible to defend. They barely had time to size up their enemy and the layout before rounds from one or both of the FBI men cut them down. Their lack of strategy made it clear they hadn't expected this sort of resistance.

Four bodies lay within a twenty-foot radius of the main door. There was no further motion from outside. The smoke of spent ammunition rose as a fog around the top of the platform. Savas started to rise, but Miller held up his hand.

"Not yet!"

"You think there are more?"

"Maybe this was a feint. Stay low."

"But Fawkes isn't there!" hissed Savas.

"We don't know that. Can't see their faces."

"He's not there," said Poison, looking down on the corpses. "He's no Johnny Rambo."

"Don't shoot!"

A cry rang across the warehouse.

"*That's* Fawkes," said Poison.

Miller peered over the crate in the failing light. He strapped on a set of night vision goggles and adjusted them.

"I don't see anything, John. He's still outside."

"Fawkes!" cried Savas. "If that's you, come in with both hands high in the air!"

There was a pause. "No way! You'll shoot me!"

"Paranoid to the end," whispered Poison.

"That's not our plan!" yelled Savas again. "You're useless dead. We need you to fix this shit!"

Another pause. "Is she there? Poison?"

Savas made to speak again but was cut off by the girl.

"Fuck yeah, you piece of shit! All this is because of you! And you *bugged* me, you fucktard? Seriously?"

A dark form ambled into the warehouse from the door, his head covered by a hood. His hands raised above him.

"Turn around," called Savas. Fawkes obeyed. "Now close the door. All the way."

Fawkes grasped the handle of the sliding door and yanked. At first it didn't move and he lost his balance. After several hard pulls and better planting his feet, he managed to scrape it across the floor to the staccato bursts of metal on cement. A fifth jerk slammed it shut.

"Now back around with your hands high." Fawkes complied and Savas stood slowly and turned to Miller. "I'm going to bring him up. He tries anything, end him."

Cohen turned to Poison as Savas descended. "Will he try something?"

The hacker shook her head. "Are you kidding? He wasn't even good at first person shooters. Your man's safe."

Miller watched tensely as Savas reached the hacker. Fawkes offered no resistance, walking slowly in front of the FBI man. Savas pushed him forward with his gun, and the pair navigated the obstacle course toward the platform. Finally, the Fawkes scaled the ladder as Miller trained his weapon downward. The pair reached the platform without incident.

Poison laughed. "You still have the fucking mask. *Seriously.*"

Fawkes stood shivering in a wet trench coat, water beading and running along its contours. Contrasting the black of the fabric was a white mask—the goateed, smirking visage that had come to haunt too many of their nightmares.

"Fawkes," Savas said, stepping forward. "Miller, the extra set of cuffs?"

Miller handed Savas the restraints and he bound Fawkes' hands behind him.

Fawkes looked to Poison. His voice was heavily muffled. "Looks like they're still treating you well."

"So that's it? That's all you had left to come rescue me?" The masked man said nothing. "What a sad way to go out, Fawkes."

"It doesn't matter anymore. They can't stop things now."

Cohen kept her weapon at the ready, her eyes on Poison as she spoke. "I wouldn't count on that, Fawkes. We have a plan to stop you."

"You mean the little bald girl in the cellar?" The mask laughed. "I have a larger team taking care of her now. That's over."

"You son of a bitch," Miller said, advancing on the man.

Savas held him back with his arm. "It will be hard on you if something happens to them."

"Gonna be hard on all of us soon, Special Agent. But really it was the only way."

"Only way to what, you sick bastard!" hissed Miller, a fire in his eyes.

"Can't tell you or you'd just laugh. But really, it's for the best. The things you don't know and can't believe—well, it's like a mountain. The lies you live, the truths you hold that really hold you mockingly. Your ideals and systems. *All lies.* You are slaves to masters that count on your good intentions and low intelligence. There is a world order you don't understand and can't perceive."

Savas looked at Poison. "Is this the genius you mentioned? This nutcase?"

"Low intelligence?" Poison scoffed. "You know, they played you from the start, you dumb ass. And you bought it! You took it all in your little shark mouth and they reeled you in! All those torture videos? Interrogation scripts? They were faked!"

"I know."

"What do you mean, you know?"

"Players play the players because the play demands it."

"John—" began Cohen.

"Okay, enough of this crap," said Savas. "Let's see what you really look like."

Cohen furrowed her brows. "John, wait a minute. Something's not right."

He ignored her and grasped the bottom of the mask. Looking through the eye-slits, he stared inside. "Anonymous no more, Fawkes."

He pulled. The mask didn't move.

"What the hell?"

Reaching around, he yanked the hood back, revealing a head

covered in black leather straps. The Guy Fawkes mask was fixed tightly to it, concealing a bulk beneath it.

"Gas mask!" cried Miller.

But it was too late. Fawkes squeezed his shoulder blades together and there was a click, followed by the sound of two metal canisters crashing and ringing on the platform surface.

They exploded.

62

Fred Simon was blown backward and slammed into a wall, dropping to the ground unconscious. Debris flew across the room, smashing into the racks of computers, pocketing the overturned table, and coating everything with a thick layer of dust. Within seconds, several armed men stormed through the hole breached in the doorway, crawling over the pile of rubble from the collapsed wall, trying to get their bearings in an enclosed space choked with smoke.

Gunshots blasted from behind the table and one of the men staggered, grabbing his chest. He fell to the ground. The second began a spray of automatic fire aimed wildly in the direction of the table, but a series of shots by two weapons behind it struck him four, five, and six times. He lurched forward, falling to his knees with a scream, and rolled over on his side moaning.

As two more men burst through the opening a chaos of weapons' discharge erupted. The NSA man beside Rideout screamed and clutched his face, blood squirting from between his fingers. He rolled on the ground, howling. Rideout slumped behind the table, blood flowing from the right side of his chest, eyes swimming. His gun dropped to the ground with a clank.

Another mercenary had fallen, but two more stepped in to take his place. The invaders advanced slowly, unimpeded. The NSA man with the wrench shook behind the server racks, his pants moist around the crotch. Several feet from him Lightfoote worked like a woman possessed, ignoring the chaos.

The three soldiers stepped forward cautiously, converging on the table and the forms of the bodies behind it. Rideout glanced upward but didn't move his head, energy evanescing from his body. They looked down on him and the flailing NSA man. Two returned their attention to the rest of the room, hunting for targets. The other fired several shots into the screaming figure. The cries ceased. He turned toward Rideout and aimed.

A series of shots roared from behind them, bullets bursting through the man's mouth and throat. As Rideout watched him fall, the two beside him spun around, firing at the bloodied shape of Simon. The old CIA man managed to empty his weapon, wounding one in the stomach, even as the assailants killed him. Simon fell against the wall, bullet holes and blood decorating the surface behind him. He slid slowly to the ground, his chest a mass of wounds, his eyes blank. He lay still.

The other NSA man dropped the wrench and walked out, falling to his knees.

"Don't shoot! I surrender! I'm not part of this group! I'm from the NSA! Please, don't kill me!" Tears stained his face as he trembled before the soldiers.

"Where's the girl?" rasped one.

"She's here. Right behind me! At the terminal!"

The soldier fired into his head, and the programmer fell. The mercenary raced forward, his companion stumbling behind, bent nearly double with his wound soaking his clothes.

The first soldier leapt around the stacks of computers and opened fire at the terminal against the wall. The chassis exploded into fragments, the continued discharge blowing it and the monitor to pieces. He ejected the magazine and reached for another.

A pair of feet swung down from the piping above, catching him square in the face. The impact snapped his head back sharply, and his arms and legs went slack before he dropped to the ground.

Lightfoote landed like a cougar, crouched low to absorb the momentum, her arm splayed to the side along the floor. The remaining soldier staggered toward her, movements sluggish and jerky, gunshots blasting wildly from the barrel of his weapon to pock the walls harmlessly.

Bright silver flashed through the air and the soldier's head snapped to the side as the wrench slammed into his jaw with a heavy crunch of bone. His body continued to the side and toppled over. Both soldiers now unconscious.

Lightfoote leaped beside them and bludgeoned each in the head. Satisfied, she raced beside Rideout, her gaze lingering a moment on the body of Simon across the room. "JP! You there?" She slapped his face.

His eyes struggled to open, a gasp escaping his mouth. "Oh, God,

Angel. Shit, this hurts!"

Lightfoote pulled off her shirt, revealing a tight sports bra. She pressed the shirt against the wound, eliciting a scream from Rideout.

She shouted over him. "JP! Listen. Here, this arm works." She pulled one of his hands to the shirt. "Stay with me! Keep some pressure there. I'm running up to get a medkit. Slow the bleeding!"

He nodded and his arm tensed against his chest. He inhaled sharply. "Angel, wait," he gasped as she turned to leave.

"What?"

Rideout stared at the blasted computers. Every terminal was destroyed. "The worm?" he managed.

She crouched beside him and kissed him on the cheek. Sweat dripped from her shoulders and arms. His blood glimmered in streaks across her scalp.

"Launched. Gone!" She smiled. "You did good. Now shut up and don't die on me."

63

THE WHITE VAPOR had nearly dissipated. The faint aroma of gunpowder and ash mixed with a sickly sweetness still lingering in the air. Hulking shapes breathed resonantly from within gas masks on the platform.

The FBI team was concentrated at one end of the structure, all of them handcuffed, soldiers in masks pointing guns in their direction. The captives were still coughing badly, tears and mucus running from their eyes and noses. Their weapons were in a pile at the feet of their captors.

The mask spoke. "So easy. Don't you guys ever play chess?"

Poison stood beside Fawkes, a gas mask around her head. She looked down at the FBI team. "What are you going to do with them?"

Fawkes cocked the smirking visage to one side. "Kill them, of course."

"Please, don't," said Poison, eyes large.

"Be grateful you aren't there with them. I should kill you as well for betraying me. But I don't have the emotional fortitude. You get to live because of my weakness. But not them. Not after what they've done."

"I told you!" she cried. "It was all fake! They didn't torture me!"

"Perhaps," said Fawkes, "or perhaps this is some demented state of Stockholm Syndrome. Did they promise you amnesty? Immunity? Do you think any of that matters now?" The mask studied her coldly.

"No!"

He turned to the FBI team. "Even if it was all a ruse, it was a very painful ruse for me. Until I figured it out, before I realized that it was all *too* easy, perfectly engineered to elicit an emotional response, get me to put myself in terrible danger—before all that came into focus I really went through the agony of watching her suffer." He extended his hand and received a gun from one of the soldiers. "And that will not be forgiven."

"Stop, Fawkes!" cried Poison, moving toward him. A towering

soldier grabbed her from behind and lifted her off the ground as she flailed.

Fawkes motioned to the warehouse floor. "Get her out of here. She doesn't need to see this."

Screaming, Poison was taken by two guards awkwardly down the ladder. Fawkes and the remaining guard stepped in front of the FBI team. The mask turned to Savas.

"It has been an interesting game, one still with several pieces in play. But here I have the King, and, I suppose, his Queen, even if by abilities I think the real Queen is lying in a pool of blood in a basement in New York City."

"Just a video game to you, Fawkes?" spat Savas. "Our lives. The nation. The world. Millions, billions of people who will wake up tomorrow back in the Dark Ages. Most of them to die."

There was a flash of lightning and a loud explosion. A deep rumble followed, shaking their bones.

"Fittingly dramatic. A sign from God do you think?" The masked man laughed. "*Live free or die.* I think New Hampshire's motto? One of those tiny states. But a slogan that is central to the value of our short existence."

He turned the weapon in his hands, removing the magazine, checking the chamber, and reinserting the box.

"Imagine a prison so intricately constructed that the inmates believe themselves free. The slaves cannot see their chains. When you're one of the few to see through the deceptions to the heart of this darkness, most of the time you go mad, or cynical, or do something stupid and get the forces in control to erase you. That was nearly my fate."

Cohen leaned against Savas and rested her head on his shoulder. Miller squirmed vainly in his restraints.

"But knowing what I know, it's clear that the infection *must* be sterilized. Like cancer, the treatment will be horrific. It may kill the patient. Indeed, humanity may never rise again. And that might just be for the better, you know? Anyway, it won't be for any of us to see, but for those a thousand years down the road. If any civilization rises from these ashes." Fawkes motioned to the guard beside him, who stepped forward and raised his weapon. "Sorry for the pain, but it will all be over quickly."

He raised his weapon and aimed at Savas. "Goodbye."

There was another bright flash and deafening sound. But this wasn't the storm.

The platform swayed from the force of a blast, the entire warehouse shuddering violently. Unlike thunder the rumbling was short lived, and debris rained across the interior, pieces of wood and metal thrown as far as the platform surface. The front of the warehouse had been torn apart, crates and other discarded elements shattered and burning. Black smoke filled the room, its turbulent structure illuminated by the raging flames.

Fawkes and the soldier were hurled to the floor of the platform. The soldier's weapon discharged wildly as he fell, but his impact momentarily stunned him and he lost his grip. The gun skipped toward Miller and the back edge of the platform, plunging into darkness below.

Miller used the chaos and struck outward with a blinding kick, catching the man's face full on. There was a cracking sound and the man screamed, rolling to his side as blood streamed into his hands.

Fawkes had stumbled forward and smashed into the railing beside Cohen, his mask shattered, jagged white pieces hanging loosely from the gas mask. Cohen smashed her shoulder into his gun hand, the impact dislodging the weapon and sending it plummeting out of sight.

Fawkes leapt backward, dodging wild kicks from Savas, stumbling into the railing on the other side of the platform. The soldier beside him pulled out a handgun and wiped blood from his broken nose.

"Kill them!" Fawkes cried.

But the soldier didn't even raise his weapon. Two shots exploded from behind them, and the man's head erupted in a soup of blood and flesh. His limp body dropped like a stone, shaking the platform.

A woman's voice called from below. "Don't twitch, masked-boy, or we'll liquefy your big brain, too!"

"Houston!" Cohen cried.

Savas closed his eyes in relief.

There was a clattering from the ladder. A soot-covered woman sprang upward, a pistol in one hand trained on Fawkes' slumped form.

"Got you covered from two angles, asshole, so think before you act." Her eyes darted from the shattered mask in front of her. "You three okay?"

"Yes!" Savas said angrily. "What about the other guards?"

"Killed in the explosion."

The jigsaw face spun toward her. "And Poison?"

"She's gone," said Houston.

Fawkes screamed and lunged at her wildly, his hands a pair of claws aiming for her face. With a pivot, she sidestepped his motion and used her gun arm to bring the butt of the weapon viciously down on the back of his head. He collapsed and didn't move.

Heavy steps sounded as Lopez awkwardly climbed the ladder with his one good arm. He landed roughly and glanced down at the two bodies. He exhaled slowly and smiled at the FBI team. "Better late than never, right?"

NOVEMBER 5

64

ARMED MEN USHERED President York down a dimly lit flight of stairs. On each side, soldiers took positions with weapons aimed upward, speaking quietly into headsets. Beside her was a lanky, gray-haired man, his face flushed, a sling around his arm. The group reached the bottom, the claustrophobic stairwell opening on a dank tunnel receding into darkness. Its opening was broad, wide enough for a vehicle to pass through. Water leaked out from it to pool at their feet.

"Madam President," said one of the soldiers, "this shaft will take you to the helicopter. Sergeants Holmes and Nesic will accompany you." Two uniformed men stepped beside the president. "We're going to stay here and blow the tunnel if we have to."

"And then what?" asked York.

"We'll hide out. No one knows these emergency tunnels like we do. Everyone made fun of the upkeep. Well, who's laughing now?"

"Be safe, Captain. And thank you. It's good to know I have supporters even in the military."

She grabbed her companion by his good arm and turned to the tunnel. The two other soldiers flanked the civilians and they moved forward, the neon green of glow sticks lighting their way.

"Elaine, how far do you think this is going to go?" asked Tooze.

"The coup?" she asked, pulling out a small handgun. "General Hastings isn't a halfway kinda guy, George. Unless someone puts a stop to him—and I'm not going to dress up what that means—unless someone either arrests or kills the man, we're heading for a full-blown military takeover."

"What will that mean?"

"God only knows," said York, shaking her head. "Kind of in unknown territory there. A centralized command for sure. Suspension of the Constitution and a streamlined civilian authority headed by military personnel. Either they'll get the governors on board or they'll install puppets to run the states—state militias and law enforcement. Once they have the guns under control everything else will fall into place. They're going to marshal the entire national machinery to their power structure beyond the military—NSA, FBI, banks."

"It's really headed toward a dictatorship?"

"It's a rare military coup that ends with a vote."

They continued walking, their shoes muddied and soaked from the brown sludge coating the bottom of the tunnel. "Until this all gets cleared up—and who knows how long that will take—they'll want an iron fist to hold the nation together. I see their point. I really do. I just don't think all of them see how things can go very wrong, very quickly. You walk down some paths and you can't go back."

"Do you think Hastings knows?"

Her eyes flashed intensely toward him. "My greatest fear is that he does, indeed. *Temporary* may be something only those around him believe. He always had a run of the crazy in him."

The tunnel opened into another cramped chamber, a dull light above revealing a rusted spiral staircase. The walls and metal throbbed from a disturbance above.

"Bird's here," said one of the soldiers.

They scaled the steps, Tooze awkward and often requiring assistance as they climbed, his wounded arm useless. The light grew rapidly near the top.

They exited the emergency tunnels through a hole at the corner of a helipad. The blades of a powerful helicopter thundered overhead, kicking dust and forest foliage into their path. The green and beige camouflage of the machine rose like a wall before them.

"Damn, that's a big one," gasped Tooze.

A soldier smiled. "Sea Stallion, sir. Big mother. She's loaded with an armored transport inside for when we drop you two off the mountain. Entrance in the rear."

The president and the Homeland Security director followed the soldiers around the churning aircraft, heads bowed, hands over their faces to mask the debris. They rushed up a ramp lowered from the back. Several officers and two civilians greeted them inside.

"Ms. President," said a boyish face in a mud-splattered suit. "Let's get you strapped in and get the hell out of here."

York quickly embraced him. "Daniel. So the Secretary of Defense is still with us. With Treasury I think we might just be able to field a government in exile." She smiled toward a statuesque blond in a badly torn white dress

"Ms. President, please," said the Treasury Secretary. "We're sitting ducks."

They made their way around an eight-wheeled armored vehicle with an enormous machine gun. Foldout seats were fixed to the sides of the aircraft. Civilians and soldiers took their places, buckling the belts. The rear door slammed shut.

The Defense Secretary spoke loudly over the growing din of the engines. "We were planning for an off-shore base, but they've seized control of the important carriers. They've got a version of events painting us in a bad light and we won't get safe passage."

"NORAD?" asked York.

"That's the goal. The military and civilian leadership is resisting Hastings there. But it's a ways and we're going to have to regroup with some of the armed forces loyal to you."

"Should I call them all Loyalists, now?"

The Defense Secretary didn't smile. "It's chaos out there, Elaine. The whole system is coming unglued. We've got anarchy in the streets and a governmental split. We need numbers and weapons to make it to Colorado."

York felt the tug on her stomach as the giant bird went airborne. "No arguments from me, Daniel. This is going to be ugly and long."

One of the soldiers gazed out of a window beside him and whistled. "Goddamn. The admin building's blown! I can see fires across Mount Weather!"

The president released her belt and steadied herself beside the young man, staring grimly through the glass. "Fighting has started."

Tooze shook his head. "I can't believe it's come to this! We're turning on each other. First the riots in Washington. New York by now, I guess. And now this."

York continued to look down at the retreat site, her words cold.

"Rome burns."

65

HOW THEY HAD made it back to Intel 1 was as much by miracle as by the muscle they were forced to use. Between National Guard roadblocks and bands of rioters roaming the city streets, they'd had to rely on force on three occasions. In one engagement, they'd killing several armed gang members who'd tried to carjack them. It was a scene Savas had never imagined living through, firing weapons in the middle of the day on mobs swarming them in the heart of the city. The relative safety of the Javits building suddenly seemed like a haven in a growing storm.

The staff left at the FBI building were frazzled and leaderless. The brass had fled, either called to other duties or frightened for their own skins in the anarchy spreading across the island. Savas pulled the remaining personnel from normal functions and organized them into guards at all entrances to the building. The last thing he was going let happen was for some random group of thugs to undo all that they had accomplished.

They had Fawkes. *Alive.* And now they were going to make him stop this unfolding catastrophe, or show them how to.

"He looks like a damn kid," said Miller, glaring at the man slumped handcuffed on the couch in Savas' office.

The masks were gone. A dark-haired cipher rested calmly before them, his eyes closed behind cracked smart glasses, his voice strangely controlled given his situation.

"How's the battle out there, agents?"

Cohen stared through the large window in the office down to the streets of New York. She spoke sadly. "People are dying. Many suffering. Some accomplishments you've racked up."

"Simon's gone," Savas said. "JP's critical. Good people you're not worthy of, Fawkes."

"I meant in the matrix. Where's that Angel girl?"

Lightfoote sat clacking over a laptop. "Here, boy-genius. Look for yourself."

She turned the screen around toward him furiously as he opened his eyes. With a groan he raised his head slightly, blood still coating the back of his neck from the blow Houston had landed.

"Nice shoulders," he said. "Drop that bikini top and we're in business."

"The red lines are my immune worms. The blue yours. Fucking kicking your sorry ass."

He lay back and smirked. "Going to go twelve rounds, I think. Fuck, that's beautiful, you bitch. Never imagined anyone would be that crazy."

Houston and Lopez entered the crowded office in a rush. "Okay, we've got people at the main entry points. But it's a weak job. Some are just secretaries, for God's sake! They'll fold quickly under any real assault."

Savas nodded. "Hopefully there won't be one. In the meantime, Fawkes, or whoever the hell you really are, we need to make sure Angel's code wins. We need you to shut your worms down or tell us how to do so." He pulled a chair up and placed a foot on it, leaning toward the hacker. "No good cop, bad cop. It's all bad, today. You don't look like you'd last five minutes with Frank."

"He wouldn't make it through one," growled Miller.

"So you're going to talk to us."

Fawkes laughed. "You think I built an off switch? You *fools*. This was *it*. This was meant to go the distance. You can kick me, drown me, get me to do whatever or say whatever. I'll even pretend two plus two is five for you. I'll get on a terminal and tell you I'm fixing everything. If you hurt me enough, I might even believe it myself. But it will be for nothing. *A lie*. Because I didn't build that worm to come home. No one can call it back."

"Son of a bitch," said Miller.

Fawkes continued. "You should *thank* me. You all should thank me for finally driving a stake into the world's vampires. You——"

"Shut up!" yelled Savas. "I'm not in the mood for more of your crazy."

"But I didn't even tell you the best part," said Fawkes, grin wide. "Paranoid? The best part is that I can *show* you."

"Show us what?" asked Savas.

"The truth. The truth I discovered hacking through the financial systems. The truth that they couldn't conceal from me. I know *who* they are. I know where they're working from!"

Savas narrowed his eyes. "What are you talking about?"

"Bilderberg." Fawkes sighed.

Cohen spun around. "What did you say?"

"Bilderberg."

Savas turned to Cohen. "What's that?"

Cohen approached Fawkes, removing her glasses. "The Bilderberg Group. It's a conspiracy theorist's wet dream. The biggest economic conference in the world. Center of Europe. Centuries old. Private. Secretive. No transcripts. No records. World leaders, industry magnates, academic powerhouses, media moguls. Bipartisan support in the nutcase-community that they are the real force running the world."

"That's the *nexus*," said Fawkes, eyes alight. He pushed himself up and stood before them, postured stooped. "But it's like an octopus. And it's real. Let me show you! Take these cuffs off. The next part is what is really—"

There was a pop and tinkling of glass. Fawkes froze, the top half of his head blown apart, a crimson spray painting the wall behind him. His mouth hung ajar, his finger raised to make a point. Instead he dropped to the floor.

"Down! Everyone down!" yelled Savas.

Miller had moved alongside the wall, weapon held beside his head. He approached the window.

"Sniper round," he said, examining the hole. "Long distance shot. A professional." He lowered his gun. "He got his man."

Houston came alongside him to get her own look, keeping her body away from the window. "Now I'm feeling a bit paranoid, myself."

"He's dead." Cohen was bent down beside the body, sidestepping the blood seeping into the carpet. "You don't think—?"

Lopez cut in. "That someone from a mysterious organization running the world killed him so he wouldn't spill their secrets?"

She exhaled. "If you put it like that—"

Lightfoote stared at her laptop screen, speaking slowly. "No, you'd need enormous resources. You'd really have to be an octopus in every major corner of the civilized world. Perhaps eavesdropping on our conversations to know how close we had come. In the middle of all this chaos."

Savas turned to his cybercrimes head. "Angel?"

"But maybe if you were a truly paranoid anarchist, you might do something strange. You might know this phantom group was after you. You might build in a contingency in case they got to you. Some kind of Armageddon fail-safe."

"What are you talking about, Angel?" asked Cohen.

Lightfoote looked up from her computer. "Got an email as few seconds after the shot," she said, glancing down at the body of Fawkes. "From him."

Savas shook his head. "How could Fawkes send you an email? He's dead."

"Read it. You'll see."

Savas took the laptop and held it up to his face. He read out loud.

"Hi Angel baby, if you got this, well, I'm toast. Linked to my heart rate, so I must be dead. I hate it when that happens! Sorry for trying to kill you, but don't take it personally: just the business of rebooting the world, you know? You're one annoying bitch. That's why this is for you. Things are much worse than you think. Only a few of us know the truth, and if you're reading this, we're all likely dead by now. Attached is an encrypted file: you might be able to crack it. If so, you've earned a shot at glory. Good luck. You'll need it."

Savas looked at Lightfoote. "Where's the file?"

"Scroll down to the end of the email."

Savas swiped his fingers on the trackpad.

"The Nash Criterion. What the hell does that mean?"

The office phone rang.

"I thought phones were down," said Lopez, removing his gun.

"This is an internal line. From the front desk. I'll put it on speaker."

A loud rasping sounded from the phone. Someone on the other end wheezed and spoke with a death's rattle: "They're coming. The stairways. Get out. They've shot everyone."

Explosions sounded and the line went dead.

"Let's move!" cried Lopez. He and Houston sprang through the doorway.

They left the body of Fawkes behind, Lightfoote pulling a USB stick out of the computer but leaving the laptop on the desk. She pocketed the stick and drew a gun.

The six moved down the hallway, passing empty offices and abandoned desks, Cohen lumbering on her crutches. They reached the center of the floor just as the elevator doors opened. A group of men in combat gear stepped out.

"Behind the cubicles!" hissed Savas.

They crouched low, Miller and Savas pointing weapons forward, Cohen looking behind them with a puzzled expression on her face.

"Where—" she began but was cut off by the blaring of a bullhorn.

"FBI Intel 1 division! We are United States forces here to apprehend you and the fugitives! Come out with your hands raised or we will be forced to engage!"

A deep stillness settled over the room. Miller touched Savas on the shoulder. "We're not going to overpower these guys, John," he whispered, his expression grave. "Whoever they really are, we're outgunned and outnumbered."

Thoughts racing, Savas considered his options. He was given little time.

"Last warning, Agent Savas. We know you have the terrorist. Hand him over, come out with your hands over your head and you might live!"

"He's dead!" cried Savas. "The hacker is dead in my office. We're coming out." He placed his hands on the weapons of Cohen and Miller beside him. "Put the weapons down. We'll figure a way out of this later."

Lopez and Houston! He had to keep them calm, stop them from doing anything stupid. He spun around, but they were gone.

His eyes met Cohen's. "Where?"

"Angel, too," she whispered. "I don't know where."

"Agent Savas, come forward with your hands in the air!"

Savas placed his weapon on the ground and stood up facing a

group of ten men. Miller and Cohen followed suit. The soldiers aimed weapons in their direction. One called out loudly as several approached them from the sides.

"Under the authority of Directive 51 and the Military Commissions Act, you are under arrest as unlawful combatants, subject to indefinite detention and a hearing before a tribunal. You are hereby stripped of your Constitutional rights and all rank and privilege. Follow all instructions precisely and rapidly or risk the use of force."

They were cuffed and led into the elevators. Frantically, Savas scanned the room a last time, desperately trying to locate Lightfoote and the others. But it was empty. He saw no sign of them.

The doors closed.

BEFORE:
THE ANONYMOUS EVENT COMMISSION

DEPOSITION IN THE MATTER OF:
UNITED STATES ARMED FORCES SPECIAL TRIBUNAL,
Plaintiff,
v.
JOHN SAVAS, Defendant
Case No. M120039E-007X

CONTINUED DEPOSITION OF:
JOHN SAVAS

CBD: And this was the last you saw of agent Lightfoote or of the two fugitives?
MR. SAVAS: That's correct.

[REDACTED]: And so we are really intended to believe that these three simply vanished before a group of trained soldiers? That you were so caught up in the moment of your arrest that you even failed to notice their departure?
MR. SAVAS: That's how it happened.

CBD: But why would they leave?
MR. SAVAS: Lopez and Houston had some good reasons. They were framed for crimes they did not commit. I think they must have thought of a way out.

CBD: How could these two know a way out of your building?
MR. SAVAS: I assume Angel told them. Probably it was her idea in the first place. There wasn't much time for decisions. And she always had a sixth sense about outcomes.

[REDACTED]: And now the explanation is that your cybercrimes head, after releasing a rogue virus through the world's computer systems, after taking secret documents with her, documents sent by the hacker Fawkes—your claim is that her escape with the fugitives was due to her magical ability to see the future! That the reason she helped the terrorists escape is due to some kind of a *vision*. A vision, agent Savas!
MR. SAVAS: I don't know about a vision. What I do know is she makes spontaneous and intuitive

choices. They are usually the right choices.

[REDACTED]: This is absurd!
MR. SAVAS: So what is the Tribunal's theory?

CBD: This isn't the time, Mr. Savas for—

[REDACTED]: Our theory is quite simple. And like Occam's Razor, is what is likely true. It doesn't involve fortune telling or wishing away the documented crimes of outlaws. It doesn't require an imaginary hacker-boogieman who single-handedly brought the world to its knees. The Tribunal believes that you and your collaborators in the NSA and CIA, along with the nation's most wanted terrorists, orchestrated an attempt to overthrow the United States government, a plan carried out under the guise of this *Anonymous* organization, but masterminded by you and your cybercrime head, Angel Lightfoote. This Fawkes was only a mask, not worn by some invented hacker, but masking your crimes, Mr. Savas. When your attempt at sedition was finally stopped by our soldiers, you allowed your fugitives and computer mastermind to escape, stalling our team while they made their getaway.

MR. SAVAS: You really can't be serious.

[REDACTED]: And now the time has come for you to confess and work to bring these traitors in, or to meet yourself the swift hand of justice.

CBD: Mr. Savas, please. Is there nothing that you can provide for this tribunal about their whereabouts? Their intentions? Their plans?
MR. SAVAS: You know as much as I do.

CBD: Anything at all?
MR. SAVAS: No.

CBD: And what about this message from the hacker, this file. What is in it? What does it mean, the *Nash Criterion*?
MR. SAVAS: I have absolutely no idea. And that is the God's honest truth.

[REDACTED]: Enough. This session is concluded. The depositions are over. We will move to the

next phase of this process. And may God have
mercy on your soul, Mr. Savas.

(THE DEPOSITION WAS CONCLUDED AT 2:19 P.M.
SIGNATURE OF THE WITNESS WAS NOT REQUESTED BY
COUNSEL FOR THE RESPECTIVE PARTIES HERETO.)

CERTIFICATE OF NOTARY
DISTRICT OF COLUMBIA

I, [REDACTED], CERTIFY THAT THIS DEPOSITION WAS
TAKEN BEFORE ME ON THE DATE HEREINBEFORE SET
FORTH; THAT THE FOREGOING QUESTIONS AND ANSWERS
WERE RECORDED BY ME STENOGRAPHICALLY AND
REDUCED TO COMPUTER TRANSCRIPTION; THAT THIS IS
A TRUE, FULL AND CORRECT TRANSCRIPT OF MY
STENOGRAPHIC NOTES SO TAKEN; AND THAT I AM NOT
RELATED TO, NOR OF COUNSEL TO, EITHER PARTY NOR
INTERESTED IN THE EVENT OF THIS CAUSE.

A penny loaf to feed ol' Pope
A farthing cheese to choke him
A pint of beer to rinse it down
A faggot of sticks to burn him

Burn him in a tub of tar
Burn him like a blazing star
Burn his body from his head
Then we'll say ol' Pope is dead.

—English Folk Verse (c.1870)

THE
NASH
CRITERION

EREC STEBBINS

The

NASH

CRITERION

Book Four in the INTEL 1 Novels

Erec Stebbins

Twice Pi Press
New York, NY, USA

Only one thing is impossible for God: to find any sense in any copyright law on the planet. —Mark Twain

This book is a work of fiction. Any references to historical events, real people, or real locales are used fictitiously. Other names, characters, places, and incidents are the product of the author's imagination, and any resemblance to actual events or locales or persons, living or dead, is entirely coincidental.

The Nash Criterion. Copyright © 2016 Erec Stebbins
www.erecstebbinsbooks.com

Unless otherwise indicated, all materials on these pages are copyrighted by Erec Stebbins. All rights reserved. No part of these pages, either text or image, may be used for any purpose other than personal use. Therefore, reproduction, modification, storage in a retrieval system or retransmission, in any form or by any means, electronic, mechanical or otherwise, for reasons other than personal use, is strictly prohibited without prior written permission.

Paperback CS   Hardback
ISBN-10: 1942360126   ISBN-10: 1942360134
ISBN-13: 978-1-942360-12-4   ISBN-13: 978-1-942360-13-1

E-book:
ISBN-10: 1942360118
ISBN-13: 978-1-942360-11-7

Published 2016 by Twice Pi Press
TwicePiPress@gmail.com

Cover designs by Erec Stebbins

Images licensed from Shutterstock.com, Pond5.com, and individual artists. Copyrighted artists Krasowit, Olga Nikonova, and isak55.

Edited by Michael Matheson.

To Pete and Michelle:
I try to keep an open mind

O Conspiracy,
Sham'st thou to show thy dang'rous brow by night,
When evils are most free?

—William Shakespeare,
Julius Cæsar

PART 1

*"Behind the ostensible government sits enthroned
an invisible government owing no allegiance
and acknowledging no responsibility to the people."*

—Theodore Roosevelt

1

"WILL THERE BE anything else, Elaine?"

Tipping her bifocals down, President York looked up from the mass of papers on her desk in the Oval Office. Before her stood a lanky man in a formal business suit, white hair and blue eyes staring back.

"No, George," she said, rubbing her eyes. "A crazy week. I'm sorry about the Senate vote. It's a slap in the face to me that they held it up as long as they did. In the end it wasn't even close. You deserved better."

George Tooze nodded. "Homeland Security is a macho position. They don't want some academic heading it. But it's done. Onward."

"Onward indeed, George," she said, gesturing to her desk.

Tooze motioned to leave but caught himself, turning back to the president.

"It was something today, Elaine. I remember when Obama was sworn in. First African-American president. Now this. No one will forget your speech. It will be in the history books."

"We've come a long way, baby. But if I hadn't been in boots and fatigues? Wouldn't have scratched that glass ceiling. So much fear out there. They don't care if you've got a law degree from Harvard, served in the Senate ten years, hell, even that your daddy was in that chamber. People need Daddy in the White House. Richard was a genius to use my military photos so much in the campaign. I think I ran mostly as a soldier!"

"You have a large base. A strong one. And we'll use that, don't you worry. We just had to convince enough fence sitters. And we did. Congratulations, Ms. President. You've earned it."

He smiled and closed the door behind him as he left. York watched him exit the White House and step toward a black town car idling in the driveway. It was good to have such loyal supporters early on. If you didn't, when things got rough, you were in trouble. And Elaine York didn't fool herself—in this business, sooner or later, things always got rough.

A large phone at the far end of the desk vibrated.

"You're kidding me."

York stared dumbfounded. The device was a military-grade smartphone, a one-of-a-kind custom gadget with cutting-edge voice and data encryption, designed specifically for one job: to serve as the President's communication device of convenience for hotline calls.

Hotline calls.

More than twenty bilateral hotlines existed between the United States and other nations. The famous Russian hotline was complimented with many spanning allies in Europe to frenemies in Asia and the Middle East. The phone was not supposed to buzz except when the White House Communications Agency had received and was routing a call from one of these nations' leaders. York felt the weight of her office descend like a mountain on her shoulders.

She grabbed the device and keyed in her unique code. "President Elaine York on Direct Link."

Static only. York engaged several additional security clearance codes. Nothing. Her heart began to pound. They checked this line every hour of every day! How could it be malfunctioning?

A pop of static startled her. A man's voice spoke.

"President York. It is so good to finally be able to speak with you."

York felt cold. She had run simulations with the hotline communication system. Procedures were followed, protocols in place. She should be speaking with White House Communications. She should be briefed and transferred to the incoming hotline call. What the hell was happening?

"Please don't be alarmed."

"Who is this? You aren't WHCA."

"No, we are not. We are not a formal part of the US government. Or any government."

York stared slack-jawed for a moment. "How the hell did you get this number? Who are you?"

"The answers to both questions are intertwined. You need to discover those answers before your presidency continues much further."

"Look, I don't know what this—"

"There is someone waiting for you underground. At the new Cogcon Line. I think that he will peak your curiosity."

"How do you know—"

"We know and we have access. Which should tell you all you need to know."

York blinked. "You have access to the train line?"

"Rest assured, Ms. York, your gleaming new railway is still a secret, known only to the proper governmental agencies. And our group."

"Who are you?"

"It is best we explain in a different setting."

"Why should I trust this? You could be luring me into a trap. I'm going to call—"

"Friendly fire, Ms. President!"

Her face paled. Elaine York stared forward wildly and swallowed. "What did you say?"

"Battle of Khafji. Terrible accident. Was it eleven servicemen died? You were assigned to that unit, weren't you?"

"In a non-combat role. Everyone knows that! Women weren't allowed to serve in combat roles then."

"But we both know the truth, don't we, Ms. York? Your actions were noble, truly. But of course it's not me you would have to convince. You and several other soldiers resisted some men in uniform who were out of control. The ensuing firefight was a tragedy." He paused. "And easily misconstrued. It would be terrible for your presidency if certain information were released to the public."

She squeezed her fingertips to her temple. This wasn't happening!

"The Cogcon line, Ms. President. Try at least that far. Someone will be waiting for you."

The connection closed.

In a near panic, York opened the trap door underneath her desk and descended into the Horsepower command post. It was empty. She searched for the Secret Service staff who manned the post, but found no one. Monitors around her displayed camera footage from inside and outside the building. Communications equipment crackled and blinked. A filled coffee pot steamed beside several unopened sandwiches.

"What the hell?"

Continuing was insane. This was an attack on the Presidency. Only an idiot would follow the directions from that cipher on the hotline.

Friendly fire.

She couldn't escape it. It would ruin her, strip her presidency of all moral authority and hand her opponents the perfect weapon to discredit her. Whoever had been on the other end of the line, they had terrible knowledge—dangerous knowledge, and the power that came with it. She had nowhere to go but forward, into the trap they had set for her.

She made her way through several of the hidden passageways leading to the classified rail line. Outside the deepest military and governmental circles, the new train was only a distorted rumor. The line served to secrete the president and staff deep underground, away from the White House in the event of a national catastrophe. As she opened the final doorway with a retinal scan, she saw the gleaming metallic surface of the presidential car in front of her, the hum of the electric motor purring softly.

A tall black man in a sweater looked down at her solemnly.

"Hello, Elaine," came his deep voice.

York stared up at the former community organizer, his hair completely grayed, his shoulders stooped and his gait limping. He looked old. He looked defeated. He looked mournful.

"Barack?"

2

"THOSE WERE *SOLDIERS!*" said Houston. "We need to go back!"

The three stood in a stairwell, two flights down from Intel 1. The hacker Fawkes had just been killed in the office of John Savas—his head blown open from a sniper shot through the window. Sara Houston and Francisco Lopez had fled along with the remaining FBI agents, only to have Angel Lightfoote pull them to the side and toward a glowing EXIT sign.

"Trust me!" she had whispered without further explanation.

For reasons Houston would never fully understand, she had. In a split second decision, she had followed the bald woman into the stairwell, Lopez behind them. They glimpsed at the last moment a group of soldiers pour from the elevators with weapons drawn.

Browning in hand, Houston began to climb the stairs. The muscled arm of Lightfoote held her back.

"We can't!" she said. "There isn't time! They'll be looking for us. They'll know soon we're not with them."

Houston nodded. "We're wanted fugitives, I get it. But they've risked everything with us. I'm not going to abandon them now."

Lightfoote shook her head. "Not for you. For me!" She removed a thumb drive from her pocket and brandished it at Houston. "Fawkes's email and attachment. They want this! We can't let them have it. Not until we know what it is." Houston's pause was all the assent Lightfoote required. "Now, let's move!"

The FBI agent bounded down the stairs like a spider. Houston glared at Lopez who shrugged, and they followed after her, both struggling to keep up.

"Subbasement?" rasped Houston, glancing at the signs over the doorways.

Lightfoote landed heavily from a jump. "Yes."

A door was ajar, the stairway ending in a dank and musty corner. The smell of rotten eggs assaulted them. Lopez grabbed Lightfoote with his good arm, the sling on the other soaked in sweat.

"Where are we going?"

Houston scowled at the dimly lit passageway in front of them. "The goddam sewers. That's where."

Lightfoote nodded. "These huge buildings produce a lot of shit. There's got to be a connection to New York's underground rivers. If we can get access, we can follow it to some of the manhole connections—maybe find one they haven't welded shut. Come up on street level somewhere a little downstream." She turned on the flashlight app of her smartphone. "There has to be an access door down here somewhere."

There was. After several tense minutes of searching around pumps and other machinery, they found an iron hatch opening to the main sewer line. It required all the strength Lopez had left to pry it open, but soon they scrambled into the dark bowels of the city. A knee-high river of waste greeted them.

"Glad we skipped lunch," said Lopez, holding his hand to his mouth.

Houston stopped Lightfoote with her hand.

"Okay, before we go any further, hacker girl, what the hell is going on? Who were those soldiers? What do you know?"

Lightfoote cocked her head to the side. "I don't know. I feel it. Fawkes opened up Pandora's Box, Sara. Bad things came out. The soldiers came out. They're part of it. We have to see what's in this file. That's what they want. That's why he was killed."

"But you don't even know what's in that file!"

"Fawkes was a crazy bastard. That's what I know. But we had a kind of sick relationship." Lightfoote stared down into the darkness of the tunnel. "Whatever's in this, it was everything to him. It's why he did it all, brought the fucking world to its knees. He was trying to kill something. Something in this file."

"This Bilderberg?"

"Maybe," said Lightfoote.

Lopez shook his head. "And you think he's right? You think his death and those soldiers are somehow related to this?"

"Yes," she said. "Let's just give ourselves the chance to find out, get a look at this, okay? Before they whisk us off to some dungeon somewhere."

Houston stared into the green eyes before her. "Some dungeon? So that's what's going to happen to them? We left them to that?"

"I don't know for sure."

"But you feel it." Lopez crossed himself. "God be with them. I know what the monsters do in those dungeons. I've seen the product up close." He passed his finger over the stigmata on his forehead.

"All right," said Houston. "Let's get out of here. Get back to the apartment in Harlem. We've got computers. Internet access—to whatever's left of it. We'll see what we can find out there. And we better find something. Or we abandoned them for nothing."

———————

An old Chinese couple crossing the street jumped backward and scampered away as a manhole cover rocketed into the air and landed several feet away from the dark hole. The iron disk wobbled like a giant coin to a ringing stop.

A bald woman in combat fatigues leapt out of the manhole, landing heavily on her feet. She drew a pistol and scanned around her, body in a tense crouch. Two others followed: a second woman covered in black, giving a hand to a large man in a flowing coat nursing his left shoulder.

Chinatown was empty, the old couple having thought better of continuing their walk. Shops around them were boarded up, many looted, debris and trash littering the roads and sidewalks. As the sun began to dip below the ridge of buildings in lower Manhattan, the three of them raced out of the road and into the alleyways, disappearing like silent shadows into the falling night.

3

THE NIGHTMARE BEGAN as soon as they exited the FBI Jarvits building. Savas glimpsed several black vans and military issue trucks parked outside, armed men lining the perimeter. Soldiers marched them in file to the convoy like prisoners of war, hostile eyes tracking their movements, weapons in plain sight and at the ready.

As they approached the vans they were separated, each directed to a different vehicle. Savas had only an instant to stare into Cohen's eyes before the men jerked fabric over his head, leaving him in claustrophobic darkness. They cuffed his arms behind him, then roughly shoved him forward. He stumbled into the vehicle, smashing his forehead. A foot thrust him tightly into the corner and knocked the wind out of him.

"Shut up and don't move, and I won't have to use this."

Savas could hear the static crackle of a Taser inches from his face.

Several heavy bodies dropped into seats around him before the door slammed shut. The engine turned over and the vehicle lurched forward into the streets of New York.

With no visual input his brain had nothing to offset the choppy movements of the drive. Growing nausea churned his stomach into a painful knot. He tried visualizing images with the movements, always a step behind, the effort hardly compensating. *God help me from getting sick in this bag.*

He tried to guess their direction, the streets taken, hoping to learn where these men were taking them. But he failed. Within minutes, the vehicle's jerky maneuvers had scrambled his sense of direction.

He guessed it had been half an hour when the van stopped abruptly, throwing his face into the chair in front of him. The impact gave him a black eye, and he tasted copper from a busted lip. Unable to wipe his face, the blood dripped through the hood.

"He's a bleeder!" cried a man standing over him.

Laughter erupted. Arms hoisted him roughly to his feet and flung him out of the van. He forced himself not to gasp as his shoulder smacked the concrete. Pulling up slowly, he spit blood. *Focus, John.* He tried to slow his heart rate. He breathed deeply.

The sea.

The thick taste of brine and marine life penetrated the hood. The gull cries and sounds of waves told him all he needed to know. He'd been taken to a port, likely in lower Manhattan given the travel time. Boots rang on thin metal as a massive object thudded gently into the space before him.

A boat.

His other senses were primed, hearing and touch sharpened. He sensed the vessel and its weight rocking on the waves, knocking against the dock.

They're taking me out to sea.

They stowed him roughly below deck, his wrists chained to the wall, the pitch of the boat sending another wave of nausea through him. They still hadn't removed the hood, the fabric now glued to his face from clotted blood. He didn't dare show any weakness or ask for aid. Whoever these men worked for, they had been instructed to treat him like the worst terrorist suspect. The implications sent a chill through him as he thought about Cohen and Miller, and what fate awaited them all.

At least he knew they would be together. The three had been split up, either for security or psychological warfare. Perhaps both. But their captors weren't careful enough. He'd heard the high-pitched sounds of a woman's voice—*Rebecca's voice*—as she cried out, an impact sounding from her hitting the deck heavily. *She's on board.* But he couldn't let himself dwell on what had happened to her. He had to focus, keep his wits about him, and discover all he could that might aid in an escape.

But he wasn't fooling himself. He'd known too many rendered terrorists, read too many reports, and could appraise professionally their situation. Statistically, escape was all but impossible. Only a handful had been recorded. As he fought off the bile climbing in his throat, he forced himself to face the truth—any attempts to escape, should they ever present themselves, would almost certainly end in failure. Probably in death.

We'll have to work with them. A recipe for Stockholm Syndrome. But the only hope for freedom, for survival, lay with their captors. Hope depended on meeting the desires of those now controlling their lives. Part of him wanted simply to resist, to find an opportunity to make a last stand and take down as many of them with him as he could.

But I'm not alone. Rebecca's here. Such a selfish death would not only break her heart, but would seriously endanger her life. He had to swallow his pride, his anger, suppress the desire to strike out. He had to act calmly. Shrewdly. He had to find a way to bring his captors to his side and convince them to release them. But without knowing who had taken him or why, it was impossible to know what to do, or how likely such efforts were to succeed.

The boat moved. He felt the random vectors of pitch, roll, and yaw from the waves give way to a clear direction. The sounds of powerful engines vibrated through the walls of the vessel. Kerosene fumes began to choke him.

The ship left the dock, but headed where, or why, he couldn't guess.

4

"HOLY SHIT! LOOK at this!"

Lightfoote leapt across the cluttered floor of the dilapidated brownstone, holding a laptop in the air as she approached Houston and Lopez.

"A second, fly-girl," said Houston, eyes focused on the deep wound in Lopez's shoulder.

Lightfoote stared at the hulking form of the former priest, shaking her head. *Damn.* Even in the middle of everything else, he *was* distracting. His shirt removed, he resembled a bodybuilder more than a former math teacher. His pecs flared and his lats striated as he tensed from the pain. She watched Houston finish applying ointment and seal the wound with taped gauze.

"Healing?" she asked, impressed with the CIA agent's field dressing.

Lopez grabbed his shirt and stood up. Houston exhaled. "Yeah, he heals fast. But it was an ugly gash. High caliber round ran like a spear through the muscle. But it's closing well. Just need to keep it from infection. Couple weeks and he'll be back in the ring."

"Well, if blowing up bad guys gets boring, he's got a career modeling for the Priest Calendar."

Lopez smirked and turned away, slipping his shirt slowly over his head. Lightfoote's gaze followed him as he walked to the window and stared outside.

"So, where's the fire," said Houston.

Lightfoote crouched and placed her laptop on the floor, turning the screen toward Houston. A series of colored strands ran across a map of the world in a diabolically complicated web. *More and more, my web.*

"Remember this map?"

Houston nodded. "Yeah, your worm versus Fawkes's. Yours were red? Looks like you've turned the tide."

"Right?" Lightfoote grinned softly. "At this rate, just a few weeks and the danger's gone. Well, millions of computers may still be infected. But my code isn't going anywhere. It'll take down any further attempts of his to spread. Best case scenario: we'll just have a few years of flare ups before we can hunt down the last copies."

"Congratulations, Angel," said Houston, rubbing her temples. "You need a medal or something."

Lightfoote breathed deeply. "Well, that's the good news."

Lopez turned around and walked over to the pair. "Sounded much too positive given current events. What else?"

"World's gone to shit. Communication's spotty from overseas. Media's mostly down and what's up is just broadcasting propaganda."

"Propaganda?" said Lopez, crouching down and looking at the screen.

Lightfoote opened a series of windows. Headlines from newspapers appeared online alongside video from ashen-faced newscasters.

"A presidential *coup?*" said Houston.

Lopez touched a window filled with text. "York claimed emergency powers and dismissed Congress? Nation-wide martial law?"

"I told you it was Pandora's Box," said Lightfoote. "Times article has the most details. York annulled the constitution and suspended civilian courts. Half the military's gone over with her, claiming extraordinary wartime powers. The other half is protecting members of Congress and attempting to end the coup." She leaned back on her hands and looked between the pair. "Basically we're in civil war, if you believe this."

Lopez eyed her sharply. "Do you?"

"There's a war on, that's for sure." She gestured at the screen. "The public opinion damage control is in full swing. But York, a dictator?"

Houston nodded, locking eyes with Lightfoote. "We met her. Only for a few minutes, but you learn a lot about someone when bullets and bombs are blasting around you. I didn't see dictator in her."

"I agree," said Lopez. "But if we're right, how do we explain this?"

"Assume there is a coup," said Lightfoote, "but not led by York.

What if in the chaos Fawkes unleashed someone else decided to play Beautiful Leader?"

"Right," said Houston. "They'd need to sell their narrative. Slander York as the rebel, turn the population against her."

"Which means they don't have her," said Lopez.

"Not yet, anyway," said Lightfoote, pleased her new companions were so quick on the uptake. "But one thing's for sure, we're in a bad zone."

Lopez cocked his head at her. "The press slant?"

"If they're being fed this shit, we're in hostile territory." Lightfoote put her hands in her lap. "You said you left York at Mount Weather. That's Virginia?"

Houston nodded. "Seemed safe at the time. Didn't count on our government eating itself."

Lopez laughed. "Maybe it shouldn't surprise us. They sure have been quick to eat their own to cover dirty laundry. We know about that." Houston winced, and he reached out, stroking her hair. Houston cupped his hand.

Lightfoote looked between the two, her voice raw. "Let's hope the battle lines are drawn there."

"And if they aren't?" asked Houston. "If York's inside enemy territory?"

"Then we'd better hope she got the hell out."

The three sat in silence for several minutes. Videos of carnage and chaos looped on the laptop screen. Lightfoote fought to suppress the vague visions percolating within her. What had Savas called it? *Intuition*. Something Kanter and Savas had found useful to the Bureau. For Lightfoote, it was something else entirely. *Hypersensitive*. As painful as it was protective. Once burned, one detected even the slightest heat. And right now, the world was on fire.

"All right, been avoiding this one. There's even more bad news," Lightfoote paused. "I've tracked our friends."

"How?" asked Houston. "Not their phones. We made sure to use phones without GPS."

"Lots of ways to triangulate if enough towers are up. They're coming back online." Lightfoote entered several keystrokes, closed other windows and opened a map of the Eastern seaboard. A white circle blinked in the Atlantic, centered in a triangle of dots. "That's Rebecca's phone. John's and Frank's aren't responding. I assume they were taken, probably destroyed. Maybe Rebecca managed to hide hers, stow it somewhere."

"A bit of luck in a sea of disaster," said Lopez. "And speaking of *sea* —what the hell is her phone signal doing there?"

"Remember Fawkes?" said Houston. "He wanted to base his operations at sea to avoid the chaos he produced. Maybe our coup leader had the same idea."

Lopez leaned back and grunted. "But if they're out there, it's not on an armored yacht. If this is a military coup, our friends are likely secured on a naval destroyer."

"Complicates a rescue mission," said Lightfoote. Her stomach churned.

Houston shook her head. "Makes it *impossible*, Angel." She placed a hand on Lightfoote's shoulder. "I'm sorry."

Lightfoote stood up and removed the thumb drive from her pocket, pushing the conversation from her mind. "So we deal with this, what we can. Maybe it's the key to solving our crises, and finding our friends."

"Assuming you can get into it," said Houston. "Didn't Fawkes taunt you that it was encrypted?"

"I've tried. It's not going to be easy." Lightfoote set her jaw. "But I've got some ideas. In fact, a bunch of people have a bunch of ideas."

5

THE ENGINES SHIFTED to different pitch, the powerful thrust easing as the ship slowed to a stop in the dead of night. Savas remained handcuffed to the wall in the bowels of the boat. He'd seen no one in the hours since they left him there and heard no sounds but the machines churning around him.

The nausea had passed, his body having adapted to the ship's rocking. Exhausted, unable to sleep or relax with his hands chained high on the wall, he stood upright, muscles ceaselessly contracting to keep his balance, his body unable to rest a moment during the journey. His wrists bled from the repeated trauma of rubbing against the cuffs, blood trickling down his arms. Classic protocols designed to strip him of any power to resist.

And it's working.

For the first time in many hours, he heard human sounds. Footsteps clanged along a metal stairwell somewhere near his cell, boots banging down the outside corridor. A door opened with a grating wail. His hood was yanked off, the clotted blood ripping like weak glue. Light assaulted him.

"That's the one," came a voice from the blinding radiance.

Before he could discern more than the blurred outlines of bulky forms in front of him, they slipped the hood tightly over his head again. Strong arms grasped his wrists, unlocked the shackles, and twisted his hands painfully behind his back, cuffing him again.

"Move!"

They shoved him forward harshly through the doorway. And kept shoving him forward until he ran his shoulder into a metal bar. His ankle felt a platform. *A stairway?*

"Climb!"

Awkwardly, blind, he stretched out his foot and planted on the first step. He ascended by sense of touch alone, slipping on several occasions only to find himself shoved upward from behind, once with the barrel of a weapon placed against his neck.

"Stop!"

He'd reached the top of the stairwell. Heavy vibrations on metal accompanied the sounds of more soldiers approaching.

"What the fuck, Harrison? Haven't you ever taken prisoners before? Cuff the hands in front, dumb-ass! How the hell are we going to link the chain?"

They freed his hands and moved them around to his belt buckle, cuffing him again with a heavy chain latched to the restraints. The first tug nearly sent him sprawling, but he stumbled forward, trying to keep slack in the chain.

"Keep up, traitor! Or you're going overboard to the sharks."

The roar of the sea overpowered him—the crash of waves against the hull of the boat. Wind kicked up wildly, spraying sea across his hood. They'd reached the deck.

Denied vision for so long, his other senses began to paint phantom portraits. He sensed something looming over them as they dragged him forward, images of high walls and cliffs forming in his mind. The wind blew from the opposite direction, blocked completely by something massive and tall, a thing so large it seemed to block the sounds of the waves and reflect it back into their faces. He began to perceive a deep throbbing as if building from within his bones themselves—a gigantic motor churning beneath the waves.

A loud crash startled him, and the deck shook.

"Walk!"

Pushed forward, he stepped off the deck of the ship and onto another metallic platform, a gangplank of some sort. It bridged the gap between the boat and something far larger, a sea-going island of metal approaching like the mouth of a cave.

He toppled down, the plank ending without warning and an empty space swallowing his foot. He stumbled onto a much more solid surface, the sound of movement and laughter above him.

"Enough!" came a commanding voice. "Get him to the brig!"

Arms hoisted Savas, then pushed him forward down a secession of stairwells, through a series of heavy doors sealing like airlocks, and finally into a tight space with grill-work for walls.

The brig.

Again they left him cuffed to the wall, the chain hanging heavily along his arms, hood still cloaking his vision and nearly suffocating him. He wondered if the others would be brought here as well, but he knew it unlikely. Protocol isolated terrorist leaders, interrogations conducted without the opportunity to communicate. Standard operating procedure for these types of renditions.

A creaking metal hatch groaned and several pairs of boots tromped toward his cell. Keys unlocked the door in front of him and someone yanked the hood off. He had to turn his face from the light and shut his eyes.

"Well, you son of a bitch, you look about as fucked up as you ought to right now."

A hand grasped his chin and jerked his face forward. Savas squinted into the painful glow, a chiseled jaw and cold blue eyes staring at him.

"And I can tell you right here, right now—it's going to get a hell of a lot worse. Real soon. We're gonna make you wish you'd never been born, never dreamed up in that diseased head of yours to betray your nation. And before we kill you, kill your scumbag friends as well, you're going to tell us every goddamned thing you know about this cybercriminal."

"Fawkes?" muttered Savas.

The man struck him with the back of his hand.

"Fawkes? Who the hell is that? *Lightfoote*, you bastard. Your cyberterrorist whore! The one who let that damn worm loose!"

Lightfoote? It didn't make sense. These men had it all wrong. But he knew better than to try to explain. The tribunal had made it clear —someone had engineered a witch-hunt. He spit blood and ground his teeth.

"Go to hell."

"Oh, sweet Mary Sue, we got ourselves a tough guy." The man snorted. "Well, boys, we're gonna have us a good time breaking this bronco." He leaned in and whispered to Savas. "And we got all the time in the world to explain things to you."

6

"THREE CARS HAVE pulled up outside, Francisco!" Houston held the Browning beside her temple, parting the yellowed curtains as she stared through the window. *Things are moving too fast!* Already a noose was closing on them. "Two vans. A black town car. They're pouring out like roaches, heading for the steps." She darted away from the window and ran to the center of the room.

They'd killed the lights. The musty brownstone in Harlem was strobed by headlight beams darting through the windows. She saw the broad form of Lopez drop a laptop into a backpack and drape it stiffly over his shoulders. *He's still in pain.* He picked up a pump-action shotgun from the floor, catching and holding her eyes for an instant. A sheen of pale skin gleamed as it moved through the light streaming through the window. Lightfoote stood beside him with a drawn pistol, bald head and piercings flashing.

"They'll send a few round the back, coordinate the entry," said Houston. "We've got thirty seconds."

Lightfoote checked the display on a smartphone. "Getting a signal from the sensors—back and front. Right on the money, Sara. Let's see if they're ready for this."

"Watch for debris!" cried Houston. *I never get the damn yields right!*

The three crouched behind overturned boxes and furniture. Dust from the long-abandoned building filled the air with fine snow. The front doors rattled violently from a sudden blow. Lopez raised a metallic box in one hand.

"Now!" cried Houston. She ducked as he pressed the button.

Two explosions rocked the building. The front door erupted in a fireball, launching wood and metal in all directions. Several windows near the entrance shattered, exploding outward. Poorly maintained sprinkler systems sputtered, rusty water haphazardly raining across the interior, smoke-stained rivulets running across the floor.

"Go!" yelled Houston. She leapt forward.

The three sprinted, weapons pointed toward the shattered doorway. Mangled bodies were strewn across the brownstone steps, blood black with soot, dripping like molasses to the street below. A driver gawked at them from one of the vans, the door half open, his body tense and frozen in shock.

Use it. Houston set herself, firing two shots before he could react, and he toppled to the ground. The door slammed in the other van. The engine coughed and raced as the driver gunned the accelerator, the gears popping loudly as he shifted. The van lurched forward.

A shotgun blast from Lopez burst the back tire. The van pitched as the driver tried to turn sharply. The right side elevated off the ground and the van flipped violently onto its roof. It landed with a shattering of window glass and crunching metal on the left side. The front end plowed into a lamppost. With a single beat of silence, a fire ignited in the engine.

An empty car waited beside the entrance. Either the driver had fled or been killed in the explosions. Houston waved them to the vehicle. *Did any survive the rear blast?* If so, they had only seconds. "I'll drive. Move!"

The three dashed down the steps and into the car. Houston in the driver's seat, Lopez and Lightfoote aiming their weapons out the rear windows. The car jumped forward with a squeal and raced into the streets of Harlem.

"Damn that was fast!" Houston gunned the engine and aimed for Harlem River Drive. "Backtrace said an hour?"

Lightfoote shouted from the back, the air rushing through the windows mangling her words. "Barely! The NSA is back. Their fingerprints are all over the trace. But that fast? That wasn't a general scan. We're their target—they *know!*" The waterfall of sound stopped as the back windows were shut.

"Jesus!"

Lopez grimaced and placed the shotgun on the floorboard. "That was a strike team. Serious players."

"But not after *you*," said Lightfoote. "They don't even know you two exist."

Houston nodded, steering roughly, the tires screeching as she ran a red light. The relative quiet felt unnatural, adrenaline still coursing through her veins. "I'm getting a little tired of running like this."

Lightfoote swung away from the window and set down her gun. "We're going to have to be a lot more careful. They *really* want this damn file."

"Then it's important," said Houston, darting onto the highway. Taillights flashed past her, horns blaring.

"Whatever's in it," said Lopez, "must be bigger than we can imagine. They've taken the FBI team captive. They're tracking us with the full power of the NSA, sending professionals after us. We need to figure out what it is we have."

Lightfoote sighed. "That's what I was trying to do, dammit!"

"Well, your hacker friends are going to have to work faster," said Lopez. "We barely got out of that."

Houston turned toward the Willis Avenue bridge. *I have to think clearly.* "I'm going to avoid the toll stations. Take us on I-87 into the Bronx. Disappear this car as soon as we can. Steal another one. Angel, we need to get you online again. You need to find this hacker collective."

"I've got to warn them," said Lightfoote. "If they tracked us, they can track them. They've got to take measures to prepare. Disappear and arm themselves. They're going to be risking their lives to do this."

"But will they?" asked Lopez.

Houston cursed as a delivery truck weaved in front of them. "Francisco, she's a hero in the hacker underground. You saw those chat rooms, the messages she got."

"People worship a hero from a distance. Not many want to be heroes when the bullets fly."

"We'll see," said Lightfoote. "Maybe not for the good of it, or for me. Maybe for the challenge of Fawkes's encryption. Something Big Brother wants us *not* to see. Maybe they want to see it as much as we do. Maybe they want to be the ones to spill the secret."

"Maybe," Lopez muttered.

"Either way," continued Lightfoote, "we need to come up with a new plan. Digital security for sure. We'll need every anonymous protocol around. We'll need to move frequently. No more than a few hours at any connection. We need decoy stations to mimic our profile, lock those down and have them waste manpower checking them out."

"And we need to distribute the file."

"Yes, get it out to every hacker with a functioning processor. Parallel processing. Together, we can crack it."

"You sound confident," said Houston. "How can you be so sure?"

Lightfoote stared forward into the red taillights in front of them.

"Because we have to."

7

SAVAS FELT HIMSELF scream again, but his body had been pushed far beyond conscious control. He could only react to the waves of torment and panic. The survival machine encasing his consciousness performed desperate actions shaped by millions of years of evolution.

The cry exploded from his lips without volition, drowned in the waterfall pouring into his lungs. Strapped to a wooden board, a partially permeable fabric tight over his mouth, only a fraction of the liquid penetrated, but it triggered thrashing and an adrenaline response. The rest spilled over his face, completing the illusion of submersion, dying, suffocating, and strangling to a final end. His muscles convulsed as he struggled against the restraints.

It ended and a boot plunged into his left side to cast him face first onto the wet metal. The impact registered as a small gnat in a hurricane of agony. Fabric fell from his mouth and he coughed violently, puttering out small sprays of water. Too little to have actually killed him, the volume still set all his physiology of imminent death into motion. He gasped for air.

"You're just making it harder on yourself. As well as the others," came the cold voice that had begun to haunt his dreams.

Savas coughed roughly. "Others. No. What—"

"How long will you make us work her over, Savas? Just tell us the truth and her pain can stop."

"I've told you everything!" He didn't recognize his own voice. The words were the cries of an asylum inmate.

"*Where* is Angel Lightfoote? Tell us and you can go. She can go. It's that easy."

Savas struggled to hold back tears.

"*Please*. I don't *know*."

"What was in the email? Tell us that then. Was it another worm you would use to attack the country?"

"We didn't *attack*."

Savas cried out as a boot toe speared him in the side. The kick lifted him off the floor, and he moaned.

"Stop insulting us. Do you think that mock tribunal is going to get you out of this? You'll be convicted, I have no doubt. But even if you aren't, there's no way—*no* way—you traitorous scum, that I'll let you leave this place alive. Do you understand? You aren't going to walk out of here after what you've done. Maybe, just maybe if you play ball, and help us track down these terrorists, your precious Rebecca might live."

"Please, don't hurt her. I've told you everything I know."

A hand reached down and pulled his head back by the hair.

"What is the Nash Criterion? What does it *mean?*"

"Don't. Know." He gasped. "Fawkes. Last email. Death trigger. No time."

The hand smashed his head into the metal grating. The room spun. He couldn't focus on the words. Strong arms dragged him from the room and down a short hallway, grated metal cages lining each side. Faceless forms slung him into one and he landed heavily on his shoulder, a stab of pain jolting him conscious.

A broad shape stood silhouetted in the doorway, the outlines of the man's face barely discernible. But the Voice—everything had mutated into a voice now. No eyes, no face, no person. Just a hateful Voice that meant pain and impossible requests. The Voice dragged him and others through hell and back, teasing them with relief that came in the form of unscalable mountains, nonexistent answers, locks that could never be opened, and pain that would never end.

"This is really going nowhere," said the Voice. "It's time you thought carefully about giving us some of those answers, agent Savas. And soon. Your friends don't have much time left."

"I told you *everything.*"

"You can do more. And I know just the ticket. We'll resume our discussions soon and we'll let you in on some of our work with the others. Maybe we'll let you sit in and watch as we work on your sweet Rebecca? Would you like to see her?"

"No, please—"

"I can see it would mean a lot to you. We don't usually have an option like this for difficult prisoners. Can you imagine all the work we put in only to have some motherfucker like you die on us? What a waste of our time! But bring in a child, or lover, and these tough men break like china. I think you're one of those men, Savas. I think when you've seen enough of what we'll do to her, you'll shatter like a plate and tell us what we want to know."

"No, please! I'll tell you now! Everything, I promise. Whatever you want to know." He would lie. He would make up any story. Find one they could accept. Anything to stop them.

"Now, that's very helpful of you, John. But it's just lying desperation. I've seen that, too. No, no—only when you're truly broken will you skip the lies and get to the truth. I just hope that point comes before your dear Rebecca is too damaged to be worth anything to you anymore."

"No!"

Another kick to the face cut short his scream. The door slammed shut as he rolled away from it, nauseous and dizzy.

Footsteps and laughter poured like acid over his fading consciousness.

8

FRANK MILLER STOOD upright, his shirt removed to reveal enormous musculature. Wires were taped to heaving pectorals that dripped with sweat. His arms were pulled out to the sides, clamped tightly. His pants stained with sweat and urine, blood dripping from his lips, teeth marks in the torn flesh. He panted with his head cast down.

A man beside him turned a knob, generating a throbbing hum. Miller screamed, his entire body convulsing. His eyes rolled back involuntarily in his head. The electrical jolt ended quickly, but it demanded a high price. Miller slumped forward heavily, the restraints on his broad arms groaning.

The blue-eyed man stepped beside him and pulled his head back by the hair.

"We've got juice to do this every day for the rest of your life. Right now the damage is minimal, whatever the pain. But the more we fry you, the more cells will burst in your tissues, the more nerves will be damaged. First, you'll lose feeling in your extremities, your fingers and hands. Coordination. Then eyesight. Brain damage is next. Agent Miller, after all you've done, this is hardly the way to end your life."

Miller drooled to the floor, his mouth twitching. Words slurred with spit and blood escaped as a whisper: *"Fuck* you."

The inquisitor sighed and rubbed his temples. He looked toward the man at the controller.

"Call it a day, Rice. The specialist arrived an hour ago. Tell him he's up."

"Yes, sir," said the man, exiting the room quickly.

"I don't have time for heroes, Miller. I need results, and I need them now. Fortunately, technology is on my side."

The soldier Rice returned, the door groaning as he opened it. A bald, thin man followed him with two large duffel bags, his expression detached.

"Ah, here he is. Dr. Kuriyan." The blue-eyed man examined the bags. "That's all you need?"

"Yes," Kuriyan said, removing wires and electrodes, drills, scalpels, and power sources. "Designed for any environment. You already have him immobilized, so I'll just add this."

He removed a metallic skull cap encased in a cage. Sizing up Miller, he nodded.

"He's big, but it will fit."

"You've come highly recommended."

The visitor plugged in power supplies and set his tools along a small table. "I'll need ten minutes to prep him, once he's properly restrained. Once I've located the brain regions and tested the voltages in the tissue, you can proceed. He'll answer truthfully anything you ask. Cognitive function will be minimally impaired." He looked over the wires connected to the prisoner. "Assuming it hasn't already been. I'll need all that disconnected."

"Rice—do what he says."

The soldier nodded, eyes wide. He rushed to remove the wires from Miller's chest and arms, ripping the tape, tearing hair and skin in the process. Miller didn't flinch.

"He's nearly unconscious," muttered Kuriyan as he fiddled with the skull cap. "My technique is far more useful with a prisoner in his right mind."

"Your technique is here to get a job done. We need information yesterday. We expect you to get it."

Kuriyan frowned and continued to adjust the equipment. "All right. I'll need you to hold his head against the board," he said, indicating the metal stand on which Miller was strapped.

The blue-eyed man nodded and the soldier grasped Miller's head and pushed it backward.

"Easy, his muscles are slack. Don't want to break his neck. Keep him facing forward—yes, like that. Good. Now," he stepped forward with the caged skull cap. "I'm going to fit this over his head, clamp it to the metal behind, and then tighten it over his skull." He scanned the room. "I'll need that chair to stand on."

The blue-eyed man pushed a metal chair loudly across the floor.

Kuriyan stepped on it, ducking slightly under the low ceiling, and raised the cage over Miller's head.

"Hold him steady. *There.*"

Miller's eyes flashed and his head darted to the right. His forehead smashed Rice, who stumbled against the wall, holding his eye and cursing.

The leather clamp on Miller's right arm groaned and popped, the material failing as he brought his arm around and struck the visitor in the mouth, sending him careening from the chair. Rice had regained his footing and charged, but Miller swung his arm again, connecting violently with the soldier's head. Rice's head jerked backward, eyes empty and unfocused, before he plunged downward. His head struck the side of the metal table, wrenching his neck to the side and he lay unmoving on the ground.

Miller reached out for the blue-eyed man, fighting against the remaining restraints, fingers clawing the air in front of him.

Three shots roared off the small room's metal walls as the interrogator fell away from Miller's grasp, gun in hand. The first shot sent sparks and metal shards flying behind Miller. The other two buried themselves deep in Miller's chest. Blood misted into the air and spilled down Miller's torso.

"Shit!" cried the blue-eyed man.

He moved quickly to the fallen soldier, keeping a careful eye on Miller. He placed his hand at Rice's throat, checking for a pulse. He pulled it away scowling and glared at Miller.

"He's dead, you son of a bitch. Broke his damn neck."

Miller gasped and choked, blood frothing at his mouth, eyes swimming.

"You better not fucking die on me yet."

He kept his weapon trained on Miller and circled around him to the crumpled form of the doctor.

"Doctor Kuriyan," he said. "Are you all right?"

The doctor groaned and stumbled against the wall, bracing one arm against the corner. The other cradled his jaw. He pulled his hand away, tissue and teeth floating in a red pool.

"Jesus," said the interrogator. "Go get cleaned up, and send a medical crew in here." The hatch clanged open, and several soldiers with raised weapons entered.

"Sir, we heard shots!"

The blue-eyed man waved them away. "Get our visitor some attention. And send a crew down here to save this motherfucker." Miller continued to thrash weakly before them. "Tell them I want him alive and conscious long enough so the doc can drill into that stupid skull of his and place his wires."

He turned to them, holstering his gun, eyes frigid.

"I want some fucking answers, goddammit!"

9

A RUSTED SUN set through the clouds over vandalized cars and buses littering the streets of Queens. A lone figure stepped around a corner, a swollen backpack over his shoulders, two heavy bags in each hand. Dark sunglasses and a newsboy hat concealed his features.

Lopez scanned the deserted street in front of him and placed the bags on the ground. Reaching around his oddly flowing robes, he removed a handgun and checked it, replacing the firearm quickly. He took up the heavy duffels again and made his way cautiously across the street.

As he approached a towering apartment complex, he made his way down a tight alley filled with piles of rotting garbage, the reek potent even in the cold December air. Near an overflowing dumpster he walked up to a small door that angled sideways, the hinges ripped from the wall. He kicked softly and it swung from a remaining hinge near the top. He entered.

He moved directly to a dim stairway and descended quickly, breath strained and broad shoulders bowed by the weight he carried. Three flights down the stairwell ended at a door with a shattered EXIT sign, one bulb still flickering. Glass crunched on the ground under his feet. He placed the bags down again and removed the pistol, opened the door quickly, and spun toward a dark hallway with the firearm aimed in front of him.

He saw no one in the corridor. Grabbing the two bags with one hand, he grunted from the pain to his shoulder, but kept his weapon ready, shuffling awkwardly forward. He passed a janitor's closet, the door smashed open, broken items inside strewn haphazardly. He dropped the bags in front of a small door with a faded label reading: TELCOM CLOSET.

He rapped a brief pattern on the door and it opened to reveal Houston's piercing blue eyes.

"Damn, Francisco," Houston said. "*Three hours.* You had me scared. We need to find chargers for these phones."

"Tomorrow." He entered quickly, dragged the bags inside, and dropped the backpack on the ground with a loud impact. Houston locked the door behind him.

The three of them repositioned awkwardly in the cramped room, the space hardly larger than a suburban wardrobe closet. A single incandescent bulb lit the space in a soft yellow, revealing a spaghetti of wires spilling from opened pipes above them. Many of the wires ended at several computers placed in a row along a rusted table. Lightfoote danced around the laptops like a grandmaster playing simultaneous games of chess.

"She getting anywhere?" Lopez asked.

"Angel is in the room and can hear gossip about her," said Lightfoote, not taking her eyes from the screens or fingers from the keyboards.

Houston smiled. "Yes. Brief you in a minute. She did get a message out to York. Had to hack through a bunch of defense computers. If she's picking up, York will get the last coordinates from Cohen's phone. A brief message about what we saw."

"She owes us one."

"She does. Meanwhile—what's the loot?"

Lopez grunted. "Just about everything is gone out there. People fled and took out almost every shop. I'll be damned if I know where they all went, or when they're coming back." He opened the duffel bags. Metal disks glinted softly in the dim light. "Cans. Mostly vegetables. Some fruits. Guess people don't like to eat healthy when civilization is collapsing around them."

"It'll do," she said. "I'm famished."

He dragged the backpack beside her.

"But there is *this*."

He unzipped it, and a pile of boxes spilled out of the bursting fabric and slapped heavily on the ground. One opened and numerous bullets rolled across the floor.

"Now we're talking." Houston kissed him and smiled. "How the hell did you find it?"

"They've cleaned out the gun shops—I wonder how many of those idiots end up shooting each other? But they didn't think to look for storage. Or maybe they couldn't get through the locks. Big megastores have shelves of ammunition and some firearms. No weapons we don't have. Lots we wouldn't care for. But the ammunition—we're low after that raid."

Houston pulled a box out of the bag. "Holy shit, Francisco—.45 ACP?"

He smiled. "Yeah, I figured you'd be glad to see those."

"You bet your ass." She removed her Browning. "Mama's got some milk for you, baby boy. Thank God. Now I won't have to be shooting one of those plastic toys people insist on calling guns."

"Hey, Glock's a good friend," muttered Lightfoote, clacking the return key emphatically and looking in their direction. "Might save your life someday."

Houston shook her head. "Maybe. What now, FBI girl?"

"Now, we wait. I've done all I can. We've got more bandwidth here than we can use. The entire complex seems abandoned."

"Those gangs didn't count?" said Lopez.

"Not in my book. Not enough fight. Anyway, no traffic on the inbound cables. So, I've routed the main lines to the laptops. The data is out, the hacker groups have it. I sent it through a maze of servers and TOR networks. The NSA will track it down eventually, but maybe not before we get what we need and can get the hell out of here."

"What we need is that file decrypted," said Lopez.

"Right. Whatever Fawkes did, it's good but not unbreakable. Patronizing bastard wanted it just tough enough to test us. Make sure we're *worthy*."

"What about the NSA? They've got the file presumably?" asked Houston.

Lightfoote nodded. And collapsed on a plastic chair. "Definitely. They just needed to raid my accounts. I didn't have time to wipe anything. And there are ways around that, too."

Houston stared at the rows of numbers running wildly across the screens in front of them. "So how the hell is some group of distributed hackers going to out-muscle the computational power of the NSA?"

"They can't," said Lightfoote. "Our only hope is to be smarter. More clever."

"And if we aren't?"

"Then they're going to get the information first," answered Lightfoote. "It's clear they want it. They're willing to kill for it. Even if we do break the encryption before them, they'll still get there eventually. So, if we get lucky, we're going to have a small window. We'll need to act fast."

Lopez exhaled. "And do what? We have no idea what's in that file. Maybe it's a final, insane joke from Fawkes to troll us once and for all."

Lightfoote shook her head. "I don't think so. I told you: I think I knew him in a way few did, even if we only spoke a few times. His personality stains his code, his worm. He's much too serious about all this. That file has something radioactive. Fawkes was killed for it. Our friends were snatched for it."

Houston smirked. "And we were almost killed for it, too, Francisco. She's right."

Lopez looked over to the computer screens.

"Then I hope these hackers know what they're doing."

10

THE HATCH OPENED and a figure plunged onto the floor. Long brown hair spilled in clumped knots to conceal her face. Her hands were splayed out in front of her and bound, and she struggled to use them to prop herself up. Soiled clothes hung from her frame.

"Get up, Agent Cohen," came a cold voice from behind her.

Several men entered the room alongside a short-cropped older man with ice-blue eyes. He gestured to the floor and the men stooped down and dragged Cohen to her feet. Two women stood in front of her in lab coats, a large flat-screen monitor hanging from the wall to their left. Numerous sharp objects glinted on a table beside them. They looked like surgical tools.

"Put her on the table."

The men did as instructed and tossed her harshly onto a metal slab mounted in the center of the room. Cohen groaned from the impact, hair still obscuring her face.

"We're reaching the limits of our tolerance with you and your people, Agent Cohen," said the cold voice. "We need you to understand that you don't have much more time. The tribunals have been a circus act, a show to convince you and your husband that cooperation is mandated. Those sessions failed. So, you've forced our hand. We can't let your seditious plans continue."

"We aren't traitors." She leaned forward weakly. Her eyes burned through the matted strands of her hair. "We aren't terrorists, either!"

The interrogator nodded and one of the men beside her struck her in the mouth. Cohen rolled hard on the table away from the blow, moaning. The man on the other side shoved her back in position.

"Your tired refrain angers me."

"You're monsters," she gasped.

"Do you think you're being mistreated?"

Fearful eyes stared back from the table.

"Perhaps you don't understand just how serious we are."

He nodded to a man standing guard by the door, who opened the hatch and called down the hallway. A rough scraping echoed outside. Someone was dragging a heavy object across the floor. Two burly men wedged themselves and a third figure through the hatch. They tossed a body to the floor.

Cohen screamed.

"*Oh, God*. No!"

The naked body of Frank Miller lay prone on the metal floor. Clotted and dried blood caked his torso and head. The hair had been shaved from a portion of the scalp, and three large holes had been drilled into the skull. A coating of frost melted along the grayed skin.

"No, Frank. I'm so sorry."

"Agent Miller was most uncooperative. Attacked and killed a good soldier, in fact." The cruel eyes leaned toward her. "This will be your fate soon. It will be the fate of your dear husband, Agent Savas, if we do not learn the whereabouts of your accomplices. There isn't going to be any escape. Your trick with the phone was clever. But it's over. The device destroyed. No one is coming to save you."

Tears ran down and smeared the dirt on her face.

"No. Please. I've told you everything. I'll tell you anything. I'm not holding anything back."

"That may well be true, Agent Cohen. Perhaps you were not privy to all the information. But I can't take that chance. Instead, I have found a way to make you most useful to our efforts."

Cohen blinked as the monitor across from her lit up. "John?" A guttural sound escaped her lips. "What have they done to you?"

The battered visage of Savas blinked in stunned silence, an eye swollen shut, the same side of his face cut and covered with blood. His slurred words poured from split lips.

"Oh God, *no*," came the voice from the screen. "You bastards— no! Don't do this! Please!"

The men alongside Cohen strapped her arms and legs tightly to the table.

"*Stop!*"

"Two bodies, Agent Savas, as you can see from your cell monitor. One dead." He walked up to Cohen and held up a large hunting knife, laying the edge near her throat. "The other still alive for now." He ran the edge slowly down her torso, over her breasts, to her crotch. He smiled at the camera mounted in the flat screen. "And still mostly unsullied."

"They're in Harlem!" screamed Savas, weeping. "It's a safe house. They're hiding out there!"

"John, no. Don't." Tears fell from her eyes.

"Oh, but he has to, Agent Cohen. That's what I'm counting on."

Savas continued in a high pitch. "Please. I'll tell you where it is. Where they're hiding. Everything you need to know. Let her go!"

The man spun the knife in his hand.

"Sadly, Agent Savas, that is not enough."

"*What?* Why?"

"You're too late with that information. We already discovered that lurking place. We nearly had them, but they escaped. Killing, you might want to know, several of our people. We will need more from you. Where else would they go? How can we track them?"

"That's all I know! It's the only place! There isn't any other way to track them! We used burner phones. They'll be in hiding!"

"Oh, this is terribly unfortunate." He shook his head sadly. "I am inclined to believe you. I think the china has shattered. What a tragedy you had not told me this earlier, before they could escape." He frowned. "But you had to be a tough guy."

He nodded to a man next to him, who moved toward Cohen's feet.

"These men are not soldiers, Agent Savas. Do you know why?"

Savas only stared in panic at the man.

"Most of the soldiers aren't good at this. They follow orders, but only up to a point."

"No, wait!"

"But these men," he said, "have no such qualms. They are most useful when we need to go beyond certain points." His blue eyes shown as he rolled the words off his tongue.

"I can work with you. I can help you locate them, serve as bait. *Anything.* Please!"

"Yes, Agent Savas. I'm sure you will. Once you are convinced.

When you have watched us hurt her day after day, it will seal your *honest* cooperation."

"I told you already about Harlem! I'll cooperate!"

"A sudden break. Emotional with no time to override." He shook his head. "But tracking them will take time. Weeks, perhaps. During that time, in the hours at night when you can't sleep? When you remember what has happened to you, your friend Miller here, your wife? No, you will devise some trick. We will lose time and more men." He walked up to the screen and stared coldly at it. "No, agent Savas. Too much time for you to plot. Unless you are utterly broken."

The other man reached the top of the table.

Cohen spoke firmly through tears.

"John, just close your eyes. Don't watch. *Please.*"

The blue-eyed man smiled.

"Even the blind can hear."

11

"I DIDN'T WANT to be here," said the rich baritone. "Usually the last president has to make this important transition, but with that unexpected death, well, I'll have to do." He nodded to his reflection in the window. "This way you'll trust them. They've found it smooths things significantly."

The train sped through the underground tunnel, the absence of Secret Service officers only one of many factors unnerving York. She turned toward the former president, his frame slouched and angled in the plush chairs, his gaze unfocused through the window at the blurred stone walls speeding past.

"Trust who, Barack? What the hell is going on?"

"I think we're almost there," said Obama, standing awkwardly as the car swayed. The train decelerated rapidly. He motioned to York. "You'll get off here."

She stared through the window as the brakes hissed, the cabin coming to a complete stop. "Here? We aren't at the terminal point. We're in the middle of the damn tunnel! How do we get off here?"

Obama smiled wanly. "You'll see. Come on."

The doors opened, and she followed him out of the car numbly. A small ledge rose over the tracks, a set of steps rising from it. A metal door gleamed at the top of the stairway.

"This isn't in the maps."

"Retinal scan will get you in," Obama said. "You're lucky—you should've seen the digs they had when I was sworn in. This is Madison Avenue." Again the weak smile. "It's going to seem impossible, Elaine," he said, looking down the length of the train as it curved around the tunnel. "It's like growing up, except doing it again later in life. You have to give up a lot of childish ideas that aren't true. Santa Claus. The Tooth Fairy. Of, by, and for the People. You have to accept the adult world and work with what it is, or—well, or you won't make it in that world." He put a hand on her shoulder. "The train won't leave until you go in. Good luck."

She watched in shock as he turned around and boarded the train, the automatic doors closing behind him. York glanced down the tunnel walls, along the tracks and train cars, and finally back to the doorway before her. She half-believed she was dreaming.

"Maybe it's a stroke," she whispered, slowly ascending the stairs to the gray metal door.

A lens with a red light glinted down at her.

"So, Star Chamber—all this and you weren't prepared for a short woman?"

She rose on her toes and stared into the glass circle in front of her. Seconds later bolts disengaged with clangs and the door swung inward. York stepped forward into a dim chamber that turned pitch as the outer door slammed shut behind her. The locks sealed loudly.

The walls shuddered, she felt her stomach drop, and the floor plunged downward. As she fell, her eyes adjusted to the chamber, noting metallic walls devoid of instrumentation or insignia. Void of information.

Gravity tugged heavily on her as the lift came to a stop. The door behind her hissed, and she spun around to see an opening into a room glowing with blue light.

Straightening her blouse, she exhaled sharply, staring forward with determination.

She walked through the doorway.

12

"No!"

SAVAS LUNGED forward with all his strength, but the two guards on his right and left held his shoulders down. His arms were tied harshly behind him, lashed to the chair. His feet were bound at the ankles. He could not stop the events in the other room. Forcing him to watch, the men beside him held his chin up to the screen.

Blackness. The screen popped and fell dark. A deep hum dropped through the ship in pitch until it fell out of human detection. Bass notes shook through him.

"What the fuck?" One of the guards beside him cursed, stumbling in the darkness, tripping on a leg of the chair, his body impacting the unseen wall.

"That was the reactor, Burton."

"Nuclear powered ships don't lose power, dumbass! And we've got rows of batteries. Power's cut somewhere."

"Where's the backup?"

"I don't know! Shit! Can't find the damn door. Here!"

A metallic grating screeched and a rush of air entered the room. Savas still could see nothing except the faint afterglow of the monitor. No light entered from the outside corridor. He heard muffled shouts and explosions from above.

"Holy shit! We're under attack!"

A light leapt forward highlighting the barrel of a gun.

"Burton, mount your weapon-light! It's all we have!"

The other soldier followed suit and both rushed down the hallway.

Savas closed his eyes and strained to hear. The sounds of fighting intensified. He felt the boat slowing, yawing clockwise as the engines remained quiet. He yanked at the restraints but got nowhere, and slumped in the chair in frustration. Their one chance of escape and he couldn't take advantage of it!

A thunderous blast shook him. Metal shards flew through the

hallway, clanging and slamming against the walls. Acrid smoke spilled into his room, followed by the sound of rushing boots.

A bright light shone into his eyes from the doorway. Completely blinded, Savas turned his face away, squinting.

"They're here! I've got Savas!" cried the voice with the light.

"Found the others!" came a muted voice down the corridor.

The man pulled out a stick and cracked it, and a bright blue light filled the room. He tossed it on the floor in front of Savas and switched off his flashlight.

"What the hell?" asked Savas.

The man dropped to his knee behind the chair. "We're a rescue team. Seal assault squad. We're here to get you *out!*" Savas felt a hard tug on his wrists and heard the restraints tear. His hands were loose. The man bent over to his ankles and cut the ties with a large blade, freeing him.

Savas stood up and almost fell, his knees buckling. The man caught him from behind.

"Can you walk?"

"Hell yes."

He willed himself forward. His muscles screamed, but he forced them to move, the motion and adrenaline quickly loosening the tightness.

Cold metal touched his hand. The soldier had placed a gun there.

"We might be shooting our way out, Agent."

He stumbled into the hallway. Above, the chaos continued: explosions and the sounds of aircraft and heavy guns firing. Two more soldiers stood in front of them. They were dressing a woman.

"Rebecca!"

Her head turned as he limped forward. They embraced and he wept, holding her tightly to him.

"John, no time," she said, pulling back, tears in her eyes. "We've got to move fast."

"FBI man," came the clipped voice of one of the Seals. "Off with the shoes and pull these over you. Now!"

He didn't have time to think or understand. The man handed him an oversized suit. It felt synthetic. A similar dark material covered Cohen and she held swimming flippers under her arm. The men pushed them forward as she zipped up the suit.

"You're going to go straight up the ladders. If we still have it secured, it will take you to a lower deck, near water. SDVs are there waiting with drivers. Don't hesitate. Jump in. We've got only minutes."

Another set of explosions rocked the ship. The soldier speaking to him smiled.

"At least air support is giving them something to chew on."

They reached the ladders. Cohen climbed above him, racing for the top. Savas followed closely behind.

"Rebecca, the men—"

"Not now, John. Please. They're dead."

He heard the strain in her voice. He closed his eyes and climbed.

They stepped onto the deck as salt water sprayed over them. Rough waves battered the hull, the ship no longer under power to steer. Fires flicked above as wounded men screamed over the gunfire.

"My God," Savas whispered. "It's an aircraft carrier."

The enormous expanse of a flight deck loomed several stories above him. A Seal shoved a mask into his hand and helped him fit it over his head, another strapping flippers on his feet. The man shouted through the turmoil.

"Dive in toward the SDV!" he screamed, pointing below at a dark shape. "They'll hook you up. Do what they say! Stay calm!"

The man pushed Savas forward. He saw Cohen leap into the night air and plunge into the water below. Grinding his teeth, he stepped off the deck. The sounds of battle funneled into a point over his head, and a great, wet maw opened below him, wind and waves drowning out the battle above.

His feet smacked the surface and the cold water enveloped him. Arms pulled him against a black hull and he felt someone grab his head and attach something to the back of the mask. Stale air began to flow into it.

A hand pointed to the hull, and Savas saw an opening to a hollow interior. Brown hair billowed from within as Cohen moved inside, out of his sight. He kicked with the powerful flippers and approached what looked like an oversized torpedo. Seals helped him inside and followed behind him.

He floated to the back of the chamber alongside Cohen. Bubbles erupted from behind her as she breathed, her eyes focused intensely into his. He grasped her outstretched hand.

The door lumbered shut, but the water remained, along with two Navy Seals accompanying them. Not a submarine, the interior remained flooded for the duration, air supplied by the tanks hooked up to their masks. The craft's acceleration pushed them backward. Cohen leaned her mask against his and closed her eyes.

13

He lost all track of time and sense of direction in the cramped submersible. But he didn't care at that moment. Just to be next to Cohen again, to have escaped that hell-hole—he couldn't process the miracle. He felt grateful. Delivered. They held onto each other.

Part of his mind continued to race. Who had sent these soldiers? Why had they turned on their countrymen? And who had kidnapped them in the first place, whisking them out to sea on an island-sized aircraft carrier?

He had no answers. He began to obsess about pursuit, a panic building that somehow the cold man with the voice would return, strap him down, make him scream. The carrier had seemed badly damaged and incapacitated. Had it remained so? Were small ships sent to hunt them down? He doubted this submersible could stay underwater for prolonged periods of time. Where were they headed? He stumbled from dreamscape to dreamscape.

A soldier in front of him spoke into his mask. The soldier beside him answered silently and looked in their direction, motioning with his hand to the door. Savas glimpsed a communications setup in his suit, but surrendered to fatigue and ignored it. He simply nodded back.

The other Seal engaged the mechanism and the side door opened to blackness. Savas and Cohen followed the two men outside the craft, swimming awkwardly and trying to keep up, beams from their helmet lamps strobing the water. The soldiers often doubled back to help them along.

Above, Savas began to catch a faint glow. A diffuse radiation supplemented the helmet lamps. Perhaps the moon or artificial lights. He couldn't be sure. He began to make out shapes in the water around him.

A wall.

In front of the two soldiers, a sheer rock face loomed. The men took no heed and swam straight for it. Savas and Cohen flailed forward, a dark circle growing in the surface before them.

A tunnel. Broad enough to allow them to swim inside, but too narrow for the submersible. Savas looked behind them. The craft had disappeared. They were on their own and headed into the bowels of a cliff.

As they passed within the opening, Savas saw that it was manmade. Too round, devoid of the growths and imperfections of natural formations, his headlamp revealed telltale evidence of boring machines. Someone had dug these tunnels. For what purpose he could not guess.

The Seals ahead turned in their direction. A flash of light from their headlamps pierced the darkness. The FBI agents had lagged behind, and the soldiers waved them on. A current pushed outward from the tunnel like a tide, dragging like gravity as they tried to continue inward. Their pace was slowing. They were tiring. Savas prayed they did not have far to go.

After some minutes, the soldiers stopped ahead. As Cohen and Savas caught up, he saw that the passage split four-ways. The two men discussed the different tunnels animatedly, gesturing in each direction. *Wonderful.* He saw a blue light flash from each of their helmets and what appeared to be a screen superimposed on the glass. *A frogman's heads-up display?* He hoped they had a map for these tunnels to reference. *How much oxygen is left?*

After several minutes of watching the back and forth, Savas saw them come to an agreement, settling on the rightmost tunnel. Again the soldiers waved them forward. The marathon swim continued, exhaustion beginning to take a severe toll. Cohen struggled, her eyes downcast and unfocused. His own breath filled the inside of his mask like some elephant's gasping. They couldn't go on much more.

Ahead, a shaft of light dove into the water. The soldiers aimed right for it, their pace accelerating. Savas felt his heart leap, adrenaline coursing through his veins. *The last push.*

The tunnel opened into a wide chamber, multiple other passageways underwater embedded around them. But the soldiers ignored the other tunnels and began to swim upward, toward the light. Savas grabbed Cohen's hand. Her face was pale, but her eyes glowed with hope. They kicked upward together, the current gone, the final burst of energy giving them the power to keep pace with the Seals.

The four of them broke through to the surface, artificial light reflecting off the ripples and partially blinding them. An enormous domed roof arched above them. Around the pool of water ran a stone walkway. Doors and passageways opened in different directions away from the chamber.

As his eyes adjusted, he saw figures lining the pool—soldiers, weapons in their hands, aimed in their direction. In the middle of the group of men stood a short woman, her silver hair contrasting with the black body armor she wore.

The Seals urged them forward. They covered the short distance to the water's edge, and with the help of several soldiers above managed to drag their bodies and equipment out of the water. Feeble and nearly helpless on land, others helped them out of the wetsuits, two female soldiers covering Cohen's naked form in a robe. Savas stood with trembling legs, his soiled clothes, suit, mask, and air tank at his feet. Soaked and dripping, he shivered in the crisp air.

The gray-haired woman walked forward, her gaze stern as it assessed them. She placed a hand on Cohen's shoulder as she spoke:

"Agents Savas and Cohen. I'm honored to meet you. I only wish the circumstances had been different."

"Ms. President," whispered Savas, his fatigue nearly overwhelming.

Cohen smiled wanly. "Thank you. I thought we were lost. Worse than lost. How did you find us?"

"We'll explain more soon. Right now let's get you two looked at and off your feet." She paused. "Looks like you missed the luxury accommodations."

Savas stared dumbfounded at the subterranean space, the military men, and the woman before them. *Could I be hallucinating?*

"Ms. President, please. Where are we? What is this?"

She smiled from one side of her mouth.

"Welcome to the Presidency in Exile." Her eyebrows arched. "Seven stories below the streets of New York City."

"Below New York?" he said, his eyes straying upward to the

arching supports of the towering ceiling.

"Welcome to the underworld."

14

SAVAS SAT DOWN next to Cohen outside the medical facility. They were dressed in borrowed fatigues, soldiers donating whatever they had available. For the first time in what felt like years, they were left alone. He stared at her in awe. The quiet and stillness transfigured her familiar form. She dimmed the world around him, infinitely valuable. He reached out and squeezed her hand.

"Always thought you'd look good in gear," she said, smiling.

Self-consciously, he examined the camouflage patterning, the baggy shirt sagging around his midsection. He rubbed the thick stubble on his cheeks.

"I don't get the luxury of making everything I wear look good," he said, raising his eyebrows toward her. "But thanks."

She inhaled sharply, staring into space. "We just left him there."

Savas closed his eyes. He wasn't ready to face the losses. *More losses.* A price for service that now rose beyond anything he could justify. "Yeah. I know."

"Did you see what they did? I mean, why?"

He opened his eyes but was unable to make eye contact. "I don't know, Rebecca."

"And JP? He was wounded in the firefight at the Bureau. Anything?"

"Still no word. Not sure he was even taken to the ship. He would have needed serious medical attention."

Cohen shuddered. "Just so they could torture him later?" She glanced over his bruised and swollen face. "What did they do to you?"

He squeezed her hand again. The guilt that he'd betrayed good people burned inside. *In the end, I was weak.* "Nothing good. But I'm okay. Docs say no lasting damage. The bastards knew how to work it slowly."

She stared off into the distance. "Is there nothing they wouldn't do? How can they be soldiers?"

"I'm not sure all of them were. Some were contractors. That blue-eyed monster, for one." Cohen inhaled sharply. Savas wrapped his arm around her. "What they did to Frank, his head—well, Sara had told me about something like that."

"I remember," Cohen shivered. "The CIA agent. They used some kind of brain stimulation to get him to talk."

"Yeah," said Savas, rolling his pained shoulder. "They found a dead doc. Traced him to some shady military contractors. Apparently it's the new thing. Electrodes in the brain. Turn off free will. Get answers. Less blood."

"Didn't seem like less blood to me. They *butchered* him, John. Threw him down for us to see. To hurt us. Break us. Before they—" She stopped and held her hand to her mouth.

"Stop. Slowly. Not all at once."

She nodded, holding back tears. "Right." She looked around the room. "*Jesus*. Now what?"

A firm voice answered from behind them.

"Now you get to choose." York walked in with several aides and military men.

"Choose what?" asked Cohen.

"Whose side you want to be on in this conflict, and what you want to do about it."

They stood around a map of the United States. It was displayed on a table in the middle of the subterranean lair's enormous operations center. Soldiers manned computers and communication equipment, tracked troops and intel, and spoke into headsets to contacts unknown. Along the sides of what looked to be a retrofitted subways station, wall-sized flatscreen monitors surrounded them, displaying a bewildering series of images from satellite downlinks to war-game simulations.

On the LCD screen before them, the nation glowed in blue and gray. The East Coast and parts of the Deep South shown with a gray hue. The map was colored blue in the center, a bright star flashing in the state of Colorado.

"General Hastings has most of the Navy under his thumb, except for several contingents of Special Forces that stayed loyal to my office. Fortunately, almost no one knows about this facility. It was scheduled to be decommissioned, a relic of the Cold War."

Savas shook his head. "What is this place then?"

"A local Mount Weather or NORAD. Was once intended as a governmental bunker in case of nuclear attack. A huge network of abandoned tunnels and water stations were converted to the purpose. Telecommunications, arms, food stores. You name it. It's in disrepair, as I said, headed for the chopping block, but we've gotten it up and running. Thank God the air filtration systems still worked or it would have been over before it began."

"Why won't Hastings look for you here?"

"He might eventually. That's why we can't stay long. But it's obscure and buried in archives. All but forgotten. Except for us old timers. Not high on the military priority list either, deemed too vulnerable to attack. Which it is."

"Comforting."

She looked him in the eye. "We're on a knife's edge. Every day we stay here brings the noose closer. But every day rallies more to our cause. We've managed to muster a good part of the 2nd Infantry Division from Fort Lewis. Those that didn't join Hastings's ranks, that is. I have a small army at my disposal."

"Can we trust them? How do we know loyalties?"

York frowned. "We don't. That's the hard truth. But we're doing all the PR we can. Trying to win hearts and minds. But we don't have any problems Hastings doesn't. Going to be brother against brother."

"It doesn't sound real," muttered Savas.

"The fight is up there, too," she said, gesturing toward the ceiling. "Propaganda wars before the blood is shed in earnest. People are taking sides. But the real battle will be somewhere in the middle," she said, indicating the map. "We have the Rockies, NORAD. They have the coast. Someday soon, we're going to meet up between these points. Before that, we need to get to NORAD. We need to run our campaign from there. And that's where we're headed if we can make it."

"Why risk it?" asked Cohen.

Savas saw that she was in analytical mode, but his mind refused to function when he stared at her. She still wore a blanket from the medical center. Small in the cavernous space, a petite brunette wrapped in layers of fabric, her form called to him. *Vulnerable.* He struggled to process the conversation.

"Because here, I'm just as much a prisoner as you were on that ship. It's a matter of time before they find us. Maybe days. We've secured a lot of machinery, troops. We have air attack options from several locations. We'll move soon."

"Air options," said Cohen. "I heard jets over the ship."

"Not jets. Cruise missiles. Immune to the worm. A great irony—modernizing our aircraft, we left them vulnerable. The best attack and transport craft are either grounded or too unreliable in the air. Each side is racing to fix that, but we don't have the time to wait."

Savas turned to York, the president's words focusing his attention. "Wait? For what?"

"My best strategy would be to hop a transport and fly to Colorado. But my advisors say it's too risky. Too few working planes, too few air traffic systems. There'd be no escort. Some surface-to-air missiles and it's over. Since we can't wait for the air, we move on the ground."

Cohen stared sharply at the President. "Why did you come?"

"Here? I told you. It was the only—"

"No," she interrupted. "The boat. *Us.*" Savas heard the restrained emotions in Cohen's voice as she continued. "You're running for your life while the nation crumbles. Why did you come? How did you find us?"

York smiled and put her arm around Cohen. "Because you have some friends in high places. Actually, I don't know where they are, but they reached me. Hacked into our damn servers." York laughed, moving back to the map. "Hastings's men can't find us yet but your computer girl sure as hell did."

"Angel," said Cohen.

"Don't know her name—or maybe you're being figurative? Anyway, she was with two people that cashed in a debt I owed them

—my life."

"Mary and Gabriel," said Savas, using their codenames.

"So *you* sent them? I'd guessed. No coincidences in this game. But it's good to know. And you two have my thanks as well."

"We can call it even, then," said Savas.

"Where are they now?" Cohen asked.

"Don't know. They got into our servers, routed messages directly to me, identified themselves. Sent me your profiles and GPS coordinates. Seals did the rest. Honestly, I didn't think we had a prayer. But Hastings is too confident, didn't count on a lot of things."

"Like what? How did they pull it off?" said Savas, shaking his head. Images of the titanic carrier rushed through his thoughts.

"Wasn't that hard in the end. We had some air *options*, but that wouldn't have done much with the firepower they could have launched our way. But the US military hadn't seriously considered an internal war—same team, suddenly at each other's throats, with all the codes and perfect intel on our targets."

Cohen nodded. "You knew where to hit them."

"Not only, darling," winked York, "but we also knew how to get into their onboard systems and shut everything the hell down. Turned that thing into a hundred-thousand-ton floating hunk of iron."

"They tortured us," said Cohen flatly. "Murdered our friend. They drilled holes in his head."

The President's upper lip twitched. "I've been briefed. I wish I could act surprised. This country's wrestled with some monsters, about how to deal with evil people. Hastings belongs to a wing that sees no road as too dark, no line that can't be crossed. All the more reason we need to find a way to stop him. Which brings me to your choices."

Savas barked a laugh. "I don't think we want to go back to the Hastings side, Ms. President."

"I'm sure. But you don't have to help me. You can flee. Hunker down with your families. I'd understand that. But I know who you are. I know what you've done for this country and what those you sent to help me can do. And if I understand things, it was your department at the FBI that stopped the worm that started this mess. The nation needs you. And I want you by my side."

"By your side?" asked Savas. Cohen's eyes squinted.

"Personal bodyguards and problem solvers. Heavy, I know. But there is one more piece to this puzzle you don't know about. Something that makes everything in this coup secondary."

Cohen shook her head. "What could do that?"

York exhaled. "*Bilderberg.*"

15

A SPARTAN ROOM *devoid of furniture or decoration. Twelve enormous flat screens mounted from the ceiling, forming a circle. In the circle's center stood Elaine York, marveling at the design efficiency, the brutal and humbling focus that centered the occupant in front of twelve titanic faces.*

She rotated slowly, examining each of them, feeling dizzy in the process. Eyes bored into her from every direction. God-sized faces. All strangers.

It was impossible. Here she stood, Elaine York, President of the United States, two-time US Senator, political player for most of her adult life and observer before that during her father's career—and she didn't recognize even one of the faces staring back at her. All her connections developed over a lifetime meant nothing in this dark room. People more powerful than she could have imagined surrounded her, making her question the entire world order she had taken for granted. And she knew nothing about any of them.

The door closed behind her.

"Thank you for coming, Elaine," said a voice she remembered.

York stared ahead at an ancient visage, a face from another age with blue eyes and pocked skin.

"You're the one on the phone," she whispered,

The man smiled, revealing yellowed teeth. "Yes."

"Who are you?"

"There won't be any names here, Elaine. Only yours."

A female voice. York turned to her right. Two enormous pools of brandy confronted her, keen eyes of a beautiful woman with dark hair and vaguely Middle Eastern features. Her accented English reflected her appearance.

York scanned once more the ring of faces gazing down on her. Faces from all over the world. Dark and light, old and young, men and women. She returned her eyes to the older man.

"Why am I here?"

He smiled again. "You've read some science fiction in your youth, have you not, Ms. York?"

"Yes," she said, bewildered.

"Your brother's books, I believe. Wasn't so fashionable for a young woman to have such boyish hobbies, no?"

"I'm glad to say things have changed."

"Indeed. But some things do not change. And that is why you are here." He held up a dog-eared paperback. The book on the screen loomed at twice her height. "Isaac Asimov—Foundation. Do you remember this book, Elaine?"

"Yes. One of the first science fiction books I really loved."

"Stilted, clumsy language. But it had a very interesting idea. A brilliant idea. Do you remember it? It was what the series was based on."

York felt lost. "Scientific prediction of society, of the future. Shaping society with mathematical sociology."

"Exactly!" The old man smacked the paperback with his hand. "What if I told you it wasn't science fiction? What if I told you it is possible to predict, and therefore shape, human societies and civilization through quantitative modeling?"

"That's absurd."

"Is it?" said the woman to her right. "Economists use mathematics to predict recessions, bubbles, and investments. Traders do the same to play the markets. Epidemiologists can predict the course of disease and optimal quarantine and vaccination strategies to prevent epidemic spread of pathogens. Are we not shaping our world with mathematical predictions on a constant basis? What could one achieve by integrating all these models, especially if one had the capital resources to alter the inputs?"

"That's different than Asimov's idea."

"Only in a matter of degree," said the older man, pulling her attention forward. "In fact, that's why you're here. Because the course of human events is being shaped toward a brighter future by such methods. And we are those carrying out this noble task."

York glanced around at the faces. No one smiled. No one laughed. These people appeared utterly serious, spouting nonsense.

"Looks like you're dropping the ball a bit. The world seems pretty

FUBAR to me."

"A deceptive illusion, Ms. President. Scored as a percentage of population and cultural dynamics, human civilization has achieved the highest stability ever measured in the historical record."

"How's that possible? We have four major wars ongoing, political chaos in several nations, resource and environmental problems—you name it!"

"It's a matter of perception, Elaine," he said. "Ten billion people with lightning fast tech is very different than one billion and snail mail. Most chaos is minor, blown out of proportion by crisis-driven content in the news media. Local chaos notwithstanding, as a planetary average, we exert unprecedented control."

"Unprecedented?"

The woman spoke again. "Ours is not a new organization. Faces may change over the decades. Tools modernized. But not the purpose. That remains constant. With ultrafast computers, more robust theory and modeling, we can now predict and shape the world to a degree of precision our predecessors could only have dreamed of."

"Predecessors. What the hell is going on here?"

"Very simple," said the man again, "You must accept that your assumptions about the world, how it is governed, where the power lies— they are all wrong. Power does not rest with nations or the individuals leading them. It rests with us. We have held this power for centuries, controlling economies, making kings and presidents, directing conflicts and religions. Clumsily at first, to be sure. Almost to our own extinction at several points. But no longer. The modern age has advanced the modeling of social groups to a point that, like the weather, we are increasingly accurate over longer and longer stretches of time. We have consolidated our power and influence."

York squinted at the screen. "So, you're telling me that behind all the world governments, there's a super group of individuals"—she gestured around her—"these same individuals glaring down at me, who run the world? In secret? Without anyone knowing?"

A man's voice behind her spoke. "I wouldn't say no one knows. It's a question of how much they know and what they might do about it. Rumors of us persist no matter what steps we take to erase them.

Sometimes we're Jewish bankers or cultist Illuminati. Hidden extraterrestrials or demonic forces. Vampires." The god-like faces chuckled. "Strange and inaccurate myths concocted to explain anomalies and pieces of data recalcitrant individuals obtain. Sometimes we encourage certain wild ideas to cast doubt on the real truth."

York shook her head. "How do you expect me to believe this?"

"You've seen what we can do. The power we have over your national system to bring you here. Your own former president playing the role we specified for him."

She felt like crying. It was madness. "Then what do the masters of our universe want with Elaine York?"

"Probably nothing," said the man.

"Nothing?"

"Truly, we do not wish to interfere in your service to your nation. It is likely our direct intervention will be extremely rare. It is increasingly so these days. In fact, you may never hear from us again. Our efforts are so pervasive and thorough, so long-planned, often we can allow the models of behavior for you and your political parties to play out without, shall we say, adjustments. However, should there come a time when reality and our models diverge, should our goals be threatened, we may be required to contact you. It is imperative that you then do as we ask."

"Or what?"

"You risk far more instability and harm by rebelling."

"And if I still refuse?"

The woman spoke. "The consequences will be harsh. We will be forced to remove you from office and replace you with a more cooperative politician."

"Replace me? How?"

The old man frowned. "Consider the fates of presidents throughout history who have rebelled against our requests. Lincoln and Kennedy. William Henry Harrison, Zachary Taylor, William McKinley, Warren Harding, Franklin Roosevelt."

The room felt cold and hostile. York swallowed. "These are all presidents who died in office. Several assassinated."

"Indeed, President York," he said, leaning back in his chair. "As you can see, our reach is centuries old, and we do, as they say, play for keeps."

16

I'M RANTING.

COHEN paced back and forth in the President's private office. Her mind burned. Her arms gesticulating of their own accord. She flicked glances at Savas, desperate for him to intervene, to exorcise this demon in their midst. *Say something, John!* But he sat quietly, looking too stunned by York's revelations to do anything but nurse a cup of steaming coffee.

"Then, *everything*, it's been a lie!" she cried. "For generations! Democracy's been a facade! We took marching orders from these shadows? World events, wars, millions of deaths—all controlled by these ghosts?"

York nodded from behind her desk, her fingertips pressed against each other.

"Why, Ms. President? *Why?* How could you go along with this?"

"They threatened me. They could have ruined me and others. They tried to confuse me with that bullshit about building the perfect world. But the truth was all too clear. They were dictators brutally enforcing their control. I couldn't see a way out."

Cohen swallowed bile. Anger coursed through her, but also pity. This strong woman, *a soldier*, someone Cohen had admired for years, reduced to a lackey for other powers. *Not only York.* Every president for centuries. The image of former president Obama standing in front of a train made her dizzy. Nothing seemed real. *Who can we trust?*

Cohen placed her fingers to her eyes. "Obama really met you in a secret underground railway station and brought you to them?"

York nodded. "Yes, Rebecca. And it was every bit as devastating to me as it is to you right now. But try to look beyond it. See something important. Whatever damage this Fawkes did, he provided a golden opportunity."

"Which is?" she asked.

York stood up and walked to an American flag tacked to the wall behind her.

"The country's divided. At war. But what we're *really* fighting is an enemy we've never seen before. One that's covertly controlled us for hundreds of years. Presidents cowered before them. Because we believed it was the only option." She spun back around to face them. "But Anonymous changed the ground rules, ripped the carpet out from under all our feet. They've blown the support structures and stripped them of their armor." She walked back to her desk and dropped into the chair, closing her eyes. "But they won't go down without a fight. Right now, the US command structure's in chaos. They've infiltrated every level, all the way to the Joint Chiefs. Military contractors at their right hand. Hastings their current puppet. But we have a loyal core, tough and smart. They've taken Cheyenne Mountain and set up our headquarters for the war."

"War?" asked Cohen.

The president's eyes flashed open. "The war to win our country back. Since you've been imprisoned, I've fanned the chaos created by Anonymous. It's spread. I saw an opportunity. I've rebelled against our *masters*. The first chance in hundreds of years to free the world of their control, to create truly independent nations."

York keyed in several strokes at her computer, and a flatscreen monitor on the wall to their left flashed to the blue-gray image of the US. She drew her finger across it from New York to the Rockies.

"We're not going to hide. We're going to muscle our way straight across interstate 70, and our forces are going to blow out of the sky, water, and into the earth anyone who tries to get in our way. We won't get another chance. We have to get to that mountain."

"But how can we stop Bilderberg?" asked Cohen. "Let's say you make it to the mountain, even end the coup. We're no closer to doing anything about them, knowing who or where they are. What happens after Cheyenne, Ms. President?"

"*Elaine*. Please." York put her hands on her hips. "Look, if I'm going to be first naming you two, I want it reciprocated. I need you as real advisors. People who'll speak their minds, tell me hard truths. I've got enough people to salute me."

"Going to take some getting used to," said Cohen. Discordant images of York fought inside her. Authority figure. Savior. Coward. Revolutionary. *Friend?* "Okay, *Elaine*, how can we do anything about them?"

"Right now, we can't," said York. "My first priority is to get me, what's left of the Constitutional government—the members of Congress, the Judiciary, all we've managed to round up with us—get us all to NORAD. From there we stage a war of ideas and bullets until we crush this coup once and for all. Afterward, we go after the Bilderberg Group."

"Won't it be too late?" Cohen asked, her frustration building. "Isn't it the same chaos that led to the coup that makes them vulnerable? If you win, if you start normalizing things, their power will return. They'll assassinate you like Kennedy."

"Yes, a distinct problem," York said coldly.

Savas stood up, pacing before the map. Cohen sensed his mood before he spoke, felt the rhythm of his movement, smelled the testosterone fomenting action. *Please be back, John, we need you. I need you.* He had seemed so broken.

"You said Angel was following up on the message from Fawkes?" he asked.

York sighed. "She didn't say much, but it sounded like they had discovered something important."

He turned to York. "You said you wanted advice. Well, let's start now. You've got a solid game plan for fighting this coup. God willing, you'll get to Cheyenne Mountain. But we need something else for Bilderberg. Maybe Angel and our other friends are our secret weapon. Can you get us in contact with them? We need to find out what they've discovered."

York nodded. "I can try. We have less than half the satellite networks functioning, but at least we control most of those."

Cohen shook her head. "I can't believe it. He's dead, but Fawkes is still jerking our chain."

"Yeah, maybe," said Savas staring at York. "But until today, I'd never thought to ask where the chains came from."

"Fawkes saw them," said Cohen. The mysterious hacker came into focus for the first time. "He was willing to burn down the world, cause the deaths of billions of people to break them. But no—not like that. We aren't terrorists or mass murderers. There has to be another way." She turned her gaze to York. "We have to find another way."

"Then let's start by finding out what the lunatic was trying to tell us," said York. "We'll reach out to your people. I'll make this a priority."

Cohen exhaled slowly. "And let's hope they escape the net a little longer."

17

"I'M HEARING MORE from upstairs. Looks like the neighbors moving back." Houston pressed her ear against the door of the telecommunications closet, straining to filter the muffled sounds. "Someone's bound to come down here at some point. It'll be soon."

"Doesn't matter," said Lightfoote, glancing back from her laptop. "We have to leave anyway. I'm getting hits on my sentries—NSA is poking around. I give us a few more hours before they zero in."

"Packing," said Lopez, dropping food and firearms into bags. "No need to convince me. They aren't messing around. Not another Harlem raid."

Houston walked away from the door and stood over Lightfoote, gazing at the laptop screen. A strange image glowed before her. "Well, at least we got what we came for."

Lopez barked a laugh as he zipped closed one of the duffels. "Sure. And *still* we are no closer to understanding what the Nash Criterion is all about." He gestured toward the screen. "Just look at that chaos!"

Houston frowned. *He has a point.* "Angel, nothing in that image makes sense. Are you sure it's decoded correctly?"

"Sara, if it weren't it would be gibberish."

"It *is* gibberish," said Lopez.

"No! It's an *image*. A clear image. The encryption was broken correctly or it would be total junk—no image, no text, just incomprehensible bytes. We have the contents. It's a very high-resolution TIFF file. That just doesn't pop out randomly. The decoding is correct. We just don't know what it means."

Houston pointed to several regions of the screen. "An image of an image. What is this? Some lunatic's cork artwork? What are these chicken-scratch labels on all these graphs?" She read out loud. "Epsilon-equilibrium, evolutionarily stable strategy, subgame perfect equilibrium, perfect Bayesian, Riemannian manifolds, catenary formulas, n-person games, C1-isometric embeddings—what the hell?

What does it all mean?"

Lightfoote looked at the ground. "I don't know."

Houston continued. "And this thing on the edge—gold color, half a circle, a line—looks like alien hieroglyphics."

"No idea."

"I thought you were the genius here," muttered Lopez, leaning back against the wall and closing his eyes. "Two days, no sleep. A hacker underworld. A thousand computers processing and what? This *nonsense*. This is what people want to kill us for?"

"I'm not a mathematician," snapped Lightfoote. "I don't know what this is about. Neither did any of the hacker groups."

"I taught high school math once upon a time," said Lopez. "These aren't any topics I've heard of. We're wasting time we don't have."

We're getting run down, turning on each other. Houston tried to diffuse the tension. "Maybe higher level stuff, Francisco. It reads like a graduate school math course book scribbled all over some wild cork board." She wasn't even convincing herself.

Lightfoote cocked her head to one side, staring at the screen. "Sara's right."

"I am?"

"This *is* a board. Look—the edge, *here*. That golden alien symbol —it's cut off, only part of it shown. Thumb tacks, tape. It's like something out of *A Beautiful Mind*." She began to type furiously.

"A beautiful mind?" asked Lopez.

Yes! Houston remembered—vague images of Russell Crowe, Princeton, and equations. "The movie? With the crazy economist?"

"John Nash. It was about John *Nash*. Not an economist. A *mathematician* who did economic work. Got a Nobel Prize. The file, remember? The *Nash* Criterion? Look!" Several biographical pages opened in her browser with photos of a gaunt, gray-haired man.

Lopez had joined them, staring at the screen. "That one of your cork boards?"

He indicated an image of hundreds of pieces of paper taped to a board and adjacent wall. Riotous handwriting and equations covered the scraps. Houston knew immediately they were on to something.

"My God, he *was* crazy," she said.

Lightfoote nodded, furiously scanning text. "Schizophrenia. Says here he thought aliens were talking in code to him through the newspapers."

"That qualifies," said Lopez.

Lightfoote continued. "See this timeline of his life? He was a new star in the '50s, went nuts, disappeared for *forty years*, then resurfaces half-sane to claim a Nobel prize." She read in silence down the page. "Says he's still crazy but—get this—he can recognize *patterns* of thought, split them into *crazy* and *not crazy* from observing other's reactions. Statistical analysis of sanity."

Houston was stunned. "Is that possible?"

"Hard to believe," said Lightfoote. "But this handwriting—look familiar?"

"Definitely," said Houston.

Lopez laughed. "Well, it looks like the same decorator was involved, that's for sure." Houston's head was hurting. "I don't get it. What would some insane university professor have to do with Fawkes or Bilderberg?"

Lightfoote continued to type at a mad pace. "That's what we need to find out, right?"

The haunting mask of Guy Fawkes danced in Houston's mind, along with the bloodied head of the hacker Fawkes lying face down in Savas's office. "Maybe this really is just all for the *lolz*, Angel—Fawkes with a final, last laugh at us."

An image appeared on the screen of an open space within a building, a large display surrounded by onlookers in the middle of the frame. Houston squinted. *Was that—*

"Look at this," said Lightfoote. "Maybe Fawkes *was* trolling us. But this board is *real.*"

Lightfoote zoomed into the image, centering on the display. A large cork board with numerous scraps of handwritten notes filled the screen. The extreme pixelation obscured the finer detail.

Houston felt a chill. "My God, it's the same. Where is this?"

"Nash Museum, Princeton University." Lightfoote rested her forehead on the top of her hand. "It's an exhibit—elements from his life, artifacts from his crazy time, too."

"Why would Fawkes send us a picture from a museum dedicated to the ramblings of a nutcase?" asked Lopez, his arms raised in frustration.

"A Nobel Prize-winning nutcase," said Lightfoote. "Prize in *economics*."

Houston nodded. "Fawkes was all about the world financial system, taking it down. His Bilderberg paranoia was tied up in that. Cohen's words, remember? Right before the soldiers descended. Maybe Nash knew something, wrote it down in his crazy period. No one understood."

"But only Fawkes did? Really?" said Lopez.

"He was a crazy genius too, Francisco. Maybe that's why he only gave us half the photo."

"Or maybe he wanted to make it difficult for just anyone to figure this out," said Lightfoote. "He's pushing us to go there. I can't get anything else online. Image searches only give the low res photo—can't do much with that. We need to see this thing. The whole poster board." She looked over her shoulder at Houston and Lopez. "We need to go to Princeton."

"I was afraid this was coming," said Lopez. "A dangerous journey. And, even if there is something in this, what if we can't figure it out? Maybe it's hidden in the crazy of this Nash? You're asking us to travel across a war zone—with military forces hunting us down—to try and decipher the ravings of a lunatic!" He stared at Lightfoote.

"Even Angel admits it's a strange mission," she said.

Houston reached over and touched Lopez on the cheek. "We're tired. We're fried from this and people trying to turn us into Swiss cheese. But it looks *real*. We have to figure it out." His face softened as she held his eyes.

"We might get some tutoring," said Lightfoote.

"From someone at Princeton?" asked Houston. "John Nash? He's still there?"

"Unfortunately, no. Says here he died in a car crash in 2015. Taxi."

"An eighty-six year old dies in a taxi crash?" said Houston.

Lightfoote nodded. "It's a strange one. But I meant this guy—Avi Kaplan. He runs the museum. Some ex-Nash student who was close to him for decades. Worked on many of his important papers. Helped Nash's wife during his crazy years."

"I see this is destiny," said Lopez. "When do we leave?"

Lightfoote bit her lower lip. "Tonight. Angel needs one more hack. To send a message."

Houston raised an eyebrow. "To who?"

"President York. We need to talk to her."

18

"YOU'VE MADE CONTACT?" asked Savas.

They stood in the operations center beneath Manhattan, the labyrinth of tunnels snaking away from them in multiple directions. Military personnel and civilian staff continued to work close by, frantically orchestrating the coming journey westward. Savas could hear them debating the logistics, tactics, and threats. He tried to tune out the coming storm and focus on their communication effort.

"We think so," said York. She deferred to a boyish soldier in front of a terminal. "Specialist Turner?"

"Yes, ma'am! It's a Tor-scrambled secure chat—as secure as we can make it. Your friends, if these are your friends, have an extra serving of paranoid and all the software to work this with me."

"What do you mean, 'if' these are our friends?" asked Savas.

"That's just it, sir, how do we verify? We put out the codes and information you mentioned. They must have been monitoring a lot of information, and they took the bait. They reached out to us. But could be NSA or someone else."

York interrupted. "Hastings has control of the NSA servers. They have tremendous computational firepower and are spying on every internet and cellular network. Landlines too, of course."

Turner continued. "We need something specific, something that could distinguish friendlies from hostiles. Once that's done, we can risk more channels open."

Savas shook his head. "NSA a hostile. Half the US military a hostile. What the hell has happened?"

"Let me try," said Cohen.

The soldier nodded and stood up from the chair. "It's chat. Just type. They'll respond."

She sat down and typed.

"Gabriel's brother?"

Text appeared after a short pause.

"Archangel Michael."

"Who killed the wraith?"

"Gabriel."

"Cabin. What grows on the doors?"

"Rose creepers."

Cohen leaned back and sighed. "It's them."

Savas agreed. "Definitely."

Turner's eyebrows arched, and looked at York. She nodded and he resumed his position in the chair. "Okay, then let's initiate video."

A window opened on the screen. Pixelated blurs moved as if in a strobe light. The video improved, the resolution increased and movement smoothed. A bald woman with piercings across her face stared back intensely at them. Cohen leaned down to the screen.

"Angel! Are you okay? Where are Gabriel and Mary?"

Behind Lightfoote, two faces appeared.

"Right here, Rebecca," came Houston's voice. "We're fine."

"Where the hell are you?" asked Savas

She shook her head. "Can't tell you. Can't be sure who's listening or if you're okay. Not compromised. They're after us."

"We know," he said. "We were taken. Interrogated. They were very interested in finding you. You saved our asses, tracking us. We escaped and are in hiding with the President." He inhaled deeply. *Just say it, John.* "There's bad news. Frank's dead."

Lightfoote balled her hands into fists. "How?" She glared at Savas.

Cohen spoke. "We're not sure. They—" She couldn't finish.

"They tortured him to death," finished Lightfoote. "I get it. And from the look of his face, it looks like John was next. JP? He was dying when we left him."

"I don't know, Angel," said Savas. "My guess is they would see to him, give him medical attention."

"So they could torture him later," said Lightfoote. The silence answered her question. Her green eyes flared. "Who's doing all this?"

"Bilderberg," said York, pushing her way into the line of the camera.

"Then it's real?" came the deep voice of Lopez. "What is it?"

"Something impossible to believe. I've arranged to have some files

484

sent to you. Look them over when you get a chance. But the bottom line: Bilderberg is a set of powerful puppet masters pulling strings across governments the world over. Anonymous nearly brought their system crashing down. I'm running for my life because I'm fighting it. There's been a military coup run by a high ranking soldier—Gerald Hastings. But he's only a front. The Bilderberg Group is behind everything."

"Who's in this group? Where are they?" asked Lightfoote.

"We don't know," said York. "We don't know one name or where they're located. For all we know they're distributed, all over the world. But their goal is to return the nation and the world to a pre-Anonymous status quo. In that world, they shape and guide the nations to their own ends."

Lopez spoke. "We're getting the files now. This is a little hard to believe. Tin-foil hat stuff."

"I know," said the President, "but I think the materials in those files and recent events will help things fall into place. If it helps any, I've *spoken* to them. After my election. They secretly contacted me, impressed upon me in ways I could not dismiss who was really in control of our world. For years I went along with it. Like other presidents. Like leaders across the world. I'm not proud of it, but there's no time to explain everything, what they threatened if I didn't. The consequences to me and others. But now—well, maybe we can stop them."

"Because of Fawkes," said Lightfoote. "And he's not done. He left us the file."

"Yes, John and Rebecca mentioned it."

"We've broken the encryption."

York leaned forward. "What does it say?"

"It doesn't say anything. It's an image file. One that doesn't tell us much right now. But it leads us in a clear direction."

"You won't say more?" asked Savas.

"Sorry, John. This is too important. Especially now after hearing the president."

"Angel's right," said Houston. "It's a long shot, but we need to follow up on it. We need to travel to unravel this. But we need to do it alone. We're a small group. We can hide."

"We can afford you the protection of a powerful contingent of the US military," said York. "We're going to NORAD. We'll fight our way there if we have to. Loyalists to this nation are waiting for us there. Come with us! Seek safety at Cheyenne Mountain to understand this puzzle."

Lightfoote shook her head. "Not putting the eggs in one basket. The file is leading us in another direction. We have someplace to go, and it's not the Rockies."

York frowned. "I can't spare anyone to help you, I'm sorry. And without knowing more about what you're doing, it doesn't seem wise even if I could. You won't reconsider? We can help you!"

Houston spoke firmly. "We think Fawkes gave us a key to Bilderberg, something we can use against them. But it's buried in an enigma we have to solve. We can't come with you. Not yet. Not until we know if it's useful. We have to commit to it."

Savas spoke to the screen. "Angel, you're sure about this? You really think Fawkes was on to something?"

"Definitely," she said. "Saying more might tip off our enemies. I'm sorry."

"My gut says you should be here," said York. "But there's no denying what you've done. I just wish you hadn't been so successful at stopping the worm. The one thing Bilderberg needs now is a return to normalcy. We have to prevent it at all costs."

"So now what?" asked Cohen.

"We turn these three loose," said the president. "And hope to hell they give us something to help fight this menace. Meanwhile, we muster out." She turned back to the screen. "You three stay alive and contact us when you can. The offer still stands. If you need us, if you can make it to us, we'll protect you."

"As best *you* can," said Lightfoote. "I assume Hastings isn't going to let you stroll over to NORAD without incident."

"No, he won't," said York. "But we'll be ready for him."

"Then maybe you're ready to hit him for us, too," said Lightfoote.

York arched an eyebrow. "Hastings?"

"His intel arm. The NSA. They're like ticks all over the internet, sucking info and tracking us. We were almost killed in Harlem because they tracked us. We need them off our backs, and away from the hackers that are working with us."

"You're working with hackers?" asked York.

"Parallel processing. That's how we cracked the encryption. We're counting on them. Right now, they're organizing. But it's all going to get bloody if the NSA spies keeping crashing the party."

"What do you want us to do?" asked York.

"Hit their data centers. Take them out. Fort Meade and Utah for sure."

"Isn't Utah on *our* side?" asked Savas.

York shook her head. "Not so clean cut, John. It's in our supposed range of control, but nobody has troops there and no one can commit them now. It's sided with Hastings. He's got the full power of the agency. Lots of cyberwarfare going on between NORAD and the NSA right now."

"Take them out," said Lightfoote. "Give us a chance to breathe. You don't even need to kill people. Those server farms live and die on cooling and electricity. Take out the water supply, local power stations."

"We've got the cruise missiles, but we're going to need them, too. I'll put together a team to analyze the most efficient attack, see what we can spare." York nodded, coming to a conclusion. "Actually, it will likely help our journey. Should of thought of this before. The NSA gets satellite information, monitors a lot of communications. Hastings can track us, get useful intel, just from whatever goes out from the areas our convoy passes. But not if their server farms are down. That'd jab a stick in his eye." She smiled. "Yes, Angel. I'm starting to take a real liking to your idea."

19

"GENERAL HASTINGS, YOUR first priority is to neutralize York."

The Director's rough voice spoke toward an enormous flat screen monitor, the deep bags under his eyes melding with his lined face to create the appearance of a melted landscape. The face of a heavyset man in a decorated uniform stared back, eyes darting left and right.

The general licked his lips. "We're looking at a full-fledged *war* if we continue. We risk fracturing the entire nation!"

"Let me explain the dynamics to you once again," said the Director, his voice cold. "We are at crisis point. If York solidifies her power base, and if the fugitives with the terrorist's documents survive, we risk the formation of a permanent front against our long-term interests. This would be unprecedented in recent history and could unravel decades-long efforts. We will not allow this. If you can't put an end to this rebellion, we'll find someone who can."

The general spoke through clenched teeth.

"I understand. We won't fail. But I warn you, there's going to be one hell of a mess to clean up."

"We will deal with it later. Find her, General. Kill her and her enablers."

The old man closed the connection and the general's face vanished. In its place, an array of faces appeared and tiled the screen. A woman with an Iranian accent spoke from the center of the screen.

"He is right. The simulations are in chaos. We are quickly oscillating outside our bands of prediction."

"I know!" shouted the old man, slamming his fist onto the table in front of him. "The hacker has disrupted everything. Hopefully, we can put this fire out soon and push things back into line."

"It may be difficult to do so within the models we have developed," came the clipped Germanic accent of a silver-haired man on the lower left tile. "Those models are statistically based. They rely on the *average* properties of large numbers of individuals, or, at worst, a few very well defined pressure points. The hacker was a completely random and extreme element. A *black swan*. His efforts are like a volcano erupting, scrambling all the weather forecasting. We might be basically starting over."

A man with Chinese features spoke from the wall of faces.

"We are at an inflection point. Those worst-case scenarios may not occur. Not if we end the social ripples of this *Anonymous* now. If we can bring the previous financial and political systems back online quickly, strongly suppress any deviations from it and any predictions of the past models, we may enter a quasi-stable tangent path. It will be different, but manageable. The simulations are still in flux. Nothing is fixed."

"All the more reason we must act forcefully," said the Director to the screens. "We must center our efforts on the anomaly in the United States. The other nations appear to be returning rapidly to previous trajectories in the forecasts. But not America. York is now in open rebellion against us. America is still the world's most powerful nation. Should she prevail, one hundred years of effort will be burned to the ground. She could undermine everything."

"If she prevails, we will also be hunted," said the woman.

The Director raised his voice. "I'm not worried about that! Eventually we can take her down and those who support her. Quench any investigations or covert efforts. They have nothing on us. No solid information, only the crumbs we gave her and the myths of the lunatic fringe. They will get nowhere. It is the damage to the *system* we have so carefully developed that will be devastating."

"Hastings may win," said the German. "York is vulnerable now. Unless she can regroup with her supporters at NORAD. But there is a lot of land to cross in that nation."

"We will not rely only on him. Our assassins will infiltrate the military and every local population center along her path. We are flying in teams from across the world. Some will also be diverted to hunting down the FBI specialist, Lightfoote, and the fugitives aiding her."

"Still no progress with the file contents?" asked the woman.

"No. But there is little doubt as to its contents. The mention of Nash is clear."

The woman sighed. "The social engineering. It will be spelled out."

"Yes, and in the right hands, it will be understood for what it is. Our hidden plans laid bare. Countermeasures obvious. They will be able to undo nearly everything."

The German spoke. "They are as big a threat as York."

"Yes," said the Director.

The woman leaned back in her chair, long black hair cascading behind her head. "And if York or these fugitives elude us? Or do so long enough that they begin to capitalize on their threat? What then?"

The Director sighed. "It's one thing to be set back centuries. It is another to be made vulnerable to a death blow. If Hastings and our teams do not stop this soon, if the simulations show we are losing the ability to contain this catastrophe, then we will have only one choice left."

Silence descended, broken by the Chinese man at the upper corner of the screen.

"We have rarely used a failsafe. I had hoped we were beyond such measures."

The old man scowled. "Your weakness, Yigong, has always disturbed me."

Yigong continued. "Tens of millions will die. It's not 1945! With these kinds of numbers, the ends don't justify the means. The *ends* change as well."

"As a percentage of the human population, it is little different from the series of world wars we orchestrated in the 20th century."

A man with a Spanish accent interrupted. "Percentages tell one thing to statisticians. But absolute numbers—these are human beings, Director."

The Director held his hands up at his sides. "Are we forgetting our purpose, and what we have achieved? We've raised billions out of poverty, reduced death and suffering from infectious disease, raised the world lifespan to unprecedented levels. Only because of *our* guiding hand has human civilization not torn itself to pieces, blown itself up, undoing all the progress in science and government, crashing back to another dark age!" He sighed and wiped his brow, sweat glistening on his face. "Sometimes, to maintain this historical arc of progress, thousands, even millions had to die. Those deaths improved the lives of a thousand times as many!" He scanned the faces, his expression stern. "And now we have the science to do it with clarity, to know whether the lives lost will mean something down the road. Humanity *requires* guidance. *You know this!* But our ward requires harsh treatment when ill. And right now, the world is very ill."

"And so, if the criterion is reached, amputation?" said the Spaniard.

The Director took a deep breath. "Let's hope it does not come to that. But make no mistake, we will do what is required."

PART 2

"The biggest men in the United States,
in the field of commerce and manufacture
are afraid of somebody, are afraid of something.
They know that there is a power somewhere so organized,
so subtle, so watchful, so interlocked, so complete, so pervasive,
that they better not speak above their breath
when they speak in condemnation of it."

—Woodrow Wilson

20

SAVAS STARED ACROSS the ranks of soldiers and military vehicles. Part of his mind wouldn't believe it, couldn't accept the reality around him. Rows of drab transports, jeeps and trucks, lighter armored vehicles like Humvees—some mounted with rocket launchers—churned behind them as they rode up a steep tunnel incline.

They were inside a heavily armored vehicle, one supposedly resistant to major arms fire and explosive devices, disguised as a troop transport on the outside. Marines lined the interior beside Cohen and York, along with her advisers. It looked like something from a science fiction film with digital displays and operators monitoring troop movements and communications, speaking into headsets.

He turned to the President. "How has all this remained hidden?"

"It wasn't exactly hidden," said York. "New York City crews and administrations knew of it. They had to maintain the tunnels and concealed exits. Prevent anyone from breaking in and discovering it. What likely kept the secret was that it was on its way out. Something everyone knew about but didn't talk of because, well, it was over. A historical relic. Until we set up camp, it was mostly empty."

Ahead of them an enormous doorway opened in the rock. A stone wall split in the center along a vertical axis and continued to widen, orange light from outside pouring into the shaft. The doors themselves were made of steel more than three feet thick, the outer stone a facade textured to match the bedrock.

"This exit opens on the Jersey side of the Holland Tunnel, right in a wall of rock concealed with hazard signs and fake debris. Traffic, your odd onlooker, won't see it. Undercover soldiers have been guarding it for decades."

"Wait, we just went under the Hudson?" asked Cohen. "There's another tunnel?"

"Yes," said York. "There aren't too many ways off this island, you know. You didn't think Uncle Sam would build a secret underground shelter and not have an equally secret way to get the hell out of it?"

"Are there others?" Cohen's eyes widened.

"Two," said York. "By the Lincoln and Midtown tunnels. These emergency passages piggyback off the infrastructure of the others, lying alongside like leeches. We've got decoys exiting both of those right now. Hastings will be watching. If he has hard intel where we were holed up, he might be bringing fire to some or all of them. This way we'll spin their heads a little, hopefully give us time and space to get out. But we've hedged our bets in several ways."

"How many troops does he have? Equipment?"

"We don't know. The good thing is he doesn't know what we have. Anonymous took the satellite systems down completely. Including military and governmental. They're coming back online slowly, although we've lost a few probably forever due to orbit problems. But NORAD controls most of the birds up there. And we control NORAD. We've all been blind the last few weeks, but Hastings is going to stay that way except for a few inconsequential Navy sats, thanks to Angel's idea. While our vision slowly clears."

"The NSA attack? It's set?" asked Savas.

"Timed to our exit. Missiles are on their way now."

Ahead, the light intensified as the caravan approached. Savas could see the opening clearly now. Larger than he expected, the diameter surpassed all the tunnels he knew. Of course, the Abrams tanks and other large vehicles escorting them were wider and much heavier than even the biggest civilian transports.

"We're using their blindness to our advantage as much as we can," she said. "Have a look."

The convoy burst out of the tunnel and into a sea of military vehicles. The parade pouring out behind them was dwarfed by rows of tanks, highly mobile artillery, and massive numbers of troop transports. Soldiers lined the area. Vietnam-era helicopters thundered and he glimpsed their shadowed forms overhead. Cohen gasped.

"We've been positioning our forces nearby," said York, "They've been distributed for a few days, but tonight a large contingent moved to this exit. We've got a few birds for recon, but they're old and not suitable for combat. The ground vehicles and equipment are another matter."

They joined a group of heavily armored escorts and the convoy rushed onto the lined asphalt of an interstate. Savas could see the rest of the vehicles lining up to follow behind them.

"There were some minor skirmishes, but Hastings didn't have much in place. But soon he'll know we came through here and have some sense of our strength when his forces report back to him." She closed her eyes and exhaled. "Then we'll see what he does. For now, we need to get to the interstate and rendezvous with the main bulk of our forces."

"There's more?" Cohen asked.

"A lot more," said York. "We're fifteen thousand strong. Transports. Supplies—food, fuel, ammunition—enough for the journey and several major battles. It's nearly two thousand miles to the mountain. We can run most of these vehicles at thirty, maybe forty miles per hour. Three days minimum if we give ourselves six hours per camp. Lots of time and lots of land for Hastings to mount several offensives. Thankfully, all this Armageddon solves any traffic problems."

"Jesus," whispered Savas.

"Two thousand miles," said Cohen. "One long convoy. We'll be out in the open, exposed."

"Yes," said York. "Our asses hanging in the breeze. But with both sides' air power still reeling, it's feasible. And they aren't looking for a military victory. They just want slow us down. If they can stop us long enough to find me—well, that's the goal."

"Assassination," said Savas.

"NORAD can fight this war without me," she said. "But not the war for the people. If I'm not around to put a visible face—the democratically elected face of the people—against the forces of Hastings and Bilderberg, they win."

Bright light screamed overhead, a roar rattling the air around them.

"That was low," said Savas.

Thunder rumbled from the distance.

"Missile strikes. Clearing our way. Casualties are just going to climb from this point."

Cohen grimaced, her voice rough. "Sibling against sibling. The second Civil War."

21

SARA HOUSTON STARED out over New York Harbor, a cold December wind raking harshly across the bow of the boat. Darkness shrouded Lady Liberty, the post-Anonymous breakdown of order along the East Coast leaving the statue untended. Her upraised torch only a silhouette against the setting moon. The churning water along the hull of the craft began to lull Houston, ease her seasickness, and for a moment she wished she could simply let go of the madness around them, close her eyes, and lose herself to the sounds of the sea.

Instead, she looked toward the retreating lights of lower Manhattan and the enclosed cockpit of the vessel. The windows of the stolen pleasure yacht were tinted black, and she couldn't see Lopez and Lightfoote inside. She assumed the FBI woman still stood at the wheel, Lopez struggling to come up to speed with the navigational systems to help pilot them in the right direction.

Their plan was straightforward. They would continue south through the Upper Bay, passing alongside the Bayonne peninsula. Near its tip, they would change course with a sharp westerly turn into the Kill van Kull, the three mile stretch of tidal strait between Staten Island and Bayonne. It would get them out of New York by avoiding the major land bottlenecks of bridges and tunnels. The more open sea would make it far harder to monitor and control. If all went well, they should enter Newark Bay within the hour, pass Shooters Island, and turn south toward the Goethals Bridge. They hoped to find a place to dock somewhere near Port Newark, steal a vehicle, and slip onto I-95 south towards Princeton. What could go wrong?

"Helicopter!"

She heard Lopez before she saw him emerging from the cockpit. He rushed alongside her.

"You were right about monitoring the police bands," he said, expression serious. "The NYPD and National Guard are working together. Mostly just trying to restore order, it seems. I didn't hear anything about us. But the curfew is still in force—still martial law.

They'll bring us in if we're spotted and we can't let that happen."

"Not sure we have the firepower to bring that down, Francisco," she said. "Not sure I want to unless I have to. Probably some kid's dad trying to do his job."

He sighed. "Agreed. Angel says we should go dark. It's a big pond out here. Unlikely they'll spot us in the middle of it."

She nodded and followed him back inside. As they entered the cabin, the boat shuddered as the motor cut off. Lightfoote moved quickly. One by one, the lights on the boat went dark—green LEDs marking the starboard and port sides, a white stern light, and a bright lamp on the masthead.

"Glad they modernized this one," she said. "Can you imagine trying to pilot this boat without a manual? All hail the touch screen and auto mode."

Houston gazed out the window. "Moon's nearly set."

Lightfoote followed her gaze outside. "Good thing. White fiberglass is a bad color to hide in under moonlight. Okay—she's dead in the water now. No need to drop anchor, should be a quick pass. Besides, if we're made we'll need to move fast."

Lopez stood halfway in and out of the cabin. "I can hear it." He motioned for them to follow.

The telltale rumble and thwack of the helicopter's motor and blades were carried over the water by the wind. The winking red lights on the craft were nearly lost in the blaze from a spotlight.

"Checking up on our girl," said Houston.

The helicopter approached Liberty Island and arced around it, the spotlight trained along its shores. They watched the bird do a complete revolution around the island, the light moving off the shores and onto the statue itself. Another full rotation had the craft's pulse coupled with a strobe effect from the spotlight, almost giving the towering figure the illusion of motion. Finally, the helicopter accelerated toward the Jersey shore. The light faded as it pulled away.

"Likely first of many flybys tonight," said Houston.

Lightfoote returned to the control panel and started the engine. "We need to get to the highway before sunrise. Great to hide out here at night, but we can't go dark in the day." The vessel shook to life, but she didn't turn the lights back on. "And I vote we stay dark tonight as well."

Lopez returned to the navigation system and switched the police scanner back on. "I don't know how many they have out patrolling, and there is no way to cover all the coastline. But some of this journey puts us in pretty narrow straits. We could get trapped there without many options."

Lightfoote nodded as the boat lurched forward. "Let's just hope their plate's full already."

"Going to go back out," said Houston.

"Still nauseous?" Lopez asked.

"Yeah. It's a hundred times worse in this cabin."

She opened the door and stepped back into the cold air. Immediately the wind and temperature drop began to relieve her symptoms. She walked back to the bow and leaned on the railing. Lady Liberty disappeared behind them in the blackness, lower Manhattan a foggy glow in the growing mist. Ahead, she began to see the outlines of the narrow opening to the Kill van Kull, traffic nonexistent. *Who would dare sail now, after all this?*

She hoped Lopez could get his head around the navigation. She didn't see much room to maneuver within the strait, and the sides were decorated with docks and moorings. They weren't even amateurs, and a collision could be ruinous. Ending their journey at the bottom of the New York harbor estuary was definitely not part of the plan. They had too much to do: A mystery to unravel. A shadowy organization and military coup in the United States to help thwart. And if a crazed terrorist's last words were right, in southern New Jersey an answer awaited them.

A glow flickered northeast of their position. The light revealed an approaching cloud front, dull orange reflecting off the low clouds rolling in from the northwest. The night rumbled and the light winked out.

And returned, the position slightly different, a trio of will-o-the-wisps in the far distance like someone had switched on and off several giant street lamps. An ensemble of rolling bass notes shook around them. Houston heard the cabin door open. Lopez and Lightfoote approached the bow and stood beside her, gazing north as the light and sound show continued.

"What is that?" asked Lightfoote. "Thunder?"

"It's not like any thunder I've ever heard," said Lopez.

Houston gritted her teeth. "Not thunder. Those aren't storm clouds."

"Then what?" asked Lopez.

A turbulent growl grew from the south and crackled, flashing through the air from port to starboard side. A flaming light screamed past them northwards, the rocket's burner searing streaks into their eyes. Its rumbling faded into the low throb of explosive detonations as it disappeared into the distance.

"Explosions," she answered. "From bombing runs."

Lopez placed his hand on her shoulder, squeezing firmly. "God help us."

22

HOUSTON SQUINTED THROUGH the sunglasses as the morning sun glinted off the wet road in front of them. The mists had begun to clear but left a thin layer of water on the highway. It would evaporate quickly, but the surface blinded them for the moment.

"How's the glare, Francisco?"

Lopez grunted, his eyes behind shades heavy and dark from the sleepless night. He still favored his left shoulder, but it functioned better each day, the wound closed and shrinking. Houston knew the muscle damage would take longer to heal, and one hundred percent was months away. Dominantly right handed for most activities, it would have to do.

And they would need him. She had no doubts. Desperate men hunted them, assassins who stopped at nothing to prevent them from piecing together the mystery waiting in Princeton. The priest would have to become a killer again. His inner conflict would continue.

For now, she clung to the relative peace. The remainder of their voyage through the harbor and subsequent ride down the interstate had been uneventful—if one could call wrecking a cruise boat while trying to dock it, scampering to safety as it sunk beside a mooring, and hot-wiring an SUV *uneventful*. But by the standards of the last few weeks, it was almost relaxing.

Lightfoote slept soundly in the back of the black SUV, her body splayed out across the rear-most seat like an unruly teenager. She'd pushed herself more than anyone. Houston turned her head and stared at the strange woman—hacker, FBI agent, shaved and pierced cyberpunk, as much a mystery to her as whatever waited for them in Princeton. Houston sensed a darkness hidden within her.

Within each of us.

She returned her gaze to the road. "Two more lights and it's a right on Washington Road."

"I remember," he said gruffly. "We've gone over the route ten times."

Houston leaned across the seat and placed her head on his shoulder. "I'm tired too, Francisco. But we can't get down now. Everything is on the line."

"I know. Just on edge."

"Still, when we're together—it's a shield. Makes me feel we can do anything. I hold on to that."

He kissed her forehead, returning his eyes quickly to the road.

"God, and I thought working for my boss was a Hallmark card."

The rustling of fabric against the back seats was followed by a thud and vibration in the car. Behind them, Lightfoote leaned against the door, her feet flat on the floorboard.

Houston laughed. "Up already?"

She yawned. "So, where'd you two meet? Assassin school?"

"At a funeral," said Lopez.

"Touché," she said.

"He's serious," said Houston.

"Wouldn't surprise me. What funeral?"

Lopez sighed. "My brother's. Murdered by a madman who nearly brought down the CIA."

Houston cut in. "But that was before we were paraded across the front of the tabloids as some murderous, sex-crazed Bonnie and Clyde. Before we uncovered the CIA dirty laundry that got us smeared and on the most wanted list. Before your boss helped save our asses when we were caught hunting down the *real* killer of the former VP. The same man who killed his brother."

Lightfoote whistled. "Well *damn*, girl. John never said anything. He and Rebecca were unmovable. We all knew something was going on, but this? I've got to hear this story."

"Better story to hear than live through," Houston whispered.

"No time for stories," said Lopez, the car slowing. "Washington Road. Princeton University on the right."

Lopez swung the car off NJ 1 and onto Washington Road. The car sped through a short forested region, opening into extended fields of green as they approached a stony bridge. They passed over a body of water and into a tree-lined and well-manicured region.

Lightfoote mumbled. "Einstein. Woodrow Wilson. John Nash.

Up ahead."

"On the left, actually. Faculty Road," said Houston.

Lopez turned at the junction and followed the road deeper into a forested patch. Just as they were getting used to the broken light and shadows, the environment shifted violently from pastoral to industrial and back again as they crossed railroad tracks. Lopez slowed at a sign reading Alexander Street.

"Right here, and then left on College, yes?"

"That's it," said Houston, staring at the campus buildings around them.

Ahead, a tower rose into the air. Stunted by Manhattan standards, in this rural enclave it rose majestically skyward, gothic spires and the gray stone facade giving the impression of medieval England more than southern New Jersey.

"Cleveland Tower," said Lightfoote, following Houston's gaze. "Built as a memorial for President Cleveland in 1913. Sixty-seven bells in a carillon at the top. Center of the Graduate College of Princeton University. Where John Nash got his Ph.D."

Lopez pulled the car into a circular drive in front of a row of stony buildings. He switched the engine off and got out of the car. The two women followed.

"It's completely deserted," he said. "We haven't seen a car or human being the whole way in. Where the hell is everyone?"

"A few weeks of Last Days events likely had everyone scrambling for home or the hills," said Houston. She turned to Lightfoote. "Looks like you've done your research. Where now?"

Lightfoote scanned the area. "Inside is the main quad. Tower's there on our right. The Nash Museum is directly behind it, built right beside a golf course."

Houston laughed, "So, after a hard day of schizophrenic econ, you can go tee off with the boys."

Lopez shook his head. "All right, let's go get the rest of that image."

"Don't move!" A man's voice shouted.

Footsteps sounded from behind them. They turned to see four men approaching, one with a raised handgun. Two of them seemed hardly out of high school, fear in their eyes. They dropped several bulging sacks to the ground.

A blond man walked slightly forward, the gun in his hand. A thin smile crept across his face.

"Well, what have we got here?"

23

"YOU BOYS FROM around here?" asked Houston with a smile. "We're a bit lost."

The two groups were separated by about ten yards, the car to the side. The men looked ragged, unkempt, and their thin leader stared with a wild glare. He kept moving the weapon from Lopez to Houston to Lightfoote, settling longest on the large form of the former priest.

"None of your business!" he yelled. "Who are you? Why are *you* here?"

"We're looking for someone," said Lopez. "We'll stay out of your way."

"Well, you found someone, asshole!" he barked, spittle coating the fuzz of blond hair on his chin. He inched forward, pointing the weapon at Lopez.

"Come on, Henry, we ain't got time!" cried another. "Those fucking soldiers are *here!* We got what we came for. Let's go."

Henry licked his lips. "Shut the fuck up, Nick! We're going. Yeah, we're going. We're just not going empty handed." He motioned with his gun. "Wallets. Purses. Any fucking gold or jewelry, you throw it over here."

Lopez looked at Houston. She nodded. Lightfoote said nothing.

"No problem. We don't want any trouble," said Lopez, carefully fishing his wallet out from his robes and tossing it to the feet of the man.

"You bitches, yours! Now!"

"I have to get my purse from the car," Houston said.

"No, no, no, no. Don't go near the fucking car! Got your little 22 in the glove compartment, am I right?"

"Henry, fuck it! Let's go. We got more than we can carry."

"Yeah, yeah," said Henry, a smile on his face. "We don't need no more money. But it's a long trip. Lonely trip." He waved the pistol. "You girls are coming with us."

The other three men looked at each other. Two of them smiled while Nick continued to protest.

"Dammit, no! We can't take more. We got too many already!"

Henry spoke coldly. "That's for sure."

He turned toward Nick and pulled the trigger. The weapon cracked crisply in the cold air. The teen grabbed at his throat as his legs gave way. His screams turned to gurgles as he convulsed on the ground.

"*Jesus*, man," said a man behind him, his eyes wide as he gaped at the twitching form of the dying man.

"Shut up or you're next!" Henry stepped toward Lopez. "World's gone to shit. Ain't no rules, not no more. We do what we want." He glared at Lopez. "You, wetback! You want to be next?"

With a final glance at Houston, Lopez shook his head.

"*No mas, señor.* I don't know these girls. After all the crazy, I was just carpooling with them. Not my problem."

"Down on your face!"

Lopez kneeled and fell prostrate on the manicured grass in front of the graduate college building. Houston began to cry as Lightfoote placed her hands over her eyes.

"Now, you two, this way. You run, I shoot you. You try anything, I shoot you. Look at that!" He pointed to the corpse beside him. "*See?* I will. I'll blow your fucking brains out!"

The women moved slowly forward, their bodies shaking in fear.

Henry turned to his remaining companions. "I did all the work here for you pussies. I get a go at each before either of you. You understand?"

One on his right nodded. "Yeah, man. Whatever you say. Jesus Christ. I can't believe you shot Nick."

"No rules but my rules. I make the rules." He turned to the other on this left. "You got that, Bill?"

"Yeah. You make the rules."

He looked Lightfoote up and down. "You, metal face." She stopped. "Put your hands down. Come here. I want to get a look at you."

Lightfoote walked up slowly, Houston following a pace behind.

He smiled. "Green eyes. Cool. You looked *fucked up* girl. I bet you can do some shit. Twisted, huh? Fuck me good?"

Lightfoote smiled and looked into his eyes. "Yeah. I'll fuck you up good."

Her hands shot forward and grasped the gun as she sidestepped. Using her body weight in a continuous motion, she twisted the wrist, bones snapping audibly. Henry screamed, staring down at his arm in shock, the hand wrenched at a grotesque angle to his forearm. Lightfoote crouched on one knee, his gun in her hand, the barrel pointed forward.

Stunned, the other two men barely reacted. Like a drunk, the one on the right began feeling around the middle of his lower back for the weapon tucked in his belt. His head snapped backward as a gunshot reverberated off the stone. At the same moment, Houston sprang like a panther toward the man on the left. He swung his arm in a haymaker from the side, only to find himself in her embrace as she redirected his unbalanced attack into a twist and flung him onto the grass. He landed heavily, the wind knocked out of him. He wheezed as he looked up into the massive barrel of a Browning 1911.

Henry fell to his knees. He cradled his wrecked hand.

"What the *fuck?* You broke my fucking arm!" Tears streaked his face from the pain.

Lightfoote dropped his weapon on the roof of the car with a clank. She nodded to Lopez as he stood up. "We can keep theirs as backup."

Lopez examined the gun. "Only when we're desperate. What a piece of crap. Guy's lucky this thing didn't blow up in his hand."

"He's got other hand problems," said Lightfoote.

"Who *are* you?" asked Henry.

Lopez checked the chamber and removed the magazine, continuing to examine the weapon. "We need to question them about the soldiers."

Henry's face reddened. "Always get girls to do your dirty work, Spic?"

Lopez smiled grimly and walked to the trunk with the weapon.

"Hey, I'm talking to you!"

Lightfoote struck the man in the chest with her foot. He crashed to the ground with a groan.

"You bitch, I'm going to—"

"Shut up," said Houston, kicking him lightly in the head. He shut up. Her weapon remained aimed at Bill.

Lightfoote stared down at Henry. "Your dead friend said *soldiers*. What soldiers?"

"You'll find out. Not telling you shit!"

Lightfoote sprang forward to land on his abdomen, her right hand like a claw smashing into his crotch. He screamed, began to struggle but froze, a high-pitched squeal tearing from his lips.

"Yeah, I can do all kinds of shit with your junk." Her hand pinched like a vice on his pants. He screamed. "Two little balls. So much pain." She squeezed tighter and the man's face reddened, the scream cut off, his body paralyzed. "I'm going to ask this one more time. And you're going to answer, or you're going to learn about a pain you never knew could exist."

24

"THERE'S A SHED over by those trees," said Lopez, moving in its direction. "Likely for the grounds crew. I'll be right back."

"Where is he going?" moaned Henry.

Billy and Henry were tied with hands behind their backs and set against the car. The bodies of their companions lay in the grass directly in front of them.

"Ah, God! My arm! It hurts!"

Lightfoote scowled. "Maybe we should just shoot the ass and put him out of our misery?"

"No, I like to hear him whine," said Houston, a dark look in her eyes. "Reminds me of what he was planning to do with us." She walked up to the man and crouched down. "Karma's a bitch, ain't it, asshole? If your friend hadn't sung like a bird, things might be much worse for you."

"Bad song," said Lightfoote. "Sounds like it's a scouting party. They're sweeping through Princeton, but my bet is they're headed here. I think the NSA mainframes cracked the encryption before York got to them."

"You're sure she hit them?"

Lightfoote lit up. "Oh, yeah. It's like a thousand digital gnats suddenly disappeared. I'd love to see them scrambling to get back up and running. But right now, we have our own problems."

Houston stood back up and nodded. "Yeah. We don't have much time. More will come even if we can take these out."

A strained voice came from behind them. "Let's divide this up."

They turned to see Lopez laden with a pregnant tarp over his shoulders. He bent his neck and tossed it to the ground with a heavy thud and rattle.

"You two go to the museum. Take photos of the giant cork board. We can analyze them later when we've found a place to hide out."

"What about you?" asked Houston, looking toward the bulging tarp.

He bent down and unfurled the stained fabric, revealing shovels and gardening equipment. His head turned toward the two men.

"We're going to dig two graves. Better than leaving them out to rot."

"We?" asked Houston.

"Dumb and dumber there," he said. "They'll dig."

"I'm not digging nothing," said Henry.

Lopez stood up straight and his arm pointed toward them in a fluid motion. A dark barrel gleamed at the end of it. He screwed a long silencer to the end.

"You're going to dig those graves. Or I'm going to dig all your graves. Your choice."

"You broke my fucking hand! I can't dig!"

He kicked a spade forward from the open tarp. "You've still got one good arm. Use it. Your friend will use the shovels, and I'll be keeping both of you in my sights."

The ground in front of Henry exploded, dust and rocks coating his face, snow and mud stuck to his blond locks. He screamed and turned his head from Lopez's gun, coughing as tears ran from his spattered eyes.

"And you'll do it quickly. We don't have much time."

The men nodded.

"Wise move," said Houston. She reached down with a blade and cut their bonds. Both flinched from the knife. Lopez kept his weapon trained on them. She moved around the car and opened the trunk, ducking under the lid and back out holding a red canister.

Lopez squinted. "You're going to torch it?"

"Not going to leave any clues in that place once we leave. Let those bastards spin their wheels and wonder what we found out. Bring the bodies. Save the digging."

"The older Catholic rites die hard," he said cryptically. He nodded to the canister. "That's our reserve. Hope the fuel pumps are working around here."

"I'll use sparingly," she said. "Place is full of paper. Should go up like a straw man." She jerked her head toward the tower and looked at Lightfoote. "Ready?"

The pair set off at a jog to the museum.

Lopez never took his eyes off the two men as they winced, bringing their hands around.

"Now, both of you—dig."

———————

The two men were dripping with sweat when the women returned. Henry whimpered against a nearby tree, clutching his hand to his chest. Two shallow and uneven holes had been dug and the bodies dragged into them, the dirt placed on top barely covering the corpses. A light snow had begun to fall, coating the ground in a patchwork of white.

"Got the photos, several angles to make sure," said Houston breathing heavily, bursts of fog coming out of her mouth. "It's the same board from the file photo, but we have the rest of it. Still more than half the gas in this thing," she said, shaking the canister.

"Good, give me five minutes here."

Lopez held a flat black box and removed a folded red item from within. He placed the box on the thickening layer of snow and as he stood back up, unfurled a crimson stole trimmed along the sides with golden embroidery. He placed it over his head, the two tracks of red and gold offset strongly by his black robes.

"Blessed is God, Who poureth out His grace upon His priests, like the oil of myrrh upon the head, which runneth down to the fringe of his raiment."

Lightfoote leaned over to Houston and whispered in her ear: "What is he doing?"

"Giving them a funeral."

"Why *these* guys?"

Houston shrugged. "Not running for our lives right now. Got a little time."

Lightfoote smirked. "The Priest and the Whore."

Houston didn't reply. Her eyes didn't leave Lopez. The snow had begun to fall heavily, the day darkening from the heavy clouds.

"Lord God, by the power of your Word you stilled the chaos of the primeval seas, you made the raging waters of the Flood subside, and calmed the storm on the Sea of Galilee. As we commit the body of our brothers to the deep, grant all peace and tranquility. You promised paradise to the repentant thief; here also bring us to the joys of heaven. Gracious Lord, forgive the sins of those who have perished."

The two men looked on in shock at the proceedings. Henry had even stopped his whimpering.

"Lord God, whose days are without end and whose mercies beyond counting, keep us mindful that life is short and the hour of death unknown. Let your Spirit guide our days on earth in the ways of holiness and justice, that we may serve you, sure in faith, strong in hope, perfected in love. And when our earthly journey is ended, lead us rejoicing into your kingdom, where you reign for ever and ever. Amen."

He made the Sign of the Cross over the graves.

"All a waste, you stupid priest. They wasn't even Catholic."

"That's all right. I'm not a priest." He folded the stole and replaced it in the black box. "And I'm not Catholic. Not anymore."

An orange light flickered off the low-lying clouds. The brightness intensified near the peak of the tower and cut through the heavy snowfall. Lopez approached the men.

"Now, you two are going to get the hell out of here. I don't think I need to explain that if you try anything, or if we catch wind you have given the soldiers or anyone else information about us, we will not pause to plant you in the ground along with your friends." He fit his hands one by one into a pair of black gloves. "I might not even give you last rites."

25

AGAIN HE WOKE to the sound of his own screams.

Savas sat up violently in bed, arm raised to ward off a blow. Daylight had barely begun to remove the shadows of night, but a chorus of birds piped in the surrounding forests. Muffled shouts and heavy crashing swirled around him. His breath exhaled in ragged clouds from his chapped lips as a hand reached over from his left, and pressed gently down on his arm.

"It's okay, John," said Cohen, her voice pained. She leaned up against him, tugging on the army issue blanket, brown hair tangled and strewn haphazardly about her shoulders. "Just another dream."

Savas stared blankly forward. "Where are we?"

"Mmmm. Tent on I-76, just outside of Harrisburg."

He closed his eyes. "The convoy. Right. We started to see mountains." He shook his head. "Damn. Sorry, Rebecca."

"Want to talk about it?"

"And say what?" He coughed. "Variations on the usual. Thanos died. Right in my arms. You were almost—the towers were falling on us. Cinder blocks, metal and glass pounding you and him. I tried to shield you, but I couldn't. And they kept hitting and hitting until the stones turned to fists and I was in that damned boat and strapped to that table. And you were screaming on the monitor."

"John—"

His hand made a fist. "I can't protect the people I love. No matter what I do."

She took his head in her hands and turned it to her. "No, John. You can't. Look at me!" He grimaced, the muscles tensing across his chest. "You have to accept it. You aren't Superman. You aren't a hero out of a book or a movie. We fight monsters. Someday something bad might happen to me. You have to look it in the face and accept it. Like I have for you, for a long time." Her eyes glistened. "Someday, time is going to take away as much dignity, inflict as much damage and pain, as any of these monsters could. I need you to be there and be strong, now *and* then. Knowing what will happen. I will be for you."

"You're stronger than me," he whispered. "It's easier to get angry, strike out at a threat with adrenaline coursing through you. Fighting the incoming sea without end? I don't know how to do that."

"You don't fight it," she said. "You ride it out as best you can. That's all anyone can do."

"And hope for something transcendent afterward? That this isn't it, this screwed-up world and decaying flesh?"

"I don't know, John," she said, shaking her head. "My mother always said the b'rakhot. After she died, we didn't hear many prayers. My father wasn't much for ritual."

"Yeah, me either. I wish I had Father Timothy's confidence."

Cohen ran her fingers through his hair. "No time for crises of faith. Let's see what the soldiers have us eating this morning. We're going to be moving soon."

They dressed quickly in the frigid air and stepped out into the blinding light of the sun rising over the highway. Savas marveled as he stared down an endless line of military vehicles and troops, metal gleaming, engines coughing and spewing soot into the crisp air, chatter and the sounds of mundane activities giving lie to the absurdity before them.

"They've laid out some tables over there," said Cohen.

Savas followed her lead and they made their way over to a line of soldiers waiting beside a makeshift kitchen. The smell of burnt protein and fat mixed with the cold air and stirred deep feelings within him. He put his arm around Cohen and pressed her to his side.

"FBI!" came the bark of a well-known voice.

They turned, straining to see around the jockeying soldiers scrambling for a meal. A mop of disheveled gray hair sitting at a long table waved them over. The president and her advisors were shoveling food into their mouths as they spoke over a large map.

York glared in their direction. "You two aren't good enough for the regular mess. Over here with the civilians."

Savas saw Cohen smile. He was still too shaken for such a display.

They picked their way around the bustling troops and up a short hill to the president's table. A paper map was spread out over the surface. Bowls and trays of food weighed it down in the cold wind, and various items from rocks to condiment containers were arrayed along the colored lines marking interstates and cities.

"I'm a dinosaur and prefer a hardcopy," said York, spooning a heap of eggs. "About to gouge my eyes out looking at those blinking digital displays in the command vehicle. Here, grab some *grub,* I think is the technical term. Plate of eggs and bacon and something I'm not sure what it is, but it's runny as snot."

They quickly raked the food onto a free plate and sat down across from York at the table, several aides looking askance at them. York ignored the looks and gestured over the chaos on the table.

"So, what do you think?"

Savas chewed on a burnt piece of toast and shook his head.

"I'm not sure I can make out what you're representing here."

Cohen pointed at several aggregates of items.

"Major cities on the map. These must be troop gatherings. Enemy troops, if I can say that about other Americans."

"You bet your sweet ass you can, daughter," said York. "And they have gone off and picked the wrong goddamned side of this war." The president bent over the map. "This line of rocks, that's us, this convoy. We're just outside of Harrisburg, Pennsylvania. We made pretty good time once we got rolling. Luckily, Hastings's damn hit-and-runs have been poorly executed. We're on schedule to make Mount Cheyenne in three more days. Considering the slow start out of the gate, it's not bad. So far, so good."

Cohen pointed to a dense collection of salt and pepper shakers.

"What's that ahead?"

"The bad," said York. "We've got partial satellite coverage and some imagery, also some scouting drones. That right there is Columbus, Ohio, capital of the state and fifteenth largest city in America. Right now, Hastings is fortifying it with some serious strength: infantry, heavy arms from the recon images. West of the city," she said, tapping an overturned coffee tin, "is Wright-Patterson Air Force Base. The base is his, and they are quickly turning it into a center of operations for this campaign."

"Why there?" asked Cohen. "I thought air force was useless."

"So did we," she answered. "But reports show increasing numbers of Hastings-controlled aircraft going into use."

"They've solved the worm problem," Cohen whispered.

"Yes," said the President grimly. "We believe they have. It will take them some time to get their planes online, but more and more, the longer we're out here, the worse it will be. We're likely to see some heavy assault coming from the land *and* air when we get into Ohio."

"Jesus," said Savas. "What can we counter with?"

York frowned. "Superior numbers on the ground, especially with the break-away troops from Fort Bragg that managed to rendezvous with us last night. Meanwhile, our side is working overtime to crack the digital problem with the advanced aircraft, but Hastings has the aerial advantage until we're closer to NORAD."

"So there's going to be a battle?" asked Cohen.

"Outside of Columbus it looks like."

"I hoped it wouldn't come to this."

Savas squinted down at the map. "And this tactical advantage in the air. What does that mean, practically?"

"It means," said York, glancing grimly upward, "that come this evening in Ohio, the skies are going to be raining fire."

26

THE CONVOY COMMANDEERED the entire highway.

Before sequestering within the command vehicle, Savas had stared out at the troop transports, tanks, armored trucks with antiaircraft missiles, and an assortment of different medical and more mundane vehicles pouring down one of America's most traveled civilian roadways.

The giant convoy was divided into several staggered contingents. In the far lead were a set of soldiers tasked with keeping the roadway clear. This involved engaging what foolish civilian drivers would brave the coming military force and getting them off-road as well as clearing obstacles—construction or hazards often the product of sabotage from opposing forces. More than one bridge had come under fire from Hastings, and repairs or complete detours slowed everything. Instead of the consistent jog at thirty miles an hour modeled in the underground Manhattan base of operations, they found themselves oscillating between crawling and all out sprints. The strain began to show on equipment as increasing numbers of vehicles failed and were left on the side of the roadway.

Despite the challenges, their progress managed to be significant, if in spurts. Small raids by worm-resistant, Vietnam-era aircraft or troop ambushes were countered effectively, although the intensity of some of the assaults stunned even a street-hardened, antiterrorist agent like Savas. After a particularly close explosion rocked their truck, leaving a prolonged ringing in his ears, he turned to Cohen in disbelief.

"This is what Frank dealt with for years in Afghanistan."

Cohen nodded, her face a mask of tension. "Probably worse. Fine way he was repaid for his service."

"I think worse is coming," said Savas. "Gunshots, even the explosions at the airfield in Mexico when we tracked Mjolnir—nothing like these bombs and missiles. My brain is still rattling around, I think."

"That last one was very close," said Cohen, glancing nervously toward York. "It's a dangerous shell game."

"There were what, five decoys? Five command vehicles spread around out there?"

She nodded. "I think so. And I heard the communications guy up front say one was hit earlier."

"Jesus."

"They're going to target those preferentially. And the drivers know," she continued in a stunned monotone. "Who does that? Who salutes and gets behind a wheel of a decoy knowing they're just bait to hide someone else?"

"While we sit safe in here," he said.

"Not completely. Everyone's in the line of fire. Shell game is an odds game. But our odds are better than theirs."

Savas shook his head. "An amazing job—this truck looks like any normal troop transport on the outside. But in here," he said, gesturing to the banks of military communications, computer monitors, and other high-tech yet hardened technology, "it's a different story. Thick armor cloaked by the false vehicle wall on the outside. I didn't know the army could be so clandestine."

"Thick or not, I don't think anything would stop a direct hit," said Cohen.

"Well, let's hope we don't get one of those."

They were nestled in the back corner of the truck, strapped to wall-mounted seats and staring down at the military dance of soldiers and equipment. Stiff and sore from over twelve hours of travel, they were cold even in their coats, the interior unheated to conserve fuel. York sat alongside several soldiers who manned the equipment, their fogged breath like a cloud around them. Her face was grim. She rose and headed in their direction. He guessed what she might say.

A series of blasts outside explained the situation forcefully. The vehicle heaved and rocked violently, and sent the president crashing to the floor on her hands and knees before the FBI agents. A flurry of curses sounded as Savas and Cohen helped her to her feet. A soldier leapt to her side.

"Ms. President," he said, "are you okay?"

She sat down beside Cohen and regained her bearings.

"Yes," she said hoarsely. "Getting a little old for combat, I think." She blinked repeatedly. "Get the plan in motion and I'll brief our passengers."

The soldier nodded and turned toward the front of the truck.

"Plan?" asked Savas.

"We're three hundred and fifty miles past Harrisburg, around twenty outside of Columbus. We've been positioning our forces in anticipation of what's ahead."

A whistle overhead presaged an earthshaking explosion.

"That bastard Hastings has let the dogs out," she growled. "His troops are advancing. Heavy artillery is first in line. We've also detected incoming aircraft and a few missiles already, although a last-minute sabotage of his naval assets has grounded most of his cruise missiles for the time being. "

"Cruise missiles." Savas could hardly take it in.

"The modern military is something to behold," said York. "This is not going to be easy or pretty."

Sonic booms shook the air above them as the sound of jet engines ripped through the sky. More explosions followed as did the screaming of men outside.

"What's going on out there?" asked Cohen.

"War," said York. "Better you don't see. Better none of us sees unless we have to. We need to keep our heads and stick with the plan. We stay low. We remain covert. Meanwhile, many good men are going to engage that son-of-a-bitch and die today so we can continue this journey."

She stood up and dusted herself off.

"It's going to get ugly fast. Hold on and hope for the best. If you have a god to pray to, now is a good time."

27

"Princeton's finest, and the best they had was Jack?"

Houston slurred her words, her grin asymmetric and comical. She leaned heavily against the bulk of Lopez, his dark hair spilling underneath his cap and brushing her pale cheek. The three sat huddled together in a crowded dorm basement, clouds of water vapor escaping their lips, ice surrounding a nearby water fountain from a burst pipe.

Lopez took the bottle from her and shook his head. "This was supposed to help us forget the cold, not blast us to nirvana." He smiled at Lightfoote. "There's nothing in the world this little lady can't do better than me, unless it's hold her liquor."

"Not fair," snorted Houston. "You're three times my weight."

"And you're heavier than Angel, but I wouldn't put money on me to out-drink her."

Lightfoote smiled. "Cyborg. Hyper-metabolism."

"See?" said Houston. "Explains everything." Her eyes lingered on the FBI agent. "You're some mystery girl."

Lightfoote removed a woolen watch cap and rubbed her fingers vigorously over her scalp. A red film of hair had begun to grow out. "So are you two. Tell me," she said, replacing the hat and nearly pulling it over her eyes, "what's the story on the Browning? You don't shoot anything else."

Houston sat up clumsily. "What makes you think there's a story?"

"That's not just a gun, girl. That's *your* gun. There's a story."

Houston laughed. "Fucking cyborgs. Well, my dad gave it to me. Trained me on it. Brought it back from the Korean War."

"Korean war? How old is he?"

"He would have been eighty. Died ten years ago."

Lightfoote nodded. "But he gave you his issued sidearm?"

"War changed him. Sucked a lot of the life out of him. He never talked about it. *Never.*" She grabbed the bottle and swept it away from a frowning Lopez. "They didn't have things like PTSD or therapy back in those days. He put away his uniform—*pluke*—and everything he took back from the war. Shut it all up in a trunk. *Click.* Never opened it again. I never saw it anyway, even all those years later."

"Except for the gun," said Lightfoote, staring intensely at her. "So he robbed the cradle? To have you, your mom must have been a lot younger."

"Mom. Ha. Now there are *problems.* She hunted him down, daddy figure or something she thought she needed. I don't know. Course it didn't last. She was gone like a wild butterfly." Houston watched the liquid swirl as she shook the bottle. "He was a good father. Don't get me wrong. You know, back then there weren't too many single dads. He never remarried. Never dated as far as I know. I think the only thing keeping him alive was me." She opened the bottle. "Until I left home." Her eyes flashed toward Lightfoote. "So! What's *your* story, fly girl? And don't even bother. I know there's one, too."

Lightfoote didn't smile. "Dad was a cop. Followed in his footsteps."

"No son to do it?" asked Houston, wiping her chin as whiskey dripped.

"It's more complicated."

"He teach you how to shoot, too?"

"No. Never got the chance." Lightfoote paused. "He was killed in the line of duty. Until then, I didn't want to be a cop. I had other interests. Dancing mostly. But everything changed when he died."

"Why'd that change things?" asked Houston.

"It's complicated."

Lightfoote reached for the bottle. Houston nodded and handed it over, watching her take a swig.

"Gotcha. We don't have to—"

"I saw him die," she said. "I was just a few feet away. I couldn't do anything." She took another gulp. "I knew then there were monsters in the world. I think I was a bit lost afterward." She laughed. "Make that a lot lost. But I couldn't just *dance* anymore." Lightfoote stared off into space, the whiskey bottle dangling over her raised knees, wobbling back and forth as she swung her wrist. Her eyes moved to Lopez. "So, big guy, you do the *follow dad* thing, too?"

A deep laughter rolled in the room. His deep brown eyes looked at his feet. "I wish I could have. Not remotely smart enough. My father was a NASA engineer, recruited from polytechnic school in Mexico City. Test scores off the charts. Helped build rockets in Alabama during the Cold War and Space Race."

"A literal rocket scientist!" barked Houston, nudging Lopez with her shoulder.

"I guess I did try. Ended up teaching intro calculus at a Catholic school. But that was as smart as I was going to get. No rocket science for me."

Lightfoote put the whiskey down and hugged her knees. "So why the priesthood? Visions? Voice of God?"

Lopez smiled. "I wish that as well. But, no. My motives were earthly. Rebelling against my neocon brother." He reached over and stroked Houston's cheek. "And denial of something similar inside me."

"So who taught *you* to shoot? You're the best I've seen."

"He had the best teacher," said Houston.

"You?" Lightfoote smiled. "Really? Blind date activities?"

Lopez put an arm around Houston. "When we first met, in the middle of all that crazy, it was the one thing she wouldn't shut up about. *Going to teach you how to shoot.* Drove me nuts. I'd rarely held a gun. Certainly not a man killer. I didn't want to! Violence, killing— I'd turned my back on it. I was a peacemaker, turning the other cheek." He laughed. "Before the priesthood, I'd used my fists a lot. I tried to turn it around, suppress it, have God's word my sword and shield and all the St. Paul Ephesians *Armor of God* stuff."

Houston kissed his cheek and shook her head. "Poor bastard. He had to learn the hard way to use some other armor and weapons. Bad guys out there."

"Monsters," said Lightfoote, her expression distant again.

Lopez squinted slightly at her but said nothing.

Lightfoote continued. "So, what's the plan for you two, assuming the world doesn't end soon?"

Lopez shrugged. Houston leaned back into his chest. "No idea. We're FBI most wanted, and Savas can't change that. Nobody can. Dead or alive kind of pariahs. We killed the former VP! Hundreds of government agents. Blew up a fucking police station. He's a pedophile. I don't think you come back from all that."

"So, John really put you in deep witness protection? He kept it all under wraps."

Houston nodded. "With help from CIA. Fred Simon." She looked away and closed her eyes, nuzzling into Lopez.

"I'm sorry about what happened," said Lightfoote. "We were overrun with Fawkes's mercenaries. I was lucky to get the code out. They almost won."

"Don't apologize. You stopped a madman," said Lopez. "We'll see when all this is done what kind of world is waiting. But I'm not hopeful. We've resigned ourselves to new lives, new identities. Always hiding. Always running."

"Priest and whore. Gabriel and Mary."

"Something like that, right Sara?" Houston didn't answer. Lopez looked down and sighed, brushing his hand over her head.

She was asleep.

28

SAVAS GRITTED HIS teeth as he trudged through the new-fallen snow. No longer snow, but a black slush from fires and exhaust that tainted the purity. Flames continued to lick at the metallic skeletons of blasted vehicles, chemical fumes from rubber and burnt machinery choking him.

His shoulders burned from carrying the stretcher. The medic at the other end of it walked with his head bowed in silence. Savas had lost track of the number of bodies he'd carried like this. *Less than one hundred?* It felt like more, but he knew he couldn't have managed so many. Perhaps much less. All clarity had disappeared and his mind reeled.

Savas had killed men. Had watched them die in numerous ways. He'd seen small skirmishes with terrorist groups, suffered wounds on several occasions. Had watched the towers fall in New York, mosques obliterated around the world, and witnessed a nuclear detonation over the Gulf of Mexico.

But nothing had prepared him for true war.

Bodies still littered the roadway and sides of the road. To his right he caught a glimpse of the burning hulk of a fighter jet, the shape only barely discernible from the mangled wreckage. Far in the distance, he could make out the skyline of Columbus, a small handful of skyscrapers like desolate redwoods in a devastated forest veiled in smoke.

Columbus burned.

They reached a medical tent. He knew they were close before they entered from the smell and the screaming. Hundreds of wounded soldiers produced an environmental-level impact. The snow around them was crimson as well as black.

They placed the stretcher outside the tent alongside rows of corpses. The woman they carried had died along the way. Savas had seen her injuries and known that nothing in modern medicine could have changed the outcome.

"I'm going to take a minute," he told the medic, who just nodded and went about his duties.

Savas sat down on a set of wooden boxes outside the tent. For the first time in many years, he felt an old craving, a desperate thirst for a drink that would burn and numb. It frightened and fascinated him to watch this old specter rise so many years after exorcism. *I'm more shaken than I realize.*

He turned his mind to the ear-splitting and grating sounds of metal scraping on rock, watching the engineering corps clearing the road of debris and smashed vehicles. He hadn't counted on the obstacles war would put in their way. They needed to deal with the human toll of battle, but the logistical nightmare—opening the path for what remained of the convoy—demanded attention.

He scanned the road behind them. He could not comprehend the carnage. It distorted his reasoning. He would have sworn truthfully that the overnight battle had obliterated the president's force. But as he took appraisal of what remained in the morning light, he saw it was much the reverse. The bulk of the convoy remained intact. Perhaps one in ten vehicles had been successfully targeted by weapons fire. Craning his neck, he could see that the human toll, especially on the part of Hastings's men who had recklessly assaulted their position, increased as one approached Columbus. Bodies carpeted the stretch toward the damaged city. A nightmare might surround him, but the lower levels of the hellscape awaited them ahead.

In the initial hours of the assault, he had absorbed some of the military strategy unfolding. Not a ground commander, Hastings had led his soldiers into a slaughter. Yet that assault had taken the lives of many in the presidential convoy. The air and artillery attacks had been devastating, as missiles and explosives strafed them along the highway. But the air advantage proved too weak to turn the tide on the ground. York's advisors claimed their superior numbers and far superior battlefield strategy had won the day decisively.

Abstractions. On the ground around him, a decisive victory looked more like a meat-grinder. The cries and weeping of the wounded had become a haunted chant from the plains of Gehenna in his mind, tearing at his awareness even when he was alone. Images of bodies broken, shredded, inverted in manners hard to imagine, trespassed before his open eyes. Young faces turned to cold cadavers. Voices silenced. *And voices crying out.*

As the sun crept over the fog of smoke clinging to the ground, he saw a silhouetted form ambling slowly toward him. The rhythm, the stride, the body motions—*Rebecca.* The vapors slowly revealed her sooty face as she came to take a seat on the boxes beside him. She leaned back against a tent support and closed her eyes.

"The president?" Savas managed to ask after a few minutes.

"Safe. On overdrive. She can't be human. We're going to move soon, John. I came to tell you."

"We aren't done."

"Doesn't matter. We can't wait to take care of everything."

"These are men and women here. We can wait."

She sighed. "If we do, we'll have more deaths on our hands. Every minute we delay keeps us from Mount Cheyenne. Every minute means Hastings has more time to plan another assault."

"Another?" Savas couldn't process it.

"I've been in the command module. I've seen the new recon. He fucked up here, but he's already regrouping. York says he's not stupid and he'll learn. Next time will be worse, and there's no telling how much more tech he'll have online by then."

"Where next? I mean, where are we headed? Where's the next battle?"

"Kansas City for both, unless Hastings gets a lot more creative." She placed her hand on the back of his head. "We've got to move."

Savas nodded and stood up, Cohen behind him. He looked over the battlefield once more.

"Kansas City. Another battle. *Worse.*"

She stared out toward the smoldering skyline of Columbus.

"Looks to be. Yes."

"My God, Rebecca. This is America. What are we doing?"

29

"THERE'S A CODE here," came Lightfoote's weary tones.

The three remained in the basement of a Princeton University dorm room. A wave of soldiers had come by the building, loudly thundering through several of the upper floors, but abandoned the search as they moved toward the smoldering remains of the Nash Museum. They'd ignored the lower floors.

Houston moaned and drank from a cup of cold water. Her eyes were closed. "God I need an aspirin. I'm breaking up with Jack for real this time."

"There's a primer," continued Lightfoote. "I know it. I just can't figure it out. There's a measuring stick in this mess!"

Lopez sighed. "So you've been saying since dawn. But it's a quarter to five and there hasn't been anything more. Don't you get hangovers?"

"Cyborg."

"Right. I'd forgotten."

They'd been staring at the reconstructed image for hours, assembled on the computer from several photos Houston had taken, completing the half obtained from Fawkes's file.

"What do you make of it, Francisco?" Houston had asked after they stitched the images together.

"Nothing," he'd sighed. "Just more crazy."

But from early on Lightfoote had disagreed. As the night had limped by, she continued staring at the news clippings, scrap paper, words and diagrams, equations and images John Nash had taped and pinned together across the giant poster board.

"Look. This isn't coincidence. Numbers!" she gestured to the image. "These number strings always appear over words or math symbols. It's like they're labeling them."

"But what's the significance? What does it mean?" asked Houston.

Lopez shook his head and yawned. "Modern art from a madman."

"We don't have time to sleep, priest!" Lightfoote stood up from the computer and came within inches of his face. "You're a mathematician."

"Math *teacher*. Remember? *High school.*"

"Do any of these equations mean anything?"

He rubbed his eyes and stared again at the image. "It's a chaotic patchwork. These are mathematical symbols, no doubt. But no true equations. Pieces of them, computational instruments without substrates. Incomplete. Might as well be random."

"They're *not* random."

Lopez shook his head again. "I can't see the pattern."

She turned back to the image on the computer, tapping with her index finger on the screen.

"This then. In the center. It looks like some weird symbolism. It's huge, colored strangely."

"Everything here is strange," Lopez added.

Lightfoote ignored him. "We only had half the image from the file, split down the middle. But look, here we can see it's a gold circle with a long black line underneath, and underneath that, a short gold line. *That* has to mean something!"

"Yeah, to aliens on Stargate."

Her eyes flashed. "Try, dammit! There's something here, I just can't see the pattern. Find the primer to interpret it. This thing stands out the most. In the middle. Gold on black. It *means* something."

Lopez sighed and squinted at the screen. "I've been staring at the image for hours, Angel. Yes, it stands out. A golden circle over a golden line. I don't—"

His words stopped abruptly.

"You don't what?" asked Houston, opening her eyes. They were bloodshot.

Lopez leaned in closely. "A golden circle over a golden line. A golden ratio." He laughed. "Holy shit."

"Well, coming from a priest," said Lightfoote, "that sounds promising."

"Former priest. But, yeah, maybe. Look, the gold line underneath is the perfect length to be the diameter of the circle above."

Lightfoote shook her head. "Okay?"

"The length around a circle, the circumference, divided by the diameter! It's the most famous number of all!"

"Pi," Lightfoote said.

"Yes, Pi."

Houston frowned. "Okay, so what? How does that help, even if that's what it's about? Who cares about Pi?"

Lopez continued to scan the image, tapping his fingers in several places. "Look, *here*—a large golden three over this word in a newspaper article: *External*. And, here, another golden number, 14, over this scribbled word, what is it—*Equilibration*."

"And here," said Lightfoote, "a golden 159 over the word *in*."

"You two have lost me," said Houston.

"Three point one-four-one-five-nine-two-six-five-three-five-eight...well, that's all I have memorized," said Lightfoote.

"Memorized?" Houston asked.

"Pi!" said Lopez. "The decimal expansion of the number Pi. My God, it's so simple."

Houston put her hand over the image. "Okay, geeks. Explain."

Lightfoote moved her hand and grinned broadly. "The numbers. Over the words. It's a code! The primer was the image of the circle and line. Telling us the code is centered on Pi. The decimal expansion of Pi is a series of numbers. Infinite. Doesn't repeat. Nash put pieces of the numbers over words."

"Not just single numbers," added Lopez, "those will show up again, over and over in an infinite expansion. He's used the *groupings*. The first few colored in gold to make it obvious. See, a golden three here over *External*. Three is the first digit of Pi, in the one's place. Then the next two digits, 14, again gold, here over the word *Equilibration*. We get two more gold numbers: 26535 and 89793238."

Lightfoote held up her smartphone, a list of digits running across a calculator app.

"The decimal expansion of Pi out to nineteen places. Divided into five groups of numbers. Colored gold."

"What does it say?"

"*If* we're right, the first four words of something: External Equilibration in Non-cooperative," said Lopez.

"So, nonsense?" Houston asked.

"Maybe not," said Lopez. "Sounds almost mathematical."

Lightfoote spoke rapidly. "Nash specialized in an area called Non-cooperative Game Theory. It's math meets economics. This sounds right!"

"So where is the rest of the code?"

Lightfoote frowned. "A few more golden numbers, then just... numbers. Lots of numbers. Different sized number strings."

"How to we know which clusters of numbers are next?" asked Lopez.

"Pi, of course."

He shook his head. "Yes, but which pieces of Pi. This could take forever. Unless..." He shook his head. "Golden ratio. I said it in the beginning but didn't make the connection. Nash was brutally literal in his symbolism."

"*The* Golden ratio?" asked Lightfoote. "Artistic ratio the Greeks loved?"

"Yes," he said. "But not only. It shows up in many early cultures, in nature, in snail shells, flowers. Weird Catholic and Jewish numerology. And it shows up in a series called the Fibonacci numbers."

Lightfoote nodded. "I remember. Take the last number and add it to the number before last to get the next number."

"Exactly! One, two, three, five, eight..."

"Thirteen and twenty-one!" said Houston. "Look! Here and here. Two more golden numbers, thirteen and twenty-one digits long."

"You're catching on," said Lopez. He turned to Lightfoote. "They match the next sequences in Pi?"

"Yes!" She showed them the numbers on the calculator.

"Then it all repeats, I would bet, starting the Fibonacci numbers from the beginning again. Seven golden numbers, the first seven Fibonacci numbers giving the length of the string of digits from Pi," said Lopez. "The sequence lengths would get too big, otherwise, but this way we know quickly how to order the search and compare to

Pi."

"Good grief," said Houston. "I thought you said this was simple!"

Lightfoote nodded. "It *is* simple for a code. A little messy for humans but not for any cryptographic analysis by computer. But we're going to need a lot of digits from Pi."

"But the first seven, all golden numbers. What does it say, Angel?" said Lopez.

She wrote down words and read aloud. "External Equilibration in Non-cooperative Games. John Nash." She looked between her companions.

"Oh, my God. This is it."

30

A FINE DUST circled the room. Part chalk from the nearby blackboard, part disintegration of the rows of cardboard boxes lining the walls and filled with decaying books, the floating remains testified that the Princeton study room was evaporating like so much of an older world.

Lightfoote and Houston sat together beside a laptop plugged into a nearby outlet. Both were disheveled, their clothes matted and filthy, Houston's dyed-brown hair showing her natural blond at the roots. Several of Lightfoote's many piercings showed inflammation around the holes.

"Let me get this straight," said Lightfoote, her green eyes intense. "You two chased down this lunatic to the VP's house, where he'd basically taken on a legion of secret service agents, blown a hole in a fortified bunker, rappelled down and taken on more agents, killing them all, and then killed the VP? This guy superman?"

"I got this all second hand. I was basically bleeding to death outside from the shrapnel from said lunatic's bombing of the CIA safe house. And he didn't directly kill the VP. Heart attack." Houston took a sip from a bottle of Jack Daniels.

"Thought you'd dumped Jack."

"I always forgive him." She laughed and drank from the bottle again. "But can you believe it? Ten years of revenge planned out and executed like James Bond and he's about to kill the VP, but the fuck drops over from a heart attack. Irony's a bitch."

"You realize that story is not remotely believable."

"I suppose not," said Houston nodding. "But if you'd told me back in 2000 that a bunch of Arabs trained in caves in Afghanistan by a diabetic Saudi prince would sneak unnoticed into America, train on small engine aircraft, hijack planes with fucking box-cutters and steer two goddamned jumbo jets precisely enough to hit each of the World Trade Towers and bring them both down—I'd have said you were full of shit, too."

"Point taken."

Houston offered the bottle to Lightfoote, but the FBI agent shook her head.

"I know my limits. Besides, tastes awful."

"Really? Old Jack ain't half bad, though I'm not a bourbon woman myself. Texas whiskey, now *that*'s another story."

"So the priest kills the wraith."

"Sort of." Houston pulled up from her slouch and placed the bottle on the table. "More like suicide by fugitive. Guy was fucked up good. All his targets were dead. Mission accomplished, but the demons were still inside or whatever. Basically begged Francisco to shoot him. I'm glad it was so easy. The wraith would have killed him under different circumstances."

"Your man seems a hell of a fighter."

"He is. But he's been trained up good. Five years ago, he was just a priest with a lot of untapped potential." Houston grabbed the bottle and took another swig. "We were toxic waste by then. Fingered for the veep attack and ten other things. If Savas and Simon—poor bastard—hadn't pulled us out of that war zone in Virginia, we'd be on death row or worse. Instead, we got a pretty little cabin in the mountains. Far from everything. I trained him there."

"Yeah, bet it would be fun *training* him," said Lightfoote. "You must have hated every minute of it."

"Girl's gotta do what a girl's gotta do." Houston closed her eyes. "Little stir crazy. Fucking cold as hell in the winter. And we kept switching cabins on different peaks. But better than this shit we're swimming in now."

"How'd you end up in the CIA?"

"Oh, that's a random one. I was looking at law enforcement. Never thought to be a spook, but the Agency's got eyes in a lot of places. Learned all this later. They identify possible recruits early, track them over a few months, few years. You've got to do well enough in school, show the right kinds of interest, have a clean security history—your family, too. A man came up to me at an ROTC session in college. Said he had a job proposition. Handed me a card. Happened pretty fast."

"How'd your dad handle it?"

"Same as with everything. Quiet. Supportive. Mom was something else. Hippy-firebrand-alcoholic on her fifth husband by then. She was in and out of rehab and other men's trailers." She swished the whiskey around in the bottle and looked between it and Lightfoote. "I like to live on the edge."

"She disapproved?"

"Said I was going to work for the empire and all that. Baby killers and hegemony. 'Bout sealed the deal for me. Everything that bitch said I did the opposite. And flipped her the bird." Houston sighed and stared at Lightfoote. "I'm tired of me. Your turn. Who were these monsters that killed your dad?"

Lightfoote held her gaze for a moment and turned away. "Not worth telling."

"Come on, that's not how this works, girl. My cards are on the table. Let's see your hand."

Heavy footsteps tromped outside the cramped room. Houston placed a finger over her lips, grabbed her Browning, and moved quickly to the side of the door. Lightfoote drew her gun from a hip holster and crouched behind an overturned study cubical. The footsteps grew louder.

"It's Francisco," came a deep baritone from outside the door.

Houston twisted a knob on the bolt lock and opened the door. Lopez shuffled inside and placed a gun on the top of a filing cabinet. Sighing, he dropped a large plastic garbage bag to the floor.

"No sign of the soldiers or our burglar friends. No sign of anyone." He motioned to the bag. "I raided several pantries and a few functioning refrigerators. Anything that could spoil has. What's left is mummified bread and a lot of cans."

He glanced across the study room, his eyes lingering on a blackboard full of incomprehensible physics equations.

"I wish the graduate students were still here. Maybe one of them could figure this out." He bent toward the computer screen. "Anything?"

Houston sat down in front of the laptop.

"This is it," she said, scrolling through pages of text and figures on

Lightfoote's computer. "This is the entire paper, but we're no closer to understanding what the hell Fawkes was trying to tell us."

"Fawkes? We're not even sure what Nash is trying to tell us," said Lightfoote. "Five hours of decoding and transcription and we have a Nobel Laureate economics paper we can't understand."

Lopez stared at the pages. "I recognize some of the math, but I don't know the theory, why it's being used. And a lot of the math I've never seen before. Way beyond my pay grade."

"We do have this note," said Lightfoote. She zoomed in on an image with scrawled text.

"What's this?" Lopez asked.

"We found it while you were out," said Houston. "I'm still not sure it's part of the encoded message."

Lightfoote shook her head. "Has to be, Sara. It's the last sequence of Pi on the board. The econ paper ends, one more piece of Pi sitting over this little note. Read it for Francisco."

Houston sighed. "*This is why we are not free. The puppet masters pull the strings.* There's this smudged part. Unreadable. Next, *their fingerprints are in the global numbers. Once the criterion is reached, they pull the trigger.*"

"Very different than the rational content of the paper," said Lopez. "It sounds like mad ramblings. Angel said he oscillated between lucid and insane states over the years."

"He did," said Lightfoote, "although everything claims that in his later years he was more stable than not. Got better and better at *classifying* and ignoring his crazy thoughts."

"But we don't know when this was written?" he asked.

"Well," said Lightfoote, "some of the clippings are over fifty years old. It's really old."

"He never published this? You're sure?"

"Yes, Francisco," said Houston. "Angel's gone through all the online databases. Enough are up again. We can be pretty sure this paper never saw the light of day."

He turned his palms upward. "But why? Okay, so it's old, from a time before he went nuts, right?"

"Right."

"But why not publish it later, when he recovered?"

Houston shrugged. "Maybe he'd forgotten about it. The illness and treatments erased it from his mind."

"Is that likely?" Lopez asked.

"No," Lightfoote responded. "He didn't lose the knowledge of his field in the later years. Continued to publish. I don't know why he shelved this one."

Lopez exhaled slowly. "How about this—he didn't just file it away. He *buried* it in this encoded crazy. Here is a work discussing something about the global economy, with analysis of multiple nations we can't understand. Written at the height of his productivity, the height of his powers. He never publishes it. Instead, right around the time he goes insane, he builds this Crazy Wall where he embeds the entire paper in a geometrical and numerical code. Why would he do that?"

Houston shook her head. "Like you said, Francisco, he was crazy."

"I'm starting to doubt my conclusions. I think Angel may be right —there's something important here. He was trying to tell the world something, but he couldn't do it openly. He was *afraid*."

"Afraid of what?" asked Houston.

"And what was he afraid to say?" said Lightfoote.

Lopez stood up. "Back in New York, you said his student set up this museum. Maybe he knows something."

"Maybe it's no accident this poster board ended up where it did," said Houston.

Lopez paced, gesturing. "We decoded it and hoped we'd be able to get to the root of this message. But we can't. We need to outsource —speak to this guy if he's still here. Still alive. If he'll even help us."

Lightfoote closed the laptop and stuffed it into a backpack. "*Agreed*. Sara, you still have the last address?"

Houston nodded. "It's about ten minutes from here."

Lightfoote walked to the door. "Let's move the stuff to the car. If this doesn't give us an answer, we might as well ride out and meet John and Rebecca and the fucking Presidential Caravan. Nash's student is our last hope."

31

No one spoke during the drive through the deserted township in New Jersey. Lightfoote piloted the car through tree-lined streets with the lights off. The night weighed heavily on them, each quiet and introspective, exhausted from the unending tension. Lost in thought, the address seemed to appear before them instantaneously, the time traveled like a vanishing dream. They exited the vehicle and walked up the short steps to a porch.

Lopez knocked on the creaking wood of an old door. No one answered. Houston and Lightfoote faced away from the house, weapons at the ready, scanning the dark street. He knocked again, each series of strikes against the wood harder. Frustration mounting, he struck vigorously, the knob vibrating and dancing back and forth past the frame.

"Any harder Conan and you might as well just knock the thing down," whispered Lightfoote.

"I know I saw some movement in the curtains," said Houston. "Someone's there. With everything that's happened, I can't blame them for laying low."

Lopez grasped the handle and set his shoulder against the panel. "There isn't time for norms. Angel's right—this old thing is ready to fall over."

"Got you," said Houston, pivoting and pointing her pistol at the door. "Angel, eyes on the road."

One try was enough. With a lunge his thick frame crashed into the door near the lock. The wood splintered and burst into shards, a cloud of dust following it inward.

Houston and Lopez moved in, followed quickly by Lightfoote. Creaking under their weight, a wooden floor extended down a dark corridor.

"We know you're in here!" shouted Houston. "There are three of us. We're armed. Don't do anything stupid. We're not here to hurt you. We need information."

They could hear their own breathing in the silence.

Lightfoote called out. "We're here to talk to Avi Kaplan. It's a matter of national security! Don't make us dig you out."

A muffled thump shook a doorway near the end of the hall. The three trained their weapons on the sound. The door creaked open and a trembling voice called out.

"Please, don't shoot. I'm unarmed."

As the door opened further a gaunt man in worn pajamas shuffled out with his hands in the air. He looked like an old image of Albert Einstein, complete with a shock of unruly hair and a mustache.

"Who else is here?" Lopez asked.

"No one. I live alone."

Houston walked toward the man cautiously. "I'll check him. Sweep the house."

"It's the truth," he said.

"Yeah, maybe."

Houston turned him against the wall and padded him down, glancing inside the closet and closing the door.

"Where is Avi Kaplan?"

"I'm Avi Kaplan."

"Nash's former student? The one who set up the museum and worked with him?"

"Yes, I cared for him for many years, off and on, since his, well, health problems."

"Health problems?" asked Houston.

He smiled wanly, his voice hoarse. "Who are you?"

"We'll get to that in a minute," said Houston, looking down the hallway. "That's a living room?"

"Yes."

"Okay, in there." She motioned with her Browning.

Kaplan's face tightened. "Yes, of course."

He walked in front of her, trembling. They entered a crowded room of chairs, a sofa, and boxes of papers. Houston had Kaplan take a seat on the couch, a cloud of dust rising as he sank into it. Lopez and Lightfoote returned.

"No sign of anyone," said Lopez.

"I closed the door and tied it shut with some wire," Lightfoote said. "It's busted all to hell. Won't slow anyone, but at least it's unlikely to attract the attention of an open door."

Houston turned to the old man. "Nash used to live here with you. Under nursing care."

"Yes." The old man hesitated. "That's what everyone was supposed to believe."

"Supposed to believe?" asked Lopez, holstering his weapon.

Kaplan nodded. "You said you were here for a national security concern. Regarding John Nash?"

"Yes," answered Lightfoote.

"Then surely you won't be surprised to learn that there have been forces interested in keeping John Nash under firm control."

Lopez loomed over the skeletal form on the couch. "What do you mean? The truth, and quickly."

He smiled and stared up at Lopez. "You don't scare me. I'm sure you could torture the information out of me, but this old heart would pop before you got enough pain going to open my mouth. I'm ancient, my friends. Had a long life. Seen a lot of things. Always John was with me. My last act in this world won't be to betray him. You'll have to find another way to persuade me to divulge his secrets."

"And what would that be?"

"You could start with your names. Tell me what important matter concerns my old friend. Convince me there's some reason I should trust you."

Lightfoote opened her backpack. "What if I told you we have a sixty-year-old, unpublished paper by John Nash?" She removed the laptop and opened it. "One that was encoded on the poster board in the Nash Museum."

"The fire in the news? That was *you?*"

Lightfoote marched across the room and sat down beside the old man.

"What if we told you we were pointed in this direction by a terrorist who nearly brought down the world financial system last month?"

She held the screen up to him. He squinted and read aloud.

"*This is why we are not free. The puppet masters pull the strings.*"

The three stared intensely at him as he met their gazes, one by one.

"This is supposed to impress me? He saw conspiracies everywhere. Left delusional messages in code everywhere. He was a schizophrenic, you know."

"This isn't the paper. It's only a last comment he made at the end of it." She scrolled on the trackpad. "*This* is the paper."

"External Equilibration in Non-cooperative Games?" he read slowly.

Lopez rumbled. "Look carefully. The world outside is going to hell. Somehow, the terrorist who trigged this disaster knew about this paper, this coded message from six decades ago. It's never been published. Isn't available anywhere."

"Can you increase the font size? An old man's eyes," said Kaplan. Lightfoote obliged. He scanned the text and spoke in a distracted tone. "So, you're chasing after the work of one madman on the words of another?"

"Both geniuses," said Houston. "Something's going on. This may be a key to understanding it."

The old man slowly scrolled on the trackpad, furrowing his brow. He didn't speak for several minutes.

"Yes," he nodded his head at last. "Dear God, yes."

"Yes, what?" asked Lightfoote.

Kaplan leaned back against the back of the sofa and closed his eyes. "*Tanquam ex ungue leonem.*"

Lightfoote cocked her head. "Sorry?"

"The lion is known by his claw," said Lopez.

"Indeed," said Kaplan. "You have found something remarkable. It can be no one else. The wording, the logic. This is John Nash."

"Can you explain it to us?" asked Lopez.

"Probably. But not right away. I would need days to digest this. He was the genius, not me."

Houston exhaled. "We don't have days. We have a nation falling down around us."

"And the note?" asked Lightfoote. *"Their fingerprints are in the global numbers; once the criterion is reached, they pull the trigger.* What does this mean?"

"I don't know. It sounds like too much that came from his paranoia over the years."

Lightfoote put a hand on his shoulder. "What if it's not? What if he was on to something and this paper reveals something we just can't understand?"

"Then you'd need to speak with John."

Lopez growled. "No longer an option. As you know."

The old man nodded. "Inconvenient, isn't it? As soon as I set up that museum, which contained this encoded paper, poor John met with a strange death."

"What are you implying?" asked Houston, her eyes narrowed.

"I was planning the museum for a number of years. John had become quite the celebrity. Recovery from madness, like it was some sort of twelve step program. Nobel Prize. Hollywood film and Oscar. The money flowed in from it all. We hardly had to break a sweat fundraising." He coughed, the sound ragged and ominous. "Sorry. Bad lungs. We all used to smoke in those days. Now, John begged me to include this poster in the exhibit, you know? So strange. Not the most flattering of displays. But of course I said yes. Who was I to deny him something so small at this stage?" He shook his head. "Governmental delegation swept the museum several times. Removed several items citing national security. Always passed by the poster board."

"Governmental delegation?" said Houston.

He smiled. "It wasn't the first time they had micromanaged our lives. Always so interested in John, since his consulting years. Took him away to special retreats many times. A pact with the devil. Money and support during his illness. Some kind of favors I was never privy to."

Lopez sat on the coffee table in front of Kaplan. "You sound paranoid."

"Do I? What if I told you I could help you after all?"

Lopez growled. "Then help us!"

"First—who are you? Don't lie to me. Tell me who you are."

Lopez leaned forward and looked the old man in eyes. "Here is the truth. No lies. We're fugitives: Falsely accused and judged because we uncovered something dirty in the heart of Washington. We helped stop the digital worm that has brought so much destruction. We captured the man behind it. Before he was murdered, he claimed his actions were to stop something even worse. He pointed us here, to Nash, to this encoded paper. We're trying to discover what he was talking about, and we've been targeted for death for doing so. We need your help."

Kaplan held Lopez's gaze for several seconds. He nodded and closed his eyes again.

"Truth is always in the eyes. Let me change. We'll need my car."

Houston blinked. "Why? Where are we going?"

Kaplan laughed softly. "The car accident? *A lie.* Staged. Someone felt John Nash needed to disappear. But they still needed his mind."

"Wait," said Lightfoote, her eyes widening, "you mean—"

"John Nash is very much alive."

"Where?" she whispered, her voice hoarse.

"A care facility, nearly an hour away. But you won't find it on any maps or in any directories."

"John Nash, alive," repeated Houston, her eyes locking with Lopez.

Kaplan nodded, appraising each of them in turn. His eyes lingered on their weapons.

"And you may want to bring those guns along."

32

"HOW MANY GUARDS?"

Houston stared from behind the wheel at the old man beside her. Lopez and Lightfoote were fully suited up with body armor, checking their weapons in the backseat. They'd been on back roads in New Jersey running northwest of Princeton for forty-five minutes. The ride had been mostly quiet, the directions given by Nash's former student punctuating the stillness as they drove across the rural landscape. As they approached, Kaplan had begun to describe the location.

"Not sure. More in the beginning after his death was announced. But less of late. John's weak. He actually needs a lot of the care of a nursing facility. There are many patients in case someone stumbled across the location. To keep up appearances." Kaplan pointed through the window. "Here. Left here."

"Why did they let you visit? Why let you know?" asked Lopez. "You could have blown the entire thing wide open."

"Their threats were all too clear. John's their prisoner. I'd be killing him if I spoke publicly."

"That he's in a special nursing facility is one thing," said Houston. "But why on earth is it under armed guards?"

"For reasons that only the US government knows. Likely the same reason they faked his death."

"It is starting to sound like the man's paranoia wasn't so delusional," muttered Lopez.

Kaplan sighed heavily. "It's been a world of shadows and mazes. I've only wanted to make sure John's cared for. I had to make certain compromises." He gazed out the window. "The age of the paper you brought to me tonight, it's part of this. That's when John began to lose touch with reality. It was the same time the government took such a fascination with his work. Everyone speculated as to why. That film even assumed it was part of his delusions. But no."

"No?" asked Lightfoote. She leaned forward over the seat.

"It was real. They came. John left with them on many occasions.

He was never the same after that. I never knew why. But this? Maybe there's an answer now. Maybe it has something to do with this paper. Something he was trying to tell us through it. I brought you here to seek my own answers as much as for what you hope to accomplish. Answers to a lifetime of struggle with pain and uncertainty." Again he motioned toward the window. "Okay, slow down now. It's around that bend in the road."

Houston pulled the car to the side of the two-lane country road, trees of a forested patch surrounding them.

"If you don't want them to know you're coming, I recommend approaching through the forest, on foot."

Houston nodded. "We can't bring you with us, Dr. Kaplan."

"I suffer no delusions. I'm long past my clandestine spy years." He smiled.

"We'll let you know what he said."

"Thank you. I'll try to visit him tomorrow if they allow it on such short notice. I want to talk to him in person."

They exited the car quickly, leaving the economist in the front seat. Lopez opened the trunk and removed a duffel. He unzipped it and retrieved a rifle fitted with a telescopic sight, along with several handguns. Popping open an aluminum case, he handed a large dart with a clear middle section to Houston. Liquid sloshed inside.

"Do you think the tranqs are still good?" she asked.

"I don't know. Not a biochemist. So, a test." Lopez walked to the passenger side and opened the door, brandishing a dart before Kaplan. "I'm sorry, professor, but we need to test these tranquilizers. And while your trust in us is refreshing, I'm too jaded."

"You're going to knock me out?"

Lopez nodded. "That way you don't cause us any unexpected trouble, and we find out if these things still work."

"You're going to drug the guards?" asked Lightfoote.

"Not going to kill them unless we have to," Lopez answered. "And there are a lot of variables in hand to hand. We'll see how many we spot outside, try to take them down quietly, and make our way inside."

Lightfoote shook her head. "Best laid plans."

"Yeah, I know."

The tranq worked.

Lopez lay the seat back as the old man dozed. He closed the trunk as quietly as he could. Then the three of them made their way through the forest in the direction of the nursing home, keeping the curve of the road in sight. They crested a hill that opened to a compound. A driveway off the main road ended in a circular path before a one-story building. It was surrounded by barbed-wire, several security cameras visible around the fencing even from that distance.

Houston gazed through a pair of binoculars. "Guards inside are going to spot us. Likely there's some kind of motion detection system as well. No prep on this one, Francisco. Going to be messy." She continued her reconnaissance. "Two guards at the gate, none along the perimeter. It's not much on the outside."

"Why don't you take those two down and blow the power lines?" said Lightfoote. "It will blind anyone inside."

"And signal reinforcements when the alarm system fails. Also, some of those inside might be on machines they need. Maybe Nash."

She nodded. "You're right. Not worth the risk."

"You two make a run around this hill," said Houston, "come along the right side wall by the main entrance. Try to stay clear of sensors if you can spot them. Send me an alert and I'll drop the two at the gate. You keep an eye on the main door while I get down to the gate and check them for access cards. Drop anyone who comes out. If we're lucky, one of them has a keyed access to the place and we're in without triggering any alarms."

"Good a plan as any," said Lopez.

"Okay, go!"

Lightfoote and Lopez left her side and sprinted through the trees. Houston dropped to the ground and rested the rifle on a bipod, angling herself to the scope. She rotated the butt plate and loaded the first dart, closing the housing. She peered down the barrel and adjusted the focus. An alert buzzed her cell phone and she raised the binoculars, training them on the building. Lopez and Lightfoote were positioned along the wall by the entrance.

"No alarms. No movement inside," she said, scanning the

building. "Nice footwork."

Houston texted back and pocketed the phone, lowering herself again along the rifle. She checked the gas cartridge a final time and switched on the laser.

The guards were in heavy coats, pacing along the front fence on opposite sides of the driveway. Houston didn't envy them that duty in winter without a gatehouse, but the clothing complicated her mission. The dart might not penetrate the coat, depending on its composition and thickness. She would have to hit below the coat, in the leg or buttocks.

She angled the rifle slowly, bringing up the green circle of light along the leg of the nearest guard. She estimated the distance to be about 50 yards. He paused a moment, lighting a cigarette, providing her with the perfect shot. She exhaled, paused a second with the light on his thigh, and pulled the trigger.

The projectile launched with only a swift expulsion of air into the night. She switched off the laser and blinked, peering into the scope. The figure jerked backward and grabbed his leg. The dart dangled from his upper thigh.

Reload. She ignored the form of the other guard moving toward her first target and flipped the end of the rifle butt ninety degrees. Grabbing a second dart from the case, she inserted it in the mechanism and closed the butt. When she peered in the scope again, the second guard stood over the kneeling form of the guard she'd hit, trying to help him to his feet. She fired again.

This dart struck the second guard in the ass. He dropped the first guard, who tumbled limply to the ground. Houston watched him stagger as he grabbed his right butt cheek. He fell beside the first guard. She left the dart gun on the hill and sprinted down toward the prone men.

Five minutes, a guard's keycard, and several hallways later, they stood in front of room 117. No other guards were present in the building. A handful of elderly patients slept in rooms scattered haphazardly throughout the building. A frightened nurse had been locked in a closet. A front desk search revealed a chart of patients and locations. John Nash was near the back of the building.

"All right, here goes," said Lopez, pushing the door open.

A small desk lamp beside a window spilled frail light into the room. An empty bed rested against a wall on their left, a table and sofa on the right. The lamp cast a ghostly hue on a wizened form in a bathrobe, an angular face with sunken cheeks staring with empty eyes at the wall.

The three approached the figure, geometric doodles covering the surface of the desk beside him like some mad child's scribblings. Lightfoote passed her hand in front of his eyes. No reaction. She crouched down to match her eye-line to his.

"John Nash?" she said.

The face didn't move.

"Dr. Nash? We need your help. We need to ask you some questions about one of your papers. The one you never published. *External Equilibration in Non-cooperative Games*. Please! Dr. Nash?"

The old man blinked and focused on her face. He studied the two beside her, nodding solemnly.

"Yes. Yes, I've been expecting you for a long time."

33

Lopez and Houston pulled up chairs as Lightfoote held her crouch in front of the Nobel Laureate.

"You've been expecting us?" she asked.

His lips moved in a silent mutter, his voice rising as from some dark depth.

"They said you would come. Well, of course they didn't. I know they don't exist. These creatures. So much knowledge they have! But it is suspect. Always suspect! It must always be examined, filtered. *Tested*. But they said you would come. I had to analyze. I had to distinguish the real and the misfirings of the mind. It wastes so much time, this madness. So much time. I could have done so much more."

Lightfoote looked desperately at Houston and Lopez. She continued to prod him.

"Dr. Nash, the paper?"

"Where's Alicia?"

Lopez mouthed toward Lightfoote. "Alicia?"

Nash continued without an answer. "They said she died in a car crash. I don't have enough data. Not enough to classify these voices. Lies? Truth? Is this place real? It is new. New walls. New voices. Too soon to know. Where is Alicia?"

Lightfoote continued. "Dr. Nash. The paper. *External Equilibration in Non-cooperative Games*. Do you remember it?"

A sharp bark burst from the old man's lips. "Remember it? It's the only damned thing I did of any importance in my life." He reached out a trembling arm to Lightfoote and grasped her hand. "Murdered. Killed in the womb. They would never let it see the light of day. Did they kill her, too? Can you tell me?"

Lopez leaned forward. "Who's they?"

Nash leaned back in his chair, still holding Lightfoote's hand.

"They they they they. It is the delusional pronoun. Always a *they* somewhere to do something and whisper nonsense and be the conspiratorial cause of this and that and the prime mover." He closed his eyes. "They keep me alive only for the hope of more material. I refused at first. Such a mistake." He leaned forward and stared wild-eyed. "Pain rules all things. Pain erases personality. Pain they brought and branded and cut and I could not hold. They needed predictions. I developed the theory. Never enough. They kept coming. It broke me. Into pieces. Each piece a voice. A thousand voices. From the stars and the pits of hell."

Lightfoote placed her other hand on his and looked into his eyes. "Predictions?"

Tears dripped down his face as he stared into her eyes.

"Yes, yes. I see it in your eyes. I see it in your soul. Burnt soul. You have been to hell, too. Yes, poor child. The demons have branded you. And now I know it." He closed his eyes. "She is dead."

He sat shaking for several moments weeping silently. Coughing, he pushed Lightfoote away and wiped his eyes. "Social. Economic. Population. The numbers were available to us finally. Data had been collected for decades by that point, for the first time in human history. They saw my work. Saw the embryonic theories. They knew what I could give them and the devils made me do it."

"Dr. Nash, what did you do?"

"I gave them the key to total control! Centuries and centuries, they had lumbered clumsily. But now, in an age of god-like computation, they too would become gods. Thanks to John Nash." He growled like some frightened dog. "But I had a last ace up my sleeve. My *paper*. I knew I couldn't publish it openly. They would stop me. One way or the other. But it turned hard. The thousand voices were tearing at my soul. I was going quite mad from it. But I persevered. I put it down in a way they could not see. And the voices told me, 'One day, they will come. They will understand. They will come and end it.' And here they are." His mouth opened into a macabre grin.

"We don't understand it, Dr. Nash. What does the paper say?"

He startled upright, his expression incredulous. "But it's so obvious! Any mathematical analysis of the markets with anything remotely like my models would reveal it. How can it be no one has seen it? Perhaps, yes, perhaps they were taken. They could not allow it. Yes."

"Just tell us what it means," said Lopez.

"The models are predictive. Even I was amazed how well it all worked. Socio-economic movements of populations. Market cycles. Political movements. Predictive, except that they are not!" He laughed maniacally. "How could they predict accurately when unseen hands steered all from the darkness? Maxwell's demon moonlighting in socio-dynamics!" He bent forward, his index finger extending rigidly toward them. "But put in variables to model external modulation of the models—bang! There it was! The demon hand behind history. Controlling everything. Steering humanity to their purposes. Like a closed thermodynamic system, entropy, distribution of resources. To ensure control, predictability, they needed to preserve *low* entropy. Funnel resources upwards. Vast income inequality, power imbalances."

Lightfoote furrowed her brow. "So, you are saying that—"

"Sorry! Yes. I must select the vocabulary carefully. I have to speak with the subsets of ideas that are rational. *Silence* the voices." His gaze turned distant. "I proved *mathematically* that the markets were being manipulated by a powerful influence. One outside of any of the known economic variables. Is *that* simple enough for you? But more than this. Yes, so much more. More than they understood fully. There are cycles between nations and groups, statistical mechanics, the billions making it predictable. There is a turning point that recurs with temporal predictability, a phase transition of instability. An hour of revolution when a maximum in instability is reached."

Lightfoote gasped. "The Nash Criterion."

Nash laughed. "Yes. They should name it after me. That is as good a name as any. But no one will ever know."

"We know," she said. "And your paper, it shows how to calculate it? How to determine when these instability points will come?"

"Yes. That's the whole point."

She nodded, her words spilling out rapidly. "And they want this desperately. It will allow them to know when the revolutions will come and ride them out."

He shook his head. "Too naive. Much more than ride them out.

To destroy them. Kill, and kill millions to maintain their course, their control. They only guessed I had this answer. They only had metrics for when the criterion neared. But not a predictive model. They never got it from me."

Lopez shook his head. "I don't understand. Why would you give in to their demands on all but this?"

"Because it is the key to their long-term survival, Francisco," said Lightfoote.

"A great weakness," finished Nash. "Social cycles they cannot avoid, but can control if they are predictable." He pointed with his finger. "But which their enemies could use against them if they held the predictive power."

"Are we in a cycle now?" asked Lightfoote. "The world is falling apart. They act threatened."

"No," said Nash, shaking his head. "What has happened—an anomaly. It's Asimov's Mule. *Unpredictable.*"

"What?"

"The predictions rely on statistical patterns, patterns that only exist, that are only predictable when there are very large numbers of people to smooth out the random noise. Like the thermodynamics of gasses. A few molecules and quantum chaos rules. But Avogadro's number? The gas laws are obeyed! Of course, there is always noise— individuals, small groups, doing unpredictable, random things. Random for the models. But if five billion do the predictable things, the world is predictable, the noise averaged out. Unless you have a Mule."

Lopez grumbled. "What the hell is a Mule?"

"No one reads anymore," Nash sighed. "An individual that introduces a systemic randomness. It rarely happens. So few have the ability, and they hunt them down ruthlessly now. But this Anonymous it had to be a Mule. No other explanation. Now the system is off model. The curves of prediction diverge from events. They have to steer it back. But until they do, they are vulnerable. Discovery. Intervention. Assassination. This Mule has deliberately exposed and weakened them. Now is the time to act."

Houston shook her head. "But Fawkes didn't reveal where they are."

Nash exhaled, his posture slouched. "It's in the numbers. You can't hide the source of the external stimulus. Follow the numbers back to them. It can be computed. You will find them."

Lopez threw his hands up. "Dammit, who are *they*?"

Nash turned to him and grasped the priestly robes.

"Bilderberg."

With that word the room was plunged into darkness, the central air silenced, the power cut. Everything fell still.

Nash sighed.

"Too late. Too late. They're here."

34

"DOWN ON THE floor!" cried Houston.

They dove to the ground just as the windows exploded. Glass sprayed inward as bullets whizzed over their heads. Paneling splintered, fabric burst open, and dust filled the air as shards tinkled to the ground. They rolled away from the exposed wall, gunfire trailing them and pocking the floor with holes. Lightfoote and Houston dove behind a couch, Lopez rising behind a ventilation pipe jutting out from the wall. He reached into his robes and removed two grenades clipped to his body armor. And pulled the pins.

"Frag out!"

He hurled the grenades through the battered window and turned his head. Light flashed and two thunderous claps shook the building one after the other. Dust and debris spilled into the room through the shattered window. Then silence as the gunfire stopped.

Houston cried out from behind the couch. "They'll be in the building. We've got seconds until they can pin us at the door!"

"Nash!" cried Lightfoote. Her head popped over the couch. The professor lay dead on the ground, his head a gruesome impact zone of multiple rounds.

"Tell me you have more grenades, Francisco!" yelled Houston.

"One."

He didn't need instructions. Together he and Houston darted toward the door, both unleashing a hailstorm of bullets through the window into the night. No one returned fire. Lightfoote took up the suppressing fire as the pair reached the door.

Lopez pulled the pin and tucked the grenade to this chest. He motioned downward to Houston. They both crouched.

"Now," he whispered. She turned the knob, flinging the door wide.

Lopez rolled the grenade outward and Houston slammed the door shut. The pair dove face first to the ground. An eruption of gunfire punctured holes in the door above them, the discharge terminating with an explosion.

The door blasted inward in pieces, fragments of wood and metal embedding themselves in the walls. Houston screamed out and clutched her leg. Lightfoote leapt over her body, firing into the hallway. Short return fire followed, and a guttural cry.

In the sudden silence, Lopez pulled Houston away from the window and behind the couch. He tore open the black fabric of her pants to reveal a black gash in her thigh.

"It's a nick, Sara. Shrapnel sliced you open, but nothing inside." He sliced and ripped segments of his robes.

"How deep?" she gasped as he stuffed fabric in the wound and tied a band around her leg.

"Deep enough. But the bleeding is manageable. We need to get you out. Stitched. Up!"

She placed her arm around his shoulders and neck, hopping alongside him toward the door.

"We're sitting ducks," she muttered.

"Inside is clear," called Lightfoote as she darted into the room. She glanced at Houston's leg and at Lopez. "Can you carry her? Fireman's style? We need the speed." Lopez nodded.

"Shit," gasped Houston as Lightfoote helped hoist her onto the broad shoulders of the former priest.

"All right, let's move!" said Lightfoote, dashing quickly down the hallway. Lopez followed behind, awkwardly navigating the shattered doorway. The bodies of three soldiers in gear lay strewn around the entrance. Inexperienced, or underestimating their quarry, they had foolishly made a fatal close approach. They were a horror show.

Two more bodies lay prone on the ground as he sped down the hallway, his thick frame bowed under Houston's weight, footsteps sounding thunderous to his ears. He felt his breath coming in gasps, the muscles of his back beginning to burn.

Lightfoote held up a hand as he approached the entrance to the building. Stopping on a dime proved more strenuous than the run, and he nearly lost balance.

"Dammit, Francisco!" said Houston as he slammed her into the doorway. "I don't need more damage!"

Lightfoote scanned the area outside with night vision goggles. Satisfied, she nodded to the pair.

"Can't see any movement. There might be an ambush waiting, but I'm hoping they overcommitted in there. Anyway, we don't have much of a choice. We have to go before more arrive."

"Agreed," gasped Lopez. "I've got one shot up that hill and need to take it soon."

"Let's go. You first and if you draw fire at least I'll have a chance to counter."

They ran. Lopez lumbered up the grassy hill toward the forest with Lightfoote waiting several seconds before following. No one waited in ambush. No shots were fired. She exited at a full sprint and quickly overtook them, scampering up the hill into the trees. As he crested the top of the hill, she passed him again, the goggles strapped on, and scouted the facility below. Lopez lowered himself to one knee.

Lightfoote returned. "Clear. Nothing moving down there."

"I'll need a minute," said Lopez.

"No time," said Lightfoote. "We'll make a basket."

They grasped each other's wrists in a square pattern. Houston stood on one leg and dropped into the seat. The pair hoisted her, shuffling quickly through the underbrush. Five minutes later, they had reached the car.

It was clear even from a distance that they wouldn't find Kaplan alive. The vehicle had been damaged, the tires ruptured by gunfire. Blood covered the inside, coating the windows in crimson.

"Motherfuckers," whispered Houston as she rested against a tree beside Lightfoote. She watched Lopez remove several bags from the trunk and place them on the ground. "At least they were too much in a hurry to search the thing."

"We need a vehicle," he said flatly. "We could ditch the gear, but we'll need to put some space between us and this place soon."

Lightfoote exhaled. "Those soldiers didn't teleport. There'll be a car or truck at the facility."

"Go *back* there?" asked Lopez.

"I'll run back. Either we finished them and the spoils are ours, or we didn't, in which case we're basically screwed anyway. I'll just find out before you do."

Lopez frowned. "Go. You better come back."

Lightfoote saluted and began a quick jog down the road.

"Meanwhile," groaned Houston, "get your ass over here and lower me to the ground. I'm not going to wait out our doom on one foot beside this damn oak tree."

35

MILES OF BARREN cornfields long-ago harvested surrounded them —mangled, yellowed stalks poking through a foot of snow. The convoy had halted fifty miles outside Kansas City, gleaming gray and camouflage spreading out for miles around them. In the cold December air, the president, her advisors, civilian and military, shivered around a long foldout table with a map. Beside it, a large flatscreen monitor had been erected, a lengthy power line running back to the command vehicle.

"What are the numbers this time, General Franks?" York asked.

"Double what we faced at Columbus," he said grimly, mouth drawn in a line. "Satellite data indicates they've cut off any reasonable routes this convoy could consider taking around their positions." He pointed to images on the flat screen. "You'll see they've learned from Ohio. It'll cost us to break through their lines. The only advantage I can see is that this time they've struggled to bring in the heavier artillery units. Half the number we saw before. Our guerrilla tactics and the weather have been very effective since we got some of the aircraft back online. But the increasing air power on their side might make up for it."

Savas spoke up for the first time. "So, we're looking at a longer battle, likely with far more casualties than Columbus?"

Several of the military men openly scowled in his direction. Savas knew many resented their presence at these strategy sessions, and he didn't know why York insisted they be there. But he would speak his mind while it lasted.

"Yes," said the General. "But nothing we can't take and remain fully capable of completing our journey. That's our hard assessment."

"With all the aircraft coming online," said Cohen, "is there a point in revisiting the option for the president's evacuation directly to NORAD?"

"No," cut in the General. Several of the aides and advisers nodded in agreement.

"Why not?" asked York, her sharp tone mollifying the hostile looks coming from her staff.

General Franks shifted to a more diplomatic tone. "Ms. President, while it's true the odds are better than they've been for such a mission, it is our opinion they are still far too risky, and the damage to our cause if you are lost, far too high."

"And what about the lives of the hundreds, probably thousands, of young men and women who will die at Kansas City? How high is the price on their lives?"

"It's not that we don't take into account the people serving—"

"Spare me, General. Taking their lives for granted has been a national pastime for decades." She gestured to the screen. "At this level, it's all abstract—marks on a map and numbers. And most of us here remain cocooned in our command bubble, even in this convoy placing us so close to those we're asking to die for us. To die for *me*."

The stout form of the General tightened. "We don't have the aircraft to give you a proper escort. If they were to get wind of the mission, we couldn't stop a determined sortie. Hell, some airborne or ground launched SAM could blow you out of the sky. And I don't even know what types of drone assets they have."

George Tooze, the Secretary of Homeland Security, leaned across the table, his gaunt frame trembling in the rising wind.

"Elaine, this is a hard choice. No doubt about it. But you'd be a fool to rely on a mad dash, vulnerable, exposed in an aircraft. The General and his staff say we can fight our way to NORAD. Many will die, yes, but it'll be much worse for the nation to lose you – for you to fall into Hastings's hands, and leave us without the force of your personality fighting his block. We're almost there! One more battle is all he has left in him."

York frowned and stared out over the vehicles. Savas didn't envy her. Every choice she made, even the right ones, would cost lives. Bad choices would cost more lives. He had never experienced such a burden of command.

"You're sure they can't mount another offensive?"

The General shook his head. "Not near enough time. They were stretched thin as it is here. Without compensating for the lost ground artillery with aerial power, even with their stronger positions, we're going to run roughshod over them. There's no way they manage to outflank us from here to Colorado. Not after two defeats. They can still snipe at us, but their stopping power's gone."

York nodded. She looked at Savas and Cohen. "God knows I want to spare our troops another battle. And I certainly don't want to be the reason for a single death. But we're in a war of hearts and minds as much as territory right now. I and what remains of the Constitutional government have to reach NORAD." She turned to the military men. "There'll be no evac. We face them. And goddammit, you better be sure we win this and win it big."

The meeting ended. The maps rolled up and the electronics rolled back into the vehicles. York turned to Savas and Cohen a final time, but said nothing. Then walked stiffly back to the truck.

"Looks like the weight of the world is on her shoulders," said Cohen.

"It is," said Savas. He shivered. "Let's get inside before we freeze."

36

A DARK SUV sped through the New Jersey back roads. The license plate was damaged, impossible to read. A black antenna rose from the back, thick and unmoving even as the air rushed over the roof. Opaque windows reflected the night.

Inside, Lopez gripped the wheel tightly and tuned a scanner on the dash. Harsh voices barked out coded signals in military slang. He grunted and turned briefly to the back of the vehicle.

Behind him, in the place of standard passenger seats, flat screens lined the sides of the truck, stools bolted to the floor in front of them. Racks of weapons gleamed in the back, a makeshift cot beside them. Houston lay on it with her leg propped up and her upper thigh heavily bandaged.

"How's the leg, girl?" he asked.

"Hurts like hell. Thank God for the medkit. Best we can manage now."

Lightfoote spoke as she glared at a monitor. "Pretty damn lucky find, if you asked me. Mobile command vehicle, had their positions mapped out. We'd have been caught in a dragnet if our little commando team hadn't left us this baby."

"*Had* their positions mapped out?" asked Lopez.

"Yeah," sighed Lightfoote. "We just lost the readout. Matter of time before they figured it out. Took them longer than I thought. Guess they were spread pretty thin."

Houston leaned up in the cot. "You're sure you killed our GPS?"

"Yes, or we'd already be dead," she said. "But I'm not complaining. Positions, thread the needle to get out of the net. Medkit. And now a small arms locker back there. My favorite's the grenade launcher."

"Rack of M249s looks good," said Houston. "Boxes of ammo underneath."

"We can't keep this rig," said Lopez. "They may not be able to track us, but they'll be looking for it at the major junctions. We'll have to take those soon."

"I agree," said Lightfoote. "I think we have a long trip ahead."

"Oh?"

"Results of the calculations coming in fast now. Nash knew what he was doing. I think we've found them."

"You're sure?" Houston asked. "You said it could take weeks."

"There are levels of precision." Lightfoote glanced at the laptop on her left. "Once you understand what the equations refer to, it's just a matter of number crunching. Nash couldn't do this in the day, but we have computers now in our pockets people like Nash could never have imagined. Code was easy to write. And this little baby," she said, patting the side of the SUV, "is one linked mother. Saved a lot of time. Grabbed numbers online for nation-state GDPs, population, trade—all the variables in his paper. For controls I did repeated analysis at various time points in history. Major world events—everything fit the curves of his models."

"So it means he could predict it. Like the weather?"

"Yes, but the key thing is the constraints on the system to match the curves."

"What does that mean?" asked Houston. "Constraints?"

"In this paper, Nash includes a set of equations that aren't about markets and populations and trade and all that. These equations are like some external force pushing on all these variables."

"This is Bilderberg, whatever it is?"

"Yes. That's the key. These predictions assume there's something *outside* of our societies and economies, something actively shaping the course of history. To any rational person, it would seem like madness—some divine hand. Any sensible person would just set those weird variables to zero—concentrate on those that relate to real world aspects of trade and population—then crank out the numbers."

"Except the real world doesn't agree," said Houston. "It agrees with having the outside force?"

"Right! The numbers coming out for nations, economies, populations: they agree with the equations that *have* the modifying external force. You need to tweak it, tweak the strength of those variables, but it's clear. *Something* is out there, something pulling the strings and levers, pushing the pieces across the board."

"So, back to Bilderberg. It was the last thing Fawkes said before he died."

Lightfoote nodded. "And coincidentally the last thing Nash whispered before *he* died. *Bilderberg*."

Houston sighed and lay back, repositioning her leg. "We need to find out what it is, then. Is it related to Cohen's Bilderberg group? Is that a front? Is it something else?"

Lopez spoke up from the front of the truck. "Whatever it is, whoever they are, Anonymous has them shaken. Fawkes nearly blew up the entire system they were using for—well, for whatever they are using it for. It's clear they have friends in the US government. They've taken out Fawkes, imprisoned our friends, hunted us down. This has pushed them into the open. Nash was right about that. This is our chance."

"And then there's the back-trace," said Lightfoote.

Lopez stiffened. "Did it finish? Did it work?"

"It's still computing, but it's converging on a single answer." Lightfoote shook her head. "It's amazing really. He said it could be done, and it can. Some of the variables in the external force equations are geographic. Money and power flow like a river that can be traced to its source."

"And where is it converging?" he asked.

"We need to wait a few days more to be sure, but looking at these confidence levels—I don't think the answer's going to change. It's centering on Europe. Maybe it's too obvious. Too simple. But it could end up focusing right on Bilderberg."

"But what *is* the Bilderberg Group?" asked Houston.

"Not the name. The fucking place itself."

She turned her laptop to Houston, revealing a world map decorated with thousands of colored lines. They crisscrossed the globe from city to city, nation to nation. A million small tributaries, the lines flowed from a central point, converging into a dense web in northern Europe.

"Oosterbeek, the Netherlands," she said, tapping her finger on the focal point. "Home of the Bilderberg hotel. Location of the conspiracy theorists' meetings of doom. Travel stop of dignitaries,

CEOs, Rockefellers, politicians. It's the goddamned nexus of it all."

Houston squinted at the FBI agent. "You mean it's real? The survivalist basement dwellers actually got this one right? There's really a shadowy organization running the world out of a hotel in Holland?"

"Bilderberg's looking like it might be the solution to the equations," said Lightfoote.

"Maybe so," grumbled Lopez, "but equations don't kill. Bilderberg does. We need a solution of our own."

"And a place to lay low," said Houston. "I've got a few weeks of recovery before I can be of any use. And it looks like we've got a long trip to make."

Lightfoote tapped frenetically on the laptop. "I've got something for that, too. There's a hacker underground, as you know. Well, I've been working with some of them to create something less abstract. Now there are a bunch of hackers *underground*. Outside of Newark. Abandoned fallout shelter. They've been setting up for a few weeks."

"What do you mean?" asked Lopez.

"Some who helped us with the decryption, some who believe in Fawkes's crazy quest," said Lightfoote. "Some are just anarchists who want to take down the system. They're expecting us." Lightfoote stood up and walked toward the back of the van, steadying herself on the side walls. "There's shelter and what's more some serious computer firepower. We can tap into their system and increase our attack on this problem one hundred fold. Should be able to confirm what I've done and go beyond it, narrow down the location for certain."

"You trust these people?" asked Houston.

"No," said Lightfoote, eyeing the weapons racks coldly. "But we have a tactical advantage."

37

THEY STOOD IN front of the ruins of an abandoned factory, rusted fencing and untended wild grass waist high and swaying in the cold wind. Several inches of snowfall from the night before conferred on the grounds a peace alien to the turmoil around them. In the distance, the taller buildings of Newark could be glimpsed in the morning sunrise.

Lightfoote struck the butt of a rifle repeatedly against a convex metallic plate embedded in the ground. Clouds of vapor escaped her lips. Nearby, Houston leaned heavily Lopez's shoulder, her wounded leg suspended slightly above the ground, her face a mask of pain.

"You're sure this is it?" asked Lopez.

Again Lightfoote struck the disk. "Yes," she grunted.

"You sure they're *here?*"

Before she could strike the plate again, a muffled impact rang several times from the object.

"Yes." Lightfoote smiled and lowered her weapon. A metal-on-metal screeching howled from the disk. "They're here."

The disk flipped sideways, revealing it to be a lid over a wide hole. They sprang back just in time as the barrels of multiple weapons pointed up through the opening, and one jerked back as it fired. A cloud of smoke induced a fit of coughing from inside the tunnel.

"Damn it, Morgoth!" someone choked. "Give me that gun!"

A head poked up quickly from the hole. It belonged to a heavily bearded, unkempt man in his twenties. He peered out from the hole, squinting in the morning light. He spun nearly a full circle before he saw them, eyes lingering on Lightfoote.

The beard smiled. "You Angel?"

Lopez exhaled. "Save us."

"Yeah, that's me," Lightfoote answered, stepping forward.

The man strapped a rifle over his shoulder and scampered up a ladder that extended from deep below. Behind him two men and a woman followed clumsily.

"I'm De-frag," he began, swallowing overgrown chunks of hair as he spoke. "Two dudes here are SixtyFour and Morgoth."

SixtyFour, baby-faced and gaunt, sported blond hair to his shoulders. He stooped and shuffled his feet incessantly, hiding a face pocked with acne, patches of unshaven hair scattered across his chin. Morgoth was older, graying hair trimmed to a millimeter in length contrasting with his deep black skin, a pair of smart glasses glinting in the rising sun.

"The little lady is Medea."

A heavyset woman squinted at them, hair dyed red. She wore a pair of taped glasses, a faded Wonder Woman shirt, and a suspicious expression.

De-frag continued. "We all use our handles here. We're the First Anarchists. Kinda the leaders but not really, 'cause you know there ain't supposed to be leaders in anarchy, right? But nothing was gettin' done, so we hadda come up with some kinda compromise, you see. Didn't go down great with everyone." He paused. "Sorry about the shot, yeah? No one's hurt, right?" He smiled awkwardly.

Lopez chanted under his breath. "Hail Mary, full of grace. Our Lord is with thee...."

"So," began Lightfoote loudly. "I'm Angel. It's good to meet you in the real world, De-frag. The big guy here is Gabriel," she said, nodding to Lopez.

Morgoth interrupted in a thick Kenyan accent. "And what's he supposed to be? Some priest? We don't need any priests here."

Lopez held the man's gaze. "Former priest," he growled. "Defrocked for sexually assaulting young boys and as an enemy of the state. Wanted by the FBI for multiple murders and acts of terrorism. But I am open to giving last rites over anyone I kill here. I also do weddings." The four hackers gaped. "Leaning on me and bleeding into her wound dressings is Mary. Now, are we going to stand out here, freezing and misfiring our weapons into the air, or can we get the hell inside and find her a place to rest?"

De-frag nodded spastically. "Oh, yeah, sure. Right, man! No problem."

Morgoth hissed, pointing at Lightfoote. "And that one, I don't care what you—"

"Morgoth, shut the fuck up and get SixtyFour down in the bunker." He glared at the black hacker who continued to eye Lightfoote. "Medea—how about you help Gabriel bring Mary over here and down the chute. *Now*, guys! Come on!"

Faces still in shock, the hackers obeyed. The two men entered the large entrance and bolted down the stairs. Medea walked slowly over and continued to eye the new arrivals with suspicion. She allowed Houston to place an arm over her shoulders, however, and showed surprising strength in helping Lopez carry her to the entrance.

"Holy God-damned Angel!" piped De-frag, his face exploding into a boyish grin as he stepped alongside her, watching Lopez and Medea orchestrate lowering Houston down the three-foot wide metal tube. "You and Gabriel and Mary. It's like some backwoods revival!"

"Uh-huh."

"Everyone's psyched you were coming. I mean, holy shit, it's Angel! You fucking beat *Fawkes* and let loose the most goddamned crazy code into the wild—from the fucking FBI servers! You an agent? What's your real name? You don't have to say."

"Angel," she said, her face strained as she watched Houston disappear from sight.

"Oh," he said with evident disappointment. "Anyway, like I said, you coming was *sweet!* But you fucking brought presents! The priest, ah man. Murder, terrorism, FBI most wanted! *Really?* Shit!"

"And child molestation."

His face clouded. "Uh, yeah. Um, okay that ain't so cool."

"Don't worry, that part's a lie. Big Brother. Framed."

"Really? That's even better! He must really be a bad ass!"

Lightfoote turned sharply to face him. "Look, De-frag, we're here for a reason. We need those servers you promised me. Tell me you have them."

He nodded vigorously. "Yeah, yeah. For *sure*. I mean *stability* is still an issue in this old shit hole, but mostly, *yeah*."

She held his gaze. "*Mostly?* You better not be jerking me around or that killer priest will be the least of your concerns."

He shook his head. "No way, man! But, ah, look, it's just, well—"

She grabbed his beard and yanked him toward her.

"It's just *what?*"

De-frag's voice raised slightly in pitch. "It's just that not everyone gets *why*, you know? We got all these people together—man, it wasn't easy, let me tell you—we promised them to fight for Fawkes. Help bring down the system. Dot gov, FBI, CIA, whatever, they get that. But what the heck's this Buildingburg?"

"Bilderberg."

"Yeah, that. You know, not everyone's on board. So, you know, maybe like you could smooth things over down there? Make it clear why we're all doing this? You got all kinda fans, Angel. And maybe some who'd like to take you down, too, you know? Hackers always gotta one up."

Lightfoote let go of his hair and scowled.

"Yeah, I'll make it clear all right. One way or another."

She marched off to the hole.

38

LIGHTFOOTE RELEASED THE ladder rungs and landed loudly on the metal floor at the bottom of the tube. De-frag swung the heavy lid shut with a grunt, cutting off the morning light above. Balancing on the wall-embedded ladder, he turned the wheel handle to lock the hatch shut, and the poorly oiled threads cried out and reverberated through the steel walls of the shelter. She tasted a staleness in the air as dust rained from above.

Lightfoote let her eyes adjust as De-frag climbed down slowly. Weak LEDs glowed along walls. Away from the chamber, a tunnel jutted into foggy light. Indistinct mumbling and chatter echoed down its length.

"It's down that way," said De-frag, wiping dirt from his hands on his checkered shirt. "Pretty damn big inside, actually, but this tunnel's a squeeze."

"Where's the electricity from?"

"Well, we got some big-ass batteries and a diesel generator. But we don't start it 'cause we all fucking suffocate. Morgoth wanted to put some solar panels topside, but I was all like, 'Dude, it's like an advertising sign saying we're here.'"

"You're not running this off batteries."

"Right, no. So, this thing's built close to an old transformer. Sewage line too, which helps some, you know. Some paranoid old boys back in the '50s. Russian nukes, bam! You know?" Lightfoote eyed him impatiently. "Yeah, so we got some electricians who rigged a connection. Course they're not really trained in grid-leeching, so we've had surge problems and whatnot. Lost some servers. Now we've got the boxes on layers of protectors. It's a bit ridiculous, but so far so good! Ready for the hacker-pocalypse!"

"Okay. Let's see what you've done here," said Lightfoote, and she crawled quickly down the tunnel. De-frag sighed and hefted his bulk into the tube and slowly wormed his way forward.

Lightfoote reached the end of the metal cylinder and rose to a crouch, her shaved head scraping the lip of the exit, her eyes parsing the expansive space in front of her. The entrance opened three feet above the floor of an extended corridor that ran forward for perhaps fifty yards. The height of the ellipsoidal shelter reached ten feet at its apex, but forced stooping near the sides as the ceiling tapered off. Along the length of the main hall, doorways opened to side rooms.

People milled about the space, congregating at makeshift computer tables hosting monitors and keyboards, or at a long, central table where meals were taken. The walls and floor were a hazard of cables and wires running in bundles or loose, duct-taped in place or left unsecured. Dark power cords slithered along the length of the shelter, daisy-chained with adapter cords.

De-frag thumped to a stop behind her, panting. "This is the common area. Business end's the rooms way in the back—hold our server farms, as much as we could stuff into this place. The rest are bedrooms and stuff. Have their own toilets. That's probably where they took your friend. Makeshift medical. We have a real doc, too!"

By now, the din inside had begun to taper off, all eyes turning to Lightfoote. People had stopped eating and turned from their computers as heads cocked her way.

De-frag chatted on, oblivious. "It's a functional hacker terrorist cell! We got some of the area's best. Well, and not so best, too, if you want to the truth. But man! Fawkes started it all and then you two duked it out in cyberspace for control! Country's down for a long count. This is it! Just look at it!"

A strange wind of whispers replaced the rowdy conversations, and Lightfoote could catch repeating instances of "Angel" and "Fawkes." A heavily pierced woman at the end of the table stood up and faced her. She raised her hands and began an exaggerated and slow clapping. Other's joined in, some standing, some remaining seated, and the sound swelled and accelerated. Yells and whoops topped the ovation as stomping feet climaxed to the calls of "Angel, Angel, Angel!"

She turned her head back to De-frag. "Seriously?"

He beamed. "I told you you had fans!"

39

"WELL, LET'S GET this over with."

Lightfoote coiled even tighter at the tube opening and sprang outward, the impact of her boots reverberating through the metal shelter like thunder. Hackers swarmed her as she moved toward the table in the center of the long room, back-slapping her, many with looks of awe. Behind her, De-frag lowered himself awkwardly from the tube and straightened his twisted shirt.

The crowd parted roughly. Annoyed cries were stifled, and people moved away to allow a group of men to march toward Lightfoote. At the head marched Morgoth, his expression fiery. Two brawny men stalked behind him. They held metal pipes.

Lightfoote watched them approach silently. People near her instinctively moved away, leaving her and the three men in a circle of onlookers.

Morgoth sneered. "She's a Fed. She's not one of us. *Come on,* people! She sabotaged Fawkes's code. If it wasn't for her, he would have taken the system down once and for all. She's the enemy and shouldn't be here."

The chamber echoed with a chorus of boos. But some nodded their heads in agreement. Lightfoote stared impassively at the three men.

"Aw, shit!" came the voice of De-frag, and he pushed himself through the crowds. "Morgoth, fuck this, man! That's enough! We agreed to—"

One of the large men beside Morgoth stepped forward and came at the bearded hacker with a pipe. De-frag cursed and warded off blows with his arms, but he had little fight in him. The men drove him out of the circle.

Morgoth stepped closer to Lightfoote. "This is an anarchist commune, De-frag. You can't tell me what to do. And I'm not going to let this Fed stay here." He raised a gun and pointed it at her, inches from her face. Gasps erupted like steam leaks. "You're going to leave, or I'm—."

Before he could finish the sentence, Lightfoote's torso swept left and her hands darted in a blurred motion. There were two slaps barely separated, a snap and the gun was airborne, landing with a clank on the floor. Morgoth screamed and cradled his right hand.

"You fucking bitch!" He moaned. "You broke my finger!"

Lightfoote resumed her stance in front of him. "You were saying?"

An electric buzz spilled across the crowd. Morgoth backed up, doubled over, his mouth frothing. He turned to the pipe-wielding men. "Fuck her up!" he spat.

The two men approached her warily, their steps staccato, feinting to make a strike, hopping back, repelled by some unseen force as they approached within a given distance. Lightfoote balanced on the balls of her feet, never flinching. She rolled her eyes.

"You boys just do foreplay or are we gonna get it on?"

The man on her left growled and leapt toward her, drawing the pipe behind his head. He swung, but Lightfoote sprung into him, one arm locked and outward, her shoulder impacting his arm at the elbow, dissipating the strike. Simultaneously, the other hand assumed the shape of a slab, the fingers curled tightly, presenting the knuckles. They plunged into his windpipe, paralyzing him. She slung him into the onrushing form of his partner. The second attacker stumbled backward as the first assailant dropped to the ground clutching his neck, wheezed gasps erupting like barks.

Lightfoote had obtained a set stance again, eyeing the panicked man before her. "Time to quit, asshole."

But she only riled him up. With a yell he charged forward holding the pipe over his head. Lightfoote sidestepped as he swung wildly downward, thrusting her hand to his bent form and augmenting his twisting motion. Losing control, his upper torso overturned and he flipped onto the floor, the impact knocking the wind out of him. The pipe clattered and rolled across the floor. The other man gulped awkwardly beside him, still clutching his throat in pain.

Lightfoote scooped Morgoth's weapon off the floor. She stared at him as she held it up. "Not even competent street fighters. Let's see, no bullet chambered." She ejected the magazine and pocketed it. "I wonder if you even have another mag. Can you shoot lefty?" She tossed it at his feet, glaring at him. He turned away, his appetite for conflict vanished.

"Well, if that don't beat all the shit out of a horse." De-frag wandered back into the circle, nursing his bruised forearms.

Lightfoote turned her gaze around the gawking faces. She raised her voice.

"I could have killed this asshole! But my guess is he's not the only one to think like that—want me out. So I want him and any sympathizers to hear what I've got to say." All eyes were on her. "I don't give a damn if you don't agree with me. Between me and my friend," she cast a glance toward the back of the room, "we'll put anyone who tries to stop us six feet under." Heads turned. Lopez stood silently in his priestly robes, a shotgun held across his chest.

Stunned silence greeted her.

"Now that that's clear, let me tell you why you're going to let me do what I came here to do. Morgoth said I'm a Fed. He's right."

More murmuring. Louder.

"I took down Fawkes's code because it was the wrong fucking way to fix a broken system! *I* have the right way."

"She betrayed him! Betrayed us!" came a voice from the crowd.

"I watched Fawkes die, but I didn't kill him! It wasn't the Feds, or the CIA, or the police or government."

"Then who?" came another cry.

"They're called *Bilderberg*. An organization you need to help me stop. Fawkes's last words—given to me—gave us the key. He sent me an encrypted file that *you* all helped me break. You've seen it. An image of a madman's poster board. I've seen the online discussion— none of you could figure what it's about. But we *did*. In that wall is the code to reveal the hiding place of a conspiracy that's been controlling our world for centuries."

"The Illuminati!" "Aliens!" "Fucking Jews!"

"*Bilderberg!*" shouted Lightfoote over the growing bedlam, turning in a circle. "I'll distribute to you the proof. Make up your own minds. But I'm telling you it's *real*, and it's everything the worst conspiracy theorists have feared and more. And we have a way to track them down. A mad Nobel prize-winning economist gave it to us: economic equations to trace their center of influence."

"What did De-frag promise you?" came a woman's voice.

"Your servers. I need your raw computing power. You've all been fighting a long time. You just didn't know the real target. Today, *here*, I can give you that target. We're close to finding them. You can help me. And you can do it willingly. *Or* ... we take control of this place until we're finished."

Several shouted protests.

"No, it's not fucking democratic of me! It's dictatorial. Right now we don't have time to form a parliament or play teenaged anarchist. In case you haven't noticed, the nation is tearing itself apart outside. Maybe that's what some of you want. But if so, you're gonna have Mad Max and worse. Or you can help us reboot this world, help kill a very real Big Brother, and stop people who've been secretly controlling all our destinies!" She shone with sweat, towering above the crowd. "There's no more time for debate. I've got to get to work. Who's with me?"

No one moved or spoke. Lightfoote scanned the room, jaw set, as Lopez stood silently in the back. And then, a slow chant.

"Angel."

A few softly repeated her name. Others joined a growing chorus.

"Angel. Angel. Angel."

The chant swelled and people stomped their feet or banged the table or walls. The chamber rattled and shook. Lightfoote glanced back at Lopez. He simply nodded.

Slowly, the applause died down. As the chanting stopped, Morgoth looked furiously at Lightfoote and cried out:

"She's not one of us. She's antithetical to the movement. You're making a terrible mistake!"

"Your objections are noted," said Lightfoote. "Gabriel, let's put him and his little gang into lockup."

40

SAVAS AND COHEN sat atop an armored Humvee, its surface-to-air missiles spent, the soldiers inside asleep even as the thundering roll of explosions continued around them. He shook his head. The human mind adapted quickly, even to the insane—the foundation, Savas knew, of PTSD. After a day of intense assault, counterstrikes, endless violence and death, the men were exhausted. Far behind the main battle, they could now rest as the front of the conflict moved toward the urban center of Kansas City itself.

Savas couldn't sleep. Cohen breathed slowly, her head on his shoulder, her eyes closed. He tried not to disturb her as he stared into the interrupted blackness, waiting for morning. The stars were constantly dimmed by blinding explosions, weapons' flashes, and manmade clouds rising into the sky.

He could taste it in the air: a burnt, acrid cloud the wind could never fully dissipate. It sank into their clothing, formed a thin layer of dust in the vehicles, and induced bouts of asthma in the susceptible. As if on cue, one of the soldiers within startled from sleep into a coughing fit.

It has been over a week of fighting, ten days of push and retreat, artillery and blast, carnage, and a slow victory. Their opponents had learned from the last engagement. This one had been much costlier. But finally, they held the upper hand. The president's troops had pushed Hastings' force nearly inside the Kansas City limits. Soon, they'd been assured, it would be over.

The road ahead drew his attention. A man in fatigues sprinted toward them, the cap on his head marking him an aide to the command center. *This can't be good.* He shook Cohen gently.

"Morning already?" she rasped.

"Rebecca, we got company."

Her eyes flicked open, one hand rubbing the sleep out, and she focused on the approaching soldier. His pace didn't abate, and when he finally came to a stop in front of the vehicle, he doubled over for several seconds to catch his breath.

"Evening," began Savas. "All okay on the western fr—"

"Come with me now!" he gasped out. "No time to explain. The president wants you at her vehicle immediately."

"What's going on?" said Savas. Cohen sat upright.

"I'm not here to talk or take no for an answer. *Now*, sir!"

The FBI agents exchanged glances and hopped down to the asphalt. The soldier turned and motioned for them to follow. "Double time!" He began to run.

The pair followed at a fast clip, wordless, dashing past sleeping soldiers and quiet vehicles toward the command vehicle. As they arrived, the tension spiked: high-ranking officials and military personnel were congregated around the president's war table. Soldiers inside spoke rapidly into headsets as they scanned computer screens. Faces were grim. Savas and Cohen edged closer to hear the dialogue, suppressing their gulps for air.

"If they're gonna launch," said a heavy-set general, "there's no way to clear the battlefield. It's a logistics nightmare. This many men, this much equipment, it's a day's bug out and you know it!"

"Then it has to be faster!" cried York.

"Impossible!"

Tooze leaned in. "Elaine, that's it. You've done what you could. It's time to leave. We can evac you and other VIPs on a few of the older choppers that still fly."

"It's a massacre! A slaughter!"

"If they follow through, it's already assured, Ms. President!" yelled the general.

York removed her glasses and squeezed the bridge of her nose. "Give me the assessment again."

An aide to the general suppressed a sigh. "NORAD detected SLBM activation. The boats are parked off the East Coast. For those missiles, we've got fifteen minutes after launch, less perhaps depending on trajectory."

The general spoke clinically. "They don't need precision accuracy, Ms. President. An air blast. We're not fortified. They'll umbrella the area. From the initial NORAD data, it's likely a Mark 4 type, fourteen warheads. Each is a hundred kilotons. They'll carpet bomb the convoy and surrounding area."

"We'd won, dammit!" she shouted, pounding the table, spilling small pieces marking positions across the map. "Nuke his own people? His own army?"

"It's *because* we've won," said the general, wiping sweat from his brow. "Like I told you, this was their last stand. They know they've lost it. This is a Hail Mary."

"More like a Hail Satan," she said. "NORAD can't shut it down?"

"They're still trying," came the voice of another high-ranking officer. "But there isn't much of a chance."

"Tens of thousands of our troops, this *entire* city, are going to die, gentleman. That's what you're telling me?"

"Yes, ma'am. And we can't stop it."

"Elaine," began Tooze softly, "We have—"

"Prep the aircraft," she interrupted, staring coldly at her military advisors. "Go with the Migrant protocol, worst case scenario. Get as many of the VIPs out as you can." She paused and sighed. "Don't say anything to the troops. Not yet. If Hastings steps back from the cliff, we need to hold this location. We can't afford to scatter—it could be a feint and Hastings trying to gain an edge here. But the second we have a confirmed launch—God forbid—I want everyone notified with details. Tell them the truth."

"It won't be enough to get them out."

"Maybe, maybe not. But they deserve a shot. God forgive us all for what we're doing." She looked them over. "All right. That's an order. Move!"

The military men saluted and raced off to enact her commands. Tooze remained beside her, and Savas and Cohen were slowly revealed to York as the crowd of soldiers dissipated.

"You catch all that?" she asked wearily, slumping into a foldout chair.

"I'm not sure I can believe it," said Cohen.

"I know I can't," said Savas.

"You'd damn well better believe it. What's more, you two are coming with me, part of my personal entourage when we fly like bats out of hell." They simply nodded. York closed her eyes. "Just like bats out of hell. Because hell's coming."

41

THEY SAT TOGETHER at the long table, the shelter's hackers giving them a respectful space, and dined on scavenged canned goods and a never ending soup of protein powders from a GNC store raid. Lightfoote scowled as beige goop dripped from her spoon.

"I don't know how many more artificially sweetened, vanilla-flavored amino acid blends I can slurp down." She turned to Houston. "How's the leg?"

"Wound's closed," she said. "I won't be running the one hundred anytime soon, but walking's good. Limited weight bearing drills: squats, lunges." The former CIA agent turned the bowl up and drank down the goo. "Thank God for these protein shakes. Good to rebuild the tissue."

Lightfoote frowned. "Tastes like liquid cardboard."

"Pretty much," laughed Houston. "Our prisoners won't stop whining about it."

"How secured are they?"

Houston chewed on stale crackers. "Physically, not very. We rigged some locks on the doors. But the best bars are psychological. I think you broke them. That and Francisco's silent shotgun-priest thing." She smiled. "Works every time."

Lopez cut in: "Nothing from Savas and Cohen?"

Lightfoote shook her head. "I've tried several times. I've left emails, texts, whatever I could. No response and I can't raise them on the emergency line."

"You sure you had a connection?" asked Houston.

"Not in here, but I went topside. Phone was ringing. No one home."

He exhaled. "Something's wrong. They've never gone dark so long. I'm worried."

Lightfoote nodded. "Me too. But it's getting pretty nasty out there if we're filtering the local Hastings propaganda accurately. The other hacker communities at least help with that."

"Let's see," began Houston, "after translating Pravda, what do we get? The president is leading an armed resistance. That's her trying to get to NORAD, of course. Hastings is unsurprisingly claiming she's trying to establish a dictatorship. The military is split between them. And fighting has begun. Huge battles reported Midwest, East Coast, West Cost, Philly. Our friends are likely caught up in all that insanity." She gestured around her. "Makes this shelter seem rather foresighted."

"Caught up, and how badly?" asked Lopez. "Battles like that—I don't care what your army, sometimes you don't walk away. Look at what happened in Princeton."

"Jesus," said Houston, closing her eyes. "They sterilized it. Couldn't find us, so why not burn the entire fucking place to the ground? I kind of liked the gothic look they had going on there."

"If something happened to York, we're toast," said Lightfoote. "The country will fall to this Hastings, or whoever is put in his place to pull the strings. No way out of that. And we *need* York. Especially now, right when the numbers are converging."

"Any updates?" asked Houston.

"Good news, sister!" popped in De-frag. He landed heavily at the table, a tin plate piled with ketchup-plastered beans rattling and partially spilling its contents. He shoveled several plastic spoonfuls, speaking through a full mouth. "Cause we got ourselves an answer!"

––––––––––

"Well, we kinda got ourselves an answer," said De-frag, scrolling through lines of incomprehensible output. The group sat in one of the back rooms, centered around a group of monitors.

Lightfoote leaned in and examined the screen. "What do you mean? I see a clear peak, here, Northern Europe, right where—wait a second..."

"Exactly," finished De-frag.

"How can we have other maxima?"

"Don't ask me, sister. I'm just running your code. Them's Nobel Prize equations."

Lightfoote squinted. "The second maxima is far smaller, but the statistics are good. What the hell?"

"Lay-agent translation, please," barked Houston.

"Yeah," sighed Lightfoote. "Okay, first—we got the precision convergence in Europe. And what do you know, it's in the Netherlands. In a one hundred mile radius that includes the damned Bilderberg Hotel. That's the major convergence. Cross-checked and independently verified with control data removed. All the external manipulation of the economy and political trajectories center there."

"Well, yeah, except that they don't, really," added De-frag.

"Right, except that they don't," said Lightfoote. "There's a collection of nodes, weaker, but they look real. One stands out the most—some sort of major influence is tied into this one as well."

"Well, where is it?" asked Lopez.

Lightfoote reached over De-frag and keyed in several commands. A map of the world appeared, a wild crisscrossing of lines converging on Europe and the northern United States.

"Here," she said, pointing to North America. "New York City."

Lopez turned to her. "New York? Right under your noses?"

"It might not be anything like the Bilderberg center. It's a minor peak, and maybe tied to the fact that New York is a financial and world political center, an 'echo node' that reflects its influence, but isn't causal."

"Isn't causal?" repeated De-frag.

"It isn't a power center in and of itself."

"That makes sense," said Houston. "There are minor nodes at most of the main financial centers—London, Shanghai, Tokyo."

"Maybe New York is more important."

"How can we know?" asked Houston, grimacing as she repositioned her injured leg. "Do we have two fronts in this fight? More? Do we need to take out the others, too?"

Lightfoote shook her head. "There's no way to know, and everything we're doing here is experimental, anyway." She set her mouth. "I say we ignore the weaker nodes. Everything—history, the strong signal on the Bilderberg node—it all points to Europe."

"And we don't have the resources, or the time, to make ten pit-stops," said Lopez. "I agree. Let's take out the big dragon."

"Whoa," said De-frag, his eyes large. "Take out? What—ya'll are headed overseas to, you know, *kill* people?"

Houston shot him a hard look. "We'll do what we have to. They have to be stopped."

Lightfoote stepped back from the monitors. "We've got to reach out. We need help."

"York again?" asked Houston.

"She's the only one with the resources. It will take us ages to get there. I'm not even sure *how* right now. It's not like commercial airline traffic is back up."

"Go above ground to call out," said Lopez. "We'll come and provide cover, scout the area. Stay up there all day if you have to." He stood up. "This is the endgame. If we can catch them unprepared, we might have a shot at stopping them. Once and for all."

42

THEY EXITED THE computer room and marched from the back of the shelter. Lightfoote toted a bag with her communications equipment. Houston limped behind at a slower pace, refusing any help from Lopez. De-frag trailed behind like a kid in a candy shop.

At the sight of their passing, conversation stalled and heads tracked them. SixtyFour sat in front of a makeshift security center, blond hair spilling around bulbous headphones that covered his ears. A grainy video image flickered jarringly on a monitor in front of him. It showed only static. He turned, sensing their presence, removing the earphones.

"Up?" he said softly.

Lightfoote nodded. "We're all going. Probably a long session."

SixtyFour shook his head. "Wait."

"We don't have time—" began Lightfoote.

"Hold on, hold on," De-frag cut in, his brows furrowed. "SixtyFour's quiet, so, you know, when he talks, you gotta listen. What's up, dude?"

The gaunt teen pointed at the screen. "Video's dead."

"Yeah, okay. Not the first time," said De-frag.

"Sounds," said SixtyFour, tapping the earphones. "Too much. Rustling. Impacts. Can't identify. Someone's up there. Sentry's silent."

"Sentry?" asked Houston.

De-frag looked pale. "Yeah. She's posted in the rubble, couple hundred yards out. Claustrophobic. Couldn't take this tank."

"She's actually a sentry?" asked Lopez.

"Right," said De-frag. "Chatty as hell, too. No way she went quiet. No way she wouldn't respond." He looked back at SixtyFour. "I think we got trouble."

A shout from the back of the shelter dropped all conversation to silence. Medea hustled toward them, waving her arms, a blur of dark clothing and a red streak from her dyed hair. She shouted again.

"We're blown!" Her heavy form came to a stop in front of them.

"Damn they're good! Must be NSA or something. They've traced us, ID'd our location. I don't know how. We're getting penetration tests coming up our asses!"

"I thought York had bombed them!" said Houston.

"She did!" said Lightfoote. "Slowed them, just not enough."

"They know we're here?" Houston asked Medea.

She nodded. "No way they didn't geolocate us by now."

Lopez looked into the metal tube in front of them. He removed a handgun from his robes. "That means—"

A thundering clank turned heads in the room.

"That means those aren't friendlies upstairs," said Houston grimly.

"That means we're screwed!" cried De-frag, grabbing at his hair.

A deafening hammering began above them, the sound echoing through the tube.

"Ah, man, ah man, ah man," cried De-frag, spinning in circles. "The hatch won't last long. Then what?"

Lopez steadied him with a firm hand on his shoulder. "Then, if they don't drop a bunch of grenades down here, we fight them hand-to-hand."

"Hand-to-hand?"

"Do you have weapons? Firearms?" asked Houston.

De-frag nodded. "Yeah, sure. Some brought their guns and stuff. It ain't much. We pooled them all in a locker."

"Get them," said Lopez. "We're going to be facing trained special operatives. We're going to have to organize a front to prevent any significant penetration through the entrance—trap them in the tube. It's the only hope to fight them."

"Fight them," muttered De-frag. "We got guns, man, but, you know, I don't know if we got many who can shoot straight. You know what I mean?"

"What else is there?" said Lopez.

Medea leaned in and hissed at De-frag. "Or, dumbshit, we could use the escape tunnel in the back? Remember that?"

De-frag's eyes widened. "Fuck, yeah! Why didn't I think of that?"

"Because you're too busy pissing your pants," said Medea. "We've got to get them out."

Lightfoote turned to Medea. "Take us there."

"Yeah, before half this place figures out what's going on. That's going to be a bottleneck, let me tell you."

Lopez stopped them with his arm. He glared at De-frag. "Get them armed."

De-frag looked at the blond kid. "That's SixtyFour. He's the only gun-nut here. You got this, buddy?"

SixtyFour nodded and raced off toward a row of storage lockers along the sidewall.

"Let's move!" said Lightfoote.

The group filed past. Frightened hackers staring toward the entrance tube, the hammering continuing. Medea ducked into a back room and single-handedly shoved aside a wall of servers, revealing a hatch in the wall.

"This is it," she said.

"You've tested it?" asked Houston.

"Ah, not exactly," said De-frag.

Lightfoote locked eyes with him. "Explain."

A loud explosion rocked the shelter. Screams came from the chamber outside.

De-frag shifted into a higher pitch. "Just schematics, man! It's a tunnel, leads out along the sewage line, then up and out, a couple football fields away."

"But you've never tried it?"

Medea shook her head. "Never even opened the damn hatch." Another explosion. More screams. She stepped up to the wheel and set her shoulder to it, her hands turning white as she pressed with all her strength. It didn't move.

"Move," said Lopez. He grasped the wheel in his massive hands and angled his body sideways, his legs taking the brunt of the force. Nothing happened. His broad form tensed. A wrenching scream ripped through the room and the wheel inched counterclockwise. Lopez yanked and the hatch spun inward.

"Ah, shit," said De-frag, his words muffled with his hand over his mouth.

"Near the sewage lines, huh?" said Houston. "Is this a thing with us now?"

The sounds of machine gun fire echoed through the shelter. Intermittent pops of smaller ordnance peppered back.

"Smells great to me," said Lightfoote, and she stepped through the hatch, her large bag of electronics clanging on the side of the opening.

Lopez guided Houston through the opening, turning back to the room. "Medea, come with us. De-frag, these are your people." He nodded to the chaos outside. "You can't save them all, but get as many as you can in here behind us."

De-frag looked crestfallen. "It'll lead them right to you. You won't have time. You got to stop this thing, right?"

"To hell with time!" cried Lopez. "You can't let them die." Houston called his name from within the passageway. "Go! Bring those you can here!" He ducked under the opening and disappeared. Medea followed immediately after.

De-frag stood frozen in the room, his head darting between the escape tunnel and the door to the main chamber of the shelter. Screams battered his ears. Gunfire. He looked down at the ground and exhaled slowly.

"Sorry, dudes."

He turned and grasped the hatch wheel and pushed the door until it slammed shut. The metal screamed once more as he turned the wheel several rotations. He heaved the tower of computers back against the doorway, the mainframes and metallic shelves obscuring the wall completely. Exhausted, he pulled up a chair and sat down, facing outward.

A soldier in battle armor pointed a weapon at him through the doorway. "Where are the fugitives?" the man barked.

De-frag smiled like a terrified kid plunging over the edge of a rollercoaster for the first time. He extended the man his middle finger.

"Eat it, motherfucker."

Automatic discharge exploded in the room.

43

THE PASSENGERS WERE bounced roughly. Savas, Cohen, the president's close adviser Tooze, high-ranking military officers, and other governmental officials were strapped into red seats lining the interior of the large troop transport—a hulking Boeing CH-47 Chinook from another era. Missing were any high-tech digital elements, the cockpit stripped and rebuilt only weeks before to render it invulnerable to any remnants of the Anonymous worm. The modern gear was replaced by a set of instruments and controls dating to the Cold War. Alongside an escort of Blackhawks shadowed their movements. York crouched beside the cockpit and spoke to a military man seated in the co-pilot's chair.

"How much more time?" Her voice barely penetrated the rumbling of the helicopter's engines.

"Unknown!" he shouted over the din. "Estimated launch window says ten minutes, but we don't know the trajectory. We can't accurately predict. It's a navy missile for sure, fired off the East Coast, so it's loaded and fast."

"Are we clear?"

"It depends on where they detonate! If they stick to the convoy and city, yes, we're out of the blast radius. Supposedly."

"Supposedly?"

He shook his head. "We don't have the number crunching here to check. NORAD's estimates. And too many unknowns."

"She's opened up as much as I can," said the pilot. "I've vectored us radially West from the coordinates you gave. Kansas City is behind us." Turbulence bounced them viciously, and York was thrown hard against the ceiling. "Sorry, Ms. President," he said as she regained her footing. "I don't know what they did to this bird. She's flying rough, but I'll get us there. I recommend you strap in."

Savas reached out and grasped Cohen's hand next to him. Their eyes met, but they exchanged no words.

York exhaled, rotating to the single empty red chair beside the cockpit. She shouted as she worked the restraints. "Okay, assuming we get through this, what's your plan?"

The pilot answered. "Follow yours, ma'am. Six hundred miles to Cheyenne Mountain. Running this fast, we'll need a refuel somewhere along that line."

"We're working on it," she said.

"If the duct tape can hold this old lady together, it's five or six hours. Maybe less if all goes well."

York nodded. "The other evacuees?"

"Behind but in communication. We got seven birds loaded, most a lot more packed than this one. Some with vehicles. It will slow them down."

"Can't be helped," said the military advisor. "The president's the priority. We leave anyone else behind and take the escort with us."

York turned to him. "We're looking into a contingency for—"

Her words stopped. A god's lamp was lit and the landscape around them brightened like an overexposed photo. Before anyone could process or react to the radiance, a shower of sparks burst like popcorn from the control panel.

The engines made a terrible screeching noise, and the helicopter lurched to the side. Passengers screamed. The craft dropped sharply and flailed side-to-side as the pilot wrestled with the controls.

"Putting her down!" he cried.

A shadow darkened the craft. Through the windows, the bulk of a Blackhawk could be seen dropping downward, nearly careening into their Chinook. Then it was gone, the Chinook itself quickly losing altitude as well.

"Brace! Brace! Brace!"

Passengers assumed a variety of positions, confusion and fear on their faces. Savas and Cohen brought their knees close to their chests. They continued to hold hands.

The machine slammed against the ground tail-first, the helicopter crumpling from the back like a tin can. Screams and rending sounds ripped through the air. A stomach-lurching leap propelled them back into the air before gravity jerked the vehicle down again and hammered the craft into the earth. Momentum drove it shuddering like an earthquake across the ground, the cockpit mangled, dirt and rocks breaking through the front windows and flooding madly throughout the belly of the dying beast.

And then it was still.

Savas opened his eyes, his body taut and constricted, a thick dust and smoke choking his vision and breath. Cohen opened her eyes beside him, unharmed. His eyes darted forward. Upturned earth covered the president. Savas released the five-point restraints and dashed beside her.

"Ms. President?" He shoveled away handfuls of dirt from her body.

She opened her eyes. "Holy hell," she whispered. "I hope to God you're not an angel." He stared back at her. "Heaven's gotta have better-looking ones."

He smiled wanly. "Sorry, no heaven. We survived." He continued to free her from the mud and rocks.

Cohen placed an arm on his shoulder. "We're maybe the only ones."

Savas looked around in shock. At the front of the helicopter, the pilot and advisor were crushed into the control panel. Behind them —grass and plowed earth. The tail end of the Chinook was gone, and along with it the other passengers—judges, senators, and Tooze.

"George!" cried York, and maniacally tore at the restraints, freeing herself and rushing out.

Savas grabbed her. "No Elaine! It's too late!"

Fifty yards behind them, an inferno engulfed the massive engine powering the craft, charred and mangled forms within. Black smoke vomited into the sky and spilled fuel ignited the tall grass around the amputated section.

The president stared at the raging fire in horror. Her hands shook.

Cohen whispered. "John, look—"

Savas followed her gaze. Around them like campfires were the wrecked hulks of the Blackhawk escort, the machines having struck the ground much harder than their craft. There could be no survivors in the wreckage he saw.

But Savas was no longer looking at the remains of the aircraft, but eastward, behind them, high into the sky. "Dear God." A line of monstrous apparitions sprouted into the air, dwarfing the smoking fires at their feet. Dark mushrooms tainted the blue thousands of feet above the plains, casting long shadows across miles of fields. The prevailing winds had begun to chip away at their structure, eroding the rising titans into trails of smoke billowing slowly east.

"EMP," Cohen whispered. Savas and York stared at her uncomprehending. She looked away from the nuclear blasts. "Why we all went down. Electromagnetic pulse. Fried the circuitry. Pilot lost control. We dropped."

York continued to stare at the flaming tail section of the helicopter.

Savas nodded. His jaw set. "The convoy is gone. Kansas City— gone." He looked around the carnage before them. "Our evac group —gone."

Cohen shook her head. "We got lucky."

"Not just luck," said York, finally turning her back on the flames and the remains of her advisor. "Our lift was the most outfitted to resist the worm. Engineers went back decades. Tore out the damn guts and built it back. There just wasn't as much to fry inside." With a final quick glance behind, she turned back to Savas and Cohen. "But enough to do the damn job."

"What now?" asked Cohen hoarsely.

York walked back into the shorn half of the helicopter. She grabbed several bags and weapons. "Salvage what you can. We've got six hundred miles in front of us." She glanced up to the towering smoke giants. "And a madman on our tail."

44

"ADMIRAL MYERS?"

THE voice belonged to a young officer at the door of a chaotic office. A stout man with a gray shock of hair spun around in his chair, a landline to his ear, the cord wrapping taut around a desk lamp and bottle of scotch. Both crashed to the floor.

"Goddammit, son!" The young aide rushed over and began to mop up the spilled alcohol and glass. "Hendricks? Hold on, I'll call you back." He slammed the phone down. "That was a conference call to the Canadian air defense headquarters. I specified I was not to be bothered until we square out those damn false alarms on their infected computers! This better be good!"

The young man turned pale. Blood dripped from one hand as he cradled shards of glass. "Yes, sir!"

Admiral Myers sighed. "Benson, right?"

"Yes, sir! Jeremiah Benson. Deputy Commander Duval's aide, sir."

"They promote you Canadians quickly. Benson—spit it out."

"We've had contact with a flagged name from the York party. Part of the FBI team we were briefed on."

"Savas group?"

"Yes, sir. Lightfoote, Angel, Special Agent in Charge, Intel 1 Cybercrimes."

The admiral stood up. "The worm-girl?" Benson nodded. "Team Hastings knows about her. You verify her identity?"

"She claims to know the president. She knows details of the worm."

Myers shook his head. "Not enough. It could be a phishing attempt. How the hell did she reach us?" The admiral bent down and pulled out a handkerchief. "You're a bloody mess, Benson. Wrap it off and put the damn glass down. We'll have custodial take care of this." He looked toward the ceiling. "Maybe someone's trying to tell me something about the bottle."

"God? Sir."

Myers laughed. "Or worse—internal affairs." He frowned. "Lightfoote—how did she contact you?"

"Yes, sir. Sorry. That's just it. She's *inside* the system. She must have hacked in. We're getting contacts from internal email and instant messaging servers. It's a flood!"

"Hacked in? *Jesus*. Should've had that girl do our penetration tests. Well, that's probably better than a retinal scan. I don't think there are too many cyberwarriors at that level. It's got to be her with everything else."

"Yes, sir, that's what we figured."

"We'll make sure. York gave us some security questions. We'll use those. " Myers glanced down at the shattered bottle. "Damn I need a drink." He stood up, Benson mirroring him, the aide's hand wrapped in bloody fabric. "Let's get to the floor."

A small crowd gathered around a cubicle in the Command Center inside of Cheyenne Mountain. An array of monitors tiled the walls around them showing maps of the nation and world, newscasts, and streams of data comprehensible only to analysts. Heads craned from other cubicles lining the floor space, trying to catch a glimpse or overhear what was transpiring.

Myers stared into the green eyes glowing from one of four monitors on a wide desk. The girl's face was streaked in grime and blood, her head shaved, piercings decorating her ears and nose. Beside her sat another woman, brunette with short hair showing blond at the roots. On the other side loomed a dark face, Mexican, a broad skeletal and muscular structure mostly in shadow.

Myers nodded. "So, Angel Lightfoote, and the two ciphers: Gabriel and Mary. Normally I'd call this a con-job, but, miraculously, you fit the exact profiles we were given."

"You've spoken to Savas? To York?"

"One thing at a time," he said. "You need to answer a few questions. We need to be sure you're who you say you are."

"Understood." Her gaze didn't waver.

"Uh, Gabriel," he began, looking at a piece of paper, reading glasses now sitting on his nose. His eyes wandered to Benson. "Is this some kind of joke?"

The aide shook his head. "No, sir. That's what they gave us."

"Well, how the hell am I supposed to read this? It looks like Latin!"

"Boys school, Montreal," said a lanky officer in a foreign uniform. He put his hand out for the paper.

"You know Latin, Pierre?" asked the Admiral.

Deputy Commander Duval nodded and took the paper. "But it's been a while, Jim. Let's see—*Comple in Sacerdote tuo ministerii tui summam*. And there is a final phrase Gabriel is supposed to provide."

The dark figure in the monitor nodded. "*Et ornamentis totius glorificationis instructum coelestis unguenti rore santifica.*"

Duval nodded, his eyebrows raised. "That's it. What the hell is it? Some Catholic prayer?"

Lopez rumbled over the speakers. "A blessing during the ordination of a priest."

Myers shook his head. "This one's for Mary. Javed Ahmad, otherwise known as?"

Houston replied instantly. "The wraith."

"Two-for-two. Now, Lightfoote. Five years ago you figured out a pattern. You drew it on a computer screen. It was an object pointing to a target. What was the object?"

Lightfoote's face tensed. "A hammer. *Thor's* hammer. *Mjolnir* in Old Norse."

Myers nodded. "It's them."

"Now, can we stop wasting time and get to business?" asked Lightfoote. "Where is York? Savas and Cohen? We haven't been able to reach them. We're on the run, Hastings troops on our asses. If you know about us, you must know about Bilderberg."

"We do," said Myers. "And your mission. You've found something then?"

"Yes. We have proof this group is behind everything. They've been orchestrating world events for decades, breaking international law, undermining national sovereignty. Most importantly—we now know where they are. We're going there."

"Going there?" asked Duval. "To do *what?*"

"Stop them," said Lopez.

Duval squinted at the screen. "Who are you?"

Myers cut in. "We're going on the president's word here, Pierre. York claims they're as good as a Seal commando team, and she's put them on point for this. Not that we have any real options. We can't get anyone out from here with Hastings on our asses 24/7." He gestured to the monitor. "This crew is our shadow force."

"This is insane," said the Canadian.

Lightfoote nodded. "Every bit of it. Now, where the hell is York? We need her to authorize transportation for us."

Myers exhaled. "We don't know where she is."

Houston leaned in. "What do you mean? What happened? She should be there by now!"

"They were outside Kansas City, six hundred miles out from here. Hastings put up a last stand to stop her. He lost, or was losing. Then, the unthinkable. He launched a ballistic missile and dropped a bunch of warheads on the convoy and the city. It's been radio silence since."

Houston angled back in her chair. "Oh, my God."

"We had advanced warning from satellites, and York and the FBI agents were being bugged out on an emergency flight. But before they got far the bombs hit."

"They didn't make it?" asked Lightfoote.

"We don't know. But with the EMP, there's no telling what happened. They could be alive with fried communications equipment, charred in the blasts, or pulverized when their aircraft lost power."

"EMP?" said Lopez.

"Electromagnetic pulse," muttered Lightfoote. "Nukes cause them. Supposedly fries anything except the most hardened electronics."

"Does that explain the power outages?" Houston asked.

Myers cocked his head to one side. "There were outages?"

Lightfoote nodded. "Middle of the afternoon two days ago. It's still down here. We're running off a stolen generator."

Duval leaned toward the camera. "Timing is perfect. Our reports from the East Coast are minimal—Hastings controls your territory. But that's the best explanation. We're heavily shielded here, but the pulse must have damaged more civilian equipment than we anticipated."

Lightfoote slammed her hand down on a table in front of her. "We need her help! We need a transport to get us out of the country."

"Slow down," said Myers. "We've ID'd you to our satisfaction. She's left instructions, said if you called—and I guess hacked-in counts—you'd need help. And we're here to give what we can. You say a transport? To where?"

"Europe. The Netherlands. ASAP. Bilderberg is holed up there. We know exactly where. If we can get there, stop them, we can cut the head off this beast and Hastings will be a clean-up job."

"One hell of a clean-up, by the way things are going."

"Yes!" cried Lightfoote. "But he's a puppet. Take him down and Bilderberg will replace him. Take down Bilderberg—"

"Yes, yes. We ax the puppet masters," said Myers. "I have to say, this is one of the craziest conspiracy theories I've ever heard. But I serve the president, and she says to give you what you need."

"Can you?" asked Lopez.

Myers stroked his chin. "Honestly, I don't know. You need a plane. Hastings owns the seas. But air is still risky. Ridiculously risky. Commercial traffic is grounded. Since the worm and through this civil war. We'll have to get you a military transport. But how we do that without Hastings finding out ... I don't have a goddamned idea." Duval leaned over and whispered in Myer's ear for several seconds, and the admiral nodded. "Where are you?"

"Outside of Newark. Big ass airport right next door," said Lightfoote.

"Hold your position. Monitor this feed. We'll get back to you."

Lightfoote pressed. "Can you help us?"

Duval nodded. "We might just have an idea."

45

BARRIC BOSWORTH STARED at the flaming sunset, one hand on a rusted fence post, the other fingering the butt of his twelve-gauge pressed into the ground like a walking stick. The dust particles and debris from the atomic explosions scattered the low rays of the sun into the most spectacular color show he'd ever seen in his seventy-three years. It didn't even look real but reminded him of the artificial palettes modern filmmakers were so taken by.

He scowled. Something for poets and painters maybe, but not a farmer. Nothing could erase his fury over what had happened—the anger and shock of nuclear war in his own backyard. Not even when nature turned the monstrous into something miraculous.

His scowl deepened as his eyes were distracted from the sky to the grassy fields below his farmhouse. He squinted and turned his good eye toward three shapes moving toward him up the hill. *Three people.* Trespassing on his property, coming from the direction of the blasts. As they neared, he could see they were struggling. An older woman, a younger woman, and a man. Their clothes were filthy, sooted like they'd come out of a crop-burning, their faces sunburned even in the winter chill. They were ready to collapse.

Still he didn't move. Didn't raise his weapon. He let the trio approach within twenty feet of his fence.

"All right you three, that's far enough."

The older woman stumbled. Propped up by the other two, her head hung as breaths wheezing in clouds from her mouth. The man supporting her spoke.

"My name is John Savas. These are my friends. We need shelter. Food and water. A place to rest." He spoke hoarsely through cracked and bleeding lips.

Bosworth nodded. "You come from the blasts?"

Savas nodded. "Outside the city. We've walked for two days."

"Two days?" the farmer rubbed his chin. "At the rate you were walkin', that'd put you 'bout halfway from here to the city. But you

605

ain't from 'round here."

"Our flight was knocked out of the air by the blast," said Savas, his voice weary. "We're the only survivors."

"Ain't no flights since the troubles started."

"It wasn't a normal flight."

Bosworth shifted his weight off the shotgun, his hand gripping the butt more tightly. "Well, that's what I was gettin' to. You're some VIPs, or I don't know nothin'. But what I'm wonderin' is *whose* VIPs." Savas simply stared at him. "Some are sayin' we got ourselves a civil war. Some sayin' the president's trying to take over, like Hitler. Others the military. Other's the goddamned Iranians. Even *aliens*." He shook his head. "The three of you, *flyin'*. Nuclear bomb in my home state. Just *whose* VIPs are you?"

"You gone plumb senile, Barric?" cried a nasal voice. A thin woman with wild gray hair scampered down the hillside from the house, kicking up a dust cloud, a heavily patched dress billowing around her.

"Irene! Get back in the house right now!"

She pushed past him with a grunt and bent nearly in two, squinting her eyes toward the three strangers, a clawed index finger indicating York. "I swear I'm gonna make you get that laser procedure. You're gonna give a sermon 'bout the president when she's a-standin' right there?"

Bosworth furrowed his brow and turned to York. The president looked him straight in the face. His eyes widened. "I'll be goddamned."

His hand grasped the weapon at his side firmly and he lifted it into the air, loudly racking the chamber and loading a shell. The barrel pointed above Savas's head.

His wife put her hands on her hips. "Put that damn gun down, Barric! You ain't shot it in twenty years!"

He ignored her, staring fixedly at the president. "They shot you down?" York nodded affirmatively. "Where were you headed?"

York sighed, beyond the point of disguise or deception. "To NORAD. The bunker in the mountains."

"Cheyenne Mountain?" he said, the weapon not moving.

"Yes," said York. "Government and military loyal to me are waiting. Holed up. We're trying to ride this out there. But I had to get there from Washington." She looked behind her. "It's not going so well."

"Barric—" his wife began.

"Hush, woman!" He licked his lips. "Who are these two?"

"FBI agents. Real heroes if you want to know. John Savas and Rebecca Cohen. Killed the terrorist who nearly caused a war a few years back."

Bosworth looked between the two agents. "I remember."

Savas spoke. "So, Mr. Bosworth, I think it's our turn to ask whose side *you* are on? Because if it's with our nation's rebels, you might as well shoot us now. If you're loyal to this president, to our elected government, then we need your help. President York needs your help. We can't go on much farther."

Bosworth scanned around them again, weapon at the ready. "Sons-a-bitches dropped the bomb on their own country. In *my* state." He glanced them up and down again. "You go much farther like that, they'll get you for sure." He looked at his wife. "Irene, put something on the stove. You all come on in. We ain't got much, but we got food, beds, some medicines. Maybe buy you a little time." He patted his shotgun. "And don't you worry, anyone coming after you is gonna have to get past me first."

46

NIGHT FELL, AND nothing moved at Newark airport. Planes slept along the shuttered terminals, the tower looming above as a shadow in the starlight, the runways invisible and dark. The blackness was punctuated haphazardly with the faint glow of exit signs and flickering emergency lights, the electric gasps of a region still reeling from the both the worm and the EMP.

Lopez, Houston, and Lightfoote huddled on the tarmac, three small shapes beside a broad runway racing alongside the central terminal. A blue glow blossomed as Lightfoote opened a laptop, the glare forcing the three to squint as their eyes adjusted from the darkness.

"This is the longest runway," she said, indicating a black line on a schematic of the airport. "They said it would put down here."

"They're late!" whispered Lopez through clenched teeth. "It's just a matter of time before they hem us in. We're sitting ducks."

Houston scanned the skies. "I don't know what we're looking for. They'll be flying low, trying to screw with any radar scans of the area. The airport is down, thank goodness. I don't know what else the military could have looking."

"I assume the lights will be off," Lopez said. "No runway lights. How are they going to put it down?"

"I have no idea," said Lightfoote, shaking her head and closing the computer.

The three sat in silence as the minutes dragged by. The sounds of a truck caused them to catch their breath and draw weapons, but the noise faded quickly, leaving them in the quiet of the open space.

"We ought to consider a defensive arrangement," said Houston. "If they search the airport, we—"

"Wait!" hushed Lopez, his eyes fixed on the sky. "Listen! Can you hear it?"

For a moment, the two women followed his gaze, silent, listening.

"An engine, air turbulence, something," said Lightfoote.

"There!" hissed Houston, pointing north-east and into the sky.

A hole in the band of the Milky Way yawned above them, a gap in the stars blurring its way across the sky. The sound grew more distinct, the churning of some machinery that was completely outside their experience.

"It's almost on us!" said Lopez, rising from his crouch. "It's about to land!"

The three stood back from the runway. At the far end, the shadow expanded dramatically, a shape with unfurled wings descending like a hawk on prey.

"Are the engines off?" asked Houston. "It hardly makes a sound."

Tires screeched with a quick burst of light as the plane touched down. They watched silently as the rending sound of brakes engaged and the aircraft rumbled past them, the plane slowly coming to a stop.

"It's the damn bat-plane," said Lightfoote.

The three jogged toward the craft as it circled around an end of the runway and aligned toward the other, preparing for takeoff. Drawing near, they could better make out the details of the thing. Pitch black, a coating drinking all light, sharp wings framing a blade, the plane slowed to a stop. The vertical cross section was small, the engines placed like two boxes over the wings. The sounds of a hatch opening rang in the night.

"It's a stealth bomber," said Houston, awe on her face.

"Not a bomber," came a man's voice from the vehicle. From around the nose stepped a pilot in dark gear, a broad helmet like a fighter pilot's in his hands. He marched quickly up to them.

"It's a stealth transport. A prototype from Northrop for cargo, strategic airlift capability. Bomber doesn't hold passengers." He looked at the bald head of Lightfoote. "You Angel?"

"Stealth cargo transport? What the hell is that for?"

The pilot shrugged. "They always think up uses. But never went into production. NORAD said you needed a bird and we had to get it in without being seen. And this prototype runs on some new military-grade OS. Worm-proof. There weren't too many options."

Lopez scanned the aircraft. "It will hold all of us? Doesn't look like much room."

"It's for cargo. More room than you'd imagine. It looks like a B2, but it ain't. Doesn't fly much like one either. Now, come on. Let's get you three the hell out of here."

They didn't need any persuasion. The pilot led them to the cargo entrance, and they jogged inside. Cramped and lacking much light, they stumbled to seats along the walls and strapped in.

The pilot reached the cockpit and sat next to a helmeted co-pilot. Their hands moved over the instrument panels and the cargo doors shut. The engines powered up, the interior going completely dark as the plane began to accelerate down the runway.

"Please fasten your seat belts and stow your tray tables," came the pilot's voice over speakers. "Next stop, Amsterdam."

A dark shadow leapt into the air.

47

"So, it's come to this at last."

The words were spoken by a harsh face over a computer screen, a middle-aged man in a business suit. The Director stared at the monitor from his seat underneath the Bilderberg Hotel, a panel of other monitors displaying an array of ashen faces.

"Yes, Alpha. We are in agreement," said the Director. "York has perturbed the models too much. The equations are diverging. America is lost. Europe now has a sixty percent chance of diverging from the planned curves as well. Asia will be next."

"But is York still alive?"

"We don't know. But it hardly matters now. Had we secured the nation, suppressed her message earlier, exhibited her alive or dead with the proper propaganda, it might have been contained. But through NORAD and their broadcasts, it went on for too long. The Nash Criterion has been reached."

"And you have confidence in the metrics of this madman?"

"This is what we do, Alpha. You have trusted us and been amply rewarded by our numerical simulations. The Nash Criterion was always a calculation for *in extremis*, more to calibrate the models with a high bound. We never believed the model fluctuations could reach this point. The hacker has been a disaster. There is now no way to salvage the global trajectory without dealing with America."

"Amputation?"

"Surgical intervention. Enough to render its world influence minimal, to absorb its economy and government into that of nations to be appointed as guardians over what is left. Otherwise, the equations can't be balanced or normalized. We will lose control."

"And you estimate Europe and Asia will fall back on path even after this drastic event?"

"Yes." The Director wiped sweat from his brow. "The models show a strong attractor to the established trajectories. A high confidence for stabilization within the envelope of error. But only if

America is neutralized. The parameters are tight. Too large a strike and we risk major secondary effects, climate the most significant. Such disturbances could also doom us. Too small, and the divergence will not be contained. We have a set of models for minimal, decapitation strikes of government and industry. Strong ripples are unavoidable, but we believe they can be managed while putting our past models back on track."

Alpha nodded on the screen. "Zero has decided. Do it."

The Director glanced at the screen in horror. "Of course."

"We remain in control over the required systems?" asked Alpha.

"We have verified several times over the last few days. Launch codes, missile command and control servers, and our personnel—everything is in place, as well as other nations' systems to avoid panicked responses."

"The university is on the target list."

Alpha frowned. "You don't need to explain the obvious. You aren't going to impact America without a strike here. We will dismantle everything in New York and evacuate. We need several days to manage the logistics."

The Director looked down to his desk and shook his head. "After so long. Such a perfect disguise. We won't find another like it for some time." He returned his gaze to the monitor. "What of the scientists?"

"Them? They are only a front. Mostly a pack of Nobel-chasing sheepdogs imagining themselves to be prima donnas. They are no longer needed."

"And Zero?"

"His plans will remain hidden, even to you, Director. When we've completed our transition, you may learn more. Now, prepare everything and wait for our final contact."

The screen turned black and Alpha disappeared. The Director placed his hand to his temples.

"God help us."

PART 3

"The real truth of the matter is, as you and I know,
that a financial element in the larger centers
has owned the Government
ever since the days of Andrew Jackson."

—Franklin D. Roosevelt

48

"I still can't get used to the quiet."

Lightfoote stood in the middle of the stealth transport cargo bay. A constant purr and muffled sound of wind filled the cramped space. A black SUV with tinted windows sat chained to the floor several yards behind them, the vehicle unusually long with a substantial bed. The glow of a laptop screen painted the dim interior in a ghostly sapphire. She stared up at the surrounding walls, her body still. Her computer rested on a makeshift table culled together from small boxes. Lopez and Houston sat on either side, watching her quietly. After several more seconds, she shook her head and sat down with them.

"Invisible to radar and hardly makes a sound. Pretty amazing." She looked at Houston who grimaced while repositioning her leg. "How's the thigh?"

"Better, but crouching in this black box isn't doing wonders for it." Lightfoote continued to stare. "I'll kick plenty of ass when we get there, little girl. Don't worry."

Lightfoote half-smiled. "You better. Looks like we're going to be hitting a fortress."

Lopez pointed to images on the monitor. "So, these are aerial images that see underground?"

Lightfoote nodded. "They're brand new. NORAD moved fast on our request, using some of the newer imagining satellites. Infrared. Archeologists love them—found new pyramids buried in the sands in Egypt. Pretty powerful and high resolution."

"Looks it," he said. "More than one floor underneath, I think. It's at least three times the size of the above-ground structure."

"And it's not a parking lot," said Lightfoote. "I couldn't find anything about underground structures associated with the Bilderberg Hotel. As far as the internet is concerned, it's just a simple four-story structure in Oosterbeek."

"Can we get a sense of the security?" asked Houston.

"The resolution is good, but not miraculous," said Lightfoote. She switched to regular aerial photographs. "Nothing topside to raise any suspicions. But there has to be something serious given what we're dealing with. I assume it really starts near the entrance to the underground bunker."

"But we have no idea where that might be," said Houston. "We're going to be awfully exposed hunting around for that."

"Yes," said Lightfoote. She bent over, staring at the screen. "But maybe we can make some educated guesses."

"The power lines?" asked Houston.

Lightfoote nodded. "A hotel that size doesn't need so many cables. And look at the asymmetry here. A few lines to the main structure, and then what, *five* running where? To this wing only. What the hell is going on there? Stadium lighting?"

"You're right," said Lopez. "The entrance is there." He pointed to the satellite imagery. "The forest comes close to the extended wing *here*. If we can make our way to this point, we can recon the wing. Maybe remain unseen until we move on it. I bet there's a network of cameras sweeping the place."

"I wouldn't assume the forest is safe, Francisco," said Houston.

His face darkened. "Haven't forgotten, Sara. We've seen a few examples of paranoids wiring nature to hell and back. Still, I think it's the best approach. Remember, it didn't save the occupants we came across."

Houston nodded, her eyes distant, remembering. She snapped back. "I agree. We conduct sweeps through this sector. If we identify surveillance, we avoid or deactivate."

"We might alert them," said Lightfoote.

"We might," replied Houston. "But we don't have too many options coming in this fast. Unprepared."

"I also had NORAD compile the satellite imagery over the last few weeks," said Lightfoote. "I've strung the frames together, run it several frames per second. Watch."

She double-clicked on a file and a video player opened, displaying a still frame of the top of a building surrounded by land and roads. She pressed play. Cars and trucks came and went at blinding speed, shadows running across the frames right to left, repeating over and over. "Their birds get several photos a day. Notice anything?"

"Deliveries?" asked Houston. "Guests arriving? What?"

"The number of trucks is pretty low. About enough to handle a hotel that size and not much more. Unless they have an underground railroad bringing in supplies, what you see is what they get."

"They're minimally staffed," said Lopez. "We're not going to hit an army."

Houston smiled. "You're right. It's the best news we've had yet."

"I'm not sure why it's so minimally guarded," said Lightfoote. "I sure as hell hope we aren't wrong."

"The Nash equations? A huge and secret underground bunker with a massive supply of electricity?" Lopez shook his head. "*Something* highly unusual is being hidden there. We aren't wrong."

"Maybe they never feared discovery," said Houston. "Maybe automatic security systems with a few guards seemed enough. If they've been around as long as they have and never discovered, they might have gotten cocky."

"Maybe," said Lightfoote. "But let's keep our eyes open. I don't want any surprises."

Houston smiled. "I don't either, except the one we're going to drop on them."

49

BOSWORTH OPENED THE front door, using his foot to kick the scuffed wood at the bottom to force it through a sticking point. He lost control of the handle and the door swung wildly on its hinges, slamming into the wall behind it.

"For cryin' out loud, Barric! You 'bout gave me a heart attack." His wife stood in an apron over a gas stove. "I've told you to fix that damn door!"

"Have a seat," he said, ignoring her. He placed his shotgun beside the door, drawing the shades to the windows.

As Savas helped York through the entrance, he noticed the wall behind the doorknob had numerous indentations. Mr. Bosworth's kicks over the years had made their impression. The house was built of knotted planks of wood, stained a rich honey, the polish long worn away. A small fire crackled on the right side and helped to dispel the cold air invading from outside.

"We need to use your phone," said York. "I've got to contact NORAD and let them know where I am."

"Honey, the phones have been out since that interweb virus thingy shut everything down," said Mrs. Bosworth. "And look at this, my computer." An older model desktop PC sat with a dark monitor on a table by the wall. It appeared to be covered in dried foam. "Soon as the bomb went off, every damn thing with wires 'bout caught on fire. My computer did, sparks flying everywhere."

"Irene had to pull out that old extinguisher," laughed Bosworth. "Miracle it still worked."

"Laugh all you want, Barric, but it had all our records."

"I don't think Uncle Sam'll be feeling up to any audit right now," he replied

York looked between them. "So, no computers. No landlines. Cell phones?"

Mr. Bosworth shook his head. "We ain't got one, but I heard they're all down, too. Stuff takes longer to fix out here. That's why all the kids leave."

"So we're completely cut off," said Cohen.

"Welcome to the prairie," said Mrs. Bosworth. She looked at Cohen. "Your name again, honey? I can't remember my own, somedays."

"Rebecca."

"Rebecca. Nice church name."

"I'm Jewish."

"So was our Savior, honey. So was he. Can you hand me some of those candles on the shelf there? Night's gonna fall soon and there ain't been electricity for weeks."

Cohen reached behind her and grabbed a sack of candles, walking them to the old woman. "How do you keep warm?"

Mr. Bosworth grunted. "Battery back-up for the furnace helped, but course it wouldn't last. Couple of days we lost heat. That weren't no fun, let me tell you. I switched off the A.C. to the furnace and wired up a nine volt in place of the normal one. Fooled the damn thing. Gas valve opened and furnace started fine. To get things flowing, I popped the inspection cover. No fan running, but we got a good bit of heat. With the fireplace over there, everything was fine. Well, the blower safety switch kicks out and shuts things down every now and then and we got to let everything cool down. But it works. Until the gas supply quits."

Irene snorted. "That makes as much sense as government cheese. Just don't get him started."

"I was only answerin' her question."

Irene huffed and placed several candles on a long wooden table in the middle of the room. The light had begun to fail outside, and already the warm radiance of the fireplace and candlelight tinted the room orange. She placed a fat kettle of soup on the table.

"Haven't had guests for years." She looked at York. "Last gov'ment man we had was Jim Wilson from the local IRS in KC." Her face darkened. "I guess he's dead too now, 'long with that pretty family of his. I never was much for hostin', and we ain't got nothin' proper for a president. Anyways, come eat up. You look starved."

Eagerly, the three descended on the table, the first nourishment in days drawing them greedily. Conversation halted for several minutes as the famished visitors devoured the broth.

"Sorry to say, ma'am, I didn't vote for you," said Mr. Bosworth, opening conversation.

York laughed. "Well, that's quite all right, sir. I don't take opposition personally. Unless they're shooting at me."

"It weren't that I *opposed* nothin'," he said.

Mrs. Bosworth shook her head. "He just don't want to say he thinks a man ought to be in the big chair."

"Now, Irene, I never said—"

"Never said! You don't have a thought in your head I don't know beforehand, Barric."

York helped herself to a second bowl. "You have no idea how nice it is to think about someone voting against me rather than trying to kill me. It's what all this is about, you know." She wiped her mouth with a napkin. "Some people want to take your say out of what the country does. They want to rewrite the rules, remove the people opposing them. As you see, they'll stop at nothing."

"I knew you were tough as any man for the job," said Mrs. Bosworth. "I kept telling Barric during the election. 'She's army! What else you want?' Pair of dangling ovaries I guess."

Mr. Bosworth didn't answer but shook his head, slurping loudly with a spoon to his mouth. Cohen turned to the president.

"How did you end up in Iraq? Can't have been too many women serving in combat areas back in the nineties."

"There weren't," said York. "It's a long story, starting with enlisting. And it never would have happened if my father hadn't been so damn pushy for me to enter politics." She laughed. "Try to imagine a young girl flipping her big name politician dad the finger and signing up for the army. Boy, was he pissed. Had the roadmap already laid out for me, probably when my mom was in labor. I was determined to blow it all to hell. Of course, he did spin it for the press and gained some points for his patriotic children."

"And yet," said Savas, "after it all ended, here you are. President of the United States. Dad would have been proud."

"Life's never short on irony. But right now my title is on the ropes." She placed her spoon down in the empty bowl. "And what about you, Agent Savas. Your father an officer of the law, like you?"

"He did clash with the mob," said Cohen, smiling.

"Sounds promising," said York.

Savas shook his head. "The last thing my father wanted was to be part of the law or crime. Now, my paternal *grandfather* is another issue entirely. I really don't want to know what he had to do to become one of the biggest shipping magnates in Asia Minor."

"So, you're from money?" asked York.

"Could have been. But there was too much chaos in the Balkans those decades. My grandfather lost everything, every boat he owned during the Greek genocide a hundred years ago."

"Greek genocide?" asked Mr. Bosworth. "Ain't never heard of it."

"Yeah, not as well advertised. And like the Armenian genocide, the Turkish government would like to keep it that way." He stared off into the distance. "But more than a million perished, the entire Hellenic population in Asia Minor either killed or driven West into Greece. An entire culture perished. So did my grandfather's boats and our family's wealth."

"That's a horrible story," said Ms. Bosworth.

"Just one of thousands in Europe of the last century. Genocide after genocide. Ethnic cleansing—love that word. Like they gave all the Greeks a bath or something. Not as civilized as we like to pretend we are."

York exhaled. "No need to remind me."

"Afterward, my family settled in northern Greece. A piece of land belonging to three different countries off and on before my father was twelve. For the next Balkan wars, he was conveniently drafted into three different armies. My grandparents put him on an Italian boat to the New World."

"At twelve?" clucked Ms. Bosworth.

"He did pretty well. My father was a charmer and entrepreneur. By the time he reached New York, he was fluent in Italian and had a Sicilian girlfriend. Ran a restaurant under the Brookline Bridge for more than thirty years."

"And the mob connection?" asked York.

"Getting to it. He refused to pay the protection money."

"The money you pay the mob to protect yourself from them," said Cohen.

Savas continued. "They set fire to his restaurant three times. Three times he borrowed, built it back, and had better digs than before. I guess they finally just gave up."

"Amazing," said York. "But now I see why you joined the police. You were police before FBI, right?"

"Does it show?"

York smiled. "I've been around a lot of law enforcement. Got a good eye."

Mr. Bosworth nodded. "So how'd you get from the police to the FBI?"

Savas tensed but forced himself to relax. "My son followed in my footsteps. Joined the NYPD a little before the World Trade Center attacks. He died as a first responder." All eyes were fixed on him. "I joined FBI counterterrorism afterward."

Cohen reached over and put her hand on his shoulder. Savas drank down a glass of water quickly as she spoke.

"My story's similar," she said. "I had a lot of relations killed in Israel. Bombings. I remember as a kid my mom coming to me. 'Aunt Yael won't be coming to visit this year.' 'Cousin Ziva got hurt.' I was precocious: I watched the news. Looked things up in the papers. I loved detective stories. I decided before I was out of braces that I would be a detective."

York stared intently at the pair. "Your division has a lot of people familiar with trauma."

Savas nodded. "No accident, as you might have guessed. Intel 1 was set up by a man who had a dark but effective vision. He recruited some characters, including one who's now with the pair who rescued you in Washington. He felt we'd be highly motivated."

"If he could keep you sane," said York. "This was Larry Kanter?"

"Yes," said Savas. "Killed by Mjolnir five years ago. Blew his house up."

Mr. Bosworth stared at Savas with his mouth agape. "Well, goddamn, son. Sounds like you've gotten the tour of hell."

"More like he's been stationed at the turn off to hell, Mr. Bosworth," said York. "He and the others have had to stand in the heat and steer the rest of us away from it."

Savas put his spoon down. He smiled at Ms. Bosworth and changed the subject. "This meal has been as close to heaven as I could imagine food to be. And as thankful as we are for all of it, we need to consider soon what we're going to do next. The president can't stay here. Seeing what's happened, you shouldn't want her to stay here for long, unless you like a big bullseye painted over your house. We've got to get her to NORAD."

"I've been thinkin' on that," said Mr. Bosworth. "You need something you can hide out in. Car or truck, you're open on the road. You've got to find a place to sleep. You can't count on motels or anything. Most are closed. But I've got an idea."

"You don't mean that old camper?" asked Mrs. Bosworth.

"I surely do," he said. "I've got me a nineties Coachmen Leprechaun. She still runs."

"And smells like a swamp inside."

"She'll keep you on the road, out of sight, no need for doing much but driving—straight shot to Colorado on I-70 should run you a day, and if you need more, motel goes with you. I ain't got no more real use for it. You want it, she's yours."

Savas stared at him. "It will get us six hundred miles to Colorado?"

"No promises," he said. "But I've kept her in shape. I ain't no mechanic, but I can tinker the hell out of things. Like the heater. I wouldn't push her too hard: Keep an eye on the temperature. Stay under sixty. She should get you there."

"Beggars can't be choosy," said York. "We'll have a look. But we might just take you up on your offer, Mr. Bosworth. The nation doesn't have much more time. We have to end this conflict soon."

He nodded. "Nothin' truer said. We can fill you up with a few days' supplies. You shouldn't need more than that to get there." He stood up and walked to a floor-to-ceiling cabinet, pulling a key from several on a chain. He unlocked it and swung the doors open. "And we can supply you with more."

The interior of the cabinet was lined with shotguns. Boxes of shells were stacked along the bottom.

"Barric's been a collector for years," said Mrs. Bosworth. "'Bout drove me nuts with guns all over the house. Different makes, special handles, all kinds of money thrown away. I always said: 'What are you buying all these for, a war?'"

Savas stood up and walked alongside the cabinet, examining the interior.

"Well, Mrs. Bosworth, it looks like he was."

50

"OKAY FOLKS, TIME to take your positions," said the pilot. "Here comes the crazy part."

Houston and Lightfoote walked to the large SUV and opened the doors, entering the dark behemoth. Houston sat shotgun. Lightfoote took the back seat, spinning to look on the forms of two compact motorcycles strapped in the back, then turned back and belted herself in. Outside, Lopez looked over the vehicle, examining the chains and their attachments to the floor. He called up to the cockpit.

"These will release automatically?"

"Yes," said the pilot over the speakers. "Once the ramp is lowered. You follow it down, accelerating out and clear the aircraft. Then we're gone."

Lopez nodded and stepped into the driver's seat, slamming the door behind him. He pressed a button on the dash. "You picking us up?"

"Roger that," said the pilot through some static. "We're on approach, monitoring all frequencies. The airport is still shut down for all commercial flight, but they've started bringing in cargo planes and military aircraft. We've got some heavies around. Air traffic control can't see us, and as yet we've only had one pilot call in a UFO. It's getting dark, so—hold on. Make it two UFOs. Word's getting out."

"Jesus," said Houston. "How are we going to land in this mess?"

"Hold on!" cried the pilot.

The plane banked sharply, throwing them sideways. Lopez slammed into the glass, and nearly pitched to the other side of the SUV when the stealth craft leveled off, only his grip on the entry assist handle keeping him in position. He quickly buckled himself in.

"Looks like we land dangerously," said the pilot. "An Airbus Beluga super transport at takeoff. A flying whale for sure. Just missed it. *Jesus!* Okay, hang on, coming behind another plane on approach.

Prep for wake turbulence. This is it!"

Their stomachs dropped as the plane descended rapidly and the stealth aircraft was pummeled and shaken violently. Lopez grabbed the wheel instinctively as the SUV convulsed around them. He could hear the crates of weapons and ammunition rattling loudly from behind.

Then a kick in the gut as the plane slammed onto the ground. The landing gear miraculously held together as they were yanked mercilessly forward. The pilot decelerated the aircraft forcefully, and they felt him struggle to keep the plane from pitching. The brakes screamed, and the smell of burnt rubber filtered into the SUV.

"Prepare to detach!" cried the pilot.

"Roger!" called back Lopez.

He released the brake and put the vehicle in neutral. Despite slowing, the plane still moved quickly on the runway. The failing light of dusk streamed into the dark cargo hold, a slit in the floor growing in front of them. The ramp lowered, the tarmac below racing madly past.

"Go, go, go!"

There were several loud pops, followed by the rattling of heavy chains. The SUV pitched forward down the ramp.

"Brace!" Lopez cried out.

The vehicle slammed onto the asphalt as he gunned the engine and accelerated, sparks flying from the ramp behind them as it scraped the ground. He quickly angled away from the runway.

"Clear!" he yelled.

A strained voice came over the speaker in the SUV. "We see you. Accelerating for takeoff." They heard the black plane scream into full throttle. "We aren't coming back. Good luck! Always check your six."

"Thanks, and get the hell out of here."

He steered toward the main terminal as the stealth craft rose into the air. Lopez scanned the planes and crew around him, dodging obstacles and bewildered workers.

"Map's a bit blurry in my mind. We head for the main terminal, then west, and the highway?"

Houston nodded. "Right. No one seems to have picked us up yet.

I'm sure they were a bit distracted by the unexpected landing and takeoff. But it won't last forever. There, Francisco! Ahead. Follow the green line."

Lopez flew past parked airplanes, approaching a gate surrounded by booths.

"Boom barrier ahead. Arm's down. We ram it?"

Lightfoote leaned up from the back, straining against her belt. "No choice. Look!"

Bright red and blue lights began to flash from outside the SUV. Sirens howled.

"Police," said Lopez. "Well, that didn't take long." He shifted and accelerated, grinding his teeth. "Okay, hold on!"

"Guards! Take cover!" cried Houston.

Lopez had a millisecond to process the scene in front of him before he aligned the car to the gate and ducked. Two dark figures stood at either side of the barrier. They opened fire.

Impacts struck the front window, the shatter-resistant glass forming circular craters around the bullets. Other projectiles banged across the hood and roof of the car. The passenger side mirror exploded.

They crashed through the barrier and the shots momentarily ceased. Lopez jerked up, desperately steering the SUV out of the oncoming lane and onto the right side of the road, narrowly missing several cars approaching the gate. Horns blared. Several shots chased them, two thumping against the rear doors. But they were through!

Lopez gunned the SUV down the road and approached a turnoff to the main highway. He glanced in the rearview mirror, flashing lights from police clearing the gate in the distance behind them.

"Anyone hurt?" he cried out. Sweated beaded on his forehead.

"I'm good," said Houston, exhaling slowly and leaning back into her seat.

"Ditto," said Lightfoote. She laughed. "Your man can drive, sister."

"That he can," said Houston. "We clocked a hundred before we kissed."

"Don't get too excited," said Lopez, the SUV screeching as it rounded the exit ramp. "We're going to have the entire Dutch SWAT brigade on our asses in ten minutes."

51

"MAYBE TRAVELIN' BY night might be more secret," said Bosworth, eyes squinting. Wisps of breath escaped from his mouth.

Savas shook his head, pulling the hood down behind him. "It might call attention. Typical RV is going to drive by day, stop at night. We'll leave as soon as we're packed, be out of here by sunrise. Should be in Colorado by nightfall."

"Don't think any vehicle on the road these days will look normal. Everyone's shut up. Fuel's mostly gone. I'd vote for night. At least then it's hard to see you."

"We'll need lights. It will stick out for sure."

Bosworth nodded. "There's that."

The two men stood beside the dingy sides of the old camper, its once-white paint chipped and yellowed, dents spread haphazardly across the vehicle. The garage was spacious yet crammed with tools and a small hydraulic lift. A rusted pickup truck was on the other side of the RV. The faint first light of morning began to glow through small windows in the structure.

Cohen and York stepped out of the camper, discussing what they had found inside. Mrs. Bosworth shuffled across the oil-stained floor loaded down with heavy bags. She set them down in front of the RV.

"You two look twenty years younger," she said, her eyes twinkling.

"Miracles of food and a shower," said York.

The old woman nodded toward the interior of the vehicle. "So?"

"You weren't wrong about the smell," said Cohen.

York smiled. "It's not Air Force One, but it'll do."

"Might lose your appetite, but here," she said, indicating the bags. "Some food and supplies. You won't be needing much for this trip. Maybe Barric's gun collection might prove more useful. But it's nothin' we can't spare."

"Thank you," said Cohen, grabbing the bags and heading back into the RV.

York stepped up to the two men. She pointed under the truck to a large metal box. "The auxiliary tank?"

"Yes, ma'am," said Bosworth. "It's not Department of Transportation approved, mind you. Set it up myself. But served well for a lot of trips. You got fifty-five gallons in the main tank and forty more there in the reserve. That's a good seven, eight hundred miles. Unless you do something stupid, you won't have to even stop."

"We don't plan to," said Savas. "Stop or do anything stupid."

"What we plan and what's happened haven't always been in perfect alignment," said Cohen, returning.

"You got that right, girl," said York. "But we'll go with the plan. Dawn to dusk, straight shot. I-70 is likely mostly clear. Hope for the best."

"Not much else you can ask for in life," said Mrs. Bosworth.

"I still think you're gonna be the only ones out on the road," said Mr. Bosworth. "If they're looking for you, it's got to call their attention."

"Maybe," said York. "But we can't wait. And most of Hasting's troops were at Kansas City. Don't know what he has left out here."

"Hastings," echoed Mr. Bosworth. "The general you mentioned?"

"That's the one."

Bosworth shook his head. "Bombed his own *troops*. His own *country*. What kinda man does that?"

"One we need to stop," said York.

The five of them stood silently before the large vehicle for several moments before Mr. Bosworth cleared his throat.

"I wasn't for your politics, Ms. President, but I have to say you make a good impression. My money's on you for this fight. God speed to you and I hope you make those bastards see justice."

Mrs. Bosworth flicked her hands at them. "Okay, get, all of you. Come back some day and see us. You're good company, and we want to find out how it all ended."

"And you two stay safe," said Cohen. "We don't know how long it will be until things return to normal."

"We'll do fine," said Mr. Bosworth. "Got supplies laid up through this winter. If'n things ain't better by the next, country's lost anyway. We've seen a lot of good. Feel bad for the young ones."

Savas slapped the old man's shoulder and grabbed a shotgun on the back bumper. "Thanks for everything." He glanced at Mrs. Bosworth. "We won't forget. Don't worry."

The three said their goodbyes and boarded the RV. York slid into a booth in the middle of the vehicle, unfolding a large map in front of her. Savas placed his hand on Cohen's shoulder.

"You sure you want to drive?"

She nodded. "If anything happens, you two are the gunslingers." She looked at his weapon. "Sit. You're shotgun."

"All right. Let's pray I don't have to chamber a single shell." He eased into the passenger seat, pointing the weapon to the floorboard.

Cohen started the RV, the old engine coughing loudly and catching, the entire vehicle shuddering. They'd agreed to leave off all climate control, both to save gas and not to risk overtaxing the engine. They sat in poorly fitting coats, Cohen's fingers poking up through finger holes in a set of frayed gloves, the winter gear supplied from the attic trunks of their hosts. She checked the mirrors, adjusting the rearview, and looked out the window. The garage door was opening, the pale light before sunrise spilling in. A light snow had begun to fall, the air dancing with ice crystals.

The Bosworths walked alongside the camper and stepped outside the garage as the door retracted. Standing motionless by the left side, their expressions were inscrutable. Cohen waved and shifted, the RV rumbling forward and onto the driveway, bouncing clumsily on its poor suspension. They left the farmhouse behind, the front lawn passing on the right, two stony protrusions marking the entrance to the property. She turned right and onto a local road.

"All right," she whispered, clouds escaping her lips. "Here we go."

52

Lopez accelerated to over ninety miles per hour. They passed the early morning traffic on the highway out of the Amsterdam airport like the cars were tied to the road. With five lanes and little congestion, he easily picked his way around smaller vehicles.

"What the hell does this thing have under the hood?" asked Houston. "It's as big as a bus with two cycles in the back!"

Lightfoote hung her arms over the two front seats. "And what was the military doing with it? Urban warfare?"

"Later," snapped Lopez, dodging a blaring commuter bus. The speedometer hit ninety-five. "Status of those blue lights?"

Lightfoote spun back around. "No visual, but you can bet they're in pursuit. They've likely radioed ahead. They're going to set up road blocks soon."

Houston laughed and glanced at Lopez. "Sound familiar?"

"Too familiar. Angel, the turnoff should be close! You have the maps?"

Lightfoote stared at her laptop, open on the seat beside her. "Saved by the bat-plane satellite internet. Take the next one. Puts us in some small town—not going to try to pronounce it. They sure like lots of letters here. Narrow streets. It's perfect." She paused to glance through the back window. "Update: We got company. Good half mile, but I can see the flashy lights. A lot of them."

Lopez growled. "This is going to be close."

"We need to be clear enough so they don't see the bikes," said Houston, "or else it's just another chase."

"I know," said Lopez. The speedometer read one hundred.

"That's it, *there!*" cried Lightfoote, again leaning into the front space, her arm pointing to the right.

Several signs indicated an approaching exit ramp. The beginnings of a town could be seen along the roadside. Lopez swerved toward the rightmost lanes, accelerating even more to pass several vehicles lining up for the turn, horns protesting loudly behind them. Once he hit the exit lane, he floored the brake, pitching them forward in the cabin, cycles rattling loudly behind them.

They swerved into the turn far beyond the recommended off-ramp speed, Lopez fighting the wheel, G-forces slamming them toward the left side of the SUV as they whipped around the curve. Bags beside Lightfoote thudded into the left door as she clung to the headrests of the front seats. Exploding through the turn, Lopez raced through a stop sign, narrowly missing several cars crossing the intersection. Tires screeched in their wake.

"Awesome!" cried Lightfoote as they bounced through a narrow road, old buildings rising like walls on either side of the car.

Lopez continued to decelerate. Already the highway was lost to sight. As they approached a four-way, he turned left and brought the SUV to a stop on a deserted street.

"Move!" he yelled, opening the door and leaping out.

Houston followed, her limp nearly gone. Inside, Lightfoote bent over the back seat, reaching toward the flatbed. She worked frantically at the restraints on the cycles. The back doors opened, and Lopez slung several heavy bags to the ground.

"Sara, set the charges," he said as Houston caught up, then leaned into the SUV interior. "Angel, are they free?"

"Yes!"

"In three, two, one!"

Lightfoote grunted inside as Lopez pulled on one of the bikes. The motorcycle rolled backward and careened out of the truck. He steadied it as it hit, wheels bouncing on the cobblestone road inches from Houston's face as she crouched over a large, black bag, a detonator in her hand.

"Number two!" cried Lightfoote.

The second motorcycle bounced down onto the street, Lightfoote following it out. Both vehicles were pitch black, even the metallic elements covered in a dark matt material. Black helmets were snapped into holders near the back of the seats.

Lightfoote leapt on one cycle, quickly donning the helmet. "The bat-bike!" she called.

Lopez handed her a heavy backpack, and she strapped it on. He swung his leg over the other cycle, handing the second helmet to Houston as she exited the van.

"Ready?" he asked, motioning toward the SUV.

She nodded, strapping on a second backpack, and taking the helmet from him. "Where's yours?"

"They didn't plan for three. Don't worry—likely the safest thing we're doing this week."

Lightfoote laughed. "They're quiet too. Light. Stealth Harley's next."

Her engine was running, but the sound was minimal. Lopez pressed a button and started his cycle, hardly feeling the motor.

"Electric, remember? More than enough juice to get us to Oosterbeek." His head whipped to the side. "Listen!" The unmistakable sound of the Dutch sirens wailed from the distance.

"Let's go!" cried Lightfoote, gunning her cycle and ripping off down the street.

Houston wrapped an arm around Lopez, her other grasping a small metallic box. "Go, Francisco!"

Their bikes raced past the SUV and down the hill. As they approached an intersection, Lightfoote banked left and turned, soon lost from view. Houston held up her free hand, the other anchoring her to Lopez, a red light winking in her palm barely visible in the growing sunlight. As they turned the corner, she detonated the charge.

The SUV exploded. A fireball rose into the air, fragments of the vehicle raining around the ancient street along with smoke and ash. Blue flashing lights approached the raging fire from down the road, the police vehicles slowing to a stop. One officer opened his door some fifty meters away and gawked at the inferno in front of him.

Racing back onto the highway, the two motorcycles merged with the rest of the morning traffic. Houston turned her head and stared behind them. A cloud of smoke rose from the receding town and into the sky.

"Tracks covered," she said, flipping a black sun visor over her eyes.

They raced south.

53

"WE'RE BARELY HALFWAY through Kansas and the engine's overheating?"

York stood near the front of the RV, gazing down on the gauges. The engine light flashed while the thermometer danced in the red.

"We shouldn't have pushed it after we saw the helicopter," said Cohen, the RV's speed now dropped to fifty-five.

"It was definitely checking us out," said Savas. "I'm glad there's a little more traffic out here than Barric predicted."

"At least he got *something* right," said York. "I think his opinion of his mechanical skill is a little inflated. This thing's held together with wire and string!" Her lips pursed. "We're going to have to pull over, check the engine coolant, radiator. We can't have the damn thing blow on us. We'll be stuck."

"Pull over?" said Cohen.

"I think so. Do we want to risk losing the RV?"

Cohen looked at Savas. "What was it I said about plans?"

He ignored her. "Last sign said there's a stop a few miles down the road. We do it like a pit stop. Off road to a garage, have someone look at it, assuming anyone's there. Otherwise we do our best. Anyone a grease monkey? No? Wonderful."

"We don't have a choice, I'm afraid," said York. "We'll risk exposure, but nothing like the exposure we'd get broken down on the side of the road."

Several miles later, the dilapidated RV exited on a curved ramp and spiraled to a red light, gas stations and restaurants surrounding them. Savas pointed to a large station with a visible garage, and Cohen steered the camper to the lot on the light change. To their great surprise, they saw a crowd of people there.

"I don't get it," said Savas as Cohen stopped the vehicle in front of the empty garage. "No cars. The pumps are out. Look—a sign says *No Gas*. What's going on?"

"Phone!" said York. "Inside, through the window. A woman is

talking on the phone."

"The line is for the phone?" asked Savas.

Cohen nodded. "Of course. The Bosworths said everything was down. Cells, landlines. Looks like this place has one of the few working lines around. And everybody knows about it."

A rap on the window startled Cohen. She spun the handle and rolled down the glass to stare at an older man in a greased jumpsuit.

"Overheating?"

Cohen smile. "Yes, how'd—"

"These old campers are awful. Hundred dollars says it's a coolant hose."

"Can you fix it?"

"Well, I'll have to take a look. But likely, ma'am. We got a lot of rubber that will patch you for a while until you can get it looked at properly."

York leaned over and whispered to Cohen. "Get her fixed. I'm going to that phone."

Savas turned to her. "What?"

"A working phone, John. I can reach NORAD. If I can, I *have* to. Tell them I'm alive. Where we are. That we're coming. To send *help*."

"You'll be recognized."

"Possibly. I don't have my TV crew to doll me up, and I've lost some weight from this adventure. But maybe. I'll have to risk it."

"Jesus." He looked at Cohen. "We're way off plan. All right then, Ms. President. You're the Commander in Chief. But I'm going with you."

The pair left Cohen with the mechanic, the hood already up and his torso obscured within the engine. The line stretched outside the convenience store and around the station, stragglers converging from random directions to extend the line on a regular basis. Ignoring hostile looks, Savas pushed his way through the store doors and walked past the line to the register. York held up her hand and he let her approach the counter.

"Excuse me, sir," she said, her voice ringing with an authority and grasping the clerk's attention.

A young man with several days' worth of stubble walked over.

"Sorry, ma'am," he began, "no service. We're out of everything."

"I need your phone. It's an emergency."

The clerk's face darkened. Grumblings came from the line. "Well, ma'am, lots of folk got need of that phone. It's the only one east of Colby that's workin'. We got a line."

"It's a matter of national security," said Savas.

The grumbling became much louder.

"Yeah, right!" laughed one.

"Back of the line, grandma!" someone shouted.

"My son's sick!" came a woman's voice.

"It's York! It's President York!"

The room fell silent. All eyes centered on her, the clerk squinting and leaning forward.

"I'll be damned," he said.

Whispers ran like a wind hitting a wall of trees. York turned to face them, the oversized coat from the Bosworth attic swallowing her like a steal from a thrift shop. Savas instinctively backed away, giving her the spotlight.

"I *am* President Elaine York."

Savas let out a soft whistle and turned away from the crowd. He angled his body to York and whispered. "Might as well throw up a sign that says 'Bomb here.'"

York ignored him. "I am your elected leader. I'm here right now because there's been a military coup, one you've likely heard something about. I fled Washington, chased by the same people who bombed Kansas City." People murmured. "I'm going to Cheyenne Mountain, to the NORAD bunker to lead a resistance. But I'm not there yet. I need your help. I need that phone to reach them. They need to know I'm alive, that I'm on my way. I need them to send help." She walked up to the landline, a brunette holding the receiver staring at her open-mouthed. "The fate of the country might just depend on me making that phone call."

"I'm sorry, Chief Kruger, but I'll call you back." The woman hung up the phone and stepped back.

"Thank you," said York. She removed the receiver and dialed.

———

The mechanic slammed the hood down and wiped his hands on a towel.

"And that, pretty lady, is how you do it. It's a patch, jerry-rigged, but anything's better than the leaky hose you had. You'd lost most of your coolant oil. You were lucky you got this far."

"She's good to go?" asked Cohen, a growing wind tossing her brown hair across her face.

"Yep. I topped it off. You got more gas than you ought'a be carryin', so don't think you need anything else." The mechanic turned his head to look behind Cohen, distracted. "What the hell?"

York and Savas walked toward them, a giant crowd following behind. Cohen stared back and squinted into the wind.

"Oh, lovely."

The clerk raced up and grabbed the mechanic's thick arm.

"It's *York*," he said, giddy. "*President* York!"

The mechanic nodded as the crowd came to a stop in front of him. He extended his hand.

"Mighty honored to meet you, sir. Uh, ma'am."

"You get us straightened out?"

Momentarily star-struck, he tried to recover. "Um, yes ma'am. Busted hose like I thought. You're all set."

York turned to the crowd. "All of you, I'm going to repeat what I said. Don't follow us. Don't tell anyone you've seen us. I mean it. We have killers chasing us. The same killers who murdered half a million people in Kansas City. People some of you knew. If they find us, they will kill us. If you follow or speak about us, it will make it that much easier for them to track us down." The crowd remained silent, stunned. "Whether you like it or not, you've just been drafted into a war. In wars, loose lips sink ships. Help me get to NORAD. Pretend you never saw me. Go back to the line, call your loved ones. Take care of your emergencies. I promise you, I will fight to get this country back, and to bring justice to those monsters who have violated every decency."

The crowd applauded. Savas turned away and sighed.

"Great. Let's just send up a flare to attract more attention."

York waved quickly and stepped into the RV. Savas and Cohen followed. The crowd inched forward, unconsciously attracted to the vehicle.

"Try not to run them over, okay Rebecca?" said York.

"You reached NORAD?"

"Yes," York replied as she buckled in behind the booth. Savas lingered at the rear window, gazing outside. "They know the key details—what happened, where we are, where we're headed and how. I didn't dare stay on longer than to get a promise they'd pull out all the stops to help us."

Cohen nodded and started the engine. "Readings look good. Let's try to meet them halfway." She pulled out and turned onto the road, heading for the on-ramp to I-70. "I have to say, that was something. *Uplifting*. To find so many people behind you, supporting you."

"Not everyone," said Savas, his brows furrowed as he returned to the front.

"Trouble?" asked York.

"Several characters left soon after you were revealed to the crowd. They slunk out the back. Didn't look like their roots were in Kansas. When you were in the middle of that nice speech, an SUV with tinted windows pulled up across the street."

Cohen checked the rearview. "It's behind us!"

Savas grasped the handle of the shotgun by his side. "We've got company."

54

THE DIRECTOR OF the Bilderberg Group lay back in a plush chair, his head indenting the black leather, eyes closed. His heavy jowls hung slack, his mottled skin resembling some snake's hide in the dim light. Flashes of light splashed across his dark features as an alert tone sounded on the computer in front of him. Slowly, struggling to summon the energies of motion, his eyes opened, the gray eyebrows twitching, and for several seconds he simply stared at the blinking light. Then he leaned forward and pressed a key.

"Director," he rasped.

Static hissed over the speakers, and a snowy image of a man with a chiseled jaw appeared on the screen.

"Fox team beta, sir. We've found her."

The Director raised a pair of eyeglasses to the bridge of his nose with a shaking hand. "What? *York?* She *survived?* Are you sure?"

"We have two confirmed sightings by assets on the ground and we pulled the surveillance video from a gas station near Colby, Kansas. That's about an hour from the Colorado border. There's no doubt."

"My God."

"It's worse, sir." The snowy reception garbled the man's words and face. "There was a working landline, one of the first restored to service. We intercepted transmissions over the local network from your monitoring stations. She's contacted NORAD. They know she's coming."

"Dammit!" The Director pounded his armrest, falling back into his seat and closing his eyes.

"We have a vehicle in pursuit and several more en route. It's four hours to Cheyenne Mountain. That's a lot of time to handle the problem, sir."

His eyes remained closed. "Call in all available assets. Pull aircraft off anything else. If we have a fighter plane left I want her blown off the highway."

"Ahead of you, sir. The front is decimated. NORAD controls most of the airspace and we can't launch anything without them knowing."

"There must be something. We need something in the air."

"We're working on it. We might can commandeer local craft. It's our only option."

He sat up and rubbed his eyes. "Do whatever you have to do. Run her off the road. Firebomb her car. *Anything*. She can't be allowed to reach the mountain. Terminate with extreme prejudice."

"Understood, sir. Will keep you informed."

The image clicked off and the Director sighed. He initiated another video call, and the Middle Eastern woman appeared on the screen.

"Director," she said, her hair full and uncombed behind her, a silk evening gown on her shoulders.

"Maryam, the news is bad, it seems—"

"A moment." She stood up, carrying the camera with her, the figure of a powerfully built man naked in the bed. A door closed behind her, cutting off the bedroom. "Good morning."

"Morning for you. It hasn't quite arrived here. And there isn't much good to be had." She remained expressionless. "They've found York. She's alive and making a run for Colorado."

Her dark face turned to the side and she cursed in a language he couldn't understand. "Is there no way to kill that bitch?"

"We have assets in pursuit. She's exposed."

"Yet nothing is certain."

He nodded. "The real danger is her reaching NORAD, sealing herself in the bunker, and surviving what's coming. Unless we find a way to kill her now, or cut off NORAD completely, she could wage a war of ideas against us."

"What good will it do? There will be nothing left of the nation. She can summon an army of rocks and the radiation-poisoned."

He shook his head. "That's not the danger. It's Europe and Asia. If she can reach them, she could disrupt the world with that megaphone."

"If the assets fail, can we accelerate the program? Initiate it before she reaches the bunker?"

"No," he said firmly. "Zero must be out. It takes time."

"Then we'd better hope your men finish the job on the ground today, Director. I will brief the others."

She smiled coldly as the connection closed. The old man exhaled and once again crashed backward into his chair.

Damn these women.

55

"THERE'S A SECOND one!" shouted Savas from the back of the vehicle.

The RV screamed as Cohen pushed it past seventy. She glanced down at the gauges.

"We're running hot again!"

"How bad?" shouted Savas, moving to the front of the camper.

"Just in the red. But she can't take much more of this."

York loaded shells in a pearl-handled, double-barreled shotgun from the Bosworth collection. "No choice, sister. Those two trucks aren't looking to parlay." She slammed the barrels shut with a snap.

"Absolutely not!" said Savas to York. "Put the gun away. If they make a move, you're going to stay out of sight. You're the target. Don't be crazy!"

"We're not going to let them make a move," she said. "We're going to move on them first."

"Elaine—"

York looked sideways down the window along the side of the RV. "Your husband always have this problem with authority?"

"Pretty much," said Cohen.

"You want to let me drive, Rebecca?"

"I'm the analyst. He's Rambo."

"Then it's settled," said York. "This rig won't auto-pilot. We need as many guns as we can. I'm shooting."

Savas sighed. "Perfect."

"Second one is closing. It's going to be soon. Since you're worried I'm too delicate for combat, you take the rear window and I'll cover our flank."

"Back window is jammed, remember?"

York cocked her head to one side. "What do you think the shotgun is for? Bosworth will understand."

Savas moved quickly to the back as York rolled down the window beside her. The roar of rushing air thundered into the RV. He kept to the side of the window to avoid being seen by the SUV tailing them. Crouched beside it, he signaled to York with his fingers, and mouthed, "Three, two, one..."

He sprang backward, aiming the gun, and turned his head. A deafening explosion roared through the vehicle, dust and debris clouding the air. Most of the blast carried outward, slamming into the onrushing SUV. The truck stuttered and swerved, the driver nearly losing control. Savas pumped the action.

"The other's overtaking us!" cried York.

He pulled the trigger again, aiming the twelve-gauge through the window as the pursuing vehicle closed the gap. The front windshield of the SUV shattered directly in front of the driver, a hole the size of a fist punctured in the glass. A cloud of red burst inside and coated the windows, the truck veering violently to the right. It flipped, rolling wildly, and was quickly lost to sight as it smashed to a stop.

Two blasts in short succession followed from the front of the RV. Savas heard a tire explode, followed by the careening form of the second SUV veering into the median and plowing into the concrete separator.

"Good shooting, agent Savas!" cried York triumphantly.

"Two more trucks!" cried Savas. He dove to the floor and yelled to York: "Down, down, down!"

York dropped underneath the booth table. Bullets exploded through the camper. Windows shattered, glass fragments raining on the ancient carpet and upholstery. Cohen cried out as the rearview mirror popped. An engine roared and as the blade beats of a helicopter boomed from the left Cohen shouted again. Instinctively, she swerved to an approaching off ramp, trying to slow the RV and control the exit.

"Sorry!" she screamed. "I thought it would ram us!"

"Forcing us off the highway," cried Savas, rushing to the back of the camper. "Got a little distance, but the SUVs are following. Helicopter is banking for another pass."

"Can you get a shot at it?" cried York.

"Maybe," he said, "but they've got automatic weapons. I won't last long enough to aim."

York turned and looked ahead through the front window. "Where are they herding us?"

Cohen sounded defeated. "Local road. Two-lane. Nothing but farms and fields."

"Take the on-ramp?" called Savas. "Quickly!"

Cohen turned sharply right onto the two-lane road. "Can't! Black SUV at the bottom of it waiting!" She accelerated, the lumbering vehicle rocking back and forth.

"Our bird is back," said York, grimacing. "What the hell is it doing?"

The craft sped in front of them, passing overhead and down the road for some distance. It turned and banked sharply, half a circle until it had aligned itself with the road again.

"Oh, shit," said York. The helicopter dropped altitude and hovered just a few feet over the road. "John, those SUVs still behind?"

"Closing the gap. It's going be a shooting gallery in a few seconds!"

"What do I do?" cried Cohen, the bulk of the helicopter approaching quickly.

"Side road!" shouted York. "There!"

Cohen swerved. Dust clouded the air behind her as the RV skidded on the dirt and pebble road. She fought the wheel and centered the vehicle, catching her breath as the uneven surface flung them up and down.

"SUVs following!" cried Savas from behind. He hung on like some trapeze artist to the bunk beds as the vehicle lurched side to side.

"That house," said York, top of the hill. "If we can make it we can go to ground there. Fight them off."

"It's too far," whispered Cohen. "We're too slow on this road!"

"Hush, child! Don't think! Do!" York stepped up and strapped herself in beside Cohen. "Gun it! Make for the driveway. Ram the gate!"

The sounds of the helicopter had returned, higher but still in pursuit.

"They're almost on us," yelled Savas. A shotgun blast sounded from the back. It elicited return machine gun fire, strafing the top level of the camper.

York pointed forward. "Rebecca, look out—"

The camper pitched forward. Savas was thrown toward the front, his form flying through the corridor and slamming into the back of the passenger-side seat. The RV shuddered, the nose diving down, the windshield darkening and shattering like a spider web. They reeled sideways and the camper fell on its side, sliding to a rending stop in a fog of dust and raining pebbles.

"John!" cried Cohen as she fought with her seatbelt. She crawled along the left wall of the camper, coughing in the thick dust. He lay unmoving, blood covering his face. A strong reek of gasoline filled the air.

York called, "We've got to get out! The front glass—it's peeled half back. Help me out!"

Torn between the unconscious Savas and York, Cohen paused, paralyzed. She turned to the front. York was suspended sideways above her in the passenger seat, the belt the only thing keeping her from tumbling down. Cohen braced the president's form with her shoulder and wrapped her arms around her.

"Release the belt," she said.

The belt clicked and the full weight of York's body pushed Cohen downward. She cushioned the older woman's fall with a grunt. They turned and kicked violently the remaining sheet of shattered glass, peeling it further from the window.

Dirt continued to spill slowly into the camper, and they could see an abandoned, unplowed field in front of them. York grabbed her gun and turned to Cohen.

"Pull him out," she coughed, the fumes thick and pungent. "This thing could go up like a bomb any second. Those bastards are likely right outside by now. I'll do my best."

Cohen stared at her in disbelief but needed no prodding to turn back to Savas. The old woman groaned as she wedged herself out the empty window frame, the gun dragged behind her.

The air above brightened with a flash of orange, and a rending, ground-shaking explosion shook the RV. York squinted, adopting a bent crouch, the gun aimed as she pivoted to survey her surroundings. Off to her right, a fireball plunged from the sky and exploded a second time on impacting a neighboring field. A powerful engine rushed over her head, and the shadow of a muscular aircraft darkened the sun. The wreckage of the helicopter burned in front of her.

When the plane had passed, York turned to look behind the camper. The men were rushing back to the SUVs, planting themselves behind it for cover, aiming machine guns upward. They opened fire as the engine noise returned. York followed their aim. Swooping in over the field like some demonic crop duster, a plane rushed right toward them, heedless of their gunfire.

York gasped. The plane opened fire from the nose, a trail of light spewing from a hunting dragon. A deep grating sound battered her ears. The SUVs and men around it simply exploded.

Not from a bomb or missile, but from the impact of thousands of rounds of heavy ammunition. The bodies were blown apart in puffs of red, flesh and limbs spraying behind them. The vehicles similarly disintegrated, metal filleted off the chassis, the gas tanks igniting and torching the remainder.

The aircraft passed over the scene of destruction like a bird of prey, and banked once more, coming in low over the neighboring field with wheels visible. It was landing.

York lowered her shotgun and leaned against it, sweat and grime smearing her clothes. "About damn time."

56

THREE SHADOWS CROUCHED in the thick foliage at the forest's edge, a manicured expanse of green erupting before them and crashing into a white and gray chalet-style structure. Bright walls trimmed with dark balconies and rain gutters were offset by a purple-tinged shingled roof. Two prominent gables fought for attention along the front of the structure, one centered over the window-studded ground floor entrance, large words in cursive script decorating its center: *Hotel de Bilderberg*.

Lightfoote placed a hand on Houston's left shoulder. "And you're sure that's the last of the security?"

Houston nodded. "Key was taking out the central power line. We could have played peek-a-boo with those motion sensors and cameras all day and still been spotted. But they didn't wire it redundantly. So, *pop*, find the main power line and cut it before it can branch out. Forest goes blind."

"I really need to hang out more with you two," said Lightfoote.

"We've seen a little more of this than we'd like," said Houston.

On Houston's right, Lopez scanned the grassy field in front of them through binoculars. "Any minute now they're going to notice the system's down. The security on the building is still doing fine, I'm sure."

"So we wait for them to come to us," said Houston.

"Then what?" asked Lightfoote.

"We'll see," said Lopez. "We'll either get a leg up or have to make a mad dash, and then all hope for surprise is gone. It'll be a first-person shooter at that point."

Houston took the binoculars from Lopez and made her own appraisal of the grounds. "Let's hope a leg up. And look, just in time." She offered Lightfoote the lens.

Lightfoote focused below. "Two redshirts."

"Redshirts?" asked Lopez.

Lightfoote looked over the binoculars at him. "Star Trek?

Security guys that always beam down but don't beam up?" Lopez shook his head and shrugged. "Never mind." She turned her attention back to the approaching figures. "Two men. One's muscle. Well trained, fit, and he's packing. The other's not. He's clumsy. A technician I'd bet."

Lopez spoke to Houston. "Charges prepped?"

She nodded. "It's modified. More flash than bang."

"Assuming you got it right." He looked at Lightfoote. "She's our resident *untrained* explosives operative."

Houston shoved him upright. "Not by choice. Now, let's get in position."

Each grabbed a bag from the ground. They moved quietly twenty yards to the right, hugging the forest edge and keeping the two guards in sight. As the men reached the woods, the three of them lowered to the ground behind a large bush and fallen log. The power line snaked into the forest in front of them.

The Bilderberg workers approached. A heavyset man kneeled before the main cable, shaking his head and gesturing to a frayed gap in the line. A short conversation followed, the features of the trim man clouding with concern. He nodded and reached into his pocket and retrieved a mobile phone.

"Now, Sara," whispered Lopez.

"Look away!" she hissed back.

They turned their faces and shut their eyes. A blinding flash and a sharp crack sent the two men falling to the ground, writhing and moaning.

The three figures in black pounced: leaping over the fallen tree, they fell on the prone figures like tigers. After a brief contest, the two Bilderberg agents lay incapacitated and unconscious, hog-tied and gagged with duct tape.

"Got his cell," said Houston, tossing a roll of tape onto a black bag beside her. "Any of you understand this?" She held the phone up.

Lightfoote shook her head. Lopez laughed. "This is our lucky day. Guess the unemployment rate is pushing people out of southern Europe." He took the phone from her. "It's Spanish."

Houston smiled. "I think what he was planning to write was *shut the outer security system down.* Power linkage, need to isolate systems. Sound believable?"

"Maybe," said Lopez. "Let's see how it works."

As Lopez texted, Lightfoote continued to search the men, pulling out IDs and weapons. She called up to Houston. "Cards are magnetized. Might get lucky with them inside." Houston nodded. Lightfoote held up a black gun. "Another pistol."

"Looks like a Walther," said Houston. "Standard issue police pistol in these parts. German made."

"Good," said Lightfoote removing a shoulder holster from the man and fitting it to herself. "Never know when you're going to need a good German pistol."

"And the ruse pays off," said Lopez, shaking his head. "They're dropping the system for five minutes. They're sending backup. Guess they're nervous."

Lightfoote stood up and smiled. "A leg up."

"Maybe two," said Lopez. "Let's go."

They zipped up the backpacks and strapped them over their shoulders, leaping out of the woods and down the steep grass incline. Houston trailed behind, her leg slowing her pace. Pistols gleamed in their hands, eyes flashing between the ground and the door to the extended wing of the hotel to keep balance.

Lightfoote and Lopez reached the side of the building first, and the former priest reached into his black robes to remove a metallic canister, spraying black the lens of a camera mounted on the wall. Houston caught up with them, her face dripping with sweat. She placed her back along the wall, gun held to the side of her head, aimed up.

Lightfoote backed away from the hinges, hugging the wall as well. "Opens outward," she whispered. "I hear movement. They're coming."

At her last word, the door to the hotel swung toward her, and two men in suits exited. Each had a wired earpiece and showed a firearms bulge in their tailored jackets. They never got the opportunity to reach for them.

Lightfoote and Lopez caught them utterly flatfooted, a fury of disabling strikes bringing the pair down. The man beside Lightfoote had taken a heel to the back of his head and lay sprawled in front of her. Lopez followed a split second later, a powerful punch to the abdomen loudly cracking a rib, his target doubling over. He grabbed the man's head with his other hand and drove it into his knee. The body fell heavily to the ground.

Houston had already darted inside. "Clear!" she said, waving them in. "Francisco, get those bodies in here before we attract attention. Angel—"

"The transformer. On it." Lightfoote removed a gray block and set of wires from a bag and sprinted along the side of the hotel.

As Houston kept watch, Lopez dragged the unconscious bodies inside. The door opened to a small vestibule, revealing a second doorway. He tied up the pair and sealed their mouths with tape. His eyes darted sharply as the inner door clicked. Houston stood beside it, an ID card in her hand from one of the employees, the door open.

The building shook violently and a blast ruptured the air around them. The lights inside cut, the door making a loud and final metallic clip. The hallway behind it turned red from emergency lighting.

Houston tossed the ID to the floor. "Glad I tried this before Angel blew the thing."

Lightfoote bounded through the doorway panting. "Main transformer's down. Unless they've got a backup generator, power's dead for a good bit."

"Power looks out here," said Lopez, checking the mag on his sidearm, "but you can bet what's below has a redundant source. Question is how stable, and how long until it kicks in."

Houston moved down the hallway. "It won't matter if we don't find a way to get down there. This was the wired wing. The entrance is here, somewhere."

A sound of scraping metal screamed from the corridor, and they instinctively crouched and aimed. Two men bounded into the hallway space, weapons drawn, seeming to materialize out of the wall itself.

A storm of gunfire greeted them. The three invaders held the advantage, the Bilderberg guards shaken from the blast and orienting to the hallway. They were hit with multiple gunshots before they could even pinpoint the location of their attackers. One managed a wild shot into the ceiling. Their bodies fell heavily to the ground, groans escaping from one of them.

Three panthers bounded forward. One of their targets was clearly dead, two shots having struck him in the heart. Lightfoote crouched beside the other who moaned, crawling forward, a crimson soup pouring from his stomach and neck.

"He's bleeding out." She rose. "We move."

Blood splattered the corridor walls but for an opening in one panel, revealing a passageway down. A set of spiraling metallic stairs raced away from them into a red light that dimmed to a fog below. Shouts and the sounds of running feet echoed upward from the stone walls.

A door beside them opened, and the terrified countenance of a black woman stared at them. Houston pointed the barrel of her gun down the hallway. "Go," she said. The woman tore down the plush carpeting, dodging the bodies in front of her.

Lopez removed a pair of grenades. "Clear."

The two women stepped backward and away from the opening as he pulled the pins. He dropped them immediately along the sides of the stairwell, a two-foot buffer between the railing and the wall allowing them to fall without impediment nearly the entire depth of the shaft. He jumped away from the opening, placing his back against the wall.

Loud clanks followed, a cry of surprise from below, and two nearly simultaneous explosions vibrating the walls. Smoke poured up through the shaft and into the corridor. Screams of pain came with it.

"Leg up," said Lightfoote, stepping through the opening. She descended rapidly.

57

"BAD TIME FOR a selfie?" mumbled Savas. Blood stained his face and clothes, gauze and tape in and around his swollen nose.

"You might say," said Cohen, her tone flat as she tossed aside several bloody tissues.

"Camper packs a hell of a right hook," he said.

He looked up to the crowd around him—Cohen, the president, and an Air Force pilot in heavy gear. An oak tree towered above him, the broad branches spreading over their heads like an umbrella. Behind them gleamed the hull of a powerful aircraft. Several hundred feet to his right, a foul smoke continued to poison the air from the flaming remains of the vehicles. A blue commercial helicopter thundered in from the west.

The Air Force pilot turned to face York. "We've got to get you out, ma'am."

"On that?" asked York.

"All we had," said the pilot. "Not much of a selection out there right now. They called us in from across the front. Mopping up any of Hastings forces that didn't surrender and survived the bombing. I was given your vehicle description and told to neutralize anything else."

"You sure as hell did that," said York.

He indicated the approaching helicopter. "That bird was the only thing near enough—my Hog's a single seater."

York nodded. "Too bad. Yours is the plane I want."

The pilot smiled. "Smart call. She's a fortress. But I'll be escorting you if that helps."

The noise from the helicopter became deafening as it touched down several hundred feet from their position.

"Can you get up?" Cohen asked Savas.

"Have to," he groaned, grasping the tree trunk and rising unsteadily to his feet. She helped steady him as he grabbed her shoulder. Savas nodded to the pilot. "Fire her up. I'm coming."

The pilot instead escorted York directly to the helicopter. Savas and Cohen passed the huge airplane, the rugged exterior impressing upon them a lethal practicality. The hull and cockpit were heavily armored with thick plates of metal. Two hulking engines were mounted just in front of the tail, disproportionate to the body. The wings themselves were unusually thick and extended, housing underneath five or six missiles. Several slots were empty, the pilot likely having launched some of his arsenal already. An enormous Gatling gun was embedded in the nose of the plane.

"What the hell is this thing?" said Savas.

York climbed into the helicopter. The pilot turned back toward Savas, following his gaze to the plane. "A-10 Warthog. Hell of a fighting machine."

"That's a big gun."

He smiled. "Yes, sir. Made confetti out of your friends over there."

Savas looked slowly toward the skeletal forms of the SUVs. "Damn," he said, grabbing his neck. "I'm all kinds of beat up."

"Let's get you in the air, sir." With the pilot's help, Cohen eased Savas into the helicopter and he took a seat beside York. They buckled in, the A-10 pilot slamming the door shut and waving. He turned to jog back to his plane.

York spoke to the FBI agents. "Some interesting news from the pilot while John was down. We have assets in the Netherlands."

"They reached you?" asked Cohen.

"Not me, NORAD. Same folks as called in our escort. Seems your hacker busted into their system and demanded to speak to the brass."

"Angel. Then they're okay?" asked Savas roughly.

"They were, but all bets are off now. They tracked Bilderberg down. Called in my directive to back them. Military and some remaining CIA support got them on the ground in Europe, flew them past Hastings. Now NORAD's lost contact. But they were headed to the hotel."

"Things move fast," said Cohen. "I hope they're right, and they can do something."

"We could use some victories right now," agreed York.

"Zhanna Mouradian, your pilot." A woman's voice came from the cockpit, her helmeted face briefly looking back into the cabin. "US Geological Survey, actually." She turned back to the controls and began to lift the craft off the ground. "Nothing to do with the pterodactyl over there. Called me in for my National Guard service. Proud to be carrying you, Ms. President."

"Just get me to the mountain," said York. "This bird can make it?"

"Yes, ma'am. We got about two hundred miles to travel and we're fully fueled. No problem."

York smirked. "Don't be so sure. There's been nothing but problems on this ride. Combat, nuclear weapons for God's sake. And firing shotguns out of an RV like it was some damned Old West wagon chase. Take *nothing* for granted. Some nasty folks want us dead."

The ground receded behind them and the helicopter banked sharply west. The roar of the A-10 rumbled around them as the airplane managed a takeoff from the empty fields behind. They watched the armored bird of prey gain altitude and turn in their direction.

"Well, ma'am, we've got the flying Terminator behind us, if it counts for anything."

The helicopter continued to climb rapidly. As the ground receded, the trio squinted into the bright light of the setting sun ahead of them. In the distance, the horizon blurred, a smear rising from the ground. Peaks formed at the top of the blur, some dusted with a faint white cap.

The Rocky Mountains.

58

WEAPONS AT THE ready, they rushed down the spiral staircase, the smoke thickening as they descended. Fires flickered from where the blasts had ignited materials below. As they neared the bottom, Lightfoote stopped and held a hand up to stop Lopez and Houston.

"Ladder's disengaged."

The stairs stopped abruptly, exposing a ten-foot drop to the floor below. A ladder lay among the still forms of several bodies, its latch to the stairwell damaged by the explosions. A flashing red light from an alarm system strobed the walls around them.

"Watch the hallway."

Lightfoote holstered her pistol and turned her back to the passage. Bending and placing her hands near her feet, she grasped the edge of the last stair and swung down. Her hands anchored her to the stairwell for one swing before she let go to land a foot beyond one of the bodies on the ground. She drew her weapon and turned to the hallway, still crouched.

"Next!"

Lopez followed, his descent less acrobatic, his landing far heavier. While Lightfoote kept watch, he reached up and helped Houston down, softening the landing of her weak leg. Lightfoote moved toward a small booth. The window glass had been blown inward, a bloodied figure inside slumped over a security system. She reached in through the narrow doorway and pulled him off the chair, the corpse falling against the back wall.

The shattered remains of a panel of five monitors coated a long desk, only one still operating. It showed multiple camera views of the underground bunker. Lightfoote sat in the chair and put her pistol on the table surface, pulling a keyboard up from under the counter. Her hands flew over the keys, opening command line prompts, navigating her way through the system. A map of the structure's below-ground levels appeared, and Lightfoote had the video cameras zoom in on each room in succession.

"Only two floors," she said as Lopez and Houston looked on. "Look at this. It's like one giant server farm. Especially the second floor. Hundreds of computers stacked to the damn ceiling. The whole floor below is nothing but computers and this one room at the far end."

A plush office centered on the screen, three figures within it. A smaller shape moved arthritically but with authority. Beside him, two hulking men with wide stances stood at attention, one holding a weapon. The old man spoke on a telephone.

"If this were a video game," said Lightfoote, "he's the Big Boss."

Houston scoffed. "Camera's labeled *Director*."

"Other guards?" asked Lopez.

"Not finding any," said Lightfoote, racing through the feeds from different rooms. She paused on the stream from a large room, the space packed with office cubicles.

"Who are these guys?" asked Houston.

"Don't know," she said. "Room's right down the hall, though. We'll check it out." She squinted at the screen. "What are they doing?"

"Looks like they're hiding under their desks," said Lopez. "I don't think we'll need to worry about them."

"You were right about the security," said Houston as Lightfoote continued to roll through camera views of different rooms. "I don't think they had more than ten guards."

"For the seat of global power, this place is a little disappointing," said Lopez.

Lightfoote stood up and grabbed her gun. "I guess it's white collar crime. Push the banks, pull the politicians. Throw money around. All the dirty stuff happened outside these walls."

"Not anymore," said Houston. "Time to visit *The Director*."

Lightfoote nodded. "The map shows a stairwell in the middle of the hallway. Let's sweep this floor and make sure there are no surprises, then down."

"We should hurry," said Lopez. "Didn't see any other exits on the map, but the longer we wait, the longer they can plan for us below."

"Or bring in reinforcements," said Houston.

The three stepped back into the corridor. They formed a staggered line, spaced apart and giving room for each to react and maneuver. Lightfoote ran point, swinging into rooms in succession, verifying they were empty. Lopez took the middle, prepared to back Lightfoote if confronted by a hostile. He carried a pistol in his right hand, and with his left continued to spray the cameras along the way, cutting off any surveillance the Director might have from below. Houston brought up the rear, spending half her time pivoting to defend against an attack from behind.

The largest room on the floor waited at the end of the corridor. A sheet of glass took the place of a wall from waist high, revealing workers inside. As the camera had shown, they cowered in a packed office space littered with cubicles and desktop computers. Whiteboards full of scribbled equations lined the walls inside.

"What the hell is this place?" asked Houston from the hallway. "Some economics crisis center?"

The workers would not have appeared out of place in a Silicon Valley programming company or a mathematics department at an Ivy League school. Behind their cubicles, many flinched as Lightfoote entered.

"Who's in charge?" she barked, her weapon aimed slightly over their heads. Lopez stood behind her to increase the show of force as Houston continued to watch the hallway. "No one?" She fired a shot into the ceiling. People screamed.

"Gelieve, ons niet doden! Wij zijn slechts werknemers hier!" cried a man on her right.

"English! Who's in charge?"

"The Director!" came his accented voice. "The Director is in charge!"

She leveled her gaze at him. "And in this room?"

The man swallowed. "Ah, I am."

"What do you do here? Tell me now or I'll fucking end you!" She aimed her weapon at him.

The man began a high-pitched info download. "We run models! Economic models, world politics, national power and resources for the Director! We predict the nations, world economy!"

"Stop!" cried Lightfoote. "You run simulations on the servers? Models for Bilderberg?" He nodded. Lightfoote turned her head to Lopez and Houston. "This is it. These are the fucking Nash equations incarnate."

Lopez shook his head. "You mean the world's being run by a bunch of nerds crunching numbers?"

Houston laughed softly. "Plus the money and mercenaries."

Lightfoote turned back to the room. "Access codes, to all your systems."

"We can't give those—"

Lightfoote's pistol blasted an empty terminal beside the man.

"Godverdomme!" He screamed, his khaki slacks darkening around his crotch.

"I'm not asking. Last chance."

He grabbed a sheet of paper and scrawled madly on it. As he wrote Lightfoote walked up to him, keeping her gaze across the rest of the room, coming to a stop with her gun inches from his head. "Show me."

"Show you?"

"I see the codes. Log in. Show me what I'm getting. They better not fail."

The man sat down in front of a monitor and moused the screen saver away. He opened a series of windows, entering in usernames and passwords for each.

"The first is the modeling system, *ja?* I have root access, I can access all inputs and results, all weights and fundamentals."

"The others?"

He swallowed, opening a window. "Bank access. National intelligence systems. Ah, other things." Sweat dripped from his face.

Lightfoote stared at the screen, her eyes wide. "Is there a terminal that gives me access below?"

"Yes, at the control desk for the farm."

"The backup power—how long will it last?"

The man looked like he wanted to cry. "I don't know. This has never happened."

Houston cried from the hallway. "Let's move, Angel. Seal them inside. I've rigged a little deterrent."

"One more thing," she called back to Houston. Lightfoote went to the main power strips, following several cables to sockets in the walls. She spoke over her shoulder to Lopez, "Watch them." Placing her gun on the ground, she removed a sharp knife from her belt. One by one, she removed the plugs and beheaded them, cutting off the pronged ends. A minute later all the monitors in the room were dark, the computers without power. She tossed the plugs out in the hallway.

"Your mobile devices. I want to see each of you bring me one. And I don't want to find out that even one was left out." She placed an empty box on a table and turned to the man in front of her. "Explain it to them."

He did. Eagerly, with terrified expressions, the workers brought smartphones and tablets and dropped them into the box. After the last, Lopez carried it into the hallway.

"We're going to go down this stairway, but I wouldn't recommend trying to follow us or go get help. Sara?"

Houston banged on the glass and the heads of those inside darted toward the window. Her muffled voice spoke from the hallway. "This is a *detonator*. It's tied to a block of explosives right there," she indicated, pointing behind the wall. "When we close the door, don't open it! It will trigger the bomb. *Boom*." She paused for effect. "You'll all go home to mother in a bag."

"Now, under your desks! And stay there!"

The figures didn't need to be told twice. They scrambled to move chairs and fit themselves within the cubicles. Lightfoote closed the door and examined the wires Houston had rigged. The detonator didn't connect to anything.

"I thought so."

Houston raised an eyebrow. "You didn't think I'd risk sealing off our only exit?"

"And we might need the explosives below," said Lopez opening the door to the stairwell. "Here we go."

59

THE STAIRS OPENED to a dark room punctuated by thousands of blinking lights and a heavy hum. Seeing the server farm on the cameras was one thing, but standing in the midst of it like Theseus in the labyrinth plunged them into an electronic sea. The individual servers, their fans and hard drives, the electrical coils and transformers used in power supplies and motherboards, even the vibrations of the metal chassis, multiplied by thousands of units created a strong, constant wind modulated by a droning heartbeat.

A clear corridor through the server racks led straight ahead and Lightfoote followed the path toward the center of the room. They passed numerous rows fanning sideways, the passageways lined with rack after rack of processors, resembling a cybernetic public library. Overhead, air conditioning vents blasted air into the frigid space, as if the units funneled the wintery chill outside directly into the building.

The canyons of computer racks stopped abruptly and they stepped into an open space. A large table with numerous monitors greeted them. Uneaten food and coffee mugs sat perched at the sides, one still steaming.

"Looks like the techies made for the hills," said Houston.

Lopez scanned around them and up to the ceiling, moving quickly to spray-paint a camera above them. "This place is an electricity black hole. They have to have other generators somewhere."

"I'm going into their system. Keep an eye out." Lightfoote sat down in front of the keyboard. She placed the paper with the scrawled codes on her left and began to type furiously.

Lopez and Houston kept vigil, back-to-back with weapons out. In the white noise and hum, they began to lose their sense of time and space. Each found themselves anchoring their position on the other, the table beside them, and on the repetitive clacking of the keys.

"This is amazing," called out Lightfoote. "They have direct links to the major world financial centers, biggest banks, trading floors, the Federal Reserve. I mean superuser type privileges, complete access and control. Right here I could change money flow across continents, manipulate stocks and trading. It's all automated, the Nash equations steering everything to preset ends, but I could also go in manual, too."

"Chase Bank, account 5748395033. I'd like to be a billionaire please," said Houston, her eyes on the passageways in front of her.

Lopez mirrored her scanning. "Darling, don't you remember, Uncle Sam froze all your accounts last year?"

"Those bastards."

"Listen!" said Lightfoote. "It's not just the banks and exchanges. That neckbeard was right. They have access and control of intelligence, even *military* systems. It's a click away—Homeland Security, DOD, CIA. Records, accounts, agents in the field." The clacking continued. "Oh my God." She pushed the chair back from the table.

Houston turned toward her, lowering her sidearm. "What, Angel?"

"Holy shit. They're plugged into the fucking nuclear arsenal. NORAD, submarines, satellites. They have the president's *access codes*, complete targeting control. They could launch a nuclear war against anyone they wanted."

"That's about as bad as it gets," said Lopez.

"Actually, it isn't," said Lightfoote, back at the keyboard and squinting at the screen. "Because if I'm understanding this readout, they *are* launching a nuclear war. Right now."

"What?" said Houston, her face incredulous.

Lightfoote continued to type. "There's access to multiple silos in the US, upload of target coordinates. Some kind of timer waiting for a signal."

"What signal?"

Lightfoote shook her head. "I don't know. It's not clear. Waiting for some kind of communication inbound."

"Trigger what, exactly?" asked Lopez, leaning toward the screen, his face grim.

A list of names and numbers scrolled before them. "Armageddon," said Lightfoote. "New York, Washington, Chicago, LA, Houston, Philly." The list continued to scroll. "*Jesus,* it must be twenty or thirty sites. Key population centers, government, military targets, oil, gas, mineral deposits. It's a crippling strike. From within. With our *own* missiles. USA cluster*fucked*. Gone."

"For God's sake, why?" asked Lopez.

Lightfoote shook her head. "I don't know. Only, look. Something here in the modeling programs. See? Two networks of lines in this global map. The gray web looks like what we calculated in the hacker bunker—Bilderberg at the center, nodes at major centers of power. But look—here in color, like some new world order, the web is broken. The New York node is gone. *Nothing* connects to the US. The other nodes re-balance with different weights and connections."

"It's like they're cutting off the United States," said Houston. "Putting it in a coma."

"Which is exactly what you'd expect to happen if there were a nuclear decapitation strike," said Lightfoote.

Lopez looked around. "We don't have much time. We've got to get to the office and capture the Director, whoever he is."

"Agreed," said Houston. "We've given him too much time, already. And maybe he knows how to stop this. Come on!"

"No!" said Lightfoote glaring up at the pair. "You two go. This is too close. Once a signal is sent, whatever it is, there isn't much time to stop it. I've got to see what I can do here while I still have access. Before they lock me out or this server farm fails."

"Or before someone comes up and shoots you in the back of the head," said Houston.

"You think you can stop it?" asked Lopez.

"I don't know!" said Lightfoote.

Houston gestured around them. "You'll be blind here, Angel. Vulnerable."

"Gotta risk it," she said turning back to the screen, her fingers working the keyboard. "It really looks like these maniacs are serious."

Lopez stared at Houston, who reluctantly nodded. "If you think you've got a chance to interfere with an attack, do it," he said. "Sara and I will take care of the Director."

Lightfoote shot them a quick glance. "Be careful! I don't want to save the damn world again if you two aren't going to be in it."

60

"WE'VE LOST TWENTY-three silos!" came a voice from the back of the Command Center.

Admiral Myers' thick hair danced in disarray, the gray like an explosion from a geyser. To exacerbate the chaos, he repeatedly grabbed chunks and yanked them mercilessly, glaring down at the terminals in front of him. "I can't believe this is happening. Morris—anything on the subs?"

Another voice called out from behind him. "Negative, sir. All the boats are quiet."

"Any targeting info?"

"No, sir. Not yet. We're getting the data now, but so far, just the silo readings. And things are definitely powering up."

"Sir, we've got a live stream from Montana."

"Put it up."

Myers glanced up to the giant monitors in the front of the Command Center. A grainy video appeared on one of them, the image of two men in a small room furiously working the control panels. Some panels had been torn out, wires dangling.

"These boys trying to sabotage the thing?" asked Myers.

A man below him at the desk looked up. "Believe so, Admiral."

Deputy Commander Duval walked into the Command Center trailed by three others. He headed straight for Myers.

"Any pattern?" he asked the Admiral.

"Nothing. Seems random. Silos here, silos there. Most of the arsenal is still under our control. These others—Christ Almighty. *Charlie Foxtrot.*"

Behind Duval were York, Savas, and Cohen. Filthy, clothes soiled and torn, scrapes and bruises covered their exposed arms and faces. Savas was the worst, a shattered nose red and swollen, dried blood caked around the nostrils, the entire middle of his face a violet patch. Myers turned to the trio and shook his head.

"You three look as bad as we feel. Sorry to welcome you here under these circumstances, Ms. President, but I'm glad you made it." He saluted.

York saluted back. "Duval tried to brief us on the way up. You've lost contact with several nuclear missile silos, I understand?"

"Not exactly," said Myers. "See there? We've still got video feeds and communications with the operators. But a lot of good it's doing us. The missiles are severed from their control. No presidential orders. No football bag with codes. No two-man rule. Someone else is running this show. The damn things are going into a pre-launch state, signals from the silos indicating they've been prepped and target coordinates uploaded."

"Impossible," whispered York, staring at the frantic efforts of the men on the screen.

"God knows I wish it were. It's spread all over our Minutemen locations, across multiple states simultaneously. Seemingly random except in each case the silos are also sealed off from the rest of the facility. We can't get anyone near, and we don't have the personnel to go after each one on the outside. Although we're putting it in motion."

"Hackers?" asked York.

"These systems are dinosaurs, Ms. President. Hell, they run off nine and a quarter inch disks. They're not even networked." He shook his head. "No, this has got to be far older."

Cohen whispered, "Bilderberg."

Myers and York turned to her, but a loud voice from in front interrupted.

"We've got coordinates on ten missiles! Going to the monitors."

Numbers rolled across the screen along with associated map names. Gasps vented across the Command Center.

"All the targets are internal," said York.

"All targets identified!" came the voice. The numbers and names continued to pass by on the screen.

"NORAD?" asked Myers as a map of the nation appeared, red circles indicating the missile targets.

The man at the station in front of him spoke. "No, sir. Doesn't seem so."

He shook his head. "I don't understand. If it's Bilderberg, why not us? We're the enemy, not the rest of the nation!"

Cohen spoke. "NORAD's a very hard target. Too buried. Too ready. The other targets are soft."

York turned to her. "It's *madness*. Why? And how?"

"I don't know how," said Cohen. She looked at Myers. "You said this wasn't hackers, it had to be something old. Probably something long in the planning and maintained. Think about what Bilderberg is, what they've been doing for decades: pulling all the strings at every level. Why would they leave control of the most powerful weapons on earth out of the equation?"

"And the why?" asked York. "This isn't Hastings trying to take me out. This is the end of the nation!"

"We need to reach Angel," said Cohen. "They're at Bilderberg. They might have found something out!"

"We've been trying to contact them for days," said Myers. "Nothing. Only static since they touched down." He turned back to the screen, staring at the soldiers in the silo. "Besides, it's not gonna matter much *why* if we don't find a way to stop it soon."

61

THE DIRECTOR SCREAMED on the phone, his bodyguards flinching and tense, the air in the room stale and claustrophobic. He gestured to a computer screen in front of him, the emergency lights bathing the lush office in flashing bursts of red.

"There is no choice!" he screamed. "We're completely compromised, main power cut, security neutralized. Our computer system is infiltrated. I don't know how! But I'm locked out. They have access to everything. They could shut the entire program down!" A voice shouted indistinctly from the speaker. "Correct. We need to accelerate the launches. We need to amputate this node and transfer control to another. Yes, long term. Don't you understand? We're completely blown. Bilderberg is finished!"

One of the guards leaned toward the Director. "Sir, we've lost another camera." His gun was out, and he assumed a crouched position behind the desk. The other guard mirrored him.

"I've got invaders approaching as we speak, Alpha. We don't have time to argue. Yes, I *know* you and Zero are not out! So we spare the New York node, at least for now. Damn the simulations! We don't have time to check the repercussions." More shouts from the speaker. "And we don't have time to confirm or debate. If we don't launch now, we could lose the opportunity forever!"

The Director glanced at his screen. The monitor was tiled with squares. All of them were black but one, a camera looking toward the server farm. Two dark shapes sprinted toward the lens, one reaching a hand toward it. The last video feed went black.

"Damn!" He pulled out an ancient looking revolver. "They're standing outside my office door. This is it, Alpha. Transfer control to Maryam. Abort the New York warhead. Then launch the rest."

The guards aimed toward the door as the Director placed the receiver down on the phone. He checked the bullets in his revolver.

"We don't know their numbers, but if—"

His voice was swamped by a thundering roar, the door blasting inwards, debris and dust slamming the three men backward and against the wall.

"Shit!" said Houston as the she turned toward the Director's office. The door was gone. Along with it a portion of the wall, an enormous dust-choked hole opening its maw toward them like a hungry beast. "I never get the damn yield right. We need him alive!"

The pair jogged forward cautiously, weapons raised in front of them. Darting into the wrecked room, they approached the three bodies behind the desk. It was as they had seen in the video feeds—the old man and two guards. Now coated in dust and pieces of rubble, their weapons flung against the wall and out of reach. The guards opened their eyes.

"Barrel on each of you!" yelled Houston. "Don't even—"

The men leapt at them, one throwing a large wooden plank at Lopez, forcing the former priest to deflect it, and preventing him from firing. Houston pulled the trigger twice as her target crashed into her and sent her sprawling. Dust kicked up in the scuffle. But her shots had flown true, and the assailant was badly wounded. The wind knocked out of her, she managed to pull herself to a crouch, gasping for air and steadying her aim as the guard in front of her rose clumsily. Her third shot struck him in the forehead, the body hanging in the air, paralyzed, then dropping like a rag doll.

Lopez had tried to reorient after deflecting the projectile, but he didn't have time to aim and the shot went wide. The guard slammed into him and they toppled backward. Lopez rolled with the motion, drawing his knees to his chest and propelling the attacker over his head and behind. The man's momentum did most of the work, hurling him against the wall, before crashing to the ground.

Lopez flipped to his feet and spun around, a fire in his eyes, his feet planted in a fighting stance. Disoriented, the man braced himself with one hand against the wall, and rose as well, turning with his fists raised to engage.

He never threw a punch.

Lopez darted forward, closing the distance with a step, nearly inside the reach of the guard. The first impact came from his knee into the man's groin. The guard's cry was stifled by the second blow, a double strike from each hand to the side of the head as Lopez swung his arms like a pair of short fighting sticks. The impacts were titanic. The man's jaw cracked loudly. He dropped to the floor unconscious.

"Leave the weapon!" cried Houston.

Lopez spun around. She pointed her gleaming Browning at the Director. The old man's arm was reaching up the desk to his handgun. Lopez walked toward him, bent and retrieved his own weapon, and took the revolver as well.

"What have you people done?" moaned the old man, silt crusting his lips and face, like macabre makeup for the dead.

Houston righted a fallen chair and sat across from him, careful to remain out of reach. Lopez trained his weapon on the Director.

"The question is what have *you* done, you crazy fuck. Nuclear war?"

"You understand nothing, nothing of what we have accomplished, what your dear president York had gone along with for years."

"She didn't have much of a choice, I'd bet. You people had your hands in every pot, on all the dirty laundry. Did you think you could try to control us all forever?" She brandished her weapon. "Now, we're going to have a little chat. About the nuclear silos and how to shut that shit down."

The man said nothing but brought his hand to his mouth.

"Sara! Stop him!" cried Lopez.

But it was too late. The heavy jowls bit down and a liquid flowed out from the sides. The Director swallowed as Houston rose, a grim smile on his face.

"Poison," said Lopez, a disgusted scowl on his face. "You son-of-a-bitch."

"It's a special blend," choked the Director, foam beginning to burble in his mouth. "High dose. Very...fast. Acid adjuvant."

He doubled over wheezing, the foam more prodigious. His body convulsing. Lopez and Houston watched in horror, powerless to stop the inevitable biochemistry. The convulsions continued for several minutes, increasing in severity, and the old man toppled over on his side beside Houston's feet, unmoving.

"Well, fuck." She turned to Lopez. "Now what?"

62

A VOICE CALLED out over the loudspeaker system in the NORAD Command Center.

"Repeat, all silos restored to base control. Ten are non-operational due to damage. The remainder are responding to operator commands."

NORAD staff dashed around the center, data flying over the giant monitors, those at desks on the phone or working their computers furiously. The room stank of tension, men visibly sweating even in the air-conditioned environment.

Admiral Myers sat down and hung his head. "Jesus Christ. Thank God for deliverance."

York frowned at the screens. "You still don't know why we're back in control?"

Myers shook his head. "No idea. And *yes*, it worries me. But right now, with those birds shutting down, I'm going to take five minutes and count this as a win."

Cohen turned to York, her brown eyes sharp. "It's got to be Angel and the others. Too much a coincidence."

York nodded. "We need to reach them as soon as possible."

"We're on it," said Myers. "Still reaching out. Still nothing. They're either really busy—or dead, sorry to say." The old man closed his eyes and leaned back in the chair.

"Keep trying," said York. She put one hand on Savas and the other on Cohen and led them forward. "Meanwhile, you two come along. They've set out a little office for me down the hall, and we need to talk."

———

York closed the door to the office, the noise and frenetic chaos of the crisis center muted behind the glass and wood. Photos of a man and his family decorated a desk in the center. Savas and Cohen rested in two chairs facing inward, and York moved behind the desk and

685

took a seat, staring across the cluttered surface at the FBI agents.

"This may or may not be over," she began. "We may or may not contact your friends overseas. This war with Hastings might be ending or gearing up to another round. Either way, I've got to plan for our next steps." The pair watched her expectantly. "We need an anchor on the East Coast. The West is ours, and that won't change unless there's a dramatic shift in the balance of power or those nukes finally do fly. But the East is still enemy territory." She leaned forward, holding their gaze. "I've lost all my advisors, some also my close personal friends. After what you and I have gone through, after I've seen you in action, I trust you. I value your advice. Since Kansas City, you've been my road advisory council."

Cohen fidgeted uncomfortably. "An honor, Ms. President."

"What kind of anchor?" asked Savas.

York leaned back in the chair. "We need a second base of operations until this war is over. Something secure that's right in Hasting's side of the court, under his nose. A place we can store troops and equipment, launch guerrilla attacks. One that can be defended against anything but the most powerful assault."

"The Manhattan bunker," said Cohen.

"Exactly."

"But we abandoned it," said Savas. "It could be in Hastings's hands now."

"It could," agreed York, "but it isn't. You might remember we left a contingent to try and hold the base? Not many. They couldn't have held it if Hastings had gone after the bunker seriously. But he didn't. He figured the real war was out on the plains—and he was right. But he's been handed devastating losses and left himself open for an attack from within. We're going to be flying several secret missions to bring the fighting numbers up at the bunker. Personnel to make it a base of operations." She smiled. "What I need is someone to run the place. People who have shown the strength and character, creativity and courage under fire it will take to make that base work. People I trust."

Savas and Cohen glanced at each other, and back at the president.

"Elaine, if you're thinking to suggest—" began Savas.

"I'm not suggesting. This is an Executive Order. From this point, until I deem it no longer necessary, I hereby appoint both of you as the civilian heads of the Manhattan bunker. You will have authority over everyone there, including armed forces personnel. You will be charged with getting the location back up to speed, readied for an extended war campaign if necessary. I will of course provide you with military advisers, logistics support and a contingent of Special Forces troops."

"Ms. President!" began Cohen.

"Never interrupt the Commander in Chief," said York. "I know you both are tired. God knows, I am. Half the staff out there are ready for early retirement after this. But it's *not* over. I, this nation, needs our best people and everything they have."

"We aren't qualified to serve in a military capacity," protested Savas. "Whatever you think of us, we aren't ready to be put in charge of such an important operation and given the power over soldier's lives."

"Let me be the judge of who is ready for such duty," she said. "Your command there will violate a hundred regs and piss off a lot of people. But that will all go on the back-burner. Because right *now* we have a *Last Days* problem on our hands." She stood up and put her hands on the desk. "You'll leave within the hour."

"What?" said Cohen.

"Several Special Forces teams will accompany you. They're prepping a transport and fighter escort for you at Peterson right now. This can't wait. We have Hastings on the ropes. You're our left hook."

York walked to the door and opened it. The flood of noise swept over them again—calls on the loudspeakers, machinery, the incessant drone of the fans pumping air into the underground buildings.

"Take a few minutes to gather your thoughts. Then meet me back in the Command Center. Myers will have people ready for you." The president turned and strode down the hallway without looking back.

Cohen frowned at York's retreating back. "Well, John, I can't wait for the hazard bonus."

63

"DON'T YOU TWO know how to knock?"

Lightfoote stood inside the cavernous hole blown in the wall, her gaze tracking the circumference of it. She carried a black backpack with her.

Lopez stood over a body on the floor, wrapping the man's arms and legs in duct-tape. Houston sat on the edge of a damaged desk, padding her neck and chin with a bloody cloth. A long abrasion ran down her chest.

"The Director's dead," said Lopez. "Suicide. We'll get nothing from him to help stop the attacks."

Lightfoote walked in through the rubble and stared down at the crumpled body of the old man. She dropped the bag on the floor and turned to look behind Lopez. A soft moaning came from the floor beside him.

"You roped that calf?" she asked. Lopez nodded. "Okay, well, the good news is I managed to fry their controls on the silos. Irony! I used some of Fawkes's leftover code on their systems, subroutines my immune packets hadn't completely erased. I modified a few and set them loose on their command and control code. They're not going to be using it again for some time."

Houston cocked her head to one side. "I didn't think missile silos were networked like other things."

"They aren't," said Lightfoote. "Irony number two. To keep control of them, Bilderberg had to link them. So, Uncle Sam at NORAD was out of the loop and could do nothing while Bilderberg pulled the strings. But their links, on modern servers, exposed them to hacking."

Lopez clapped her on the back. Houston smiled broadly. "Damn, girl, you *did* just save the world again. Or maybe a hundred million lives."

"I think it was definitely a team effort," she said. "So, now, the bad news."

"I'm looking for the mission when we stop hearing that," said Lopez.

"Bilderberg—whatever this place is, or was—it's not what we thought. Not the whole beast, but just one part of it."

What do you mean?" asked Houston.

"Bilderberg has been the nexus for decades. Maybe centuries. Who knows? But whatever this organization is, it's a hydra. Many heads in different parts of the world."

"The nodes in the computer simulations?" asked Lopez.

She nodded. "The Nash equations were incredibly predictive. They've locked me out of the system now, totally wiped it, probably amputating this node. But not before I found connections to the other locations. They're subservient, taking orders from here, but active, focal points for local manipulations of markets and politics. Each had a different name, its own contact, its own infrastructure and power base. I was going to save all the data, transfer it, so we could chase them down and figure it out, but they trashed the server before I could."

"So, the New York cluster is real?" asked Houston.

"More than that," said Lightfoote. "It's the heart of it all."

"I thought this place was," said Lopez.

"Bilderberg was a *front*. It's so devious. For the simulations and string pulling, this served as a focal point. If anyone came looking— really came looking like us—they'd be drawn here. But it's *not* the puppet master. Bilderberg's strings, and the strings of the other nodes, are all being pulled from New York. By *Zero*."

Lopez furrowed his brow. "Zero?"

Lightfoote shrugged. "These guys like drama. But that's all I have. A name. *A handle.* The records didn't spell anything else out. Just Zero."

"What do we do with that?" asked Houston.

"Well, there *is* more," said Lightfoote. "More on the location, anyway. They set up the perfect facade to hide him. While the conspiracy theorists of the world had their eyes on Bilderberg, the real puppet master was hidden away, completely unsuspected, in a green, intellectual oasis in Manhattan. A place standing unimpeachable, working for the 'benefit of humanity,' while it served in the shadows as the beautiful mask to hide the hydra. Whoever Zero is, he's there, at a biomedical center called the Ramsey University."

"The what?" asked Houston.

"I didn't have much time to look it up. Little I got said it was founded by the Ramsey family in 1901 along with some other oligarchs. People thought it was a tax shelter with some 'give back to the world' guilt down payments for the tycoons. But it looks like the story was just social camouflage. The place was set up to hide something very different, much darker."

Lopez shook his head. "You mean Bilderberg *isn't* the center of power? But this Ramsey University is? How?"

"I don't know," said Lightfoote. "But that's where this Zero is. A place no one would think to examine, with Nobel Prize winners, disease cures, a research hospital. And it's been the center of power for over one hundred years."

"The name Ramsey raises some red flags," said Houston.

"More conspiracy theories," said Lightfoote. "But yes. It's all starting to feel very eerie." She shook her head as if to clear her thoughts. "Back to the nukes for a minute. We need to contact NORAD, get them to move on the silos to prevent this from happening again. I'll walk them through it."

"You can do that?" asked Houston.

"Should be able to. Their control system was all spelled out in the connections here. It's not magic. I think we can wall them out forever."

Lopez turned to the receiver on the old-style landline. Dust slid down the sides of the plastic handle as he raised it to his ear. A dial tone spilled from the speaker. "Still works."

"Good," said Lightfoote, retrieving her laptop from the bag and laying it beside the phone. "One more piece of critical intel. Zero is *still* in NYC. The missile launch was only to be triggered by his command. The silos were prepping and on standby, firing once he bugged out."

"Wait, are you serious?" asked Houston.

Lightfoote nodded, opening her computer. "Probably who Mr. Cyanide here was talking to before he offed himself. We've wounded them terribly, but we didn't get the queen bee. But maybe we can. Zero is leaving NYC within the next twelve hours."

"What can we do about it?" asked Lopez "We're here. I doubt anyone has any available assets in the area after all the chaos. No one will get there in time."

"We have to try," said Lightfoote. "Another reason to get NORAD on the line." She scrolled her fingers on the trackpad. "Here's the protocol York gave us for calling in." She picked up the receiver and entered a sequence of numbers, followed by several pauses and three more number sequences. "This takes forever if I remember. They filter and trace the hell out of the calls."

Finally, there was an audible click.

"Yes, this is Angel Lightfoote. I'm here at the Bilderberg hotel with Gabriel, Mary, and a lot of dead guys. I need to speak to Admiral Myers."

64

"Agent Savas? Agent Cohen?"

A soldier peered into the back cabin, pulling back a makeshift privacy screen to see inside. Savas opened his eyes, rising on an elbow from the seat. Cohen slept unmoving in the chair beside him.

"I'm sorry to wake you, but there's an urgent call."

Savas shook his head. "Can barely breathe through this damn nose. Can't sleep."

The soldier motioned to him. "It's the president on the secure line."

A minute later both he and Cohen were huddled together in the chilly transport, Cohen yawning and still half asleep. Savas spoke to York on a video screen.

"Slow down, Elaine. One thing at a time. My team, they're alive, unharmed?"

York nodded. "They're worse for wear, but no major injuries."

"They really did it. The missile aborts, the silo shutdowns."

"Yes," said the president. "Lightfoote's fingerprints all over it, of course. But their team had to infiltrate the hotel underground. We don't have time, and I'm not clear on all the details, but it looks like Bilderberg was running some sort of science fiction population simulation, shape world events by using computer models."

"And this all had to do with this Nash figure? Fawkes's file was about some econ genius and his work?"

"Yes," said York. "Frankly, I'm skeptical until I've learned more. Sounds ridiculous. But they're sure. They're meeting with local CIA and US military representatives in the area now to lock the site down. But they saved our asses."

Savas bowed his head. He couldn't help but feel both relieved and proud. "Okay, so how does this relate to New York and this university?"

York sighed. "It's all moving so fast we can't hope to verify everything. So we're going on trust, John. Do you trust your people?"

"With my life. Looks like we all did."

"Well, what your people are saying is there is more to this than simply Bilderberg. Bilderberg was only a center of operations, but the organization is spread around the world. Most importantly, a key figure, maybe *the* key figure, is right in front of your plane in New York."

"At the Ramsey University," said Cohen.

"Yes. Angel Lightfoote was sure of it. She begged us to get someone there, to stop him."

"Stop who?"

"All they had was an alias. *Zero*."

"Someone in New York at a biomedical institute running the damn world named Zero?" said Savas. "You know how this sounds?"

"Of course I do! So I ask again—do you trust your people? And do you trust us? Because there's more. We've done some of our own digging based on Angel's data. We think we know who this Zero is— Luc Osomer-Levitt, the president of the university."

"Wait, I've heard of him," said Cohen. "Big time pharmaceutical player. A scientist I think. Was embroiled in several financial controversies but nothing ever stuck."

"That's him," said York, static partially garbling her words. "But a little digging into government databases reveals some very interesting coincidences. Like invitations to the annual Bilderberg conference, to begin."

"Gets my attention," said Savas.

"How about the funneling of huge amounts of money from some of the most powerful families in the world to the university? Charitable donations on paper but the numbers don't add up. Finally, NSA data on communications between his corporate offices and seven of the Bilderberg nodes identified by Angel."

"That's no coincidence," said Cohen.

"Unlikely. Angel claimed she had information that Zero's on the move, bugging out of New York in a matter of hours. He might already be gone."

"Leaving from Ramsey?" asked Savas.

"Best intel we have."

Cohen nodded. "All right. Send in a strike force. Take him into custody."

"*You* are the strike force," said York, her expression grim. "We don't have the skill set in the staff left in the Manhattan bunker."

"Us?" said Savas incredulously.

"Your special ops teams are perfect for the job. This could be the kill shot to Bilderberg. You both *have* to be there." Her face stared unblinkingly at them through the screen. "We've uploaded what known schematics of the place are available—campus map, entrances and exits, buildings. But there's likely to be a hidden layer, like at the Bilderberg Hotel. There may be levels and structures buried in the bedrock we know nothing about."

"And we have no sense of how fortified they are. We could be walking into a shooting gallery," said Savas.

"Yes, you could."

He placed his hand on his bandaged face. "Okay, how do we get there? I didn't even think this through when we boarded the damn plane. Are the airports open? LGA is close."

"Negative. Hastings controls it. Or did. It's chaos on the ground still. Airport isn't operational as far as we can tell."

"Then what?" asked Savas, holding his arms in the air.

"Sergeant Williams, would you introduce yourself?" called out York loudly.

"Yes, ma'am," came an authoritative voice behind them. A tall black woman stepped toward the screen. "HALO specialist Aisha Williams."

"HALO?" asked Cohen.

"High Altitude Low Opening."

Savas looked at the video feed. "You aren't serious?"

Williams continued. "We'll jump about thirty-five miles out from the island, sir. At forty thousand feet and this airspeed, we'll need a good distance to land on target. Give it three to four minutes for the drop. But it keeps the aircraft out of SAM range and minimizes possible flak."

"In case Hastings is watching," added York over the speakers.

"Jump?" Cohen asked, her eyes widening.

"Three teams," said Williams. "You'll both have chaperones. They'll steer you with the groups until we touch down." Savas and Cohen simply stared at her. "We've only got an hour to the drop point, and we need to get you both on oh-two as soon as possible."

"Oxygen? Why?" asked Savas.

"Purge the nitrogen from your blood, sir. You can't just jump at forty-K. Pressure's too low. You'll get the bends."

Cohen turned an incredulous look to Savas. "Nitrogen bubbles in the blood," she said, swallowing.

"Hurts like hell, sir, and could kill you."

Savas stared at the soldier. "And assuming we survive this madness, where are you intending to put us down?"

"Central Park," said Williams. "Lots of open space there."

"Surrounded by skyscrapers," he said.

"We've done worse, sir," said Williams.

Savas stared toward the ceiling. "You've got to be kidding me."

York smiled on the screen. "Good hunting, all of you. Bring us back a trophy."

65

THE JUMPSUITS WERE ungainly, awkward for the untrained bodies of Cohen and Savas. They breathed deeply from the oxygen tanks, a helmet fitted over their heads and a fighter pilot style mask to their mouths. In theory, the enriched gas was slowly pushing the nitrogen out of their bloodstreams. A second tank of oxygen would accompany them on the way down. Savas struggled to breathe regularly through his bandages.

"Remember," said Williams, momentarily repositioning her own mouthpiece and shouting over the din in the aircraft, "you're jumping at commercial airline cruising altitude. It's minus sixty out there or worse. You can't breathe the air. Stay with your chaperone. Keep repeating the thumbs-up sign if all is good. Stay calm. They'll guide you through the jump at each step. The chutes will deploy toward the end of the jump, controlled by your chaperone. We'll steer you to the target site."

A sturdy Special Forces soldier crouched behind each agent, checking their suits and tanks. They were strapped lightly to their charge. Both reacted to the coming leap into the sky as a routine day at the office and treated the FBI agents as just another package they had to deliver. Savas couldn't decide if that was comforting or alarming.

A red light began to flash above them, signaling the approaching jump point. Williams motioned for them to stand, and together with their chaperone they moved to the back of the troop transport, the bay doors opening and the loading ramp pointing downward.

The early morning light spilled brightly into the aircraft, a waterfall of sound churning from the wind turbulence around the opening. An abstract patchwork of boxes and lines passed below, different colored shapes separated by highways and intermittent urban clusters. A deep red ball rose over the horizon.

Williams waved her arm several times. "Go, go, go!"

One by one the soldiers stepped to the edge of the ramp and

toppled over calmly, performing a short somersault before zipping from view behind and below the aircraft. At the line's end, the FBI agents were positioned at the edge, Cohen briefly turning her helmet back to look at Savas, her eyes and face obscured by the tinted wind guard. The soldier pushed her forward, and she dropped, racing away toward the other members of the parachute team.

Soldiers guided Savas to the edge. He looked down, the height deceptive, the seven and one-half miles between him and the ground not registering to a mind utterly unused to such vertical distances. He felt a pat on the shoulder and gave the thumbs up. A push drove him forward into an explosion of white noise. He was flying.

Or falling. The sensations were overwhelming. First the noise hit him. The churning air racing against his plummeting form roared like an engine, nearly blocking out his ability to think. The vibrations were powerful, the air beating against the fabric of his suit and helmet, the invisible medium hardening into something powerful and tangible, slapping strongly across his body. The rising sun blinded him, even through the tinted visor. He could barely stare forward toward their destination and was forced to look straight to the onrushing earth.

He hardly noticed the soldier strapped to him above, his senses numb. Another series of hard pats on the shoulder reminded him he hadn't signaled. He put out his hand and did the thumbs-up. He felt no nausea, no dizziness, the pummeling he took from the battering wind and sound overpowering all other sensations.

A line of skydivers approached ahead. He had lost all sense of time. The divers maintained a separated distance. Williams had said it would create a low radar profile. An obese shape trailed the others ahead of him. He realized it must be Cohen and her chaperone, and that he likely presented a similar image. Considering the enemies lurking below, he hoped they were indeed as invisible as the soldier predicted.

Down they were yanked by earth's pull, their velocity now constant, the force from the air they pushed against equal to the force of gravity. *Terminal velocity*, thought Savas. Williams had said it would take only minutes to complete the jump, but it felt like they'd been falling for hours before he finally saw the jagged landscape of

Manhattan. They plunged through a layer of clouds, momentarily blinding him, but he saw the chutes in front of him deploy. A second later, the soldier above him pulled the chord, and Savas was yanked upward harshly.

Their fall slowed dramatically, but the approaching skyscrapers only intensified the sense of plunging recklessly forward. The group of jumpers passed over the lower tip of Manhattan, the Statue of Liberty a flattened speck below, the Freedom Tower reaching upward toward their feet. Ahead the white, snow-covered rectangle of Central Park loomed, the chutes angling steadily toward it. Adrenaline coursed through him as they approached midtown, their height appearing to put them on a collision course for many of the taller buildings surrounding the park. But they skirted over them, the penthouse balconies a short drop below, the barren trees of the park rushing up to greet them.

The soldier slapped his shoulder three times. The signal for landing. Savas looked down and set his legs, the trees inches below. They exploded over a wide space, descending rapidly over a field of bright white. His feet slammed roughly into to the snow-covered grasses of the Great Lawn.

They maintained their balance, and the chute collapsed neatly behind them. Savas removed his helmet and exhaled deeply, relieved to be on the ground and to see Cohen disengaging from her chute. While cold, the air tasted fresh compared to the bottled gas from the tank. He squirmed out of the jumpsuit and let it fall to the ground. The Special Forces soldiers were grouping together. Savas and his chaperone jogged up and joined them.

Williams pulled out a GPS device. "We have the coordinates of the target here. We'll make as direct a course as possible through the park and city to that location."

"Don't bother," said Savas, interrupting her. The eyes of the other soldiers turned to him in surprise. "No need for GPS. This is my city. Follow me."

66

THEY STOOD AT the bottom of a large hill, a twenty-foot arch with the university's name and logo engraved on the side. Towering metal rods barred the entrance, the gate locked in place. A gleaming set of turnstiles occupied the space on the right and left, refusing entrance without an activated ID card.

The young man stared intensely at Savas, his eyes nervously darting to the crowd of armed soldiers behind him. He licked his lips and grasped the security badge on his uniform.

"I'm sorry, sir, but I can't let you in the university unless you have an invitation. Now, we can try to call—"

"Let me repeat," said Savas. "This is a matter of *national security*."

"You have no ID, you're armed. I'm sorry, sir. Now, I'm going to call the police if you don't move on."

Savas laughed. "Seen much of the police these last few months?" The man said nothing. Savas motioned to the soldiers who stepped closer, their weapons aimed slightly over the head of the guard. "Now, look. We can do this easy," he growled, "or we can do it *real* easy."

The security guard stared at the soldiers, his eyes wide.

"Richard, what the hell is going on here?" A tall black man with a thick Jamaican accent rounded the security booth and stared through the gate's bars at the assembled teams. "Who the hell are you?"

The young gate guard spoke, wiping sweat from his forehead. "They claim they're sent from the *president*. President York. They don't have *any* clearance. No invite. *Nothing.* They have guns."

The older black man nodded. "Yes, son, I see those guns. Do you know what they do with those guns?" The young man swallowed. "Those are Special Forces. Look at those insignias. Rangers, Seals, Green Berets." He looked at Savas. "Why are you here?"

"A matter of national security. We have to see the president of this institution. Immediately."

The older guard nodded, a last look at the weapons removing all doubt. "Good enough for me." He punched in a code inside the booth and the mechanism for the large gate engaged, the two halves swinging back and in. "But you better hurry. Something strange is happening. All the docs running to the tunnels, following the president."

Savas turned to Cohen and the others. "He's rabbiting." The doors opened and the troops moved in. Savas turned back to the guards as he headed up the hill. "You made the right call. You have access to the security system?"

"I do."

"Shut it down. Shut every camera in this place down."

"Yes, sir," said the guard. He pointed up the hillside. "To Patron's Hall. Building at the top. Left stairs down to the tunnels."

Savas nodded and turned to sprint up the hill, catching up to Williams.

"Heard him, agent Savas, but slow it down. We're going to treat this as hostile territory. Move smart."

"We might not have much time!" he seethed.

"Better late than dead, sir. We can't do nothing if we're dead."

Cohen grabbed his arm and stared at him. Savas exhaled. The soldier was right. Given what Hastings and Bilderberg had at their disposal, a squad of mercenaries wouldn't be out of the picture. This invasion could end before it began.

They reached the hilltop, the Special Forces group moving cautiously, examining vulnerable angles and approaches. A six-story building from another era rose before them, a set of marble stairs leading to a set of glass doors. Around them, the campus was utterly deserted.

A different welcome greeted them in the foyer. The armed team of soldiers burst through the doors in tactical formation, weapons aimed forward, their posture aggressive. In front of them stood a buzzing crowd of older men and women, many in ill-fitting suits or lab coats, pacing the marbled room. At the sight of the soldiers, they fell backward, eyes wide and fearful, conversation extinguished.

"Where is the president?" asked Savas, stepping forward and acting as the group's spokesman. No one responded. "This is a matter of national security. Where is your president?"

A rotund man with a beard, resembling some baron in an Armani suit, stepped toward them authoritatively. "I'm Joac Ratkvetch, Full Professor and Head of Laboratory. We need some answers. Are you with the police?"

Savas motioned to Williams. "The stairway. See if it leads to the tunnels." Williams and several soldiers moved to their left and a doorway to a set of steps leading down.

"Tunnels," said Ratkvetch. "Yes, it most certainly does. Our president went that way, but seems to have lost his mind."

"Explain," said Savas.

"First tell me who you are? You wouldn't believe how we have been treated these last days. Herded, shouted at! Can you imagine—"

"*Explain,*" growled Savas.

The professor startled. "Well, he came here with *armed men.* They've destroyed the president's office, all the records. They've stolen important samples. The noise brought us all here. We know something terrible is happening. He's heading to the river campus access."

"And so?"

"To escape the island! The war is coming here, no? You have to get us out!"

Several heads nodded as the university professors crowded around Savas.

"We're important people!" cried one.

"I'm Michelle MacKinnon, Nobel Prize winner."

"Korgie Barfmour," cried a botoxed blonde.

Two men stepped forward. "Seth Burley and John Harrison. We need protection!"

Pandemonium erupted.

A burst of automatic gunfire exploded. Marble chips and dust rained from the ceiling. Williams stood at the stairwell, her weapon smoking. Savas nodded to her.

"Stairwell's clear," she said.

Savas motioned to the rest. "We move. To the tunnels."

The tall blonde grabbed his collar. "And what about *us?*"

Savas swiped her hand away and continued to the door. "Write your damn memoirs or something. Stay here and panic. I don't give a damn. Stay out of our way or you're going to get a bullet."

She gasped, and fell back with the others. Williams led the way down the stairs, Savas and Cohen behind her, the remaining soldiers following closely.

"Little harsh, John?" asked Cohen with a raised eyebrow as they rounded a turn in the steps.

"*I have a Nobel Prize.* What a bunch of self-important blowhards."

The stairs ended, the passageway opening to a broad tunnel leading down into the bowels of the island.

"Why does a university have a series of underground tunnels?" asked Cohen, staring in disbelief as the passageways plunged down in front of them.

"For something that needs to hide underground," he mumbled. He drew his sidearm and began to head down the tunnel. He felt a firm hand on his shoulder.

"No disrespect, agent Savas," said Williams. "We're all combat vets. Seen more tunnels than we'd like to think about. We'll take the lead here."

Savas nodded, stepping to the side. "You have point, Sergeant. We'll stay out of your way and watch your back."

"Glad you're not going to go alpha on me," she smiled, moving forward.

"Too damn tired for that, ma'am."

Williams turned around and motioned the soldiers forward. They swept into the tunnels.

67

THEY DID NOT get far. The group had been moving cautiously down the main tunnel passage, ignoring side branches and the many closed doors and hatches dotting the walls. Most of those were locked on examination, and the maps York had provided indicated none led to anything more interesting than storage or machinery rooms. The maps did not show where the main path ended, which was all the suspicion they needed to continue following its course.

The temperature within the tunnel spiked dramatically as they moved forward. Enormous steam pipes ran overhead and alongside the walls, the thermal energy radiating outward and noticeable from a few feet away. After less than ten minutes, having seen no one and no clues, the passage began to slope upward and a large opening to another building came into view.

"Damn," said Williams. The extended line of soldiers stopped along with Savas and Cohen in the back.

"The new research building," said another soldier, pointing to the map. "The tunnel connections fade out in the middle, but we've just gone from building to building. No secret lair. No escape route."

"He had to go somewhere!" Williams said. "What did we miss?"

"About fifty doorways that aren't on the maps," said Savas, moving toward the front of the group. "And that might have something else behind them the maps don't show."

"We go back over it, carefully this time," said Cohen. "There's got to be more to this than a simple passage between buildings."

"We're running out of time," said Savas.

Cohen nodded. "Then let's work fast."

Williams moved through her team and toward the FBI agents. Savas interrupted her.

"No disrespect, Sergeant, but this is where we take over."

Williams smiled. "Touché."

"Only Rebecca has point, and we give her some cover. She's the real sleuth."

Williams positioned men at the beginning and end of the tunnel, blanketing all entrances and exits. She and another soldier accompanied Savas as he followed behind Cohen while she meticulously swept along the tunnel walls. Her deliberateness was painful. Time was running through their hands, every second an hour. When she stopped in front of a rusted door, he checked his watch, surprised only five minutes had passed.

"This is it," she said, crouching and touching the ground.

Williams shook her head. "This is what? What do you see?"

Cohen held up a finger, a dull orange powder coating her skin. "Rust," she said and stood up, gesturing to the door. "This thing's been here a long time. The metal's built up a layer of rust ignored for years, maybe decades. But look. Around the handle and the hinges, the rust is disturbed. Some scratched, some cracked. It fell to the floor here," she pointed to a thin film of red on the rock below.

"There's a shoe print in it," said Savas.

Cohen nodded. "Not from your team," she said to Williams. "I got a lot of looks at the boots from behind. Not John or my shoes." She placed her hands on the door handle. "Someone's opened this door very recently."

Williams called the soldiers back from the tunnel extremities. They took positions near the doorway as Cohen yanked on the handle. It didn't move. Savas stepped up and together they forced the rusted hinges to yield, a screeching sound echoing around them.

The red glow of emergency bulbs lit an empty passage. The rank smell of sea and grime spilled outward, and the shoe prints continued into the thick muck coating the floor. But the prints were far more numerous, a confused stampede of footsteps preserved.

Savas checked the map. "Definitely not a machine room. And judging from all these prints, it looks like the president has a few friends."

Williams motioned to her team. "We move in separated pairs. Khyber spacing."

A soldier stepped forward and into the tunnels. "Back in the hellholes, snake-eaters," he said and disappeared. One by one they entered, and again, Savas and Cohen were relegated to the rear.

Moving through the hatchway Savas nearly struck his head on the low ceiling, the sounds of footfalls ahead of him echoing in the concrete tube. The red emergency lighting painted an infernal glare on the roughly hewn stone surrounding them.

The sounds of pounding metal reached his ears. The tight tunnel opened broadly to reveal a small chamber, a ladder racing upward, a four-way intersection of passages running from the focal point. The twelve soldiers were spaced to cover the passages, several training weapons on the ladder.

"Now what?" asked Cohen. "Four possibilities."

"This doesn't exist on the maps," said Williams. "We'll have to split up."

Savas felt his stomach drop. Too much time wasted, and now their forces thinned.

The soldiers conferred, pairs moving down the three new tunnels. Williams pointed to the ladder.

"We'll leave two here to guard against someone coming up our ass from the first tunnel. Leaves us four and you two to try this ladder. Here's what—"

Her words were cut off by gunfire. Echoes rang from the passageway in front of them. "Found them! Henson, Ripley, hold this point. The rest of you, with me!"

The automatic weapons discharge continued, and Williams and three other soldiers sprinted down the tunnel. Savas turned to Cohen.

"I guess we stay—"

Above him, metal screeched. Savas glanced up to see a hatch over the ladder open briefly, and momentarily caught a glimpse of a face. The man vanished, omitting to even seal the hatch, panic in his eyes.

"John, no!" cried Cohen.

Savas leapt onto the metal rungs and raced upward, thrusting his torso through the opening, weapon raised. A blurred shadow turned a corner down a narrow hallway, and Savas vaulted from the ladder to sprint down the passage. As it veered left, he spun quickly, gun raised, poised to engage.

He found himself in a claustrophobic space hewn carelessly out of the bedrock, a wall of guns aimed his way. Light poured from a broad opening behind the mercenaries. A brief glimpse showed Savas a short ramp leading down to the East River. An armored yacht approached on the water.

A thin man, in a suit, his hair graying, stepped forward. He held up a hand to the four bodyguards who had trained their weapons on Savas.

"A firefight at this juncture would be most unwise," he said to them, his eyes darting behind him.

"Luc Osomer-Levitt," said Savas, refusing to lower his weapon. He recognized the face of the Ramsey president from the last-minute dossiers York had sent them. The man appeared even more robotic in person than he did in the still photos, his face hardly displaying a flicker of emotion. "Or should I say: *Zero*."

"Agent Savas," he said. "I'm impressed, but please put your gun down before someone gets killed."

Savas heard the sound too late, distracted by the men in front of him. A heavy blow struck the back of his head as he tried to pivot. The ground raced up surreally. On his hands and knees, the world spinning, his gun kicked across the floor, powerful arms raised him to his feet.

"We wondered how you escaped," said Osomer-Levitt. "You live up to your reputation."

His head exploding, the figures around him only slowly returned to focus. The arms dragged Savas before the man. He winced as a gun pressed against his head.

"How do you know..."

"Who you are? Don't be coy, agent Savas. If you're here, you've clearly put together enough to know I have been involved in your capture and interrogation. I took a very personal interest in everything you and your Intel 1 group had to say."

"You bastard," Savas managed, his head pounding. "You have my people's blood on your hands."

"Collateral damage is such an unfortunate part of war. And this has been a war, agent Savas. Anonymous nearly destroyed us, and your cybercrimes head had radioactive material we could not allow to be released. We had no choice."

"The Nash Criterion."

"Yes. That madman was a double-edged sword for all of us. Useful for his time, but it's over now. Your people have put the planet on a course of self-destruction. We may not be able to fix this."

His fogged head still couldn't process much of his surroundings, let alone rebut the man. Adding to the confusion, a new voice spoke from behind the phalanx of guards

"Bring him forward. Let me see him."

The voice rasped and carried a striking tone of authority. For the first time, Osomer-Levitt's mask cracked, and concern flickered briefly over his features. The guards instinctively shifted, opening a small wedge to what lay behind. Savas strained to focus, the blurred outlines of a short and squat figure refusing to clarify. A grotesque form rolled forward, the legs swollen beyond possibility. Unless...*wheels!* The figure sat in a wheelchair.

Osomer-Levitt spoke. "We don't have time. There may be others with him. At the least his agent wife."

A woman's voice came from behind him, and Savas flinched.

"Too late," said Cohen. "She's already here."

Savas's head throbbed as he looked over his shoulder. Cohen stood alone, an army-issue coat wrapped around her, eyes trained on Osomer-Levitt.

"Time for parlay," she said.

68

"Parlay?" scoffed the Ramsey president. "I have your husband at the barrel of a gun. You are unarmed. What can you possibly bring to the table?"

"You're talking. You're hesitant. What are you afraid of, Luc?"

Osomer-Levitt licked his lips as Cohen stepped several paces closer. Savas looked on helplessly, trying to organize his thoughts for some sort of attack. Cohen simply stood there, her arms awkwardly out from her sides, her eyes fierce. *What is she doing?*

"It wouldn't be the figure behind you, in the wheelchair? Or the ship coming into dock?"

"You both should have never come looking."

Cohen stepped two more paces forward, now only feet from the group of men.

"Did you think we would simply turn our backs on what's going on? We stopped Anonymous, Luc. We saved your little plan."

"And then blew up our base of operations."

"None of our people."

Osomer-Levitt smirked. "Such coincidences do not happen. You have shadows we can't uncover. I commend you for that. But it has York's fingerprints all over it."

"The boat is about to dock!" cried out one of the mercenaries.

Osomer-Levitt shook his head. "You have no idea what you have done. You think you are saving the world, but you are dooming it to repeated cycles of dark ages."

"And only your tyranny could save us all from ourselves? That's why you nuked an entire city? Were about to nuke the entire country? This is your enlightened march to global civilization?"

"A *necessity* because of the terrorist Fawkes. Had we been left alone, the course of human history would have only been forward. But you are too trapped in your primitive tribal systems to see it." He pointed to one of the guards. "We'll take them with us. When we are secured, we'll deal with them in a controlled fashion."

"Don't count on it." Cohen smiled as the guard approached her. "A little trick I learned from a hacker frenemy."

Cohen raised her arms out from her body. Savas's blurred vision leapt back months to a warehouse in New Jersey, the motion and similarities triggering the deja vu. Two metal canisters clanked on the ground, rolling forward toward the group. The men instinctively looked down, their weapons aiming toward the floor. The gas bombs ignited.

Even without shrapnel, the compressed air blast stunned Savas and the guards. Then, the chemical concoction attacked. He felt his lungs and eyes burn, his breath hellfire. He fell to the floor coughing violently.

A short spurt of automatic weapons fire erupted behind Cohen. *The Special Forces soldiers? More mercenaries?* Time ticked languidly. His body heaving, he crawled blindly to find some escape from the gas. Someone grabbed his head. He couldn't resist. He felt a bag yanked over his face. No, *a mask*. A short blast of fresh air purged the toxic fumes. He breathed wildly like a drowning man.

"John! Slow down! Breathe slowly." *Rebecca*. He grabbed her arms, opening his eyes. A masked monster from World War I stared back at him. Inside the goggled eyes were brown irises, threads of brown hair. He staggered to his knees, leaning against the wall. A pair of strong arms helped him to his feet. *Sergeant Williams*.

"The boat!" she cried, darting past him into the room.

Weapons fire erupted again. He turned and limped through the dissipating gas, bodies of mercenaries littering the floor. Among them, the blood-stained suit of the powerful president of Ramsey University, Luc Osomer-Levitt. His eyes stared vacuously toward the ceiling.

Savas watched as Cohen holstered her Glock pistol. He looked between her and Osomer-Levitt. "You?"

She nodded. "Got it when I need it, John. Just next time, don't run off like an untrained monkey after the bad guys. Okay?"

He nodded, turning his head to the East River below them. Williams and the other soldiers returned from the ramp, their eerie masks still in place. She spoke loudly through the plastic.

"It's gone, dammit. We took out some windows and maybe punctured the fuel tank, but not enough. We need to get assets on the river and ocean before they disappear."

"The man in the wheelchair?" asked Cohen anxiously.

"What wheelchair?" said Williams.

"There wasn't an old man in a wheelchair? He's not in here. He got to the boat!"

"Who got to the boat?" Savas asked.

Cohen's shoulders slumped. "The kingfish. *Zero*."

Savas stared into her mask. "That old man was Zero? I thought it was Osomer-Levitt!"

"I don't think so, John. Osomer-Levitt was taking orders. One more facade in this cursed house of mirrors. And Zero escaped."

"All the more reason to get on the COM and call this in." Williams left them and consulted with her team, several of them accompanying her outside with a backpack.

"Let's get outside," said Savas, "and get some real air."

The pair walked outside. Already the soldiers had removed their masks, and Savas and Cohen followed suit. One of the men had placed a portable radio on the ground, quickly working the device. Savas bent over and coughed, breathing in the crisp winter air, the cloud of water vapor heavenly after the chemical fog.

"Jesus, John, you've got blood all over your neck." Cohen removed a scarf from inside the heavy coat she wore and pressed it to the back of his head.

"Easy!" said Savas, pulling away. "Damn, that hurts."

"Sit still. You always find a way to bleed on these missions." He sat down as Cohen applied pressure to the back of his head. She shook her head. "You need stitches."

"The old man—Zero?" he sighed. "Who was he?"

Cohen looked out over the water, a mist rising off the river, no sign of the boat or other activity. Across from the university, Roosevelt Island ran along the water like a thin canyon wall.

"I have a theory," she said.

"Yes?"

"There is one name that comes up over and over in all this. A key member and organizer of the Bilderberg group meetings. A well-known proponent of a one-world government, on the record as preferring it and that it be run by a small group of financially aware people. The key figure funding this university, selecting its leadership, and whose family set the entire project in motion."

Savas grimaced as he turned toward her. "You mean?"

"And of the right age and health to be trapped in the constraints of a wheelchair," she ended.

"Daniel Ramsey."

Cohen nodded. "I didn't get a good look at him, and I wouldn't likely recognize him anyway. Like the old Soviet leaders, he's been rumored to be dead fifty times. He's over one hundred years old."

"One hundred?" asked Savas. "How?"

"Through his nineties publicly active. I don't know how. Ramsey biomedical science miracles?"

"This is crazy."

"I agree. And I'm sure it's not over."

The heavy boots of Sergeant Williams tramped down the wooden ramp toward them. She crouched beside the water.

"Reached a relay. NORAD's in the know. New intel: Hastings is dead. The coup had its own coup. It's chaos over on this side of the country right now, but the president is moving fast to reassert authority. Looks like this might be over soon."

"The boat?" asked Savas.

Williams shook her head. "Not many assets in the area we can use. They'll do what they can." She fixed her eyes on them. "But I think it'll be long gone before they do."

69

"I like what you've done with the place." York sat down in a chair beside Cohen, the cluttered surface of a desk separating her from Savas. The newly outfitted office smelled of wood finish and plastics. "This is yours, John?"

Savas nodded. "Rebecca's is down the hall, next to the data centers. She wanted to be close to the raw intel."

"You two look a thousand percent better." The president smiled. "I think John's nose almost looks normal."

"We've all recovered a good bit since Ramsey," said Cohen.

"At least physically," said York.

Savas shifted uncomfortably. "Still nothing on our Zero?"

"No," said York. "Coincidentally, the Ramsey family has let it be known that Daniel passed away peacefully during the crisis. A funeral attended by big names will occur soon. By invitation only."

"Amazing," said Savas.

"Could be true," Cohen said. "He was over one hundred. Maybe the stress of what happened at the university? Or should I even call the place that?"

"A university?" asked York. "It certainly was a research institute handing out PhDs, did real science. But it was a golden facade over a skull. While you two were holding the East Coast together, I turned loose some less gifted detectives. Their job wasn't hard, once we knew where and what to look for. The place was a cesspool of corruption and fraud. Researchers bought like free agents, showered with insane amounts of money. Biotech and Big Pharma on their leash. Oligarchs laundering support for Bilderberg through the financial ledgers. Nobels bought and paid for. All to construct an unassailable reputation, one that would shield the university from all prying eyes."

"How on earth do you buy a Nobel prize?" asked Cohen.

"Like anything else. Meet the market price. You don't think the old farts in Sweden handing those things down are the Twelve Disciples?" York smiled ruefully. "They even had one poor researcher on ice for days, hiding his death from the world. Paying off the hospital and doctors for a week until the prize was announced."

"Why in the world?" asked Cohen.

"Nobel Prizes only go to the living. And Ramsey had put a substantial down payment on this one and wanted to get the return on his investment."

"I expected something more," she said. "A lot more. Science is supposed to be about truth."

"A hundred years ago, Alfred Nobel dumped a ton of money on the prize. Money spoke loudly then. It speaks loudly now. Always has, always will." York laughed. "You wouldn't believe the email exchanges the NSA dug up. The Nobel committee's a tired group of Swedish has-beens, mostly unknown in the world, even in the fields of science. Poor bastards are charged by history with the important yet unrewarding task of bestowing the ultimate scientific prestige on others. Think of the power they hold. Think of the *temptation* to make that job a little more *rewarding*. Many had their price. And Ramsey had the means to meet *any* price."

"This is science, not politics!" said Cohen.

"My dear, everything is politics. And with so much power and money involved, bring in the plumbers. Because you've got a nasty brew. Priests, senators, and scientists—dirty laundry all the same. Human nature." ·

"They should be held to higher standards."

"They are. Just means the price goes up. Ramsey had more than enough to shape things as he wanted. And those investments did bring a return, a shield of false honor. Behind it Bilderberg operated with impunity." She shook her head. "It's so ironic. Nobel and Ramsey were rivals for the world's oil supply before the Communist Revolution. Some accuse the Ramsey family of funding that coup. It blew up the oil region, and Nobel suffered a crippling loss while Ramsey locked in control of the world's petroleum supplies. Nobel actually had to sell his remaining shares in oil companies to Ramsey! *Humbling.*"

"You know a lot about this," said Savas.

"Former law and history teacher, John. Also, it's been an eye-opening read of the intel reports the last few months."

"So, Daniel Ramsey inherited a Nobel Prize that owed his family deeply," said Cohen. "Zero had a lot to work with. A brilliant use of resources."

"Assuming Zero *is* Daniel Ramsey," said Savas. "With his disappearance, or perhaps death, we might never know. Meanwhile, with or without him, Bilderberg will be regrouping."

"With Angel's data, it's not going to be easy for them," said York. "We've busted four of the sites on her list, apprehended several powerful and shadowy figures. The others managed to make a getaway, but their organization is trashed, their web of influence shredded. They've got *a lot* of rebuilding ahead of them."

"And so do we," said Savas.

"We do." York looked them in eyes. "I won't forget what all of you went through for me, for this nation. I won't forget what you lost." She pulled out a set of papers and placed them on the desk. "Here are the orders for the Presidential Medal of Freedom. Frank Miller and Jean-Paul Rideout. Congress has too much on its plate with elections and reconstruction. Had to go executive order for the funerals."

"Without the bodies, it's a hollow ceremony," said Savas.

"Not at all," said York. "Funerals aren't for the dead. The dead get nothing from them. They're for us, the living. For grief and something even more important—for memory. It's what holds our society together. That's why we need them. And that's why I'm going to make sure these men are remembered well."

Savas didn't yield. "Even so, they deserved better."

"It's all very much appreciated, Elaine," said Cohen, reaching across the chair and squeezing the president's hand. "John never really lets go. It's why he's up at 3am too many nights. But he does appreciate what you're doing."

"I know he does," York said, smiling toward Savas. "It will be a beautiful service in DC. Many of the cherry orchards survived the riot fires. They're beginning to bloom. Colors everywhere."

"A rumor of spring," said Cohen wistfully. "This bunker has some strong downsides. Most of us don't get out for weeks at a time. It's a problem for morale. We need to schedule more frequent top-side rotations, even if it means some risk of exposure."

"You're the bosses," said York. "But I think you're right."

Savas shifted in his chair. "On that point, Elaine—the coup is over. The military and civilian leadership stabilized. We still have distribution problems, but beyond the function of this bunker. I think we've done our job in the crisis."

"Indeed you have, John. And it's been a critical one to getting things back on track quickly. You two have coordinated a truly remarkable East Coast intervention."

"Then we're wondering what the end game is. We need to get back to Intel 1, to the FBI. I know there's an interim leadership in place, but I'm anxious to make sure things are done right."

"Anxious to get your crime-fighting division back into the game?" asked York. "After all this, you're not looking for a break or early retirement? You could ask for a helluva severance package."

"You have to ask after Kansas City?" Savas shook his head. "I don't think I'll pass any emotional quotient tests or whatever they're called. My therapy is work, the only one I've known or will know. Work to protect this country. Over and over again I've seen how much needs to be done. What's happened hasn't changed that. It's only strengthened it. And I'm not done with Bilderberg quite yet."

"And you?" she asked Cohen.

"This is what we do, Elaine. This is what we love to do. At least when we're not getting shot or tortured for it."

York nodded. "Well, you're right. The need for this Manhattan bunker is coming to an end. Fawkes and his brand of Anonymous are gone. Bilderberg is on the run. The country is coming back online."

"I'm glad you agree," said Savas, relief evident in his voice.

"I do. And that's why I'm here today. Canceled some terribly important and boring meetings with Congress to make it." York stood up and looked through the window to the hive of activity outside the office. "You've taken a decayed infrastructure and turned this bunker into a formidable enterprise. Of course, you had ample funding and top personnel we supplied. But give people a mound of clay and only a few can turn it into a masterpiece." She pivoted back to them. "This site is too valuable to simply shut down. Our world has changed, my friends. Become too fragile, at the mercy of poorly secured systems and encircled by terrible weapons too easy to use. And we know too well that powerful forces want to control our destiny beyond the will of the people. After what's happened, after we nearly lost our nation—well, I think this place needs to go on functioning. But perhaps in a different guise."

Cohen arched an eyebrow. "What kind of guise?"

York sat down again, placing her fingertips together in front of her face. She stared intensely at the two agents.

"Well, that's what I really came to talk to you about."

———

The construction vehicles passed by the unusual military checkpoint, a wall of concrete slabs and scaffolding obscuring what lay behind. Alongside the checkpoint, cars continued to rumble through the Lincoln tunnel, traffic beginning to pick up again in the intervening months since the crisis ended. All was not back to normal, as the armored Army vehicles lining the toll booths testified. But for many, normal appeared to be on the horizon at last.

Lopez and Houston sat in the far back of one of the beat-up vans passing through the hidden entrance. They wore laborer's work gear —boots and blue jeans, yellow hats on their laps—distinguishable only by the looming bulk of Lopez behind the other workers.

They passed under the archway in the bedrock, the van rocketing down an orange-lit tunnel under the Hudson. The driver spoke. "Clear of the final checkpoint. We'll be at the facility in five." The passengers relaxed, some loosening and removing the hot costumes, revealing other clothing beneath.

"So, the bat cave?" said Lopez, his large hands spinning the hard hat. "Are we sure about this?"

Houston shook her head. "I don't think so."

"Good answer."

She whispered to him privately. "Look, Francisco, cons: we're disappearing again, giving up the hope of a pardon or vindication.

Getting a new set of laundered identities."

"I love it when you talk dirty in my ear."

"Shut up." She smiled. "York was right. Her political situation is too fragile right now. The country is barely on its feet again. We're too radioactive. But the pros! We get to fight bad guys with people we trust and believe in, with ridiculous, *presidential* resources to conduct investigations."

"Doesn't this secret presidential force scare you a little?"

She looked out the window at the rock walls speeding by. "It does. Sounds a little too much like something Cheney would have done. *Or did.* Don't forget his secret assassination squads. But, I trust York. More than most, anyway."

"Maybe more than you should."

"Maybe. But she's proven to me where her heart lies. She could have *been* Hastings, held on to power, been Bilderberg's puppet." She exhaled, a smile on her face. "And Intel 1! John, Rebecca, and Angel —we've been through fire with them, more than once. I'm alive because of them."

"That I don't forget," said Lopez, running his hand through her hair.

"They're gold in my book. Besides—all of us, we did good. We did *damn* good. I don't know, but if we're gonna get the bang-bang toys and put on a fucking cape, who else would you pick for your team? I trust them. Not just to do the job, but to do it honorably."

The orange light began to fade, replaced slowly by a sterile fluorescent glow. Through the front windshield, they could see the opening in the tunnel and large underground lot that lay behind it, two monstrous metal doors swinging inward to allow their passage

"I hope you're right, Sara. Good intentions and the path to hell and all that."

Houston stared forward, the vehicle passing through the blast doors. She set her jaw. "You know, Francisco, so far every damn road we've been on has been to hell. We might as well do what we want while we're traveling."

Lopez grunted. "And Angel? You think it's wise to put it all in her hands?"

Houston sighed. "I don't know. Power for good or for evil. Crazy stuff. If you had sole control of the plans for the atomic bomb back in '45, what would you do? Turn the tech loose on the world? Destroy it? Either way you play God. I don't want that kind of responsibility. Do you?"

"No," said Lopez. "I'm glad I'm not able to make the choice. But two times she's held the fate of the world in her hands. Now a third. I hope she makes the right choice." The van pulled to a stop and the giant doors slammed shut behind them. "Whatever it might be."

70

THE SETTING SUN burned a potent crimson through the glass, backlighting the explosions of spray from the massive waves pummeling the rocks below. Lightfoote stared out toward the craggy rocks and the expanse of the Pacific racing to the horizon. Her scalp was freshly shaved and gleaming, her bare arms like Greek marble against the dark fatigues she wore. One hand played with an eyebrow piercing while the other drummed along the thick glass. Around her, the floor-to-ceiling windows of the restaurant offered stunning panoramic views of the ocean, the Seal Rocks, Marin coastline, and the entry to the Golden Gate Bridge.

It had been a peaceful day, but she experienced it only as a bizarre and unnatural event in the context of the last six months. At dawn, she had begun at one end of the San Francisco Zoo, walking leisurely west toward the shore. No animal, no botanical arrangement was too inconsequential for her time. She lingered at each exhibit. Her eyes drank the miraculous life forms around her like balm poured over a burnt wound. By the time she reached the jutting outcrop of rocks thrusting the restaurant over the churning waves, the day had almost ended and the sun had begun to dive toward the water.

Her laptop was open on the table, an untouched plate of food and full cup of now cold coffee on either side of it. She refused to look at the screen again. Its contents were memorized, seared into her mind from hours of obsession. The final code was ready. Looking at it wouldn't change anything. Her problem now wasn't technical—it was moral, and she struggled to make a choice.

Press ENTER, and let loose a modified version of Fawkes's code, one that would leapfrog over the duct-taped patches placed across the world's computers to block it. Code that would take her still ranging immune worms weeks to recognize and erase. By then, the task would have been completed, every trace on the computers of the Bilderberg group wiped clean of the Nash equations. The power to scientifically model human populations and manipulate them would once again be relegated to science fiction, the can kicked down the road to some near future when the ideas were rediscovered. Gone would be that temptation to tyranny, to the godlike powers offered. Gone also would be the ability to correct societies that had gone wrong, to use reason to try and steer the mad human course on Earth toward something less self-destructive.

All she had to do was press a button.

Lightfoote had already erased the files Fawkes had sent to her, the images of the mad cork board she and Houston had reduced to ash. Gone too was the decoded text of Nash's paper. With the murder of Nash and Kaplan, the last human beings able to resurrect that work had perished as well. All that remained were the computer servers of the scattered Bilderberg group. As Fawkes had shown, they hadn't adapted to the new realities of the digital realm. Her code would hunt them down faster and more effectively than any governmental agency. It would complete the destruction of this terrible knowledge.

And all she had to do now was press a button.

"I'm sorry, ma'am, was there a problem with your meal?"

A young waitress looked down anxiously at Lightfoote and her plate, her bulging chest and tight clothing contrasting oddly with her customer's militarized appearance.

"That's all there are," said Lightfoote. "Problems."

The woman smiled weakly. "I can get the manager."

Lightfoote stared through the woman, turning her head in a slow arc, taking in the restaurant, the clientele of tourists and Silicon Valley entrepreneurs. She frowned.

"You know, we're just not ready. It's too soon."

"If you want us to bring it out later, I can have another—"

"Not *mature* enough. Monkeys just knocked out of trees."

The waitress took a step back, her eyes darting. "I'm sorry?"

Lightfoote raised her index finger and struck a key on her laptop. She stared at the screen, ignoring the waitress for several moments.

"There," she said at last. "Yup. It's all done. *Cleaned up.* We'll be gods another day." The waitress looked on in bewilderment. Lightfoote stuffed her laptop into a bag. "Can I have the check, please?"

"If Bilderberg meetings are just talking shops, why do the most powerful figures from around the world bother to attend? What other summit of world leaders in politics, finance and business would go completely unreported in the mainstream media such as the BBC? It's impossible not to reach the conclusion that the non-reporting of these events is anything other than a conspiracy between the [Bilderberg] organizers and the media. It merely confirms the belief of many that the hidden agenda and purpose of the Bilderberg Group is to bring about undemocratic world government. It's a disgrace that the European Commission is colluding in that."

—Gerard Joseph Batten, British representative to the European Parliament, 12 September 2011, at the European Parliament in Strasbourg, France

"For more than a century, ideological extremists at either end of the political spectrum have seized upon well-publicized incidents such as my encounter with Castro to attack the Rockefeller family for the inordinate influence they claim we wield over American political and economic institutions. Some even believe we are part of a secret cabal working against the best interests of the United States, characterizing my family and me as 'internationalists' and of conspiring with others around the world to build a more integrated global political and economic structure — one world, if you will. If that is the charge, I stand guilty, and I am proud of it."

—David Rockefeller, *Memoirs*

"We are grateful to The Washington Post, The New York Times, Time magazine and other great publications whose directors have attended our meetings and respected their promises of discretion for almost forty years. It would have been impossible for us to develop our plan for the world if we had been subject to the bright lights of publicity during those years. But, the world is now much more sophisticated and prepared to march towards a world government. The supranational sovereignty of an intellectual elite and world bankers is surely preferable to the national auto-determination practiced in past centuries."

—David Rockefeller, purported remarks at the Bilderberg Group meeting in Baden-Baden, Germany in June 1991 (published in *Hilaire du Berrier Reports*), considered apocryphal despite widespread dissemination, as no written or audio evidence has been presented from this meeting.

ABOUT THE AUTHOR

www.erecstebbinsbooks.com

Erec Stebbins is a biomedical researcher who writes political and international thrillers, science fiction, narrated storybooks, and more. He was born in the Midwest, his mother a clinical psychologist and his father a professor of Romance languages at the University of Nebraska in Lincoln. His father's specialty, old Romance languages and their  literature, is the source of the unusual spelling of his middle name: "Erec." It is an Old French spelling, taken from an Arthurian romance by Chrétien de Troyes written around 1170: *Érec et Énide*.

He has pursued diverse interests over the course of his life, including science, music, drama, and writing. His academic path focused on science, and he received a degree in physics from Oberlin College in 1992, and a PhD in biochemistry from Cornell University in 1999. He has worked for several decades studying the structure of biological macromolecules involved in disease.

Book 1 in the Intel 1 Novels

THE RAGNARÖK CONSPIRACY

A Western terrorist organization targets Muslims around the world, and FBI agent John Savas must put aside the loss of his son and work with a man who symbolizes all he has come to hate. Both are drawn into a race against time to stop the plot of an American bin Laden and prevent a global catastrophe.

"Fortify your shelf of Armageddon thrillers with this promising newcomer."-*Library Journal*

"What a debut! A heart-pounding tale of terrorism sure to be controversial, **turns the genre upside down**." -*Internet Review of Books*

"A taut tale of international intrigue with a **unique twist**." -*The Washington Times Communities*

"An **enticing and much recommended** addition to thriller collections" -*The Midwest Book Review*

"A new thriller with an **unusual depth**" -*BiblioBuffet*

"Unlike most 'war on terror' thrillers" -*Publishers Weekly*

"Fans of the Vince Flynn books will enjoy Stebbins' take on terrorism with a twist." -*Booklist*

"Stebbins has his finger on the pulse of greed, disillusionment and the search for redemption in this **pulse-pounding debut**." -*RT Book Reviews, Four Stars (Compelling-Page-turner)*

"Outrageously entertaining: epic, explosive, subversive, engaged and compassionate, like a Michael Bay movie written by Aaron Sorkin." -*Chris Brookmyre, author of Where The Bodies Are Buried*

Book 2 in the Intel 1 Novels
EXTRAORDINARY RETRIBUTION

MURDER, TORTURE, AND VENGEANCE COLLIDE TO THREATEN THE HIGHEST ECHELONS OF POWER.

"Startlingly dark" -San Francisco Book Reviews
"A labyrinth of highly charged action" -Tome Tender
"A plot that never stops" -ForeWord Reviews

Evil is not born of madness, but madness of evil.
Follow a rogue CIA agent who uncovers a shocking conspiracy deep in the intelligence community. But a shadow follows the investigation: a killer bent on a revenge so terrible, it is only matched by the crimes committed against him. In the end, no one escapes unscathed, no beliefs will go unchallenged, and no wrong will escape the terrible, final, and *extraordinary* retribution.

"Stebbins nails it with this book. Just when you think you have the recipe down for international thrillers, an author upends it and creates multifaceted characters and a plot that never stops. Intrigue, murder, ethics, religion, romance, an international setting...the author has packed everything" **-ForeWord Reviews**

TRILOGY

Daughter of Time, Books 1-3

"Stebbins has a penchant for the unexpected, even for the genre. These are works that nurture wonder and sometimes break hearts." —Foreword Reviews

READER, WRITER, and MAKER: Omnibus of all three novels of the trilogy. A single book (and eBook), both paperback and hardcover. Speculative fiction with time travel, alien Armageddon, metaphysical mysteries, action, adventure, cosmology, cybernetics, religion, and romance!

The Caterpillar and the Stone

Once upon a time in the middle of a beautiful garden, there lived a Caterpillar and a Stone, and they were very much in love. A fairy's tale of love, loss, and beauty for not quite grown-ups. Presented as an illustrated, full-color love storybook. Author narration available on CD and digital music files, as well as integrated into a multimedia iBook®.

www.ingramcontent.com/pod-product-compliance
Lightning Source LLC
Chambersburg PA
CBHW030736030726
47497CB00001B/10